WEST FROM YESTERDAY

RANDOLPH CARTER HARRISON

ISBN: 1492115843
ISBN-13: 9781492115847
Library of Congress Control Number: 2013914831
CreateSpace Independent Publishing Platform
North Charleston, South Carolina

To blood kin, true friends, good dogs, and blind luck.
No man was ever more blessed.

BOOK ONE

On the ninth day of June 1864, in an atelier overlooking the rooftops of Paris, Tucker Lightfoot Clairborne, tangled in lavender-scented bed linen, completed a joyous, perplexing, long-anticipated rite of passage.

At its conclusion, the young woman, whose last name he never learned, rested her curls on his chest. He contemplated her face. A bridge of pale freckles across her pert nose connected high cheekbones. Her lips were slightly parted. Using a corner of the embroidered pillowcase, he dabbed the perspiration dotting her upper lip. The labors of love had fatigued him to the point that the young Virginian gave no thought to what his parents, particularly his mother, would think should they learn of his most recent experience in the third year of his residence in Louis Napoleon's France. His seventeen-year-old body seeming to melt into the bedding, Clairborne shifted his gaze to the open window, where lace curtains undulated in the breeze. The pale orange bottom of a single distant cloud announced arrival of a new day in Paris.

Forty-eight hours later and an ocean away, his older brother, Captain Payton Clairborne, was cut in half by a twelve-pound shot fired from a Yankee Parrot gun at a rural Virginia crossroads called Cold Harbor. The top of the Confederate captain's body cartwheeled into the air, spraying its contents on the emaciated, barefoot, caterwauling rebels the young officer was leading against solid masses of entrenched blue-clad Union troops.

It took two full months for the word of his brother's demise to reach the ancestral home of le Compte d'Argenteuil, whose hospitality Tucker Clairborne had enjoyed since shortly after the beginning of the War between the States. Reining his lathered mount at the chateau entrance, the postillion handed the letter to the estate chamberlain, who took it to Tucker Clairborne at his breakfast table.

The young man reacted to the news with panic, bolting to his room, throwing random items into his valise, and shouting orders for the groom to bring a carriage at once. It was simply not possible to remain in France an instant longer, even under the benevolent, indeed affectionate eye of the count, his father's close friend and frequent prehostilities visitor to Warwick, the Clairborne plantation on the James River southeast of Richmond.

As Clairborne paced the ancient stables waiting for the horses to be harnessed and the footmen to load his baggage, his host appeared at the door, his elegant form cast in silhouette by the morning sun.

"You would leave without bidding me adieu?"

Distracted with worry, Clairborne was unaware of his host's arrival and jumped at the sound of his voice.

"No, monsieur, I'm sorry that I gave you cause to think I would be ever be so impolite. I must return home as soon as possible. I have learned just now my brother has been killed.

The Yankees killed him at a place called Cold Harbor. Anyway, monsieur, I must take my leave."

Saying nothing, the count reached into the pocket of his fawn-colored waistcoat and withdrew a folded letter. Clairborne recognized his family's creamy, embossed bond.

"Tucker, I have here a letter from your father I received two months ago," the count said, handing him the envelope.

Clairborne was suddenly confused. His host had never delayed sharing any communication from home and family. Why now?

As he looked at the letter and beheld his father's handwriting, it hit him. "It's all gone."

The Yankees had been occupying Warwick for two full years now. Adjacent to Berkley Plantation, the Union Army headquarters for its ill-fated campaign to take Richmond, Warwick provided first Union General George B. McClellan and then his replacement with splendid comfort during the effort known as the Peninsular Campaign that had become such a disappointment to Lincoln. Clairborne's mother wrote letters urging him not to worry, as the Yankees were mostly respectful and his younger sister was beyond their gaze, living in the southwestern part of the state that remained "free and unoccupied."

The letter was from his father and was addressed to "My Dearest Friend Gilles."

"Knowing my boy as I do, I am certain he is becoming more restive, more determined to return and join the fray, but I beg you, Gilles, prevent this from happening. It is clear to me that you have become quite fond of the boy, and few things have ever given me such pleasure, knowing how impeccable are your standards.

"It is therefore all the more difficult for me to say—nay, to beg—that even should you have to physically restrain him, do not allow him to leave France until you hear from me that it is time for him to come home.

"His brother and Tucker are my only hopes to restore Warwick and our family to its status quo antebellum. Should he return before the hostilities are concluded, I would lose him on the battlefield; of that I am certain. I am equally certain I could not bear the loss. Save this letter until you need to convince him that my prayers are for us to restore our home, our family, our fortunes, and our beloved Virginia when this plague of death and destruction is finally ended.

"My deepest affection, respect, and gratitude to you, Gilles, for all you have done and continue to do. That my son is safe with you provides the only solace I know, and I will never forget it.

"Your humble and obedient servant and comrade, John."

Clairborne folded the sheet and turned his blank gaze to one of the stable's cats as it stalked a mouse hidden in the hay.

"So you see, Tucker, it is your father's most urgent desire that you await his summons to return. I must honor his request, and you must understand why reason and obedience must prevail over emotion and anger. Will you obey your father's wishes?"

Reluctantly, he had. But the ensuing months were sheer agony unaffected by his host's unfettered hospitality and futile attempts to provide diversions.

And now, nearly a year later, another dispatch rider pounded up the poplar-lined parkway to the chateau.

Within minutes, Clairborne's host appeared at the door to his room. Before a word was spoken, Clairborne knew from the count's expression and his form that yet another disaster had struck. His host didn't make immediate eye contact. His broad shoulders were rolled forward and downward, and he was not immaculately attired—all of which told Clairborne in unmistakable terms that something terrible had happened. Where it had happened was not a mystery. It could only be Virginia.

"I'm so sorry, Tucker, so very sorry to have to tell you that your father has died."

Once, years ago in Virginia, Clairborne had fought his older cousin in what began as a contest of young male wills but quickly turned into a fervent, mutual desire to hurt each other. In the melee, his opponent grabbed a pick handle and swung it at Clairborne, who managed to duck just enough to partially deflect what would have been a mortal impact. Instead, the blow broke three ribs, knocked the breath from his lungs, and rendered him unconscious.

In the instant he heard of his father's demise, he recalled that body blow that stunned him to incoherence.

Then his father's image appeared in his mind's eye. Tall. Elegant. Smiling. Deep lines radiating from the corners of gray-green eyes. Strong chin accentuated by a neatly trimmed beard flecked with gray. The eyes did not blink. At the touch of the count's hand on his shoulder, Claiborne flinched.

"How? In battle?"

The count responded by handing him the letter from his mother.

Typhoid fever. Disease. Death by bad water.

The impulse to crush the letter was instantly overridden by his desire to preserve it to read in full at some other time, just not now.

Without looking around, he sat on his bed and stared at nothing.

"I must go home. My mother and sister need me," he said softly.

"There is something else," said the count. "Something that might make it easier for you to return quickly."

Clairborne looked up at his host. "The war is over, Tucker. Lee surrendered. The news arrived with the letter."

Clairborne shifted his gaze from the count to the ancient portraits on the bedroom wall. He wondered how long ago they were painted, how many tragedies had occurred since then.

"All for nothing. For nothing. I must get to Cherbourg or Brest and book passage on the first ship for America, anywhere in America," he said as he stood.

He began pacing nervously, watched by the count, who said nothing for long moments.

"Of course, Tucker. But may I suggest that you permit Henri to pack your belongings while I determine which ship will get you home most quickly. As impatient as you are to leave, a little investment in time might actually get you there sooner."

Clairborne knew his host was correct and indicated so by a nod, a gesture that seemed to break the dam of reserve and lead to a convulsion of sobs and tears.

He was only vaguely aware that his father's friend and his host for the last three years responded with a firm embrace.

Later, they sat in the drawing room, which smelled of wax, tobacco, and leather, while Clairborne's possessions were prepared for the journey home. The count turned to him and waited to speak while the manservant moved silently across the polished marble and thick carpet to refill the snifters with cognac.

"There are so many things that should be said at this time, Tucker. I will endeavor to say only that which I deem most important. I want you to know this. Shortly after you were born, I encountered a series of financial reverses. Your father found out, and to put it succinctly, he saved me from ruin. Ours is more than a friendship. Since then we have been business partners. Now with his passing and the loss of your brother as well, you and I will carry on that partnership. Do you understand?"

Clairborne did not. Not fully. His world had never required any effort on his part to understand the means by which Virginia soil and the work of others supported his life. As the second son, he knew he would never inherit Warwick, but he was equally certain his brother Peyton would ensure neither he nor their sister Amelia would ever want for material comfort. Of course there were slaves and crops and foremen and overseers—and lawyers in Richmond and London and, oh yes, bankers, all of whom came to Warwick every other year. But no, he did not fully understand the significance of what the count was saying.

Nor did he care. But this was something he decided not to say lest he hurt the count's feelings and appear insensitive to what he knew was yet another example of the counts' largesse.

"This is all that I want you to remember," said the count. "Here in France not long ago, a way of life ended, a very ancient way of life, and it ended in oceans of blood, most of it the blood of innocents."

The count looked out the tall windows at the immaculate lawn and fountains.

"You must accept that everything you held dear is no more. It is over, the way of life since your ancestors' time. So what is ahead of you? Pain. Pain and struggle. The victors will try to destroy even what is left. But if you decide to, you can prevail, my son. You can prevail and restore Warwick, and I will help you do it."

LEAVING

June, 1, 1868

This is my last night in Warwick. I cannot sleep. Indeed I do not want to since sleep would deprive me of the scent of the James, the soil, and the plants, the sounds of the birds, the sounds of the house itself as it cools after a hot day. Never in my twenty years have I been so riven by conflicting emotions. The sadness that has been so prominent in my life of late is even more pronounced at the thought of leaving my family home. For 147 years, Clairbornes have lived on this spot, 135 of them in this house. My ancestors who started building it could never have conceived that it would eventually become one of the grandest homes on the James River. In the vestibule, there is an etching of the home as it was 110 years ago: a single-floor structure, mostly of wood and some brick, chimneys at both ends, flagstone steps with wrought-iron railings. It doesn't show the smithy, the stables, or the slave quarters, but as early as I can recall, Clairborne children have had to learn the layout of the entire estate as a primary component of our education, including which crops are rotated among which fields.

As amazed as those ancestors would be to learn what had risen from those rude beginnings, my more contemporary kin would be distraught to see what it has become in less than a half decade. In *the three years they were quartered here, the Yankees destroyed the slave quarters and two of the barns, ate all of our chickens, pigs, geese, and cattle, stole most of the horses and mules, nearly all of my mother's Limoges and Waterford, all of her silver services, and even some of the quilts sewn by house servants and given to my ancestors to mark births and weddings.*

From here on the second floor, I cannot see the James because of the blanket of mist rising from its torpid surface. Before the night is done, it will cover the main house and will stifle all sound from the barn and the stables and the forest on the north side of the property. As I write, I hear my own voice asking me, "Why are you leaving?" Perhaps it is just an echo of all the other voices that have asked me that question since I announced my intentions to my mother, sister, and (I predict) soon-to-be brother-in-law. More likely, the voice reverberating in my head is not my own but rather those of my father and all the Clairborne fathers before him. It would be inconceivable to any of them that a male Clairborne of sound mind and body would simply up and leave.

The persistence of the question forces me to answer myself.

I leave because I am not up to the challenge of taking Warwick from its present state of disrepair and debt to its rightful state of prominence and productivity. I have essayed these three years since my return from France to make sense of the past-due taxes and the need to identify a source of manual labor now that we have no slaves. But how can anyone pay for work when there is no money? And unless there is work, there are no crops, and unless there are crops, there is no money.

I know of no estates in our beloved Southland that have come up with an answer to this conundrum, which is made all the more devilish by the fact that our European markets for tobacco and cotton have been replaced by tobacco from Turkey and cotton from Egypt and shifts in commerce required by the Yankee blockade that forced our clients to find new, more reliable sources for what we used to supply.

The legislature in Richmond is no help. Full of assorted scalawags and "freedmen" elected to office by fellow former slaves who can neither read nor write, it provides planters no sympathetic ear, much less active assistance.

Yet as angry and frustrated as I am, I cannot participate in the new movement called the Ku Klux Klan started by General Forrest. It seeks to use terror to restore what is gone. While its growing ranks here in Virginia include some true gentlemen and friends of mine, most of the Klansmen I have met are ignorant ruffians with whom I would never otherwise associate—and certainly would never introduce to any gentlewomen acquaintances.

I have paused to collect my thoughts and raised my eyes to the stars so brilliant above the low-lying mist. All of what I write about our miserable circumstances is true. But what is also true is that I am weak. I am not strong enough to see this through, to struggle with books and numbers, to plead for more time, to find new markets and crops. To find money. To see my beloved Warwick partitioned into farm plots is more than I can bear. I swing between rage and suffocation.

A stronger man would wait and hope and fill the interim with hard work and hope. But not me. I am leaving. Staying would crush me. Leaving is an act of desperation, but I cannot deny that it also exhilarates me. I am heading west—to end up where, I have no idea. I will become a new man, a different person than I am this night, a man unencumbered by obligations to ancestors, neighbors, and this sacred soil. At least that is my hope.

I dread the dawn and the tears I know it will bring from Mother and Amy and pray with all my heart I will be able to restrain my own at least until I am out of sight.

I must turn to practical matters and compile an inventory of items to bring.

LIST OF ITEMS FOR THE JOURNEY
Three pair wool socks
Three pair drawers
Three handkerchiefs
Three linen shirts
Two suits w/waistcoat
Two cravats; one black, one maroon
Two pair gloves (dress and riding)
Two pair riding breeches

Blanket
Folding knife
Bowie knife
Father's flask
Peyton's copy of The Odyssey
Coffee cup
Flint/steel
Compass
LeMat w/100 rounds
Parker w/20 rounds
Pencils
Journal
Money belt (contents to be secured later—I hope)

The last entry caused Clairborne to smile. He had exactly $19.47 cash to his name after paying the train fare from Richmond to Saint Louis for himself and his two horses, one of which carried him and the other his possessions.

He scanned the room to see if he could identify something else, something small, a keepsake of all that he was about to abandon. Opening the drawer of the nightstand, he saw the *Book of Common Prayer* given to his then-twelve-year-old father to mark his confirmation and first communion in the Episcopal Church. Opening the Moroccan leather cover, he read his father's handwriting on the flyleaf:

Strawberry Plain
July 16th, 1826
May I be worthy.

Slipping the book into a pocket of his jacket, Claiborne looked out the window and said aloud, "May I as well...."

———ᴧᴧ———

The soft knock on the door told him Samuel was performing his duties still.

"Master Tucker, I have your coffee. Master Tucker, you awake?"

Samuel, head of the house servants, had been serving the family since twelve years before Clairborne's birth in 1848. With emancipation, Samuel and the rest of the slaves whose toil enriched Warwick Plantation were free to leave, and most had. Since April 1865, some had returned, unable to find work, housing, or scattered relatives, and that was a major part of the challenges Clairborne chose to leave behind.

How to pay for work that slaves once provided in return for the "cost" of housing and food? How to put workers in the field to grow crops for which there did not seem to be any demand? How to keep workers at Warwick through a growing season when they could leave at will for any reason, including rumors that some other planter was paying more, and more regularly, than the owners of Warwick?

But Samuel and Ellie and Nancy and her son Moses never left. Clairborne realized as he thought of them that they had provided the only continuity in a world gone mad, ripped apart by the forces of war and hunger, political impotence, and humiliating poverty.

For an instant, Clairborne wondered if he could take Samuel with him, or maybe Moses. The companionship and familiarity would be an anodyne to the ache of parting, but just as quickly, he recognized the impracticality of the concept.

"Come on in, Sam."

The door opened, and Samuel entered, his white linen shirt crisp with starch and his black trousers creased and clean. His yellow-and-black-striped waistcoat bore no trace of stains or evidence of the work required to keep Warwick as clean and comfortable as circumstance allowed.

Backing through the door, Samuel carried a plate of bread and honey in one white-gloved hand, a cup of coffee in the other. No silver service bearing ramekins of jams and sugar; no sterling creamers, butter dish, or spreading knives; and no gleaming pot of Jamaican coffee—all to fend off a young man's hunger until breakfast was served in the dining room an hour or so later. The silver services were long gone, scattered in single spoons and saucers into the trunks of Yankee officers or the knapsacks of their enlisted men.

"Master Tucker?"

"Yes, Sam."

"You still leaving this mornin'?"

"I expect so, Sam."

"Master Tucker, mind if I ask you a question?"

Clairborne put his cup down and looked directly into his servant's rheumy eyes, knowing the query he was about to receive would be asked in the spirit of these new times when servants could ask personal questions of the men and women they served. To his quiet amusement, Clairborne found himself thinking, "And why the hell not?"

"Sam, these are new times. You sure as blazes have earned the right to ask me just about anything." Holding up his hand to show he had more to say, Clairborne closed the steamer trunk, pointed to it, and said, "Sit down if you will, Sam. I want to tell you something first.

"I'm all topsy-turvy, just like everyone else these days. I don't know what's coming down the pike in next hour, much less in the next day or month. I just know a couple of things for sure, for absolute certain.

"The first is that the Lord is punishing my people. None of this could happen unless it was his will. There's an awful lot of folks up north of here who say what's happening to us is nothing more than the wrath of God, the wages of sin brought down on us slaveholders."

Samuel was silent but held Clairborne's eyes with his own steady gaze.

"I can't say for sure I know what's right or wrong anymore. I just don't know. But I know for sure that I want you to know how much I..." Clairborne looked away, his throat constricted by a painful knot.

Samuel said nothing.

Clairborne waved his hand and blurted, "I can't tell you how much I appreciate your loyalty, Sam. Without you and Ellie, my mother would have died, and there would not have been anything left of this place. But because you took care of her and of things around here, she could make some decisions to save what she could. If ever I was cruel to you, or uncaring, I'm sorry..."

Samuel stood and said, "No sir, you were never—"

"Please let me finish, Sam. I...we just took everything for granted. We didn't ever think about you being slaves and all. It seems like we should have, but the fact is, we didn't. I just want you to know that I don't take for granted all that you've done for me and my family these long, long years, Sam. I wish things were different and I had some way to reward you, but I don't. Other than words, I've got nothing to give you."

Clairborne extended his hand to his former slave, who regarded it for a long moment before taking it in a firm grip.

"I was going to ask you if you had any particular things you wanted me to watch out for after you leave, Master Tucker, anything you can't ask anyone else to stay up on?"

Clairborne shook his head at the latest example of this bond no one else could understand.

"Yeah, actually Sam, there is," Clairborne said as he took his servant's hand in both of his. "I need you to take care of yourself. I need to know that you are going to be around for a long time to come. That's what I've got to know: that you will take care of yourself."

—◊◊◊—

As she waited for her son to come downstairs, Mary Clairborne was not at all certain she could behave in the proper manner. Pacing the polished hardwood floor that gave off the faintest scent of beeswax, she told herself that she was confused because there was no precedent for her. Everyone she knew with male relatives had lost someone to war-related events, be they deaths from battle or disease.

But this was different.

Her healthy son had returned from his European sojourn, stayed home for almost three years, and was now about to leave of his own volition. Not only did she not know where he was going, apparently he didn't know either, beyond some irritatingly vague "out west..."

Since she learned of his intentions, she'd thought of nothing else but had made little effort to change his mind despite the raft of reasons why it was a bad idea and the paucity of reasons why it was a good one. She tried not to think of the impact her son's departure would have on her personal situation, telling herself that to do so would be selfish. She simply could not imagine life without a male presence. Her forty-eight years were full to overflowing with patriarchs, most of them *patera familium* in the true Roman sense of the words.

Tucker shrugged when she tried to corner him into confronting his responsibility to his family, his ancestors, his neighbors, his posterity.

A wan smile shaped his face. "Mother, haven't you recognized by now that I am not up to running this place, that I just don't have it in me?"

He kissed her hands.

"Amy is the one who will take care of Warwick, Mother. She's far more capable than I will ever be."

In a flash, she realized he was right. Her daughter had effectively been running the place for years, helping her make decisions she would not have made without her daughter's advice.

But she still could not come to terms with Tucker's leaving. And she recognized that what most bothered her was the suspicion that her son was leaving because he was a coward, that he simply lacked the essential grit and gumption needed to confront the difficulties ahead.

She wondered how much of that was her fault. Had she mollycoddled him to the point where she emasculated him? There were so many instances of her making excuses for his behavior and so many more of her making sure her husband never learned of their youngest boy's latest transgressions.

And now, in a matter of moments, he was leaving. She might never see him again, and that, ultimately, determined her demeanor. "I don't want his last memories of me to be clouded by my anger or criticism," she told herself.

So she glanced once more at the full-length mirror in the vestibule by the front door, returned to the parlor, and sat down on the horsehair stuffed divan. She ran her hands over nonexistent wrinkles in her black silk widow's dress, one of three she had been wearing for more than three years and would continue to wear for another three. She tried not to look around and assess how things had changed since all five of them were last together in this room.

Tucker entered and embraced his mother, holding her firmly and long enough to tell her he was securing the memory of her, particularly her slender form and her scent.

Clairborne could only think of one thing to say. "It's time, Mother. Will you give me your blessings?"

"Yes, Son, and I'll give you more than that," she said, turning to retrieve a linen-wrapped bundle on the sideboard.

"These are some things that belonged to Clairborne men that I want you to have. Don't open it now. Some are practical.

Some are just sentimental, but they all have meaning, as I hope you'll agree when you see them."

Clairborne tucked the bundle under his arm, took her hand, and led her to the front steps, where his sister and her fiancé waited by his horses.

Amy clearly had been weeping. Dark circles beneath her gray eyes looked almost blue, and she wore no powder or rouge. The lace handkerchief clutched in her dainty right hand was soaked with tears.

"Oh, Tucker, you just don't have to do this. You don't have to go anywhere, and I still can't understand why you are leaving." She grasped his arms. "Will you not stay at least through the growing season?"

Clairborne shook his head.

"Amy, Amy, it would just be delaying the inevitable."

Then he turned to his mother and to Amy's fiancé, Tom Breckinridge. "I've said this to Amy and to each of you individually. Now I want to say it again so you all hear it from me at the same time.

"Amy is more capable of managing Warwick than I will ever be. That's just a fact. And when you two finally tie the knot, Tom, Warwick and your lands will have the best chance of returning to the way this place was before.... I honestly believe this is best for everyone. I do."

He embraced his mother and then his sister. He shook hands with his future brother-in-law. He turned to face the servants. He embraced them in turn—Samuel, then Ellie, then Nancy. Moses was holding the reins of his horse. Clairborne took the reins, said thank you, and mounted. He checked the lead rope to his packhorse.

He took off his broad-brimmed gray hat, swept it downward in his best cavalier salute, turned, and rode off, not once looking back.

—⁓—

June 8, 1868

I killed a man last night.

I took a man's life because of a pocket watch.
Although he threatened to "geld" me if I failed to hand over my treasured Breguet, it still comes down to the fact that I killed a man rather than part with a piece of jewelry.

He appeared to be drunk. He held his knife in such a manner that it seemed he did not know how best to use it. He clearly didn't know I had my Bowie under my coat. I don't believe he knew what happened to him. I still do not fully understand it either.

No one saw or heard, so no one seeks me. I wish for the company of Reverend Simmons. What would he say of this deed? What would my father say? I cannot contemplate what God's judgment will be.

I must try to think of something else for a while.

—ᵥᵥᵥ—

The Louisville & Nashville express train for Saint Louis pulled out of the Nashville station spewing clouds of steam and smoke, notifying all within earshot of its bell and whistle that it was only three minutes behind schedule.

Clairborne sat on a bale of hay in the freight carriage, where his two horses and one belonging to someone else were tethered. The car smelled of fresh hay and coal smoke. He had it to himself at least until the first water stop on the sixteen-hour trip to Saint Louis. The L&N freight agent and his assistant rode in the express car, sorting mail and the baggage tags bearing the destinations and owners of the trunks and the freight—bales of catalogues, crates of corsets, bullets, window panes, paint buckets, and printing press components—bound for towns and homes west of Saint Louis. He absent-mindedly stroked his horses' velvet-soft muzzles, his thoughts consumed by the events of the previous evening.

The details were clear enough.

He had been returning to the rail yard where the freight car with his horses waited on a siding. Like all railroads, the L&N had designated areas in its major stations where passengers shipping horses could unload, exercise, water, and feed them during scheduled breaks in their journeys. The agent had recommended a hotel restaurant within five minutes' walk, and Clairborne had surprised himself by deciding to make the trip on foot. He had exercised, groomed, and fed his horses as soon as the car was moved to the siding, so now that his horses had stretched their legs, he would too.

A glass of sour mash, followed by terrapin soup, roast duck, ham croquettes in a white sauce, candied sweet potatoes, biscuits and honey, a slice of chess pie with a glass of sauterne, and a black coffee combined to put him in a better mood than he had known for days. As he paid the $1.47 tab and pulled a cigar from his leather holder, Clairborne smiled, recognizing that he had just spent most of his dinner thinking about the future rather than dwelling on the past. It made him feel good.

At the intersection leading downhill to the station, he noticed an alley bisecting the brick warehouses on his right and knew that the alley must connect to the square in front of the station. He took the shortcut. The darkness was disconcerting, for although residual evening light remained on the street, the alley was pitch black. It was not fear of thieves or ruffians that caused him to pause. It was fear of stepping into the human feces he couldn't see but the odor of which nearly made him gag. So he stopped to let his eyes adjust. "Of course," he thought. "It's like any other city in the world. People defecate in alleys. No surprise."

He moved forward slowly down the grade to avoid both stepping into something or tripping over something else.

He sensed the other person before he saw him, and when he did, Clairborne knew instinctively there was going to be trouble.

The man approached him oddly, rapidly but out of kilter, slightly clumsy. Clairborne initially thought the man was a cripple, but when the man addressed him, his words and the slur that rounded the consonants filled in the picture. The man was drunk.

"Gimme that watch, you sumbitch. Gimme that goddam watch, or I'll geld you like 'at fine bay horse of yourn," the man said.

"How in the hell did he see my watch in this darkness, and how in the hell does he know anything about my horses?" Clairborne wondered. "Easy, mister," he said.

"Go to hell, you fancy turd," the man yelled. "Gimme that goddam watch 'er I'll cut yer nuts off right now."

It was the voice of the stable hand who had delivered the hay to the baggage car. The only thing he had said to Clairborne earlier in the day was, "That'll be two bits" and "Nice watch."

And now, three hours later, the bastard was drunk, demanding his watch, and threatening to castrate him. It was too much.

Clairborne abruptly moved toward his assailant until he was close enough to see the cheap skinning knife the drunk held awkwardly, blade down, his right hand wrapped around the handle.

Clairborne had not a minute of instruction or experience in knife fighting, but he had begun mastering the epee when he was eight. Until now, it was an entirely academic exercise, something expected of most landed gentlemen, something his father had definitely required of him and his brother.

"The watch, you lily-livered pri..."

Clairborne reached under his coat, but instead of retrieving his father's engraved Breguet, he slipped his brother's Bowie from its sheath.

He stepped toward his assailant and slammed his left arm down on the drunk's right wrist. His opponent, holding his blade downward, couldn't parry the blow.

With his right hand, Clairborne jammed the Bowie into the man's stomach, turning slightly to his left as he did. The double-edged blade entered an inch above the navel, and when he swiftly extracted it, the result was precisely what the knife's inventor, brawler and adventurer James Bowie, had in mind. The wound doubled in size.

The drunk bent over, and a muffled, inchoate sound, half belch and half scream, bubbled from his open mouth. Slippery, steaming intestines tumbled from the gaping wound. Clairborne brought the Bowie straight up into the soft tissue between the man's chin and Adam's apple, the blade tip making a muted popping sound as it emerged from the greasy curls at the top of the man's head. Clairborne yanked the blade out as the man silently collapsed on his own entrails.

Clairborne stepped away.

The man's legs twitched wildly, and his arms flopped on the filthy cobbles for a few seconds and then stopped.

Clairborne became aware of a nauseating stench rising from what seconds ago had been a live human. It reminded him of the stink emanating from the entrails of deer he'd killed and dressed.

He looked around. No one.

He knelt beside his assailant, who was lying face down in a pool of blood and coils of gleaming gut.

Clairborne wiped his blade on the back of the man's filthy shirt, and even in the poor light, saw the blood on his own coat, trousers, and the part of his shirt his coat didn't cover.

He wiped his blade again and then stood and looked around. No one.

He looked at the body.

"Damn you, sir," he said, stepping over the motionless form and walking to the rail yard.

———∿∿———

On his return to the car, Ajax, his bay gelding, shied at the smell of blood and offal on his clothes. He stripped and soaked his clothes in the galvanized water tub. He decided they could get through the night without water.

Changing into a fresh union suit, shirt, socks, and pants, he slipped the braces over his shoulders and decided that he would also wear the belt and sheathed Bowie. If there was one lesson from this night, it was to be prepared. A shiver went through him. He looked at his horses. They were gazing at him.

He remembered the bundle his mother had handed him on the steps as he left home. Retrieving it from the neatly stacked pile of his possessions by the car's unused stove, Clairborne contemplated the linen-wrapped package and wondered what his mother had selected. Would it be of sentimental value? Practical? He recalled how many times his mother had surprised the men in the family with her common sense and her ability to make important decisions "without a lot of female dithering," his father had noted on one such occasion. And yet she was nothing if not the paragon of refinement—genteel, elegant, demure, and patient.

That he might never see her again intruded on his thoughts. To get away from such unpleasantness, he quickly untied the heavy twine.

Inside were a number of items: his father's ivory-handled straight razor, sterling-silver shaving mug, and boar-bristle brush; his brother's harmonica; the travel chess set, its pieces exquisitely carved ebony and ivory. It was his mother's gift to her husband the last Christmas they were all together at Warwick.

Also among the keepsakes was a sealed envelope bearing the writing of both his mother and his sister.

The front of the envelope read:

Tucker Lightfoot Clairborne
from
Mother and Amelia

Clairborne hesitated to break the wax seal, recalling the discussion of whether the family should order replacement sealing wax from London or attempt to make their own. They had opted for the latter, and he smiled at how well it had turned out. The seal bore the family crest: three demi-lions rampant over the motto "vincit qui patitur": "He conquers who endures."

He broke the seal and unfolded the letter.

Dearest Tucker,
By now you are far from Warwick, but you will never be far from our hearts and our thoughts. There is nothing we can say that will cause you

to be safe. We know we can scarcely conceive the perils you will face. In our discussions of what we could do to provide you with the means to surmount these challenges, we identified the need to give you options.

We have learned these painful years past that the world in which we now live cares little for blood lines and the accomplishments of ancestors. Instead, it places a priority on debts paid promptly, the yield and market price of this year's crops, and the likelihood of financial gain in all fields of endeavor.

Therefore, we want you to have a reserve upon which to draw for whatever reason, be it an emergency or a fanciful notion. Please do not fret about this, as it involves no sacrifice on our part. It is your share of this year's profits from the Nanticoke. Your father's half ownership in the ship and his partner's recommendation to register it in France has proven to be an invaluable and, we must say, unexpected source of revenue.

To that end, we have established an account in your name at the Mercantile Bank of Chicago and deposited therein the amount of $500.

Again, Dear Tucker, this is your share. Receive it in the certain knowledge that we send it with our abiding affection and our prayers for your continued safety.

Love forever, Mother and Amy.

He gently folded the letter and turned his gaze to the horses, who were still looking at him, ears erect.

He was unable to place anything in context. He had known of the half ownership of the brig called the *Nanticoke* but was unaware of its returning a profit. Had he just ignored a letter from their shipping agent? Had he read the report and just not realized the significance of the columns of numbers? How could he have been unaware of profits when the very existence of Warwick had been under a veritable financial siege for years?

No answers surfaced in the turbid pool of his confusion, but one thing was clear.

He had killed a man and been rewarded with wealth, all within a single night.

It made no sense.

———※———

From the train station to the eastern bank of the Mississippi, Clairborne studied the sprawling city on the opposite shore of the continent's biggest river. It took a moment for him to put his finger on what Saint Louis reminded him of. Then he had it: a recumbent sow nursing a huge brood of piglets, or maybe a bitch sprawled on her side with an enormous litter suckling a fantastic array of teats.

Rising gently from the river, the first several yards of the bank were paved with cobblestones, and for more than a mile upstream and down were hundreds of boats—side-wheelers, stern-wheelers, lighters, barges and here and there, some old-fashioned keel boats, all nosed into the shore, loading or unloading cargo composed of every conceivable artifact of human existence. It was a phenomenal sight.

He felt himself drawn to the eastern shore, which was almost as frenetic as the Saint Louis side. It took him less than five minutes to find a ferryman, pay his fifty-cent fare, and load his horses. He asked the ferryman about the massive bridge under construction to the north, the first to cross the Mississippi. "Goddamned waste of money," he snorted. "Rich bastard railroad men gonna own the world and put everyone else out of business. Hope the damn thing falls in the river and takes them with it...."

The closer he got to the western bank, the more interesting the city became. The sheer bedlam of hissing steam engines, shrieking whistles, cursing stevedores, yapping strays, and shouting teamsters made normal conversation difficult.

Nearing the western bank, the ferry nudged a bloated horse carcass carried southward in the caramel-colored current of the river the Indians called the "father of waters." No one paid it any attention, occupied as they were with preparations for disembarkation. Clairborne was the only one of the eleven passengers looking at the cityscape, which was so clogged with people and animals, carts, wagons, coaches, and cabriolets that he wondered how he would ever locate a decent place to stay, a bank, and an outfitter who could be trusted not to cheat him. He was aware that he had never been any place like this. He understood that along with his excitement came the need for caution to counteract the danger oozing from the ground like the rank stench of the riverfront itself.

As he offloaded, his horses reacted to the crowds, the noise, and the smells with snorts and nervous tugs on the reins and lead rope. Clairborne stroked their muzzles to calm them. A barefoot, filthy urchin, his shaved head bearing the tattoos of ringworm, appeared at his elbow.

"I'll help you with one of them, mister. Only a penny to walk with you till we get to where you can mount," the boy said with a lisp.

"Nah, that's all right, sonny. I can make it."

"Don't look like it to me. You ain't been ashore more 'n a minute, and somebody already cut your pack open."

Clairborne turned and beheld a shirt sleeve hanging from the bottom of the pack saddle straddling Ajax's broad back. Someone had neatly slit the heavy canvas, tried to remove the contents, and slipped away when it snagged, foiling the robbery without his even being aware of it.

He tucked the shirt into the pack and rearranged the canvas. Turning to the boy, he said, "Don't suppose you saw who did this?"

"If I did, I wouldn't tell you 'cause you didn't lose nothing," he said.

"Guess you're right at that. What's your name?"

"Toby."

"Well, Toby, tell you what. You escort me up to where I can mount, and I'll give you a nickel for your services," Clairborne said with a grin.

"Why'd you do that, mister?" Toby said, cocking his ear to consider what he clearly thought was an oddity, even for a place as full of them as the Saint Louis riverfront. "Never heard of nobody payin' more 'n they had to."

"Well, just consider it a reward for warning me about the theft," Clairborne said. "Now, we got a deal or not?"

"I reckon. Where you headed? You want a woman? Whiskey?"

"Dang, boy," Clairborne said. "You're a tad young to be pimping, aren't you?"

"You a goddam missionary, mister? What the hell business is it of yourn what I do or sell?"

"Whoa. Watch your language, young man. I don't take kindly to needless profanity from anyone, least of all from somebody still wet behind the ears," Clairborne said.

"Fuck you, mister," the boy said as he spun on his bare heel and walked away.

Clairborne watched him walk into the crowd. Once the boy had moved beyond Clairborne's reach, he turned around and held up a short knife blade, which Clairborne instantly realized the urchin had used to cut open his pack. Clairborne smiled and said, "Welcome to Saint Louis."

At the top of the embankment, the crowd thinned out enough for Clairborne to mount. He rode across the tracks of the Saint Louis and Iron Mountain Railroad, which paralleled the river. Turning west on Choteau Avenue, he observed the gradual transition from jam-packed streets and low clapboard-and-canvas structures to the more spacious, refined, and permanent, all directly related to height and distance from the river. Choteau Avenue was lined with multistory structures of stone and brick as finely designed and constructed as buildings in any city he knew. The primary difference between those places and this was the weather. Europe and Virginia got hot and uncomfortable every summer, and the streets of all urban centers reeked of unwashed bodies and the urine and feces deposited by oxen, dogs, horses, mules, and men.

Saint Louis was simply sweltering, and it was only June. There was not so much as a breeze to dissipate the miasma that enveloped him. This was weather you wear, he observed to himself, weather that gets between the skin and clothes, that occurs only at the high ends of temperature and humidity extremes. This was weather that either triggered torpor or evoked anger. Retrieving a handkerchief from his coat pocket, he removed his hat and mopped his brow and hair, noting with mild disgust the spreading sweat stain on the hatband. He decided to ignore decorum and removed his coat, folding it over the saddle in front of him. He unbuttoned his vest halfway. His linen shirt clung to his frame, soaked through with perspiration across his back and under his arms. Without further thought, he unbuttoned the shirt at the neck and sleeves, which he rolled up his forearms.

Moving away from the river took him to surprisingly broad streets lined with hotels, banks, saloons, and a number of law offices. Dotted among these were gunsmiths, outfitters, and shipping agents. The crowd was dense and mostly afoot. At least a third were black laborers. There were almost no women to be seen. Every hotel had a watering trough and hitching rails, and all had youngsters posted to watch the clients' horses. Some of the more expensive-looking hostelries had canopies shading the windows fronting the street and the lobby entrances.

Pulling the watch from his vest pocket, Clairborne realized he had not eaten anything since a meager and highly unsatisfying dinner in Illinois the night before, followed by two cups of black coffee at the ferry landing this morning before he crossed the Mississippi.

At the spur of the moment, he decided to spend some of his financial windfall on a hotel, a good hotel with a bath, a dining room, and a saloon. He would use the time in Saint Louis to actually think a bit, to plan what would come next and where he would go from here. He realized with a start that until that moment, he had not given his future much thought beyond simply heading west with a vague notion that he might look up family acquaintances and seek their advice about how a young man should best pursue his fortune.

At the corner of Choteau and Ninth Street, his gaze fell on the granite facade of the "Excelsior Hotel—Saint Louis' Finest." He stopped and nodded to the liveried doorman. As the doorman approached, Clairborne put on his jacket, dismounted, and handed over his reins.

"Welcome to the Excelsior, sir. Would you like your horses groomed?"

"Yes, and give 'em some oats. Haven't come all that far today, but it won't hurt them."

The doorman handed the reins to an even younger member of the Excelsior staff. "We'll have your baggage brought to your room, Mr....?"

"Clairborne."

"Mr. Clairborne, of course. The stable we use is less than three minutes from here, down that alley and then two blocks to the left. Jameson's, it's called. First-rate facility. All included in your room payment, sir."

"Fine," Clairborne said. "Just be careful untying the pack. Some young ruffian down at the landing tried to lighten the load for me."

The doorman shook his head. "I'm sorry that was your welcome, sir, but it's good you learned early on that there's a need to be circumspect in our town."

"Circumspect? That's a word I wouldn't expect to hear," Clairborne thought, leaving off "from a hotel doorman." He untied his saddlebags and watched as his pack was unloaded, placed on a brass cart, and wheeled inside. "I'll keep these," he told the doorman, who had reached for the saddlebags. "Thanks just the same," he said, handing him a quarter.

"Thank you, sir," the doorman said with an emphasis that showed his appreciation for Clairborne's generosity. "I know Saint Louis well, sir, having lived here these ten years, so if there is anything that you'll be wanting or needing to know that you may not feel like asking about at the desk, sir, you just let me know. Name of Frank, sir. At your service."

"I'll keep that in mind, Frank," Clairborne said, turning to enter the Excelsior's dark, spacious lobby—which he immediately noted was significantly cooler than the street.

The hotel's assistant manager, who introduced himself as Basil Snyder, escorted Clairborne to his room, expounding the hotel's attributes on the way to the second of four floors.

"The upper floors get pretty warm this time of year, so that's why we've put you on the second. And since it faces east, away from the street and toward the river, you won't be bothered by the smells. And if there is any breeze at all, you'll get the full benefit," he said. A full six inches shorter than Clairborne, the manager wore his black, heavily pomaded hair sharply parted in the middle. His mustache was waxed and pointed at the tips, which moved in synch with the man's constant banter.

"Will you be needing anything, sir? Your clothes laundered, a bath or shave?"

Clairborne paused. "Well, I don't see much percentage in taking a bath before noon—not with this heat—but I might just take you up on that before dinner. I would like to get some time with your boss, come to think of it," he said.

The assistant manager jerked his head around to face Clairborne. "I hope I've not caused you offense or inconvenience, sir."

"No, no, not at all. It's just that I don't know this town all that well. Don't know it at all, really, and I need some recommendations for certain business arrangements," Clairborne said as he hung his hat on the oak rack standing beside the marble-topped washstand.

"Of course, sir. Of course. Mr. Rathbone would be most happy to consult with you on any such matter. Shall I tell him what time would be most convenient for you, Mr. Clairborne?"

"Any time it's convenient for him," Clairborne replied as he pulled a fifty-cent piece from his vest pocket and handed it to the assistant manager. "Fine place you have here, and thanks for your service," he said.

Without looking at the coin, Snyder said, "Most gracious of you, sir, and please let any of us know if there is anything we can do to enhance your Saint Louis sojourn."

—◦◦◦—

The meeting with Arthur Rathbone went well. A tall, thin Englishman with an aquiline profile, Rathbone melded British reserve with American openness to produce a demeanor well suited to the hospitality business. He told Clairborne that he had been in Saint Louis for eleven years and had chosen the city as his ultimate destination in America while still in his native Manchester. His father and uncle owned two successful hotels and encouraged his pursuit of fortune in America with a modest bankroll. Rathbone had parlayed his bankroll into a one-third interest in the Excelsior, the other two-thirds being held by a Pittsburgh banker who was married to Rathbone's first cousin. All of this made him a fortunate pick for Clairborne in terms of connections, knowledge, and experience.

After shaking hands in the lobby and adjourning to Rathbone's small but tastefully furnished office, Clairborne noted approvingly that Rathbone directed him to a padded, green leather settee and then sat himself in a chair across a low table rather than behind his walnut desk.

Rathbone offered him a drink, whiskey from a crystal decanter, and a smoke from a selection of hand-rolled cigars from a cherrywood humidor inlaid with some of the finest marquetry he'd ever seen.

"I must say, sir, that this whiskey and the cigar are excellent. May I be so bold as to ask whether they are products of my home state of Virginia?" Clairborne asked.

Rathbone laughed. "Indeed they are, my good man! You know your whiskey and tobacco. The cigars are Lawrence

Brothers, and the whiskey is from Virginia, not Tennessee or Kentucky."

Clairborne returned his host's smile. "Few people know that bourbon was actually invented in Virginia, back in the 1600s on an estate adjacent to my family's. It was then called Harrison's Landing, but now it's known as Berkley."

"Ah, then, that explains your tastes. So how can I be of service, Mr. Clairborne? I sense you are a man with something in mind."

The impact of the ninety-proof bourbon on Clairborne's empty stomach, or more precisely on his mental state, produced a reply more candid than he would otherwise have given.

"No, actually I don't have specific plans for much of anything, but I've recently realized that I should. I'll be honest, Mr. Rathbone. I am not, as the French say, *un homme d'affairs*. Never had any interest in money or how to make it." Clairborne sipped the bourbon and considered his words before continuing.

"Before the war, my family was wealthy. Now we are not. In fact, truth be told, we are poor. Perhaps not destitute, but we are...ah...should I say, of limited means, and I must come to terms with that reality and build my future upon it. I hope my candor does not make you uncomfortable."

Rathbone shook his head. "On the contrary. I am honored that you should confide in me to this degree. It is one of the things I so like about America," he said, leaning forward and putting his glass down on the table's tooled leather top.

"Americans are so open. It makes business discussions so much more efficient. Allow me to simply say that I am interested in the opportunity to offer my counsel as well as the services of this establishment," he said.

Clairborne nodded and smiled. "Thanks. Not to change the subject too abruptly, but since you come from England, doesn't this heat bother you? I find it oppressive, to say the least."

Rathbone pointed to a painting in an expensive gilded frame hanging on the walnut-paneled wall behind Clairborne's head.

"Are you familiar with India, Mr. Clairborne? Specifically its climate and the British presence there?"

"Ah, not really, beyond its location and the Taj Mahal, tigers, and all that. I will say that at my brother's recommendation, I started reading about the raj early on. My family is full of anglo-philes, to say the least."

"Capital," Rathbone said as he poured another finger of amber corn whiskey into Clairborne's crystal tumbler.

"The reason I asked," Rathbone said, "is that my family lived there for sixteen years. Father was a civil servant. If you are familiar with India at all, you know that the British literally flee Delhi for Dharmsala in the Himalayan foothills when the dry season arrives. It's an entire way of life." He paused for a moment and then said, "May I share an idea with you, Mr. Clairborne, one that I've not shared with many others, but I must admit that I am so taken with it that it is difficult to contain."

Clairborne was mildly surprised at the Englishman's excitement but found it contagious. "Of course."

Rathbone stood and began pacing. "Saint Louis is the fourth largest city in the United States behind New York,

Philadelphia, and Chicago. More than 310,000 people already live here, up from 160,000 just ten years ago. When one considers our location at the confluence of the two mightiest rivers on the continent, the rail lines coming here—you saw the Eads Bridge under construction—and the unimaginable wealth that lies to the west of us yet to be tapped, Saint Louis will soon enough be the nation's third or even second largest. It is absolutely inevitable."

Clairborne nodded politely.

"So what, you may well ask, does all this have to do with your question about the weather? That is where my idea becomes relevant." He leaned toward Clairborne and lowered his voice to an almost conspiratorial tone. "Have you heard of the Ozarks, my good man?"

"The Ozark Mountains? Of course," Clairborne replied.

Rathbone smiled as he sat down. "Truth be told, anyone who has seen the Himalayas, Alps, or the Rockies would chuckle at the presumption of calling the Ozarks mountains. But they rise high enough to be much cooler in the summer than Saint Louis, and they are only two hours from here by train—two hours! Do you know how long it takes to get to Dharmsala from Delhi? Eighteen hours! And that's on an express."

Clairborne grinned and said, "Oh, so that's the idea. Buy land in the Ozarks and promote it as a haven from the heat—like Dharmsala to Delhi."

"Oh capital, capital! You have the very essence of it," Rathbone said. "Tell me, does it not attract you, cool breezes scented with pine? Clear lakes brimming with fish and towns with rail connections and modern facilities, telegraph, some already even with elevated sidewalks?"

Clairborne found himself more intrigued by the thought of Saint Louis becoming the country's second largest city than by an oasis in the Ozarks. But he recognized the reality of the forces behind Rathbone's vision and felt himself lifted on a wave of enthusiasm that had begun rising when he first saw the city from the Mississippi's eastern bank.

As Rathbone expanded his vision, Clairborne studied his whiskey and wondered how much of the euphoria he felt was due to the liquor and how much was attributable to rekindling fondness for his country, a nation that had destroyed one way of life but now seemed hell bent on revealing another. He could have been angry about the fact that Saint Louis was thriving while Richmond, Atlanta, Savannah, Charleston, and others were still squirming under the weight of Yankee occupation. He mentally shrugged and made a fundamental decision on the matter, telling himself, "I don't care about the past."

—◆—

Journal entry
June 13, 1868

When I try to think of how best to describe my situation, the word that comes to mind is "turmoil." It bothers me because the word has a pejorative connotation that doesn't square with the excitement I have felt since I arrived here. I had heard that Saint Louis was one of the most vibrant cities in the world, and my experience to date has confirmed that.

Rathbone has introduced me to Henry Figgleston, atty-at-law; Joseph Schwarz, outfitter and owner of one of the largest dry goods emporia in town; and Bryce Morton, president of the First National Bank of Saint Louis. As a result of these fortuitous meetings, I now have letters of introduction to prominent men residing in a number of locales west of here; cash in my pocket made possible by something called a wire transfer of funds; a new suit, slicker, duster, and gauntlets; a brass telescope, and a coffee grinder.

Perhaps the most unlikely "acquisition," however, is a partnership in a business venture. Rathbone also introduced me to a fellow Virginian, Archer Nickelsby, who hails from Winchester in the northwestern part of the state and does not come from a family known to me. Nickelsby is the source of Rathbone's whiskey and cigars and is raising capital to vastly expand his reach into what he called "the pots of gold" developing all over the west. His enthusiasm for the potential gains to be realized by providing quality tobacco and alcoholic spirits to newly wealthy westerners proved so irresistible that I asked for the chance to invest. He seemed surprised, I assume because Rathbone may have told him I was not in possession of significant capital, but we quickly agreed on terms that resulted in my investing $100 in the Great Western Supply Co., Purveyors of the Finest Spirits and Tobacco.

I sent Mother a telegram telling her where I am and that all is well. I declined to provide any information about my business dealings.

Too hard to do in a telegram, so I'll have to figure out what to say and how best to say it in a letter.

—∿—

By the afternoon of the third day at the Excelsior, Clairborne felt renewed. The combination of successful business meetings, good meals, a bath and haircut, two shaves, and clean clothes to replace the bloodied garments he'd thrown from the moving train had significantly improved his mood. As he descended the staircase into the lobby, Rathbone approached him, a grin spread across his lean face.

"Excellent news, Mr. Clairborne. At dinner last evening, I met a gentleman whom I think you would find rather interesting, to say the least. You may have heard of him—Nolan Caudill?"

Clairborne shook his head. "Sorry. I haven't."

Rathbone waved his hand and said, "No matter at all. Mr. Caudill is a Texas cattleman, one of the better known, one whom folks talk about along with Shanghai Pierce. A truly remarkable individual even by Texas standards.

"He is here after completing a drive that brought more than four thousand cattle to Sedalia. Unfortunately, he's staying at the Regent, but my friend runs it, and he invited me to dinner with Mr. Caudill and his son." Rathbone lowered his voice and leaned forward. "Can we continue this conversation in my office?"

As they entered the office, Rathbone closed the door.

"I took the liberty of mentioning your name, and I told him you were very interested in furthering your prospects, that you were considering the cattle business. I endeavored to give him some information about you—I assure you I was discrete—and he asked me to pass along an invitation to meet him, should you care to." Rathbone leaned further forward and said, "I hope I didn't exceed the limits of discretion in doing so."

Clairborne laughed. "Heavens no. I am indebted to you, sir. It is the very thing I would have asked had I known of the opportunity."

"Excellent. Could you dine with them this evening?"

"I could, and with pleasure."

Rathbone leaned forward and said, "I have a favor to ask of you."

"Ask away."

"Would you be amenable to inviting the Caudills here?" Rathbone held up his hand and continued. "I would pick up the bill entirely. It's just that I know our fare is superior to the Regent's, as are our rooms. If I could get someone like Caudill to select our hotel, it would be a major feather in our cap and well worth the cost of a dinner. What do you say?"

Clairborne's first thoughts were along the lines of instant and unconditional agreement. Then a cloud passed over his enthusiasm.

"It seems a fine idea, but isn't there the chance that Caudill might misunderstand my...ah, financial situation if he thinks I could throw such a party? I mean, after all, I'm just looking for a job."

Rathbone stroked his chin. "Hadn't thought of that. Well, why don't I just go straight out and make the offer myself? He'll understand my aim without my having to be so uncouth as to articulate it. Would that be acceptable?"

Clairborne nodded. "My friend, it would be more acceptable than I can say. Now, what time will we meet, and can I get my shirt laundered and a cravat pressed in time?"

"But of course. And if you have time, we can also go over some things about Mr. Caudill that I think you should know.

"First, as is the case with every Texan I've ever met, he is indefatigable, a force majeure, as our French friends would say. In the last ten years, he has lost his wife and two of his three sons. His youngest, Sam, is with him here, and he dotes on the boy. I think he's about seventeen. Second, Mr. Caudill has on at least two occasions that I know of been financially destroyed, again within the last decade. Once by drought and once by Indians. Third, he is considered a leader in a land of very independent people. Texans tend to follow men like Caudill when it comes to times of crisis, and I would say that by eastern standards, every day in Texas presents some kind of challenge.

"Lastly, Mr. Caudill is very, ah, religious, and he is quite focused on saving souls, so you can expect him to inquire about yours."

Clairborne shifted in his chair, grinned, and said, "I assume we'll be drinking cider tonight, then."

"I'm afraid so, although he does like his cigars. You should also know that he knows Chisum and is friends with Loving and Pierce and Goodnight. They all shared the work of civilizing Texas, and God knows that task is large enough to challenge even those four.

"Like Goodnight, Caudill was a Texas Ranger, at war with Comanche and Kiowa as well as white and Mexican desperadoes while most went to fight for the Confederacy. His sons were with John Bell Hood when they died within a week of each other. I hear that loss was more than Mrs. Caudill could bear.

"As to the cattle drives, I don't know why Caudill and the others use different trails to move cattle north, but it might prove interesting to ask."

"Anything else?" Clairborne asked, his interest in the dinner conversation piqued by what he had just heard.

"Actually there is," Rathbone said. "It's well known that Mr. Caudill is quite fond of Shakespeare."

—∿∿—

The dinner proved to be one of the most fascinating of Claiborne's life to date.

Caudill and his son were extroverted, articulate, and gracious, albeit just a bit rough around the edges. Both were short in stature but projected such vigor that they seemed larger than they were. Caudill the elder wore a beard of biblical patriarch dimensions. His son's visage featured a downy mustache struggling to darken his upper lip. The father was rounder than the son, but the father also gave the impression that his shape stemmed from decades of exposure to the elements and the grinding vicissitudes of frontier life rather than the sedentary accumulation of lard.

Both wore expensive black broadcloth suits. Caudill the younger differed in that his vest was dove gray rather than black like his father's. And both men's faces were the color of hand-rubbed mahogany except for the portion of their foreheads covered by their broad-brimmed hats. That part of their faces was as white as a fish belly.

The only negative thing Clairborne noticed in the course of the five-hour evening was what he considered to be a rather glaring hole in the Caudills' dining etiquette. Both attacked their plates with a two-fisted intensity more appropriate to a competitive sport. Caudill Senior used his napkin almost enough to keep up with the soup, bread crumbs, and gravy accumulating in his beard. Caudill the younger used the flat of his butter knife to deliver candied sweet potatoes to his mouth, noisily sucking them off the blade.

Small points, Clairborne told himself later as he sat on his bed reviewing the evening.

The main thing was that Caudill had offered him a job. All he had to do was show up at the Caudill's Rocking C Ranch in west Texas. It was not clear exactly what he would be hired to do. They had talked extensively about cattle drives and the growing market for beef in cities east of the Mississippi. Caudill spoke enthusiastically of how the arrival of railroads at Kansas trailheads would facilitate movement of the more than three and a half million cattle from Texas plains to eastern dinner plates.

And he insisted that there were fortunes to be made for the daring—"and the lucky, which I count myself to be."

"Lucky?" Rathbone asked. "Surely, sir, your name has been made more by perseverance than by good fortune."

Caudill laughed. "Let me give you an example of luck." After wiping his mouth on an embroidered napkin and downing several swigs of cider, he half turned in his chair to face his host.

"Everyone knows about Texas cattle fever," he said. "Mr. Clairborne...?"

Clairborne had never heard of it. "No, sir."

"Well, last couple of years, Texans, me included, have driven our herds to Sedalia here in Missouri and other railheads around there." His face reddened. "Now some dastardly folks are denying us the right to bring our herds here to Missouri. They say our stock brings fever with it, kills the local cows. Last year, there was shooting. This year, the Missouri legislature passed a law against us."

"So where does the good luck come into this?" Clairborne asked.

"Dang good question, son," Caudill said. "Sounds pretty dang grim so far, don't it?"

"Yes sir."

"Well, here it is, then. The railroads are heading west. Every season, they come hundreds of miles closer. Next year, I'm driving my herd to Abilene, Kansas. Ever heard of it?" Caudill asked with a sly smile.

Clairborne thought for a moment.

"No, sir. Can't say as I have."

Caudill threw back his head and laughed. "That's 'cause the place didn't even exist until about six months ago. Fella named McCoy from Chicago bought up a bunch of prairie along the Union Pacific right-of-way and made a fine railhead out of the place. Got cattle pens that'll hold thousands of head right next to the tracks."

Caudill leaned back, put his thumbs under his vest lapels, and smiled broadly. "So if Missouri doesn't want our money, we'll just have to spend it in Kansas."

Rathbone looked as if he'd swallowed a turkey bone. "Oh sir," he exclaimed. "I do hope you'll leave some pocket change to spend on Saint Louis hospitality!"

Spearing a chunk of roast, Caudill waved it in front of Rathbone and replied, "My good man, for a meal like this, I'd ride to Chicago. Fortunately, I don't have to."

What Clairborne later recalled most clearly was the part of the evening that focused on him. He knew he must have made a good impression or he wouldn't have been offered a position—pay and precise job to be determined later—with the Caudills' Rocking C Ranch.

"We've got about five hundred thousand acres, more or less," Caudill said, glancing at his son, who nodded in agreement. "Sounds like a heck of a lot, but it takes at least ten acres of grass to support one head of cattle for a year if the grass is good, and most of it ain't."

It was midway through the meal that Caudill brought up religion, and he did it directly.

"Mr. Clairborne, are you washed in the blood of the lamb?"

Despite Rathbone's warning, Clairborne had not given a lot of thought to how he should answer.

"I am a Christian, sir. I was instructed in the path as a child in the church my great-great grandfather built. I believe Jesus Christ is my savior, but I also believe that my relationship with my creator is private, and I recall distinctly my father's admonition to be wary of those who talked publicly about their own piety. He often cited Matthew five six as his reference."

Caudill reacted to Clairborne's answer with a guffaw and a slap of his leathery hand on the starched tablecloth.

"By heavens, sir, your father was right. It's the deed that gets recorded in the golden book, not jawin' about deeds."

As the conversation shifted to a discussion of the individual cowhands Caudill and the other emerging cattle barons employed, it quickly became clear to Clairborne that he lacked a number of what prospective employers considered basic job skills.

"How are you with a lariat, Mr. Clairborne? Most hands use a rope way more'n they use anything else, including a firearm."

Clairborne swallowed before answering, assuming his answer would kill any chance of getting hired. He decided to tell the truth, knowing that if he didn't, he would be proven a prevaricator the first time he threw a rope in front of an audience.

"Can't say I've ever touched a rope, sir. Sorry, but it's true."

"I assume, being a Virginia boy, you can stay on the hurricane deck of a pony trying its best to give you a taste of gravel?"

Clairborne recalled countless fox hunts in Virginia and stag hunts in France, galloping full tilt through fields, vaulting his mounts over fallen trees and streams, stone walls, and hedgerows.

"Yes, sir. I believe I can ride with the best. I know my horses and what it takes to care for them."

Caudill took a break from the assault on his dinner plate and leaned back in his chair. "Well, Mr. Clairborne, are you in possession of any other attributes that commend you to the cowboy life with all its vicissitudes?"

"I understand, sir, that my accomplishments are modest and my experience is thin when it comes to the hard life you've been describing." A small smile spread across his face. "I guess I would say that I am an excellent shot with a long gun, that I am a man of my word and have a fair singing voice."

Clairborne paused.

"I understand not much of that cuts the mustard when it comes to cowboying, but if I can memorize Shakespeare's sonnets, I figure I'm a pretty quick study, and I sure want to see the elephant and make my mark..."

He caught the quick exchange of glances between the Caudills at mention of the Bard.

"Shakespeare, huh? Don't know what good that would do you on a drive, but it sure is a good thing to know when you're hunkered down for months in the winter. How good are you with numbers?"

While considering his response, Clairborne decided to couch his answer in terms of relevance. He was quite certain that as basic as was his knowledge of algebraic equations and Pythagorean theory, it was way, way more than that of most men chasing beeves around the prairie.

"Yes, sir, I believe I can navigate numbers better than most," he said.

"Well, that's good," Caudill said. Turning to his son, he added, "Sam, what do you think about Mr. Clairborne here taking care of the calf wagon until he learns a mite about ropin'?"

His son nodded his approval while demolishing a third of an apple pie a la mode. Caudill looked at Clairborne and said, "Boys that can throw a hoolihan are about a dime a dozen, but somebody who can sit a horse and not get lost in account books is kind of rare. You show up at the Rocking C, and we'll find something to keep the dust from settlin' on your sombrero."

After dinner, Rathbone led the group to an elegant room featuring French doors leading to a small formal garden at the rear of the hotel. There the men selected cigars from Rathbone's humidor, participating in the quiet ceremony of lighting each other's smokes before taking their seats on the carved stone benches and wrought-iron chairs lining the crushed-gravel paths.

Examining the ash of his panatela, Caudill turned his head and said, "Mr. Clairborne, you were not in the war, as I understand."

"No, sir."

"Have you ever seen a dead man, a man die a violent death?"

Clairborne's memory flashed to the Nashville alley. He wondered if there was any possibility Caudill somehow knew about what happened there. He decided there wasn't.

"No, sir, I haven't," he lied.

Caudill slowly exhaled a cloud of blue smoke and watched it hang in the still night air.

"Reason I ask is that out on the plains, things can go sideways faster than greased lightning. Men can be at their worst same time others right beside them are at their best. Hard to tell who's gonna go which way most of the time."

"Yes, sir."

"You have a firearm?"

"Yes, sir, my father's Parker double sixteen and my brother's LeMat."

Caudill nodded. "I assume you know how to use both. Want some advice?"

Clairborne leaned forward and nodded. "I certainly do, sir."

"You'll do well to acquire a rifle as well. Single shot'll do. Repeater's probably better if'n you can afford it.

"Main thing is stoppin' what needs to be stopped. If'n you can do that with one shot, fine. If not, may want to invest in a repeater." Shifting his cigar to his left hand and pointing his right at Clairborne, he said, "You understand I'm talking about people as well as critters such as snakes and bears. You ever seen a grizzly?"

"No, sir, but I sure would like to."

Caudill smiled. "They ain't as many of them as they used to be, but trust me on this: you want to see a grizz, you go to a zoo. You don't want to run into one in the wild.

"So here's my advice," Caudill said, leaning forward and stroking his beard with his gnarled right hand. "You'll find most folks are good, hard-working, generous, like I said. But there are some of the baddest actors on earth west of here, and there ain't no law most places. That means you have to be ready at all times to take care of yourself."

Turning his face upward toward the crescent moon, Caudill said, "Son, we live in hard times, and Texas is a hard place—mebbe the hardest—but a man who ain't afraid of honest sweat and occasional disappointment can find Texas a fine place to spend his allotted time.

"But..." Caudill paused, and for a moment his lips trembled, and Clairborne thought the patriarch of the plains might be about to weep. "But you got to earn Texas. You got to be worthy of what it has to offer. If you aren't, Texas'll kill you and scatter your bones to the wind.

"So here's my last word on it. Hobble your horses at night. Keep the LeMat within reach and your long gun across your saddlebow. Try not to travel solo, but be dang good and careful who you do ride with."

Caudill turned back around, took another deep draw on his cigar, and paused again. "Mr. Clairborne, hope you don't take offense, but you're as green as my mother's eyes, so you'll do best to watch out for desperadoes and ne'er-do-wells of all stripes. And one more thing..."

"Sir?" Clairborne said.

"Was I you, I'd put that fancy watch where nobody else can see it. You sure as blazes won't need it on the plains, and wearin' something that shiny'll draw bandits like road apples draw blow flies. Hope you don't mind me saying so."

Clairborne leaned back in his seat and looked at the ash on his own cigar for a long moment. "Not at all, sir. I'm thankful to be reminded of just how much I don't know."

—◆—

After the Caudills' departure, Clairborne and Rathbone shared some vintage port and light banter, most of which focused on the guests of the evening. Later, Clairborne knew better than to try sleeping. His mind was so busy; there were so many things to decide that he knew sleep was not possible. On the matter of rifles, Clairborne faced the fact that while

Caudill's advice was undoubtedly sound, he, Clairborne, was running low on cash reserves.

Recognition that he was again considering budgets and personal finances brought a smile. Never in his life had he cared about money. He had always considered himself to be a man of modest material desires, unlike most of his peers in both Virginia and France who insisted on the latest in horses, fashion, and firearms. He, on the other hand, had always been content with whatever his brother handed down to him or his parents provided. Of all the material possessions he'd owned, the only thing he could recall purchasing for himself was a Wilkenson epee and scabbard he'd seen in a Richmond shop when he was fourteen.

Lying on his bed with his hands behind his head, he made a decision. If he could find a cartridge-firing rifle and fifty rounds of ammunition for not more than thirty dollars, he would buy it. If not, he would rely on his LeMat and the Parker double for protection and meat.

As the morning light came up and his energy wore down, he heard a soft tapping on the door. Opening it, he was surprised to see Rathbone holding an envelope.

"This wire just arrived. Hope it's not bad news." He excused himself after handing Clairborne the yellow paper and saying, "Don't hesitate to let me know if there is anything I can do."

Clairborne used his finger to open the envelope.

DEAR TUCKER - STOP - MY MEETING WITH GOV. GENERAL SCHOFIELD RESULTED IN RETAINING WARWICK - STOP - HIS BROTHER IS COL. GEO. SCHOFIELD, CMDR OF FT.

LEAVENWORTH - STOP - WISH YOU TO THANK COL. SCHOFIELD FOR HIS BROTHER'S ASSISTANCE - STOP - LOVE, MOTHER, AMY - STOP

The telegram created more confusion than clarity. Why had his mother sought the "assistance" of the Yankee general who was the Union's proconsul in Richmond, exercising life-or-death decisions over every aspect of contemporary Virginia? The victorious Yankees called it Reconstruction, appointing a military governor for each of the former members of the Confederate States of America. These men were all active general officers in the Union Army, presiding over the punitive measures enacted in Washington to dismember the society that had risen in rebellion.

So what had caused his mother to seek assistance from this sworn enemy? Why had this same man apparently provided that unidentified assistance to his family?

Downstairs in the lobby, he encountered Rathbone seated in an alcove, enjoying his first cup of coffee. As usual, Rathbone had a pragmatic approach to Clairborne's problem. He suggested they visit an editor friend at the *Saint Louis Post* to see what news had come from Virginia that might be relevant to Clairborne's situation.

The meeting was both enlightening and embarrassing for him.

Enlightening because there had been a series of articles printed in both editions of the paper over the last two days that fleshed out the telegram with relevant detail. Embarrassing because his ignorance of the articles illustrated his disdain for current affairs, even as they affected his home.

Boiled down to its simplest elements, it seemed that the military governor of Virginia had vetoed a state legislature attempt to confiscate all land holdings larger than twenty-five acres. His decision stunned not only Virginians of all stripes but also sent shock waves across the entire country, the northern portion of which was angered by his "softness" while Southerners who faced similar threats in their states rejoiced in this unexpected example of "fairness."

It was further reported on the front pages that the general in question, John Schofield, was a Missourian who had risen to fame in the Union Army and in the last twenty-four hours had been named by President Andrew Johnson to be the new secretary of war.

After reading the articles and dispatches, however, Clairborne remained ignorant of the role his mother had played in bringing about this legislative coup.

Before agreeing to meet with Mrs. Mary Bassett Clairborne, Major General John McAllister Schofield requested and received a thorough vetting of the lady in question. He already knew she was the wife of a fellow graduate of West Point. Captain William Clairborne had been his first commanding officer after Schofield's June 1853, graduation and subsequent assignment to the artillery. He recalled those distant days with deep affection. Clairborne was one of the best commanding officers Schofield ever had, a role model in the truest sense—stern but fair, demanding but flexible, good with his subordinates, and first and foremost, a leader in deeds, not just words.

The bald but heavily bearded Schofield knew of the Clairborne connection to Virginia when he took the office of the state's military governor. He also knew of the deaths of William and Peyton Clairborne. He was thankful he'd never faced his former commander on any of the war's battlefields, an occurrence all too common for the brethren of West Point who found themselves on the opposite ends of the guns during the organized slaughter ironically known by the oxymoron "Civil War."

Schofield made it a matter of policy not to mix personal relations with official duty, so he had not called on the Clairbornes even though their residence was less than a day's ride from the repaired Richmond mansion he occupied.

When his aide brought him the letter from Mary Clairborne requesting an audience, he promptly acquiesced knowing that failure to do so would be an egregious breech of etiquette.

His decision was also facilitated by the secret knowledge that he was about to be named as the new secretary of war in the Johnson cabinet.

The incumbent secretary, Edwin Stanton, a radical Republican outraged by Johnson's refusal to impose more draconian measures on the South, had simply worn out his welcome in the administration of the man who had become president when an out-of-work actor fired his Derringer pistol into the head of Abraham Lincoln.

Four days after Schofield received Mary Clairborne's letter, an aide announced her entrance to his splendid office.

Mary Clairborne still wore the black widow's weeds required by the loss of her husband. She affected no makeup other than light powder—no rouge or lip color. Her scent was subdued. Her brown hair, threaded with silver, was parted in the middle and pulled back to a tight bun that supported her black bonnet. She removed her black lace glove to shake hands with the governor, who advanced from his desk.

"My dear Mrs. Clairborne. Allow me to tell you how sorry I am for the loss of your husband and your son. I so regret the deaths of such men, not only for the pain it causes their kin but also for the impact on our nation."

She curtsied slightly and replied, "How very gracious of you to say so, General."

They took their seats around the low, glass-topped walnut table, and servants poured tea from sterling sets.

"I know you are a very busy man, General, so I will be as direct as possible," she said. "I hope that my brevity should not be seen as discourtesy. I suspect you are subjected to a steady stream of visitors importuning you for one thing or another."

Smoothing nonexistent wrinkles on her dress with both hands, she continued, "I don't presume to speak for anyone else, although the situation in question affects scores of others. As a woman, I would never be elected to present this case to you, but I do so because I despaired of my male counterparts ever arriving at consensus on a common approach to the matter. I assume you are aware of certain draft legislation aimed at breaking up large land holdings in Virginia?"

Schofield put down his cup and said, "Indeed I am, madam."

"I am here to ask you to exercise your veto power on that legislation for three reasons, each of which I believe to be compelling."

Her hands folded in her lap, light brown eyes locked on his, Mary Clairborne said, "First, the measure would utterly destroy any chance of the state recovering its economic health for decades. The legislation does not define what happens to the land after it is confiscated, and it contains no provisions for assistance to new owners for things like livestock and seed.

"Second, it completely ignores the state of flux regarding markets for Virginia's agricultural products."

Keeping her hands in her lap, she leaned slightly forward and said, "And third and most compelling, General, is that passage of this infamous act would do more to fill the ranks of the Ku Klux Klan than any conceivable act of man.

"I will not presume to tell you what your duty is or to whom you owe it, sir, nor will I presume to tell you how odious are the acts of many Klansmen or that desperation and fear are the Klan's prime recruiters. I believe, sir, the Klan is today only a flickering flame, but passage of this act will ignite a conflagration that will consume us all, evil and good, lawless and law-abiding."

Standing and extending her hand, she said, "I am unable to articulate my appreciation for your time, General. In leaving, I will also tell you that I decided to try to see you because I believe you to be guided by the same motto that guided my beloved husband. I speak, of course, of the words engraved on the granite walls of Thayer Hall: 'Duty, Honor, Country.' I bid you good day, sir."

With that, Mary Clairborne curtsied, turned, and walked from the room, head erect, leaving in her wake a stunned silence finally broken when Schofield said to his young aide, "Mothers like that, my boy, are what made Southern men so strong in battle...."

In his last act as military governor of Virginia before departing for his new post in Washington, Major General John MacAllister Schofield vetoed the Land Redistribution Act, sent to him by the Virginia legislature. Explanation of his decision was contained in his handwriting on the cover page of the bill.

"This act would do more harm than good. John M. Schofield. Military Governor, Virginia."

———

Descending the stairs from his room to the lobby, Clairborne was glad but not surprised to see the smiling face of Arthur Rathbone.

"You're up mighty early," Clairborne said.

"I wanted to see you off on your adventure. You're probably in a hurry, but I wondered if I could provide you with a good breakfast and the best coffee you're likely to enjoy for quite a while," Rathbone said, taking Clairborne's elbow and steering him to a splendidly set table at the back of the empty dining room.

After they'd finished the omelets, ham, bacon, pancakes soaked in sorghum syrup, and biscuits with peach preserves, Rathbone leaned away from the table and wiped his mustache with the starched white napkin bearing the hotel's embroidered monogram, "Mr. Clairborne—" he began.

"Sorry to cut you off, but the fact is that I feel we have become friends. Please do me the honor of calling me Tucker."

"I would be honored indeed, Tucker, and your saying that reinforces what I was about to say."

"Pray continue," Clairborne said with a nod.

"It may be entirely presumptuous of me to address my concern explicitly, may even be a touch insulting to you, but be that as it may, I feel compelled to caution you about some of the specific hazards you may face as you travel west of here."

Clairborne toyed with the handle of his butter knife. "Are we talking about weather, animals, or humans?" he said, grinning.

"Actually, the last. I assume you have heard of the James Brothers, Jesse and Frank?

"I have indeed. Who hasn't?"

"Well, you should understand the risks of riding directly into the heart of their 'territory,' so to speak." Rathbone sipped his coffee before continuing. "And it's not just the James brothers. They really don't seem to bother individuals. But to be blunt, western Missouri is literally crawling with outlaws and road agents. Many of them are like the James brothers, former Confederate irregulars who rode with Quantrill's Raiders who cannot adjust to peace—or who prefer the outlaw way of life."

Everyone knew of the bloody history of the region, even young Americans who had been living in France during the Civil War. The conflict between pro-slavery Missouri and pro-emancipation Kansas erupted long before the first cannon were fired at Fort Sumpter and had produced atrocities so terrible they became the stuff of conversation even in Europe.

Clairborne knew why the authorities had been unable to capture the James brothers. Since their first big bank robbery in February of 1866, they roamed across the region with apparent impunity, evading posses and troops of cavalry alike. And the reason for their slipperiness could be found in the lubrication provided by the local populace. In the minds of most in western Missouri, the James brothers and the young men who rode with them were "local boys," and their attacks on banks and, lately, railroads, were attacks on wealthy "outsiders." Fear and sympathy, Clairborne knew, were the best guarantors of security, just as was the case with the Ku Klux Klan back east.

"Based not only on what I've read but also on what I've heard directly from my guests, you would be well advised never to ride alone. It simply isn't safe, Tucker. And the road between here and Fort Leavenworth is heavily traveled enough that finding someone reputable to ride with shouldn't slow you down."

"I appreciate your counsel, Arthur," Clairborne said as he pushed back from the table and stood. "It's been very good of you to see to my needs so completely." He extended his hand. "I look forward to seeing you again, my friend, and I wish you good fortune." As they shook hands, Clairborne added with a grin, "And who knows. If I make my fortune, I may just be looking for a cool, calm place to retire, some place in the Ozarks perhaps..."

Outside in the overcast dawn, Clairborne was not surprised to see his horses waiting for him, packed, fed, watered, and, sensing travel ahead, stamping feet impatiently.

He double-checked his bridle, cinch, saddle, and saddlebags on Bucephalus and then examined the lead rope, bridle, and the diamond hitches that secured the pack on his other horse, Ajax. He found it to be perfectly tied and tightened, the canvas folded to drain rainwater to the bottom of the pack instead of trapping it next to the items it covered.

Turning to the bellboy holding his reins, assistant manager Frank, and Arthur, Clairborne dispensed a dollar to the boy and a fiver to Frank—understanding in so doing why their eyes bulged at his generosity.

"You folks took care of me. I appreciate that." He swung gracefully up to his saddle and adjusted the belted holster housing the massive LeMat revolver under his coat. Touching the brim of his hat with his right hand, Clairborne said, "Adieu, my friends," turned his horses, and rode west down Choteau Avenue.

The choice of trails and byways west from Saint Louis offered Clairborne options ranging from the volume of fellow travelers sharing the turnpike in question to the likelihood of finding acceptable accommodations along the way. Before departing, he decided to spend most of his journey acclimating to the environment and learning from experience what he needed to know about taking care of himself, his horses, and his kit without assistance from anyone else. Increasing independence was a major component of his excitement about what lay ahead. It was for that reason that he also opted to take the least-heavily traveled route. It was not so much that he sought solitude per se, he told himself, it was the fact that he had already taken a hardy dislike to teamsters, whom he considered loud, crude, smelly, and incredibly profane.

They jammed the main thoroughfares of Saint Louis, and most of them heading west took their eight-mule, double-hitched rigs on the turnpikes that either crossed the Missouri at Saint Charles or followed the river on its south bank through Jefferson City.

Heading southwest from Saint Louis, Clairborne spent the first night in a small but lively town called Fenton. It was an easy twenty-two miles and boasted a clean hotel. The more circuitous route Clairborne chose west from Fenton took him through the uplands that bordered Rathbone's favored Ozarks. He hoped this less-direct route would be cooler and offer more solitude and fewer teamsters.

The second day of the trip began with an early start, no particular end point in mind, and cool, cloudless skies still strewn with morning stars when he mounted and swung west on the pike.

A little after noon, it began to drizzle. Clairborne put on his waxed canvas slicker while his horses drank at the ford of a small creek. Midway through the afternoon, the drizzle turned to rain. By evening, the rain turned to a torrential downpour.

Observing that the storm soaking through his slicker at least lacked lightening, he sought the cover of the largest tree he could find adjacent to the trail, eventually selecting a huge oak. Its canopy provided only partial relief from the pounding storm, but a little was better than none, so Clairborne set about reliev-ing his horses of their respective loads, feeding and watering them and finally tying them to a picket line he set up between two stout saplings at the edge of the oak's canopy.

Then he set about taking care of his own needs, quickly recognizing that a fire was out of the question and that the only thing worth the effort was avoiding as much of the streaming downpour as he could. Minutes later, sitting under a tarp already sagging ominously from the weight of the water accumulating on it, Clairborne smiled at his situation.

It was simply the worst physical discomfort he had ever known. He looked at his horses. Both were still steaming. Clairborne wished he could rub them down with a dry cloth and get them under better shelter. Ajax regarded him with a look Clairborne interpreted as a rebuke, recognizing that this was also the first time either horse had been subjected to such prolonged exposure to inclement weather. He also noted that Bucephalus was studiously ignoring him. Clairborne decided his black mount was concentrating on how best to extract vengeance from his rider for this thoroughly unpleasant experience.

The rain continued without cessation for the next two days.

Wet to the bone, hungry, and more tired than he had been in his life, Clairborne decided to seek a homestead, a farm, anything that would provide cover for him and his horses. So thick were the clouds that darkness came much earlier than would have been the case on a clear day.

If he hadn't glanced to his left, he would have missed the pinprick of light in the distance, light that could only mean one thing: other humans residing in a structure they might share.

A half mile off the pike, he approached what turned out to be a small farm with two outbuildings, one perhaps serving as a barn, although it was more of a shed. The other was a lean-to sheltering a paltry collection of equipment, the largest of which was a plow. To the right of the one-story clapboard, unpainted house, a field of young corn rows marched down a slight grade to the forest edge. A pig studied Clairborne's approach from beneath a wagon. A rooster emerged from behind the barn and clucked aggressively, equally upset at the intrusion of the stranger and the indignity of being wet through his green-black plumage.

A fitful curl of smoke emerged from the squat stone chimney, but since it drifted away from Clairborne, it brought no hint of what might be warming on the fire inside. Two mottled curs howled at him from beneath the porch, fangs bared, backs and legs rigid with aggression.

Clairborne's shouted "Hello the house!" increased the canine chorus and drew the smaller of the two into the rain, where it overtly challenged the newcomers.

Watching the planked door fastened to its frame with leather hinges, he saw it open just enough to expose the twin black eyes of a double-barrel shotgun staring out at him from the gloom within.

"Whatch'you want, mister?" a reedy male voice inquired. "And who the blazes are you comin' up on my land in the darkness?"

"I'm just a traveling man headed west. I'd surely appreciate a chance to get out of this rain for a while, tuck my horses under a roof if I could."

"Well, you ain't gonna get that around here. You could be some damn road agent far's I know. Now you get the hell of my land 'fore I decide to ventilate you proper," the voice said.

"Sir, I'd be willing to pay for some time in your shed yonder. Don't even want to come into your home. I just want to get out of this downpour for a while," Clairborne said. He simply could not believe such a reasonable request for hospitality could be denied. "This is all some kind of misunderstanding," he told himself.

"You deaf? I said get off my land." The octave of the voice went up along with the shotgun muzzles, which moved from the unseen man's waist level to being sighted at shoulder height.

"All right, all right, I'm going," Clairborne said in disbelief. "I hope the Lord softens your heart, mister. Good day," he said as he turned and started down the path away from the farm.

Halfway back to the road, his anger at the inhospitable treatment mounting, he heard a voice from behind him. Turning in his saddle, he saw a barefoot boy splashing through the mud as he ran after Clairborne from the house.

"Mister, my ma got after pa, sayin' it ain't Christian to turn you out. They say it's all right for you to put up for the night in the barn. I'll take you back and help you with them horses. Only thing is, pa don't want you in the house."

"Sonny," Clairborne said, "I'm so dang glad to get out of this rain, I'd stay put in a pig pen if it were dry. Swing on up here, and let's get out of this before we both drown."

The barn was surprisingly neat, and to Clairborne's delight, it didn't leak. Two mules and a jersey cow regarded his arrival from their stalls, their fresh manure adding a pungent edge to the aroma of sweet hay in the loft. Hanging on the plank wall were a whipsaw, a sledgehammer, two drawknives, a pair of tongs, a shovel, and a pickax. The loft above half the floor space was full of hay, and beside the ladder leading to the loft was a worn pitchfork.

After stripping the pack from his bay and removing the saddle from his mount, Clairborne rubbed the horses down with handfuls of straw and then fed and watered them from buckets he filled from the rain barrel outside under an eave. His horses cared for, he unfolded the canvas covering his pack, spreading it out to expedite drying and noting with satisfaction that the contents were only damp, not soaked through as he feared they would be after the three-day downpour. Opening his valise, Clairborne recovered dry clothing, stripped off his wet attire, and chafed his skin with the wool blanket he planned to wrap around himself in a few moments when he finally lay down to rest.

As he pulled dry trousers over his fresh long underwear, the barn door slid back to reveal the boy and a man. The boy carried a bowl with a blue-and-white-checkered gingham napkin covering its contents. The man carried the double-barreled shotgun. Of indeterminate age, the man radiated displeasure as he stood by the door and watched the boy approach Clairborne with the food.

"Ma wanted you to have somethin' to eat. It's good mush, 'n they's a chunk o' cornbread," the boy said as he placed the bowl on a log round that served as a seat and a base for splitting firewood.

"Well, sonny, that's right Christian of your ma. You tell her how much I appreciate her kindness. Especially since I haven't had a hot meal in three days," Clairborne said. Nodding to the man, he added, "And thank you, sir, as well. I sure appreciate getting out of that dang rain."

"You can save yer thanks, mister," the man said as he spat tobacco juice on the packed dirt floor. "Was up to me, you'd be riding that fancy horse o' yourn' down the pike a piece."

"Well, thanks anyways, mister. I'll get out of you hair at daybreak," Clairborne said, instantly wondering if the already illtempered host would be offended by reference to hair when his head clearly lacked any.

Turning to leave, the man said, "Tommy, you bring the bowl and spoon back to the house soon as he's done, y'unnerstan'?"

Without looking at the man, the boy said "Yessir" over his shoulder and continued to contemplate Clairborne as he ate.

"Mighty fine mush, sonny. Your ma's a good cook. I'll be done in a minute so's you can get on back to the house like your daddy wants," Clairborne said as he wiped his chin with the napkin.

"Ain't my daddy. My daddy's dead and gone. Abe's my stepdaddy since about two months ago," the boy said as he sat down on the straw-covered dirt floor.

Clairborne paused. "Sorry to hear about your dad. You got a nice home here, though."

"Nice enough, I reckon. You a lawman?" the boy asked, resting his head in both hands, elbows on the patched trouser knees.

"A lawman? Heavens no. Why'd you ask me that?" Clairborne said, putting down the bowl.

"'Cause Abe said nobody uses the road much 'cept neighbors and outlaws, and you was too fancy to be a outlaw, so you must be law. Said far's he's concerned, that's as bad as you bein' a bandit."

"Well, sonny, I'm surely neither," Clairborne said as he resumed eating. "I'm just a traveler heading west."

"How come you're on the Sedalia road 'stead of Columbia pike like most folks?"

"To tell you the truth, that's why. Lots of teamsters and lots of traffic on the main pike," Clairborne said, shaking his head. "I just wanted a little more solitude, that's all."

"What's solitude?"

"It means being by yourself." Recalling Rathbone's warning, Clairborne asked, "Lots of bandits around here, are there?"

Without hesitation, the boy nodded and said, "Yup. Sure are." He stood up and looked around as if to see whether his stepfather had returned. Approaching Clairborne, he held out his hand and said, "I'll take that if you're finished. Got my chores to do 'fore turnin' in."

Clairborne gave him the bowl and wooden spoon. "Thanks again to your ma and to you too."

The boy turned and left without another word.

Clairborne stared at the barn door, wondering why the initially friendly youngster so suddenly changed moods and departed. It occurred to him that the change happened when the subject turned to outlaws, clearly a sensitive topic hereabouts, considering as well the singular focus on that topic evinced by the boy's stepfather.

"Where there's smoke..." Clairborne said to himself as he climbed the ladder to the hayloft. Burrowing into the aromatic hay and pulling his blanket over his bare feet, Clairborne reveled in appreciation of his new condition; warm, dry, and full was good. Cold, wet, and hungry was bad. Before surrendering to the tug of soft slumber, he resolved to put such elementary notions much higher on his list of priorities than they had been up to now. Then he fell asleep.

—— ∿ ——

Amazed at what a difference a day made, Clairborne opened his eyes to see the bottom of a shingle roof, his nose suffused with the sweet smell of hay, his ears noting the absence of rain pounding on the shingles.

Yesterday, his existence was defined by physical misery. Today, astride his black, his belly full of cornmeal mush, a biscuit, and a cup of coffee, he was again headed west under a cloud-filtered morning sun, cosseted by a freshening zephyr. The forest closed in to within a few feet of the rutted roadway. The large oaks, beeches, and elms that dominated the woods were a paradise for songbirds, cardinals, grosbeaks, robins, and finches, each intent on establishing its territory or attracting a mate. Two hours into the ride, his mount snorted and pricked its ears. Something was ahead.

The something turned out to be two horsemen who rounded a bend at a canter less than twenty yards away. Both riders were young and lean, clearly not city boys. Both wore unbuttoned wool coats, and the older of the two wore a long feather, almost a plume, sticking out of the gray silk hatband surrounding the rounded crown of his broad-brimmed hat. The younger rider's hat was not as flamboyant. Both were clean shaven. Both tucked their trousers into high, muddy boots. Only the younger one smiled as they approached.

The older one spoke first. "Howdy, stranger. Fine day for riding, ain't it?"

Clairborne reined in his mount while a twenty-foot gap remained between them.

"It surely is, 'specially compared to the last few days. I thought I was going to drown while I was still astride," Clairborne said, removing his hat and running his hand over his hair.

Both riders chuckled and then leaned forward, resting their forearms on their saddlebows.

"Where you headed?" the older rider asked.

"As many times as I've been asked, you'd think I'd have a better answer than just 'heading west,' but that's about all there is to it."

"That's a fine-looking mount, mister," the young one said. "Matter of fact, both of them horses is fine looking, for sure."

"Thanks," Clairborne said.

"You ain't travelin' light, are you, taking a packhorse along with you an' all," the young one said.

Before Clairborne could respond, the young rider added, "That's a nice watch chain you got, an' I'll wager there's a mighty fine watch attached to it. What do ya' think, Frank?"

"Bet you're right, little brother," the older rider said.

At the mention of his Breguet watch, Clairborne's mind raced to a killing in a Nashville alley and a dinner table warning in Saint Louis. He silently cursed himself for continuing to wear the watch in a place where time, as measured in hours, minutes, and seconds, no longer mattered. He wondered if he could get to the LeMat in its holster under his coat and quickly recognized that retrieving his side arm in a timely fashion was not an option, ensconced as it was in the army holster that covered the gun with a large flap. The flap and the brass stud that secured it were designed to protect the gun from the elements and to prevent it from falling out of the holster during a full gallop. It also prevented anything approaching a rapid retrieval of the weapon in emergencies—which Clairborne's intuition told him was quickly developing.

"Mind if I take a look at that watch of yourn?" the older rider asked.

"Yeah, actually I do," Clairborne said without thinking—then said to himself, "Oh hell, things are going to get ugly again over my damn watch, and this time it'll be the death of me."

"Now, how about that Jesse," the older rider said to the younger one. "Don't that beat all. I just want to look at the man's timepiece, and he don't want to let me."

"Strikes me as downright hostile," the younger one said, maintaining his smile.

"Gents, I surely don't mean to come across that way at all," Clairborne said, mustering a smile of his own as he absentmindedly passed his left hand over the vest pocket holding the Breguet. "It's just that this was my daddy's, and it's the only thing of his I still have, so I'm kind of careful about it. Maybe too much so, I admit, but that's just the way it is."

The older rider leaned forward as Clairborne's hand passed over the watch.

"Careful, there, mister," he said. "Careful where you're putting your hands. We don't want a misunderstanding about your intentions now, do we?"

Recognizing the riders could have interpreted his movement as reaching for a weapon, Clairborne used the index fingers and thumbs of both hands to pull back the edges of his jacket.

"Gentlemen, as you can see, I'm heeled, but not in a way that would allow me to draw without giving you about ten minutes' notice."

Again the riders chuckled.

"Dang boy, I like your style," the older rider said, slapping his thigh. "Say, is that a Confederate buckle on that gun belt?"

Clairborne looked down at the buckle bearing the large engraved letters CSA at his waist. "Sure is. Belonged to my brother."

"Why ain't he wearin' it then?" the younger one asked.

"Yankees got him at Cold Harbor," Clairborne said.

His answer quieted the two riders for a long moment. The older turned to his companion and said, "Well, what do you think, Jesse? Should we let this ole Southern boy take his daddy's watch and ride on?"

The younger rider contemplated Clairborne for another long moment.

"You know who we are, mister?"

It was at that moment Clairborne realized he knew the answer to the young rider's question. "Well, I heard you call him Frank, and he addressed you as Jesse, so if I were to bet, I'd wager your family name just might be James."

"Well, you'd win the pot. That's who we are," Jesse said with a lopsided grin. "Now here's the bargain me and brother Frank are going to make with you. You ready to bargain?"

Confronted by two of the most famous outlaws of the age, Clairborne didn't waste time asking himself why he deserved such bad luck. Instead, he felt himself calming down, taking a deep breath to best face what was coming. He was pleased and surprised that considering the imminent violence he felt was inevitable, instead of panic, a wave of serenity washed over him. He looked up at the leafy canopy, heard the call of a mocking-bird, thought of his mother, and said to himself, "What the hell? This is as good a place to die as any."

Turning his gaze back to the James brothers, he said, "Sure. As long as I'm not bargaining with my honor, I'm game."

Slapping his thigh again, Frank said, "Dang, I do like his style, Jesse."

Jesse maintained his grin. "If you swear you won't tell nobody you talked the James boys out of robbing you, me and Frank will bid you adieu and farewell. What do you say to that, Southern boy?"

Relief flooded through his body, and Clairborne tried his best to maintain his composure. He smiled and doffed his hat with a cavalier's sweep. "A capital idea, gentlemen."

"Well then, adieu and farewell," Jesse said.

Frank and Jesse James wheeled their mounts off the road and entered the forest, but not before Frank turned in his saddle, waved, and shouted, "I do like your style!"

—⁓—

At twilight camp, Clairborne finished his beans and bacon, threw more wood on the fire, and retrieved his father's flask from the valise. The sips of bourbon he allowed himself slid down his throat and percolated into his system. Resting against the mammoth trunk of a splendid sycamore, he still could barely believe he had emerged from an encounter with Frank and Jesse James not only with all of his physical possessions but also with his body intact, and he wondered if the stories he'd heard about the two were true before deciding they couldn't be, not completely.

What he'd heard about the James boys before he met them—that they were cold-blooded murderers and plunderers—simply didn't square with the two men who not only let him go but did so with a sense of humor. They struck him as two wild fellows having a whale of a good time. But he also recalled Frank James's keen attention to hand movements as well as the way he and Jesse wore their weapons. Both rode up with their coats open to allow unfettered access to their side arms. On reflection, Clairborne realized Frank's holster was unusual because it seemed to be cut down in front to fully expose the hammer and trigger guard of what appeared to be an 1860 Colt Army .44 caliber. Contemplation of how Frank James wore his side arm reminded him that the flap covering his own LeMat made drawing it quickly an impossibility. Reaching down beneath the wool blanket covering the lower half of his body, Clairborne pulled the holstered LeMat into view and studied the holster and gun belt without removing the gun. Speaking out loud to his brother's pistol, he said, "You're not going to do me a whole lot of good if I can't lay hands on you when I need you."

Removing the massive LeMat from its holster, Clairborne ran his hands over its European walnut stock and its blued octagonal barrel. He turned the cylinder to examine each of the nine .44 lead bullets it held and then accessed what was considered to be the defining characteristic of the handgun that had been a favorite of Confederate soldiers fortunate enough to own one: beneath the main barrel was another cylinder holding a twenty-gauge shotgun shell. The shell was stuffed with buckshot, chunks of lead that on their way from muzzle to target made a distinctive sound. Yankees called it "the blue whistler." The total firepower of the LeMat was greater than that offered by any other handgun of the era. Combined with its balance and reliability, the LeMat's lethality made it the most valuable of Clairborne's practical possessions. The fact that the gun had been his brother's only deepened his affection for the weapon.

Raising his eyes to the night sky, Clairborne smiled at the memory of his older brother and wished he could recount to him the events of the last twenty-four hours. Then he initiated what would become an inflexible routine in the life of Tucker Lightfoot Clairborne. Instead of returning the pistol to its holster and then putting the rig away for the night, he slid his pistol under the saddle serving as his pillow. Without a conscious decision, he slowly moved the hammer to half cock and placed the gun where he could instantly retrieve it when and if this western adventure produced a threat that would materialize with little or no warning. He stroked the LeMat's cool metal surface and was reassured by its mass, its history, and its proximity.

A moment later he retrieved his oil-cloth-wrapped journal, opened it, sharpened the pencil with his pocketknife, and collected his thoughts.

———

Clairborne had tried everything he could think of to get comfortable sleeping on the ground. Eleven days into the journey, he was out of ideas and very tired. Eleven days with only one good night's sleep was enough to get anyone out or sorts. He verbalized this opinion to himself while trying to rationalize yelling at Ajax. A good, reliable animal, Ajax nonetheless had picked up the annoying habit of expanding his rib cage when Clairborne tried to secure the pack by tightening the cinch.

Bracing his right boot on the horse's flank, he tugged on the cinch and yelled, "Damn it, Ajax. Don't you blow on me. Damn it! Quit that."

Tucking the cinch under itself, Clairborne stepped away from both horses.

"Swearing at my horses. That's something new."

He walked back to his campfire, removed the coffee pot from the coals, and poured the remains of his morning brew into the blue-enameled cup he'd bought in Saint Louis. He ignored the fact that it was already chipped and sipped the steaming, syrupy liquid. It was nearly an hour since he had placed the pot in the coals. In the interim, he'd repacked his bedroll and prepared both horses for the day ahead. Savoring the last cup, it occurred to him that before this journey, he would never have accepted coffee that looked, tasted, or smelled like this. And the fact that he could chew the grounds that washed into his mouth with each sip only made his changing culinary standards more ironic.

He took off his hat. The sweatband was doing its job. Dark yellow stains circled the silk lining and had spread to the bottom front of the crown where it joined the brim, turning the gray beaver fur felt a deep black. Not long ago, indelible sweat stains would have been just as unacceptable as terrible coffee. The hat would have been thrown away—or given to a house servant—but no more. This was the only hat he had, and he recognized that it was going to get a lot nastier in the not-too-distant future what with all of the dust and sandstorms he'd heard about. He rubbed a finger over the gold lettering of the monogram still visible on the right side of the sweatband, remembering the day he got the hat. He put it back on his head and realized he had no earthly idea how long Toltan Hats had been providing well-made, fashionable hats for Richmond gentlemen—or whether Toltan still had his shop at the corner of Cary and Fifteenth across from the Saint Charles Hotel. He hoped so.

Holding the cup in his right hand, he absent-mindedly reached for the small of his back with his left hand and rubbed the tender spot just above his belt. Only old men were supposed to have sore backs, he told himself, wondering if there was some secret to sleeping comfortably in the open air, some trick to waking up refreshed known only to Indians, trappers, and seasoned cowhands.

At the first fork in the road, the appeal of sound sleep led him to take the branch heading slightly to the northwest, which a hand-carved sign promised would take him and his aching back to the town of Sedalia.

—*ᴧᴧ*—

Pancakes. Pancakes and syrup. Pancakes, syrup, and bacon. And good coffee.

Until the last few weeks, Clairborne had not given much thought to food. He had always enjoyed his meals, particularly when they included good company. But he had never found himself envisioning specific foods, contemplating their consumption or recalling specific details of how he preferred them to be prepared or consumed. His stay in France had enhanced his appreciation of how good food could be, had in fact elevated his gustatory lexicon to include the concept of "cuisine." Still, he was amused by the realization that for the last day, his thoughts had been focused on a stack of buttermilk pancakes so warm from the griddle the butter slathered on each layer melted almost immediately into clear yellow pools. He thought about how the melted butter facilitated absorption of the sweet sorghum syrup poured over the stack, which was then cut into bite-sized sections. He told himself it was easier to spear the pancakes before the bacon. Otherwise, the bacon mashed the pancakes and made them hard to retrieve.

As he rode, reveries of pancakes and bacon led him to aromas, the best of which, he decided, were, first, morning coffee; second, cooking bacon; third, freshly mown hay. What about a good cigar? A fine Bordeaux? The smell of a horse?

Then he wondered why his list didn't contain the scent of a woman. "Do I really like coffee more than females?" he asked himself, deciding not to answer the question right away but to keep it in mind for further consideration, maybe after dinner some dry, cool evening—if such a blessing were ever again to be granted.

In the distance, he spotted a wagon occupied by two males headed in his direction. Pulled by two muddy mules, the wagon was loaded with sacks and boxes and appeared to be leading a Jersey cow.

As he drew closer, Clairborne saw that the man who had been holding the reins passed them to the boy seated beside him and reached into the wagon boot, from which he withdrew what appeared to be an army surplus rifle. Single shot, muzzle-loaded, and accurate up to 150 yards, the weapon fired a .54-caliber lead projectile called a Minié ball, after its French inventor. It was in fact not a ball but a conical projectile, which, coupled with rifling in the weapon's barrel, made it a significant contributor to the carnage of the conflict that had recently ripped the country in half.

"Howdy, friend," Clairborne yelled, waving his right hand to show he had nothing in it while the left held his reins.

"Hello there," the man answered as the boy pulled back on the reins. The mules slowed to a stop, and the man subtly shifted the rifle muzzle to retain its aim at Clairborne.

"Say, you folks know how far it is to Sedalia?" Clairborne asked.

"Why, sure. Just come from there. You should make it by sundown," the man said. "You headin' there to see the hangin'?"

"Hanging? No. Lord no. No, I've no interest in such activity."

The man spat a prodigious stream of tobacco juice and didn't bother to wipe the residue from his prominent chin. "Me neither, though anyone kills a child deserves to get his neck stretched."

Changing the subject, Clairborne said, "Don't suppose you could recommend a hotel or good boarding house, could you?"

That caused the man to guffaw and spit another steam of tobacco juice into the mud.

"I look like the kind o' rich man can spend money on a bed, mister? Tarnation, I ain't got but a straw mattress on the floor for my whole family. Dang if that ain't a dumb question, if you don't mind my sayin' so. No offense meant, y'unnerstan'."

Clairborne smiled. "Nah. None taken. I suppose I can find a place to eat and somewhere to sleep on my own."

"Oh there's plenty of places. I just ain't got enough cash to spend on any of 'em. Don't know that I would even if I could since most of 'em is true dens of iniquity. Yessir, you'd be right smart to avoid most of 'em places for sure," the man said. "Mebbe when they finish building the railroad in a year or so, all them riff-raff'll go build the next railhead and leave Sedalia like it used to be, but I don't think any town ever gets nicer. Always seems to go t' other way."

"Can't argue with that," Clairborne said. "Good day to you, sir."

"And to you too, sir," the man said. "You might want to be careful, mister. They's some bad actors hereabouts. One less after the hangin', but still too dang many. Thought you might be one of 'em, to tell you the truth." Turning on the wagon seat, he yelled, "That wide spot on the road you come to next is Otterville. Sedalia's 'bout fifteen miles ahead of you. Good luck."

The image of Sedalia Clairborne carried as a result of his chat did not square with what he saw as he rode into the outskirts of the town. He spotted small farms, most neatly tended, with groves of trees and glistening oval ponds punctuated with geese and ducks. Sunflowers gazed at him as he rode past.

Clairborne noticed that folks tipped their hats when they looked up from their labor, while most of the roadside curs ignored him completely. The farmsteads gave way to clapboard houses, almost all of which featured front porches, and all of the porches had either a swing or a rocking chair. Some even had both. Dark morning glory vines embraced white picket fences.

"Sure doesn't look like a den of inequity to me," Clairborne said to his horses.

That religious theme segued his thoughts to the string of churches he passed on both sides of what had become a crowned road with drainage ditches on both sides: Baptist, Lutheran, Presbyterian, Methodist, Pentecostal, and Roman Catholic. Lo and behold, even an Episcopal church—slate roof, stone walls, stained glass, and a dark red door mounted on large, black, iron hinges. Episcopalian substantial. The neat black script on the white sign next to the flagstone walk identified the edifice as Saint Andrew's and further informed that Father Gregory Michaels presided over services Sundays at nine in the morning and three in the afternoon while prayer services were held Wednesdays at six in the evening.

Without a conscious decision to do so, Clairborne swung into the churchyard and dismounted, tying his horses to the hitching rail on the right side of the flagstone walkway leading from the road to the church door.

Removing his hat as he entered, Clairborne was pleased with the symmetry of the nave, the comfort derived from the similarity between this small Episcopal church and those of his Virginia home, particularly that of Saint Phillip's, built by his great-great-grandfather and attended faithfully by his family ever since.

Clairborne took a seat in a carved oak pew halfway to the altar, flipped down the kneeling pad, and knelt, head bowed, eyes closed, hands clasped to his lips.

He opened his eyes to see what he assumed was the priest (what was his name again?—oh yes, Father Gregory) face the altar and bow his head. For several minutes, the priest went about his routine without acknowledging Clairborne's presence, and then, after completing the ritual, he turned and caught Clairborne's eye, smiled, and walked through a doorway between the altar and the choir stall.

The lamp representing the Holy Spirit glowed red in the cool, dark interior, and shafts of late afternoon sun slanted through the stained-glass image of Christ triumphant behind the altar. Tranquility reigned. He reached for his watch only to remember he had moved it to an inside coat pocket, away from the view of anyone who might have more than a casual interest in the Swiss chronological wonder.

Thoughts of the watch instantly took him to the Nashville alley. Clairborne looked up from the stone floor and saw the priest sitting across the aisle, his head down, eyes closed, apparently in prayer. His immaculate white surplice covered an ample frame, evidence that the priest enjoyed his meals. His bald head was fringed with gray, close-copped hair, and the lower half of his pink-cheeked face was covered by one of the longest beards Clairborne had ever seen. His visage conveyed benevolence and intelligence, all before the priest spoke a word.

"Good evening, Father. You have a beautiful church."

The priest stood and extended his large right hand. "Thank you, my son. You are new to Sedalia. Welcome to Saint Andrew's. May I offer coffee, Mr....?"

"Clairborne. Tucker Clairborne of Tidewater, Virginia, Father. Please call me Tucker, and yes, I'd like that very much."

The priest led Clairborne to a small but cozy office lined with leather-bound books at the back of the church. The room amplified Clairborne's sense of comfort, his sense of being in familiar environs for the first time in weeks.

"You are a sojourner on your way west, I presume," the priest said as he poured coffee into a china cup on a saucer of the matching pattern, which Clairborne recognized as Royal Doulton. "Sugar, cream?"

"Ah, neither, thank you. I used to use a lot of both. I guess that's one of the ways being on the trail can change you," he said with a smile.

"Ah yes. The simplicity of necessity, as our Quaker friends would say. You are a member of our church, Tucker?"

"Oh yes. Confirmed by the bishop when I was twelve."

"I assumed as much when you said you are a Virginian."

As the idle conversation continued, Clairborne's thoughts focused on a looming question. Why did he turn into the church, and why did Nashville come so quickly and compellingly to mind?

"Father, there is something I would like to discuss with you. I know you're bound to respect the privacy of my words, but I need you to reassure me nonetheless."

The priest maintained unblinking eye contact and nodded.

Father Gregory retrieved the coffee pot, refilled Clairborne's cup and his own, and returned to his chair, which creaked under his weight.

"I, I ah...Father...there's no other way to say this. I killed a man. I stabbed him in the stomach, and then I stabbed him in the throat." Clairborne lowered his head.

"He died right away. I just walked away from him, left him there in that alley." Clairborne looked up. "I don't feel bad about doing it—killing him, Father. I sleep all right. Never lost my appetite. I don't dream about it or anything, but Father, I surely did kill him. I gutted him like a pig."

"Did you attack him without cause?"

"Oh no, Father. He was trying to rob me. He wanted my watch, my father's watch. He was drunk, I think. He had a knife. I won't tell you what he said he would do to me if I didn't give him the watch, but I really thought he would do it. I mean I *knew* he would do it."

Clairborne put his cup down and put his hands together as if in prayer.

"Father, I broke the most important commandment, didn't I? It says, 'Thou shalt not kill,' but I surely did."

Despite the fact that killing the man had affected neither his sleep or his appetite, a surge of emotion rose from his belly. His body trembled. The priest reached over to Clairborne with both hands, placing them on Clairborne's forearms.

"First, my son, you must indulge me in some theological semantics," he said quietly. "Will you humor me for a moment while I share some insight into the commandment in question?"

"Father, I'm interested in anything you can share with me on this. Believe me."

"I, and many, many others in both the Christian and Hebrew faiths believe the commandment does not say 'Thou shalt not kill.' Do you recall in your confirmation classes any references to the Vulgate translations of biblical texts used as the basis of the Saint James version of the Bible?"

Clairborne did not and was mildly embarrassed by inference that he should and his failure to do so. "No sir, I honestly don't."

"You see, Tucker, there are a lot of very wise, very pious people who have spent their lives in pursuit of holiness and knowledge of God's ways who believe the commandment is not 'Thou shalt not kill,' but 'Thou shalt not *murder.*'"

Clairborne instantly understood the semantic difference but just as quickly wondered why this was the first time he had heard it articulated by anyone, especially a churchman.

"He was trying to rob you? He threatened your life, and you believed him?" the priest asked.

"He came at me with a knife, Father. It wasn't just words. He came after me."

"Tucker, you remember your Old Testament, the slayings, the battles, the epic conflicts of the Israelites with their foes."

"Of course, Father. My favorite is David and Goliath. My father told me that faith in God allows believers to defeat nonbelievers even if the foes are mightier in the physical sense."

The priest smiled. "We can talk later, if you like, about that specific message. I don't want to offend you, Tucker, but you might want to consider how it came to pass that the South, with all of its strong Christians, lost to the Philistines from the north, but that is a whole different subject."

Before Clairborne could admit that he was flustered by that very issue, the priest continued.

"The Old Testament's stories of deaths that God approved are the reason so many of us believe that the word 'murder' is the more accurate and relevant. It's all based on ancient Hebrew—which I learned before I went to Palestine to study. The Hebrew word for kill is '*harog*.' The Hebrew word for murder is '*retzach*.' So why does this matter, you may ask? In ancient Hebrew texts, the commandment is written '*lo tirtzach*'—'Thou shalt not murder.'"

The priest leaned forward and said clearly, "That phrase, '*lo tirtzach*," is repeatedly cited as the prohibition against unjust killing, not as some kind of sweeping injunction against all killing. Think of it. It's irrational. Would Abraham have been guilty of murder if he carried out God's command to take his son's life? What about all the slaying and the taking of life on the Bible's battlefields, Sampson, King David? The word '*retzach*' is never used.

"No, Tucker. From the bottom of my heart, I don't believe you committed murder if what you say is true, and only you know that for certain. If it is, a just God will not send you to damnation for what you did. But you will benefit from earnest prayer for the soul of the man you killed...and your own as well. Nothing is more serious than the taking of life, justified or not."

―⁓―

Clairborne spent the next three days as a guest in the Saint Andrew's rectory, sleeping in a feather bed and eating excellent fare prepared by Mrs. Patrick, the priest's elderly, widowed housekeeper. Clairborne attended the Wednesday prayer service, placed a dollar in the collection plate, and sang familiar hymns in a tenor that brought approving glances from worshippers in the pew around him.

When it came time to leave, a vague sadness settled over him. He would have enjoyed more of the priest's company, winter evening dinners with good wine and even better conversation. At the churchyard gate, he noticed the road was jammed with all manner of people heading in the same direction—toward the town center, drawn by the hanging. The mood seemed positively jovial, people calling to one another, laughing, and wearing their Sunday finest.

He rode beside a man on muleback, not speaking until they had to stop because of the crowd massed in front of them.

"I heard the person to be hanged is a boy," Clairborne said.

The man on the mule didn't turn his head to face Clairborne when he responded.

"Yep. And good he's gonna hang afore he gets older and continues his murderin' ways, says I."

"He was caught robbing a bank?"

"Uh huh. Them Creeches got to thinkin' they was the James boys. Tried knockin' off our bank couple weeks ago. Couldn't even knock off a ole tar-paper bank like that'n. Got all crossed ways with the town folk. Marvin Hayes—he runs a dry-goods store, old Marvin took one in the knee, had to cut offn his leg."

"So they're hanging this Creech fellow because he shot a citizen?" Clairborne asked in a conversational tone.

"Hell no. They're gonna stretch his neck 'cause what he done to little Katy Schenk."

Before Clairborne could ask, the man said, "Trampled that child tryin' to get away. Just a damn shame what they done to her, and her only seven years of age. Seen her remains myself over to the church. Why, even the undertaker couldn't fix her up. No sir, Billy Creech is gonna burn in hell for that."

Clairborne made no conscious decision to watch the execution. He just became a bit of flotsam floating on the tide pulled by the gravity of the gallows erected on the other side of town.

His mind's eye pulled up the memory of a photograph he'd seen a while back, a photograph that disturbed him as no other had. It recorded in sharp focus the death by hanging of the four men and one woman the Yankees charged with President Lincoln's assassination. He'd never seen the like. A row of soldiers silhouetted on the Fort McNair prison wall like so many crows on a telegraph line. The white-coated, straw-hat-wearing hangman adjusting a noose, the disconcerting open umbrellas shading whom—the executioners, the about-to-be executed? Both? He refused to show it to his mother and sister, hiding it

93

in a bottom drawer of his wardrobe cabinet where, he realized now, it would be found sooner or later.

What he recalled most vividly were the white bands wrapped around each conspirator's legs and the cloth sack over each of their heads. He'd shivered at the thought of someone slipping a bag over his head, blocking out the sun or moon, a robin or a stray cat in the execution yard. Astride Bucephalus, riding into Sedalia on a sunny morning, he trembled at the thought of darkness descending over him before a stout length of hemp broke the fall through the gallows trap door.

"You mentioned the Creech boys," Clairborne said. "Are they only hanging this Billy Creech? What happened to the others?"

Another spit.

"Got away. Posse couldn't catch 'em. One got found later. Hiram. Dead. Gut shot. Billy swore it weren't his horse trampled little Katy, but there was witnesses—not that it matters."

Clairborne estimated there might have been as many as five hundred people gathered in a festive ring around the raw-wood gallows. He engaged in small talk with the family standing in their wagon next to him. He accepted their offer of an ear of roasted corn and a tin cup of lemonade. At the base of the gallows, a brass band stood behind a sign identifying them as the Sedalia Marching Society. Children cavorted in the space between the band and the crowd, some strutting to the marching tunes. Clairborne noticed the rooftops of the nearest buildings, both substantial brick affairs, were occupied by rifle-bearing men, one of whom held his field glasses in the direction of the open ground beyond the town limits.

The band stopped playing, and a buzz like the sound of hundreds of bees, industrious rather than angry, moved over the gathering. Like wheat in a wind, heads turned to the left, where, Clairborne saw from his mount, four men and a boy approached on foot; the men clad in black suits, two of them holding double-barrel scatter-guns across their chests as they walked slowly behind the bare-headed, manacled boy in the middle. Leading the procession, a tall, bearded, frowning man Clairborne thought could have been an Old Testament patriarch clutched a Bible in his left hand, his right holding a Remington Navy pistol in .36 caliber.

The quartet moved slowly, not out of reverence for the solemn nature of the occasion but because the boy, hobbled by massive leg irons, couldn't move any faster. His irregular, hopping pace triggered tittering from some of the spectators. The tittering led to catcalls and jeering. Someone threw an apple core. The patriarch stopped and said something Clairborne couldn't hear. Silence, total and unsettling, enveloped the scene; even the wind ceased and the noose stopped swaying. Horses, mules, and oxen stilled their movements—no snaffling, no rattling, or clanging of halters or bridles or whiffle trees broke the silence. Women stood on tiptoes, tottering toward the procession. Fathers lifted their children to their shoulders. A baby cried out and was quickly shushed.

Clairborne expected a speech, at least from the patriarch, whom he realized might not be the town's senior law dog as he'd assumed. He might be a judge or the mayor, either of whom would seize the opportunity to make points with the electorate.

He was wrong about the speech.

After the quartet mounted the stairs, one man handed his shotgun to the other and moved behind the boy, reached up for the noose, and handed it to the patriarch. "Here comes the black sack," Clairborne told himself, a surge of pity bolting through his guts reflexively followed by disgust at his weakness.

But there was no sack for Billy Creech. The patriarch placed the massive noose around Billy Creech's neck and adjusted its thirteen coils behind his left ear where it would snap the slender neck when the boy ran out of rope. Clairborne saw that the youngster's shirttail hung over the back of his trousers. His hair was combed down from a part in the middle of a head mounted on skinny neck sprouting from narrow shoulders. The boy's expression had remained constant from the moment he'd ascended the gallows. His beardless chin angled upward, his eyes unblinking.

The patriarch retrieved his pocket watch, observed it for a moment, and then slid it back into his vest pocket.

The patriarch leaned close to the boy's left ear, adjusted the noose again, said something so quietly that not even the two scatter-gunners could hear him, and then leaned back. The boy awkwardly turned his face toward the patriarch as if to study him for a moment, his range of motion restricted by the noose. He turned to the crowd.

"I ain't no child killer. I ain't." His high, clear voice was more defiant than fearful or apologetic.

The patriarch nodded. A mechanic standing beneath the gallows threw his weight behind a four-foot lever, and Billy Creech plummeted through the trapdoor. Recalling the scene later, Clairborne was certain he heard the distinct snap of the boy's vertebrae.

The crowd dispersed quietly, its energy drained by the clinical precision of the execution. No gagging, kicking, or writhing. Having refused a last meal, the boy had not even soiled his pants when he bounced once, oscillated twice, and then stopped dead. The carnival atmosphere evaporated more quickly than dew in the morning sun.

———

Again, Clairborne selected his route west from Sedalia to Fort Leavenworth so as to avoid as many fellow travelers as possible. He accepted the fact that he enjoyed—in fact, preferred—the solitude, especially after the hanging. He also told himself that despite the unlikely encounter with the James brothers, bandits frequented the well-traveled roads for the simple reason that they had more opportunities to ply their trade there.

For the next two days, his trail took him up gentle slopes, down to streams and creeks, and then up again through a forest of large hardwoods. Clairborne was beginning to look for a suitable campsite for the coming night when he noticed Bucephalus's ears flick forward. He turned to see Ajax also on alert. Something or someone was ahead in the trees.

Clairborne reined in, pulled back his coat, unsnapped the flap covering his LeMat, and drew the hefty pistol from its holster. He rotated the cylinder lock, shifting to the twenty-gauge shot-filled round. If he was going to be unpleasantly surprised, better to spew several chunks of lead at an enemy than a single bullet.

He listened, focusing his eyes and ears in the direction both horses were studying with equine intensity. He heard nothing. The horses were absolutely still, no stamping or snorting. "Probably not a horse," Clairborne thought. "That means it's either a critter or a man. Whatever it is, it isn't making its presence known, and that's not a good sign."

He silently berated himself for not checking his pistol's charges. Hadn't done so for a few days. "Stupid and lazy," he thought. He envisioned pulling the trigger on a bandit only to hear the muted pop of the percussion cap followed by silence instead of a roar because the damp powder refused to ignite. "Would be my own damn fault," he thought.

A moan floated out of the trees ahead, followed immediately by another, louder and more urgent. He gently kneed his horse forward and quickly emerged into a small, cool glade bisected by the trail. Twenty feet from the tree line, a dapple gray gelding lifted his head from grazing to watch Clairborne's approach, black leather reins hanging down from the bridle. A roan gelding packhorse also watched him from the far side of the dapple gray. Beyond the horses, something was on the ground, something that looked in the failing light like a pile of rags or a dark tent canvas.

Clairborne dismounted and looked around at the trees, LeMat moving in synchrony with his eyes.

Nothing.

He slowly approached the object on the ground and saw it was a man. Facing away from Clairborne. Tan, broad-brimmed hat lying on the ground six feet from the body. The body was lying on its right side, right arm twisted awkwardly behind its back. Left arm lying limply on the ground. No movement.

A sudden groan startled Clairborne and his horses, which snorted and backed away. Clairborne slowly walked around the body to see its front side. The right side of the man's face was contorted by the ground. A ginger-colored mustache flowed over the man's mouth, which was open and half filled with dirt. The eyes were closed. The man looked dead.

Judging from his clothes, his horses, and their tack, the man was a person of substance. His nicely cut black coat was made of expensive light wool with satin-faced, peaked lapels. Beneath the coat, Clairborne could see a paisley-patterned silk vest in muted gray and burgundy and, under that, a white muslin shirt. The tip of a black silk cravat was visible beneath the man's chin, which was covered by a light-red stubble matching his mustache and the long, wavy hair disheveled by his fall. Clairborne also noticed the man wore elegant gray leather gloves. His gray trousers were tucked into nearly knee-high black leather boots adorned with European-style spurs. As he looked more closely, Clairborne detected the distinct shape of a holster under the coat. Gently reaching down, he took the edge of the coat and drew it back, revealing a slim, finely stitched, black leather holster embossed with a rosette. That the holster was on the man's left hip and appeared to be facing backward caused Clairborne to assume that violent impact with the ground moved it to the left from its usual position on the man's right hip.

The pistol the holster normally contained was on the ground with only the muzzle protruding from under the man's body. Clairborne noted the weapon's expensive silver finish and the equally expensive engraving on the portion of the barrel he could see. On even closer examination, he saw that the silver plate around the muzzle was worn, as was the engraving closest to the barrel tip. This weapon was used. A lot. Another groan, this one rising to a near shriek, proved the man to be alive.

Clairborne holstered the LeMat and squatted by the man.

"Mister? Mister? I know you're hurt, but I can't see blood. Are you shot?"

The left eye opened and focused as best it could on Clairborne, who reached over with the fingers of this right hand to remove dirt from the man's mouth.

The man groaned again and closed his eye.

"Thank Jesus. Thank Jes..." the man sighed without moving.

"How can I help you, mister?"

The left eye opened and beheld Clairborne for a long moment before the man spoke.

"I'd be obliged if you'd shoot me."

Clairborne jumped to his feet.

"Lord. I...I.... No sir. I cannot."

"Are you going to help me, boy?"

"Sir? I..."

"I asked you to shoot me. Are you going to help me or not?"

"Lord God, sir. I cannot. I just can't do that. I'll do anything to help you, but I'm not going to do that. No sir. Not that."

"Shit," the man said. "Well, shit."

Clairborne looked over his shoulder at the man's packhorse then looked at Ajax and ran through a mental list of items he possessed that might be relevant in this situation.

"I'll try to make you comfortable. Maybe make a fire and some coffee or—"

"Goddamn it. I'm dying, boy. I didn't know a man could hurt this much. Just take my .44, put it to my temple, and pull the goddamn trigger."

"No, sir. That's not going to happen."

"Son of a bitch," the man said with surprising vehemence. "If I could move, I'd get up and stroke you to your knees, boy, I'd...."

The howl that exploded from the man sent Clairborne tumbling backward.

The howl subsided and the man repeated, "Oh, oh, oh, ahhh," and then went silent.

Clairborne turned in near panic to the horses. Knowing he had nothing in his own kit, not even whiskey, he ran to the man's packhorse, frantically untied the hitches, and unwrapped the pack. He remembered that he had a nearly full canteen, turned and looked at the man, and decided that he could not pour water into the man's mouth. He continued to unpack.

On either side were matching black leather valises bearing the monogram GJM in brass letters. The corners of the luggage were reinforced with brass, and the large locks on each appeared to be brass as well. "Where are the keys?" he wondered as he fumbled with one lock to find it flipped open at the touch of his fingertips.

Flinging aside long johns, nightshirts, socks, shirts, handkerchiefs, a pair of heavy leather gauntlets, and a pair of lace-up shoes, Clairborne was looking for something like a medicine kit or a whiskey flask, something that might reduce the man's pain.

Nothing in the first valise.

The search of the second seemed to be as futile as that of the first until Clairborne neared the bottom, where he discerned two matching boxes. At first he thought they were humidors, a notion he quickly dismissed on finding that one contained paper, envelopes, two pens, and a bottle of India ink with a waxed-cork stopper.

The second box was the bonanza for which he was hoping: a medicine kit.

Bandages. Scissors. A blade that looked like a scalpel. A needle and a bobbin of catgut for sutures. And a small brown bottle bearing the label "Bromley's Tincture of Laudanum."

He grabbed the bottle, stood, and sprinted to the recumbent figure.

Kneeling down, he extended his arms toward the man and then hesitated. He still didn't know the nature of the man's injuries. Nashville flashed again. What if his right side was opened from armpit to hip? What would happen then if Clairborne rolled him over? "Everything inside will come out, that's what."

"God in heaven," Clairborne mumbled. He stood and looked around, turned and ran to the man's gorgeous gray mount. As quickly as he could, he removed the saddle and saddle blanket and carried them over to where the man lay in silence.

Clairborne positioned the saddle as close to the man's head as he could and then moved to straddle the man's head and shoulders.

Grasping the right shoulder of the coat, Clairborne tried to lift the man, which elicited another howl of pain and failed to move the body an inch.

"If I don't move him, I can't help him, and if I can't help him, he will be dead weight sooner than later," Clairborne said aloud.

Bending down and grasping the same points of the man's body, Clairborne heaved. The body moved over and back, coming to rest with the middle of the back on the saddle's fender and seat, the head drooping backward for lack of support. Clairborne quickly balled up the saddle blanket and wedged it under the man's neck and head, raising it to the same angle as the rest of his body.

He looked for wounds and found none except for the massive, yellow-edged purple contusions and dirt-filled abrasions on the right side of the man's face. It occurred to Clairborne that the injuries were internal, the result of falling or being thrown from the horse.

Standing to admire his work, Clairborne realized that the wrenching movement had elicited not a sound from the well-dressed form in front of him.

"Lord, have I killed him?" he wondered as he kneeled and placed his right forefinger on the man's carotid artery. It pulsed. The first attempt to move him must have produced such excruciating pain that the man lost consciousness.

Clairborne looked around and asked himself, "What now?"

A fire. Cover the man with a blanket. Erect a tent-half to protect him from the elements. Make some coffee. Care for the horses. What else?

Laudanum.

Get some laudanum into him.

How much?

A lot.

No spoon. He ran to his own kit and extracted his stew spoon.

Pouring the viscous, gray concoction, Clairborne wondered if it would choke the man or kill him outright and decided immediately to give him two spoonfuls and a little water. For reasons he himself didn't understand, Clairborne gently stroked the man's throat with his left fingertips as he emptied the spoons of laudanum and drops of water into the man's open mouth.

The man swallowed without choking or gagging.

Clairborne stood, looked around, and realized darkness had fallen. Above him, stars littered the sky. He dropped slowly to his knees.

"Please give me the wisdom to help this man. Please don't let me hurt him," he said aloud. For a few moments he remained on his knees, head down, eyes closed. Then he stood up, turned around, and got to the business of making camp.

———

Journal entry
June ? 1868, Western Missouri

This evening about dusk, I encountered a badly injured man lying on the ground near his horses. It seems he was very badly hurt by the fall from his horse, but I am unable to determine the nature or extent of his injuries. I can find no blood on him any-where. He seems to be paralyzed by pain and, with the exception of a few seconds of consciousness, has been mute and immobile.

He is clearly a man of substance, as all of his possessions and cloth-ing are expensive and well cared for. His mount and packhorse are Morgans, the mount being one of the most beautiful horses I've even seen. A gelding, black maned, dapple gray. The tack on both horses is finely embossed black leather with silver snaffles and furniture.

On his person (actually, on the ground under his person) I found a silver-plated, heavily engraved 1860 Colt Army cap and ball in .44 caliber. In a shoulder holster under his coat, he carries another fancy Colt of the same caliber, but this one has had the barrel cut down to about three inches. In his kit, I found two more Colts, one with an eight-inch barrel as well as another three-incher. All of his guns are finished in silver and beautifully engraved, and the guns with the three-inch barrels have had the front sight removed. The two eight-inchers also appear to be named. On the backstrap of the one I found beneath him is engraved the word "Thunder," while the other has the engraving "Lightning." They are consecutively numbered.

He also has two long guns in his kit, two model 1866 Henrys, one a rifle with an octagonal barrel and custom sights and the other a carbine. Oh, yes, he is also carrying a bone-handled Bowie on his right hip, so perhaps he was carrying the holster on his left side.

I am wracking my brain to see if there is something more I should be doing to help him. The Christian thing would be...

"You writing a book?"

Clairborne started when he heard the voice from his ward. He moved to the man, who regarded him with hooded eyes and an ever-so-slight smile almost hidden by his mustache.

"How do you feel?" Clairborne asked.

"Well enough for a dying man."

"Dying? Why do...you seem OK now, mister. Why do you think you're dying?'

The man blinked slowly.

"Because I know what happened, and I've seen men die of a fractured pelvis, and mine's busted up pretty fair."

"Pelvis?" Clairborne asked, instantly recognizing that the man was right. Next to outright death or a broken neck or back, a fractured pelvis was just about the worst thing that could happen to a man thrown from his mount. Clairborne's heart sank. There was no recovery from a fractured pelvis. In addition to the literally incredible pain erupting from shattered bones rubbing and penetrating nerve ganglia, he knew that the man was bleeding to death internally even though no blood was visible.

Clairborne didn't know what to say.

"Your name, boy?"

"Clairborne, sir, Tucker Lightfoot Clairborne."

"I can see you're not from around here. Good manners normally preclude me asking personal questions, but this situation isn't exactly normal, is it?"

"No, sir."

"You give me laudanum?"

"Yes, sir."

"From my pack?"

"Yes, sir."

"There's a good boy," the man said and started to nod, but even that slight motion elicited a sharp hiss and clamped eyes. He was quiet a few moments.

"How long ago you give it to me?" But before Clairborne could answer, the man smiled and said, "Oh hell, it's not like I have to worry about addiction. Give me some more. Please."

Clairborne poured two more spoonfuls into his mouth, followed by some water from his canteen.

"I don't suppose you know who I am," the man said.

"No, sir."

"Well, no real reason why you should, being an easterner and all. From the South though, right?"

"Yes sir. Virginia."

"Good. Thought so. Good. I'd hate to have a Yankee put me in the ground. Where in Virginia?"

"My family has a place called Warwick on the James southeast of Richmond although there's not much left of it anymore."

Both were silent for a while, and then the man chortled, grimaced, smiled.

"Damned if this don't beat all. Wild Bill Martin done in by his horse." He closed his eyes. "I guess it's better than getting killed by some damn fool bushwhacker. At least this way nobody can ever claim their gun hand done in Wild Billy Martin. You never heard of me, you say."

"Ah, no, sir."

"Well, let me ask you this: You ever hear of Wild Bill Hickok?"

"Oh, yes, sir. I sure have."

Visibly agitated by that answer, the man looked up at the night sky and loudly said, "Goddamn it. I knew it. You know where I was headed when this happened, boy?"

Before Clairborne could answer, he said, "Kansas. I was going to Kansas to confront that goddamn usurper and shoot him if I could. Shoot him in the heart in a fair fight to show the world who the real 'Wild Bill' is. That's me, goddamn it. Not that long-haired showboat."

Exhausted by his expostulation, he closed his eyes and unclenched his fists lying at his sides on the blanket Clairborne had tucked under his body.

In a voice so low Clairborne had to lean over to hear it, the man asked, "You know what his real name is, boy? It's James Butler Hickok. Not William nor Bill nor Billy. When he was riding with the Red Legs, they started calling him 'Duck Bill' on account of his big nose. He didn't like that, so after he killed a couple of folks, he took to calling himself 'Wild Bill.' That was a damn long time after folks started calling me 'Wild Bill,' I can tell you that. It just rankles the hell out of me."

Another long silence ensued.

"Was that my writing material you were using?" Martin asked.

"Oh no, sir. It was my journal. I'm just keeping a journal as I move along."

Martin's eyes opened wider than Clairborne had seen. He stared at the young Virginian before saying, "A writer. A record keeper, are you?"

Clairborne responded, "Well, I'm not really all that disciplined about it and all. Not like Pepys or some of the famous diarists anyway."

Clairborne became aware that Martin was studying him. Clairborne didn't know why or what to say, so he said nothing.

Martin raised his right hand a few inches from the ground. "Take my hand, son."

Clairborne knelt and took Martin's hand as requested.

"I want to tell you some things. I guess this is about it for me, and you being here and all is beginning to seem like a blessing, kind of like a gift. When I think of what would have happened if you didn't just come along, or if some damn hothead showed up instead of you.... You religious?"

"Yes, sir. In a manner of speaking."

"Well, I haven't been for a long while, but I see God's hand in this turn of events, son, I'll not deny it. Will you bear with me while I ramble a bit?"

"Yes, sir."

"Well, here's the deal. My name is Gillaume Jean Martin, and I'm from Louisiana. Born to Francois and Lizette Martin in Bossier Parish, year of our Lord 1836." Martin looked up and said, "What did you say your name was again, your surname?"

"Clairborne, sir."

"Oh. With an *r*. Reason I asked is that one parish away from Bossier is Claiborne Parish. Thought there might be some connection."

Martin took several shallow, rapid breaths.

"I have to cut to the quick, son. I can feel darkness descending. I said I was on my way to find Hickok. I was coming from Bossier Parish. I went back after being gone all these years to kill the man who killed my love. I left her long ago and told her I'd return. Wrote her for a while and then stopped. She married a man I always hated. Didn't know if she did it to spite me or what. Anyways, I got word he beat her pretty often. Not even in private. Slapped her around in public even. Had money and land, so nobody tried to stop him.

"Couple of months ago when I was up on the Platte, I heard tell he hit her again, and I just turned old Hammer around and rode for home. By the time I got there, Ellie was dead. Said she died of consumption, but sure as hell, getting beat on didn't help her any. I found the son of a bitch, called him out, and shot him. Just once. A .44 two inches above his belly button. It come out just about the top of his right kidney. Maybe took a chunk of it even. Anyways, I watched him kick and crawl and bleed out in the dirt, and I cursed him for a goddamn coward and a black-hearted cur, and then he died.

"Now I'm going to say some things I'd like remembered, OK?"

"Yes, sir."

"I never, never back-shot anyone, you hear?" When Clairborne didn't immediately acknowledge, Martin raised his voice. "You hear? I never back-shot anybody. You hear somebody say I did, you tell them they're a goddamn liar."

"Yes, sir."

"I never, never shot anyone wasn't heeled. I been shot three times myself, and that can't happen if you're getting tangled up with anybody that ain't heeled."

"Yes, sir."

Martin took several more rapid, shallow breaths.

"Need a tad more of that joy juice, son."

After swallowing another sip of laudanum and waiting for its mellowing effect, Martin looked up at Clairborne.

"I have to tell you something. I can't rightly figure out how to say this, but I have to tell you that I feel right strongly about you. It doesn't make sense, I know. But I feel like you are some kind of angel—now listen to me—some kind of angel sent at my last moments on this mortal coil. I truly believe that, and I thank God for sending you to me."

Clairborne tightened his grip on Martin's hand and said nothing. He had no idea what to say, how to respond to being called an angel by a man who was a killer, but he sensed the man's need to express his feelings. He wished to God the man would not die. He wanted to get to know him.

"Now, quickly. Couple of more things. Give me a sheet of paper and my pen and something to write on—your journal will do."

Clairborne complied, and Martin covered two sheets with his writing, a laborious process culminating with his telling Clairborne to put the paper into an envelope, on the back of which he scrawled, "Last will and testament of Gillaume Jean Matin written by his own hand this day in Missouri; Y.o.O.L 1868."

"You don't happen to know the date, do you?" Martin asked, to which Clairborne responded, "No, sir, I sure don't. I think it's a Tuesday, though."

"Well, it doesn't matter. Put this into my coat pocket for me. Now in case somebody questions this, wonders if it's really writ in my hand, you tell them to get in touch with Judge Isaac Parker over to Saint Jo. Worked for him awhile and signed affidavits and other such papers. He'll vouch for it, and sure as hell, nobody is going to challenge his word," Martin said.

"OK. Here's some things I've learned I want you to know so maybe you won't have to get shot three times to learn 'em."

Yes, sir?"

"Don't ever hand your gun to anyone. Just don't. Ever. Shoot a lot. If you intend to go about heeled, you must know your pieces and how to handle them. Practice. Every damn day if you can.

"Protect your back. Look around. In towns and open country. Look around and ask yourself was you a critter or a bad actor, where would you wait to jump somebody?

"Always expect the worst, and you'll never be unpleasantly surprised. If you prepare for emergencies, you'll probably never have them." Martin smiled and added, "Unless you fall asleep in your saddle and your horse sees a damn serpent and proceeds to crow hop all over hell and half of Missouri."

Clairborne smiled, his affection deepening for this man who could ridicule himself at death's door.

"Oh yes. You're in a town and trouble's coming, get a shotgun and open the ball with it on the ones you think are the toughest customers. Take them out first."

It went through Clairborne's mind that Martin was assuming he would take up the mantle of shootist and build a reputation on the basis of Martin's practical wisdom. Just as quickly, Clairborne decided there was no harm in pocketing these hard-earned, rough-cut gems. In fact, it would be stupid not to. He would write them down. Later.

"And one more thing, there, Tucker."

"Yes, sir?"

"You ever meet a good woman, you come to love her, and she cares for you..."

"Yes, sir?"

Clairborne raised his eyes to Martin's face when Martin didn't finish the sentence. Tears coursed down the creases of sunburned skin fanning from the corners of Martin's tightly closed eyes.

"You stay with her and make her happy." His voice was low and hoarse. He opened his eyes and tightened his grip on Clairborne's hand. "That's the most important thing of all, son. The most important of all."

Clairborne lost track of the time as he sat holding Martin's hand. The fire died. Dew settled on the ground, the horses, and the two men. Clairborne entered the realm between wakefulness and sleep, visions came and went like chimera, some strikingly familiar and relevant, some so ethereal and abstract his subconscious questioned their meaning.

He emerged from this uncharted domain at the squeeze of Martin's hand to see that an oily luminescence was sliding into the recesses of the forest and spreading over the glade.

"Tucker, I need you to do one more thing for me, son."

"Yes, sir."

"Now listen, son. I don't want you to argue with me. You're a savvy young man. You know what's happening here, what's going to happen to me. So here is my request."

"Yes, sir."

"Go get Thunder and bring him to me. Then get on your mount and ride off for a while, a half hour or so."

"Sir, please don't ask me to..."

"Tucker."

"Sir?"

"Tucker. You know this is the best thing to do, and you know it needs to be done now. Don't you?"

Clairborne focused his energy on defeat of the tears searing his eyes. "Yes sir. I do. It's just that, it's just that..."

"Come on, son. Please."

Clairborne stood, walked to the pile of Martin's possessions, retrieved the silver Colt, returned to Martin, and holding it by the barrel, handed it to him.

Martin used both hands to hold the weapon while he gazed at it for long moments. He lowered the revolver to his blanketed chest and looked up at Clairborne.

"Now I need you to saddle up and ride off for a while. Just for a while."

Clairborne saddled his horse and led it back to where Martin lay.

For a moment neither said anything, and then Clairborne knelt and placed his right hand on Martin's forearm. Martin smiled.

"You are my angel, son. Thank you and God Almighty for letting me go this way. Now I bid you my fondest adieu. Farewell, Tucker Clairborne of Virginia."

Impulsively, Clairborne kissed Martin's forehead and brushed his tousled ginger hair from his brow.

"I wish I'd known you longer, Wild Bill. God keep you."

Clairborne mounted, wheeled his horse, and trotted out of the clearing into the trees. He reined in twenty yards down the trail, torn by an overwhelming desire to return to the glade and to.... "To what?" he asked himself, and just as he answered, "Just to be with him a while longer," the hollow pop of a pistol shot startled horse and rider, and Clairborne knew it was too late.

He sat his horse for nearly an hour, overcome with dread of the task ahead. Then he turned and rode slowly back to the clearing.

He did not want to look at Martin.

Anticipating the effect of a .44 ball—210 grains of solid lead—fired into the head at point-blank range made his stomach turn. He pondered how to wrap the body in the tent half without having to look at it any more than he had to.

Reentering the clearing, the first thing he noticed was that Ajax was gone. Both of Martin's horses were still tied to the picket. A quick sweep of the tree line showed his packhorse moving toward him from the forest where it had fled the sound of gunfire. He dismounted and tied both of his horses to the picket, studiously avoiding the body that lay mere feet away. He packed his personal items, took a long drink from his canteen, and sat down on the grass, arms on his knees, back to the body.

He removed his hat and lay back, resting his head on his hands. Ragged wisps of cloud bore the faintest blush of pink on their bottoms, evidence that the day was still young. How long before rigor mortis set in? Would he be able to put the body over a saddle if that happened? If not, what then? He reached for his watch to figure out how long it had been. Remembering that the watch was in an inside coat pocket, he decided he didn't need it to know it had been more than an hour since Martin died. It was still cool, but summer heat was implacable in its advance and would claim the clearing within an hour.

No choice. It had to be done now.

He stood and walked to where Martin lay. At first, the only difference he saw in Martin's position was that his head was turned to the left. Then he noticed the color, or rather the lack of it. Martin's face had been like that of any man who spent his life outside: his forehead was creamy white where his hat blocked the sun's relentless rays. From midforehead down, it had been the color of a brick. Now it was pale white tinged with green shading to yellow.

As he got closer, Clairborne saw that Martin's features were distorted as if he were made of wax and the wax had melted and succumbed to gravity's tug. The upper portion of Martin's head was twisted to the right away from his jawline.

Clairborne saw the wound, gagged, and spewed bile on his boots. He'd not eaten in two days. He retrieved his canteen, drained it, and swished the last dregs in his mouth to remove the taste of revulsion.

Rather than looking at the corpse or trying to do anything with it, he took down the shelter half and placed its edges along Martin's sides, tucking it under the body as far as he could.

Blowflies swarmed around Martin's open mouth, half-open eyes and the clumps of brain, hair, and skull lying on the left side of the distorted head. Clairborne swatted at the luminescent blue tormentors but quickly accepted the futility of the effort. Reluctantly, he again looked at the terrible, ragged, nickel-sized hole halfway between the ear and eye, flesh and hair in a circle around it burned black by powder flash.

The hideous wound galvanized him to cover Martin and get him up on the horse as quickly as possible. It took every bit of his strength to get Martin over his shoulder. Carrying the corpse the fifteen feet to Martin's horse wasn't all that hard, but when Clairborne tried to shift the body to the horse's back, the animal snorted with fear and shied, causing Clairborne to lose his balance and drop Martin's remains to the ground, where Clairborne landed with a grunt on top of him.

"Son of a bitch!" Clairborne yelled at the top of his lungs as he rolled away. "Son of a bitch!" Clairborne caught his breath, sat up, and looked at the canvas-wrapped corpse.

"I'm sorry, Bill."

When he approached Martin's mount, it reared again, pulling loose from the picket and trotting into the trees. Clairborne considered the situation. Perhaps he should put Martin on Ajax, who seemed to be the most phlegmatic of the four horses. Realizing there was no guarantee any of the animals would accept the fearsome burden, he decided to retrieve Hammer and get on with it.

It took another hour, and when it was done, Clairborne's clothes were soaked with sweat. The heat and humidity of late June Missouri had returned in full force, evaporating the memory of the cool night they replaced. He looked around to see that he had recovered everything and realized he had one remaining task.

Walking to the spot where Wild Bill Martin had shot himself in the head, Clairborne used a stout branch to bury the largest chunks of tissue and bone and scatter the rest. He threw the stick as far as he could before mounting and riding on.

—⁓—

Last Will and Testament of Gillaume Pierre Martin
also known as (the *original*) Wild Bill
I, Gillaume Jean Matin, being of sound mind, if not entirely sound body, do hereby bequeath to Tucker Lightfoot Clairborne, late of Warwick Plantation, Virginia, all my goods and worldly possessions.

I do so knowing that Mr. Clairborne is unaware of my actions, which I take at death's door. Mr. Clairborne has succored me in my final hours, showing a Christian care for a man he does not know.

Said goods and possessions include but are not limited to:
My horses and tack

My Colts (4 in number) and any credit remaining in my dealings with Colts Firearms, Hartford, Conn., whose work has provided me with the means to successfully defend my life against assorted villains and assassins.

My two Henry repeaters and my two Derringers

My pistol belt and holsters, clothing to include boots and hat

Cash money in the form of seven $50 gold pieces in my cartridge money belt and one $20 gold piece in the sleeve in the top of each of my boots.

I also leave to Mr. Clairborne my 50 percent ownership and share of profits in the Bon Ton Saloon, the adjacent Palace Hotel, and any other properties acquired by my partner, Marcus Price, whom I ask to recognize Mr. Clairborne as my legal heir in that regard.

Finally, I bequeath to Mr. Clairborne the responsibility to ensure my reputation as the original Wild Bill is duly recognized.

I wish all men of good will to honor my last wishes, as Mr. Clairborne has treated me in a good Christian manner and I am comforted by his attentions.

Signed this day in early July, year of our Lord 1868.
Gillaume Wild Bill Jean Martin
Born May 22, 1836, Bossier Parish, Louisiana

—◦◦◦—

July 2, 1868, Independence, Mo.

I have come to loath reporters and their vile trade. A more worthless, contemptible bunch of lying miscreants has never existed. These vultures simply have no concept of decency or honor. They cannot believe a man would tell the truth about a given turn of events simply as a matter of course. Because of these jackals, it is taking all my effort to avoid being labeled "the man who killed Wild Bill Martin." It seems few, if any, are inclined to believe he died from injuries sustained when he was thrown from his horse. I have stopped reading the articles concocted of the most wildly inaccurate fabrications. Even worse, many are written by people I have never even met.

The situation is infinitely complicated by the fact that Billy left everything he owned to me and that there was a lot more than I ever figured. Two days ago, Sheriff Thomas took me in to see Judge Maynard Coughlin, who is handling the case. The judge asked me if I knew Billy's plans to make me his beneficiary, and I told him no. Then he asked me if I knew what all Billy had to leave. Again, I said no, but I had a pretty good idea what his horses and guns were worth.

I wish I could have seen my own face when he asked me about the cash and property. It seems Billy left me half interest in a hotel and saloon in some place called Rawlins in Wyoming territory. It also seems Billy had seven $50 gold pieces in his gun belt and two $20 gold pieces in his boots. My respect for Judge Coughlin and Sheriff Thomas is great in that they are going to pass the windfall on to *me when they could well have kept it to themselves, and I would never have known about it.*

Judge Coughlin has counseled me on all related matters. As a result, I must wait here in Independence until the will passes through probate. The facts that the will was not witnessed, Bill left everything to me, and I brought in his remains combine to mean that the normal process will move even more slowly. When I reacted to the news that Billy left everything to me by telling the judge I didn't want his possessions, he told me straight out that if I didn't take them, they'd wind up getting scattered among various flim-flam artists and carnival barkers who would used Bill's stuff to make money, and if that was OK with me, he'd let it go at that and I could leave.

Well, it isn't OK with me, so here I sit for what I hope will be a short while.

My enforced idleness does give me time to consider my state of affairs and to contemplate how it came to pass that I have become a wealthy man with:

> *about $400 in the Mercantile Bank of Chicago*
> *a half interest in Great Western Supply as a result of a $100 investment*
> *$390 inherited from Billy (to be retained in gold, not deposited in any bank)*
> *half interest in a hotel and saloon (value unk. at this point)*
> *four horses (two American Saddle Bred and two Morgans)*
> *five handguns, two long guns, and one shotgun*
> *assorted tack and equipment*

I have just decided that my enforced idleness shall not be worsened by self-enforced isolation. Despite my concerns about encounters with members of the press, I am going to go downstairs, have a drink or two, and then dine at the best restaurant I can find.

July 2, 1868, Independence, Missouri

> *Dearest Mother and Sister,*
>
> *My life has been so full of surprises and events that I've found myself swept away and almost without the ability to control where I go and what I do. This last week is a good example.*
>
> *First, I happened to find a man who had been severely injured in a fall from his horse. I tried to comfort him and stayed with him until he expired. I have since learned he is a well-known gentleman around these parts. I took his remains to this town, which is a fine place with all of the excitement and energy so common out here. Anyway, the undertaker discovered a will on the man's person. He left all of his possessions to me. Can you believe it? He left me not only his horses and hardware, his clothes, and his cash ($390), but also half ownership in a restaurant and hotel in a place called Rawlins, Wyoming Territory. I have never heard of the place, but they tell me that the Union Pacific Railroad will reach the town this very month.*

Becoming the beneficiary of this man (I should have mentioned his name, which is Gillaume Martin, from Louisiana) has caused me to revisit my Texas plans, but I want you to know that I still intend to honor your request to pay our respects to Col. Schofield. Fort Leavenworth is only a couple of days from here, so I should be able to arrive there within the month once all the legal things get done. I have telegraphed the Col. but have not yet had a reply.

Mother and Amy, in closing, I must admit that I am at a loss to explain these windfalls that have taken me from poverty to comfort within the space of a few months. My faith in humanity has been elevated, first due to Mr. Martin's astonishing decision and then to the fact that the subsequent characters in this drama—the undertaker, sheriff, and county judge—have proven to be men of sterling honesty and responsibility. I must also say that even before these latest events, with the knowledge of my share of profits from the Nanticoke, *I was able to endure exposure to the elements knowing that if I wanted to, I could seek the creature comforts of civilization.*

I must tell you both that I am now in a situation that allows me to assist you with meeting financial obligations at Warwick. I consider it my duty to do so, and it would give me the greatest of pleasure as well. I will not belabor this point, but I expect you to be straightforward with me on this matter.

So, in closing, dear ones, please know that I am truly well and blessed beyond my ability to comprehend the Lord's design. I miss and love you both, Tucker

Along with the letter to his mother, Clairborne also sent a telegram to Col. Schofield at Fort Leavenworth in which he briefly identified himself and requested a meeting "should you have the time to meet with this traveler on his westward journey." After an afternoon full of meetings with the judge, two notaries, and a magistrate—meetings during which he nearly fell asleep—Clairborne went in search of a good drink and a better meal. There was no peace and quiet to be found in Independence, Missouri, in 1868. All day, all night, the hours were filled with comings and goings of businessmen, teamsters, lone riders, families arriving, and families leaving in covered wagons, carts, buggies, and on foot. Nor was there a moment free of drunks and carousers looking for the next saloon, trying to find their way home, or getting run over by freight wagons when they passed out in the street.

It was nearly 9:00 p.m. when Clairborne walked into the smoke-filled, crowded saloon, which, according to the gilded sign above the front entrance, was known as the Rondeyvoo. Tobacco smoke obscured the back of the room. Clairborne caught fragments of Brahms floating up from a piano at the end of the bar, but the shouts, laughter, and conversations of those trying to be heard drowned out all but the few high notes. Ornately carved, mirror-backed bars lined both sides of the room. Four bartenders struggled to keep up with the demands of thirsty patrons lined up two and three deep, those at the front resting their muddy boots on the brass footrails. Clairborne noticed immediately that the spittoons spaced along the floor seemed to be missed as often as they were hit. Gobs of tobacco and saw-dust stuck to patrons' boots and streaked the plank floor. He wondered how anyone could drink and chew at the same time and decided he didn't really want to know.

Working his way into the room, he noticed that almost every table hosted a card game or some other type of gambling. Two thoughts shot through his mind. "Somebody is making a lot of money with this place, and I'm never going to gamble." He reasoned that the professional gamblers were just that: professionals. "So for me to sit down with a professional cardsharp would be like giving my money away. Not going to do it. Ever."

He found a chair lying on its side, picked it up, sat down, and surveyed the surroundings more closely. No one paid him any attention. There were no women in sight. He wanted a drink but didn't want to stand in line at one of the bars. He decided to leave and get a drink and dinner somewhere else.

Clairborne was halfway to the exit when a man tapped him on the shoulder. When Clairborne turned, the man who tapped him said to his drinking companion, "I tole you it was him. Pay up."

The second man looked at Clairborne a moment before asking, in a voice blurred by too many shots of beer and rye whiskey, "You kill Wild Billy Martin?"

Clairborne was instantly irritated.

"No, I did not. Nobody killed Will Bill. His horse threw him, and he died because he got all broken up inside. I did not kill him. I found him."

The man who tapped Clairborne said, "Easy for him to say, no witnesses and all." Then he took a drink from a half-empty mug.

Clairborne regarded him for a moment. Battered derby hat. Greasy collar open at the neck. Old stains dotting the shirtfront. Sleeves rolled up. No jacket. No weapons visible. Shorter than Clairborne by a full head. And just about drunk.

"Are you calling me a liar, friend?" he said in a lowered voice, leaning forward to close the distance between them.

The other man swayed, shrugged, and said, "Shit. He only said weren't no witnesses, so who the hell knows what really happened, that's all."

"Well, you see. That's where you're wrong," Clairborne said. "I just got through telling your smelly, ugly, stupid friend here exactly what happened, and he seems inclined to publicly call me a liar." Turning to the first man, Clairborne said, "Right?"

"Who the hell you calling ugly and stupid?"

"Ugly, stupid, and smelly," Clairborne corrected.

He felt his heartbeat accelerate, pounding in his ears. He knew the surge of adrenaline coursing through his veins would soon make his hands shake. Clairborne recognized the signs that he was losing his temper. "Think," he told himself. "Don't have even my Bowie on me. Stupid. Don't know how many friends these two have here. In the middle of the room so can't protect my back. Don't die in a saloon because you got mad at a couple of drunks."

"I ast you a question, mister. Who you calling stupid?" the first man said, his foul breath causing Clairborne to involuntarily lean back.

"Tell you what," Clairborne said. "You apologize, and we'll just call it quits."

"Me apologize? Me apologize? Why, don't that beat all," the man yelled. "This sumbitch calls me a name and wants me to apologize."

His yelling attracted the attention of others within earshot, who turned to identify the source of the commotion.

They saw Clairborne's right fist come up under the man's chin, snapping his head backward, flipping his battered hat forward to the floor. They saw Clairborne follow up with an equally vicious left fist to the jaw of the second man. Both dropped to the sawdust-covered floor, spilling their drinks and scattering bystanders.

Before either could rise, Clairborne kicked the first man in his crotch, turned slightly to his right, and pounded his right fist into the nose of the second, leaving both writhing and howling, knocking over hurriedly emptied chairs.

Pain from the knuckles of his right hand shot up his arm to his elbow.

He pointed to the men on the floor and said, "You bastards ever call me a liar again and you'll get worse than that, so help me." He looked at the circle around him; silent men, many of them smiling, waited for the next event. He decided there was nothing else worth saying, reached over and righted a chair, nodded at the nearest man, and walked from the room.

Journal entry, July 5

Everyone whom I have asked here in Independence tells me the army unit based across the river at Fort Leavenworth, the Tenth US Cavalry, is composed of "niggers." When I pressed for clarification, I learned the Tenth Cavalry, along with a sister regiment, the Ninth Cavalry, is composed entirely of Negroes—with the exception of the officers, all of whom were white. So now, not only am I going hat in hand to a Yankee officer, but the Yankee in question leads a unit of Negroes, some if not most of whom probably came from the South and are former slaves.

I am seriously thinking about skipping the whole thing.
What I don't know:
If Col. George Schofield is even at Ft. Leavenworth.
If the esteemed colonel would deign to see me if he were in residence.
The details of what transpired in Virginia other than the general did something significant and the Clairbornes benefitted. What, why, and how are complete mysteries.

Then there is the conflicting information to be considered.
The locals say the Tenth Cavalry is commanded by the well-known Col. Benjamin Grierson, who rode to glory with his 600-mile raid into the heart of the Confederacy. And Col. Schofield? Seems he is

only a major, maybe Grierson's deputy. Maybe not. "Ain't my job to keep track of them blue-belly bastards," one man told me.

I am very tired, and my hand hurts.

—◦∿∿◦—

The next morning, Clairborne slept in. Heat of the night and lingering pain in his knuckles kept him tossing and turning until just before dawn. He awoke as light limned the room in gray, used the chamber pot, and crawled back into bed, pulling the sheet up to his chin and sinking immediately into deeper sleep.

Soft tapping awoke him just before ten a.m.

"Mr. Clairborne? This is the hotel manager, sir. You have a caller, an official caller, downstairs. Should I tell him to come back later?"

Clairborne yanked on his trousers and ran to the door in his nightshirt and bare feet. The hotel assistant manager, Mr. Aloycious Gunderson, stood in the carpeted hallway, wringing his pale hands and sweating nervously.

"I'm so sorry to bother you, sir, it's just that we don't often have to deal with soldiers, and the lieutenant insisted I give you his compliments and his card and request that you meet him in the lobby at your earliest convenience. Again, I'm very sorry to disturb your rest, Mr. Clairborne."

Clairborne rubbed his sleep-swollen eyes and accepted the proffered calling card, the engraved letters in the center of which told him his caller was

Sylvester L. McGinnis
Smaller letters in the lower right corner of the card added
2nd Lieutenant
10th Cavalry Regiment
United States Army

"My compliments to Lieutenant McGinnis, and please tell him I will join him in a few minutes. If you would be so kind as to ask him to meet me in the dining room and to put a pot of coffee out for us, I'd be obliged."

"Oh, of course, Mr. Clairborne. I'll do so forthwith," Gunderson said, obviously relieved his client was not angry.

As Clairborne closed the door and doffed his nightshirt, he realized the lieutenant's presence was in response to his telegram requesting a meeting with Major Schofield. He was impressed with the promptness of the response. As to whether that promptness boded ill or well, he was undecided.

—⁓—

Pimples. And a pathetic attempt at a mustache.

The first impression of Second Lieutenant Sylvester McGinnis was not favorable as he sat at a table in the dining room sipping the coffee Clairborne had provided. When Clairborne approached and extended his hand, Sylvester stood, saluted, and shook hands.

"Lieutenant McGinnis at your service, sir. Major Schofield sends his compliments and directed me to extend his invitation to join him at Fort Leavenworth at your convenience."

Clairborne's incubation and subsequent life in Southern mores had implanted in him an ear for tone of voice innate to aristocracy everywhere. To Clairborne the words meant one thing, but the tone dripped disdain. He regretted that he had not shaved, for if he had, there would be one less obvious reason for the Yankee jackanapes to regard him as a lesser being—which he clearly did.

As the lieutenant spoke, Clairborne took his measure: several inches shorter than Clairborne's seventy-two inches. Prematurely thinning brown hair close cropped on the sides and parted in the middle. Gray eyes rimmed in red lids. His dark-blue tunic immaculate except for the light dusting of dandruff flakes. Epaulets on each of his narrow shoulders were cavalry-yellow with embroidered yellow silk lieutenant's bars on each side.

His black Sam Brown belt gleamed, as did the covered holster on his right hip. A patina of dust accumulated on the morning ride did little to dull the shine on his high black boots.

Clairborne gestured to the seats, and as they sat down, McGinnis said, "There is some urgency in the major's request since our regiment is leaving Fort Leavenworth soon for a new post."

"Oh really," Clairborne said. "When?"

"Later this month. We are to move to Fort Riley, Kansas, so your timing is fortunate."

"Is there a particular reason for the move?" Clairborne asked.

The lieutenant's response and the superior tone in which he delivered it intensified Clairborne's initial dislike for the young officer with skin problems.

"I can assure you, sir, that the United States Army would not undertake such an endeavor on a whim. That said, I am not at liberty to discuss such matters with civilians."

A lifetime of lessons in civility, some of which were emphasized with a willow switch wielded by his father, caused Clairborne to word his response with studied precision. Rising from the table, he said, "I apologize, sir, if I inadvertently implied that so august and respected an institution as the United States Army would be guided by whim in the place of grand strategy.

"Please convey to Major Schofield my appreciation of his gracious offer and assure him that I shall call on him as soon as possible. Is there a particular day of the week that would be more convenient?"

"Thursdays are intentionally kept more open," McGinnis replied.

"Today is Monday. I shall arrive at Fort Leavenworth Thursday next in the morning. Please be so good as to let the major know," Clairborne said. "Now, I bid you good day."

Clairborne's tone and the stiffness of his posture mortified the young officer, who belatedly realized that he'd insulted the civilian, triggering the distinct possibility—if not likelihood—that Clairborne might inform Major Schofield of his breach of etiquette. The lieutenant stood and stammered, "Oh, sir, I didn't for a moment wish to cause you umbrage."

"Not at all, Lieutenant," Clairborne said as he nodded in a perfunctory bow. "Not at all." But as McGinnis looked around and saw other diners studiously examining their late morning meals, he recognized that everyone within earshot knew he had insulted someone practiced in the skills of delivering ostensibly innocent words in a wrapping of tone and body language that conveyed a distinctly different meaning.

Back in his room, Clairborne steamed. The irritation he felt with the lieutenant shifted his focus to the forthcoming meeting with the lieutenant's superior officer. Clairborne knew there must be no such breach of etiquette, actual or perceived, on his part. Not only was he representing the Clairborne family to this Yankee officer, he also was simply compelled to underscore the ingrained nature of Southern civility, a responsibility so deeply ingrained it was normally not necessary to think about it—which he told himself was in stark contrast to the Yankee officer, who probably learned the basics of etiquette in classes at a military school.

Fort Leavenworth was a day's ride away, but because he said he would call on the major in the morning hours, Clairborne decided to leave Independence immediately, find decent lodgings in Leavenworth near the fort, and spend Wednesday evening preparing his clothing, his mount, and his mind for the encounter. He wished he knew more about what had happened in Virginia. Looking into the mirror on the washstand, he shook his head and said aloud, "I surely don't like being unprepared. I surely don't."

⎯⎯⎯

Astride Bucephalus a few hundred feet from the main gate, Clairborne observed the post for almost an hour and was reassured and discomfited by what he saw.

The army post's order and immaculate cleanliness were more impressive than he'd expected. The stone and log structures, beginning at the busy main gate, implicitly spoke of permanence and purpose. Fort Leavenworth was the oldest army post west of the Mississippi, and since its founding in 1827 on the west bank of the Missouri River, the fort had played a pivotal role in the development of the frontier. And in the forty-one years since troopers directed by Colonel Leavenworth began cutting trees and laying foundations, the post had assumed an aura of impressive gravity and order. His eye for architecture told him enough time had passed for essential pragmatism to be overlaid with aesthetic touches such as the white picket fences in front of the suttler's store and the neo-gothic main chapel.

Clairborne's discomfiture arose from observation of the soldiers manning the guard posts, performing the menial tasks beyond the gate, and practicing both cavalry and dismounted drill on the broad parade ground. Most of them were Negroes. There were some all-white units, all of them a good distance from the Negro elements. As he had heard in Independence, the officers in the Negro units were all white, but he could not take his eyes of the black soldiers themselves.

He quickly realized he was not seeing what he had expected to see.

As he leaned forward in his saddle, Clairborne mentally made a list. First the horses. Each unit had the same color mounts. He could see three distinct units, two large groups he took to be troops and one smaller one he thought was called a detachment. The chestnut and gray horses of the individual units gleamed in the early morning sun. There were well groomed and beautifully muscled.

Then the men themselves. It didn't take a practiced military eye to know discipline when it was this obvious. The men moved in unison, close-order drill on horse or foot, showing countless hours of practice. And when a rare breach of drill was perceived by the Negro sergeants conducting most of the exercises, Clairborne saw swift corrective action.

When he arrived at the post in the early morning, he heard the clarion notes of a bugle and soon understood that bugle calls on an army post had the same function as church or cathedral bells in cities: telling everyone within earshot not just the time of day but what was expected of them at that time as well.

He recalled his father's stories and realized that his father had deeply loved his years in the same uniform worn by these men at Fort Leavenworth. He also remembered that his father was torn between his duty to the army and duty to his family, the latter winning out when the death of Tucker's grandfather meant the responsibility of managing Warwick fell on his father's shoulders.

Pulling his father's Breguet from his vest pocket, Clairborne decided the hour of observation had settled his frame of mind enough to proceed with the encounter.

It was a different lieutenant who rode up to the main gate guardhouse to escort Clairborne to his meeting. This one, who introduced himself as First Lieutenant Schuyler Fenton, was the picture of a cavalry officer: broad shoulders; narrow waist; long, curly blond hair brushed over his ear beneath his kepi, on the top of which gleamed a polished brass badge featuring a pair of crossed sabers. Tanned, blue-eyed, and in possession of the whitest teeth Clairborne had ever seen, Fenton radiated an ebullience aligned with his recruiting-poster appearance. Clairborne liked him immediately.

Fenton and Clairborne rode a quarter mile into the immaculately maintained post, passing individuals and groups of soldiers engaged in a broad range of activities, the most interesting of which for Clairborne were what appeared to be open-air classes. The latter, conducted under canvas screens, included basic literacy. Fenton said the classes were not mandatory or part of the scheduled activities. They were for soldiers who wanted to learn reading and writing, and they used their personal time in the pursuit. The classes, like all the other activities Clairborne observed, were strictly segregated by race.

Clairborne was mildly surprised by the amount of manicured grass he saw around the buildings, flagpoles, and other structures. Across the parade field, a bright palette of colors at the base of handsome, two-story stone and brick homes spoke of women's presence in the section of the post called "officers' country."

They pulled up in front of a two-story, slate-roofed, yellow-brick building fronted by a stone porch that ran its entire length. Nearly twenty horses were tied to hitching rails on either side of the broad stone steps leading to the porch. Soldiers occupying benches on the porch and those standing by the horses cut off their conversations and sprang to attention at the approach of Lieutenant Fenton and his civilian guest.

An impeccably groomed private stepped forward and snapped a salute. Fenton returned the young black soldier's salute and said, "As you were, Johnson. We'll be at least a couple of hours with Major Schofield. See that Mr. Clairborne's mount is watered, and, Mr. Clairborne, oats for your mount?"

"No, thanks. He's fine with his morning feed at the hotel."

"Just water then, Johnson."

A second round of salutes, and Johnson lead Bucephalus to the stone trough at the side of the building.

The orderly room was the model of cleanliness, as was everything else Clairborne had seen that morning. Clerks in tunics and polished "low-quarter" shoes sat at desks around the perimeter of the large room, at the back of which was a huge, now-cold stone fireplace. On one side of the fireplace were the regimental colors and on the other, a large, glass-fronted case housing a display of memorabilia collected over the decades by soldiers long since departed.

A mustachioed, gray-haired Negro whose sleeves bore embroidered yellow silk sergeant's chevrons sat at a desk in front of the door leading to Major Schofield's office, and at the approach of the lieutenant and his charge, he stood and said, "Major Schofield would be delighted if you would join him in his office, Mr. Clairborne."

Fenton stopped, removed his kepi, and shook hands, saying to Clairborne, "Delighted to meet you, sir, and I hope to see you again."

"Likewise for certain, Lieutenant."

Then Clairborne crossed the threshold into the domain of Major George Wheeler Schofield, United States Army, Bureau of Ordnance.

⸺◈⸺

The man who rose to meet Clairborne was of medium height, attired in a double-breasted, dark-blue uniform coat, the brass buttons of which were obviously polished every day. A slight bulge at the waistline indicated the major was spending more time behind the mahogany desk than on his McClellan saddle. The most impressive aspects of the major's appearance were the magnificent sideburns cascading down the sides of his face to his collar and the deep-set, piercing, pale-blue eyes from which emanated a gaze so fierce it was almost disconcerting. Even as he extended his hand, Clairborne found himself pitying any junior officer having to deliver a negative report to this man.

The major's smile and hearty greeting belied his steely countenance.

With his left hand, he directed Clairborne to a horsehair settee and seated himself beside his civilian guest.

"May I offer you a cigar, coffee?" he asked.

"Coffee would be very nice, sir, thank you."

Clairborne hadn't been aware of the enlisted man standing at attention just inside the door. At a nod from the major, the man turned on his heel and left, only to return in less than a minute with a sterling-silver coffee service. The tray and pot bore the regimental crest, as did the creamer, sugar bowl, and china cups.

"Are you sure you wouldn't care for a fine Havana to accompany the coffee?" the major asked.

"Actually, I would," Clairborne replied and selected a robusto from the proffered polished walnut humidor. After the perfunctory cutting and lighting ceremony, both men leaned back and emitted a small cloud of rich, blue smoke.

"I must compliment you on your coffee and cigars, Major. They're excellent."

"Why, thank you, Mr. Clairborne. We live hard in the field, but we see no reason for privation in the garrison. Now what brings you to Kansas from Virginia?"

Clairborne laughed. "I wish to heck I could give you a good answer, Major. To put it in the proverbial nutshell, my mother asked me to pay my—or rather our—respects, in gratitude for something I believe your brother did, but to be quite honest, I don't know exactly what that was. I only got a telegram with no details."

"Ah," the major said as he exhaled and contemplated his hand-rolled smoke. "Perhaps I can enlighten you. It seems that my brother, in his capacity as military governor, vetoed a piece of legislation that would have confiscated every land holding over twenty-five acres in size."

Clairborne knew that from the articles he had read in Saint Louis. Before he could ask, the major added, "John was leaning toward veto anyway, but your mother called on him to make the case personally. And apparently," he paused, smiled, and fixed Clairborne with his piercing gaze, "apparently my brother was quite impressed with your mother and her argument. I assume that doesn't surprise you."

They both laughed.

Shaking his head and thinking about the diminutive woman walking into the governor's office to present a case none of the male planters had the courage to make, Clairborne said, "No, Major. When I think about it, it doesn't surprise me one bit."

Their shared amusement at the imagined scene broke whatever social ice remained between them.

Over the next hour and forty-five minutes, they discussed the coming regimental relocation to Fort Riley and the desperately thin ranks of the army tasked with defending the already huge and expanding frontier. After such relevant topics had been thoroughly parsed—actually Clairborne asked questions and listened to answers—Clairborne decided to venture into the issue most intriguing to him.

"As you know, Major, my family owned slaves for generations. I grew up surrounded by slaves. I never knew a single free Negro, so I am fascinated by what I see here, by these Negro soldiers and, frankly, by what seems to be their discipline and their fine appearance."

"You say that as if it surprises you, Mr. Clairborne, as if you didn't think Negroes capable of such achievements."

Clairborne paused and studied the pattern of the oriental carpet under his boots.

"I believe it accurate to say, sir, that my experience with Negroes is such that I never had the opportunity to see them in any situation other than slavery.

"I also believe it is accurate to say that while it was not discussed much, and certainly never discussed in the presence of womenfolk, Southern landholders, slave owners, were always aware of the potential for rebellion, or for another slave revolt such as that lead by Nat Turner. So to see hundreds of Negroes riding fine mounts and wielding modern firearms takes some getting used to. I make no bones about that."

"I appreciate your honesty, sir. Permit me to tell you my sentiments on this topic. They are simple, really. I never gave the issue much thought before the war aside from a general sentiment that slavery was evil. I joined the army to preserve the union, not to end slavery. But my experience with the Negro soldier has made me aware of just how fundamentally unfair their continuing treatment is. I will state flatly that these are as fine, as capable a group of fighting men as I have ever served with, and I have served with the best. You seem discomfited by my position, Mr. Clairborne."

"No, sir. I'm just trying to reconcile the conflict between what I know from my previous life with what I am seeing—and hearing—here. I hope you will understand that such a wide gap cannot easily be closed."

"Mr. Clairborne, it occurs to me that there may be an opportunity here for you. Are you interested?"

Not knowing what the officer had in mind but intrigued nonetheless, Clairborne nodded. "Of course, Major. What do you have in mind?"

"First I want to share something with you. You may have already heard this. Do you know the primary reason we are relocating to Fort Riley?"

"I assume to get closer you your operational area as the frontier expands."

"That is the official reason, sir. On paper, that is how the move and the expense are justified, but it is not the fundamental reason."

"And that is...?" Clairborne asked after sipping his coffee.

"The reason is that our regimental commander, Colonel Grierson, is in constant conflict with our post commander, our host, if you will, Colonel Charles Damon, who, to put it mildly, despises Negroes. It would be one thing if his hatred were a private matter, but it is not. He has gone out of his way to make life as difficult as possible for the Tenth Cavalry— everyone in the unit, white and Negro. It is to the point where regimental relocation is the only answer to maintain unit cohesion. The situation here is simply intolerable. So we are leaving."

Clairborne was simultaneously surprised, saddened, and confused by the revelation.

"I, ah, find it hard to understand. I mean I assume this Colonel Damon is a Northerner."

Schofield nodded and tapped the ash from his cigar. "He is."

"I also assume his sentiments are known to his superiors if they are as public as you indicate."

"Correct again."

"Then why, if I may ask, is that tolerated? I mean, if Washington believes in these Negroes enough to raise several regiments, with all the attendant expense, surely such overt..." Clairborne paused while searching for the best word.

It was supplied by Major Schofield. "Attacks?"

"Yes, sir. He seems to be attacking, undermining Washington's policy. How could he get away with that?"

Schofield contemplated Clairborne. "Does your question imply that you think his sentiment might not be justified?"

Clairborne was startled.

"I, I...I just know that I am seeing things, lots of things, that I never imagined before. I still think about slavery. I even had a talk with a priest, an Episcopal priest back in Sedalia, about slavery and about whether it could be God's punishment of us, the war and all, because we had slaves. I'm stumbling around here, Major, because I still don't really understand what happened to the South. I guess more to the point, I don't understand why it happened. Every single person I know there is a God-fearing Christian, and yet...." Clairborne shook his head and shrugged his shoulders.

"Are you still interested in the opportunity I spoke of?"

"Indeed."

"I propose to give you the opportunity to see for yourself what caliber of men these are. We move in two weeks. The advance party leaves in six days. I invite you to stay here on post until then, observing our activities, and then ride west with the advance party, which I will command. What say you, sir?"

Clairborne didn't hesitate. "I would be honored, Major. Honored. It's passing strange that I came to thank you for something your brother did for my family, and now I am obliged to you for this marvelous opportunity, this adventure."

"Mr. Clairborne, if I can cause one American to understand what these soldiers are doing for our blessed country, I will be duly recompensed, believe me."

A gentle rap on the frame of the open door came from the Negro sergeant.

"Begging the major's pardon, sir, but Colonel Grierson sends his compliments and requests your presence."

Schofield stood and extended his hand. "A fine talk, my friend. Please join us for dinner at the officers' mess this evening, and by then you should be able to retrieve your belongings from the hotel and stow them in our guest quarters. Welcome to Fort Leavenworth."

Clairborne shook the major's hand. "Major, the pleasure is all mine. I'll see you at dinner."

—◌◌◌—

July 9, 1868
Fort Leavenworth, Kansas

Even though I admit that my thoughts are diluted in drink, I must enter my recollection of this evening before retiring for the night. I cannot recall another such event. Again, I am conflicted between what I think I should feel and what I actually do feel about this night and the characters who populated it.

Yankee officers all. Yankee officers. I was just feted by fourteen US Army officers who treated me as an honored guest instead of a member of the class that fought them so long and hard.

Among the most astonishing things in an evening replete with same, Major Schofield raised a toast to my father, a toast to which the collected fellows responded heartily with "Hear him!" "Well said," "To the Colonel," and other resounding affirmations of the major's words. I was so taken aback by the gesture that I fear I shall not recall verbatim what was said, but I must try to get it down.

Rising and holding up his glass of port, Major Schofield said, "Gentlemen, our guest tonight is the son of one of the finest officers to serve in the United States Army, Colonel John Clairborne, late of the Army of Northern Virginia. It is three years since the conclusion of that saddest episode in our nation's history, and yet we still smart from the wounds sustained in those years of bloody strife. For our country's sake, we must move on. I tell you, my brother, whom, you know, has just assumed the position of secretary of war, has told me more than once that Colonel Clairborne was the very model of an officer. In the name of Colonel Clairborne, a distinguished graduate of West Point, let us recall the years of service to the United States and discard to the winds of change all lingering bitterness over divided loyalties. So, gentlemen, I give you Colonel John Clairborne, husband, father, and distinguished fellow officer."

At the conclusion of the meal, several—but not all—of the junior officers told me how glad they were to make my acquaintance and extended an invitation to join their respective troop as a guest.

Earlier this week, I decided I would never gamble, knowing I lack the skills to win at games of chance, but that said, I would have wagered every cent I own that something like this evening's revelries could never have taken place, and I am dumbfounded by it all.

I simply cannot comprehend the cascade of unlikely events that have carried me along these last few months. I don't know where they will ultimately take me. I don't know how long this exhilaration will last. I only know that more surprises have happened to me since I left Warwick than in all the years until that point.

I do not regret leaving and striking out on my own.

July 10, 1868
Guest Quarters
Fort Leavenworth, Kansas

> *Dearest Family,*
>
> *There are two things I wish to share with you, the first of which is to assure you I am enjoying the most robust health of my life to date. I surprise myself by saying that since less than two weeks ago, I was acutely uncomfortable, exhausted, hungry, and feeling three times my age. I attribute that sad state to the fact that in my life to that point, I had enjoyed a degree of privilege that I was unaware of in many respects. I knew, of course, that my domicile, food, education, clothing, and possessions were virtually unattainable—actually unimaginable—to most folks. You and Father ensured that I never took that for granted and that I was always aware of my duty to God, Virginia, and family in return for those blessings. I am aware, Mother, that I have not measured up when it comes to the last of those three, and that is a burden I will endeavor to rectify in time.*
>
> *The health I referred to involves physical discipline. I know that you and Father made decisions to shelter me from life's vicissitudes. I would do the same thing as a parent. The point is that since I have had to sleep on the ground for weeks on end,*

feed myself, and care for myself entirely without assistance from anyone else, I have become a stronger, dare I say better, person.

Mother, Amy, you will recall that in the days before I left, you both asked me why I was so bent on departing, what I hoped to gain. I was unable to answer you then to my own satisfaction, much less to yours. Now I know. I sought independence, and I have found it. Please do not be hurt by these sentiments. I do not mean that the family bonds that I feel more strongly than ever were cloying, restricting, or negative. I mean rather that my life at Warwick was so privileged that I'd become dependent on others to do virtually everything for me, even after the late unpleasantness so dramatically changed our lives. Now I have put myself into a position of having to do everything for myself, and I am the better for it.

I do not know what experiences lie ahead, but I know that life west of the Mississippi is even harder than I imagined, so I know there are many, many challenges to come. Rather than dreading them, I have come to anticipate them, to prepare for them on the basis of knowledge I have gained from experience and through conversations with men who have already survived tests of will and wit beyond telling.

I want you to know, to believe, that your son and brother is doing very well by himself.

Now for the second topic.

By my address you will doubtless know that I reside these last two days at Fort Leavenworth as a guest of Major George Schofield. Not only has he proven to be a boon fellow, but for some reason, he seems to believe I am good enough company to warrant an invitation to accompany him and a troop of his cavalry to Fort Riley. The Tenth Cavalry, in which Major Schofield serves (as regimental ordnance officer, not as commanding officer) is being relocated. The reasons for this major undertaking are many and varied, some making excellent sense in the military rationale, while others are neither rational nor clear to me.

Let me share some numbers with you for context of what follows.

At the end of the late unpleasantness, the Union Army had more than 1,300,000 men under arms. Today it has less than 30,000, the majority of whom are garrisoned east of the Mississippi. That means that the frontier, more than two million square miles, hosts fewer than 15,000 soldiers. There are about nine regiments out here. Four of them, including the Ninth and Tenth Cavalry, are composed of Negro soldiers. I find this astonishing in itself, but I must confess to being almost as confused by what I have observed since my arrival here. While I have been around them only these few days, I am compelled to tell you that I am rather impressed with the discipline and the appearance of these Negro troopers.

The regiment was created under the auspices of Colonel Benjamin Grierson, who remains its commanding officer. Yes, Mother, this is the same Colonel Grierson who made his infamous "ride through the Confederacy" in 1863 as part of Grant's Vicksburg campaign. I suspected there would be some awkwardness in our initial meeting, but that proved to be an unfounded fear. The good colonel is an excellent host and, to my surprise, has spoken not infrequently of his regard for the officers and men of the CSA.

He and Major Schofield have also told me privately that many of the white officers with whom I socialize were assigned to this unit against their will, seeing service at the head of Negroes as a step down in their career. I find it very interesting, however, that after a short period of service here, most of the officers become both proud of their regiment and sensitive to slights of its reputation, real or perceived. That brings me to the salient point of this topic.

I have been told on reliable authority that the real reason for the transfer of the Tenth Cavalry from Fort Leavenworth to Fort Riley is to remove the regiment from the odious influence of Col. Charles Damon, who in his capacity of post commandant has elevated his antipathy for Negroes to such public prominence that the situation has become untenable.

My host officers of the Tenth tell me Col. Damon and the Tenth Cavalry commander, Colonel Benjamin Grierson, have nearly come to blows over public statements made by Col. Damon regarding the Negroes. They also tell me that this has corroded the ranks of the post's officer corps to the degree that officers from the Tenth are virtually castigated by officers from other regiments and that fisticuffs have become the rule rather than the exception at the post officers' club.

I find it very ironic that I feel such sympathy to these men and their officers, and to be truthful, I don't understand why I feel this way. The men are almost entirely former slaves. Most are illiterate, but army discipline has apparently given them a means to separate themselves from their past as slaves and to create a new life in service to the powers that freed them. Major Schofield also told me the Negro reenlistment rate is much higher than that of white soldiers, while the desertion rate is lower. I have yet to see them in action against hostiles and may never have that experience, but again, the officers tell me these Negro troopers are at least as steadfast under fire as are their white counterparts.

I simply must consider all this as I endeavor to adapt to my life as a westerner. I know how difficult it must be for you to understand what I am feeling

and seeing here. It just seems that these Negro soldiers are so different in their bearing and conduct
from the Negroes we know in Virginia that I must
understand why this is so.

Before I close, I must share with you the best
experience I have had. At the end of last night's
dinner, at which I was the honored guest, Major
Schofield raised his glass to "a distinguished fellow
officer," Col. John Clairborne. He urged the officers
present to understand how much men like Father
contributed to our country and never to question
their honor. As you can imagine, tears welled up
in my eyes when I heard these blue-coated soldiers
praising Father.

Well, I will close now, as it is past midnight and
the bugle will blow in less than five hours. I think of
Father and Peyton often and have come to recognize why they were drawn to army life. The sense of
purpose is palpable.

I wish I could give you an address to use for return
correspondence, but alas, I do not know one. What a
thing to say. Let me restate that in a way that might be
less alarming to you. I know where I am going (Fort
Riley), but I don't know either a post office address for
that place or how long I will be there.

Finally, Dear Ones, please know how very
much I care for you and how I cherish memories
of Warwick. It is because of you and Warwick that
I can venture out of the familiar to discover new

*places, and, honestly, more about myself. Also,
please know that I will always, always endeavor to
make you proud of me.*

Love and affection, Tucker

———✧———

Four days later, Clairborne received another surprise from the officers of the Tenth Cavalry. He was asked to join the regiment's command and staff element in the position of honor as the advance party "passed in review." Astride a gleaming Bucephalus, beneficiary of a solid week of US Cavalry grooming and feed, Clairborne took his position between Lieutenant Fenton, adjutant to Major Schofield, and Lieutenant McGinnis, who served as the ordnance officer.

The regimental band, arrayed in dress uniforms replete with gold braid and plumed helmets, formed up to the left of the command element. A series of shouted commands followed by different bugle calls led to the regimental adjutant trotting up to the regiment's commander, Colonel Grierson. The adjutant swung his saber hilt to his lips, blade vertical, and announced in a shout, "Advance party, Tenth United States Cavalry, all present and accounted for, sir."

Colonel Benjamin Grierson saluted in return. "Very well. Advance party shall pass in review."

The adjutant wheeled his horse to face the regiment and repeated the colonel's order to the regiment.

Clairborne felt his pulse quicken at the spectacle unfolding in front of him. He knew the adjutant's saber movements were an ancient form of salute called "present arms" and that it, the review and many other aspects of army life, had originated thousands of years earlier, before the age of chivalry, the crusades, the Romans, or even Alexander the Great.

Slanting rays of summer sun glinted off polished brass and silver. The jingle of bridles and spurs and sabers, the pounding of drums and hundreds of hooves, shouted commands and blaring trumpets, pennants flapping in the dust-thickened breeze redolent of horses and leather and men generated a unique and ancient aura. Bucephalus twitched and stamped in excitement matching that of his rider. This was pure spectacle. It was what career soldiers remembered after trading McClellan saddles for rocking chairs. It was what his father and brother loved. The undulating, synchronized mass of men and horses, wagons, field howitzers, and their caissons rolled across the parade ground toward the gate and the plains beyond. Clairborne felt his very soul was linked to Charlemagne and Richard the Lion Heart, George Washington and Jeb Stuart. He found himself thinking about joining the army, becoming a permanent part of this brotherhood, but as soon as the concept formed in his mind, he shuddered, reality clarifying his thoughts. "Brotherhood?" Brotherhood with the white officers or with them all? Brotherhood with those Negroes. "No," he decided. "Don't get carried away here. All of this is designed to do exactly what it's doing: spread a thin layer of pageantry over a life of mud and boredom, blood, sweat, and fatigue. No. Not for me, but I sure enjoy the show."

Every night of the subsequent march west was the same. In point of fact, every aspect of every day of the march was virtually identical to the day before and the day to come. "Routine, thy name is 'military,'" Clairborne mused. This could be stifling or reassuring, depending on the frame of mind and purse one brought into the situation. He also recognized the logic of it all. It is simply impossible to efficiently do anything involving more than two individuals unless there is order, structure, and discipline. And here on the seemingly infinite prairie, there was an abundance of all three.

There was a well-established trail to Fort Riley Schofield's unit could have followed, but he explained to Clairborne that taking a different route gave all involved, down to the lowest ranks, an opportunity to enhance their knowledge of the terrain. Clairborne observed the morning and evening meetings, where the officers perused their maps to compare what they'd expected to what they'd actually encountered. The advance party was preceded by a smaller party that ranged up to five miles ahead of the main column. It served primarily to detect any potential threats. It was also responsible for finding suitable locations for water and rest breaks, noon meals, and ultimately, evening camp. On the second day, the advance party was augmented by "screens" of troopers riding on the flanks of the main column, just beyond the limits of sight. Schofield explained that while there were no known hostiles in the area, Indian raiding parties ranged hundreds of miles, and the cavalry's hundreds of horses would be a lure impossible for them to ignore.

"I'm not worried about Indians inflicting casualties on us so much as their making off with our mounts and mules. It's happened too many times to recount, and few things end a promising career as quickly as losing horses to Indians without a shot fired," he said with a grin.

Camps were chosen for their proximity to water when possible, and when not, high ground was selected for the human camp while the horses were concentrated in hollows, where they could be most easily guarded. While most of the men tended their mounts, cook fires and campfires flared and flickered, each tended by enlisted men assigned duty as kitchen police, a much-hated job that required peeling potatoes, scouring pots, and doing whatever the mess sergeant demanded of them. In fair or foul weather, officers' tents were erected by work details of enlisted men who also positioned wagons in designated areas to facilitate their use as defensive positions if needed.

Meals on the march were the most basic of fare. Officers and men alike ate salt pork or bully beef, bacon, beans, and biscuits. In garrison, breakfasts featured pancakes and eggs, but in the field, "gut busters" and "rooster bullets" were a memory of easier life. Coffee was the only beverage, morning, noon, and night. Mere possession of alcohol was a punishable offense.

On the third evening, as dinner drew to a close and individual officers excused themselves to perform their rounds, Schofield asked Clairborne if he would care to "take a turn around camp." For several minutes, they walked in silence, absorbing the ambiance of an army camp at a prairie dusk. Murmurs of conversation punctuated with not-infrequent laughter eddied out from knots of blue-clad men clustered around fires the smoke of which rose slowly in the still, warm air, the calm punctuated by the hammer blows of farriers using the dwindling light to make one last repair of a wheel rim or a loose horseshoe.

To the west, low-hanging thin clouds sandwiched iridescent slices of sunset above the black horizon. Within minutes, a single evening star, a harbinger of a rainless night, was joined by swaths of light points and celestial dust that never failed to humble Clairborne and remind him of his first night at sea.

As a three-quarter moon peeked over the eastern edge of Kansas, Schofield directed Clairborne to a knoll just beyond earshot of the nearest soldiers. He sat down and took a deep breath, removed his campaign hat, smoothed his hair, and retrieved a black leather cigar case from his tunic pocket. He offered Clairborne a panatela, which he clipped and lit before performing the same routine for himself.

"So what do you think of my army so far, Mr. Clairborne?"

Clairborne had sensed a query like this was coming but considered his answer for a few moments nonetheless.

"Well, sir, I'll tell you. I had a tutor back in Virginia who told me once that 'creativity lies on the cusp between chaos and order.' I mention that because I find myself pretty evenly split between admiration and confusion. I mean, how can you admire something that confuses you?"

"You are confused by what you see?"

"Yes. Well, sort of," Clairborne said with a shrug.

"Mind if I make an observation, Mr. Clairborne?"

"No, of course not. Why do you ask?"

"Well, you might take this the wrong way, but you've said that about yourself rather often since we met, that you are 'confused' by your experiences and what you see. Is that fair to say?"

Clairborne was embarrassed. He liked decisive people, particularly decisive men. He thought of himself as decisive but realized that the major was right. He had probably been more confused by things in the last four months of his life than ever up to that point. He also realized that during the liquor-lubricated evenings since his arrival at Fort Leavenworth, he had probably spoken too often about the intellectual and emotional conflict between his past and present experiences.

"I have a recommendation to make," Schofield said.

"And that would be?"

"I'd like to commend you to Lieutenant Rall. You've met him. Commands E Troop. Good soldier. Why don't you ride with him for a few days instead of with us in the command element?"

"I'd like that if it's all right with the lieutenant."

Schofield smiled. "Oh, don't worry about that. I've already taken the liberty of suggesting it to him, and he has expressed his enthusiasm for the idea. Not that he had any choice, of course."

The two chuckled, and Schofield added, "I want you to pay particular attention to Sergeant Herman, Sergeant Titus Herman."

"Any particular reason?"

"Well, no, not really. I'd just like to know what you think of him after riding with his troop for a few days."

If there was one thing Clairborne had learned about Major George Schofield, it was that the good major rarely, if ever, did anything without a predetermined purpose. He was pretty certain this was the case with the major's suggestion this time as well, but he decided to see what that might be through observation rather than interrogation.

"Starting tomorrow?" Clairborne asked.

Schofield stubbed out his cigar. "Good a time as any, I suppose."

"Well then, tomorrow it is," Clairborne said as Schofield rose and turned toward the camp.

"I'd like to stay here a while longer, Major, if I may," he said.

Schofield responded with a wave and walked away.

The next morning was a scorcher even before the soldiers broke camp. Clairborne mopped his brow before mounting and wondered how a spot so far from a large body of water could still be so humid. At breakfast, he introduced himself to Lieutenant Ludwig Rall. Of medium stature, Rall sported a fashionably long, full mustache that didn't connect with curly sideburns or the pointed van dyke accentuating Rall's already strong chin.

Rall's gray eyes radiated a sort of perpetual glee and interest in everything around him that, at first, disconcerted Clairborne with its energy. All officers wore bespoke uniforms and boots, but Rall's bore the distinguishing marks of the very best in material and expensive tailoring.

The explanation came soon enough once the column resumed its movement and idle conversation began to flow.

Rall was Austrian. Third son of an ancient and noble family. His family divided its time among their country estate near the village of Lofer, a palace in Vienna, and a castle outside Salzburg. After nearly three years in France as the guest of French aristocrats, Clairborne recognized the social stratum represented by the dashing lieutenant at his side. As the third son, Rall had no chance of inheriting any significant land or property. He would be expected to join the church or enter some form of service such as the military or Austria's large diplomatic corps. If he didn't go the church route, an arranged marriage was in store as part of a highly structured, predictable, and very comfortable life.

But Rall had rebelled.

Years of training as a cadet in the Austrian cavalry confirmed his predilection for the military. His father, who held the title of count as well as the rank of general, was sent to the United States as military attache at the outset of the Civil War and had brought his youngest son along as his aide. Within six months of his arrival in America, the younger Rall privately decided he would stay, that here he would make his own fortune and accumulate experiences unimaginable at home.

There had been a predictable, prolonged row with his father. His mother sent scores of increasingly emotional pleas to return to kith and kin, all to no avail. Rall's decision was enforced when his father disclosed the identity of the girl deemed a suitable matrimonial match, "a simply ugly woman with no redeeming social graces, all duty and no humor," Rall said with a laugh.

Clairborne had met some Germans in Europe, but no Austrians until Rall. He had heard that there was a distinct difference between the two nationalities in that Austrians were much more gay and animated than their Teutonic relatives to the north. Rall certainly seemed to bear that out.

He dismissed concerns about advancement so common to fellow officers in the tiny postwar American military. "I'm here for the adventure, not the money," he said with the studied insouciance of a young man who, despite disappointing his parents, had not been disinherited.

During the first day, Rall introduced Clairborne to the other white officer and to the troop's Negro noncommissioned officers, including Sergeant Herman. Clairborne's first impression of the man Major Schofield asked him to observe was that he was both taciturn and intelligent, as well as young to be the troop's senior enlisted member. He also found it interesting that Herman maintained eye contact when addressed. The Negroes Clairborne had known did not.

It was after dinner on the second night together that Clairborne found the opportunity to ask the question most prominent in his mind since meeting Rall.

They made the last-light rounds of Rall's troop and then retired to a position outside the camp perimeter to enjoy the day's last tobacco: a cigar for Clairborne, a meerschaum pipe featuring a carved turk's head for Rall.

"I've been curious about something, but I must admit that it's rather sensitive," Clairborne said.

Rall turned to study the young Virginian and said, "Delightful to have a subject of interest to discuss on such a good evening as this."

"I learned right away that many of the officers in the Tenth didn't want to serve with Negro troops. They saw it as bad for their career. I heard that some even saw it as punishment, so I'm curious about how you wound up so far from Austria as an officer leading Negroes on the Kansas plains."

"Good question, that. Good question, and the answer is simple. I prefer challenges as a matter of course. I prefer to ride saddles rather than chairs, and field assignments are very hard to get in America these days, so if one wants a command of any kind, one can't be choosy. So here I am, my friend."

Clairborne liked listening to Rall's grammatically correct English sharpened by the throaty edges of a native German speaker.

"One other thing," Rall said. "With your education, you probably know that in Europe, the tradition of hiring mercenaries to fill out the ranks is quite common. In our wars with the Turks, we have always had thousands of men under our banner who were neither Austrian nor even Christian. Riding with them," he said, pointing at the enlisted men with the stem of his pipe, "is not so very unusual for a European as Americans may believe."

Clairborne understood the analogy to Europe. It was not far-fetched at all, although in every case he could recall, those mercenaries always had their own officers, but it was a hair he declined to split.

"Now I may ask a sensitive question of you?" Rall said.

"Sure."

"How are you feeling about being around so many of these Negroes? Your family had slaves, yes? That must make it rather interesting for you."

"Yes. Interesting to say the least," Clairborne said. After a pause, he added, "I really still have not decided what I think about the whole thing."

"Well, I would be rather suspicious of someone who could make such big decisions very quickly. I mean, we both come from backgrounds shaped by traditions and privilege and power. It is hard for me to imagine what I would feel if all of that went away in a few years of my life."

Clairborne regarded the profile of the young Austrian beside him.

"I thank you, sir, for your understanding. It is comforting to know that someone else has more than an inkling of the issue."

Rall turned. "Inkling? What is this 'inkling'?"

Clairborne chuckled. "Oh it's a little insight, a, ah, a suspicion if you will."

"I-n-k-l-i-n-g?" Rall spelled out loud.

"Exactement, mon ami," Clairborne said.

"Well, it is a good day indeed when you learn a new word. I will remember this 'inkling.'"

Clairborne tried to think of the French word for inkling but couldn't find it. The fact that he was even discussing semantics and vocabulary at all in the middle of a cavalry camp on the Kansas plains gave him a quiet pleasure. He looked up and reminded himself to remember this moment when he said his prayers later that night.

Rall returned to his tent, but as he had on previous evenings, Clairborne lingered outside the camp perimeter.

He lay on his back with his hands under his head. Heat from the sunbaked soil radiated into his muscles while above him, a silent shower of meteors streaked the indigo Kansas sky. Hours at a telescope aimed by his tutor slipped into mind, time when acquisition of knowledge was his only real duty. Such a blissfully simple time of hot chocolate brought by silent servants, his mother bringing him a jacket on the coldest and most crystalline of nights.

The same stars he studied in Virginia, counted on a ship to France. The same stars scattered above him in Kansas.

With his eyes closed and the warmth of the soil caressing his back, Clairborne wandered into the netherworld between slumber and wakefulness, a realm of images both new and old. The Kansas prairie beneath him didn't smell like the rich loam of James River bottomland, and the trampled tall grass emitted a bouquet different from that of the freshly mown hay of Warwick's fields. And yet, his reveries led him over the knoll that hid the slave quarters from the big house, and there were faces he recognized: Sam, Moses. They'd gathered around a low fire, some standing, some leaning against the rude structures that were their homes. Others sat on stumps or overturned buckets. All stared into the flames, and Clairborne wondered what caused their sadness. The songs, the rhythmic rolling of their deep voices, caused him to search for the name of what he realized was a hymn, their version of a hymn sung in his family church. The harmony washed over him like a cool stream, lifting sadness and loneliness from him. He was home again.

But he was not.

His suddenly opened eyes beheld the Kansas heavens above him, not Virginia's. He sat up and looked around. The sound of voices singing reached him from the soldiers' camp along with the pungent smoke from their buffalo dung fires. A deep bass sang, "I looked over Jordan and what did I see," and a chorus of soldiers answered "Comin' for to carry me home." Again the bass: "A band of angels comin' after me," and the chorus reaffirmed, "Comin' for to carry me home..."

Clairborne stood and moved to where he could see the singers. The solo bass emanated from Sergeant Titus Herman.

Although he faced Clairborne on the other side of the campfire, Sergeant Herman seemed to take no notice of the white civilian known by all of the regiment's enlisted men to be a slaver.

———

As he sang, the sergeant's mind was filled with the face and form and feel of a woman he hadn't seen for five years, a woman he would have married had matrimony been permitted to slaves.

If he had asked, which he did not, Clairborne would have learned that Titus Herman began his life at a rice-and-indigo plantation outside Charleston, South Carolina, called Brenmore. Born to a woman assigned to prepare meals for field hands, Titus Herman was sent to the stables when he was six to serve the needs of the grooms who cared for the master's hunters and the ladies' palfreys.

Because of the value his white master placed on livestock, slaves who tended it ate marginally better food and enjoyed better living conditions than those who worked from before dawn to after dusk in the fields. Herman, whose father was Mbundu, a people of the Ndongo kingdom ruled by the ngola, and whose mother was born on the Gambia River, "learned horses" quickly. He developed the ribboned musculature forged by hard labor and nearly decent food. By thirteen, he was a groom with specific responsibility for the mounts used for the master's fox and deer hunts. The position meant that he was one of the exactly eleven out of Brenmore's fifty-seven male slaves known by name to the owner and his family. On hunt days, when wealthy, landed whites from all over the region gathered at Brenmore, he was given a liveried uniform and boots to wear when leading the horses to the main house from the stables. It was during one such day when he was fourteen that he was first impaled on the beauty that was Irene.

Irene. A young house servant whose comeliness was the subject of constant conversation among the male slaves of all ages. He had seen her before when he brought horses to the big house, but it was often months between occasions for mutual consideration.

On that particular autumn day, Titus was holding the reins of his master's hunter, a tall Morgan named Zeus, when Irene emerged from the house carrying a tray of drinks and cakes.

"Good lord, she's changed. She's grown. No child no more. That's a woman for sure," he thought as his mind churned over how to finagle a meeting. His plans were interrupted by the voice of his master, the corpulent, sybaritic Thomas Herman.

"Titus, you going to hand me the reins or stand there like a statue? Come on, boy." Before Titus could answer, Thomas Herman followed his line of sight to Irene, who was blissfully unaware of the attention about to focus on her.

"Oh, so that's it," he laughed. Pointing his riding crop at Irene, he said, "Gentlemen, it seems my groom here has been struck mute by the blackamoor beauty yonder."

The boy nearly bolted on recognition of what he so inadvertently had done.

As the plantation master's male and female guests turned to identify the object of his gesture, Irene began trembling so hard she nearly dropped the heavy silver platter and its accouterments.

Mrs. Mildred Herman was not amused.

"Irene, put the tray on the table before you drop it," she commanded. Then, turning to her younger husband, whom she scolded with a sour tone intended to conflict with her innocent words, "Thomas, my dear, shouldn't you and your beau cavaliers be pursuing some small furry creatures rather than mocking the servants?"

Herman roared with laughter, stood in his stirrups, and bawled, "Master of the hounds, away, away," his calls triggering notes from the hunter's horn and the rush of thirty-eight dogs and twenty-seven horsemen from the manicured side gardens toward the fallow fields and the forests beyond.

Left standing in an empty courtyard, the young groom lifted a surreptitious gaze to the flustered house servant he had mortified with his attentions. As she scraped crumbs from the starched linen tablecloth, Irene stole a glance at the groom.

On any plantation or locale housing slaves, an efficient clandestine network carried information about arrivals and departures as a result of sales, punishments, affairs, births, and deaths to all members of the slave community, regardless of their station.

Irene had heard about the boy called Titus early in her life at Brenmore, although it wasn't until she was seven that she first saw the stable hand, who was two years older. He accompanied his mother to the detached structure that served as the kitchen for the big house. His mother, Penny, needed her son's assistance to carry buckets of scraps, rejects, soup bones, and old fruit to supplement the fat back, hominy, peas, and greens she prepared for the field slaves.

Irene and Titus never spoke. They didn't have to.

As soon as the initial attraction manifested itself in their adolescent souls, both became aware of a sort of low-grade permanent fever of worry afflicting all those living in servitude who shared bonds of affection more powerful than even the legal ties to their masters.

"What if he is sold?" Irene worried at night.

"What if the master takes her?" Titus asked himself, immediately answering, "I'll kill that fat bastard then kill myself," knowing that taking his own life would prevent both a lynching and the torture that would precede it.

For the next year, Titus kept clear of the big house, seeing Irene only twice from a distance.

Then came the war. Within months of the onset of hostilities, Titus Herman and the other slaves at Brenmore observed the steady departure of white males into the apparently insatiable maw of the Confederate Army. Few returned. They also noticed the steady increase in the number of white women wearing widow's weeds.

Virgil Hamilton, overseer at Brenmore, enlisted in the Confederate Army in the spring of 1861. He was replaced by Ezekial Throckmorton. Nineteen-year-old Zeke Throckmorton returned to South Carolina after being invalided out of the gray-clad ranks of South Carolina General Bernard Bee.

At a Virginia crossroads called Manassas, Throckmorton was next to Bee's bay mare ramming a charge down his musket's barrel just as the general pointed his sword at a writhing mass of men shrouded in gun smoke and dust. Throckmorton heard Bee yell, "There stands Jackson like a stone wall! Rally on the Virginians!" Then something smashed him so hard it knocked him off his feet. Sitting up as his colleagues rushed past him, Private Throckmorton couldn't rightly place what was going on. He wasn't exactly hurting. He just couldn't catch his breath. He was thirsty. He reached for his canteen with his right hand and tried to remove its cork stopper with his left hand. Only he couldn't. He looked down. No left hand. No left arm. The left sleeve of his light brown homespun shirt hung in blood-drenched ribbons from just above his elbow down to the cuff. But the sleeve was empty.

"Now where's my dang arm?" Throckmorton said before he passed out.

His subsequent arrival at Brenmore changed things for the slaves. Throckmorton was less attentive than his predecessor. His charges quickly adapted with an awareness of the opportunities this change presented along with an intuitive understanding of the need for caution to preserve the fissures in the walls that so completely proscribed their lives.

It was this change that allowed the groom Titus and the house servant Irene to meet more often and for longer than either of them had dreamed possible.

Clairborne knew nothing about the world of Titus Herman. What took place in slaves' quarters or in illicit trysts was as alien to him as the far side of the tarnished silver moon above his Kansas camp. But inconceivable as those events in South Carolina were to the Virginian, they had already begun to shape his life in ways he would find even more inconceivable, if that were possible.

———✺———

C Troop was riding at the head of the column stretched out more than a mile over the Kansas plains. The six-man scouting party was two miles ahead of the troop. At this point in his experience with the army on the move, Clairborne became preoccupied with not falling off his horse. The heat, the monotony of the landscape, and the slow, rocking motion of the horse beneath him presented a pathway leading from torpor to drowsiness, from fatigue to oblivion, dulling his senses, pulling down his eyelids, sliding his thoughts into mysterious reveries of oddly juxtaposed people and places. It was usually the specter of Wild Bill Martin that dragged him back from the edge of what would have been a humiliation—falling off his mount in front of hundreds of soldiers.

It was slumber in the saddle, after all, that had done in the Louisiana pistolero.

Clairborne found himself urgently seeking something to distract him, something to pique his interest and focus his wandering mind.

He tried estimating distances. Too hard.

He thought of his weapons and his lack of skill with them. Too unsettling.

He knew he should be shooting the inherited pistols, but he declined to do so in front of the soldiers during their target practice—again, not wanting to be embarrassed by inaccuracy that could only be attributed to the shooter since the weapons were so obviously excellent.

What then? Prairie dogs? He was past interest in the rodents he'd quickly understood were hated by horsemen. Blundering into a prairie dog town at a full gallop could only lead to disaster—unavoidable disaster for the horse, highly probable disaster for the rider.

What then? He found himself thinking of his tentative objective: finding the Caudill ranch and hiring on to drive cattle north across these same plains to a railhead town. He began to have second thoughts. "Lord, if I can't stay awake heading south, what makes me think I'd be able to going the opposite direction?"

Clairborne was aroused from his torpor by the Austrian lieutenant at his side.

Raising his right gauntlet above his head, Rall yelled, "Column halt!" The command was echoed by each soldier with command responsibility behind him.

Rall withdrew a telescope from his saddlebag and stood in his stirrups.

Clairborne looked at Rall and then turned his gaze in the direction of Rall's focus.

Far ahead, a column of black smoke slanted in a breeze, its origin obscured by terrain and heat haze. Clairborne surmised that the dust cloud close to the smoke was the scouting party returning at a full gallop to the main column.

A surge of energy coursed through every man and mount. Something was up.

Anticipating the need for quick decisions and equally fast communications, Rall kept his telescope on the horizon but yelled, "Bugler, sound officer's call."

The sharp notes carried to the rear of the column. Officers leaned forward in their saddles, slapping reins against horses' flanks, spurring their mounts from a standing start to a pounding, clod-throwing gallop to the head of the column.

"Gentlemen, the scouting party is returning with an urgency that tells me something drastic has occurred to our front. I thought it more efficient for you to hear Corporal Johnson's initial report at the same time I do."

The junior officers arranged their horses abreast of Rall and his civilian guest and waited silently for the six minutes it took for the scouts to close the distance, rein in their lathered mounts, and watch as their corporal saluted and made his report.

"Corporal Johnson reporting, sir. We observed the remains of two men I believe were buffalo hunters. They were ambushed by Comanche, at least twelve. The hostiles departed to the southwest. The fire is from the cart the hunters were using for their gear and their hides. It looked like one or more of the hostiles might be wounded, judging from the blood trail, sir.

"No weapons of any kind at the site. Everything of value taken—horses, equipment—but they killed one of the mules hauling the cart. I believe the attack happened within the last two hours, three at the outside, sir."

Rall nodded. "Good report, Johnson. Damn it to hell. Comanche, you say?"

"Yes sir. Could be some Kiowa with them, too, but definitely Comanche, sir. I think Kotsoteka."

Rall looked at Clairborne. "We're just at the northern edge of their territory. This is definitely a raiding party." Rall turned to look back at the main column only then appearing over the top of a small hill.

"Mr. Markham, you will assume command of the advance party while I report to Major Schofield. Advance to the site at the trot, and be very careful about ambush. Secure the site and wait for my return. Understand?"

"Yes, sir."

"Very well. Mr. Clairborne, you may remain with the advance party if you care to."

"I do."

Rall wheeled and left. Markham raised his fist and said to Sergeant Herman, "Advance at the trot."

Herman stood in his stirrups, turned to the column, and bellowed, "Advance at the trot, ho!"

As he spurred his horse to hold his place in the column, Clairborne understood that the trot was the most efficient pace for covering distances, faster than a walk but less demanding of horse and rider than canter or gallop.

The buffalo hunters had camped in a bowl formed at the bottom of three hillocks. Before the column arrived at the scene, the breeze shifted, bringing with it the greasy, roiling residue of flames consuming wooden cart, leather traces, buffalo hides, and human bodies. Clairborne felt bile rising in his gorge at the fetid, curiously rich odor of burning skin, fat, and bone.

As the column approached the knolls, the source of the fire still hidden from sight, Markham turned to Sergeant Herman.

"Sergeant Herman, send a detachment to establish perimeter security on the heights. Maintain visual contact with the main element."

Herman wheeled and rode off with men selected on the fly to occupy the low heights surrounding the killing ground. Then he rejoined the main column as it ascended the hill and rode over the top and then down the grassy slope.

Most of the cart was gone, consumed by thin orange fingers of flame still stroking the charred planks. Wheels canted inward, only the stout hubs and the iron rims recognizable. Heaps of hides smoldered in what had been the cart's bed, their mass preventing the fire from consuming them completely. On top of the hides were what remained of the hunters; one face down on the hides, the other face up on top of his comrade.

Clairborne and Markham rode as close as the heat would allow.

Clairborne vomited on himself before he could raise his hand to his mouth or lean away from his body. He looked away. Markham had pulled his yellow silk scarf over his mouth and nose. Clairborne involuntarily looked back at the conflagration and heaved again.

He looked up to see Markham holding out a handkerchief. "Thanks, but I don't want to foul your linen," he said as he retrieved his own. A wave of embarrassment washed over Clairborne as he noticed the soldiers studiously ignoring him.

"Sergeant Herman, pull that cart apart and put out the fire. Be as careful as you can with the remains of those folks," Markham said.

Clairborne forced himself to watch the work. The soldiers looped a rope around the charred foot of one of the hunters, but when they tugged on it, the leg separated from the corpse where it had been slashed when the hunter was castrated.

Clairborne rode over the small hill, dismounted, and used water from his canteen to clean his shirt and trousers. He was still cleaning himself when the main column arrived.

The regiment's commander, Colonel Grierson, led the column. They halted at the edge of the bowl and surveyed the scene.

Grierson shook his head. "Well, gentlemen, this will provide us a little diversion from the routine of march. I want a twenty-man detail from B Troop, four days' rations, fifty rounds per man, ready for pursuit in ten minutes. Mr. Rall, you will take C Troop with the same supplies and follow the detachment within the hour. If you fail to make contact in four days, you are to proceed to Fort Riley. Questions?"

"Yes, sir," said the lieutenant who would lead the pursuit element. "Prisoners if possible?"

"Always. If possible, lieutenant. Just remember that your mission is punitive. So if there is resistance, crush it. Anything else?"

"No, sir."

At the exchange of salutes, Grierson said, "Good hunting."

Clairborne dismounted with the officer contingent. It took nearly an hour for the burial detail to dig two six-foot-deep graves in the hard soil. A corporal fashioned two crosses from the charred remains of the buffalo hunters' cart and pounded them into the dirt. Grierson read passages from *The Soldiers' Book of Prayer* while his officers and men of the burial detail stood at the gravesite, heads bowed, hats removed. Before he remounted, in a voice so low only Clairborne and those closest to him could hear, Grierson said, "We'll get them. Sooner or later, we'll get them. I give you my word."

At dinner that evening, Grierson was unusually animated. The discussion focused on the continuous conflict with the Indians and the inevitability of their defeat.

"We all know the outcome is preordained, gentlemen," Grierson said. "The question is how long before it happens, before the Indian is completely subdued and civilized."

Clairborne would later recall that Grierson's next statement was the first time he had heard an army officer articulate what would soon become the grand strategy designed to secure the American west from Canada to Mexico, the Mississippi to the Pacific.

"You all know that two months ago, General Sheridan convened his field grade commanders in Chicago to discuss the Indian matter. You also know that Washington is divided between those who feel that only force will succeed and those who believe a mutually agreeable peaceful settlement with the Indian can be accomplished. I will tell you what my flamboyant friend George Custer and I recommended.

"We jointly proposed what we believe is the best of strategy— in that it is both long term and simple. The plains Indian, specifically the most troublesome tribe, the Comanche, cannot survive without two elements: horses and buffalo. I believe he must be denied both, and I expect that to emerge as official strategy within the month."

The officers responded with loud cries of "hurrah" as they slapped the mess table in approval of what they had heard.

"Those of you who have served with me for a while know that I believe in sharing information and experience with my officers to a degree not many of my peers are willing to do. I do so in the interest of ensuring that your independent decisions are based on the most complete understanding of the objective and the situation as possible. It is in that regard that I will read to you the words of General Sheridan at the close of the conference." Grierson sipped his coffee, withdrew a piece of paper from his pocket, and unfolded it slowly. The only sound was the ever-present wind.

Clearing his throat, he began. "The buffalo hunters have done in the last two years more to settle the vexed Indian question than the entire regular army has done in the last thirty years. They are destroying the Indian commissary. For the sake of lasting peace, let them kill, skin, and sell until the buffaloes are exterminated. Then your prairies can be covered with speckled cattle and festive cowboys, and all will be well."

Grierson refolded the notepaper and returned it to his pocket. "I will tell you, gentlemen, that it's virtually impossible to apprehend the Indians who murdered those hunters. I won't bother saying why since you already know. So why chase them at all? you may well ask. The answer is that I want them to see a pattern of futile pursuit by the army. I want them to think they can always get away from us. Then, when there is a large enough concentration of them to warrant the effort, we will surprise them not only with the relentlessness of our pursuit but with the manner in which we conduct it as well. And when we do catch them, those we don't kill on the spot will walk back to prison and reservation because we will kill their ponies. All of their ponies. The Comanche in particular is defined by his horse herd. Deny him that and you deny him mobility. Deny him mobility and you deny him his manhood."

As they walked to their tents, Clairborne stopped and faced Schofield. "A question?"

"And it is?"

"Colonel Grierson said you all knew that catching them was...I think he said it is 'virtually impossible.' I don't understand that."

Schofield stretched his arms over his head. "You are a gentleman familiar with horseflesh as a matter of your upbringing."

"Of course," Clairborne said.

"Ever heard of the Barb, then?"

Clairborne searched his memory for the word and latched on to the word "berber," which connected him mentally to "Barb."

"The breed from North Africa, the one the Arabs bred for the desert," Clairborne said. "Or was it the Berbers who bred them? I can't recall which."

Schofield nodded. "Good, good. It doesn't matter, Arab or Berber. The point is that the barb was bred for the desert. Incredible endurance. Doesn't need much water. Eats anything that grows."

"OK. So the connection to the Comanche is what?" Clairborne asked a little impatiently.

"The connection is the Spaniard, my friend. The conquistadores rode barbs into the new world. Over time, many got loose or were stolen or taken in combat. The Comanche—all of the plains Indians, in fact—are riding these wonderful horses whose bloodlines go straight back to the Sahara.

"On a tactical level, it means Indians riding horses with barb bloodlines can go farther and faster on less water and fodder than army horses. We carry fodder with us because our horses can't thrive on local grasses. That means we're slower. It's that simple." Schofield scuffed the turf with his boot. "They also ride one horse for distance and lead as many as three or four others for either the hunt or battle. You wouldn't believe how far and how fast they move. And, my friend, of all the plains Indians, the Comanche has evolved as the true master of the horse. They dominate all the others: Sioux, Arapaho, Cheyenne, Apache. All the other tribes. Absolutely dominate them. And, I might add, so far they have effectively dominated us as well. And the Spaniards, the Mexicans, the French, and the British. For almost four hundred years, as a matter of fact."

Clairborne silently absorbed the information.

"Four hundred years?"

Schofield smiled. "Precisely. They have established an empire as real as that of the great Khan, Tamerlane, or Xerxes. The Comanche have absolutely dominated the center of this continent, millions of square miles, for hundreds of years. I would match their skills against those of any Mongol at the gates of Europe."

"So how will the army beat them?"

"The best strategy is the simplest, but just because it is simple doesn't mean it will be easy or quick.

"Intelligence is the key. Knowing where your enemy is and what he is thinking. Knowing what he wants to do and what he can do. We will accumulate that knowledge and use it in concert with the tribes that hate Comanches and who will ride even with whites if it gives them a chance to settle old scores. We will strike when intelligence tells us it is time. It will also probably involve winter campaigns. They can't move as well in winter."

"When do you think that will be?" Clairborne asked.

"Years from now, I think."

"At the risk of displaying my ignorance, just how will the army come by the intelligence you need?"

Schofield smiled. "Same way Alexander got his. Turning the tribes against one another. The antipathy, the rivalries, or feuds, whatever you want to call them, between the Lakota and the Crow, the Comanche and the Apache, the Apache and the Navajo are old and enduring. I think you'll see us taking advantage of that. My point is, they all hate the Comanche because the Comanche rule the roost."

Schofield shook his head. "No. I correct myself. Not all of them hate Comanche. They all fear the Comanche, but some tribes, the Kiowa most of all, are allied with them, a kind of reliable 'auxiliary,' if you will."

Schofield stopped, removed his campaign hat, and ran his hand over his head.

"As a cavalryman, there are two things I love about being here on the frontier. First is the opportunity to see the plains Indian on horse. They're the finest light cavalry since Genghis

Khan. Second, the spaces here are so vast that the American cavalry operates in a theater unmatched anywhere I can think of, certainly unmatched in Europe. Maybe Russia is similar with its steppes. But here the tactics—even the weapons—are new. They're being developed right now, as we heard at dinner. Don't you find that exhilarating?"

After a moment, Clairborne said, "I do, actually."

"So much of the military elsewhere is tied up in tradition, but here on the prairie, things change almost every day, and individual officers like me have a chance to make those changes," Schofield said. "I'm even working on a concept for a new pistol that will revolutionize our tactics. It is a fine time to be a cavalry man."

Fort Riley, Kansas, was not all that different in appearance from Fort Leavenworth except that it was newer, a little rawer, and a little less painted. Spread out over a broad, rolling junction of the Republican and Kansas Rivers, Fort Riley had been hosting army units since 1853 and had taken on the same air of permanence that graced Fort Leavenworth.

The process of locating and occupying all of the facilities designated for the Tenth Cavalry was, in Clairborne's opinion, barely controlled chaos. Elements of the advance party moved into and out of the same buildings two or three times before final decisions were made. During that time, Clairborne noticed that the senior officers reacted to the bureaucratic muddling with a controlled irritability, the junior officers griped openly among themselves, and the Negro noncommissioned officers and enlisted men seemed stoic and bemused by it all.

Four days after the arrival of the main party, things began to settle into a routine, and Clairborne began thinking more about his next move. Texas seemed a long way away, and the thought of crossing the "empty" spaces between Fort Riley and the Caudill Ranch was increasingly daunting, to say the least.

On the basis of the constant references of his officer hosts, Clairborne began to think of that space as "Comanche country." He learned that of all the tribes occupying specific sections of the Southern Plains, the Comanches dominated military concerns. When he considered the journey south, Clairborne was pretty certain he didn't want to encounter any of the Indian tribes, at least not on their terms and certainly not in a meeting for which he could not adequately prepare himself.

Then there was the matter of a half interest in a hotel and saloon in Wyoming Territory. He could take a train to Rawlins, since the Union Pacific tracks should arrive there this very summer. How much money had he earned on his half-interest in the last month since he inherited? Did his ostensible partner even know he had a new partner? Should he telegraph the man to establish contact or just show up and, after a suitably polite interim, ask to see the books?

In the back of his mind, as he considered the options, was the gnawing realization that he had told Caudill he would come to Texas, that he would arrive at the Rocking C and help take cattle north this autumn. In Clairborne's mind, accepting Caudill's invitation was virtually the same as giving his word, which pretty much settled it. After a few more days of killing time at Fort Riley, Clairborne reluctantly made his decision. It was on to Texas. "And God help me."

—◆—

On the stone porch of the regiment's new headquarters, Clairborne stood with his hands in his pockets and leaned against a roof post. In front of him, lined up parallel to the building, were five large tandem-tongued wagons, each pulled by six army mules. The wagon masters gathered in small groups and chatted while they waited for orders. He had quickly learned that the army looked at idleness in biblical terms—as in providing the devil with opportunities. The correlation from the perspective of enlisted men was simple: "Never stand when you can sit. Never sit when you can lie down, and never stay awake when you can sleep." And the related philosophy was: "Always look busy, and never volunteer for anything."

His observations were interrupted by the arrival of Lieutenant Fenton, who came out of the orderly room, nodded at Clairborne, and stood silently beside him for a few moments.

"Know what's in those wagons?" Fenton asked.

Clairborne ran his eyes up and down the line of canvas-covered rigs.

"No."

"Care to hazard a guess?"

Clairborne scratched his chin. The wagons were going to be off-loaded to the regimental headquarters. "Let's see," he said. "What does the army need to do its job? Bullets, weapons. food, clothing, medicine. Well, I know this isn't the armory, so it shouldn't be carbines or pistols. It's not the mess hall or the infirmary, so it's not beans or bromides. I give up."

"Mr. Clairborne, you are looking at the Tenth Cavalry's heart and soul, the things without which no army can function." Fenton flashed his white teeth in a smile that conveyed an underlying message.

After another pause, Fenton leaned toward Clairborne and whispered, "Paper. Paper, Mr. Clairborne. Forms, documents, rosters, records, manuals, inventories, articles of war. We brought only two wagons of medical supplies but no less than five wagonloads of paper. If this is what it takes to run a regiment, just think what it takes for a division, an army... and the mind truly boggles at what it must be like at the War Department."

Fenton waved his hand at the wagons. "It may be heresy to say it, but I have no ambition to rise in rank to the point where I spend my days in a chair shoveling paper rather than astride, leading men."

Abruptly taking Clairborne's arm, Fenton said, "Heavens, I nearly forgot why I came out of the orderly room. Major Schofield sends his compliments and asks that you join him at your convenience."

Schofield's office was completely furnished and looked as if he had occupied the stone-walled room for years instead of days. Even the oriental carpet and horsehair settee were in place opposite his walnut desk.

Rising from his chair, Schofield walked around the desk and directed Clairborne to take a seat.

"What do you think of Fort Riley?" he asked.

"Well, it's only the second army post I've seen, but it does seem rather similar to Fort Leavenworth. I guess that makes sense in that there are obviously common requirements for all posts."

"Indeed," Schofield said while offering Clairborne a cigar.

"Mr. Clairborne, I will apologize in advance for my brevity, but I face a rather daunting list of chores today. There is one pressing matter that I wanted to address with you."

"Of course, Major."

"We have not really discussed your plans to ride down to west Texas."

"No sir. I didn't presume to bring it up, there being so many other things on your plate."

"Actually, there is something on my plate that is relevant to your plans. You recall I suggested you pay particular attention to Sergeant Herman?"

"I do so recall, and I have observed him closely, sir."

"And your opinion?"

Clairborne considered his response. From Schofield's first request during the march, Clairborne had been curious about Schofield's motives. His answer was aimed as much as possible at Schofield's clear respect for Sergeant Herman.

"He seems quite capable. Very capable, in fact. It also seems that both your officers and the enlisted men respect Sergeant Herman. I saw your officers asking his opinion on a number of occasions, and I never saw any enlisted men question his orders. He is also a fine equestrian, no doubt about that."

"Well, if your were one of my officers, Mr. Clairborne, I would say 'excellent report.' Now allow me, if you will, to tell you why I wanted you to observe Sergeant Herman. Did you know that he has a wooden leg—his left leg, to be precise?"

Clairborne did not know that and performed a quick mental review of Sergeant Herman's movements. He did recall a very slight limp but hardly what one would expect from a cripple with a wooden leg.

"He certainly carries it off pretty well. I had no idea."

Schofield smiled. "Capital. Capital. I wanted you to think of him as fully capable. You see, Mr. Clairborne, Sergeant Herman is mustering out of the army. He requested an exception to the regulations requiring him to be pensioned off as a result of his wound—in the line of duty, by the way, and Colonel Grierson and I endorsed his request. Alas, the review board did not concur. Next Friday at retreat ceremony, he will muster out."

Clairborne felt himself saddened and was surprised at his sentiment. When Schofield said nothing further, he asked, "So if I may ask, Major, what is the relevance of the sergeant's retirement to my ride to Texas?"

"Just this. I'll be blunt. The territory between here and west Texas is as fraught with hazard as any stretch on the face of this planet, and you are unlikely to make it to your destination alive. We—all of us—believe that is the case, sir, and even had we not come to enjoy your company, we would be obliged to dissuade you from undertaking such an endeavor.

"Mr. Clairborne, there are no fewer than four separate tribes, perhaps as many as seven, that are hostile to white men in that country. It is sheer folly for you to try to cross it alone. In fact, it's unlikely the best troop of this regiment could make that march without casualties.

"The army doesn't have the authority to stop you, but it is within my purview to most strongly recommend that you make your journey to Texas in the company of Sergeant Herman. He is heading there as well for reasons he has not disclosed."

Clairborne was shocked at the suggestion. On the one hand, the sergeant was as close to an expert on the terrain, the Indians, the horses, all of the relevant factors, as one could hope for in a companion.

On the other, he was a Negro, a former slave. To Clairborne's mild amusement, he found himself wondering not whether he could accept the sergeant's company but rather if Herman's life as a slave meant he would eschew the opportunity of prolonged, isolated, hazard-filled time with a former slaver.

"Would he agree to ride with me, Major?"

"You mean because you were a slaver?"

"Yes. He's a free man with no obligations to anyone but himself. He may not cotton to the idea."

"You'll never know unless you ask. I will leave it up to you from here on out, but I will tell you again, as clearly as I can, the journey to Texas from here is fraught with hazards beyond telling. You would be most wise to avail yourself of Sergeant Herman's company," Schofield said.

"If he is willing," Clairborne responded.

"Yes. If he is willing."

At the conclusion of the conversation, Schofield directed his first sergeant to find Sergeant Herman, tell him to saddle up, and escort Mr. Clairborne for a short ride around the post perimeter.

Fifteen minutes later, Herman walked into the orderly room and approached the first sergeant, whom he had known for years.

"What's going on, Top?"

"Can't tell you, Sergeant. You just need to accompany Mr. Clairborne on a ride this afternoon. Don't know anything more than that. The major probably doesn't want his tenderfoot guest to get gored by a buff. Anyway, it's nothing big. Be here at 14:00."

Clairborne and Herman had ridden in silence for ten minutes beyond the gate when Clairborne reined in at the top of a rise. Beyond them, the Kansas plains swept to a dun-gray horizon that seemed both close enough to touch and infinitely distant.

Clairborne's mind had been spinning since his talk with Schofield. He considered multiple approaches to the subject, finally deciding that nothing was as relevant and effective as straight fact.

"Sergeant Herman, I know you must be wondering what's going on, why you were told to ride out here with me today, so here it is."

Herman said nothing and maintained his focus on the horizon.

"I'm leaving shortly for Texas—southwest Texas, to be exact. Major Schofield says you may be heading in that direction too. He very, very strongly suggested you and I discuss riding together. I am amenable to that idea. It seems to me that the dangers ahead almost require travelers to seek safety in numbers—even if the number in question is only two."

Clairborne hoped his little joke would elicit a response. It didn't. Herman was silent. Clairborne's hackles began to rise.

"Damn it. I'm the one who should be hesitating to ride with him," he thought. "Instead, he's keeping me on tenterhooks. Well, to hell with this. I'm sure as blazes not going to beg him."

Just as Clairborne was about to wheel his mount around and ride back to the fort, Herman spoke while continuing to study the horizon.

"You were a planter," he said to him in a tone that could have been both a statement and a question.

"I was."

"How many slaves your family own?"

Not knowing the precise number, Clairborne decided citing a specific guess was better than saying he didn't know.

"Forty-seven."

Herman said nothing and didn't move. Clairborne began to wonder how long he should remain by the sergeant's side.

Still looking into the distance, Herman said, "Next Friday'll be the first time in my life I won't have to answer to anybody but myself. I'll not be anybody's servant ever again."

"I'm not looking for a servant, Sergeant. I'm looking for a riding companion, nothing more."

Herman turned his horse to face Clairborne. "You given any thought to what you need to pack? It's not going to be easy. You going to bring that bay packhorse?"

"I am. What about you?"

"Been trying to figure that out. I don't want to spend all my savings on beans and bullets, but I'd rather have enough than not enough."

"Well, why don't we try this then, Sergeant? I'll come up with a list of what I have. You do the same thing. We'll meet in a day or two to compare and see what else we need." As his words left his lips, Clairborne wished he could recall them. What if Herman couldn't read or write? Had he begun this tenuous relationship by embarrassing the man, and if so, how far should he go to rectify the ill-defined situation?

Again, Clairborne opted for directness.

"It may have been presumptuous of me to assume you can write, Sergeant. I could gin up a list for both of us."

"No, sir. I can do words and numbers. I learned to write, and I can read maps as well," Herman said. He reflected that his "no, sir" was habitual and that if he were ever to approach equal status with this or any other white man, he would have to be more selective in using the word "sir" in his conversations. There would always be times for it, just a hell of a lot fewer than in any part of his life up to next Friday afternoon.

"Well then, Sergeant. Do you have any questions of me, anything you need to know to help you decide on your course of action?"

Herman had been in the army a total of five years, counting his time as a laborer, but he still paused every time a white man asked him for his opinion. Once his reputation as a good soldier became known in the regiment, white officers—the good ones—began to solicit his opinion more and more often. His strong and instinctive interest in not only the flora and fauna of the plains but also in the human inhabitants formed the basis for his unique understanding of the environment. Herman was one of only nine men in the entire regiment who had learned sign language, the lingua franca of the continent's vast midsection. His illicit hunts as a boy in South Carolina, efforts to supplement slave rations with protein provided by venison, possum, squirrel, and duck had long since taught him to observe animals, to learn their ways in order to kill them. Almost immediately after joining the Tenth Cavalry, Herman was assigned to hunting parties sent out to supplement meager army rations. The food supplied to the postwar soldier was always both of poor quality and meager to the brink of scandal, and Negro units usually got whatever white soldiers rejected.

So his Negro noncommissioned officers and their white commanders soon recognized Recruit Herman as someone to watch. He and a small number of fellow recruits were given more opportunities—to fail or succeed—than their peers. Within six months of his enlistment in the Tenth, Herman was promoted to corporal, thanks to both his innate abilities and the need of the new regiment to fill vacant positions. The two gold stripes he sewed onto his sleeves and the extra two dollars a month that went with them gave Herman a sense of pride he had never known, but it was a pride he carried inside and never articulated to anyone.

He proved to be an apt student when it came to regulations and army protocol, formal or informal. Then there was his knowledge of horses. In a cavalry unit, literally nothing else was as valuable as understanding the horse. Herman had been around or responsible for the care of horses for more than twenty years, since he was six.

The Tenth Cavalry Regiment was first and foremost a fighting unit. It existed to execute the orders it received from Washington via Sheridan's headquarters in Chicago.

Executing orders on the American plains frequently involved fighting, and how a man fought was the most important consideration of all when it came to the opinion of peers and superiors. Herman showed from the beginning that he was a fighting man.

All of this experience and knowledge would have marked him as worthy of promotion in any case, but it was his skill and courage under fire that eventually added the third stripe to his sleeves, a full ten more dollars to his payday, and the title of sergeant to his name.

The violent encounters in question were never as grand in scale as the battles he survived as a private in the Grand Army of the Republic's Fifty-Seventh Volunteer Regiment of Colored Troops. The carnage and chaos resulting from collisions of tens of thousands of soldiers, cannon, and cavalry in the Carolinas and Georgia were simply never approached in magnitude by what the army referred to as "skirmishes" with Indians on the Central Plains.

But Herman and his comrades knew that a rifle bullet could blow off a man's jaw or tumble his guts into the dirt as readily in a fight between ten people as it could in a battle involving ten thousand.

Reflecting on his past, Herman realized he had not answered the white civilian's question.

"I'm sorry, Mr. Clairborne. I was thinking about something else. Your question again?"

Clairborne had begun to be irritated by Herman's silence but repeated his question.

"I thought you may have something you wished to ask me, to know about my situation, before you make your decision."

Without thinking, Herman said, "Do you want me to go with you?"

Without hesitation, Clairborne responded. "Yes, I do. The more I think of it, the better an idea it is, actually."

Herman resisted the urge to smile and shake his head in wonder. "How things can change," he thought. He felt like praying. He felt like an Israelite. His mother's faith surged within him. "From slave to this, to this slaver asking me to ride with him. Not telling me to. Asking me to. Lord, lord, how things can change."

"Well, Mr. Clairborne, I'll tell you. I know you can ride, but I've never seen you shoot, and I don't know—I hope I don't insult you—but I don't know if you can fight. Thing is, between here and Texas, there're going to be scrapes sure as sunrise. I just wish I knew more about how you handle yourself in a scrape." He paused before adding, "Horses and men both. If they ain't got sand, if they ain't got plenty of bottom, they won't make it out here. Even if they do, it's no guarantee they won't wind up under a pile of rocks with no marker."

Clairborne understood the primal logic of Herman's concern. He wanted to blurt out that he knew how to handle threats better now than ever before in his life, but he stopped that train of thought before it took him to an alley in Nashville.

"That is the question for sure, Sergeant. I could say just about anything, but you and I both know that words don't amount to a hill of beans. It's just deeds that matter, and I surely don't have the store of them that you do."

"Well, Mr. Clairborne, I'd like to chew on this for a while. Can I give you an answer tomorrow?" Herman asked.

Clairborne was disappointed and more than a little disconcerted by Herman's hesitation. He'd assumed Herman would go with him and had begun to adjust his thoughts about the journey to accommodate the presence of the Negro soldier. The possibility that the man would not ride with him knocked Clairborne's confidence.

"Sure. Take your time," he said. "Guess I'd better be getting back to get ready," Clairborne said as he nodded and wheeled his horse around to head back to the fort.

Herman said nothing, watched the rider depart, and then turned to face the prairie, his thoughts moving in several directions. "What choice do I have?" he asked himself. "Ride alone or ride with him. Unless he's completely useless, it's better to ride with him, especially if he listens to me. No way to know that without trying."

The decision was one best made with all of the cards on the table and all of the experience available brought into play. There was only one man Herman respected enough to seek his counsel: Sergeant Major Ezekial Jones, the Tenth Cavalry's senior noncommissioned officer. Whatever the sergeant major advised would determine Herman's ultimate course, and Herman would be comfortable with it.

As he passed through Fort Riley's main gate, Herman felt a stab of nostalgia and loss knowing that in a short while, he would leave all this forever, one way or the other.

In addition to being the regiment's senior enlisted man, Ezekial Jones was also one of the biggest and strongest of its members. His height, his biceps, and his barrel chest combined to make the sergeant major so imposing that he rarely had to raise his voice. Unless, that was, he was in front of formations on the parade ground. Then his commands carried from where he sat upon his horse to the most distant soldier in the rear ranks. The decorations he rarely wore but everyone knew about also contributed significantly to his authority. Won in battle at Fort Donaldson and Fort Pillow, Jones was the only man in the regiment, with the sole exception of Colonel Grierson, to have been awarded his medals by General Ulysses S. Grant in his capacity as commander of the Army of the Tennessee. The aura naturally generated by such men was accentuated in Jones's case by the fact that his only known vice was his evening pipe of Virginia tobacco. He didn't drink, curse, or womanize. Many of his men thought that to be both amazing and more than a little strange. But they would never so much as hint at such opinion while in his presence.

Herman was recruited by then-First Sergeant Jones when the Tenth Cavalry was being raised at Fort Leavenworth. Colonel Grierson personally reviewed the record of every prospective recruit and the recommendations made by his renowned first sergeant. The job of filling the new regiment's ranks was made easier since for every position there were six or seven applicants, many of whom were veterans of service during the war.

Herman's unusually rapid promotions made it professionally acceptable for him to legitimately claim the regimental sergeant major as a friend.

They sat on a half-log bench against the exterior stone wall of Sergeant Major Jones's quarters. Herman passed his tobacco pouch and waited until both pipes were filled and lit. The aromatic smoke hung in the still afternoon air, mixing with the post's permanent bouquet of sweat, dust, and horse manure. Herman pulled a faded bandana from his trouser pocket and wiped the dust from his knee-high riding boots.

"You know anything about Mr. Clairborne asking me to ride down to Texas with him?"

"Nothing official."

Herman knew the code for that statement. It meant that the sergeant major had not engaged in either verbal or written formal communication on the topic—but that he knew all there was to know about it nonetheless.

"OK. Let's hear what you can tell me unofficially."

"Well, both the colonel and the major believe Mr. Clairborne doesn't really understand just how hazardous his trip will be."

"Probably doesn't, being a tenderfoot and all," Herman said.

"They think you being with him improves his chances of getting there with all that long hair of his still under his hat instead of at the tip of some buck's lance."

"Probably right again," Herman said as he used a nail head to tamp the tobacco more tightly into the bowl of his corncob pipe.

"Give much thought to how riding with him might help you?" Jones asked.

"Not really."

"Well, think about this. Being with a white man instead of alone is going to make it less likely that any white boys you run into are going to do something bad just for the heck of it."

"Hadn't thought of that."

"And word has it Mr. Clairborne is heading to west Texas because Old Man Caudill invited him to come down and hire on."

"Heard that."

"Well, if you was looking for a job, showing up with a man who has an invitation and, assuming you make it together, will recommend you, might be about as good as you could hope for. Seems to me, anyways."

""Not sure I'd want to stay in west Texas," Herman said.

Jones paused to consider his pipe.

"You don't know exactly where in Texas she is, do you?"

"No. It just seems likely, from what I know, that the only Texans that owned slaves were in the eastern part, not out west. Up around Louisiana, not out in the Llano," Herman said.

"Probably right. But you still got to get to Texas one way or another, and we both know a lot of black men are getting hired to push cattle, so you'd be among your own kind."

Another prolonged silence.

"So you think I should go with him?"

"I do. Been watching that boy since he showed up. Family's from a big place on the James south of Richmond. He's a slaver, no doubt about it. Was a slaver. But I admire the fact that he left all that. Whatever happened to his home, it still has to be an easier life back there than out here, and I've heard him asking more questions about army doings and buffalo and Indians than any man I've ever known. Shows me he wants to learn and isn't shy about asking. That's good."

Herman understood that Jones's last statement was one of the longest he had ever heard from his friend. That meant the sergeant major placed great importance on the subject.

"Well then, I guess I'll ride with him. Worst thing that could happen is he loses his nerve in a fracas. Everything else he can learn. Guts can't be taught."

"Um hum. Looking forward to hearing how it works out," Jones said as he regarded the young sergeant beside him.

"So am I, Sergeant Major." Herman said. "So am I."

—◦◦◦—

Clairborne stopped shaving and opened the door to see who had knocked. It was Herman.

"Sergeant Herman. You're up early. Come in."

"Ah, thanks, but I'd rather talk outside, if you don't mind," Herman said, consciously deciding not to use the word "sir."

"OK. Let me finish scraping my face, and I'll be with you shortly," Clairborne said as he closed the door. Taking the last swipes at the lather, Clairborne regarded himself in the mirror above the marble washstand and decided Herman's message was no. Why else would he want to talk outside, where there would be less likelihood of an argument or a display of pique?

Opening the door, Clairborne found Herman standing under the porch roof, gauntlets in his left hand slowly tapping his leg.

Motioning to the bench beside the door, Clairborne said, "Care to take a load off while we talk?"

"Mr. Clairborne, I don't want to seem unfriendly and all, but, ah, I'm still in the army, and it wouldn't look right, me sitting down with you here in officers' country."

Clairborne felt relieved at the understanding of Herman's formality.

"Of course, Sergeant. I hadn't thought of that. Have you made your decision?"

"I have. It seems a good idea. Saturday morning departure?"

"Ah, yes. Saturday morning," Clairborne said, somewhat taken aback by the brevity of Herman's communications on a subject he had assumed would involve much more discussion.

"You mentioned comparing lists of supplies and equipment, Mr. Clairborne. When would you like to do that?"

"Well, let's see. Today is Wednesday. If we meet tomorrow morning, we'd still have almost two days to secure what we don't have. Is that convenient?"

Herman surprised Clairborne with a broad smile.

"I don't know how much last-minute fuss there'll be mustering out, but if I know the army, Mr. Clairborne, there'll be plenty. How about seven in the morning?"

"See you then."

Clairborne ran his hand over his freshly shaven chin as he watched Herman walk away. His limp was amazingly minimal considering that his left leg was wood from midcalf down. Clairborne wondered about the prosthetic—what it looked like and who had made it. Whoever it was had to be a master craftsman. In postwar Virginia, Clairborne had seen countless soldiers hopping around on crutches, a trouser leg pinned up to keep it from flapping. Some had peg legs, mere wooden stumps strapped to what was left of the leg in question, but none moved as close to normally as did Sergeant Herman. His range of motion was so good, it had almost won him permission to remain on active duty.

"I wonder how long it will be before I get a look at it?" Clairborne asked himself.

Observing army routine from his vantage point on the guest quarters' porch, he realized something that startled him, something so basic that he was chagrined for not thinking of it before. He had not fired more than one load of ammunition from the guns he inherited from Wild Bill, despite his benefactor's insistence and despite the fact that Clairborne understood and agreed with that admonition.

Back in his room, he strapped on the gun belt, slid the silver Colt engraved with "Thunder" into the slim, tooled holster on the belt's left side, and regarded himself in the mirror. He recalled thinking that Wild Bill's impact with the ground was the reason his holster seemed to be on the wrong side. He'd long since learned that carrying a pistol butt-forward on the side opposite the shooter's strong hand was the style preferred by many, including some of the best-known shootists. West of the Mississippi, there was constant debate about the tools of the trade—firearms, saddles, ropes, even horse breeds. All were vital to westerners, be they cowboys, soldiers, buffalo hunters, lawmen, or outlaws. Clairborne had already learned that depending on opportunity and circumstance, it was not uncommon for westerners to dabble in all five occupations during the course of lifespans usually both hard and short. Some of the most well-known names belonged to men who divided their time among hunting camps, cattle drives, gaming tables, or enforcing whatever law existed in frontier settlements, written or otherwise.

After loading each of his weapons, Clairborne retrieved his horse from one of the huge stables. He rode to the regimental orderly room, dismounted, and went inside, where he encountered Lieutenant McGinnis wearing the sash that marked him as the unit's officer of the day.

"Good morning, Lieutenant," Clairborne said stiffly. "I understand the army likes to keep track of its guests when they leave or enter the post, so I'm letting you know that I intend to ride out for some target practice. A couple of hours, maybe three, not much more than that."

"You could use one of our ranges if you like. Save you the ride," McGinnis said.

Clairborne had anticipated the offer and decided that when it came, he would decline. He didn't want to embarrass himself in front of anyone, particularly soldiers who might be amused by the accuracy of his shooting. He had not fired the weapons enough to know just how good or bad he was. That he was within hours of committing himself to months of riding across arguably the most dangerous place in the world underscored his desire for privacy. If he couldn't hit anything, he didn't want anyone else to know, particularly Sergeant Herman.

Thirty minutes east of the main gate, Clairborne found himself so alone that from where he sat, he could not see even the smoke from Fort Riley's kitchens or the chimneys of the civilian dwellings and businesses that clustered around army posts like so many ticks on a hound.

Sweat trickled from his hairline down the back of his neck. He removed his gloves, wiped his face with a handkerchief, and then turned to survey the terrain in all directions.

"Not a damn thing between here and Texas except a river or two."

He wondered if any Indians were watching him. He remembered the burning bodies of the buffalo hunters and how the leg separated from one of them when the soldiers tried to drag them out of the fire.

Adrenaline burst in his stomach, bringing with it the acid taste of brass on the back of his tongue. His heart began racing, and he opened his mouth to breathe.

"Dear Jesus. What have I got myself into? What...why am I doing this? I don't care about Texas or cattle or Caudill. Lord above, these men have been telling me over and over I need to be thinking about Comanches. Why didn't I? Why? Why?"

He shouted "Goddamn it" so loudly he startled his horse. He dismounted and sat abruptly, holding the reins in his left hand, rubbing his face with his right.

"This is just crazy," he said aloud. "I don't want to do this. Hellfire, I don't have to do this. I've got money. I have enough money to last me for years, especially if I do something with it, and now I'm likely to get killed in the middle of nowhere for nothing."

A fat slab of contrition dropped into to the emotional stew bubbling inside him. He shifted to his knees and brought his knuckles to his lips.

"I'm sorry for blaspheming, Lord. I'm sorry. Forgive me for my profanity. Just let me know what to do."

He held his position for long moments, standing only when pain from pebbles under his kneecaps interfered with his meditation. He hadn't expected a response to his prayerful request and didn't see or hear one. Even the wind remained constant— no tempests or dead calms to be interpreted for divine guidance.

The soft muzzle of his horse, sniffing its motionless master, tilted Clairborne's hat forward.

"OK, Buck. I'll get on with it," he said. He took off his coat, retrieved a picket pin from his saddlebag, screwed it into the turf, and tied the reins to its loop. He pulled the Henry rifle from the scabbard and laid it on a blanket and then secured a box of .44 cartridges from the opposite saddlebag. He took a long swig from his canteen and picked out a likely target.

Clairborne elected to practice with his pistols first. Everywhere he had gone since he inherited his guns, there had been great interest in them, particularly on the part of Major Schofield. Examining one of the Colts while Clairborne related how he got them, Schofield whistled and said, "Lovely. Works of art, these implements."

Schofield went on to tell Clairborne that the pistols were custom made, that there were no others like them in the world. Schofield speculated that Wild Bill must have engaged someone at Colts in Hartford to produce the unique set of pistols combining deadly functionality with refined aesthetics. Schofield had regaled him at length about the accelerating pace of technological advancement in the field of firearms, how newfangled metallic cartridges like those in his Henry rifle would soon render obsolete the percussion cap and ball arms that had dominated the field for the last two decades.

"I'll tell you this, Mr. Clairborne," Schofield had said. "I am devoted to prodding the army to adapt this new technology as soon as possible. Do you have any idea how much cartridge guns increase an individual soldier's firepower?"

Clairborne did not. He did comprehend, however, that the Colts he possessed were more valuable than he ever imagined when first he saw them.

Now, as he stood alone on the prairie, Clairborne knew he had to learn his weapons. His life literally depended on knowing how to extract the full capability of the firearms he would carry from this day onward.

He pulled the hammer back to half cock and rotated the cylinder to check each of the six percussion caps on the "nipples" connecting them to the powder charges packed into the chambers of the cylinder. He lowered the hammer.

He returned the pistol to its slim, soft leather holster and looked around. A rock the size of a pie pan caught his eye. Maybe fifteen yards away. Should be easy. He drew, turned slightly to his left as he raised the Colt, and moved the hammer to full cock with his thumb. When eye, muzzle, and target aligned, he squeezed the trigger ever so gently. He learned the first time he fired Wild Bill's weapons that each had a modified hair trigger, inordinately sensitive to pressure.

Ignition of twenty-three grains of black powder sent a blast of flame and a plume of gray smoke from the muzzle, obscuring the target. Clairborne waited for the wind to carry away the smoke and saw no evidence that the 210-grain lead ball had impacted the stone. Right arm extended, he raised the pistol and fired again. No hit. The dust cloud dissipating in the wind told him the round had struck the dirt somewhere in the stone's vicinity. He needed to know where it had hit to adjust his fire.

After firing all six rounds, Clairborne saw that he had missed six times. He reloaded and moved five paces closer. The second round fired produced the reassuring twang of a ricochet and a white scar on the stone's gray surface, but at the lower left edge rather than the center. He held Thunder at the one-o'clock position on the stone and fired again. A hit, but not dead center.

Clairborne looked up at the sun. "Good thing it's morning. Looks like I'm going to be here all day."

July 12, 1868
Fort Riley, Kansas

At times such as these, I wonder why I bother to keep a record of my thoughts. It seems a useless exercise. Reading what I have written to date usually serves to make me sad or remorseful. I realize that most of my entries are usually either immediately before or immediately after some significant event, and tonight is no different.

Tomorrow, I embark on an endeavor I am relatively certain will be the death of me. I have not slept these last three days. Perhaps that is the reason my anxiety has transformed into resignation. I am so physically and emotionally fatigued that my senses are, I think, numbed to the point of being virtually deadened. I move about as though in a torpor. Schofield and Rall have asked me about my health, and I have caught both of them studying me out of the corner of their eyes.

The ride across the plains should be an adventure. Or perhaps the correct thing to say is that it should be thought of as an adventure. Instead, I think of it almost as one who faces a terminal disease, so certain am I that death awaits me somewhere out there. How can it not? In addition to the hostiles we doubtless will encounter, there is a virtually infinite list of natural hazards we face as well: starvation, thirst, venomous serpents and insects, riding accidents, gun accidents.

Such trepidations should prevent me from this undertaking, but pride has overcome those fears. I simply cannot face these men, Sergeant Herman in particular, and tell them I have changed my mind. They would know why.

I have been thinking a great deal about my traveling companion and our shared circumstance. It is the sense of complete irony that provides the only lightness in my mood, the irony of my facing such challenges in the company of a man who used to be a slave. From the opposing poles of our lives before the war, we have come to this situation. Both of us will ride west in the company of a man we neither know nor trust and for whom we feel no bonds of comradely affection. I know this is true because I have tried to understand why he would agree to take on the company of a man untested on the field of battle or by prolonged suffering. I've learned that here *in the west, there are many names for men like me: greenhorn, tenderfoot, tyro, pilgrim, greener, juniper, dude. All are at least mildly derogatory, and all imply that the person in question is not to be trusted with any significant responsibility until he has amassed a quantity of proven experience.*

Yesterday was memorable for both of us. Sergeant Herman was given the place of honor next to Col. Grierson at retreat formation, during which he was awarded his second medal for valor and a Purple Heart for the wound that cost him his leg. In a private ceremony after the troopers were dismissed, Grierson, Schofield, and the regiment's other senior officers gave Herman impressive gifts they had evidently paid for with their own money. These were a new Henry rifle in .44 caliber and a pair of field glasses. In a most extraordinary gesture, Herman was allowed to retain both his favorite horse and his Colt service revolver by dint of some bureaucratic legerdemain. It was clear the sergeant was nearly overwhelmed. He rarely lifted his head and mumbled, "Thank you, gentlemen" over and over.

At dinner last night, I was the object of many an oratorical exercise, although the two that I shall remember should I be granted long life were those of Major Schofield and Lieutenant Rall. The major said he admired my sense of adventure and found in me the essence of the "American character," which he defined as a willingness to leave behind the old, unsatisfying ways and boldly seek a new life, ever westward. My friend Rall took a more lighthearted approach, gently chiding me for my naiveté. Then he said what struck me the most. Standing with his glass held high, he faced me and said, "Your future is rife with challenge and, I daresay, hardship, my friend. I urge you to do one thing for our great country. Do not allow the difficulties you face to erode the civility, the appreciation of culture that is your heritage. This country needs boldness and strength just now, but soon enough, it will need law and learning, literature and music and art to shape this wild land into a place for civilized society. You must contribute to that end. Gentlemen, I give you Tucker Lightfoot Clairborne, a friend of the cavalry, a true gentleman and a man of destiny."

In four hours, I will mount my horse and ride west with Sergeant Herman. (Am I to continue to address him using his military title after he is mustered out of the army?) I am resigned to considering each sunrise and sunset as a blessing from God, whom I beseech for the one thing I require to see me through whatever lies ahead: courage.

———

Clairborne and Herman met in front of the post stables at dawn. Clairborne saddled his black, Bucephalus, and led Ajax, his bay gelding packhorse, back to his quarters to pack his belongings and supplies. Herman placed his army McClellan saddle on his gleaming chestnut gelding named Billy and led a sturdy mule he called Stumpy back to his barracks to complete preparations for the long ride. They agreed to meet at the main gate in an hour.

In their discussions to plan the journey, Clairborne quickly and effortlessly shifted to the role of a student. It was a matter of simple logic, he told himself. Herman had recommended a number of things Clairborne realized were valuable ideas.

Every weapon was kept loaded at all times.

Oats for the animals would be rationed. "We can't carry enough grain to last the whole trip, so we got to gentle them off a little at a time. The grass should be pretty good this early in the summer," Herman explained.

He recommended that Clairborne pack a crock of honey, which Herman did as well. "It doesn't spoil, makes almost anything taste better, and it's good for wounds and scrapes."

Both pack animals carried equal loads of the same items the two riders would share: ammunition; hardtack biscuit; dried beans; dried meat; tarpaulins and Sibley tents; and small medical kits containing needles, cat gut sutures, tweezers, and linen bandages. Each man carried his own currycombs, spare horseshoes, tongs, hoof pick, nails, and hammer. The packing plan addressed the possibility that one of the pack animals would be lost in a crisis.

Each man would also carry personal belongings in pockets, saddlebags, and packs. Clairborne carried his copy of Homer, eating utensils, cigars, and matches in an empty brass shell case; coffee beans; and a box of balls, powder, and caps. Herman stashed away twists of pipe tobacco, a sewing kit the soldiers called their "housewife," twelve ounces of pork, twelve hardtack crackers, coffee beans, and a bar of lye soap.

Despite his anxiety, Clairborne rode to the officers' mess, where he wolfed down what he knew would be his last good breakfast for a long while. The eggs, bacon, biscuits, butter, sorghum syrup, and coffee sated and calmed him, as did the idle banter and good-natured joshing from the surprisingly large number of officers who joined him this early in the day.

Across the post in the noncommissioned officers' mess hall, Herman tucked away his last army meal as well. He tapped his fingers on the plank table, his booted right foot on the stone floor, fidgeting in a way that was new to him and his comrades.

"Looks like you can't wait to bust out of here, Titus, you getting nervous and all," said his friend Joseph.

"Tell you the truth, I just want to get going is all. Seems like I'm wasting daylight," Herman responded.

He was mildly surprised that Clairborne was waiting for him at the gate, holding his hat in his gloved right hand. Clairborne's gray wool coat was wrapped in his yellow fish-skin waterproof slicker on top of his bulging saddlebags. His gray vest was half unbuttoned, and a maroon silk scarf hung loosely over the banded collar of his white muslin shirt. An ivory-handled Colt rode high on his left side, butt forward, and an edge-tooled leather scabbard holding a bone-handled Bowie was looped over his heavy belt on his right. Clairborne wore tan trousers with a cavalry-style canvas panel sewn into its crotch and thighs to mitigate months of saddle chafe.

Clairborne studied Herman as he rode up facing into the slanting rays of morning light, noting the functionality of Herman's civilian and army attire. He had learned a great deal about army clothes and equipment during his time with the Tenth. Their wool tunics over flannel shirts were too cold in the winter and too hot in the summer. Soldiers and officers alike had to pay for their uniforms. Officers usually paid cash to their tailors. Enlisted men had their pay docked each month.

Replacement clothing came from auctions or from the foot-lockers of deceased comrades. Herman's attire and tack was a pragmatic mix of what was available and what he could afford. A battered, broad-brimmed, sweat-stained campaign hat rode low on his brow. At his neck, Herman wore a red-and-white cotton bandana. His torso was covered with a deerskin shirt, the sleeves of which sported short fringe. His trousers were army issue, faded blue with a thin gold stripe down the outside seam and tucked in to government-issue boots adorned with army spurs.

Herman's pistol was covered in a regulation flapped holster on his right side, while on his left side, the stout black garrison belt supported Herman's own bone-handled Bowie. Tucked into a leather scabbard under his right leg, the walnut stock of his new Henry rifle gleamed under layers of hand-rubbed linseed oil.

Each side of Herman's saddle pommel sported flap-covered bags containing field glasses and spare pistol.

With little more than a nod, they turned their horses and headed for the gate.

At the massive stone-and-timber structure, the two privates on sentry duty snapped their Springfield trapdoor carbines to the vertical position called present arms. The sergeant of the guard, Phileas Gerber, one of Herman's best friends, stepped in front of the sentries.

"Who goes there?" he called in keeping with regulations.

"Former Sergeant Titus Herman, requesting permission to quit the post on completion of his enlistment," Herman replied in his best command voice.

Gerber raised his white-gloved hand to Herman, who shook it slowly.

"Best of luck, my friend. Best of luck," Gerber said. He faced Clairborne and said, "To you as well, Mr. Clairborne. Good luck."

Gerber stepped back beside the sentries standing at rigid attention, raised his right hand to the gleaming black brim of his kepi, and called, "Sergeant Herman and Mr. Clairborne may pass."

Herman and Clairborne spurred their mounts to a trot. Behind them, the rigid, familiar routine of garrison life. Ahead, a sun-bleached abyss.

Clairborne hadn't thought much about sleeping on the ground. The interlude on mattresses and under sheets had dulled his memory of sleeping in the dirt. The first night on the trail to Texas, Clairborne delayed preparation of his bedroll to watch Herman.

The ground was flat, open, grassy, and bleached. The campsite offered only two attractions: a small, stagnant pond rimmed with limp cattails and a copious fuel supply in the form of buffalo droppings desiccated by the summer sun.

Hovering just beneath the awkward silence was the need to establish camp protocol—who did what. Normally, determining such things as gathering water and fuel, starting and tending the campfire, cooking, and cleaning skillets and plates was a simple matter of agreement based on personal preferences, known skills—such as food preparation—or something as arbitrary as a coin flip. But the backgrounds of the two men setting up camp meant that such customary practices were irrelevant.

It soon got to the point of awkwardness, and both men realized it.

"Well, probably ought to work out the chores. Got any preferences?" Clairborne asked.

"Don't mind cooking. Not all that particular about scouring skillets though," Herman responded.

"All right. I'll start a fire," Clairborne said.

Both men unsaddled their mounts and pack animals and fed, watered, curried, and then hobbled them before turning to their own needs for the night.

Clairborne filled their canteens and gathered buffalo turds in a canvas tent half, not knowing how many were needed for cooking and the rest of the evening. As he stooped to pick them up, he wondered if the food would reflect the flavor of the fuel used to prepare it. "Makes sense. Applewood or cherrywood's good for roasting things. What the hell," he thought. "Not much choice."

Herman interrupted his culinary work with some unsolicited advice.

"Might want to kick those turds over before you pick 'em up. Scorpions like to hide out under 'em for sure."

Clairborne paused and pondered the bison pie under his hand. "Wonderful."

An hour later, after scouring the utensils with sand and grass, Clairborne reflected on the meal as he reclined against his saddle. He noted Herman's use of dried peppers and a drop of honey to turn their meager fare into something actually tasty.

"Say, I've got to tell you, that meal wasn't all that bad. Done that a few times before, have you?"

"Yep. Few thousand, I reckon, give or take five hundred or so," Herman said as he arranged his bedroll.

Herman wrapped his buffalo robe and a thick wool trade blanket with a canvas tent half, laid it on the ground, and then covered himself with a gray wool army blanket with a large "US" woven into its fabric. Lacking a buffalo robe of his own, Clairborne stuffed his thickest blanket into his tent half and spread it on the ground on the other side of the campfire.

"One thing you ought to watch out for is snakes," Herman said as he lay down. "Thing is, they like the warmth of your body, and sometimes they just kind of snuggle up next to you without you even knowing it."

Clairborne wondered if Herman was joking. Just how much of it was initiation of the tenderfoot into life on the plains? If Herman wanted to unsettle his companion, he had succeeded. Clairborne looked around. First scorpions, now snakes. "Wonderful."

Herman stretched his arms over his head and scratched his armpit. "Some say putting a hemp lariat on the ground around your bedroll'll keep 'em off you, but it won't."

"You know that, do you?" Clairborne asked.

"Yep. Bivouac on the Brazos a year or so ago, saw a private named Henderson wake up with a big old diamondback on his blanket beside his leg. He got all panicked and jumped up, and that old rattler bit him good. Knew he was a goner right then. Tried to get the poison out, but he died three days after."

Clairborne was pretty sure Herman wasn't joking, but his attention was drawn away from serpents and focused on Herman as he pulled off his boots. Finally, he would get to see Herman's wooden leg.

It was an amazing piece of work. Leather straps secured it to the top of his calf muscle just below his knee. The prosthetic was made of a straight-grain hardwood, elm or oak. Its exterior was carved to the shape of a calf muscle. The interior was hollowed out and padded with leather to fit Herman's stump. The most amazing aspect, though, was the metal hinges connecting the upper and lower sections at what would have been the ankle. The lower section was very much like a shoe tree, carved with such precision Clairborne could discern an arch and a distinct heel.

"Pretty fine work, wouldn't you say?" Herman asked, massaging the skin at the bottom of his severed calf.

"You can say that again. That is just an amazing piece of work."

"Yep. I'm lucky the regimental surgeon wasn't drunk and my buddy was a cabinetmaker when he was a slave. Not many hit by a .44 in the shin can still walk and ride good."

Clairborne nodded in agreement, got up, and walked over to Herman. "Mind if I look at that?" Turning it over in his hands, Clairborne was puzzled by the fact that he had neither seen nor heard of such work despite the plethora of legless veterans hobbling around the country on crutches, peg legs, or both.

"Where in blazes you get this?"

"Like I said. Buddy back in D Troop. Used to be a cabinet maker."

Clairborne shook his head. "No, what I'm getting at is, there are a heck of a lot of men in need of this, and I don't understand why it's not in wider use."

"Two things, Mr. Clairborne. First is it wasn't all that long ago, about nine months, when he made it. Second is he's a black man, so he couldn't just set up a shop and hire folks."

Clairborne's head spun. There was something wrong with this. Thousands and thousands of men could benefit from this piece of wood and metal he held. He handed it back to Herman. "Makes me feel bad knowing so many need this and won't get it. Kind of like to help this fellow start a business. Could make a lot of money helping a lot of folks."

"Could if he was still alive. Died two months ago of the cancer. Buried at Fort Leavenworth."

Herman reattached his prosthetic and pulled on his boot.

"Got to sleep with it on. Too much trouble to strap it up in the middle of the night if something happens."

He reached over to a pile of buffalo chips, placed two of the largest in the fire, repositioned his holstered pistol on the ground close to his side, laid back on his saddle, and pulled his blanket up to his chin.

"You might want to shake your boots out before you put 'em on in the morning. Might be some scorpions or spiders or snakes crawled in. Never know," he said.

Clairborne was pretty sure Herman wasn't joking. He looked around in the darkness, trying to determine from which direction such annoyances might come. Seeing nothing specific, he lay back on his saddle, his hands beneath his neck.

Above him, the Kansas sky filled with stellar dust and glowing nebulae. Clairborne searched for Orion, the Hunter, before realizing his favorite celestial character was a winter phenomenon. "Probably went somewhere doesn't have snakes and scorpions," he muttered to himself and then turned on his side to wait for sleep to remove such concerns.

—◦◦◦—

They rode in silence for several hours. There was nothing much to discuss—nothing, that is, that was socially acceptable to both of them. Each wanted to know more about the other. Each had questions to ask: family, economic status, aspirations, all things that might have been discussed had they been either of the same race or economic class. They rode in silence because it was considered rude to ask questions about another man's background, and most men weren't inclined to talk about their previous lives for a variety of reasons.

Shared experience shaped relations more than any other factor except reputation. Exceptional behavior of any sort was primary fodder for saloon and campfire banter. Since the two shared nothing in terms of background, Clairborne and Herman could build opinion based solely on experience, so it would be some time before either would understand how much or how little he could rely on the other. Neither minded the silence. It allowed each to consider the environment through which they rode, their respective pasts, and their plans for what was to come insofar as they could shape events to fit their hopes.

Herman saw it first. He stopped his horse, and Clairborne followed, his focus to the southern horizon, where a massive cloud of ochre dust seemed suspended in the late morning heat.

"Buffalo?" Clairborne asked.

"Could be. Only other thing would be people, lots of people. The Arkansas is down that way. No wind, so whatever it is must be stirring the dust. Could be people and buffalo. Hunting."

"I can't tell if that dust cloud is moving. Doesn't seem to be," Clairborne said.

"It's heading northeast, kind of toward us. Tell you what, that's a big bunch of something. Let's just give it some time. Might as well rest the horses."

They dismounted. Herman drew his Henry rifle out of its scabbard and worked the lever action, catching and reloading the bullet ejected in the process.

"I might just do a little practice," Clairborne said. "Think whatever it is would hear?"

"Nah. Too far yet."

Clairborne realized he had committed to shooting in front of Herman and mentally shrugged off the possibility he would not do well.

A shallow dry wash angled away from them at a distance of twenty feet. The bank was laminated with layers of gravel. Clairborne selected the largest stone he could see. He paused to think about the process and decided that just maybe he was thinking too much, that maybe he ought to just shoot more and think less. He withdrew the Colt from the holster, thumbed back the hammer, and in one fluid motion aligned eye, gun barrel, and rock, and then pulled the trigger.

As soon as the smoke cleared, he fired a second round and then a third, after which he lowered the smoking revolver to his side. It was obvious that all three had smacked the stone close to the same spot. Clairborne smiled.

Herman was silent, but what he thought would have pleased Clairborne had it been articulated. "That boy can shoot," Herman said to himself. His opinion of Clairborne immediately ratcheted upward. "Hope he shoots people as good as he shoots rocks"

Clairborne thought about stopping after three successful shots. He decided to expend all six, then to shoot six rounds from his other long-barreled Colt, and then to empty his Henry as well.

The second three shots from Thunder impacted an area of less than five square inches. He moved to his saddle-bag to retrieve Thunder's engraved mate, Lightning. He paused. "Better not empty both pistols at the same time," he thought.

Herman watched approvingly at what he thought was an example of Clairborne's ample experience with firearms, not suspecting he was observing a work at the beginning of progress rather than one well underway.

To Clairborne's surprise, Lightning seemed to shoot better than Thunder. Its trigger pull was identical in feel, as were the grips, but the hits were even more tightly grouped and rapid in succession. Clairborne felt a powerful and positive physical sensation course through his body. He reloaded the Colt and returned it to the saddlebag, then took up his rifle. Years of instruction and hunting in Virginia and France provided a store of experience with long guns greatly exceeding his familiarity with pistols.

A stubby brown bush with a stout trunk more than fifty yards away provided the only possible target worth the effort. As he raised the rifle to his shoulder and pulled back the hammer, he reminded himself that he was about to fire this particular rifle for the first time. "Take your time. Breathe. Squeeze." The blade of the front sight filled the notch in the rear, forming a straight visual line to the center of the plant's trunk. The recoil was familiar and comforting, as was the impact exactly where Clairborne intended it. He fired nine more rounds at the progressively smaller pieces of wood shredded by the 210-grain lead bullets.

It was an effort to restrain himself. Clairborne wanted to shout "Damn!" but instead he rubbed the rifle's brass receiver with his gloved right hand and then reloaded. After sliding the Henry back into its tooled leather scabbard, he took a long swig from his canteen. Reclaimed confidence about his marksmanship allowed him to shift to more mundane issues such as the need to clean his weapons. Black powder was corrosive and, if not removed from metal surfaces in a timely manner, would not only pit and ruin the barrel's rifling but congeal into a grimy mass, gumming up the trigger mechanism and the pawls and ratchets that rotated a pistol's cylinder or a rifle's lever action. Clairborne decided he would wait until evening and then apply the same logic to cleaning he had used for firing: disassemble, clean, reassemble, and reload one weapon at a time and keep the others loaded and ready. Once again, he found himself thinking of a phrase that was becoming smooth from use since he had left the banks of the James: "You never know," he told himself. "You just never know."

He glanced over his saddle at the dust cloud and recognized that it had moved farther north.

Herman remounted, retrieved his field glasses, and stood in his stirrups to get the maximum elevation possible on the table-flat terrain.

Clairborne waited for a report. It wasn't forthcoming, and Clairborne felt a minor irritation at the silence. Just as he was about to ask, Herman said, "Only a herd could make that much dust. Gotta be a big herd, and it's the right time for them to be moving. We need to be careful. Bound to be people somewhere around that many buffalo."

As Herman dismounted he said, "Since we're heading that way, might as well just wait here till we can swing south around 'em. OK with you?"

"How long?" Clairborne asked.

"About an hour."

"Well then, I think I'll run a swab through my Henry so I won't have to do it tonight," Clairborne said, eliciting a nod from Herman.

As Clairborne ran a series of mattress-ticking patches through his rifle's bore to remove the powder residue, Herman sat facing the dust cloud, knees drawn up, a stem of prairie grass in his teeth.

"Know what a buffalo hunter told me about cleaning rifles in a pinch?" Herman asked.

Clairborne saw the opportunity for conversation, idle chat to fill countless hours ahead. "No."

"He said he learned from an old mountain man—you know, a free trapper—that you could piss down a rifle barrel, put your thumb over the muzzle, and shake it up to break up the powder residue."

"Ever try it?"

"Well, I told my first sergeant about it, but he didn't think much of the idea, at least not testing it on an army-issue piece. Idea is that if you're doing a lot of shooting, like at a herd, you can clear out the rifling quicker by pissing down the barrel than by breaking out the cleaning gear."

Clairborne thought for a minute. "That might work in a hunt. I don't think it'd work in a fight. Leastways, I'm not sure I'd want to stand up and unbutton, pee down my piece, and shake it up."

He and Herman chuckled at the image. "Me neither," Herman said. "In a good fight, I can't even spit, so I'm pretty sure pissing would be out of the question."

Both men laughed.

Clairborne looked at Herman in profile. He felt good about the man.

At Fort Riley, Herman had suggested they go through a place called Abilene. Clairborne recalled at the time that Caudill had mentioned Abilene at dinner in Saint Louis, telling Clairborne that the town hadn't existed until a little more than a year ago. But by the summer of 1868, Abilene, Kansas, was burgeoning into what would become a phenomenon called a cattle town. Caudill told Clairborne that a Chicagoan named Joseph McCoy started buying up land around the hamlet a little over a year ago.

"There were less than forty people in Abilene, and now I hear there's more than a thousand," Caudill had said, shaking his head in admiration for what he deemed an exercise in initiative.

Herman was intrigued with Abilene as well. "When we rode through a year ago, the place only had four buildings, and they were just shacks. Now, I hear they got a hotel called the Drover's Cottage, too many saloons to count, three dry goods stores, two stables, and a church."

Clairborne knew from his conversations with old man Caudill that the cattle business was based on the premise of "free" wild cattle roaming the Texas plains being rounded up and moved north to the new Kansas settlements served by the expanding railroads. Caudill and his Texas friends John Chisum and Charles Goodnight understood the opportunity presented by the combination of free beef, cheap transportation, hungry easterners, and the hard work it took to connect all three.

Curious to see such a phenomenon firsthand, Clairborne quickly agreed with Herman's suggestion that they stop at Abilene for a good meal, a drink, a haircut, and a bath before they entered the region inhabited only by bison, wolves, and Indians.

The dust cloud they were watching seemed to be moving on a path that intersected their own route to Abilene, which they estimated was less than two days' ride to the west.

"Know how many cattle went through that place last year?" Herman asked.

"No. I just know last year was the first time big drives from Texas made it there."

Herman pointed his finger at the dirt for emphasis. "More than ten thousand head. Don't seem possible to move that many cows that far, but they did it."

"That's why they need men down in Texas and why others like that fellow from Illinois, McCoy, smell money," Clairborne said. He looked at Herman and added, "I deem it fitting and proper that two men such as ourselves should get a share of all that wealth."

Herman returned Clairborne's look. "Yes, it is. Let's go."

As he climbed into the saddle, Clairborne was seized by excitement over a possible business deal. Herman said Abilene had "too many saloons to count." Where did they get their alcohol and tobacco? "If I can get some of them to order from Great Western Supply, I can make a good return on my investment," Clairborne thought. "If there's a telegraph, I can arrange it all with Nicklesby. This could be a success. It could be my first commercial success," Clairborne told himself, his heartbeat reflecting his enthusiasm.

—⁓—

July 20, 1868
Abilene, Kansas

For all I heard about him, I must admit that I wasn't all that impressed with Mr. Joseph McCoy. Short in stature, pinched features, slack chin, and skimpy whiskers. Truth be told, I wasn't all that impressed with Mr. McCoy's town of Abilene either. At least not at first. It smells of equal parts freshly sawed lumber, turpentine, horse droppings, coal smoke, dust, and sweat. Its one street is lined with tents, most of which are saloons, and an array of raw-wood false-front structures catering to the needs of cowboys descending on this place in waves like hordes of Huns.

The noise is constant. When you can't hear people hooting and yelling, you can hear the braying of thousands of head of longhorn cattle penned up in acres and acres of corrals next to the railroad sidings. Somebody told me that last May, the population of Abilene was about 900, but now that the second year of cattle drives is fully underway, more than 3,000 people crowd the street and all of the structures designed to hold them.

If I were going to invest in anything here, it would be bathhouses, barbershops, and dry goods stores. Yesterday I watched cowboys fresh off the trail standing in line for a bath, shave, and haircut followed by a visit to one or both of the dry goods emporiums, where the money flowed like water for everything from hats to boots. Fancy silk scarves seem to be a priority for these young men, even more than new guns, which surprises me.

I had no trouble getting to meet Mr. McCoy, and I must say, my initial plan looks like a very good one indeed. He introduced me to the manager of his hotel, called the Drover's Cottage, as well as the men who run the seven other saloons he either owns outright or has a controlling interest in. Every one of them expressed interest in doing business with Great Western Supply, and I am anxiously awaiting Nickelsby's response regarding prices. Even a couple of deals would be manna from heaven in terms of unantici-pated revenue.

Tonight I am to dine with Mr. McCoy as his guest in the unfin-ished but already impressive Drover's Cottage main salon, which features oriental carpets, a crystal chandelier, hardwood paneling, and a surprising bill of fare that apparently includes fresh oysters from time to time, all thanks to the railroad connecting this prairie palace to the Atlantic Ocean.

It just occurred to me that I haven't seen Titus since about an hour after we got here. I've got to find him to coordinate our depar-ture, but I don't know where to begin. There are many Negroes in Abilene, many more than I expected to see but still in keeping with what I was told about the number of them already working vari-ous aspects of the cattle trade.

I must close to prepare for dinner. The only thing that detracts from the atmosphere is, well, the atmosphere. It is stifling. Impossible to maintain clean linen, but one does what one can to maintain decorum.

Joe McCoy waited for Clairborne at the bottom of the car-peted staircase leading to the guest rooms from the lobby of the Drover's Cottage. "Hope you brought your appetite, Mr. Clairborne. We just received a shipment of Maine lobster, and Klaus is whipping up a hollandaise sauce that'll fill the bill."

Clairborne smiled and shook his head.

"I never would've believed it possible to eat fresh seafood in the middle of Kansas, and call me Tucker if you would, sir."

As the liveried waiters held their chairs, Clairborne looked around with a growing sense of awe. The back of the room was covered by a floor-to-ceiling canvas hiding the section still under construction. The rest of the dining room could have been an expensive eatery in Saint Louis, Chicago, or New York.

"Well, what do you think of Abilene now that you've had a little longer to look around?" McCoy asked.

"Never seen anything like it. Hard to believe there was nothing here a year ago. How many cattle have you shipped already this summer?"

McCoy didn't hesitate. "Twenty-three thousand, four hundred and sixty-three. And there are at least three more herds headed here that we know of."

Clairborne waited for the waiter to finish pouring his whiskey into the cut-glass tumbler, whiskey McCoy said was from his "private stock."

"Ever heard of a fellow named Caudill?" Clairborne asked. "Nolan Caudill?"

"Yep. Sure as shootin'. He's one big fish I'd like to land. My family's been in the stock business for two generations back in Chicago, so we pretty much got a handle on anyone with as many cattle as Mr. Caudill," McCoy said as he considered the color of his whiskey backlit by the chandeliers.

"He hasn't brought his herd here?" Clairborne asked.

"No. Last year he took 'em straight to Kansas City because we weren't ready yet. This year, don't know what he plans, but he sure is up there with Chisum and Goodnight and Pierce when it comes to putting herds together."

Clairborne waited to consider how he would reply.

"Would it be helpful to you if someone told him personally about the advantages of Abilene, what it could mean to his pocket?"

McCoy's business acumen sensed a proposal in the offing from the callow but well-dressed youth across the table. He smiled.

"It surely would. It would indeed."

"Well, sir, that's where I'm headed—the Rocking C, at the express invitation of Mr. Nolan Caudill himself, and I bet he'd be right interested in a proposition that would cut time out of the drive and pay more for his cattle. Of course, I don't speak for him. It just seems pretty likely he'd feel that way."

McCoy leaned back in his chair. His eyes narrowed as he put his fingertips together in front of his face.

"I would appreciate it if Mr. Caudill got the word that I'll guarantee rail cars will be available to move his beeves east within two days of his arrival in Abilene, that his beeves will have priority on holding pens and shipping, and that he can count on anywhere between fifty cents to a dollar more per head shipping from Abilene than he'd get driving the herd east. You'll tell him that, will you?"

Clairborne sipped his whiskey, put the tumbler down on the starched white tablecloth, and nodded. "Absolutely."

Neither man said anything for a moment; then McCoy said, "Aren't you going to ask for something in return for doing me this favor?"

"No. Getting contracts to supply your needs for spirits and tobacco is enough for me, I think. I'm not greedy, and truth be told, I want to be able to tell Mr. Caudill I have no financial gain to be made from his decision."

McCoy studied the young Virginian closely. His instincts honed by years of cutting deals, including deals shaped by Chicago ward politics, told him he was in the presence of an honest man. Naive perhaps, but honest nonetheless—at least for the time being. But there was one thing McCoy didn't understand about Clairborne's stated plans.

"Tucker, you have a deal," he said as he extended his hand. "I'd like to ask you a question about your plans if, I may."

"Shoot."

"You mind telling me what you plan to do for Mr. Caudill? What job it is he offered you?"

"He didn't exactly offer me any job. Just said that if I showed up, he was pretty sure he'd find something for me to do."

"Like cowboying?"

"Yeah. I guess."

"You know much about that, do you? Cowboying?"

Clairborne fidgeted. "No. Not really. I can learn, though. I'm a pretty quick study when I want to be."

McCoy leaned forward and lowered his voice. "Tucker, cowboying is brutal work. It doesn't pay worth a damn; pardon my profanity. A dollar a day for eating dust as well as sleeping in it, drinking bad water, getting shot at by rustlers and Indians—hell, I could go on till breakfast," he said, shaking his head and nervously scratching his prominent cheekbones.

Clairborne looked down at his china bowl of oyster soup.

"I'll cut to the chase, Tucker. You're sophisticated, a tad green maybe, but you got more education than any ten men on the street. I could use a man like you, right here in Abilene. And..." McCoy stopped and looked around, "helping me with other ventures that are coming along." He spooned his bisque and continued. "It'd be a damn waste for a man like you to die or get permanently stove up out there on the prairie. I'm offering you a job with me. What do you say?"

Clairborne was stunned. He had not anticipated any such turn of events. Visions of riding in posh railcars instead of months in the saddle whirled through his head. Crisp, clean sheets and fresh underclothes, cool wine in the evening and hot breakfast in the morning cast a powerful and compelling allure.

"I, I, ah, I'm honored, sir. I truly am but, honestly, I'm not prepared to respond to such an offer without some time to consider it."

"Of course, Tucker," McCoy said with an expansive wave. "You think about it as long as you want. The offer stands. More I think of it, the more sense it makes for both of us. Now I say we cease all talk of commerce and concentrate on the lobster Mack and Franz are about to serve."

Clairborne turned to see two waiters pushing a serving cart through the doors from the kitchen. Massive silver serving dishes accompanied by condiment containers and crystal decanters of wine gleamed in the candlelight. His stomach growled in anticipation of an encounter with crustaceans and French vintages in the year-old boomtown that was Abilene, Kansas.

—◊—

Something was terribly wrong.

Clairborne awoke in a sweat and tried to put things in context. A roiling, painful, living entity lurched about in his bowels. Instinctively, he squeezed his sphincter lest he foul the sheets. He tried to recall where the privy was, and when he did, he wondered how he would make it down the back stairs and out to the four-seater outhouse ten yards from the Drover's Cottage back door. A needlepoint of pain flashed through his abdomen so intense it created a mental image of something in his guts clawing its way out through his navel.

To move or not to move? If he didn't get to the privy, he'd probably lose control of his bowels in the hotel. If he tried to move, he was pretty sure he'd lose control of his bowels in the hotel.

As wretched as his condition was, he had sufficient mental capacity to begin the hunt for the culprit, it and it didn't take long to find one: lobster. And hollandaise sauce. And too much white Bordeaux. Way too much.

"OK. OK. I have to think. Maybe I should crawl. Nobody's up, so nobody'd see me. Too slow. Gotta try walking. Who am I kidding? If I stand, it'll be a race to get to the privy before I blow up. Sweet Jesus."

He almost made it. After an hour in the outhouse, he was sufficiently empty to venture back to bed. Thank God he'd changed out of his long johns and into a nightshirt before turning in. The thought of wrestling with an array of buttons front and back during the panic-stricken rush to the privy was too ugly to consider.

Clairborne crawled into his bed wondering if he should seek out a doctor and instantly dismissed the idea. "What kind of doctor would be practicing medicine in a place like Abilene, Kansas? One who got run out of every respectable town east of here." As the weight of utter fatigue dragged him into oblivion, Clairborne thought of two things. It didn't matter where Herman was because there would be no riding west tomorrow. Then he tried to recall what his mother used to administer when his youthful overindulgence in sweets induced a round of the "green-apple two-step." He couldn't remember. "I'll think about it more tomorrow," he told himself. "If I'm still alive."

—◦◦◦—

The July sun crept through the opening between the bottom of the shade and the windowsill, sliding up Clairborne's face to his tightly closed eyes. His confusing dreams featured a bonfire so bright it caused him to squint, although he felt no heat from its flames. Then there was a drumbeat, irregular and irritating.

Clairborne opened his eyes. The rays of the Kansas sun hit his retinas so hard he winced. The drumbeat of his dreams morphed into a knocking on his door and a soft but insistent repetition of his name. Clairborne stood and fell backward on the rumpled bed. He ran his hands over his face and hair and stood up again.

"Just a minute. Just a minute," he yelled, instantly regretting the reverberation inside his cranium. "Sweet Jesus," he said.

Which was worse, the state of his brain or that of his bowels, which rumbled and lurched? He opened the door just enough to see the face of the assistant manager, a young man with a manner so deferential it seemed almost feminine. His eyes widened when he saw Clairborne's face. As used to seeing hungover cowboys as he probably was, Clairborne's visage must have been alarming.

"I'm so sorry to bother you, sir but there is someone downstairs who insisted I contact you. I wasn't inclined to allow him upstairs, but he said he knows you, and—"

"Big Negro?"

"Ah, yes. He said—"

"Send him up."

"Oh my, I, ah, I'm afraid I can't do that, sir. We have a policy that Negroes, Indians, and Mexicans are not permitted in the hotel."

Clairborne opened the door and regarded the messenger.

"I really am sorry, Mr. Clairborne. If it were up to me, I'd—"

"It is up to you," Clairborne said, holding up his hand to cut off the manager's immediate protest. "It is up to you. You are the manager on duty, and I want to see him. He's my traveling companion, and we need to talk. That's about all the explaining I feel like doing. Send him up. Thank you," Clairborne said as he closed the door.

He crossed the room to the washstand and emptied the porcelain pitcher into the basin. Looking into the mirror above it, he stared at the face in the beveled glass. "Lord, you look like you've been dragged backward through a hedge."

Just as he finished putting on a shirt and tucking it into his trousers, he heard a knock at the door, which he opened to find Herman standing next to the assistant manager.

"Thanks. This is the gentleman I was looking for," Herman said.

The manager looked down the hall and rubbed his hands together, clearly uncomfortable with the thought of leaving Herman.

Clairborne stepped back, motioned Herman into his room, turned back to the assistant manager, and said, "Thanks, and send up a pot of coffee and a couple of cups." Without waiting for a response, he closed the door and turned to Herman, whose face bore the faintest of smiles.

"Go ahead and say it," Clairborne said. "I look like death chewing on a piece o' hardtack. I know it. But I gotta tell you, I think it was bad food at least as much as too much to drink that's brought me low."

Clairborne sat down and lowered his head between his knees, instantly regretting it as his brains felt as if they were about to explode from the top of his skull.

Herman sat on the bed and silently regarded Clairborne.

"Bad as I feel now, it's better than I felt last night," Clairborne said. "Think I might just be ready to leave town tomorrow after I rest some more today."

"You mean tonight?"

"Huh? No, I mean I'll rest this morning and see if I feel good enough to square my bills and get the horses ready to leave tomorrow," Clairborne said.

"You do know it's almost evening, don't you?" Herman said gently.

Clairborne was totally disoriented by the question and its implication that he had slept all day and had confused the evening sun with that of the dawn. But there was no sense denying it.

"Hoowee. This is the worst off I've ever been. Damn. OK. Let's figure this out. Can we wait another day to start, or should I try to tie things up tonight?"

Herman smiled and said, "Don't think a day would make a difference one way or the other."

"OK, let's head out day after tomorrow," Clairborne said.

Herman stood, walked to the door, and opened it just as a waiter was about to deliver the coffee.

"I tried to find you yesterday just to hook up, but I couldn't locate you. Where'd you go? How can I find you tomorrow?" Clairborne asked.

"Oh, I'll be around. Don't you fret," Herman said as he moved down the hall.

Clairborne watched him go and then turned to the young man holding the coffee service.

"Changed my mind. What I really want is the biggest jug of lemonade you can find," Clairborne said, suddenly overcome with thirst so total he felt he could spit dust.

"If you can bring it in less than five minutes, I'll give you a dollar."

As bad as he felt, Clairborne smiled at the results of his incentive. He could not have imagined it possible for a person to run as fast as the young man did without spilling a drop of coffee or either of the two porcelain cups balanced on his silver tray.

Lying back on his bed, Clairborne tried to recall what was said by whom at the dinner. What he could retrieve from the alcoholic haze was disconcertingly incomplete.

Another thought quickly overrode his efforts to recall details of deals made over tainted lobster.

"What if I'd been that damn drunk and someone wanted to do me in?"

He knew the answer. He'd be a dead man. He decided that nothing poured from a bottle would ever again render him defenseless if he could help it. And he could.

—*∿*—

Staring at the pressed tin ceiling of his room, Clairborne considered staying in bed awhile longer. Two days of being mostly prone had not alleviated his physical misery. Sitting, then standing, caused him to swoon. He cursed himself for being weak and unable to bear the consequences of what he believed was clearly moral weakness, the inability to limit his consumption of rich food and alcohol. The word "stupid" had been prominent in his waking thoughts. Spending days on end drinking nothing but coffee; eating beans, bacon, and biscuits; and then stuffing himself with rich European fare was simply stupid. The resultant pain and embarrassment were nothing more than due retribution for stupidity and self-indulgence.

Time to get on with it.

He shaved, dressed, and packed. He went to the livery stable to check his horses, pay the bill, and see if Herman was around. He wasn't.

On his way back to the hotel, he felt as if the sun were pounding his skull through his hat. There was no shade, man made or natural, anywhere in sight unless he went into one of the tents or structures forming Abilene's main street. He had to sit down, so he stepped into the nearest tent saloon. It featured a hand-lettered sign identifying the place simply as Leonard's.

The interior was warmer than the street. The heavy canvas supported by two poles separated by thirty feet effectively blocked any breeze since there was only one point of entrance or exit. On the left, dirt-floored Leonard's featured a bar consisting of planks supported by barrels. Two kegs of beer and four smaller casks of alcohol were spaced along the backbar. Across from the bar, another series of barrel-supported planks provided the faro table, behind which sat a thin, pinch-faced man wearing a top hat, silk vest, and black tie. His efforts at sartorial correctness were completely undercut by the dark-brown circles radiating from his armpits. The three other "tables" were nothing more than upturned barrels with a motley array of chairs and stools arranged around them.

Four customers, two at one such table, the other two sitting alone elsewhere, idly examined their beer mugs or shot glasses. None paid any attention to Clairborne. Unlike the other saloons he'd seen in Abilene, there were no women present.

At first, he thought of turning around but decided to stay when he balanced Leonard's austere nastiness to the pain inflicted by the sunshine. He sat on the three-legged stool closest to the entrance flap, hoping to catch a breeze. The fat, heavily bearded bartender didn't ask if he wanted anything and continued wiping glasses with a filthy towel.

Clairborne studied the small casks on the backbar. He could not discern any name, any brand, and wondered about their origins and contents.

After a few minutes during which his eyes adjusted to the darkness, Clairborne walked over to the bar and said, "Mind if I ask you a couple of questions?"

"'At's what I'm here for. Pourin' alkyhol and swapping stories," the suddenly garrulous bartender said.

"I'm interested in your product there," Clairborne said with a nod at the small casks. "I assume they're whiskey, but where's it come from?"

Rubbing a shot glass with the stained towel, the bartender turned to regard the object of Clairborne's query and then turned back and said, "Why'd you ask?"

"Oh I'm kind of in the business, that's all. Mostly, it's just professional curiosity."

"You don't look like a whiskey drummer, and if you was, we don't never pay others for what we can make ourselves."

Clairborne's curiosity was piqued. He fished a dime out of his vest pocket and said, "Let me try some of it. Any recommendations?"

The bartender snorted in laughter. "Hell, mister, they's all got the same stuff," he said, filling the shot glass he was "cleaning" with a cloudy, brick-colored fluid from the nearest cask.

Raising the glass, Clairborne instantly regretted indulging his curiosity. The chemical smell assaulting his nose set his stomach in motion and amplified the pounding behind his eye-balls that had just begun to abate.

Placing the glass on the bar without sampling its contents, he asked, "Where you ship it in from?"

Again, the bartender hooted in laughter. "Ship it in— that's rich. We ship it in from the back of the property about twenty feet thataway," he said, nodding toward the back of the tent.

"Mind if I take a look? Just curious."

"Hell no. It ain't no secret recipe," the bartender said.

Behind the tent, Clairborne beheld a rather crude still, a set of pipes and pots and low fires. It was tended by two men, both sweat soaked and filthy. One fed scrap lumber into the glowing bed of coals beneath the heavy ceramic pot topped by a coiled copper wire. The other man stood over an open barrel, a stirring stick in one hand, a small tin cup in the other.

Clairborne's instinct told him to take a friendly, positive approach. "Howdy. Bartender said you boys'd show me how you make your whiskey. Never tasted the likes of it."

The stirrer responded. "Ain't much different from anybody else's coffin varnish," he said with a shrug of his bony shoulders. He dumped the tin cup's contents into the barrel and stirred.

The fire tender stood and regarded Clairborne through crusted eyelids and wiped his hands on his soiled trousers. "Stagger soup's pretty much stagger soup no matter where you find it, friend. Just depends on what you got handy," he said.

"Now you take this here popskull we're a-making. You start with creek water, add some turpentine, then a little burned sugar. Let it settle awhile, mebbe twenty minutes or so, then you add a twist or two of shredded tobacco, mebbe some peppers, and bang, you got a fresh batch of tonsil paint," said the stirrer.

"There's some 'at say addin' a snake head'll give it a tad more pop, but then you gotta get a snake first, and I don't much feature goin' out of my way to find Mr. No-Shoulders," he said.

"OK, now I understand why the Indians call it 'firewater,'" Clairborne said.

"Me and Clyde used to make trade whiskey up to Bent's Fort till they run us out," the stirrer said. Turning away from the barrel, he squirted a stream of tobacco juice into the dust and didn't wipe his chin before continuing.

"'Em Injuns know sometimes white traders water down their hooch, so they'd spit the first mouthful into the fire, and if it didn't flame up, they wouldn't trade," he said.

"Yeah, and sometimes they'd lift the hair of them that tried sellin' watered-down hooch, so we always put a little extry turpentine in ours. Got good trade for it every time," fire tender said.

Clairborne had heard enough. If this was the competition for good sour mash or rye, he figured his investment in Great Western Supply was bound to bring fat returns. His headache felt better.

"You want to wet your whistle, mister?" the stirrer asked.

"No thanks. Appreciate the offer, but I had a little too much last night."

"Hell's bells, mister. You need a little hair of the dog 'at bit you," the fire tender said.

Clairborne waved as he turned to leave.

"One more bite of that dog'd be the death of me," he thought, "and I'd deserve it."

On his way back to the Drover's Cottage, where he planned to finish packing, Clairborne ran into McCoy. The first thing he noticed was that McCoy was gray and drawn.

"My friend, I fear I owe you an apology," McCoy said. "It seems you and I are victims of food poisoning. I assume you suffered the same gastric turmoil as I did, although the fact that you're ambulatory is encouraging," he said with a wan smile.

"Well, I'm better today than yesterday, and if I'm better tomorrow than today, I'll be leaving Abilene. And I do appreciate your hospitality, Mr. McCoy, despite our mutual experience."

"Gracious of you to say, my good sir, but surely you'll give me a chance to make up for our unfortunate meal before you depart?"

Clairborne shook his head at the prospect. "Thanks for the offer, but I'm going to limit my intake to biscuits and coffee for the next day or two."

"Perfectly understandable. Perfectly. But allow me to ask if you're aware of a good remedy for stomach ailments of this nature. You've heard of laudanum?"

Clairborne was surprised, and his expression conveyed that before he said so.

McCoy held up his hand. "I know, I know. You believe it useful only as a pain-killer of last resort, but it's also quite effective against loose bowels when taken in very small doses—a drop in a cup of tea. Since we don't yet have a doctor in Abilene, I've had to bring along my own little pharmacopeia from Chicago. It was put together by our family physician, one of the best in the city. I've an extra bottle I'll give you to take on your ride south."

Clairborne considered the offer and found it interesting that laudanum was entering his life for the second time in less than two months when it had never been more than an academic factor before then.

He accepted both the laudanum and McCoy's invitation to a "light" and early dinner.

Seeking to avoid direct exposure to the intense afternoon rays, Clairborne returned to his room along the shaded side of the street. Passing one of the new wooden structures, he saw something he had not noticed since he entered Abilene: women outside. Three women. And there was no question what kind of women they were.

They stood at the back of the building at the bottom of a stairway leading to the second floor. Two were smoking cigarettes, something Clairborne had never seen in his life up until then. Each wore brightly colored satin dresses short enough to expose their ankles. The two who were smoking wore their hair down, another unusual sight, and on closer look, they also were standing outside in a public venue with unlaced bodices.

A flash of heat surged through his loins. It was a long way to Texas, and there were probably no women there or between here and there, he thought. It was more than three years since he'd shared a bed with a woman, and those few experiences in France had become some of the fondest of his memories. He knew now and had suspected then that the Parisian dalliances with a fair, young courtesan named Marie had occurred with at least the tacit approval of his host, if in fact they were not arranged by him. Standing in the dusty, dung-littered Abilene street, he recalled intimate details of those idyllic interludes: silken bedsheets; clean, lightly scented skin and hair. There was also a great deal of patience on the part of his partner, patience with his awkward initial intimacies.

Reveries of his few but ever-so-sweet romantic trysts tipped the scales and pushed him toward the trio of soiled doves.

The closer he got, however, the greater were his reservations. None of them were attractive. One was simply plain; the other two were simply ugly—ugly and bloated. Their satin bodices were darkened by horizontal strata of sweat stains marking the creases formed by excess flesh.

Clairborne wanted to turn on his heel, an urge heightened by realization that if they looked as bad as they did, the odds were high that they harbored some exotic pox as well, perhaps several.

The women noticed Clairborne at the same time, each surveying him with a practiced eye.

He was not a cowboy. Eastern cut to his clothes; refined, bespoke-tailored. Riding boots instead of cowboy boots, a tie instead of a scarf. The thin, plain one picked up on the pistol belt and the slight bulge under the coat, studied his angular young face graced only by a wispy brown mustache and thought "shootist," although he seemed very young.

"First dibs," said sweaty Elenor, stubbing out her hand-rolled smoke on the bannister.

"Like hell," said Julie, the other large woman. "I got him 'cause I ain't had a customer today and you two have. Back off."

Clairborne couldn't hear the words, but he knew what was happening and was even more hesitant to proceed. But how to disengage? Without breaking stride, he walked up to the slimmest girl—plain features and a much cleaner dress.

"Hello," he said.

"Well, howdy there, handsome," said Julie, grabbing Clairborne's right wrist, his gun hand. Without making eye contact with her, Clairborne removed her hand with his left. The plain one introduced herself as "Willie, short for Wilhamena."

Smiling up at Clairborne, she said, "Let's go somewhere we can talk," and without waiting for an answer, she led him up the stairs.

Entering the second floor, Willie held on to Clairborne's hand and apologized for the sawdust, explaining that while the place was still under construction, her "crib" now had walls and a door instead of just the canvas tarpaulins hanging on ropes that sectioned off the rest of the working areas.

Clairborne noticed there was no lock on the door to Willie's room and on entering was glad it faced away from the sun and had a wide-open, glass-paned window.

The room featured a small, iron-frame bed on which rested a thin, straw-filled mattress partially covered by a rumpled gray sheet. The single pillow was shiny with hair oil and dried sweat. Beside the bed, an upturned produce crate supported a burned-down candle and a water jug. A three-legged stool and an open valise completed the furnishings.

"Take a load off, there, mister," Willie said, pointing to the bed as she loosened her bodice. Clairborne sat and looked around, wondering what to say.

Willie walked up to him, removed his hat, and took his face in her surprisingly cool hands. She stooped to kiss him on the forehead and in so doing allowed him to look at her breasts, unencumbered by anything but a thin chemise under her dress.

Clairborne's reservations were now matched by his desires. Inside his head, a raging debate was going on. "This is sheer madness," he told himself. "Just grab your hat and bolt." But the pounding in his ears overrode the voice of reason.

Willie sat on his right knee. She took his left hand and raised it to her small, firm breast, slid her hand to his crotch, and kissed his right ear. Even though her breath was foul and her scent was equal parts dried sweat and the cheapest of acrid perfume, Clairborne was aroused. As the pressure of her hand increased, so did his sense of stark terror. "I can't do this. I can't do this," his mind repeated as his heartbeat accelerated.

Willie started unbuttoning his fly, maintaining the pressure and rhythmic movement of her hand.

"Oh no, oh no," Clairborne moaned aloud and tried to stand. But it had been too long, and the pent-up pressure proved too great to constrain.

When he opened his eyes, Willie's face was only inches from his. She smiled.

"Been a while, huh? Well, now that we took the edge off, let's have some fun."

Clairborne abruptly stood. The first thing through his mind was whether there was visible evidence of what just happened. He decided that even if there was, his coat was long enough to cover it. Then he realized he had not removed his coat, his boots, or even his gun belt. He didn't know whether that was funny or humiliating—or both. He was very certain, however, that he didn't want anyone else to know about this turn of events. Ever.

"Tell you what," he said, fishing coins out of his vest pocket. "Here's twenty dollars. Let's just call it even. And I'd appreciate it if we just kept this little episode between us, OK?"

Willie looked at Clairborne and then at the gold coin in her hand. She gasped and then laughed.

"Hell, mister. It happens all the time. Only nobody's ever been this generous afore. Don't you worry about nothin," she said as she closed her fist around her windfall. "No sir. Don't you worry about nothin."

⸻

Back in his hotel room, Clairborne tried put things in perspective. On the one hand, he stood to make a tidy and unexpected sum from arranging sales of whiskey and tobacco from Great Western. On the other, his Abilene encounters with lobster and whores made him want to flee as soon as possible. The immediate problem was that he had no idea how to find Herman. After packing and leaving a note for McCoy expressing regrets for a change of plans, he went to the stable to retrieve his horses and leave word for Herman to meet him at the Drover's Cottage. Entering the stalls, he saw his traveling companion sitting in the straw, his back against a post. Herman's horse and mule were ready for the trail.

"Just need to throw my gear on Ajax and saddle up, and we can get shut of this place," Clairborne said.

Thirty minutes later, the two cleared the limits of Abilene, Kansas, ill-defined as they were, and headed southwest. As they expected, the thousands of cattle coming in the opposite direction had left a trail a blind man could follow, even in the weak light of summer dusk. After two hours in the saddle, they stopped at a stream, where they camped for the night.

At first light the next morning, Herman said, "Got a suggestion."

"What's that?"

"What do you think about not staying directly on this trail but maybe riding in the same direction, just a mile or so off the to the side?"

"Why?"

Herman took off his hat and ran his bandana over his face and hair, wiped the hatband, and patted his horse's flank.

"Just seems that way we'd have a better chance of spotting bandits or Indians before they spot us."

Clairborne looked around at the almost flat, featureless terrain covered in knee-high grass and distant stands of cottonwood marking water sources. He knew that as open as the land seemed, experienced hunters of men and animals could find a thousand good ambush sites out there. He recalled Wild Bill's admonition to always look around and anticipate where potential foes might lurk.

"Make any difference which side we take?" he asked.

"Always think it best to take the harder route," Herman said. "The folks we want to stay quit of expect everyone to take the easiest way."

Clairborne considered Herman in profile for a moment. Such practical wisdom was clearly hard earned. The decision to ride with Herman looked better and better.

"Before we start, mind if I take a little practice?"

"No. I'll ride out and look around while you shoot," Herman said, nodding at the small rise a hundred yards away.

Clairborne noticed that as he rode off, Herman drew his yellow boy from its scabbard and cradled it across his saddle pommel.

"Another good idea," Clairborne thought. "Have it out and ready. Ready, ready, ready. That word seems a lot more relevant out here than it ever did back east."

He dismounted, picket-pinned his horses, then slipped the Colt from its holster, raised it, and fired in one fluid motion. Reloading the empty chambers, he glanced at his horses and realized another advantage of his regular practice. The horses had become so accustomed to gunfire, they no longer spooked when Clairborne filled the air with flame and smoke. He wished he had sugar lumps to slip into their soft muzzles. As he untied the reins and lead rope, he stroked each horse and murmured, "You boys are fine company." He remembered the stables at Warwick, then Joshua, the groom, and stable boys Luke and Matthew. Clairborne turned to look at the knoll where Herman waited. He could not see his riding companion because Herman had tied his horses below the crest and was lying on his stomach, surveying the surrounding terrain with his new field glasses.

Clairborne wondered if Joshua, Luke, Matthew were as capable as Herman and, just as quickly, understood that until now, he had never given that question any thought. "Probably should have," he told himself as he mounted. "Wonder where they are now?"

They rode at a steady, sustainable pace for three days. Routine established itself without conscious effort by either rider. Shortly after they saddled up on the fourth day, Herman pointed to an obvious game trail and said, "I knew there were buffalo around here. I could just smell 'em."

Before Clairborne could ask, he added, "It's a small herd, maybe fifty or so, drifting north." He leaned over to examine the trampled grass. "They're close. Want some fresh meat for dinner tonight?"

"You bet," Clairborne responded, recognizing he had yet to taste bison meat in any form. He wanted to know how Herman knew the approximate size of the herd, its direction of movement, and how long it had been since it passed, but decided to continue his established practice of doing most of his learning by observation rather than interrogation.

"OK. We gotta be careful from now on. Don't want to spook 'em. We'll stay below high ground and off to the side of their trail. You ready?"

Clairborne grinned. "For fresh meat and a little fun? You bet."

Two hours later, their collective patience and Herman's tracking skills paid off. As they lay in the aromatic tall grass at the top of a low rise, a herd of less than a hundred bison grazed and ambled slowly north.

"How 'bout that big old bull?" Clairborne whispered, nodding at a huge, shaggy, dust-covered male less than two hundred yards away.

"Well, he's an easy shot," Herman whispered back. "But that young female closest to us'd be better, I think. Meat from that old bull'd be tough as boot leather. That female's young, and we're only going to take the hump and tongue."

Clairborne considered what he just heard. The concept of waste was entirely new and to his mind irrelevant. The plains were literally covered with bison, millions of them. What the hell difference did one or two make in the grand scheme of things? But toughness of the meat—now that was different. No sense chewing on tough when you could chew on tender.

"Mind if I take the shot?" Clairborne asked.

"Figured you might want to. Shooting from this distance won't spook the herd. Not that it matters since we're only taking one, but that's how the hunters get so many at once. Shoot from two-fifty to three hundred yards out, and the herd won't stampede. Just kind of mill around in confusion."

Adjusting the sights for elevation, Clairborne considered asking if the best target for bison was the same as for elk or deer—center mass just behind the upper portion of a front leg, a shot that would put the chunk of lead straight into the lungs, ensuring if not a one-shot kill, at least a short chase to finish the job.

He decided not to ask.

Sighting down the Henry's blued octagonal barrel, he moved his eyes away from the target for a last moment check for wind. The grass between him and the grazing, unsuspecting prey bowed under the slight breeze wafting toward them from the herd. Nothing that should affect the shot.

He squeezed the trigger, felt the impact of recoil, and instantly worked the lever to bring another 210 grains of lead into the Henry's chamber, all without taking his eye off the bison, which stumbled to its foreknees, recovered, and began to run.

"Good shot," Herman said without lowering his field glasses. "Got her in the lungs." But his last word was lost in the report of Clairborne's second shot, which dropped the animal to its side.

Clairborne leaped into the saddle and raced to the fallen animal. He dismounted fifty feet from the kicking, thrashing, shaggy mass trying to regain its footing. He raised his rifle and walked closer, intending to administer a coup de grace. Faster than he believed possible, the bison leaped to its feet, turned to face him, and charged.

"Jesus," Clairborne exclaimed aloud, astonished that the bison could still attack with two .44s deep in its lungs. He cursed himself for being so stupid as to approach the bison on foot. He was unlikely to drop the animal with a shot to its massive skull. That meant he was about to get gored, trampled, and turned into a grease spot in the dirt.

"Can't run. Steady. Steady," he said to himself. His next shot broke off the charging bison's right horn and did no further damage. The fourth shot skimmed its jaw and plunged into its chest just below its lowered head, severing an artery before the expanding soft-lead bullet exploded the beast's massive heart.

The bison collapsed and skidded forward, its momentum and mass causing it to roll over and careen toward him on its left side even after it died. It came to a rest less than five feet from Clairborne, who took a few steps backward.

He raised the Henry, walked up to the bison, and put a round into its head between its right eye and the base of its broken right horn. Lowering the rifle, Clairborne felt his legs go weak and wanted desperately to sit down before he fell down. His heart roared in his ears. His mouth felt as if it were stuffed with cotton, and his breath came in rapid, shallow pants.

Clairborne couldn't think of exactly what to do next. He knelt and looked into the still-open eye of the bison female and wanted to caress its face. Instead he absent-mindedly reached for his Bowie knife and turned to Herman.

"You going to help dress it?" Clairborne asked matter of factly.

"Sure," Herman said as he rode up and dismounted, thinking all the while that what he had just observed was one of the most amazing combinations of stupidity and courage he had ever seen.

———

They rode for hours without speaking, and it didn't bother either one.

Day in, day out, for four days since the buffalo hunt, Clairborne and Herman stayed in the saddle from daybreak to dusk, giving their mounts a break every two hours or whenever they happened upon potable water. The terrain subtly changed from flat and featureless to increasingly rolling land creased by creeks and washes, many of which were already dry. Herman was cautious when approaching water, and Clairborne quickly appreciated the wisdom inherent in being very careful about proximity to a scarce and vital resource. Everything needed water, and the scarcer it became, the more likely it was to be contested.

Five days after the buffalo incident, Clairborne and Herman awoke to an oppressively gray and muggy morning, the air thick with the scent of impending rain. The slowly intensifying prairie light illuminated blue-gray, slanting shafts of downpours to the southwest. Both retrieved and donned their waterproof slickers before the rudimentary cleaning of eating utensils. As they finished securing packs with diamond hitches and readjusting saddle cinches, Herman turned to Clairborne and gestured in the direction of travel.

"I think we're about two days from Spanish Wells on the Canadian. Good water all year long, shelter in the ruins of a couple of buildings the Spaniards built a long time back. Nobody lives there, but there's usually somebody around. Buffalo hunters, Indians. We get close, I'll ride ahead to see who's there."

Clairborne understood that Herman was making a statement and, even though it contained no questions for him, he could ask for clarification or expansion if he wanted to without Herman taking offense. There was no need to. In few words, Herman covered the direction of march, relevant details of their objective, and a cautionary note about what to expect when they got close.

Clairborne nodded and swung into the saddle. As he had been doing since the first day out of Abilene, he withdrew his Henry, lowered the lever action just enough to visually determine that a .44-40 round was seated in the chamber, closed the action, wiped some excess oil from the side of the hammer, and rested the rifle across his saddlebow. Herman did the same.

They'd ridden for less than two hours when they flushed a large jackrabbit. Clairborne's horse reared. In the same instant, Herman whipped his Henry to firing position and picked off the zigzagging rabbit with one shot.

He rode over to where it lay, dismounted, picked it up, and returned to where Clairborne sat his horse. Herman's .44-40 bullet had hit the rabbit in the middle of its body, nearly blowing it in half. "Was trying for a head shot," he said as he used his thumb to remove its intestines, then its hide. Tucking the shiny carcass into his saddlebag, he said, "A little more fresh meat's better than none, I guess."

Clairborne nodded. "Nice shot, anyway."

At midday they stopped at a small, stagnant spring to rest the horses and make coffee, saving the rabbit for dinner. As Clairborne went to retrieve his coffee pot, Herman said, "Let's not start a fire."

Clairborne looked at Herman over the back of his packhorse and saw that Herman hadn't dismounted and was standing in his stirrups. But instead of looking through his binoculars, Herman was apparently smelling the air, his eyes closed, his head back.

Before he could ask Herman what he was doing, Herman turned and asked, "You smell that?"

Clairborne looked around and sniffed. "Can't say as I smell anything all that unusual." And in an attempt at humor, he added, "'Course, it's kind of hard to smell anything other than horses and arm pits..."

Herman neither smiled nor acknowledged anything Clairborne said. Instead, he continued to stand in his stirrups, facing their direction of march for a few more moments. He dismounted and led his horse and mule to water.

Removing his hat and scratching his forehead, he said, "I thought I smelled smoke's all." Turning to Clairborne, he added, "And Indians."

"You sure?" Clairborne asked.

"No. Not sure, but I just...I don't know, I just got a feeling we need to be extra careful. Tell you what. I'm going to ride ahead for a look. You mind staying back for a while?"

Clairborne reflected that, actually, he wasn't all that comfortable with the idea of being alone while his companion went off to determine whether or not there were hostile Indians in the area.

"No, go on ahead. I'll picket Ajax and Stumpy and wait for you up yonder under that cover," he said, nodding to the closest rise, which bore a crown of scruffy bushes.

"Use a slipknot in case it turns out we gotta leave in a hurry," Herman said as he placed the strap of his field glasses around his neck, retrieved a box of cartridges from his saddlebag, and divided its contents among his pockets. He also took off his waxed yellow slicker. "Kind of sticks out," he said to Clairborne as he turned it inside out and secured it behind his saddle.

Clairborne watched him ride away. He tied up the horses where there was the most forage, took his saddlebags, his Henry, both Colts, and the LeMat and walked up the rise to the brush cover. Clairborne perused the area and was not reassured by what he saw. He was on the lowest of a series of hillocks rising to the southwest of where he lay, effectively blocking his view of Herman's path. He considered moving to one of the higher elevations and then decided against it since doing so would require moving the horses as well.

He looked at the sky. Still angry and dark. No downpour yet, but it would come sooner or later. Clouds so solid, there wasn't even a hint of what sector of the sky the sun inhabited.

Time seemed to congeal. It irritated him that his Breguet might as well be back in Virginia for all the good it was doing packed away on Ajax. It irritated him that swarms of gnats ignored his swats and found their way into his nostrils, mouth, ears. The very dirt on which he lay irritated him, its irregular surfaces rubbing his kneecap, his elbows. "Son of a bitch." He had forgotten his canteen and decided that as punishment for his oversight, he would not abandon his post to get it no matter how long he had to wait for Herman's return.

He realized he was also irritated with Herman but recognized how stupid, how petty were those thoughts. Herman was exposing himself to danger, the worst danger of all: danger of the unknown, and instead of being grateful, he was irritated with Herman for leaving him on the bug-infested prairie. "Unworthy of you, boy. Ought to be ashamed," he said in a low voice.

After an extended period of discomfort, he fell asleep.

It wasn't a conscious decision to nap; rather, it was one that occurred when sleep crept up on tiptoes and pulled his eyelids down without his being aware of its approach. With his left arm under his head and right arm cradling the Henry, neither the cloud of insects nor the beads of sweat dripping off his nose into his stubble kept him awake, alert.

He didn't know the name of the woman he addressed in French, only that she was the most beautiful creature on earth. Beneath the plumed triumph of the Parisian milliner's art, her face was fashionably obscured by a gossamer veil. Her tiny hands, wrapped in pale-yellow silk gloves, slowly twirled a folded green parasol that complemented her sea-green voile dress, most of which was hidden from view by the black varnished side of her cabriolet. She accepted his invitation to dismount and walk with him on the crushed-gravel paths of the Tuileries. But when he tried to open the carriage door, his left arm would not rise to the polished silver latch, and he looked at his recalcitrant limb with alarm and frustration, aware that the vision of beauty was amused by the jejune, literally maladroit American boy seeking her approval and company. He considered yelling at his disobedient appendage, commanding it to do his bidding, but it continued to ignore him.

Clairborne's eyes snapped open, triggering seconds of sheer panic compounded by utter confusion. "Who was the girl? Damn! I fell asleep." He bolted upright and collapsed into the dirt when he tried to support himself with his left hand, which like the rest of his left arm was totally numb. Rolling to his right, he pushed up with the Henry, and on gaining his feet saw Herman riding rapidly toward him. Clairborne was mortified by the thought that Herman had literally caught him napping.

Herman dismounted.

"Well, this ain't good," he said. And before Clairborne could inquire as to the nature of the problem, Herman said, "At least two to three hundred Comanche bucks camped about three miles from here. They're looking for trouble, war paint. It's a war party for sure. No women, kids, old folks, dogs. We got a problem."

Herman retrieved his canteen and gulped its contents. Clairborne said nothing but realized how dry his mouth had become.

"I think they're looking for anything and everything to hit," Herman said. "I bet they're going to Spanish Wells because they either know somebody's there or they think somebody is, like maybe buffalo hunters, just like we're thinking might be."

They walked quickly to the picketed horses and mule.

"Any ideas what we ought to do?" Clairborne asked.

"We got two choices," Herman said quietly. "We can either try to ride as far away from them as we can and hope we don't run into any other parties riding in to join them, or..." He drank again. "Or we can just skirt them and ride to Spanish Wells. If there's anybody there, we got a better chance of defending ourselves behind walls than anywhere in the open, and there'd be more firepower too. And if there's folks there, we ought to warn them. That's what I think."

"You think we can get around them with them not knowing, do you?"

"I do. There's a big coulee about two miles east of their camp. Sandy bottom."

Clairborne secured the lead to his packhorse and tightened every cinch and tie-down. He swung into the saddle and rested the Henry on the bow. He considered the wisdom of riding toward the very place they thought the Comanche also had in mind. He worried about attempting to pass within a couple of miles of the Comanche camp. But he decided Herman was right. Better to fight behind a wall with a water supply than out in the open at a site determined by either pure chance or the foe with no cover, no water.

Turning to Herman as he mounted, Clairborne said, "After you, my friend."

They rode at a steady canter, stopping at irregular intervals to look and listen. Each time they did, Herman pointed to some distinctive terrain feature the army called rally points and said, "Cover if we need it."

Clairborne concentrated on each of Herman's selections with an intellectual intensity. Why there? Why not over there? Which way would we face? What if we have to cover each other? Woven thickly through his thought process was a persistent appreciation of Herman's knowledge and experience. Gnawing at the edges of his awareness was a mild but growing agitation that he was relying on this former slave to guide him through a land as wild and as dangerous as he had imagined. More so, actually. He did not like this feeling of obligation toward Herman, but not liking it didn't make it go away or even reduce it.

Herman slowed to a stop in a featureless spot.

"Let's walk them awhile." They did, in silence, for nearly thirty minutes.

Clairborne considered his feet. They hurt. He looked down at them and observed that sweat stains had worked their way through the fine leather at the insteps, leaving dark, irregular blotches. He was also aware that his bespoke riding boots were not made for walking. The heels were wearing down, and the soles were on the verge of surrendering to pebbles, stones, and cottonwood branches seeking to penetrate what was never designed to keep them out.

As his focus turned to consideration of how he could patch the inevitable holes in his soles, they stopped.

Without a word, both retrieved slices of jerky from their saddlebags and stood by their mounts, silently chewing. Clairborne theorized that the leather of his custom-made boots was softer than the jerky. He just hoped he'd never have to confirm his theory out of necessity.

"I'm thinking we ought'a just keep on going till we get there," Herman said after taking a swig from his canteen.

"How far you think it is?"

"Mebbe another fifty miles or so. Not more'n seventy."

"Woowee. That's a long way to go without stopping. You think the horses can make it?"

"Well, we'll rest now and again. Just no fire and no sleep."

Clairborne thought, "I can do it if you can" but said, "All right."

They remounted and continued for the next twelve hours, three of which were in a steady downpour of a storm heading in the same direction they were. Every hour or so, they walked the horses for what was deemed enough time to rest their legs.

Clairborne knew the rain was a blessing for three reasons: It cooled the air. It filled dry holes. And it hid them from view.

Sometime after the tenth hour, Clairborne and Herman were afoot, and Clairborne was looking down at his boots when he realized he had been paying no attention to their route of march, that he'd been merely following Herman.

Fatigue seemed to be a large but painless wound from which his strength drained into the soil beneath him. Fatigue seemingly wrapped his intellect's sharp edges in wool, dulling his thoughts to a pale gray matching the dank prairie dawn. He raised his head to note that it was slightly lighter than it had been minutes ago, although the solid cloud cover diluted the sun's rays so effectively Clairborne could not determine which way was east. He had never been so hungry. Never. It occurred to him that he had not had a bowel movement in two days and didn't feel as if he needed one.

About to fall asleep on his feet, he prodded his memory to find the perfect word to describe his motion. "Stumbling?" Not yet. "Meandering?" No. One could meander purposefully and when refreshed. Ah, "plodding." That was it. Plodding. Why did it take so long to think of such a simple word?

He plodded, reflexively putting one foot in front of the other without thought, without any idea of how long he could continue beyond "not much damn longer."

"Can you dream while plodding?" he asked himself. "If not, why am I lying on the floor in front of the kitchen hearth, watching the flames under the stock pot?"

He stopped walking and emerged from the hallucinatory torpor he'd been wearing like a cloak for hours.

"What?" he asked, looking at Herman.

Herman smiled a smile conveying fatigue and happiness. "Mount up. We're there."

They had been walking up a slight grade for so long Clairborne no longer realized the uphill march had contributed to his fatigue. Turning his head to survey the terrain, he saw nothing that indicated the presence of other humans or man-made structures. Then he smelled wood smoke. And bacon. And coffee. Herman, already in the saddle, spurred his horse into a canter, and Clairborne followed as quickly as he could. Less than a hundred yards later, they crested a rise and accelerated their downhill race toward the collection of large cottonwoods, ruins, wagons, carts, horses, and men clustered in untidy knots around at least seven separate campfires, each of which sent a column of scented smoke up through towering trees into the morning air.

Twenty yards from the nearest group of men, Herman began yelling, "Hello the fire, hello the fire," which caused the few still wrapped in their bedrolls to sit up and those squatting around their fires to stand and face the newcomers.

Herman and Clairborne halted and dismounted.

A tall, bearded man with patched knees and a coffee cup in one hand and his Remington Rolling Block rifle in the other approached and said, "You boys are kind 'a lathered up for this early in the day, ain't you?"

Clairborne responded, "Mister, you may soon have cause to get lathered up yourself, depending on how close behind us those Comanche are."

Mention of Comanche produced the same effect as poking an anthill with a stick. Jumping to their feet and instinctively retrieving their weapons, the hunters gathered around Clairborne and Herman like dogs to soup bones.

"How many?" "Which way?" "War party?" they yelled over one another until the first man to approach them turned to his comrades, raised his hand, and bellowed, "Shut the hell up! You're acting like a bunch of goddamn women. Shut up."

Extending his dirt-encrusted hand to Clairborne, he said, "Silas Beekman."

Shaking Beekman's hand without removing his gloves, Clairborne said, "Tucker Clairborne, and this is Titus Herman. Might want to ask him what he saw yesterday."

"All right," Beekman said. "You boys look plumb wore out. Let's get you some coffee and grub whilst you tell us what you seen."

By the time they reached Beekman's fire, most of the other men at Spanish Wells were also present, drawn by the daybreak disturbance of hunt camp routine.

Clairborne and Herman sat on kegs and accepted coffee and plates of beans and bacon, which they balanced on their laps as they slurped the near-scalding, thick, black brew.

"About sixty miles northeast, there's a party of maybe four hundred. War party for sure. Painted up. No women, dogs, kids, old folks. Got a remuda of maybe six hundred to eight hundred, maybe nine hundred. No tepees," Herman said. "I'd guess most is Katsoteka, but there's a lot of 'em are Tenawa, and there's a mess of Kiowa as well," he added.

Clairborne looked at Herman. "I thought you said they were Comanches."

Before Herman answered, Beekman interjected, "They are. Different tribes, but all, 'cept Kiowa, is Comanch. Katsoteka means 'Buffalo Eaters,' and Tenawa means 'Liver Eaters.'"

One of the hunters poking his ear through the crowd said, "How'd you know they's Katsoteka and Tenawa? How's a boy like you know so much about Comanch anyways?"

Clairborne looked at the grimy man, whom he instantly disliked. "Because this man's been fighting Comanche for years, speaks some, and knows sign. Because he probably knows as much about Comanche as anyone else here, I expect."

"Buffalo soldier?" Beekman asked Herman.

"Yep," Herman said.

"He was a sergeant till he mustered out and we agreed to ride down to Texas together," Clairborne added.

"Shit. If that don't beat all," said the filthy hunter who had questioned Herman's information. "A nigger sergeant. Guess the army's even more fucked up than we thought, boys." A few of the hunters chuckled. Beekman was not one of them.

"Charlie, why don't you shut your mouth. I don't care a good goddamn whether he's black or green, but I sure as hell care about what he's telling us, you dumb-ass." Beekman shifted his rifle to his right hand and pointed his left index finger at Charlie for emphasis. "Unless you got something worth hearing, keep your mouth shut."

Turning to Herman, Beekman said, "You think they'll hit us?"

"I do," Herman said. "You probably know as well as I do that war parties that big hit everything they can. Everyone knows about Spanish Wells. They probably already scouted the place. Expect they'll hit tonight at the earliest. Tomorrow night at the latest."

"Makes sense," Beekman said. Looking around, he said, "OK, boys. Seems to me we gotta plan a reception committee. If'n they don't come, we just get a day or two more of laying around, but if they do try to take us, this way we'll be ready. Anybody got anything to say?"

A short hunter in a patched, blue-and-white gingham shirt stepped forward.

"Ben?" Beekman said. "You been through this kind of thing more than most of us. Whaddya think?"

The man named Ben spoke so softly Clairborne could hardly hear him even though he was just a few feet from where Clairborne sat.

In a soft rasp, Ben said, "Horses and hides. We gotta protect our horses and kill as many o' theirs as we can, and we ought 'a use the hide bales as cover. It ain't that they'll try to kill our hosses." He spat into the dirt. "Fact is, our horses is prob'ly the most important thing to 'em. Next to our scalps.

"Every man needs to look to his water supply so's he don't have to do without or break cover to get some if this goes on for more 'n a day or two. Which it will," he whispered.

"All right, here it is then," Beekman shouted. "Ben says we need to do as much as we can to protect our horses and kill theirs. We'll empty the wagons and turn 'em on their side and use the hides to fill in breaks in the wall. Make sure you got water for a two- or three-day fight along with the ammunition you'll need.

"We're already spread out pretty even, so each party just start fortin' up where you are. You know what to do."

As if at a signal, the onlookers broke and walked quickly back to their fires and possessions. Clairborne was impressed with the sense of purpose the hunters exhibited. No panic, just efficient movement to unload bales of buffalo hides and pile them into thick fortifications.

"Why don't you two join me and my partner," Beekman said as he led four horses from the water back to the center of the compound, where efforts were underway to increase the height of the ancient and incomplete walls that formed the perimeter.

"Fine with me. Thanks," Clairborne said, glancing at Herman, who nodded agreement.

Beekman's partner turned out to be a man almost as muscular as Beekman, but where Beekman was almost dour, his partner radiated irreverence and humor.

"Padraich O'Connor at your service, gentleman," he said with an ostentatious bow accompanied by a sweeping wave of the battered derby that normally covered his fiery red curls.

"I'd offer you scones and marmalade, but we're fresh out, and that blackhearted maid ran off with a tinker from Ulster, don't you know."

He shook hands and said, "We're going to pile all the supplies on the ground, then turn the wagon over on its side in front of the supplies. That way, we'll not want for nothin' while it is that we're dealin' with these savages."

In less than fifteen minutes, their position was ready, and they moved to work on the makeshift fortifications linking each of the hunting parties.

Clairborne was strongly impressed.

Food, water, ammunition, every weapon loaded and carefully placed. Horses and mules corralled in the center of the site, many of them apparently trained to lie down cavalry fashion as he'd seen troopers training horses at Leavenworth and Riley.

Herman rolled out his blanket behind a hide bale and laid out his weapons and supplies in priority order: bullets closest, followed by water, then food. Clairborne looked around and saw a likely spot for his own contribution and copied the preparations of others. Lying down on his blanket when he finished, he surveyed the surroundings, and as he contemplated the battle to come, one thought dominated all others.

"Whatever happens, remember you're a Clairborne."

—◦◦◦—

Nobody expected much warning.

Whether the Comanche would send some warriors to surreptitiously approach Spanish Wells or the whole raiding party would blow over the surrounding ridges was a matter of conjecture. There was no discussion about the need to carefully watch their horses for signs of alertness. Regardless of the direction the wind was blowing, the Comanche horses would be sensed by the buffalo hunters' animals long before they came in sight. Beekman reminded his colleagues of the tactics they should expect.

"They like as not won't rush us. They'll ride around testing, comin' in and out to see what we got. Just make damn sure of every shot, boys. Horses first, then the bucks."

Resting on his blanket, his Henry rifle lying across his chest, Clairborne whispered loudly to Herman just after midnight.

"You awake?"

"Yep."

"They won't attack us at night, will they?"

"Why not?"

"I thought Indians didn't fight at night. Something about their spirits getting lost if they die during darkness or something like that."

Herman smiled to himself. "Well, maybe east of the Mississippi they don't, but I sure wouldn't bet my scalp on it out here. Don't know if you noticed, but there's a full moon tonight. Know what they call it out here?" Not waiting for an answer, he said, "Comanche moon because the Comanch just dearly love to raid during a full moon. They think it downright advantageous."

"Advantageous?" Clairborne thought. "Wonder where a slave learned a word like advantageous?"

Exhaustion encumbered everything Clairborne did or tried to do, such as staying awake and alert. He reminded himself he'd not slept in more than forty-eight hours and wondered if he could just grab twenty or thirty minutes sleep without jeopardizing either his own or the collective security. He never made a decision. The third time his eyelids met, it was as if someone blew out a candle and plunged him into dreamless sleep so deep he resembled nothing so much as a corpse. But not so deep that he didn't snap awake at the scuffling sound of Padraich O'Connor's approach.

"Billy's onto them. He saw them coming up the wash on the other side of the camp. I'm makin' certain everyone's got their eyes peeled. Oh, and another thing: Ben wants everyone to stay in position no matter which side gets hit." O'Connor scrambled away before either Herman or Clairborne could ask who Billy was or, more important, where this Billy was in the perimeter.

The war cries cut off such extraneous thought.

Scores of mounted Comanche warriors poured over the rises east and southeast of Spanish Wells, flowing like a multicolored lahar down the slopes and accelerating across the flats separating the barricades from the heights.

Clairborne dragged his eyes away from the swarm racing toward the other side of the compound to survey the terrain in front of him.

Over his own heartbeat throbbing in his ears, Clairborne heard the shrill chorus of shrieks and howls and the pounding of hundreds of hoofs growing louder, more insistent by the second. Sweat stung his eyes and blurred his vision. A hurried wipe of his brow had no effect on the flow of perspiration. With a start he realized that something was missing; a major component of the fray was terrifyingly conspicuous by its absence. As of that moment, not a shot had been fired by a defender of Spanish Wells.

As if to counter his concerns, a deep and rolling roar erupted around him. Clairborne was alarmed by the solid cloud of gun smoke obscuring everything except the legs and boots of some of the hunters.

"Christ! How can they see anything through that?" Clairborne asked himself, half expecting a Comanche brave to come bolting through the gun smoke straight at him.

"Here they come..." Herman said.

Clairborne whipped around. Less than two hundred yards away, mounted Comanche swarmed out of a shallow wash that roughly paralleled their perimeter.

"Sweet Jesus, we're dead," Clairborne thought. Cutting down the mass of men and horses careening toward them at a mad gallop was simply impossible, he told himself. For a moment, he could not select a target. Too many. Too fast. He considered simply aiming in the general direction of the charging horde and just as quickly chided himself for not making the most of the time available to kill as many of his potential killers as he could before they killed him.

A beautiful piebald with a blue handprint on its chest and an eagle feather flapping in its braided bridle came into focus over his rifle barrel. He squeezed the trigger and reflexively worked the lever to eject the empty shell casing and replace it in the smoking chamber with a live round.

He shot another brown-and-white horse in the chest and fired a bullet into its tumbling rider, hitting him by sheer luck in the right knee, causing him to pitch forward face first into the dust, where he writhed in agony while Clairborne swung the Henry to the next target, less than fifty yards away. Which he missed, at least with the first round. But the second shot took the rider in the chin, which caused Clairborne a fleeting second of pride.

"Head shot. Damn!" he said aloud, but he was not able to hear his own voice even if he were listening for it.

He dropped two more horses before scrambling to his feet to fire at their fallen riders over the top of the stacked-up barrels and boxes.

"Son of a bitch, son of a bitch," he shouted, calculating the speed of the Comanche advance against the volume or fire from the makeshift fort divided by the remaining distance between the two hostile entities.

He didn't like the answer. He fired again and again into the mass of horses, not wasting ammunition on their riders.

"Son of a bitch," he croaked, dropping the empty Henry rifle and retrieving the Henry carbine, which he emptied as fast as he could work its action. Then he dropped it and retrieved his Colts.

He was vaguely aware of snapping, buzzing sounds. Pointing Thunder at a befeathered Comanche astride a line-back dun, he thumbed the hammer and pulled the trigger a split second before the rider could do the same with his army-issue Springfield trapdoor carbine. His bullet caught the warrior at the base of his neck between his clavicles, blowing his body back over the horse's rump.

He raised Lightning and put two rounds each into two more Comanche horses and one round each into their fallen riders. Realizing he had missed one of them, he swung Thunder to his left and fired its sixth and last bullet into the naked warrior painted brilliant yellow from hairline to moccasin-clad feet. The Comanche's impact with the rock-hard ground shattered bones, yet he still moved toward Clairborne as fast as he could with fractured femur and broken wrist. He sat suddenly in the dust and looked at the hole in his pectoral muscle. Dazed, he tried to rise on the wrist smashed by his fall but reduced to blue-white bone shards; it collapsed under his weight. He looked up at Clairborne's head protruding from the barricade ten feet from where he sat.

Clairborne saw rage erupt in the man's eyes as he rolled to his strong arm and pushed up.

"Uh oh," Clairborne said, realizing his Colts were empty and useful only as clubs. He looked down and saw his brother's massive LeMat, raised it, and cocked the hammer. Nine shots. Nine .44 balls and one twenty-gauge shell. He'd saved it for last, thinking that if he had time to reload, dropping preloaded and primed cylinders into the Colts would be faster. Clairborne realized he had not fired the LeMat more than five or six times and that the process of converting it to discharge the shot shell required sequential steps he was not sure he remembered. "Great. Just great," he thought. Then he put down the LeMat and retrieved the fowling piece his father had ordered from Parker Brothers in London for his son's fifteenth birthday, the shotgun that had delivered many a wild turkey, many a migratory goose and mallard to the Clairborne table.

Raising the richly engraved epitome of the gunsmith's art to his shoulder and pulling back its hammers, Clairborne quickly calculated the damage the heaviest of bird shot available could do to the man crawling toward him.

"Head," he said, pulling the first trigger even as he thought about saving the remaining charge for his own head as a guarantee he would not feel his testicles being sliced off, wouldn't gag when they were stuffed in his mouth. He didn't need for the smoke to clear. The range was too short for the effect to be anything but lethal.

Only then did he look over to Herman.

Seeing Herman standing on his toes, swinging his head from side to side, Clairborne considered the field of battle before him.

The last of the withdrawing Comanche were headed toward the gully. Some turned to raise their weapons in defiance, screaming curses and imprecations at the unpenetrated makeshift fortifications.

Between the walls and the retreating warriors, wounded horses writhed in agony or stood on three legs, the fourth shattered by bullets or falls or both. The Comanche had done a remarkable job of recovering their dead and wounded. Clairborne and Herman's quick visual sweep discovered only two bodies, evenly spaced between them and less than five feet from the barricade. Clairborne could not locate the yellow warrior's body.

The compound was silent. Looking around, Clairborne saw every man busily reloading. Herman sat with his back against a keg doing the same.

"Good idea," Clairborne thought, sitting and momentarily fumbling with the components. His breathing was uneven. His hands trembled from the overdose of adrenaline, scattering grains of black powder into the dirt instead of into the Colt's chambers. He took a deep breath and exhaled. The trembling eased.

Christ, but he was hungry. And thirsty.

Clairborne looked over at Herman.

"Think they'll come back?" he asked.

"Yes, I do," Herman said. "Yes, I do."

And they did. But not during the ensuing daylight hours.

And not before the defenders prepared a surprise.

After nightfall, Beekman and the gravel-voiced hunter named Ben convened a meeting in the center of the camp attended by all present except for the four hunters assigned to watch each quadrant of the perimeter.

"Here's the deal, boys," Beekman said. Nodding to Ben, he continued.

"We're of a mind that they's so many comin' at us, we ain't gonna be able to shoot enough to stop 'em next time. These bucks didn't circle us the way Comanch usually do. They come straight at us. We think they broke off 'cause we must o' got a chief or a medicine man. Anyhow, we gotta figure they're gonna try something different, so here's what me and Ben come up with."

As Beekman spoke, Clairborne looked closely at the man and each of the others gathered around him. Had the situation not been fraught with such imminent peril, he would have broken out in laughter, for it was only then, in the ambient light, that he realized every one of them, doubtless him included, were as black as Titus Herman. Every inch of skin was covered with a thick patina of gunpowder residue, making the defenders of Spanish Wells look more like a band of riverboat minstrels than the desperate killers they were.

"We got lots more gunpowder than we'll need, even if they just try to starve us out, which ain't their style. We can outlast 'em if they do that since we got plenty of grub and water.

"So we're going to take some powder kegs and crawl out a ways, cover the kegs with rocks and such, leave a powder trail back to the camp, then touch 'em off when they're chargin' up. What do ya say?"

A short, bald man spoke up immediately.

"Too tricky. Odds against timing the fuses just right are too high. Won't work."

Nobody else spoke.

"Snake, you're right," Beekman said. "The thing is, we're looking to give 'em a surprise, something that might slow 'em down, as much as we are to kill a whole slew of 'em. Anybody else?" Beekman asked.

The man called Snake scratched the back of his neck but said nothing.

"All right then," Beekman nodded. "Let's get to it. Paddy, Lars, Ben, and me'll put 'em out and light the fuses. Rest of you get on back and rest up for the next fandango," Beekman said, flashing his teeth in a grit-enhanced smile.

Clairborne and Herman walked back together.

"Think it'll work?" Clairborne asked.

"No, but I don't have a better idea. He's right, though, about them trying something different after losing so many the way they hit us earlier." Turning to take his position, Herman added over his shoulder, "No reason why we shouldn't try something different ourselves."

Four hours later, a simultaneous, well-coordinated eruption of the best light cavalry in the world swept over and down the surrounding heights before dawn. It was a brilliant tactic for two reasons. Darkness was the best possible counter to the extraordinary accuracy of the shooters and weapons arrayed against them. And attacking from 360 degrees also denied the defenders the ability to concentrate on specific sectors of their fortifications.

Inside the walls, the inhabitants of Spanish Wells were as ready as possible.

Somebody shouted, "Start shootin' now, boys. Just aim low..."

Clairborne recognized the wisdom of the anonymous directions.

Start the killing, the rapid firing into massed enemy as soon as they were within range—which was right now—rather than awaiting closed distances that permitted aimed fire at individuals.

The attackers' tactic was confounded by topographic reality and human nature. While the Comanche braves were spread out with as much as fifteen feet between them when they formed up on the reverse slopes, by the time they descended and accelerated across the flats, they were virtually knee to knee, congealing into a wildly churning mass.

Clairborne had again laid out his Henry rifle and carbine, his Parker double, and his pistols. The only difference was that after yesterday's assault, he realized the short-barreled Colts were ideal for the closest of close combat, so he stuffed the snub-nose pistols into his waistband. He also stood from the beginning. He shot better prone but couldn't move as quickly as when he was standing.

Subconsciously, he also wanted to die standing on his feet rather than lying on his belly in the dirt.

Within seconds of the defender's first volley, gun smoke absorbed the faint light and plunged the camp into utter darkness split by muzzle flashes.

Somewhere inside the perimeter, a chaotic shout resulted in snakes of flame racing outward from the walls along the ground, until each united with the mound of rock and rubble-covered gunpowder.

Of the six such devices laid out by the defenders, only two erupted as the wave of Comanche swept over them. The other four ignited within a second after the racing, screaming, furious attackers had passed.

Circumstance—some call it luck, a factor given far too little credit by scholars of conflict—produced better results than the defenders could have hoped for.

The flashes illuminated the entire formation of Comanche horsemen, providing an invaluable reference to the defenders. The two eruptions that occurred directly under the horses wreaked predictable havoc and literally stunning carnage.

Entire quarters of horses flew into the air. Pieces of the riders went even higher. Horses not fatally injured, some not injured at all, reeled and swerved, reared and skidded to a halt so abruptly that their expert riders catapulted over their heads.

The Comanche already beyond the powder blasts nonetheless slowed and turned to see what had happened. Many of their horses shied as well, forcing their riders to shift their concentration from leaping walls and killing white men to regaining control of their mounts.

All of which gave precious time to the defenders pouring aimed fire into the Comanche. The unanticipated but logical benefit of the gunpowder explosions came in the form of grass fires consuming desiccated prairie vegetation, starkly backlighting the mounted—and unintentionally dismounted—warriors. Flashes of light, shifting smoke from grass and guns, clouds of dust randomly exposed, then shielded, the combatants' surreal and deadly encounters.

Clairborne was down to a short-barreled Colt and his LeMat.

He fired the Colt first, furiously cocking the hammer and pulling the trigger as fast as possible. The Comanche closed the distance, seemingly without suffering any effect from his shooting. He despaired. "I'm dead," he thought, steadying himself and aiming at a warrior careening toward him.

An unexpected calm descended over him. He was sad for his mother. Very sad. All the Clairborne men dead and gone. He dropped the empty Colt and adjusted the LeMat to fire the shot-filled cartridge.

It hit the Comanche brave, who leaned forward until his head was below that of his mount, at his hairline slightly to the left of center. Entering his skull in a tight grouping, the soft lead shot expanded as it plowed through the frontal lobe, angled downward and exited slightly below and behind his right ear, taking with it brain tissue, neck muscle, and a three-inch-wide section of skull.

The warrior flipped backward off the horse, but the horse carried forward, leaping the buffalo-hide barricade and galloping across the enclosure, where it jumped the opposite wall and disappeared into the dust and smoke.

But not before it slammed into Clairborne, dislocated his left shoulder, and sent him flying into an ammunition box. The empty box broke and slid away on impact rather than resisting the force of Clairborne's head with its own mass, rendering him unconscious rather than dead.

The next warrior to clear the barricade made the mistake of attempting to rein in and wheel his plunging warhorse to engage Herman. The effort took all of his energy and attention and less than three seconds. It took Herman only two seconds to react. His first shot grazed the warrior's lower back. Reacting to the searing pain, the warrior turned to face Herman, whose second shot entered the warrior's abdomen an inch below his bottom left rib.

Herman didn't wait to see the warrior fall before turning back to the perimeter, noticing Clairborne's recumbent form in passing. Knowing he had only two shots left in his pistol, Herman began calculating the odds that he could get to Clairborne's shotgun propped against a wagon ten feet away. He decided he couldn't make it.

The dust and smoke combined into a solid mass. He expected Comanche to emerge in sudden explosions of fury, leaping the barriers with contempt for the puny effort at fortification.

For long seconds, nothing happened.

Herman heard war cries and shouts from somewhere inside the gray-brown pall in front of him. He bit his lip to prevent himself from overreacting to what he thought he heard: the war cries and defiant screams seemed to be going away instead of coming closer. Was he hearing the sound of retreat? He wanted to turn and look around inside the compound to see if some unaccounted-for Comanche was doing mischief, maybe even approaching him on soft-moccasin-clad feet. But he couldn't turn away from the field beyond the walls.

"Sweet Jesus," he said aloud as he began edging toward Clairborne's shotgun.

From the other side of the compound, he heard first one, then two, then a chorus of whoops and yells. Dawn weakly illuminated details closest to him. Herman felt something on his cheek. A breeze, ebbing and flowing like water, slowly dissipated the smoke and dust cloud, sliding it sideways like a theater curtain drawn open to disclose some playwright's imagined hell.

No imagination, however, could conjure up what Herman beheld. Not even the Comanches' vaunted skills and warrior ethos had recovered all the dead and wounded. Warriors and pieces of warriors, horses and pieces of horses, were scattered across the expanse of grass between the barricades of Spanish Wells and the base of the surrounding low hills. Some horses, stunned but not visibly injured, stood with their heads down, while a few others walked slowly away from the flickering grass fires.

The Comanche Herman had shot twice was still alive, barely, but was clearly moving on his stomach toward the war club he'd dropped. Without moving from his position ten feet away, Herman methodically reloaded his Henry, aimed at the Comanche, and shot him in the head. Another warrior had fallen outside the barricade between him and Clairborne. For whatever reason, perhaps hearing Herman's shot, the warrior had stopped moving, and Herman had trouble locating him among the other bodies. Herman waited, peering through his sights at the spot he thought was occupied by the wounded foe. Movement, slight but distinct, four feet to the left of where he'd been looking, caused Herman to slowly swing his rifle, aim, and just as slowly, squeeze the trigger until the Henry bucked into his shoulder.

From around the compound, he heard other shots.

Then the voice of Silas Beekman boomed across the compound.

"Every second man check around for wounded and get fresh ammo for his self and his partner. Let me know how many dead and wounded we got."

Herman looked at Clairborne, looked back over the barricade, and then moved to the Virginian lying immobile on his back.

Breathing. Blood on the back of his head and down his neck from where he had fallen on something. No blood on his front. Herman tried to roll him over to check his back, putting one hand on his hip, the other on his left shoulder.

"Uh oh," Herman said aloud. "That doesn't feel right."

He laid Clairborne down on his back and opened his grimy shirt to behold a dark purple mass covering the upper left portion of Clairborne's chest and shoulder. Herman had seen enough recruits thrown from their mounts to know a dislocated shoulder when he saw one. He lifted Clairborne and gently ran his fingers under Clairborne's shoulder, determining in the process that the ball was completely out of and to the front of the socket, but his experienced fingers detected no breaks in the muscles and ligaments.

He looked around to see if anyone was available to help and, seeing no one, proceeded on his own.

He sat down on Clairborne's left side and placed his left boot in Clairborne's armpit. Grasping Clairborne's wrist in both hands, Herman tugged lightly to see if just maybe the shoulder would pop back in place without further effort.

"Aw, too bad," he whispered. "Sorry, friend. I got to do this," he said as he pulled the arm straight toward himself.

The eruption of pain scorched Clairborne's unconscious mind and launched a ragged scream from his parched throat but didn't restore him to lucid awareness of his predicament.

Herman considered his work. He ran his fingers lightly over what seemed to be a normal configuration of skin, ligament, and bone beneath badly bruised flesh. "Damn. Not bad, if'n I do say so myself," he said aloud as he ripped Clairborne's shirt into strips. In less than five minutes, he'd bound Clairborne's left arm to his chest, immobilized the shoulder, propped him against a saddle, and covered him with a blanket. He considered trying to get some water into him but decided that pouring water into an unconscious man was not the best idea. On the other hand, pouring water into his own parched mouth and throat was a very good idea.

Herman drained his canteen and then walked to the center of the compound, where the other men had gathered, arriving in time to hear Beekman shout, "Boys, we're all going to be famous, I guaran-goddamn-tee it!"

Each of the assembled hunters carried his reloaded rifle. Herman was the only one not carrying a buffalo gun. The long, octagonal barrels of several of the big buffalo guns, weighing twelve pounds when empty, were still smoking. One hunter stripped the smoking, checkered-oak forestock from his Remington and dropped it in a water bucket. "Damn," he said. "You boys see that? God-danged barrel got so hot it like to lit up the stock."

Some of the men were laughing, giddy with disbelief. Others looked around and shook their heads.

Turning to Herman, Beekman said, "Well, Sergeant Herman, I guess we all owe you. You and your partner hadn't given us some warning, I ain't at all sure any of us'd be wearing our hair just now. "

O'Connor slapped his back. "And how's your friend? Under the weather, is he?"

"Separated shoulder and a banged up head's all. He'll live."

O'Connor put his hand on Herman's shoulder and surveyed the scene. "It appears we all may be so lucky as to live awhile longer." He smiled and said, "This mornin' I didn't think I'd see the moon again, that's for sure, but now I'm thinking my belly needs fillin' and my thirst needs quenchin'. Everything's back to normal, don't you know."

"Not just yet," a tall hunter said. On the highest of the ridges surrounding Spanish Wells, a lone Comanche brave sat his horse and waved his rifle, undoubtedly screaming imprecations at the white men, but his cries did not carry the distance to their ears.

Maintaining his focus on the distant warrior, Beekman said, "Lars, what do you think?"

"Yah," was all the man called Lars said in response.

Herman watched as the man walked to the nearest barricade and rested his Remington rolling block .45-70 on the hides. He adjusted the tang sight mounted on the wrist of the walnut stock, sliding it a series of notches, each representing ten yards of distance.

"At least nine hundred, Lars. Prob'ly closer to a thousand," Beekman said.

"Yah."

The Comanche continued to wave his rifle from his stationary mount.

The Remington belched flame and smoke. Lars stood up.

"One a t'ousand, two a t'ousand, three a t'ousand..."

On the distant slope, the Comanche whirled and fell from his horse, which scampered away.

"Damn!" Beekman yelled as he slapped the back of the shooter.

"I'll tell you, boys. We're all gonna be famous, but with that goddam thousand-yard shot, this old Scandahoovian here's gonna be the most famous of all..."

———

July 1868
Spanish Wells, Indian Territory (Texas?)

I am certain that this vicious, two-day confrontation in the middle of nowhere warrants not so much as a footnote for veterans of the War between the States. My father and brother were involved in battles that stretched into campaigns lasting for weeks or even months. By that standard, what happened here is nothing. For those involved in the battle of Spanish Wells, however, it might as well have been Gettysburg or Waterloo.

It never got to hand-to-hand combat, rolling in the dust, stabbing, choking, gouging. It was not Thermopylae or Agincourt or Jerusalem. It was what I guess scholars of such things would call a classic example of mounted attackers against dug-in defenders.

We lost no one. Not one single member of our band of thirty-three was lost. We counted nine Comanche bodies around our makeshift walls. Those who know say the Comanche pride themselves on recovery of their dead, so the actual number of slain Indians is doubtless much higher.

How can this be?

It was scores against tens. Many, including the cavalry officers who were my hosts of late, say that the Comanche are simply the finest light cavalry since Genghis Khan's Mongols. And yet we defeated them. Thirty-three men firing from behind bales of buffalo hides stopped two charges with no losses. One of those thirty-three, I had no experience in anything like this, so I must have been the weakest link in the chain, and yet I think I held up as well as could be expected. Herman and two of the others believe both assaults ultimately failed because we shot a chief or a medicine man, maybe both. Otherwise, the Comanche would surely have swept us into oblivion.

When it began, I believed my death was inevitable and imminent. I also realized that my ultimate desire was not to survive. It was to conduct myself in such a manner that no matter what the outcome, men would say I died with honor, I wanted them to say, "That Clairborne fellow fought well." I wanted my father and brother to embrace me in heaven and tell me our family name was still intact as a result of my actions.

In the same split second that death seemed inevitable, I thought of mother, but rather than feeling paralyzing terror, I felt sadness, sorrow that this woman would have to endure the loss of her last son.

And as to the foe, again I am surprised by my feelings. As I walked among their fallen, I was struck by the beauty of their weapons—lances, war clubs, quivers of arrows, and firearms, each and every one decorated with intricate symbols I do not understand but which clearly carry significance for the individual warrior. Those men not rendered into small pieces by our efforts in many instances lie as if in repose, some without even visible wounds until they are turned over.

I find myself studying them. I marvel at their audacity and wonder what amazing force drove them to such frenzy, such irrational assaults, not once but twice. Such men doubtless expected victory when they contemplated their first attack, but what did they think were their chances of victory, of survival, as they mounted the second?

My brother wrote of his amazement at the Union Army's simultaneous stupidity and tenacity as they assaulted Southern positions at Maryes Heights outside Fredricksburg. He said many in the Southern ranks were moved to cheer the Yankees' courage and discipline even as they mowed them down from behind stone walls.

What makes men act this way? Why do they engage when they know they cannot succeed?

I stood over the body of one warrior who lay on his back. His long hair was fanned out beneath his head; what appeared to be an eagle feather was woven into it above his left ear. His broad chest was covered by an intricate assembly of beads and small bones. His legs seemed skinny and bowed. His brown eyes were open, as was his mouth. I squatted and studied him, mesmerized *by proximity to something I do not understand, a representative of a culture as alien to me as would be the ancient Persians under Xerxes or Darius.*

Did I kill him? Was it my Henry that made the small hole in his stomach and the larger hole in his back? Am I sorry if it was? I think I should be, but I'm not. It was battle. He would have killed me without remorse, of that I am certain.

———

There was a heated discussion about what the defenders of Spanish Wells should do next.

Some thought it best to leave immediately. Proponents of departure said it was wise to take advantage of the confusion and disarray the Comanche foe would inevitably be feeling after the traumatic defeat.

Others argued it best to stay at Spanish Wells for a while, a few days. The proponents of staying believed that disposing of the remains of horses and humans by fire would protect the purity of the region's primary reliable source of drinking water. They also argued that sending out scouting parties would provide intelligence on which to make further decisions.

Ultimately, the defenders of Spanish Wells were a democracy. So they debated, then voted. Even in the society of buffalo hunters, there was a hierarchy. The hunters literally called the shots. Their skinners did what they were told, but everyone got a vote when lives were at stake.

From his position resting against a wheel of one of the righted wagons, Clairborne observed the debate with fascination. Factions formed and faded, most of the men were silent or confined their spoken words to monosyllabic affirmations or disagreements of positions stated forcefully by a small minority.

Beekman and Charlie Guthrie, the man who had questioned Herman when he and Clairborne arrived, were the two most passionate and vociferous. Beekman wanted to stay. Charlie Guthrie wanted to "light a shuck outta here."

For Clairborne, it was very clear very quickly after the debate started that Beekman and Guthrie hated each other.

"For all we know, them redskin bastards is bringing in more men to hit us again. It ain't like them to quit, so why sit on our asses just waiting till it suits 'em to come back?" shouted Guthrie, waving his arms at the surrounding hills.

Beekman didn't respond immediately. Then he shrugged, turned, and took a seat on an empty powder keg.

"Tell you what, Charlie. I think you're right. I think we'd all be better off if you and your partner just took off. Get the hell out of here, and the sooner the better—before the Comanch come back to eat our livers.... Go on. Saddle up and get out. Ain't nobody gonna stop you. Matter of fact, I'll help you pack your gear."

Guthrie looked around, surprised by Beekman's suggestion.

"You know damn good and well me and Fritz ain't goin' out there by our lonesomes. We all need to travel together is what I'm saying."

"Charlie. I'm done arguing," Beekman said, slowly taking his feet. "Everybody thinks we oughta quit this place right away, raise your hand."

Guthrie shot his right hand into the air and looked around. His skinner Fritz was the only other man to signal agreement with departure, and Fritz raised his hand very slowly.

Beekman smiled at Guthrie.

"Like I said before, Charlie. Ain't nobody stopping you from going. But here's the thing. You stay, you work. And you keep your mouth shut, no yammering nor bitching, or so help me, I'll take it personal."

"Aw shit," Guthrie said, turning on his heel.

Clairborne had long since noted that Beekman was a natural leader. In a group of strong if not prickly independent individuals, Beekman articulated decisions the rest followed willingly or with minimal debate. Clairborne also noted that much of what Beekman did, he did by seeking confirmation of what he thought best rather than issuing edicts.

"OK, boys," Beekman said after Guthrie stalked off. "Way I see it, we got two chores ahead of us. We gotta get rid of them piles o' guts out yonder, and we gotta see what we can find out about the Comanch. Anybody got other ideas?"

Nobody did.

"OK. Who scouts? Seems to me it oughta' be the best, and whoever it is, better scallyhoot out o' here pronto."

Herman stepped forward. "I'll go."

"I was hopin' you would," Beekman said. "Who else?"

Three other men stepped forward or raised their hands.

"I'll go with him," said a short, bearded man whose skin was noticeably darker than the others, even taking into consideration the effects of gunpowder, buffalo blood, dirt, and sun. He nodded at Herman. "Esta bien contigo?" he asked Herman.

Before Herman could answer, Beekman said, "Sergeant, this here's Luis Baca. Best tracker here."

"Good enough for me," Herman said, extending his hand. "Vamos." Watching the discussion from his vantage point under a wagon, Clairborne thought, "Well, I'll be. He speaks Spanish too."

"Where you boys headed and how long will you be out?" Beekman asked the impromptu group of scouts.

"One party east, the other west. We ride clockwise till we cross our starts or pick up clear sign. Maybe two days, three to make sure," Herman said.

Beekman grinned. "By then, oughta have this place cleaned up enough for a church social."

Before he began his preparations for the ride, Herman stopped by Clairborne's position and knelt down.

"How's the shoulder?' he asked.

"Well, I'm not going to be hanging wallpaper any time soon," Clairborne responded.

Herman grinned. He lowered his head and looked directly into Clairborne's face. "Well, you must've took a pretty hard shot to your head. You still got one eye bigger'n the other."

Clairborne understood that Herman was speaking of his irises, that his impact with the ammunition box had rattled his skull enough to produce a concussion. He knew about concussions from a boyhood incident involving revenge for being slammed with an axe handle.

Then-fifteen-year old Clairborne encountered first-cousin Carter Byrd three months after Byrd had broken Clairborne's ribs in a boyhood scuffle that turned vicious. In the Warwick stables before a fall fox hunt, Clairborne had attacked his cousin with such ferocity that his older brother Payton physically intervened to stop the fray—but not before Clairborne seized his cousin's ears and smashed his head against the flagstones of the stable floor, producing an injury his furious father said was a concussion. Now it was his turn to be concussed. Rubbing his temples, he recalled that Carter Byrd, his first cousin and perennial arch foe of childhood, died at age seventeen at a place called Chancellorsville. Recalling his cousin, it occurred to him that his life was being defined by death and loss. He counted the number of kith and kin dead and gone in just the last five years. Then he added the drunk in Nashville, Wild Bill Martin, and the dead Comanche being piled on funeral pyres in front of him.

Closing his eyes, he thought of some men as plows turning virgin soil into productive fields. Others were tempests, ripping crops out by their roots or washing them away in angry torrents. George Washington was a plow, leaving the legacy of a new nation. Robespierre was a cyclone, destroying whole societies and leaving blood and destruction.

And most men? Seed corn. Dropped into the soil by circumstance. Maybe there would be rain or irrigation. Maybe the soil would be tilled, cared for. Maybe not. For most, probably not.

The individual kernel had no control over the dirt into which it was sewn.

"That's what's wrong with me," he thought. "I'm defining myself by how I fight. I should be studying the classics. I should be buying new land for Warwick or at least figuring out how to pay its taxes. I should be married. And instead I'm lying in the dirt in the middle of nowhere."

There was nothing positive about his state. "Except that I'm breathing. No. That's not all. I have money. In the bank, in my investment, in property, in my gun belt. Hell, I even have money in my boots," he told himself with a grin.

He shifted his rolled-up blanket to the shade beneath the wagon, crawled into the slightly cooler space, and promptly fell asleep.

When he awoke, it was night.

He stood, gripping the wheel to steady himself as he slowly arose. He scratched his matted hair and noisome armpit. He shook out his boots before pulling them on with one hand and then retrieved his hat. Inside the still-standing barricades, campfires were down to embers, fluttering circles of soft orange light marking the locations of each team of hunters. He spotted six men spaced around the camp, facing out, two sitting, the rest standing, each cradling his heavy-barreled rifle across his chest.

Beyond the walls no fewer than seven huge fires illuminated circles of prairie forty feet in diameter. Pops and crackles launched sprays of sparks.

Was each spark a soul, a life-force rising to the heavens?

He raised his eyes to follow them upward. The unusually dry, clear air intensified the light of incalculable legions of stars strewn from horizon to horizon.

How was each new arrival assigned a space in those celestial ranks?

Were the brightest above the names he knew? Achilles. Alexander. Arthur.

Were the lesser lights, the barely visible, the unknown hoplites and illiterate privates missed only by their mothers but embraced by God nonetheless?

"Is this where warriors go, their martial spirit unextinguished, inexorable, in storage until God plucks it out and puts it into the heart of an unborn combatant?"

Clairborne stood transfixed. His eyes brimmed. His neck ached.

"My father is up there. Payton too. Send me a sign so I'll know where, Father. Please."

The only change he became aware of was a slow but undeniable increase in the number of celestial bodies he could see the longer he beheld the heavens.

"OK," he said softly. "OK."

He picked up his Colts, stuffed them into his waistband, and walked to the nearest sentry. Paddy O'Connor heard his approach and turned to greet him.

"Back from the river Styx, is it?"

"You want me to spell you, take the rest of your watch? I haven't done much to help, so go ahead and catch some sleep."

"And that's just what I'll do, then. You're sure you're all right?"

"Can't handle a long gun just yet, but my eyes are OK, and that's what really matters, right?"

"So it does. So it does," O'Connor said with a smile bright enough to pierce the darkness. "I'll be in the arms of Morpheus just over there," he said, pointing his Remington at embers of the nearest campfire. "But I'll be at your side before you can hammer back the second shot from that hogleg of yours."

Clairborne watched O'Connor drop down on his robes and wrap his left arm around his rifle as if it were his recumbent lover.

He turned to the perimeter and realized he needed to avert his eyes from the funeral pyres lest they destroy his night vision, his ability to see movement in the darkness beyond them.

He looked up at the stars once more. This time his thoughts were not about kin or ancient warriors. He wondered where Herman was and how soon he would return.

—⁖⁖⁖—

Herman and Luis Baca rode slowly toward the camp at Spanish Wells at dusk the next day. The other scouting party had returned in midafternoon.

Both groups reported the same finding. The Comanche had dispersed, ridden off in small parties, leaving behind clear evidence that they had suffered significant loss of men and horses.

Their reports lifted a weight from the defenders, sparked backslaps and hoots and impromptu jigs.

After tending his horse, Herman carried his tack to a spot near Clairborne and collapsed on his sweaty saddle blanket.

Tugging his battered campaign hat over his eyes, he muttered, "I'm about plumb wore out. Can't recall being so bushed."

Clairborne felt guilty. He'd been resting, sleeping while Herman had been in the saddle without a break for two days.

"Want some coffee?" Clairborne asked.

"Yep."

Not knowing where Herman's cup was stashed, Clairborne got his own, walked to the communal coffee pot, and filled it with the thick, bitter brew, put it down beside Herman, and sat down.

He wanted to interrogate Herman about what he'd seen, what signs led to the conclusion the foe had quit the field of battle for good. Herman's snores prevented further conversation.

Drawing his knees to his chest, Clairborne retrieved his coffee and sipped, instantly regretting not blowing to cool it first.

From somewhere behind him came the distinctive whine of the man called Charlie. Complaining, grousing, cursing, his voice reminding Clairborne of an ungreased gate hinge, metallic, grinding. Irritating.

Charlie was berating his partner Fritz. Clairborne wanted to hear Fritz's response, wanted Fritz to tell Charlie to shut the hell up. He heard nothing, nothing but Charlie's nonstop harangue. He turned around enough to observe other hunters within earshot of the obnoxious Charlie. Everyone seemed to be ignoring him. Clairborne could not. He tried to simply close his mind to the aggravation and, failing that, stood and walked away. At the base of a cottonwood, he turned and regarded the camp. He thought about confronting the man, provoking him, calling him a jackass to his face.

His thoughts shifted to his pistol. He withdrew it and checked its loads. He reinserted it into the holster he wore on his left hip under the sling that supported his left arm. With his right hand, he lifted the sling enough to test the motion of his left shoulder, knowing instinctively he had to move it often to keep muscles and tendons from stiffening despite the pain such movement caused.

He heard fiddle music.

Darkness comes to the midsummer plains as either a veil, slowly lowered, or as a door, suddenly slammed. Today, a sunny, hot day in July, it slipped into Spanish Wells, gently nudging light and heat to wherever it is such elements go for the night.

Clairborne caught the scent of roasting meat and frying fat carried to him on the lightest of zephyrs. His stomach growled and moved, reminding him he hadn't eaten in more than thirty-six hours.

The central campfire, the smell of cooking, the joyous fiddle music drew him to the middle of the camp but not before he woke Herman to ask if it was safe for them to join the festivities. Herman sat up and sniffed the air. "Hump roast and fry bread." They retrieved their tin plates, their two-tined forks, and enameled cups and ambled to the cook fire, joining the growing circle of hunters, many of whom also toted ceramic jugs of whiskey, which they shared without ceremony.

Clairborne was not surprised to find O'Connor on the working end of the fiddle, but he was surprised to see Fritz walk up with a banjo, sit on a keg beside O'Connor, and join the spirited rendition of "The Mason's Apron." It was the first time he'd seen Fritz smile. He looked around to locate Charlie and found him on the periphery, jug raised, dirt-caked Adam's apple bobbing almost in time with the music. "Well, that's going to be trouble sooner than later," he told himself as a hunter next to him handed him a brown jug, the contents of which caused Clairborne to gasp.

With his Abilene observations on western whiskey in mind, Clairborne raised the jug again but compressed his lips to restrict the flow into his mouth. He didn't articulate his reasoning to himself. Had he done so, it was that he wanted to stay sober despite a strong desire to celebrate being alive after the battle of Spanish Wells. Just why he wanted to retain a clear and quick mind didn't occur to him. It just seemed like the best course of action.

Three hours later, full stomachs, physical fatigue, alcohol-soaked brains, and emotional relief produced predictable effects.

Eighteen men were sprawled in the dirt within the circle of firelight, their snores sounding like a chorus of broken buzz saws punctuated by the grunts of mating bullfrogs.

Seven others engaged in spirited discussion of topics ranging from how many grains of powder to use in loads meant for buffalo to the best care of lame horses to the virtues of women—and how to determine a true love from a fortune seeker.

Six had returned to their respective bedrolls.

O'Connor and Fritz continued to play, shifting their repertoire to ballads, the words of which were known and sung by almost all still awake, including Clairborne.

At the final chorus of "Green Grow the Violets," Herman stood, sipped the last drops of whiskey from his cup, and stretched. "Think I'll call it a night," he said.

"Hey, I got a question afore you go there, boy," said Charlie, his cold voice penetrating the good cheer like a flow of ice water from under the wagon where he'd been sitting and drinking.

"Just whose ass you kiss to get sergeant's stripes, anyways?" he said, moving into the light three people away and to the right of where Clairborne sat.

Charlie's voice and presence was as unwelcome as a viper.

"Charlie, goddamn it, why don't you crawl back into your hole and just shut up," Beekman said, shaking his head.

"I guess I can ask him anything I want. Seems a fair question, since I was four years in the by-god army and never got no stripes."

"That's cause nobody'd trust you to empty a bucket of piss with the instructions painted on the bottom, you horse turd," Beekman said to roars of laughter.

Charlie ignored the taunting and his obvious unpopularity.

"You gonna answer me, nigger?"

Clairborne snapped his head around to see Herman's response.

Herman stood silently for a long moment then turned slowly and walked away. "No," he said over his shoulder.

Clairborne detected movement on his right.

All of the hunters had their rifles within reach during the festivities.

As he turned to determine the source of the movement, he saw Charlie swing the inch-wide muzzle of his buffalo gun to the midpoint of Herman's back.

Hunters yelled and scrambled. Herman flinched. Clairborne withdrew Thunder and brought it to bear as Charlie thumbed back the massive hammer with an audible click.

The report of Clairborne's Colt .44 was much louder.

The bullet struck Charlie a quarter-inch to the left of his Adam's apple and, encountering no bone or hard tissue, continued upward through his neck until it impacted the bottom of his right jawbone. The lower right side of Charlie's face detached from his head and broke into two main pieces, but not before sending shards of shattered bone into his brain and out of his right eye socket, spraying scurrying hunters with fragments of flesh, blood and bits of brain.

Charlie's malevolent spirit had flown before he collapsed into the compacted dirt beneath him.

The ensuing silence was complete.

Finally, a stunned Silas Beekman murmured, "Sweet Jesus. Sweet Jesus," to which O'Connor added, "Mary and Joseph, I've never seen the like."

Heads turned to Clairborne. Herman straightened and turned to him as well.

Clairborne's right arm was still raised, smoke still drifted from Thunder's muzzle.

He lowered the pistol and slid it into its holster. He unfolded his legs and stood, pulling himself to his feet with his right-hand grip on the wagon wheel against which he'd been resting.

Beekman stared at him, mouth slightly agape.

"So that's it. You're a shootist. I knew there was something different about you. You're a shootist. How come I never heard your name before?"

"I'm not a shootist, Beekman. That's why you never heard of me, and I don't wish to be called such, if you don't mind."

Beekman stood and shook his head.

"Maybe you weren't a shootist before, but you sure as hell are now, and there ain't nothing you can do about it," he said as other hunters stood and wiped dabs of Guthrie from their buckskins and boots.

Clairborne sensed Herman at his side and turned to face him. They nodded, said nothing, and walked to their bedrolls.

———

Fritz spent the morning hours digging a grave for his partner. "He was not a good person, but he was my partner," Fritz said to the few who brought shovels with them.

By noon, everyone seemed in a hurry to leave Spanish Wells.

As Herman and Clairborne packed, Beekman walked over and sat on a keg, sipping his coffee while he watched. After a few moments, he said, "I meant what I said last night, Clairborne, about you being a shootist, whether you like it or not. Know why I'm telling you that again?"

Tugging on his horse's cinch, Clairborne didn't turn around and said simply, "No."

When Beekman didn't say anything, Clairborne finished preparing his tack, slipped his Henry into its scabbard, and turned to the unofficial leader of the defenders of Spanish Wells.

"You've not asked for my opinion, I know. But I also know you are new to this country, so you may not understand what will happen as a result of what you did. Well, maybe it's not what you did but how you did it."

Clairborne walked around his horse and said nothing.

Beekman drank some more coffee.

"You see, gunplay's just about the first thing folks talk about out here 'cept for maybe horses. More 'n cattle or Indians or weather. I guarangoddamntee you that within a month, couple o' hundred men are gonna be standing in saloons from Saint Louie to San Francisco tellin' everyone about how they saw Tucker Clairborne drop ole Charlie Guthrie, how Clairborne whipped out his .44 while he was sittin' in the dirt and hit ole Charlie in the throat with one shot from thirty feet away. How Clairborne was as cool as the other side of the pillow, just slippin' that ole smoke wagon back into his holster, standin' up, and sidlin' off to his bedroll."

"Couple of hundred? There're only thirty-three of us," Clairborne said.

"Thirty-two now," Beekman smiled. "But that's the point. It's a great story. Ain't none better for free drinks and hard-boiled eggs. So people're gonna tell it like they was here, don't you see. And then the folks they tell are gonna tell it, and pretty soon in the tellin', you was three miles away from Charlie and you killed him with your frown—"

"So what do you recommend, Silas?" Clairborne said in a tone that communicated that his actual question was "What's your point?"

Beekman poured the dregs of his coffee into the campfire coals and studied the bottom of his cup.

"You gotta understand folks're going to think of you as a pistolero from here on out—good, bad, or indifferent. So was I you, I'd watch my back, is all I'm saying. Just watch your back."

"All of that based on one incident?"

"Yeah. Folks—hell, me too—don't know that something like that hasn't happened before." Beekman raised his hand and smiled, cutting off Clairborne's immediate protest.

"I ain't saying it did. I'm just saying I don't know it didn't, nor does anyone else, and they'll tend to surmise it did, and that's what I'm trying to get across to you. Like it or not, fair or not, you got yourself a reputation as a pretty fair hand with a pistol." Beekman nodded toward the others. "Lots of us are fair shots with long guns. Kinda have to be in this business. Ain't none of us can wield a hogleg like you. Just keep it in mind."

Clairborne recognized the wisdom of the buffalo hunter's words and understood why Beekman was sharing his observations. He crossed the campsite to where Beekman stood. They shook hands.

"Thanks, and I hope we meet again," Clairborne said.

"So do I," Beekman answered. "I'm bettin' I'll be hearing about just where you are, and if I'm in a couple of hundred miles, I'll look you up."

Herman was already in the saddle when Clairborne turned to his mount. Clairborne made one final adjustment of the diamond hitch that secured the load on his packhorse. He climbed into the saddle and wheeled around to follow Herman, who had already spurred his horse to the southwest.

They hadn't covered more than two miles before Clairborne, checking their back trail and seeing an isolated dust cloud, said, "Somebody's coming after us."

They halted and turned, thumbing back their Henrys' hammers without moving the rifles from where they lay across the saddles. It was unlikely the dust was being kicked up by hostiles, but you never know, Clairborne thought.

Two riders cleared the crest of the low hill separating them from Spanish Wells, and Herman was the first to identify them as they rode at a canter, one leading a packhorse, the other a big mule.

"Baca and Dornheim," he said, causing Clairborne to ask, "Who's Dornheim?"

"Fritz. Charlie Guthrie's partner. The banjo player."

Clairborne swiveled around to watch the oncoming riders and in a low voice said, "I wonder where they're going."

Neither said anything until Baca and Fritz Dornheim slowed their horses to a trot and then halted in front of the men they'd been chasing.

"We go to Texas too, along with you," Baca said. His wiry frame was draped in what had once been a short jacket of scarlet wool before years of western sun bleached it to a soft peach. His hat was equally victimized by the elements, its wide brim dipping and flapping with each breeze. A thick black drawstring secured it below his jaw. As Clairborne regarded him, Baca waved his right hand and said, "I'm from Nuevo Mexico, place called Taos. I know the trail. And I know Comanche. My people been dealing with them for three hundred years."

Clairborne did some quick mental arithmetic. His family had been in Virginia for slightly more than two hundred years, a time span sufficient to warrant widespread respect—and political power—as one of the "First Families of Virginia." Three hundred years meant Baca's lineage went back to a time before Englishmen first set foot on the swampy Virginia shore in 1607 at what would be called Jamestown in honor of the Scotsman occupying the throne.

"You know Comanch, you can parlay with them?" Herman asked.

"Yes, my friend, I had the honor of being their guest for a number of years," Baca said with a smile. "They took everyone in my pueblo prisoner when I was seven. We were ransomed back five years later."

"Lord, you were a prisoner for five years and lived to tell about it," Clairborne exclaimed.

Baca shook his head. "It's not like you think. The Comanche think of prisoners as property, like horses or guns—you know, slaves, but slaves that can work and be sold or traded if they are strong. It was not pleasant at first, but it soon became an adventure for me. And of course, I was with my mother and sisters and too young to really understand what happened to them."

Clairborne wanted to inquire about Comanche treatment of Baca's female relatives but resisted the temptation on the assumption that the answer would be shameful to any man, particularly a Spaniard.

He turned to the German. "How about you, Fritz? You really want to ride with me after what I did to your partner?"

Fritz removed his battered hat and mopped his thinning brown hair with a blue bandana.

"Ach, you had no choice. That drunken bastard was about to shoot your partner in the back. Also, I am hating him since the day I met him, but I was in debt and the only way to pay was to be his skinner. It was hell, I tell you. I myself wanted to kill him more than once for sure. I want to go to Texas. I have been hearing about Texas since before I run away from Bavaria."

Clairborne remembered gallant Lieutenant Rall. "An Austrian and a German. What are the odds?" he thought.

"You have a trade there?" he asked.

"Yah. My father was armorer for the duke like his father before him. I pass years at the forge with him before he died. I could have taken his place, but I saw my chance to go to America, and I took it." He shrugged. "Two of my uncles came here before. Both are dead in the war," he said with another shrug of his broad, sloped shoulders.

Clairborne and Herman traded glances. With the slightest of nods, Herman indicated his approval of their party's expansion. To buy time, Clairborne retrieved his canteen and drank deeply, studying the two newcomers from the corner of his eye.

The German's cheeks were permanently flushed. His hands were covered by gauntlets; his patched woolen pants and galluses seemed almost threadbare, as was his muslin shirt, patched at the elbows and repaired in a least two other spots as well. But the repair stitching was as fine as a female's, and Dornheim's tack was well cared for, his horses well tended.

And Baca?

While at first he couldn't put his finger on what it was that made him feel that way, Clairborne instantly respected the man. There was his smooth economy of movement and subtle humor. His clothing and equipment, his tack were exotic and eclectic. "That's it," Clairborne realized. Baca represented a living, breathing store of knowledge he wanted to tap. A surge of optimism flooded through him as he considered days, months with Baca, hearing more about the Comanche, about his saddle with its high cantle and prominent saddle horn, its tapaderos, about the coiled, braided rope called a *riata*.

"Well, gentlemen, we're wasting daylight. I propose we resume our meandering forthwith," Clairborne said with a sweep of his gloved right hand.

Gently spurring Bucephalus into a brisk walk, Clairborne regarded the surrounding terrain, which resembled nothing so much as rumpled burlap, brown and rough to the touch. It was still early enough for the breeze to be cool, although the cloudless sky held no secrets about the heat to come.

He smiled. There was no place on the planet he would rather be. "How many men can say that?" he asked himself. "Not very many," he answered.

July? 1868
Somewhere on the American Plains

For two days now, I've been trying to think of why, with so many subjects, so many experiences, I've failed to record things in a timely, disciplined manner.

I have paused to consider what next I write.

I must be honest with myself. My father's wisdom constantly elevates my thoughts to a higher level most consistent with my heritage and the blessings I attain from it. His favorite admonition was a line from Hamlet spoken by Polonius: "To thine own self be true." He told Payton and me so often that if we could not be honest with ourselves, we were truly lost. So it is that I must face, must put into words what I have done and what the consequences of those actions are likely to be.

I have killed men. I have intentionally killed men. First in Nashville, then in Spanish Wells. I have killed men individually and en masse, in face-to-face encounters and in battle. I must write the four words again.
I have killed men.
I feel no remorse. Would I have preferred that these actions had never occurred?
No.
There it is. I've written the word, and it is true.

Each encounter was unavoidable on my part. Each encounter was balanced in that either antagonist could have prevailed. After Nashville, I wondered why I could still sleep soundly and why I was not wracked with remorse. Now, after even more killing, I continue to sleep well. It is not that I take pleasure in these killings. It is rather that I have come to view them as a series of tests that I did not seek or expect. Passing the test means that I live, so failure is not to be considered.

I have come to accept Beekman's notion that I now wear a reputation as a gunman as immutable as the color of my eyes. I so wish I had had more time with Wild Billy Martin to absorb his experiences and the knowledge gained from each of them. I understand more fully the wisdom of what he did tell me, though.

"Practice every day, if possible. Always expect the worst. Never hand your gun to anyone. Always protect your back. Always consider a shotgun if you know trouble's coming."

And what of the admonition he said was the most important of all? "If you ever find a woman you love who loves you too, stay with her." I can only pray that God presents me with such a blessing. But out here, all things feminine are so alien, so theoretical they occupy only dreams and fantasies and, as such, they leave only sadness and longing on the scented trail they leave in our hard lives on the plains.

—◦◦◦—

There are no Sundays on the plains.

No Tuesdays or Thursdays either. Birthdays and anniversaries come and go in anonymity, indistinguishable from the day before or the day after. Clairborne's birthday slid past him even before he became aware of its proximity, blending into rituals and routines so completely it became an afterthought.

When time as marked by Europeans becomes irrelevant, time as marked by nomads and hunter-gatherers fills the void. Minutes are of no importance. Seasons require adjustments.

Clairborne came to forget that somewhere in his pack, a Breguet timepiece awaited his attention, a mechanical wonder he'd killed a man to retain.

The season was summer, still in the year 1868. The terrain had slowly changed from dry grass as high as the horses' bellies to dry grass barely to the top of their fetlocks. What had been flat, treeless prairies—the "llano," Baca called it—morphed to shrub-dotted, increasingly rolling rocky terrain slashed by ever-deeper gulleys, ravines, and, of late, canyons with striated sides punctuated by pedestals of rock the color of which changed with the angle of the sun. Clairborne learned that water, if it was to be had at all, was at the bottom of these defiles. No one had to explain to him the dangers of being down there if and when an enemy was above. He didn't question the unspoken protocol of descending to canyon bottoms two at a time, the other half of the party standing vigil above while horses drank and canteens were filled.

Sitting beside Baca, Clairborne rested his forearms on the pommel of his saddle, slowly worked his still-stiff left shoulder, and studied the land. Gnarly piñons strained upward from rocky outcroppings, emitting the pungent scent of pine pitch exuding from woodpecker holes. The land through which they rode had changed from passively pastoral to increasingly dramatic cliffs and bluffs, mesas laced with draws and coulees. Stands of cottonwood delineated water sources, however small. The farther south they rode, the rarer the water became.

Only the wind was constant.

The wildlife changed with the land. While incomprehensibly large herds of bison migrated through, they saw more blindingly fast pronghorn antelope along with deer, javelinas, and occasional elk. The hunting was good, which meant that the meals were as well.

In Virginia, Clairborne had a particular affinity for bald eagles and had spent hours watching them tend their young and steal from osprey along the James River. At dawn one day in the rocky hill country where they now rode, Baca pointed to a large, dark bird circling slowly on an updraft.

"Golden eagle," he said. "Beautiful, no?"

Recalling the fish-eating bald eagles of the James River, Clairborne asked, "What do they eat? No fish for them."

"Rabbits, even young deer and pigs, anything they can kill or they find. They are the lords of the skies. Nothing can challenge them."

The lazy loops and effortless gliding triggered momentary envy.

"How wonderful it would be to just slide over this country, to just ride the wind. No aching butt. No charlie horses," Clairborne muttered.

Baca nodded. "That is why the Indian worships the eagle like no other of God's creatures. They too envy the eagle's freedom. You know, sometimes when I watch them, I think the eagle doesn't care about humans, that we are not important to him."

Clairborne turned his head slightly to regard Baca's face, which was elevated and serene, moving slowly in concert with the distant bird. He wanted to ask Baca if he thought God was like an eagle, uncaring, even disdainful of human folly. But he decided such theological inquiry was inappropriate fodder for discussion on a rocky promontory overlooking a shallow, yel-low-sand stream.

How long had they been riding together? How distant in time was Spanish Wells? Ten, twelve days?

Baca saw them first.

"Riders," he said, nodding toward the two horsemen on the rim across the canyon from where they sat.

Clairborne knew instantly they were white men by the way they sat their mounts and the broad-brimmed hats that defined their silhouettes. These and other signs told him the riders were Americans, not Mexicans, and, he suspected, not hostile in their intentions else they would not show themselves so casually.

Herman and Dornheim joined them from below where they had been watering their mounts.

"You see our company?" Clairborne asked.

"'Bout halfway up," Herman said. Dornheim said nothing but ran his gloved right hand over the receiver of the Spencer carbine resting on his saddlebow.

"I'm going to wave at them," Clairborne said, waiting moments before removing his hat to give his companions time to object.

When they didn't, he stood in his stirrups and swept his hat from side to side above his head. The two horsemen across the can-yon both responded with hand signals clearly friendly in nature.

"Well," Clairborne said. "Let's go meet those boys, and maybe they can tells us where we are."

It took the better part of an hour for the four of them to descend, ford the shallow river, and scramble up the steep talus slope on the other side of the wide canyon. More than once,

Clairborne smiled privately at the thought of how effortlessly a golden eagle could cover the same distance. As they neared the top, they saw the riders moving to meet them.

Clairborne noted immediately the absence of packhorses. That meant they were close to a camp or maybe even something more permanent.

Herman noted the quality and condition of their horses: both excellent.

All four of them recognized that the two riders approaching them at a brisk canter were clearly cowhands. There was simply no mistaking it. Broad-brimmed hats with high crowns, faded bandanas knotted at the neck. Both wore short jackets, one light blue, the other a kind of faded green. One wore leather chaps. The other tucked his gray canvas trousers into nearly knee-high boots. They sat saddles with prominent pommels, a high horn, a latigo, and a cinch. One saddle skirt was heavily embossed, the other double stitched around its border. Spurs with large rowels protruded from the rear of the same hide-covered stirrups Baca called tapaderos.

Both had long guns tucked into saddle scabbards. Both wore handguns in slim, embossed holsters, one high on his right hip, the other on his left side, walnut grip facing forward.

Both riders were smiling.

The one on the right spoke first. "Howdy, strangers. Where y'all from?"

"Spanish Wells's the last place with a name we know of," Clairborne said.

At the mention of Spanish Wells, the two riders abruptly reined in.

"Y'all was in that shin-kicking a couple of weeks back?"

Clairborne suppressed his shock at the news of the battle arriving in wherever they were before they did.

Baca and Dornheim enthusiastically nodded. Herman smiled. Clairborne shook his head in dismay.

"Well damn, we gotta make some coffee and catch up," the shorter of the two said. He extended his hand to Baca, who was closest. "Ray Fagan's my handle, and this here butt-ugly dude's my partner, Tommy Harlan."

Handshakes and name exchanges as called for in high plains etiquette went around the circle until it came to Clairborne, sitting on the far side of his riding companions.

"Tucker Clairborne. Pleased to meet you gentlemen," he said, shaking hands after removing his right glove.

"Tucker Clairborne. Heard about you," the man called Ray Fagan said, his sun-burned face and hooded gray eyes regarding Clairborne with unblinking interest. Clairborne wanted to ask just how that could be but didn't. He sensed from Fagan's lingering look that Fagan also wanted to ask some questions and was relieved when he didn't.

In a conscious effort to change the subject, Clairborne slid his hand back into his sweaty glove and asked, "You boys wouldn't know how far it is to the Rocking C Ranch, would you?"

Fagan and Harlan looked at each other and laughed; then Harlan turned to Clairborne.

"Hell, mister," he said. "You been on the Rocking C for the last two days."

BOOK TWO

TEXAS

Weeks of sleeping on the ground made sleeping on even the crudest of beds a welcome luxury. Clairborne stretched out on the low cot, his weight sagging and stretching the woven rawhide strips connecting the sides, head, and foot of the rough wood frame. Resting his head in his hands and inspecting the beam-and-board ceiling, he listened to the bunkhouse banter and quickly and alarmingly asked himself how long it would be before what was now comfort and conviviality would mutate into boredom and irritation.

And he had only been at the Rocking C for five hours.

He argued with himself about the irrationality of thinking that a given circumstance, in this case life and work on a Texas cattle ranch, would be any less interesting and ultimately enjoyable than the journey west had been.

The other side of the mental debate was his growing certainty that he had made a mistake in verbally committing to the life of a cowboy and risking life and limb to immerse himself in a world the defining aspects of which, as far as he knew, were bone-breaking labor for dirt wages, social isolation, significant danger, and constant privation. He was also not encouraged by the conversation he had heard since arriving at the Rocking C.

It was very clear to Clairborne that his new colleagues were, for the most part, illiterate to the point of being antiliterate.

The first event he observed after arriving, unpacking, caring for his horses, and selecting a bed in the adobe bunkhouse shared by more than twenty others, was an exuberant kangaroo court in which a boisterous bunch of cowboys hooted while the "judge," a bearded, balding man called Knute, charged a diminutive and diffident cowboy named Dillon with the crime of "always using city words." While all in good humor and clearly intended as a break in ranch routine, the proceedings nonetheless impressed Clairborne as punishment of the hapless Dillon, who stood in the middle of a circle of his peers, rotating the brim of his hat in both hands while he smiled and answered his "interrogator." To no one's surprise, Knute found Dillon guilty and sentenced him "four whacks on the butt with a pair of chaps, to be done right now."

Clairborne wondered how he would react to the same "charge" and punishment and quickly decided that he needed to keep his mouth shut to avoid inadvertently irritating the characters with his vocabulary and grammar. He knew he would never, even in the spirit of cowboy shenanigans, submit to bending over a wagon tongue and being spanked. Never.

Caudill Senior and Junior and the Rocking C foreman were gone when Clairborne and his companions arrived with Fagan and Harlan. On the ride in, Clairborne learned that the Rocking C was hiring for the fall roundup and drive north. Hands were needed to accelerate the gathering of stray cattle missed in the spring roundup on the massive spread Fagan said totaled "more 'n five hundred thousand acres or so, as far as I can figure."

From Harlan, they learned the Rocking C was "a pretty good deal. We have a good gut-robber. He's a surly fellow but as good a cook as I know of."

The observation brought a nod from Fagan. "Fact is, old Stoney makes the best son of a bitch stew I ever et. I think it's the extra sweetbreads and brains he uses, but he gets real touchy when you ask him about his fixins, even if you're just trying to compliment his cooking. And you know what they say: 'Don't expect mules and cooks to share your sense of humor.'"

"Yep," Harlan said. "Stew's good, but I favor his vinegar pie. Mighty fine."

"Hellfire, Tommy," Fagan snorted. "You got such a sweet tooth you'd eat a dead skunk if it was sugar-coated."

After the discussion of the Rocking C's culinary attractions, Fagan and Harlan noted that Caudill was an absolute stickler on a number of rules, some of which were set down in writing, some of which were just known by everybody. And all of which resulted in termination if not followed.

"He's downright female about dirt," Harlan laughed. "You gotta use the privy, wash your hands, and keep the floor swept. Keeps the flies down, but it's a bother, always dancing with a broom."

Clairborne noted that the legs of every cot rested in a tin can holding an inch or two of kerosene to prevent bedbugs from climbing up the bedsteads from the floor. It also almost masked the smell of sweat and boots that had never met socks.

Dornheim observed, "It sounds like a fine place to work if Mr. Caudill is fair and pays on time."

"Oh he's fair for sure," Fagan noted. "And pay comes regular, but you better be ready to trod the straight and narrow and get with the Lord if you want to stay on Old Man Caudill's sunny side."

"What's that mean?" Clairborne asked. "When I met him in Saint Louis, he asked me about my religion, but he didn't push it."

Fagan and Harlan traded glances.

"Well," Fagan said. "You sign on, you'll have to sign the Rocking C code, which, if you can't read, he or his young'n will read for you." Fagan smiled. "It's pretty strict, and you bust any of the seven rules, you collect your wages and depart."

Harlan nodded. "And then there's the Bible-thumpers. Word's out the old man's a real Christian and wants everyone else to be. That means the Rockin' C draws preacher men and God-wallopers like moths to flame," Harlan said.

"Or flies to shit," Fagan said.

"You best be careful with that kind o' talk, Ray, or you'll be drawing your wages for sure," Harlan said, wagging his finger at his friend.

"The thing is, every Bible-thumper west of the Mississippi knows he can get three squares a day and a blanket on his bed at the Rockin' C. So be ready to get washed in the blood of the lamb real regular like. Y'all boys know any hymns?"

They all nodded.

"Well, that's mighty fine. Boss'll like that," Fagan said.

Fagan and Harlan hadn't exaggerated about the rules. As he carried his gear into the bunkhouse, Clairborne saw them nailed to the wall beside the doorframe. After stowing his things under his bed and on the spikes driven into the wall, he walked over and read the words that would define his behavior and activities for the foreseeable future.

1. No employee is permitted to carry in the residential areas, either on his person or saddlebags, any pistol, dirk, dagger, slingshot, brass knuckles, bowie knife, or any other such weapons.

2. Card playing and gambling of every description is strictly forbidden.

3. Employees are prohibited from imbibing any vinous, malted, fermented, spirituous, or otherwise intoxicating beverages during their time of service at the Rocking C Ranch.

4. Loafers, malcontents, deadbeats, tramps, shirkers, gamblers, or disreputable persons of any stripe will not be entertained at any time or place, nor will employees be permitted to give, loan, or sell such persons any grain or provisions of any kind, nor shall such persons be permitted to remain on Rocking C land under any pretext whatsoever.

5. Employees are not permitted to run mustang, antelope, or any kind of game on Rocking C horses.

6. Profanity and blasphemy of any kind will not be tolerated.

7. It is the intention of the proprietors to conduct all activities on the principle of right and justice to everyone and for it to be excelled by no other in good behavior, sterling honesty and integrity, and general high characteristics of its employees, who will be hired and duly recompensed based on their skills and attitude above any other considerations such as native language or conditions of birth. To that end, it is necessary that these rules be adhered to at all times and that violation of any one at any time is just cause for discharge.

"God help me," Clairborne thought after reading the rules. "I might as well have joined the army."

August 3, 1868
Rocking C Ranch, Texas

I cannot escape the feeling that I am incarcerated.
This despite the fact that I am a free, white, male American. I fully acknowledge that my unease is self-imposed and that I may draw my wages at any time and leave.

As much as I want to avoid what promises to be an extremely diffi-cult experience on the drive north—far more physically demanding than the ride here across the llano—I cannot.

I cannot, for doing so would simply perpetuate what I fear could become a lifelong habit of running away from challenges rather than facing them and either ultimately prevailing or being able to tell myself that I tried as hard as I could to succeed and failed after a noble if not heroic effort.

I have shared these thoughts with no one. Herman has found two colleagues, other Negroes who served in the Ninth Cavalry. I have been surprised by the fact that the Negro and Mexican hands sleep in the same bunkhouse with us and take their meals with us as well. That said, Herman and I have had very limited conversations since we arrived three days ago, and I have the feeling the friendship I felt on the trail will not develop further while at the Rocking C.

I understand there are about thirty to forty hands on the payroll. The bunkhouse has many empty cots because at least half of the men are out on the range at any given time.

The Caudills and the foreman are expected back from their visit to Breckinridge, the nearest town, any day now. Apparently, they make the trip twice a year to visit their bank and to discuss the cattle market. Breckinridge is a full five days' ride east.

What I've learned about Mr. Caudill since my arrival has elevated my admiration of him to almost a state of awe.

It seems this is his third attempt to get a going concern out here, the first two succumbing to deadly combinations of weather and Indians. Apparently, he came out here before the war, becoming one of the first, if not the very first, white man to set up so far west of everyone else. The say he had four boys and a girl back then.

Comanche and Kiowa took his cattle and killed his daughter and one son. Then the war broke out, and two of his boys went to serve with John Bell Hood. They didn't come back. He and his wife and Sam came back out here in '65, got burned out again, and that was when he lost his wife. Word is, that almost brought him low, but since he buried her here, he decided he was either going to prevail or die trying, and if the latter, at least he'd be buried next to his sweetheart.

I must say that the Rocking C is an impressive place and not just because of its almost unimaginable size. The structures are stone and adobe, all single story except the main house, which has a second floor and a kind of terrace on the roof. A separate one-story structure on the right is the ranch office and living quarters for the foreman. Our bunkhouse is a sprawling flagstone and adobe building perhaps 80 feet by 40 feet with a whitewashed interior, plank floors, and a kind of rudimentary fireplace at each end. It is connected to the kitchen and dining hall (called a chuck house) by a roofed breezeway called a "dogtrot" which, strangely enough, really is where the ranch's curs laze about. The large privies are far enough from the living area to keep the smell away so long as the prevailing westerly winds are steady, which they have been 24 hours a day since our arrival. The wells provide sweet water, and a quarter mile to the east is a stream they say flows ten months out of the year. The food is as good as or better than we were told to expect, and the cowboys keep the place surprisingly clean, in keeping with what Caudill demands of his employees. I must say that Caudill's rules contribute to my feelings of uncertainty about the Rocking C. It just seems to me that his demands are exceedingly harsh. In a place as isolated as this with life as hard as it is, I see no harm in letting men play cards or throw dice. Alcohol is another story, I agree. I am also surprised and a little puzzled by the ban on wearing firearms. I've already seen two rattlesnakes, nowhere near close enough to strike but close enough to give me the shivers.

The men seem resigned to most of the rules, although they do gamble at night with a guard posted at the door.

The fact that I keep a journal is of some interest to my new acquaintances, and while I do not worry about anyone stealing any of my possessions, we have no way of locking things up, which heightens my awareness of the need for circumspection in what I write. It is not unrealistic to believe that curiosity can be more compelling than greed, and I don't want to have to explain what I mean by any given entry.

I will say that so far, no one has asked about or made reference to my run-in with Charlie Guthrie. Nor has anyone expressed undue interest in my hardware even though nobody's firearms are as fine as mine. I have not practiced since arrival but will make an effort to do so at least once a week. We'll see what happens then.

—◈—

The Caudills and foreman Isaac Steiner arrived at a full gallop, in a cloud of dust, with whoops, hollering, and pistol shots into the cloudless sky.

Clairborne was currying his horses when another hand in the corral looked east under a sun-shielding hand and said, "Here comes the old man." Clairborne saw the dust cloud rising from the three riders and their five horses racing flat-out across the valley funneling into the Rocking C between the low hills to the north and south. Puffs of gun smoke rose above the riders seconds before the report of celebratory pistol shots carried to the ranch. He was surprised and mildly amused and pleased that Old Man Caudill evinced such exuberance.

By the time the three riders reined in in front of the main house, every man was present. Even the cook emerged from his domain wearing a frown, a stained apron, and an equally stained black derby.

Dismounting his lathered gray gelding, Caudill's smile expanded when he recognized Clairborne among those reaching out to shake his hand.

"My goodness, this day just keeps getting better," Caudill said, removing his sweat-darkened glove and taking Clairborne's hand. "I was beginning to think perhaps you had second thoughts about taking up the cattleman's life, Mr. Clairborne, especially after what I heard in Breckinridge. But I am heartily glad to see you, sir. Welcome to the Rocking C."

"Real glad to be here, sir," Clairborne said, wondering just what Caudill had heard.

Turning to his son and the tall man slapping dust from his pants with his hat, Caudill said, "You remember my son, and this is my foreman, my segundo, Isaac Steiner."

"Good to see you again, Mr. Caudill, and pleased to meet you, Mr. Steiner," Clairborne said.

"Oh heck, Tucker. Call me Sam. We're not strangers," Caudill Junior said with a smile accentuating the dust-filled creases radiating from the corners of his blue eyes.

Steiner took Clairborne's hand in a firm and lingering grip.

"Looking forward to talking with you, Mr. Clairborne," he said with what could have been a smile but could also have been either wariness or curiosity. Perhaps both.

Clairborne sensed that Steiner was a leader, that it was no fluke Caudill had anointed him "segundo," giving him authority to run the Rocking C's day-to-day operations. He thought of ancient European estates and the trusted stewards the lords and barons relied on to attend nettlesome details of management.

"Men," Caudill said, facing the crowd gathered around him, "y'all know that getting back from Breckinridge means tomorrow's payday. So everybody finish up your work today so's tomorrow after a prayer meeting, we can square the books and pay your wages. We'll have a special dinner tomorrow to give thanks for the Lord's bounty and take the day off."

Hats and sombreros sailed into the air along with a chorus of hoorahs and hallelujahs. As Caudill handed his reins to a wrangler named Pinch, he turned to Clairborne.

"Mr. Clairborne, my boy and I'd appreciate your company at dinner this evening. See you then."

"Delighted and honored, sir," Clairborne said.

Caudill walked to the house, and Clairborne resumed his currying. Across his horse's back, Steiner locked eyes with him, put his right hand to the brim of his hat, nodded ever so slightly, and walked off.

Clairborne watched him for a long moment.

"I wonder where this is going?" he asked himself.

———

A short, dark, bald man Caudill called Miguelito took Clairborne's coat and hat and then led him to the parlor on the left of the entry hall where the Caudills, Senior and Junior, and

Isaac Steiner awaited, each holding a cut glass filled with apple cider.

The house interior was impressive. The polished planks of the parlor floor featured an oriental carpet. A massive stone fireplace took up most of the eastern wall. Bookshelves filled with leather-bound, gold-embossed volumes of the classics alternated with mounted antelope, deer, and bison heads and gun racks.

A solitary sepia-toned, gilt-framed portrait of an unsmiling but attractive woman hung on a wall. Beneath it a small shelf held a bouquet of dried flowers. "Mrs. Caudill, I bet," Clairborne thought.

There was a large desk and chair in another room to the right of the entry hall. A wide, freestanding staircase provided access to the living areas on the second floor and functioned as a source of ventilation during the oven-like summer months.

The place smelled of wax and woodsmoke, gun oil, pomade, lemons, and leather. Clairborne didn't know exactly what he expected, but this was not it. Here were functional comfort and a level of refinement that was downright civilized.

He noted that the windows of the main house and every other structure on the Rocking C had heavy, hinged shutters with firing slits big enough to accommodate rifles and shotguns. That had caused Clairborne to study the layout of the buildings. Each was sited to give defensive fire to the next. Clearly, Caudill did not intend to lose the Rocking C again without a battle. And that also explained why Caudill kept so many hands on the payroll year-round. All the more to man those firing slits.

Nobody in the bunkhouse said anything about his invitation to dine in the main house, but Clairborne knew that he was permanently marked by the act—whether for good or bad remained to be seen. He didn't know which to expect, although he thought it likely to generate more curiosity than jealousy on the part of his bunkmates.

Caudill extended his hand as Clairborne entered. Behind Clairborne, a grandfather clock chimed the half hour and prompted Caudill to say, "Mr. Clairborne, I do appreciate punctuality. Welcome to my home."

Given a choice of cider or lemonade, Clairborne opted for the latter, taking his glass from Miguelito and raising it in response to Caudill's proffered toast. "Gentlemen, to good company and good food. May we enjoy both tonight."

His next words were directed at Clairborne as the four men took their seats in front of the cold fireplace.

"Well, Mr. Clairborne, it's the obligatory question, but I have to ask: What is your impression so far?"

Buying time to consider his response, Clairborne asked a question of his own. "Of my western experience to date, of Texas, or of the Rocking C in particular, sir?"

"Let's start with the Rocking C."

"Well, of course the size is pretty hard to fully comprehend. Your spread is fully six times larger than my family's holdings on the James. It also strikes me that the place is very efficiently managed. I've seen a lot of horses but hardly any cattle, and the food is better than I expected."

"Capital. Now about Texas?"

"Ah, let me think. You know, sir, it is so grand that it defies description. Even with weeks of travel, I've really seen so little of it. It is...it just impresses me as a kind of blank canvas, a very large blank canvas awaiting the work of the artists here and yet to come. And to continue that analogy, as you know, there are many different schools of art, so it will be interesting to see whose work ultimately prevails, whose brushstrokes and colors leave the enduring images."

Caudill smiled and reached over to shake Clairborne's hand.

"Mr. Clairborne, your words cause me to go straight to the reason I invited you here tonight, so let's get the hay on the ground where the goats can get to it. I thought perchance we would have this talk after dinner, but we shall discuss it now rather than later, if you don't mind."

While he didn't "mind," Clairborne was also aware of the futility of saying he did.

"Not at all, sir."

"Well then, here it is. Mr. Clairborne, when we met in Saint Louis, you were obviously not a cowboy, but not many men are when they first cross the Canadian. The question is: Now that you are here, do you spend time trying to become one, or is there another way you can contribute to the Rocking C?"

Clairborne couldn't imagine what that might be or where Caudill was headed. He nodded.

"In a short while, we will be starting the biggest cattle drive ever, more than ten thousand head, a remuda of couple of hundred horses, and more than fifty men, all headed north to Kansas."

"Yes, sir," Clairborne said. He sipped his lemonade, aware Caudill Junior and Steiner were watching him closely.

"I will not be going. Sam will head the drive, and Isaac is trail boss. The operation is big enough these days that someone needs to be here year-round, and much as I hate to say it, I'm not getting any younger. So I'm staying here, as I said.

"My point is, Sam and Isaac need someone to back them up, a 'third-in-command,' if you will, and we think you might fill the bill."

Clairborne was startled. He immediately thought of how little he knew of either cattle or the terrain, and just as immediately wondered what the Rocking C hands, most of whom were seasoned cowhands, would think of such a development.

"I...I...well, I'm honored, Mr. Caudill. I certainly didn't expect such a turn of events, but, ah, may I speak in candor?"

"There's no other acceptable way to speak."

"Well, then. I know little if anything about cattle. I know nothing about the route, and I suspect the men might be a little, ah, a little, shall we say, envious of my sudden promotion."

"Well, Mr. Clairborne, let me ask you a question in the spirit of candor before we go any further. Do you think you are up to the job?"

Clairborne didn't hesitate. "Yes, sir."

"Good. Now let's address your concerns. First, you'll be surrounded by men who know cattle, horses, and the land between here and the railhead. Second, you aren't stupid, and I expect you'll pick up on things big and small pretty quick-like. Third..."

Caudill looked up as Miguelito appeared at the threshold

separating the parlor from the dining room and said, "Dinner?" With a nod in the affirmative, Caudill rose. "Let us continue this discussion over dinner," he said.

The dining room was set in crystal, silver, and china, all arrayed on a starched, white, embroidered tablecloth. Savory steam rose from the servers lined up on a carved walnut sideboard.

Clairborne sat and after respectful silence during Caudill's benediction was surprised when asked by Sam Caudill to "share your blessing with us, why don't you?"

"God make us truly thankful for these and all thy blessings. We ask in Jesus's name. Amen," Clairborne recited from memory of countless meals at Warwick.

He was not sure how such succinctness would be perceived in the Rocking C dining room, but it was his family's blessing, so there was no alternative.

"Fine words, sir," Caudill Senior said, adding with a small smile, "and in keeping with your predilection for brevity in all things theological..."

Passing a warmer full of steaming, puffy brown biscuits the size of pancakes, Caudill said, "Now where where we? Oh yes. The matter of just how the men would perceive your position. Sam, butter please." As Caudill applied a generous slab of sweet butter to the biscuit half, Clairborne looked at the two other diners. Sam smiled when their eyes met. Steiner's hooded hazel eyes conveyed the impression of a smile, although the corners of his mouth were not upturned.

"We continue in the spirit of candor, do we not?"

"Indeed, sir," Clairborne said.

"You have earned a reputation, Mr. Clairborne—a reputation which, had I not already made your acquaintance, would have led me to avoid you altogether. But taking you in the whole has led us," he gestured at his son and foreman with a buttered biscuit, "has led us to believe that you have the spirit and the judgment to do this job which, quite honestly, most with your little time on the plains would not yet enjoy."

Caudill looked at his son. "Sam, tell Mr. Clairborne what we heard about him."

"Daddy, I think Isaac should tell him since he knows Beekman so well," Sam said, nodding at the heretofore-silent foreman sitting across from Clairborne.

"Good point. Isaac?" said the older Caudill.

"Well, the thing is," Steiner said, "Silas and I know each other well. Been through some scrapes and ruckuses together. We ran into him and his partner in Breckinridge. He told us about Spanish Wells, told us about the fight with the Comanch, and he told us about you and that fellow Guthrie. I guess the main point is he spoke highly of you. Said making you a cowboy'd be like hitching a racehorse to a plow or something to that effect. Word's pretty much out about Spanish Wells, pretty much out about you. I...we don't think you'll have too much trouble with any of the hands so long as you learn some rudimentary things before we leave, and you've got time." Steiner shrugged.

"Rudimentary things?" Clairborne said.

"Yes. Such as throwing a hoolihan and treating cows for blowflies. Recognizing a running brand from a first mark and how to manage a calf wagon, things such as that. Plus some others," Steiner said. "The main thing is judgment, good judgment.

Doing the right thing when it needs to be done. The other stuff, you can learn as you go."

"That's what I came here for," Clairborne said. "I assume, or, actually, I hope I'll remain in the bunkhouse until the drive."

Caudill Senior nodded. "You will, but why do you mention it?"

"Seems like it might give me time to get to know the hands better and vice versa."

"Mr. Clairborne, that's just why we think you are a dandy choice. Now would you please pass me the soup?"

The soup was accompanied by more biscuits with various preserves and marmalades and followed by sweet potatoes, mustard and collard greens, pickled peppers, venison, a ham hock, and roast of beef followed by still-warm chess pie and coffee. Clairborne belched on his way back to his bunk.

—◦◦◦—

Because it was payday, the breakfast bell didn't reverberate around the Rocking C until seven o'clock. In the bunkhouse, clean shirts came out of saddlebags. Straight razors and hairbrushes were passed around even though it was neither Sunday nor the Fourth of July. The formal day began with a prayer service in front of the main house, after which everyone but the four newcomers formed lines in front of two tables manned by the Caudills and Steiner. Hands with names starting with A through L lined up in front of the Caudills, and M through Z (a large German named Zimmerman) stood in front of Steiner.

Clairborne noted the infectious good humor, the joshing, and the horseplay of the Rocking C hands both before and after they collected their wages. Each man removed his hat as his money was counted, and nobody recounted his money after he got it. Most got about $180 for their six months of work as hands, top hands, or wranglers, but each man saw his net income reduced by an average of fifteen to twenty-five dollars depending on advances or fines for infractions occurring in the last half year. From bunkhouse banter, Clairborne knew that within a week or so, many of the ranch hands would be broke or close to it after emerging on the losing side of illicit games of chance conducted by the light of coal-oil lanterns or campfires. Some would stash their money away in private hide sites, and some even asked the old man to return all or most of their money to the ranch strongbox for safekeeping.

Since the nearest store or saloon or bawdy house was hundreds of miles distant, there weren't many other opportunities for the cowboys to squander their wages, paid in coin at the rate of a dollar a day.

That night, Clairborne wondered where his duties should take him.

Did the job and title Caudill had quietly bestowed on him mean that he should break up the card games and dice throwing? Should he report these activities? Should he ignore them? He chose an expedient alternative. Picking up his bedroll, Clairborne went outside and climbed the ladder to the bunkhouse roof to join the other refugees from the heat, body odor, and illicit activities that filled the interior. Lying on his back, he was again dumbfounded by the profusion of heavenly bodies strewn across the skies. A light breeze facilitated his descent into the deepest of sleep.

Two days later, after washing, shaving, and eating breakfast, Clairborne emerged from the Spartan dining hall and stood under the porch admiring the sunrise with a small group of other hands when Steiner walked up.

"Mornin' gents," Steiner said. "Harlan, how 'bout you and Clairborne riding over to Salt Creek and driving whatever you find there back to the canyon. We haven't been up there the last couple of months, so there's likely enough roamers to be worth the ride."

"OK, boss," Harlan said. Turning to Clairborne, he asked, "You ready to see some real pretty country?"

"Sure," said Clairborne.

They walked to a large corral holding nearly twenty horses that had been moved just before dawn from the other side of a small hill by two of the Rocking C's wranglers. Harlan easily threw his lariat around the neck of a line-back dun and then tied the horse on a short lead to the rail before walking to the tack room to retrieve his saddle, saddle blanket, and bridle. Clairborne looked for Bucephalus, but not seeing him in the corral, he threw a loop over the neck of a pretty bay mare that followed him to the rail without resistance.

"I surely love this part of the job," Harlan said as he hung his bridle from the saddle horn and then hefted his worn but well-maintained saddle from the protruding beam that held it. "Yessiree bob. Ain't nothin' like riding out in the morning cool, belly full o' eggs and bacon."

"We going to have some time on the way to do some shooting, some practice?" Clairborne asked.

Harlan looked over his shoulder at the newcomer and smiled. "Why, sure. Give me a chance to see you handle that fine smoke wagon of yours."

"How about you?" Clairborne asked. "Don't you want to get a little practice in?"

"No. Not today. Mayhap we just got paid, but I ain't so flush as I can go poppin' caps for the fun of it. Now, I hope you don't mind me tellin' you, but bein' as how you're new to all this, you gotta get one of them saddles over there," Harlan said with a nod toward a collection hanging on a side wall. "Them there saddles is spares, and that there eastern saddle you rode in on ain't gonna cut the mustard for cowboy'n. And while you're at it, get one of them lariats hanging on the rail yonder. Might as well start learning how to throw a hoolihan while you're at it."

Clairborne followed Harlan's advice with gusto. It was as easy an introduction into the arcane arts of cowboying as he could hope for.

"That mare you picked's a little sweetie pie, so you could prob'ly get by with just a old hackamore, but take this here split-ear bridle and that bit. You won't need more for her."

"Hey thanks, Tommy," Clairborne said. "I appreciate your breaking me in gentle-like."

"Oh heck. Ain't nothin. When I come out here, I didn't know pommel from cantle and had to learn everything the hard way. Don't make sense if you don't have to, I reckon."

"Well, thanks just the same."

They saddled their horses, led them back to the bunkhouse, and tied each to the hitching rail in front of the porch, which featured five washstands, three benches, and one rocking chair.

"May want to bring a extra canteen if'n you got one, and some jerky too," Harlan said as they entered the room to retrieve their firearms and canteens.

"Wouldn't hurt to bring my spyglass, I guess," Clairborne said.

"Heck no. At'll make it a dang sight easier to spot them critters for sure."

They returned to their mounts, shoved their rifles into the scabbards, threw saddlebags over the horse's rumps, and tied them down.

Clairborne inserted his left foot into the stirrup and lifted himself into the Texas saddle, instantly noting its comfort and utility.

Out of the corner of his eye, he saw Harlan walk around his horse, patting its rump as he passed.

Sudden movement, a sound like a watermelon dropped on a floor and a barely audible snap, pulled Clairborne's head around to behold Harlan lying on his back, dust still rising from where he had fallen. Harlan's boyishly handsome face had disappeared in a torrent of blood still spurting from his inert form. The lineback dun snorted and stamped its left rear hoof.

Clairborne leaped from his saddle and screamed.

"Help, help, goddam it! Help!"

He knelt beside the blood-covered cowboy and recoiled. Harlan's fine, symmetric features were replaced by a scarlet mass of fluid and bone and tooth. Where his mouth and nose and left cheek had been there was a deep, curved imprint, the unmistakable mark of a hoof driven inches deep into Tommy Harlan's head, snapping it backward with such force it audibly cracked two of his seven cervical vertebrae.

Tommy Harlan was dead before he hit the ground.

—◌◌◌—

The room smelled of dust and pine resin. The dust was omnipresent. The sharp, clean, sweet resin came from Tommy Harlan's coffin fashioned of boards sawed hours earlier from the store of lumber behind the large, orderly Rocking C tool shed.

The coffin, unpainted and rough to the touch, rested on two planks supported by four sawhorses. A coal-oil lantern cast a flickering yellow light supplementing the orange glow of the west Texas dusk.

Tommy Harlan was wrapped in a white muslin shroud after callous-handed cowboys working in silence washed away all traces of the effects of a relaxed sphincter and bladder.

It turned out that Tommy Harlan only had one shirt. Ray Fagan had offered one of his, but Clairborne pulled a tailored chemise from his valise beneath his cot and slipped it on the dead cowboy with help from Fagan and two others. Clairborne could not bring himself to look at what was left of Tommy Harlan's face. The silence of the storeroom-cum-chapel added to the dreamlike state in which what his hands touched was not acknowledged by his thoughts.

The words "This didn't happen" repeated continuously in his mind, even as his palms cupped Tommy Harlan's head so the French cambric shirt could be slid over Harlan's slim torso.

"What was the last thing he said to me?" Clairborne felt panic rising, fear that he could not, would not recall what it was even as he knew it was the smallest of small talk, idle banter that would be inconsequential, utterly forgettable had it not been the last sound Tommy Harlan uttered.

"He'd said, 'heck no.' He didn't say 'hell no.' He said 'heck no,'" Clairborne suddenly remembered. "We were talking about my spy glass and Tommy was glad I had one. 'At'll make it a dang sight easier to spot them critters, for sure,' he said, and he kind of laughed."

And then he was dead. Broken neck. No howl of pain or cry of regret. Just dead.

"Well, I guess that about does it," said Fagan. "As fast as death descends out here, this was sudden for sure." Fagan stood beside Clairborne, his eyes fixed on the shrouded corpse, the mangled shell of his best friend.

"I'll go tell Mr. Caudill he's ready for the service if y'all think he is," said one of the other cowboys.

"Sure, Buck. Go on ahead," said Fagan.

Clairborne stood at the side of the coffin, staring across it at the greasy, yellow flame in the lantern.

Within minutes, the cowboy named Buck returned and said, "Mr. Caudill says we're gonna have the service at sunup. Says he wants to give the boys digging Tommy's grave enough time to dig it good 'n deep."

Fagan nodded. "That's good," he said and, picking up his hat, moved to the foot of the coffin. He slowly rotated his hat in both hands in silence. Then he reached out and patted Tommy Harlan's shroud-wrapped bare feet and said, "Well, buckaroo, I surely am sorry, and I'll bet that ole hoss's sorry he kicked you too. Oh, shucks, Tommy. You were a good man to ride with. Adios, compadre." He patted the feet tenderly one more time before turning away and putting on his hat.

The cowboy named Buck walked out moments later, leaving Clairborne alone with Tommy Harlan.

Clairborne stood by the coffin for hours. He lost track of time along with his thoughts. The lantern wick guttered out, replacing its weak light with strong smoke.

Clairborne sensed someone else in the room but didn't move or try to determine who it was.

It was Old Man Caudill.

"You all right, son?" Caudill eventually asked in a soft tone barely above a whisper.

"Yes, sir. I'm OK. I just...I just...." He couldn't figure out what words he needed to say because he didn't know what he wanted to say. So he didn't say anything.

"It's good of you to keep the vigil," Caudill said.

"I can't figure out why I have to. I hardly knew him, but I can't leave him alone. Wouldn't be right."

"Reckon it wouldn't at that, son. We'll hold prayer service at sunup. I'll see you then."

"Yes, sir."

Caudill placed his hand on Clairborne's shoulder.

"I noticed you didn't have one of these, and Tommy's is a good one, so here," he said, handing Clairborne Harlan's well-worn but austerely beautiful quirt. Every single cowboy carried a quirt looped around the wrist, and Clairborne had wondered how he could get one. Riding around without a quirt was as odd as riding around without a hat.

"Thank you, sir."

Caudill patted his shoulder and left, the rough planks creaking under his steps.

A while later, Clairborne needed to look at the stars. He needed to see if Tommy was winking at him from somewhere. He desperately needed Tommy to wink at him just once.

Stepping outside, he saw it was not to be. The crystal dry west Texas August air was gone, replaced by a sullen, solid overcast no starlight could penetrate. Instead, a fat yellow moon weakly glimmered through the cloud bank, tatters of which drifted across its face. In place of the signal he sought from the crisp blink of a signal star, Clairborne felt himself mocked by the faded glow of a lantern he believed was held aloft by a lost soul trying to find its way in the gloom.

"I wish you'd give me a sign you're not mad at me, Tommy. I wish you'd let me know you're OK," he said.

He went back inside. He picked up the bucket and the sponges used to wash Tommy Harlan and carried them outside. He went back, turned an empty toolbox on end, and sat down, resting his elbows on his knees, knitting his fingers together in front of his face.

Death. Death, death, and more death. He didn't challenge God to explain Tommy Harlan's demise, to provide some flash of insight, some eventual revelation into what it all meant, why Tommy Harlan had to get kicked to death as part of the Lord's plan.

"This is the kind of thing, this test he gives us," Clairborne said aloud. "He wants to see if I'll quit him because I don't understand. I guess I won't, but I truly don't understand." Raising his head to the coffin, he repeated aloud, "I surely don't."

August 6th, 1868
Rocking C Ranch, Texas

We buried Thomas Alvin Harlan this morning. We put him six feet down in the rocky soil in the Rocking C graveyard not too far from where Mrs. Caudill rests under a granite tombstone Mr. Caudill had shipped in all the way from San Antonio. I looked at it after everyone left Tommy's graveside.

It says, "True to the Memory of My Beloved Wife Anne. Born March 19, 1818. Died November 3, 1858. The Lord Needed Another Angel, So I Gave Him Mine."

There won't be any tombstone for Tommy. Instead, he got a pine plank carved with the words:
Here Lies Thomas Harlan
a good friend, kicked by a horse.

What will my stone say? What would I want it to say? Not that it really matters to me since I won't be around to read it. No, that's not right. It does matter what folks think of you after you are gone. I want folks to think I was a good man. Maybe if I have children, I will be remembered as a good father, a good husband. That would be enough.

A Negro friend of Herman's everyone calls Bone played hymns on his harmonica at the grave before we lowered Tommy down. He played "When the Roll Is Called Up Yonder" and "Rock of Ages." We sang along. Earlier, Mr. Caudill said some words over Tommy. He said Tommy was a good Christian and a good man. He said Tommy is with the Lord and that we should accept what happened as the Lord's will no matter how rough it seems. I'm trying, but it surely is hard, especially when it seems there are so many others who need taking much more than Tommy Harlan.

After he finished saying words over Tommy, Mr. Caudill asked the assembled if anyone had words of their own to share. Without thinking, I stepped forward and said:

"Golden lads and girls all must, as chimney sweepers, come to dust."

Then I stepped back and realized everyone was looking at me. It was awkward. I thought perhaps I had not said enough, or perhaps these roughhewn sons of the soil didn't comprehend the sweet simplicity of Shakespeare's musing on death. Afterward, Mr. Caudill came up to me and said he thought my words "were mighty fine" and said, "I know they must be from the Bard, but I can't recollect just where." When I told him the quote was from Cymbeline, he nodded and said, "Oh, that explains it. That's some territory I haven't yet explored."

It seems, like most of the men around here, Tommy didn't talk all that much about family, other than to say he had a sister somewhere in Kentucky. Mr. Caudill is trying to find her so he can send Tommy's wages. We also had a kind of auction for what few things of worth Tommy possessed. I bought his saddle and bridle and his lariat and probably paid more than I should, but with the money going to his kin and me needing a roping saddle, it seemed like the right thing and the least I could do.

I can't get Tommy Harlan off my mind.

"Clairborne, Mr. Caudill'd like to see you. In his office," Steiner said early in the morning of the third day after Harlan's death.

Caudill rose from his desk chair as Clairborne entered.

"Coffee?"

"Yes, sir. Thank you."

Caudill was silent as he poured from the blue enamel pot and then said, "You take your coffee black, as I recall."

"I do, sir."

Handing the cup to Clairborne, Caudill sat down and looked at the Virginian for a while as if he were trying to identify the most appropriate words.

"I'm concerned about you."

Clairborne was surprised. "Me, sir? Why is that?"

"You seem to be taking Harlan's passing particularly hard." Before Clairborne could reply, Caudill continued. "It's not just that you seem so affected. It also concerns me that the men...well, the men might not understand. I'll be blunt, Mr.

Clairborne. They might see you as soft, as weak, and I can't have anyone in authority be seen in such a manner by the hands. It just won't do."

Clairborne found himself in a peculiar position. He agreed with Caudill's logic even though it insulted him.

"I understand," was all he said.

"Mr. Clairborne, I believe the Lord is trying to tell you something, and it seems to me that your heart might not be open to him."

"Sir?"

"The meaning of Harlan's death, so sudden and all, and right in front of you. What did the Lord mean by it? Don't you see how clear it is?"

"Uh-oh," Clairborne thought. "I sure hope this doesn't mean Caudill's going to make me his personal mission, because that'll surely sour me faster than anything else I can think of...."

"Well, Mr. Caudill, I certainly have given it a lot of thought. I wish I could tell you I was as clear about things as you are, but I'd be lying if I did."

"Son, the Lord is trying to show you how quickly he can call you home, and if you are not ready when he calls, you'll face eternal damnation as a result of choice, your choice. So I want you to think real hard about what it means to be saved. I know you've been confirmed and all, but giving your soul to the Lord as a man, an adult, is different."

"Mr. Caudill, can I ask you a question, a personal question that's got kind of an edge to it?"

"Fire away."

"Are you as interested in saving the souls of all your hands, or is it more important to you that I be saved?"

"Why do you ask?"

"Well, sir. It seems to me kind of puzzling that my soul means so much to you, and I was thinking that maybe what you'd really like is for me to be saved and set an example for the others. That maybe getting me saved is kind of more economical, in terms of energy and effort, than working on everyone else at once."

As he spoke, Clairborne hoped he would see a smile, a half grin stretch Caudill's lips in response. His hopes weren't answered.

Caudill studied his cup as he swirled the grounds. He put the cup down on his desk and rose, as did Clairborne in response.

"Mr. Clairborne, the single most important job for a Christian is that of helping others accept God's plan. I believe you have promise, promise that can only be fully attained through your acceptance of Christ, his sacrifice, without which you cannot know the Maker." Shifting his weight and turning away, Caudill said, "Thank you for your time, Mr. Clairborne," his tone conveying disappointment if not anger.

Clairborne picked up his hat and said, "Mr. Caudill, there is something, a business subject I'd like to discuss when you have time."

"And that would be?"

"Well, sir. It occurred to me that we don't know where to send Tommy's wages other than somewhere in Kentucky. It seems to me it wouldn't be much trouble to ask a man when he signs on where he wants his wages sent, his possessions, if something happens. Seems that would make things easier for you, and honestly, it might make a new hand feel even better about coming to work on the Rocking C."

Caudill smiled and shook his head.

"Well, dang me if you ain't something, Mr. Clairborne. Here I was about to demote you to hand and you come up with something as simple—and obvious—as that. I'll tell you what. You take that paper yonder and get that information from every hand, and from now on, we'll make it a part of the hiring. Good thinking."

As Clairborne reached the room's threshold, Caudill said, "But I still want you to think about the Lord's message, young man."

Clairborne nodded as he put on his hat. "Yes, sir. I'll do that."

—⁓—

The next morning, Steiner walked up to Clairborne and asked, "You met Antonio Jimenez yet?"

Clairborne had to think. Collecting the names and addresses of kin from each of the hands meant that he'd met a lot of the hands in the last day, about a third of them Mexicans. After a few moments, he recalled Antonio: a small, wiry man with patched clothes, a large mustache, and deep creases from the corners of his dark-brown eyes.

"I want you and Antonio to get on up to Salt Creek where you and Tommy were headed," Steiner said. "The advantage for you is Antonio is the best damn roper I've ever seen, and he's real patient, so you got yourself the best teacher you could get when it comes to slingin' a riata."

346

"Where'll I find him?" Clairborne asked, excited about the prospect of seeing new country and learning a new and very necessary skill.

"He's at the main corral saddlin' up and waiting for you. I told him I want you two to check up on Mr. Swan on your way."

"Mr. Swan?"

"Mr. Praxiteles Swan. Lost a leg at Gettysburg. Wife died while he was gone. Lives alone now...well, with his goats and such. We think highly of him, and Mr. Caudill wants to know he's all right."

"Sure thing."

Clairborne had never unpacked his gear after Harlan's death, so it took him no time at all to collect what he needed. But by the time he got to the corral, he didn't see Jimenez, so Clairborne went about cutting a horse from the nine in the corral. His first throw of the lariat missed, and he looked around to see if anyone had seen his embarrassing mistake.

There, outside the corral, sitting a stout little pinto, was Antonio Jimenez, arms resting on his saddle horn, small face shaded by his large black sombrero, its felt brim softened by sun and wind. Clairborne noticed that the Mexican held the lead to three horses, one carrying a pack and two others Clairborne immediately understood constituted a small "remuda," spare horses to be used in shifts during the hard work to come.

Clairborne's second attempt was successful and saddling up fast and uneventful. He mounted and selected two more mounts, both geldings, for his spares. He rode to the corral gate, which Jimenez opened for him. He extended his hand.

"Antonio, I'm Tucker. I hear you're a heck of a roper, and as you saw, I'm not. Hope you don't mind if I ask a lot of questions next couple of days."

"Señor Tucker, you would be a great fool not to."

They laughed, turned their mounts, and spurred away from the corral and toward the place called Salt Creek.

—⁓—

Salt Creek was neither.

There was no salt, and the creek bed was drier than buffalo bones.

There was a ravine, a "waddy," with a gash down its bottom made by flash floods in the spring and fall, but this time of year it contained only pebbles, dust, and some stunted mesquite bushes. Two miles west and below the waddy, a green spot marked a spring, called a "seep" by the locals.

And there were the cattle, some of the strangest-looking bovines imaginable. They had enormous horns averaging five feet from tip to lethal tip. They eyed the approaching riders with deep suspicion that no good could come from their arrival. But they didn't flee, at least not most of them. The bulls simply stood their ground, slowly chewing pithy vegetation, lazily observing the horsemen with large, liquid brown eyes shielded by enormous lashes. Outlines of ribs and hipbones protruded from hides drawn taught by life on the llano. Scrawny and scarred, the cattle held little promise of tender, juicy steaks and roasted beef.

"You got to be careful around them," Antonio said with a nod toward a knot of piebald cows watching them from a quarter mile away. "Even the cows can surprise you. Don't ride at them. You just come to the side of them, slowly. Maybe even talkin' or singin'. It's best if you don't have to even use a rope.

"If you want them to go east, you got to get on the west of them and then get them moving. You have to use the lariat on a lot of the bulls, and they'll attack any time they feel like it."

"And when they do?" Clairborne asked as he watched a bull with at least six feet between the tips of horns thicker than his biceps.

Antonio laughed. "Hombre, you get out of the way. They'll gut a horse so fast you don't know what happened, and when they finish with the horse, they come after you."

"You shoot them then?"

"Sure. You want to pay Senor Caudill, you shoot them."

"How do you know they're all his? I thought a lot of the cattle out here were still wild."

"For sure they are, but Senor Caudill says if his hands round them up and they ain't branded, they're his."

"And if they've got somebody else's brand?"

"That all gets sorted out at roundup. Oh, also, we are no taking bulls. Just cows and calves. The bulls are too hard to drive, so we just leave them for same reason we don't got stallions in the remuda. Too much trouble," Antonio said over his shoulder.

Clairborne felt a pang of anxiety at the thought of leaving Bucephalus, his beautiful black stallion, behind in Texas for the duration of the drive to Kansas.

Ah well.

Clairborne paid close attention to the cows. Slightly more docile than the bulls, they allowed themselves to be moved to a box canyon with two seeps and decent grass by local standards, enough at least to feed the gathering herd for three or four days.

It was the hardest work Clairborne had ever done. By the end of the first day, he understood why Antonio and many of the other hands wore leather chaps and covered their stirrups with leather tapaderos. The mesquite, prickly pear, scrub oak, and heaven only knows what other barbed, spiked, thorned plants snagged and tore his trousers above the top of his boots, boots made of supple, too-thin leather, fine for riding to the hounds in Virginia but unable to stand up to west Texas vegetation.

After a dinner of beans, slices of dried apple, jerky, and two cups of coffee, Clairborne sat in the failing light and considered the three ragged tears in his pant legs and the nasty cut beneath the longest of them.

"Do you got more pantalones?" Antonio asked.

"Nope. Not here."

"You got a housewife, no?"

"A housewife? Oh, you mean a sewing kit?"

"For sure."

"Yeah, I got one, but I'm not real sure how to use it."

"Better learn. I show you one time."

Clairborne recovered his tin sewing kit from the bottom of his saddlebag and handed it to Antonio.

"This thread OK for shirt but no good for pants or jacket."

"All I got."

"OK. Now watch."

With calloused but surprisingly deft fingers, Antonio quickly threaded the needle and made a knot in one end of the string. He held the tear together with one hand and pulled the needle and thread over and under the edges, finished with another knot, and bit off excess thread.

"There you go. No hard."

Clairborne was determined to sew his own pants correctly on the first try. He did so and was mildly disappointed with the absence of praise he expected.

"You better wash that cut. Seen men die from smaller ones than that. Blood poisoning," was all Antonio said before rolling over and quickly snoring.

They had agreed that Clairborne would take the first watch and at one a.m. would wake Antonio and try to get maybe four hours of sleep. Maybe.

He saddled one of the geldings and rode it to the top of a small mound less than twenty yards from the so-far-cooperative cattle. Lacking any direction or guidance on what to do for the next five hours or on how to keep the herd together and in place, he decided he would simply sit and watch and keep his movement to a minimum. Some movement was desirable to stay awake and to keep the cattle from forgetting he was there and spooking when he did move.

A few hours later, Clairborne surveyed the countryside and marveled at how much detail was discernible by the light of a quarter moon. Ambient light from the Milky Way, light seeming to radiate from the white rocks and tan dirt, provided stark contrasts with cattle and cacti.

As fatigue finally exceeded enthusiasm, Clairborne realized he didn't know what time it was, or more correctly, how to tell what time it was. His expensive heirloom was in his kit under his cot in the distant bunkhouse. He didn't want to wake Antonio too early, understanding that doing so would constitute a gross breach of cowboy etiquette.

Alternative? Err on the generous side.

He splashed water on his face from his canteen. He sang. He dismounted and examined rocks. Distant howling shot adrenaline through his system, alertness edged with fear. An hour later, his eyelids seemed heavier than his horse.

He scratched his head. He pushed down on the pommel and raised his butt off the saddle seat. He watched an owl silently swoop down on some rodent or serpent.

Then he noticed a gray edge to the horizon.

"It's got to be dawn," he thought.

Antonio rolled over before Clairborne shook him.

"Hombre, it's morning. You let me sleep the whole night."

Clairborne explained.

"Today going to be hard," Antonio said with a lopsided grin. "Tonight, I start showing you how to read the stars. You sleep first tonight, OK?"

"Sure," Clairborne said. "If I can stay awake until then. Sure." The prospect of fourteen hours like yesterday made him fairly certain there was little possibility of that.

Later, when he looked back on the Salt Creek days with Antonio, Clairborne would recall that he gained more practical knowledge in less than a week than at any other so short a time in his life.

Antonio was nothing if not patient. He taught by example, by demonstration instead of lecture.

As they headed out on the second morning, Antonio shook a loop out of his lariat, and Clairborne did the same. When it came to throwing a lariat, Clairborne learned there were more options than he could have imagined, and Antonio had mastered all of them.

Most of the cattle didn't require much rope work. They moved in the desired direction in response to the mounted rider's maneuvers, cowboy and horse moving in unison to block any bovine deviation.

When he did use a rope, Antonio seemed to throw instinctively, his accuracy and timing always perfect. Clairborne watched in amazement and knew the exhibition of roping skill was the product of a lifetime of work and that the odds against his ever attaining such skill were virtually incalculable.

"You see what I do with my riata every time?" Antonio asked in a midmorning break.

"Aside from getting what you aimed at, you mean?"

Antonio laughed. "No. As soon as the riata goes where I want, I have to do what my people call '*dar una vuelta*' but you gringos call 'take a dolly.' That means take a hitch around the horn to snub the rope. You got to do it every time, or the cow will pull you off your saddle—after the rope burns your hands real bad."

"Yeah, I noticed that."

"Keep the other end in your left hand so you can slip it if you have to. Another thing. Make sure you keep your fingers clear, or you'll lose one or two for sure."

Clairborne had had no trouble staying awake so far, but the thought of losing a finger or two in a roping accident sharpened the edge of his alertness.

His first three tries to place a lariat loop over a cow's head were unsuccessful, and his pony, a veteran of years on the llano, swung its head around to fix Clairborne with a disapproving look. It reminded him of his hunting dogs and the look of disdain they gave when, after their work to find and flush the fowl, he or his brother missed the shot. When the fourth attempt slipped over the horns and down to the neck, and he also took a quick turn of the rope around his saddle horn, Clairborne felt a surge of pride as strong and deep as he had ever known.

Antonio nodded, said "Good," and rode off to drive more strays out of the brush.

Before leaving camp that morning, Clairborne decided to make dinner that night.

He poured four handfuls of dry pinto beans into a cast-iron pot of water, where they would soak for the day, softening to something chewable from the small pebbles they were when dry. That evening, he suspended the bean pot over a low mesquite fire and carved fat slices of bacon, which he dropped into a cast-iron skillet along with a handful of dried peppers. He opened a can of peaches and, on a whim, dumped some of the syrup into the beans. He made coffee. He wished he knew how to make biscuits and decided he would learn as a matter of priority.

Antonio watched from the comfort of his thick woolen poncho, which cushioned his body from roots and rocks during the night and insulated him from the cold dirt.

The beans took the longest. When the bacon was finished, Clairborne stirred some of the grease into the beans and set the skillet at the edge of the coals to keep the fat slices warm.

He poured two cups of coffee, noting with satisfaction the viscous black brew was indeed cowboy coffee. "Drop a horseshoe in it, and if'n it sinks, coffee ain't strong enough."

He dished out the beans and bacon and peach slices and took a seat on his saddle blanket. Antonio bowed his head, said a silent grace, and crossed himself before partaking of Clairborne's first cow-camp dinner. Clairborne burned his mouth on the first spoonful of beans and then burned it some more with his first sip of coffee.

Although he knew it could be considered a breach of etiquette, Clairborne wanted to satisfy his curiosity about the virtuoso of the lariat on the other side of the campfire.

"How long you been on the Rocking C?"

"Four years."

"You must'a been one of the first hands, then. He only started building it up about five or six years ago, no?"

"Yes."

"You born around here?"

"No. Across the Rio Bravo. Old Mexico."

"Just decided to see some new country?"

"What?"

"Some new country. Ride north to see what you could see." Antonio grunted. "No."

"OK," Clairborne thought. "This isn't working, and if I keep trying to pull things out of him to get a conversation going, he's liable to take offense."

They didn't talk during the rest of the meal, nor did either speak while they cleaned the utensils.

Clairborne added some more mesquite branches to the fire and lay back down with his second cup of coffee.

Antonio stood sipping his brew and watched the herd in the draw below their camp.

Without turning to face Clairborne, he said, "They say you killed a man."

Clairborne didn't know whether it was a statement or a question.

"I did."

"Me too," Antonio said, throwing the dregs of his coffee into the dirt and turning to face Clairborne.

"The oldest son of my patron. He dishonored my woman. There was no other way, but now I can never go back. Never."

"Couldn't you go elsewhere in Mexico?"

"It's not the same as here. In my country, a vaquero, well, he spends his whole life on a single rancho, his family before and his family after. You don't get paid much money. Instead you get a place for your family to live and grow some maize, some peppers, beans, and such. It's not like here, where cowboys come and go as they please."

"What about your family? I mean what happened to them after, ah, after..."

"It was just my mother. Everyone else, even my younger sisters...one ran away. One died. The patron knows his son." Antonio shrugged. "He would have killed me if he caught me, but he knows his son, and he don't punish my mother because I did something I had to do."

Clairborne considered this new information and then said, "Don't know what you heard, but I also had to do what I did. Man I killed was about to shoot my friend in the back."

Antonio nodded. "Herman. I heard. They say you are very fast."

"Who's 'they'?" Clairborne asked, his curiosity piqued.

Antonio shrugged. "Oh just the other hands."

"Not Herman?"

"No. Not Herman. He never say anything about anything. Good with horses, though."

Clairborne wanted to ask what Antonio thought about the killing at Spanish Wells. But before the words left his lips, he realized he already knew the answer.

Antonio said what he did about his own situation to establish an understanding between them. Both had done what they had to do. And that was all that needed saying.

The next morning, Clairborne recalled Steiner's instructions to make a social call on behalf of Mr. Caudill.

"When are we going to call on Mr. Swan?" he asked.

"Ay, I forgot," Antonio said. "It's no far from here. We can't both go and leave the herd. You go. Just follow this draw up to the end, and you'll see his place from there. To the north."

An hour and twenty minutes later, just as the fat, simmering orb of the morning sun dragged itself above the eastern edge of west Texas, he topped the trail at the head of the shallow canyon, and Clairborne looked north and beheld a seemingly infinite expanse of flat, largely treeless land stretching out to the sun-bleached horizon. In the distance, he discerned a collection of mean structures

that appeared to be abandoned. As he approached, he saw a mule and a donkey, then a milk cow, then chickens, then two yellow dogs racing at him with unclear intentions.

His mare didn't like the dogs. She started to skip sideways, ears back, neck arched, snorting. He drew his pistol. "Dang, I do hope I don't have to shoot a dog to start off the day. That'll sure complicate the greetings...."

When he guessed the hounds were in earshot, he stood in his stirrups and yelled, "Howdy, pups. Hello, you old hounds." The sound of his voice brought them up short. They circled him at a distance, ears back, heads down, tails erect and rigid, legs stiff. Clairborne fetched a piece of jerky, tore it in half, and threw the meat to the dogs. "Nice little bite for you, so we can get along with business, you hounds," he said.

He slipped his Colt back into his holster and spurred his mare toward the battered shack. Someone was sitting in a rocking chair on what passed for a porch. Clairborne waved his right hand, twisted around in his saddle to note the location of the dogs, turned back, and yelled, "Hello the house."

The man in the rocker waved back, but if he said anything, Clairborne didn't hear it as he slowed his horse to a walk.

"Good morning, sir. Name's Tucker Clairborne, riding for the Rocking C. Mr. Caudill sends his regards."

The man nodded. Clairborne removed his hat and gloves as he stepped up on the porch and extended his right hand.

The wizened gnome said, "Praxiteles Swan. But I expect you already know that."

"Yes, sir."

Swan seemed ancient. He was small. On the stones beside him, a twisted crutch explained why he didn't rise to greet his guest. Swan's bald head gleamed in the morning light, and his rheumy, red-rimmed, gray eyes seemed unfocused. Cataracts. His deerskin shirt was shiny with grease. Some of the holes in his homespun pants were patched. Some weren't. His tiny foot was hidden in a battered boot, but the big toe, unfettered by anything resembling a sock, peeped through a ragged hole. "Help yourself to water. Ain't got no coffee, but if'n you're plannin' on stayin', I can whip some up."

Clairborne waved his hand and spoke up when he noticed Swan holding his hand to his ear.

"No, sir. Thanks, but I can't be staying that long. Just wanted to see how things are going's all."

"Well, sonny, you tell Nolan I'm just as fine as frog's hair and tell him any time he wants to come this way, I'll wrassle him to the ground. Always was able to best him in a wrassle fight."

Thinking of Caudill's solid mass, Clairborne didn't think so.

Looking over Swan's shoulder into the dark interior of the one-room cabin, he perceived the faded colors of a Confederate battle flag nailed to the log wall.

"You fought for the cause, sir?"

"Yup. You?"

"No, sir. My daddy and brother. Both gone. Daddy of typhus and my brother at Cold Harbor."

"Wasn't at Cold Harbor but heard of it."

"Where'd you fight, if you don't mind my asking?"

Swan didn't immediately answer.

He seemed to shift his unfocused gaze to the ill-defined horizon. Clairborne tried to imagine the scenes of hardship and sacrifice, brotherhood and savagery shuffling through the old man's mind like a deck of cards, Swan examining them one at a time, deciding which he would lay in front of his young visitor while holding the rest close to his narrow chest.

"Well," he finally said in a voice so low Clairborne had to lean forward to hear it over the wind, "we all went up to Gettysburg, the summer of sixty-three, and some of us came back from there, and that's all except the details."

Neither man said anything. Clairborne looked around.

Half blind, one legged, and near deaf. How in blazes did a man live in this hard a country carrying burdens such as those? "You deserve better than this, old man," he thought. Stepping up on the porch, he passed Swan and picked up the empty bucket by the door, then walked to the well, filled it, and placed it back by the door. He retrieved a sack of coffee beans, a can of peaches, and slices of jerky from his saddlebag and deposited both on the battered bench beside the door. One of the yellow dogs plopped down at Swan's feet. The other sat beside the rocking chair and licked its large balls. Swan reached down and worked his gnarled fingers into the hound's neck fur. Clairborne saw the dog close its eyes and almost smile with pleasure. He noted that the dogs were scarred but well fed and marveled how that was accomplished in so mean a place.

"Well, Mr. Swan, it's a pleasure meeting you, an honor. Is there anything you need before I go, sir?"

Swan's smile displayed his three remaining teeth.

"A feisty redhead to keep me warm at night."

Clairborne laughed. "Don't happen to have one, but I'll keep my eye out for you. I put some coffee beans and jerky and a can of peaches on your table. It's good jerky, sir. You can boil it for chewing. I'll open the peaches if you'd like." He did so.

"Right Christian of you," Swan said. "Don't think I et a peach in a few years now." Raising the can to his thin lips, Swan sipped the syrup slowly. It transformed him. The flinty, old gnome became a small child, flushed with an almost illicit pleasure.

"Mighty fine," Swan said as he wiped his mouth with the back of his liver-spotted hand. "Yes sir, mighty fine."

Clairborne reached over and shook Swan's hand again.

He swung into his saddle and regarded the living monument to the hard Texas life that was Praxiteles Swan. An urge to say something profound was frustrated by his failure to retrieve the words he sought.

He thought of "Parting is such sweet sorrow" but knew quoting Shakespeare would be lost and probably counterproductive with this old man who was more stone than tissue.

"Good-bye, Mr. Swan," he said.

"Adios, young man," Swan replied, holding up the can of peaches. "Come on back, and I'll wrassle you someday."

Riding away from the hardscrabble home of Praxiteles Swan, Clairborne once again wondered how this man who had ridden with John Bell Hood survived on his own. Nearly blind, nearly deaf, and nearly crippled. Hell of a combination. He pulled up at the lip of the canyon leading back to the herd and turned in his saddle to study the distant homestead. He decided Swan was about as good an example of an independent man as he had ever known—or even heard of—and most importantly, he decided that Swan didn't need any undue concern or, Lord forbid, out-right pity from anyone. He doubted Swan was even sad about his situation. In fact, he thought, Swan was probably as at peace with his lot in life as anyone he was likely to meet.

He swung around and was about to spur his mare to a canter when he noticed the western horizon.

The land between where he sat and the limit of what he could behold subtly but distinctly changed from desiccated, flat, open terrain sliced by dry creek beds to a series of low, bleached-brown knuckles of hills tenaciously gripping the thin soil from which they rose, sheer-sided and striated in layers of rust and ochre. The far distance was dominated by serrated ridges and flat-topped mesas.

In the middle distance, a dust devil belly danced across the flats.

But it was neither dust nor mesas that caught his attention. Stretching across the sky above the far-off ridges, a great smear of solid cloud rose from its violet base to blindingly white heavenly ramparts, its ragged tops sheered sideways in great, wind-eroded drifts.

The cloud mass blackened, sucking energy from the morning sun behind where Clairborne sat his horse. Pulses of sheet lightning illuminated its blue-black belly as it assaulted the mountains blocking its eastward march while above, crooked bolts leaped in erratic frenzy from one cloud tower to the next.

"Lord," Clairborne said aloud. "That's coming right for us." He knew there was no escape from the tempest about to descend on him, Antonio, and the herd. He didn't know what to do other than ride as rapidly as he could back to the draw where the cattle were gathered.

When he arrived, Antonio waved him over.

"Only thing to do is stay down here," Antonio shouted over the rising wind. "Up there," he nodded at the high ground where they camped, "the lightning would get us for sure," he yelled. "You know what is, ah, *pedrisco*?"

"What?"

"Pedrisco, *granizo*. I don't know Ingles for this word. It comes in big storm like this," Antonio said as he and Clairborne donned their slickers and pulled their hats down.

"Hail! Hail! That's it. Hail can get the cattle running and hurt us too," Antonio said.

"Wonderful," Clairborne muttered as he remounted and looked west into a wind-whipped dust cloud, a skirmish line for the torrential assault about to hit them. He pulled his silk scarf up over his nose and mouth, looked around at the increasingly restive herd, and told himself, "I wish I weren't here."

So huge, so daunting was the tempest that descended on them that Clairborne sucked in his breath as its edge roared ahead. He cringed at lightning flashes and the instantaneous accompaniment of thunderclaps. Even at the bottom of the draw, Clairborne felt the hair rise on the back of his neck. Fear of death replaced dread of discomfort.

He and Antonio rode on opposing sides of the herd at the ravine's mouth. Even knowing as little as he did about cattle, he could tell their restlessness verged on imminent panic.

The hail came first.

The initial balls of ice were small enough to sound like tentative tapping on Clairborne's hat. "Not so bad," he thought.

Half a minute later, the hailstones got bigger and the wind got higher, contributing to their velocity and impact. They started to hurt. Clairborne looked around for some kind of shelter, any kind of shelter, quickly realizing that even if he miraculously found any, he couldn't avail himself of its relative comforts. He was getting paid to gather and protect cows. He couldn't abandon them.

He looked over at Antonio and, at first, couldn't determine what the Mexican was doing. The vaquero swung his right leg over the pommel to the point where it looked as if he were riding sidesaddle. Antonio was taking off his spurs. Then he took off the belt holding his knife and hung it on a mesquite bush. Clairborne understood. Get rid of metal before the lightning hit them for real.

He fumbled with Tommy Harlan's spurs. "Damn. Too hard to reach," he thought.

He looked around as a flash of sheet lightning illuminated what could have been midnight darkness but was still morning. The hailstones got bigger, and Clairborne flinched. His mare lowered her head and twitched. A jagged fork of light and companion crack of thunder brought his shoulders forward, a futile effort to get smaller.

A ball of yellow-green light rolled along the rough surface of the ground toward the herd. He looked again at Antonio, who was removing his slicker. Why? He looked back at the herd and beheld an astonishing sight.

The horns of each animal positively glowed with a flickering lime-green light. The air smelled of sulfur. The herd seemed docile, subdued perhaps by the raging elements pounding them without remorse: wind, dust, hail, three different kinds of lightning, thunder. An instant of calm and respite from the hail vanished in rain so intense and sudden in its onslaught that Clairborne held his breath for fear of drowning in his saddle.

Then a bolt of lightning shattering a wet rock a quarter mile away, an explosion of light and sound, yanked a croak of fear from Clairborne's mouth, spooked his horse, and stampeded the herd, which tried to expand in all directions but was blocked and ultimately channeled by the sides of the ravine. So it poured its panic into the only way out.

Clairborne looked to Antonio for direction. Antonio was already leaning forward over the neck of his pinto, racing to get ahead of the herd to slow and eventually turn it. Clairborne dug Tommy Harlan's gut-hook spurs into his mare's flanks and hung on as the animal leaped into a full gallop from a standing start.

Careening over the uneven terrain, he fleetingly worried about a fall, since a step into a gopher hole, a stumble at high speed, and low visibility could hurl him under the hundreds of hooves churning the wet dirt to goo. There was no time to worry about "maybes" or "what ifs."

"Where's Antonio? Where's Antonio?" Mind racing, head swiveling. No Antonio.

"Dang!"

The land rose ahead. Clairborne spurred his mare as it drew even with the lead cattle, still barreling flat-out but, strangely to Clairborne, in silence.

He whipped off his hat and began waving it in front of the lead animals, being careful to stay ahead of them. They showed no intention of slowing.

He replaced his hat only to have it blow off.

"Son of a bitch. All the way from Virginia. Where in the hell am I going to find another hat out here?" He was that certain he'd never again lay eyes on the product of Talton & Son: Fine Hats for Gentlemen.

Anger joined his fear and frenzy.

More lightning. More thunder. Both more distant. Only the rain's intensity remained constant.

It occurred to him that the herd was headed south.

"They'll be in Mexico by nightfall at this rate," he thought.

He drew his Colt, looked around for Antonio, and didn't see him. Anger rose higher.

"Can't do this by myself, goddamn it. Where are you?"

In the dim, rain-filtered light ahead, Clairborne saw the land rise on both sides of another ravine, another waddy. He veered to the left and up the grade, turned, and saw the leading cattle start to follow.

He fired into the air and screamed. He fired again and again and saw the cattle slow ever so little and deviate into the ravine. He rode along its edge and watched as the herd compressed and slowed in the narrower confines.

Holstering his Colt, he struggled to remove his slicker, finally wrapping his reins around the pommel so he could use both hands to remove it.

Seeing that the ravine opened up ahead, he spurred the mare to get in front of the cattle as they emerged from the defile and felt affection for the tough little filly with enough bottom to accelerate at the touch of his spurs.

Emerging on the left of the herd and being right-handed, Clairborne waved his slicker to turn the herd to the right.

From the corner of his eye, he saw Antonio on the other side of the herd, which, Clairborne was astonished to see, was visibly slowing and turning to its right as well. Antonio wheeled his pinto and raced to close the gap between them, then wheeled again fifty yards from Clairborne. Frantically waving their slickers and shouting, they rode in tandem for a while before Clairborne dropped back to ensure the rear of the herd continued to follow its leaders now that they were heading in the desired direction.

The rain fell hard and thick, but the cattle stopped and lowered their heads, their flanks heaving with exhaustion.

Antonio and Clairborne rode toward each other, smiling as they placed their slickers over their saddle pommels. They shook hands.

"Well, that was something," Clairborne said.

"We got to get them back to the camp. We got enough light," Antonio replied.

Clairborne looked around at the milky, sodden luminescence. He had no idea what time of day it was, how long the stampede had lasted, or how far they'd come.

It was still raining hard, but the storm's front lines had moved east, taking its lightning and thunder artillery in its van.

Fatigue flooded through him so that he found it hard to raise his head. Every inch of his clothing and boots was saturated.

He shrugged and nodded.

"OK. Maybe I can find my hat."

—◦◦◦—

A short distance from camp, he saw what reminded him of a bull's-eye target. Clairborne didn't immediately recognize it as his hat because he simply could not believe his eyes. His Toltan & Sons hat was intact, five feet above the ground in a tangle of mesquite branches. His skepticism was so great that he approached his hat in a slow walk as if racing over to recover it might cause it to suddenly vanish into the thick afternoon air.

But it didn't, and he gingerly removed it from the mesquite bush, using his thumb to restore the contours of the crown. He looked at the trademark, "Toltan & Sons, Richmond," and recalled again when his father first took him to the shop that smelled like wet fur on the corner of Third and Cary.

As they neared what was left of their camp, his eyes caught a large cow and her calf ambling away from the herd. The mare moved in anticipation of his spurs, cutting off the cow's movement so efficiently that the cow didn't hesitate or resist. In bovine resignation, it swung around and headed back to the herd, its calf trotting alongside.

Clairborne patted the mare's neck. "Good girl. Good girl," he said softly, noting the mare's ears turning back to catch his words. Rain spilled from the brim of his hat and splashed on the mare's neck when he turned to observe the herd. It pleasured Clairborne every time. It meant he had his hat back.

There was a cold camp that night. No fire. No kindling or dry firewood or buffalo chips. Everything was saturated and would remain so until exposed to at least a half-day's sun.

"Take 'em back tomorrow," Antonio said, mounting his horse for the first shift of night watch.

"OK," Clairborne said, ending the only verbal exchange of the night.

They started the next day without even coffee since there was no way to make it. The prospect of a day in the saddle with no caffeine and no food depressed Clairborne to the point of moroseness. Antonio said little, seeing nothing all that unusual about privations that defined cowboy life and were, thus, nothing out of the ordinary.

The cattle seemed unusually cooperative. Clairborne didn't know whether it was because they were tired, had become accustomed to the presence of humans and horses, or his expanding experience and embryonic herding skills had actually made a difference. Probably all three, he decided.

He threw his lariat more than he needed to in practical terms. But each time he enlarged the loop, made a decision on the kind of throw—high, lateral—and let fly, he snubbed the rope around the saddle horn, felt the mare take up the slack, and knew he was inching closer to competence.

Watching Antonio with a lariat, he identified the specific skill that would mark that achievement when it arrived.

Once or twice, he saw Antonio flick his lariat out like a serpent's tongue, but instead of the loop settling over the animal's horns, it slipped under its moving rear feet, tumbling the animal into the dust when pulled taut. It was an amazing skill that Clairborne thought he would never master.

By midday, the west Texas sun had returned with a relentlessness that raised wisps of steam from his rain-soaked attire and the backs of horse and longhorn alike. Clairborne was nearly hallucinating with fatigue and hunger. At midafternoon, they stopped for coffee and bacon. He and Antonio said nothing, each fully understanding the division of labor worked out during the last several days.

He knew from observing the lay of the land that they were only hours from the ranch. He smiled. Mere contemplation of his spartan space in the bunkhouse, a place at a roughhewn table in the dining hall, and a change of clothes gave him inordinate pleasure. He wondered how Herman was doing.

A brindle cow sidled away from the herd, and Clairborne said, "No you don't" and rode to cut it off. The cow accelerated, and Clairborne loosened the loop in his lariat, shaking it out with his right hand, holding the rest of its length coiled in his left. His eyes noted something off to his right. Nolan Caudill sat his horse on rise watching him and Antonio work the herd.

"Give him a show," Clairborne thought as he lifted the lariat loop over his head and began to swing it. His target accelerated past some high brush that would have complicated the throw. "This is going to be easy," he told himself.

He launched the loop perfectly. Its expanded circumference sailed out parallel to the ground, settled over the horns, and slipped down to the thick, muscled neck. Clairborne quickly snapped a loop around his saddle horn and started to take another turn, another "dally."

White pain exploded from his left hand, momentarily blinding him with its brilliance. A scream started from his throat but never made it out of his mouth, colliding as it did with the air sucked in by his contracting lungs.

A second flash of pain erupted from his hand. Clairborne was totally confused. His mind screamed at him to identify the source of his agony, but he couldn't focus his eyes, his vision constricted to a velvet-black backdrop on which pyrotechnics exploded and vanished in split seconds.

He fell from his mount. Almost. It seemed he couldn't fall to the ground. Something prevented him from fully dismounting from his now-stationary horse, which maintained the tautness of the lariat, at the other end of which was the cow. Clairborne's knees buckled. Another surge of pain jumped from his left hand to the pit of his stomach. He vomited. Then he screamed.

The vermillion mist of pain lifted for a second, long enough for Clairborne to see the source of his vexation.

His gloved left hand, what was left of it, was snubbed against the saddle horn beneath two loops of lariat.

"Christ, oh, Christ. Jesus!" he bellowed.

"How...?" he flash-thought.

In situations defined by mortal pain, by imminent death, the mind works at speeds incomprehensible in normal times.

At the apogee of his agony, Clairborne understood the physics of his situation.

Clawing his way back into the saddle, he vomited again as he regained his seat.

At the touch of his spurs, the mare jumped forward, creating slack in the lariat. Clairborne's right hand loosened the loops ensnaring his left. A different kind of pain ensued—hammer blows instead of knife thrusts, but pain so deep seated and severe that he gagged yet again, although his stomach had nothing more to surrender.

He dismounted and fell in a heap, gripping his mangled hand and moaning.

Vaguely aware of someone grabbing his shoulders and drawing his body close, Clairborne heard Antonio whisper, "Madre de dios."

Blood covered both of Clairborne's hands and arms as well as the front of his shirt. Writhing around spread the sticky scarlet to his trousers and boots, mixing with the dirt to make a loathsome mud.

"Ay de mi, ay de mi..." Antonio muttered.

The edge of pain receded fleetingly enough for Clairborne to look at the sweat- and gore-saturated left glove.

Blood still flowed from the wound, but what nature of wound? Clairborne couldn't discern specifics. He swooned at the impact of another wave of agony.

Emerging from the fog of hurt and confusion, a new emotion joined the chaos swirling through his mind: anger, molten bitterness at the sudden recognition that he was permanently disfigured, handicapped, scarred for life even though he had yet to identify the precise nature of his wound.

He looked again at the hand he now instinctively held above his head to reduce the throbbing.

His thoughts raced. "Index finger. Gone?" He saw that the leather binding it to the rest of the glove was flaccid compared to that encasing his other, firmly clenched digits.

He recognized that one finger gone was better than two or three. "But how do I get my glove off? What do I do? Christ, this hurts. What do I do?" he asked himself.

With his right hand and Antonio's help, he pushed himself to a sitting position.

Clairborne pawed at the left side of his belt and pulled his Bowie knife out of its scabbard, dropping it in the dirt.

"Get my knife. Get my goddamned knife!" he yelled.

Somehow the Bowie appeared in his right hand.

"Get me rock, a rock!"

Antonio scrambled and returned with a large brown stone in his hands, looking bewildered.

"Oh, oh," Clairborne moaned. "Put it...Put it down."

He raised the Bowie, but before lowering its edge to the destroyed flesh and bone, he considered for a mere second the consequences of blindly slashing at the origin of his agony.

"Only one finger. Only one. Don't need to cut two. Take it at the lowest knuckle. Do it now!" he screamed as he pushed the razor-edged steel into the unresisting mass.

—⁓—

A whirlpool of nausea swept over him. He prayed the pain would abate. And when his pleas were ignored, he raged all the louder. Someone, something was pounding his hand. Some force beyond his ken held his hand on an anvil and smashed it repeatedly with a blacksmith's hammer in time with his accelerated heartbeat.

He choked. His lungs joined the internal fray, sending urgent messages that they needed oxygen. He choked again.

He opened his eyes. Two gray forms cast shadows as they held him. Antonio and Caudill. Antonio was repeating "Ay de mi." Beneath his black sombrero, Caudill's bearded face was expressionless. His arms held Clairborne's upper torso. "Easy, easy, easy," he said.

Antonio's broad, dark face, tears coursing from obsidian eyes through layers of dust and falling from his unshaven jaw, evoked affection from some deep and previously unknown well in Clairborne's soul.

Caudill, on the other hand, irritated him.

He wanted to yell, "Easy, my ass. This goddamn hurts, you sanctimonious son of a bitch!"

He wanted to, but he didn't. Judgment reappeared in his consciousness. Perhaps that meant his pain was becoming manageable, that it would allow rational thought and coherent speech.

Clairborne lowered his gaze to his left hand. A blood-soaked, linen handkerchief, undoubtedly Caudill's, was pressed on his wound.

"Well, no doubt about it, it's gone," he said of his absent index finger. "It really happened. It's gone for good."

The first question leaping in his thoughts involved firearms. He wondered how the wound would affect his shooting and decided the answer was probably not much, that he should be able to reload—hell, maybe even shoot—left-handed with practice.

Caudill was saying something.

"What? What'd you say, sir?" Clairborne croaked.

"I asked you what lesson you learned from this, son, what you think the Lord is trying to tell you."

374

Clairborne stared open-mouthed at his employer. Confusion wrestled with anger. "What the hell kind of question is that?" he wondered.

Shifting his gaze to his mangled hand, he thought, "There used to be five fingers there. Just a minute ago, I had five damn good fingers." Now he'd lost one in an excruciatingly painful lesson in how not to rope a cow.

"Do you know what he's tryin' to tell you, Tucker?" Caudill said again.

Clairborne looked at the bloody stump where his index finger had been and shrugged.

"Maybe that I only got four more chances to do it right...."

An explosive guffaw burst from Caudill's deep chest. He jerked his head and laughed so abruptly his hat fell off. He slapped his knee. The belly laughs pulled a sheepish grin out of Clairborne even as his pain shifted from unimaginable to barely tolerable.

"Lordy, lordy, lordy," Caudill said as he leaned over, bringing his face inches from Clairborne's. "Hoooeee. 'I only got four more chances to get it right'. I swan, young man, I never heard of anyone hurt so bad saying something so dang droll."

Antonio stayed squatting by Clairborne's side. Caudill put his hand on Antonio's back.

"Let see what we can do for this young man. Lordy, lordy, I swan....." Caudill started laughing again even as he put his hands under Clairborne's armpits and lifted as Antonio scrambled to assist.

"You boys got some honey?" Caudill asked while he unslung his canteen from his saddle.

"Yes, yes," Antonio said. He leaped into the saddle and raced back to the campsite to retrieve the suddenly valuable wild honey.

Caudill directed Clairborne to a nearby large stone and sat him down.

"Gotta wash that right quick. Gotta wash it good. Don't have another clean kerchief. Don't suppose you do?"

Clairborne surveyed his blood and dirt-smeared form and had to concentrate a moment before stating the obvious.

"No, nothing clean anywhere on me, I guess."

Caudill pulled off his coat and produced a jackknife from a pants pocket. He stuck the point of the blade through the upper sleeve of his muslin shirt and cut it off as high as he could reach.

"Better than nothing."

Clairborne held Caudill's bloody handkerchief on his wound, instinctively pressing down to stanch the bleeding.

Caudill reached over and slipped the knife blade under what remained of Clairborne's left glove and cut it off, dropping it in the dust.

"OK. Let's see what we got here," he said, bending over so that the brim of his hat blocked Clairborne's view. It was just as well. Clairborne turned his head to avoid visual contact with the results of his self-surgery.

Caudill poured water over the wound, which hurt far less than Clairborne expected. He muttered something Clairborne didn't understand and then stepped back and poured some water over his knife blade.

Clairborne didn't like the look of that at all. He stiffened and drew back.

"I ain't going to tell you this ain't going to hurt. You done a mighty fine job of whackin' off the meat and bone, but there's a few little splinters and bits of glove still left. They gotta be removed afore that gets sewed up. I wisht I had finer thread in my housewife," Caudill said as he leaned over to his task.

"I got a spool of silk thread in mine, sir," Clairborne said, thankful for something upon which to focus other than Caudill's probing pocket knife. "Antonio told me it was too fine for patching my britches," he said hoarsely, his right knee bobbing up and down.

"Well, that's good, real good, son," Caudill said. "We'll just mosey back to your camp and have you stitched up in no time." He poured more water on the wound and then cut his sleeve into patches, one of which he folded over the wound and soaked with more water.

"Gotta keep that little flap soft so's we can stitch it down."

They looked up as Antonio galloped toward them, a saddlebag clutched in this hand. He leaped from his horse and raced over. "I brought honey and your housewife, Tucker. Your thread better for stitching, I think."

Clairborne and Caudill exchanged a glance, and Caudill winked. "Mighty fine, Antonio," Caudill said. "Mighty fine."

Caudill removed the bandage. Antonio handed him the small, ridged dauber from inside the honey jar. With studied care, Caudill spread a small dollop of honey on the stump. Clairborne watched Antonio thread a needle, appreciating that he washed his hands with his canteen before starting.

Caudill looked up at Clairborne and held his gaze for a moment before turning to accept the needle and thread from Antonio.

"Now son, you need to know I done this kind of thing a couple of times. More 'n a couple, actually. I watched both my momma and my daddy stitch horses and dogs, me, my brothers, even each other. Then in the Rangers, well, you wouldn't believe how often we were a-sewing on one another. Might as well have been a dang quiltin' bee. Anyways, may not seem like it now, but I'm pretty sure this is gonna be OK. Ain't gonna grow back, but it'll be OK."

Clairborne studied Caudill's slate-gray eyes as he spoke.

"Well, sir, if I have to get sewed up, I guess I'd prefer a seamstress doing it."

Caudill laughed and shook his head.

"Darned if you ain't a shine. Well, you about ready?"

"I reckon. Don't stitch me a monogram this time, though. Mebbe next."

Caudill smiled. "Darned if you ain't a shine, son. Now let's us get to work."

Rocking C Ranch
August, 1868

My reentry to bunkhouse society has proven to be somewhat awkward. Everyone's curiosity is intense, but few, only two so far, have had the courage to ask me about what happened. No one has asked how I feel about it.

It's strange in that I began to have reservations about coming here, about how I would fit in, before I arrived at this isolated, hardscrabble work in progress, and now I know that I will never be one of them. I will never be a cowboy.

What I will be remains unclear. Whatever that is, I will be disfigured, maimed.

As I sit on my bunk making this entry, I take a mental inventory of things physical and spiritual and must admit that I am encouraged. I must be mindful of the possibility that someone will read these pages without either my knowledge or my permission, so a degree of circumspection is desirable. But the fact is that I have money: cash, accounts in an established eastern bank, and other investments, the status of which I do not know. Because I have a surprising degree of financial security, I find it ever so ironic that I have come all this way only to be inspired by Mr. Caudill. He has literally carved his home, his vast and expanding home, out of the rock and dust. He and only two or three other Texans like him are the vanguard of civilization, roughhewn as they are.

Everything is on such a grand scale out here, so vast and hard and unyielding that it's difficult to comprehend how bold Caudill and his peers actually are. He is risking everything on his vision and has persisted in the face of repeated failure, loss, and, I daresay, heartbreak. I don't know the details of his financial status, but I have to assume there is an element of debt in his equation. He faces an array of foes and challenges that would deter most men: uncertain weather, poor grass, unreliable water, and, of course, Indians,

Comanche most of all. He and the other "old hands" insist the Indian problem is greatly reduced from the early years, and they're confident of continuing progress in the effort to civilize the savage.

I am not so sure. We are so far from anywhere, so far from the army, the rule of law, courts, boundaries, commerce, medicine that it seems a very precarious proposition to invest everything, particularly one's life, in a place so unyielding and unforgiving. It makes Virginia and life there seem sybaritic by comparison.

Another reason for my uncertainty about Mr. Caudill's unqualified belief in the future of his enterprise rests primarily on his own words. He has said more than once that there are fewer Americans out here now than there were a decade ago, a decline he attributes to fear. He told me yesterday as he examined my hand that a great many folks "up and left Texas, finding it too hard a land to germinate the seeds of hope." He said the Comanche, above everything else, were responsible for the departure of so many whites. And yet, he insists, "things are better today than yesterday and not as good as tomorrow will be."

I find myself thinking that for me, one advantage of this isolation is the lack of temptation to correspond with Mother. Since there is no postal service of any kind, there is no sense in drafting letters and, therefore, no need to decide whether or not to tell her about my hand.

Ah yes, my hand. It is time to write about my hand. Despite the best efforts of Mr. Caudill, me, and a few others with some experience, it became infected. The pain and discomfort prevented sleep.

Fever soaked me with sweat. Apparently, my frequent delirium also interrupted the sleep of others in the bunkhouse, so even though I told no one, it wasn't long before Titus and Antonio, among others, knew it.

Antonio changed my bandages twice a day, and Mr. Caudill showed up at least once a day to check on me. When the first signs of infection appeared, they increased the amount of rubbing alcohol they used to wash it, but it still got infected. One night I awoke to find Antonio and Titus leaning over me. Titus said it had to be stopped quickly. In fact, he said some of the hands thought I was a dead man, that blood poisoning would take me no matter what and only amputating my entire arm would forestall such an event. As I consider these next words, I am both horrified and amused. I still find it hard to believe I agreed to a form of treatment so utterly prehistoric, so alien to modern medicine as civilized people of European stock know it.

Kneeling by my cot, Titus reached inside his shirt and withdrew a folded piece of hide, which, when he opened it, revealed three small, yellowish insects, which he informed me were maggots. He matter-of-factly told me the maggots would eat the dead flesh. When I asked if that was all they'd eat, he smiled. "That's how you'll know they done their job. When you feel them eating good skin, it means they got all the bad, and you just take 'em off." Antonio nodded enthusiastically and said, "Tucker, you don't stop that infection, you get gangrene. You get gangrene, you lose your hand, maybe your arm. That don't stop it, you die. One week, maybe two, you die."

I realized that I have come to know Titus and Antonio well enough to trust their judgment. What did I have to lose? Titus said if the maggots were put on the wound, they would do their work in a day or two. I wondered briefly where they got the insects, if they dug them out of a pile of manure or some putrid mound of rotting flesh.

As they unwrapped the linen bandage, Antonio said, "No more bandage, Tucker. The bandage make it worse. Wash with water and rubbing alcohol, then dry in sunshine."

So here I sit three days later looking at the pinkest flesh I've seen since I last beheld a newborn puppy or piglet. The last vestiges of fever and inflammation are almost gone.

The maggots caused only mild discomfort when they got to healthy flesh and were not at all difficult to remove. I took them outside and put them under the porch. It was the least I could do in return for what I believe they did for me.

Mr. Caudill was delighted and pronounced the improved status of the wound to be a minor miracle attributable to God's desire for me to be saved as an example for other mortals. Who really knows what is a miracle and what isn't? Does not the reversal of an inevitable process constitute a miracle even if the means by which it's accomplished is a loathsome insect?

As I look outside, I behold the light of a new day. The cook just emerged from the kitchen to dump a pail of water into the dust.

Smoke from the kitchen stove carries with it the smell of bacon. After breakfast, I think I will ride out a ways and unlimber my Colts.

———

He did.

After a plate of beans, calf brains, biscuits, scrambled eggs, and coffee, Clairborne went to find Bucephalus. Pinch, the lead wrangler, told him where the stallion was kept. Earlier, Pinch had succinctly amplified what Antonio had said about stallions and the rationale for the strict equine segregation practiced on the Rocking C. It centered on just how troublesome stallions could be. They fought each other. They abused geldings, and of course they pursued mares with single-minded intensity. So stallions were separated—from one another and from all the other horses unless breeding was part of the plan.

Walking away from the chuck house, Pinch worked a piece of straw into his gums to loosen a chunk of unchewed breakfast.

"Been meaning to ask you, what kind of name is Boosyphilis? You don't mind me saying so, that's a hell of a name for any animal, 'specially one as fine as that mount of yours."

Clairborne smiled. He was surprised it had taken so long. Before he could answer, Pinch added, "Hope you don't mind none, but I been calling him Buck when I been working him."

"Does he like it?" Clairborne asked.

"Seems to."

"Well then, no harm, I guess. Got one for old Ajax?" Clairborne asked about his gelding.

"Nah. Nothing wrong with Ajax."

"Fine. Bucephalus was the horse a man called Alexander rode a couple thousand years or so ago. Lots of stories about them both. Just thought that, being a big, black sassy stallion, plus being kind of bull headed, the name kind of fit him."

"Whew," Pinch said, spitting a bean skin into the dust. "At's good to know he ain't named after no disease."

"Buck" trotted across to Clairborne, who drew a dried carrot from his pocket and stroked the soft, dewy muzzle.

Twenty minutes later, they raced across the flats, Clairborne exhilarated by the feel of his powerful, beautiful, faithful legacy of a time and place so far away. He made no effort to avoid a gully, sailing over it without breaking stride. A few minutes more, they slowed to a canter, then a trot, then a walk. A small pond glinted off to their left, cattails waving in the steady westerly wind. Its water was not alkaline, so Clairborne allowed his horse to drink a modest amount before leading it off a hundred yards, placing hobbles on its front legs, and pulling his saddlebag from its back.

The two Colts had a satisfying heft. He untied his slicker from behind his saddle, spread it on the ground, and then arrayed his firearms—with the exception of the Colt named Thunder—on its waxed surface.

It was time to try something different: cross draw. While satisfied with the speed and efficiency with which he could retrieve and fire the pistol riding on his right hip, he'd never stopped wondering about the advantages of wearing it on his left, as had Wild Billy Martin, even though his collision with a horse at Spanish Wells had forced him to wear it there for a while.

He shrugged and decided to try it. Taking off the gun belt, he removed the case for percussion caps from the left side to make an opening for the repositioned holster, which he slid into place, butt forward. He withdrew it and checked its cylinders, slowly turning the weapon in his hands, marveling at the process that ended with his standing alone in west Texas, this formidable, functional, aesthetically pleasing piece of metal and ivory awaiting his bidding.

"How many lives have you taken?" he silently asked.

He practiced the withdrawing and noted it automatically caused his body to shift slightly to the left as well, which he understood reduced his profile, decreasing the target area available to a foe. Even at the same level of his hips, the cross draw seemed easier, more fluid, although it involved a lateral motion in addition to a vertical element to bring the muzzle to bear.

Clairborne looked around for his first target. A prickly pear cactus offered a pink blossom at the tip of a paddle-like appendage. He reholstered the Colt, turned slightly to his right, drew, turned back to his left, and fired. Thumbing the cross-hatched hammer, he fired again.

Gun smoke obscured his vision for a few seconds before dissipating in the breeze.

When it cleared, the target was gone, not just the blossom but nearly the whole paddle on which it grew. He was dissatisfied. Thirty feet. Should have hit just the flower. But it had been a while, almost a month since he'd last practiced, and he was trying something different, so he reconsidered.

"Like playing a piano or a violin. You don't practice, you lose it."

After checking around for various reptiles and insects, he lowered himself on a flat-topped boulder conveniently located under a large mesquite bush. Removing his gun belt and opening the heavily stitched sleeve on its interior side, he held the belt up and worked out a twenty-dollar gold piece, turning it over in his fingers. On the few occasions he had done so since receiving his unanticipated windfall, he'd marveled at both the circumstances and the result. The coin he rolled in his fingertips was freedom; beautifully engraved, small but heavy, softly and seductively glinting as he turned it over in the filtered sunlight.

The particular double eagle he held was minted in 1866. Back in Missouri, the first time he examined his fortune, he'd withdrawn all of the coins from the gun belt stash and noted that some dated back to 1852.

Studying the classical profile of a woman wearing a crown bearing the word "Liberty," Clairborne rubbed the raised surface of the face and asked out loud, "Where did you come from, Lady?" His gaze went to his patched pants and his battered boots. A sour laugh, almost like a burp, popped out of his throat.

"I look like a damn beggar man," he said loudly, causing Buck to swing his head toward Clairborne and raise his ears expectantly. He flipped the coin twice, reinserted it into his gun belt, and walked to his horse.

"No yet, you old pie eater," he said, stroking the gleaming neck muscles. "You just want to stretch your legs. You know, boy, maybe I should just mount up and give you your head and see where in the hell you'd take me."

His horse regarded him with an unblinking stare, outlandishly large, liquid brown eyes shaded by long, thick lashes.

Clairborne wrapped his arms around the stallion's neck, hugging him tightly, reveling in the animal's silky solidity, the familiarity of its aroma, the moist, glistening coat. The horse quivered slightly and swept its tail.

Clairborne stepped back, holding the bit in his still-tender left hand, rubbing the muzzle with his right.

"All right, I hear you. 'Pull yourself together and get on with the day.' I get it."

Clairborne took in his surroundings and again lowered his head to examine his clothing. This time, his emotions were clear. He was not a beggar man, so why did he look like one? Most relevant was his recognition that his condition was more than a little absurd. He didn't have to look like a ragamuffin. He had the wherewithal to walk into the best tailor shop in the world and pay cash for bespoke attire from his booted feet to his shaded head.

Instead, the only thing he was wearing that looked top line and well cared for was the pistol belt, holster, and the Colt it contained. The belt was thick, oiled, double-stitched leather. The holster was the same dark brown as the belt but softer, suppler, and tastefully embossed with a single large rosette. The Colt was simply a work of art.

He was neither a commoner nor an aristocrat, at least not anymore. What was he? He'd come west to start over. And now he looked like a vagrant, a dust-covered wanderer, a begrimed mercenary in search of a meal or plunder or both. Absentmindedly fingering the business end of Tommy Harlan's quirt, he switched his focus to the ubiquitous implement of the cowboy trade and beheld a beautiful tool—six narrow strips of latigo leather, black and russet, braided over a bone handle, long, thin ribbons of hide emerging from the braids to form the business end of the "pony accelerator," a loop on the other end securing it to his right wrist.

In the mental checklist he worked through before target practice, he'd considered removing his quirt but then decided to leave it on. Things happened so fast out here, he'd never have time to take it off before drawing his weapon, so he shot with it dangling from his wrist.

Clairborne was glad he had Tommy Harlan's quirt. He raised it to his forehead, used its tip to push back his hat, and closed his eyes. In the darkness, his life suddenly came into focus. He knew what he would do.

He would honor his word and help Caudill with the drive, then collect his wages, then buy a new wardrobe, then check on his bank balance and his investment in liquor and tobacco, then ride to Wyoming to check on his half interest in that saloon and hotel. Ride the rails, that is—horses and gear in the freight car.

He marveled at the how quickly indecision jelled into a plan, the best kind of plan: logical, simple, chronological.

Hamlet appeared in his thoughts. Hamlet was his least favorite of the Bard's works—a crown prince spending all that time wringing his hands. "Just get on with it," he'd said aloud to himself the second time he read the play about the tortured Dane.

"That's right, Clairborne," he said, rising from the shaded boulder. "Just get on with it."

He picked up his shotgun, checked its load, selected two good-sized pebbles, and thumbed the hammers back. Holding the gun across his chest with his left hand, he used his right hand to throw the rocks as high and as far as he could, then shouldered the weapon and swung it up to find the airborne stones. He caught both before they hit the ground. He reloaded and did it again. His mood improved. He judged himself "proficient" with his firearms—room for improvement but acceptable.

Mind cleared, course of action identified, and targets hit, he decided to reward himself with one of his last cigars. Digging the morocco leather cigar holder out of his saddlebag, Clairborne again took a seat on the boulder and opened the case, but instead of the pleasure he anticipated, he was greeted with disappointment. The west Texas summer air had sucked every molecule of moisture out of the tobacco, leaving his two remaining panatelas fit only for kindling to start a campfire.

"Well, damn. No cigar, and sure as blazes no whiskey," he said. Clairborne decided such petty privations would not spoil his mood. He sniffed the dry cigars, which even in their advanced state of ruin still emitted notes of cedar and spice. He dropped them in the dust. "Adios, my friends," he said.

August 11, 1868
Rocking C Ranch

The fall roundup began in earnest before dawn this morning. Reps from surrounding spreads have been arriving at the Rocking C for the last week. Their job is to take charge of the cattle bearing their respective brands, either returning them to their ranches or determining how many of their cattle will be part of the herd we take north.

When Antonio and I were rounding up cattle before my accident, he told me we would leave most of the bulls out on the range and concentrate on recovering steers, cows, and their calves. This is so the bulls can continue to breed when they can, adding to the number of cattle year after year. That means most of the more than seven thousand head we have gathered are steers, cows, and calves.

The bulls that we have brought in don't remain bulls for long. Of all the tasks one has to perform, this may be the nastiest—that is, unless the steer in question gets a postcastration infestation of blowflies. Treating for that problem requires manually applying a mixture of turpentine and axle grease to the affected area. I have yet to see a steer appreciate the care.

If there is a singular characteristic of an autumn roundup I'm certain to recall for the rest of my days, I would have to say it is the juxtaposition of chaos and efficiency, very much akin to what I witnessed while with the army. The site defies description, but I must try. From dawn till well after dusk, the fields are cloaked in a permanent dust cloud thickened by smoke from the fires used to heat the branding irons. The eye perceives constant and frenetic movement. The nose is assailed with the commingled odors of smoke, burning hair, feces, urine, blood, and sweat. The ears are battered by the squalls of calves, the bellowing of their mothers, the shouts and curses of the hands, and the occasional whinnying of an excited mount.

Most of the hands cover their nose and mouth with their bandanas, making the place look like a den of thieves and road agents.

Yet despite the apparent chaos, thousands of cattle are identified and separated into distinct, smaller herds; unmarked beasts are branded; and ultimately, order prevails.

I have learned the brands of the three ranches involved in the roundup and the drive ahead but have not yet mastered the frankly bewildering array of identifying marks consisting of specific cuts in the ears and dewlaps of the animals. The hands charged with making the earmarks and dewlap identifications do so with a rapidity that is amazing. So fast are they with their knives it seems most of the animals don't fully realize what has happened until they've been released and are trotting back to the herd.

We change horses three or four times a day, drawing our mounts from the huge remuda managed by Pinch and Titus and two other wranglers whose names I can't recall just now. Theirs is a truly Herculean labor, for they must have horses selected and available for the rest of us when we rise at dawn, which means, of course, that they start the day long before we do...and finish it long afterward, for they must return worked horses to the remuda, which is kept some distance from the roundup camp.

At least we still get to eat breakfast and dinner in the chuck house and sleep in the bunkhouse. I understand that at many other ranches, the beginning of roundup is the last time the hands enjoy such basic pleasures until months later when the drive is done.

I will not be taking Buck on the drive. No stallions are allowed. I've been told that there are so many unanticipated problems on a cattle drive that every single one that can be avoided—such as those associated with stallions—are avoided as a matter of common sense.

I have been shadowing Steiner, and the more I see of him, the more I admire the man. I have rarely seen anyone as taciturn as he, even out here where loquaciousness is viewed with suspicion by most and overt hostility by others.

He is the only person I've seen since leaving Virginia who carries a LeMat. The only time I've been able to draw a smile was in response to my query about why he preferred the piece. "More bullets, more options, and more heft than anything short of a Walker if you have to use it as a club," he said.

He, Caudill Junior, and I keep the tally books, which is how I am aware of the efficiency emerging from the chaos to which I referred earlier. We are four days into this event and have identified 4,277 Rocking C cattle, 543 belonging to the T-Bar-D and 408 from the Slash-S, a Salt River outfit.

While there is little time for social intercourse, there is a constant exchange of news and rumor, mostly involving bandits, Indians, water, cattle prices, and the availability of women at our destination. Most of the hands have not been to Abilene, and I have no desire to educate them on the basis of my unfortunate experience there.

So far as I can tell, we have at least four or five more days of work ahead before completing the roundup. Then, for two or three days, we tend to the last details necessary before we drive the herd north. That, I am told, is a journey of nearly a thousand miles that should last nearly two months.

One thing of note occurred during the midday meal. One of the newer hands rode his horse at a gallop to where we were eating and sprayed us all with dust and clods of dirt as he halted and dismounted. He should have known he was committing a grave breach of cowboy etiquette. After much yelling and swearing, he was sent back to the herd without so much as a moldy crust. Should he be stupid enough to do it again, I wager he will be severely pummeled.

I must be better in keeping my journals. I hereby swear that I will make at least two entries a week during the drive, no matter what has occurred or how fatigued I might be. That is, unless I happen to lose a finger or two on my right hand, a turn of events that would require me to learn how to write with my left, so delayed entries will be permitted.

What does it say that I can jest with myself over such an eventuality?

———

Titus Herman returned to the main area from the remuda range to see a man sitting by himself in the shade of the bunkhouse porch. The man was black and huge. He wore a high-crowned hat the broad brim of which was pushed up in front. His dark blue shirt was patched at the elbows and faded on the sections of shoulder visible outside of a yellow vest too small to be buttoned. Dark wool pants tucked into battered knee-high, mule-ear boots had a canvas insert sewn into the inside leg and crotch. He wore army spurs and a Colt Dragoon cap and ball in a holster covering his groin.

He watched Herman approach and waited for him to speak.

"Howdy."

"You Herman?"

"Yep."

The man stood and stuck out his large right hand. "Evermore Blaine. Friends call me Bear, them as I got."

Standing on the ground and looking up, Herman figured the man must be at least six feet, six inches tall, his height accentuated by his thick neck and shoulders and his narrow waist.

"You serve in the Ninth?" Herman asked.

"How'd you guess?"

"Spurs. Knew you weren't in the Tenth, so must've been the Ninth. You here looking for work?"

"Yep. And for you."

As tired as Herman was, the man's words sent a bolt through his veins. He could think of nothing that would have motivated a search for him by another black man—or a white man for that matter, since escaping slavery was no longer an offense anywhere in the country.

"Well, you found me. What can I do for you?"

"Know a woman name of Irene?"

Herman was struck dumb. It was not possible that Irene, the object of his reveries, his fantasies, and his fondest recollections for lo these last five years could simply and suddenly reappear in some tangible fashion.

He stammered. "I, well, I used to know someone named Irene. Long time back, back east in the old days." His mind raced. He found himself unsure of what he wanted the new-comer to say about the only woman other than his mother he had ever loved.

"She in Texas. Place called Emmons Landing. Near Tyler. Cotton plantation. Leastways it used to be. Ain't much now."

"How you know her? How you know about me and her?"

The man called Bear stretched his arms over his head and sat back down.

"She told me is what. I was a field hand when she showed up. Then I worked the forge. She worked the big house, but we all knew about her. She a fine-looking woman, that Irene."

Herman picked up on his use of present tense. His heartbeat accelerated.

"Heard they was work here. 'At why I headed down this way. My luck to get here when everybody's leaving since I ain't a drover."

Herman wanted desperately to get the conversation back to Irene, but he decided to be courteous, to see if he could help this bearer of the best of news. He was not surprised when the very large man answered his query about what skills he did have. "Blacksmith. I'm best man around a forge you ever saw."

Cowboys were men of many individual skills, including blacksmithing, but a large spread like the Rocking C was in per-petual need of new ironwork or the repair of everything from gate hinges to wagon-wheel rims.

"You might just get some work here," he said. "Only one man works the smithy permanent, and he's going on the drive." His mind whirled with the concept of seeing, touching Irene. "I'll put in the good word for you, you want."

The newcomer nodded and didn't return to Irene, so Herman did.

"What's she doing now?" Herman didn't want to know Irene was married or had a man even though he understood how likely that had to be.

"She doing what she has to, just like the rest of us. Mostly laundry for white folks that can pay for it. She cooks some too. "

He had to know. "She got a man?"

Bear's smile was marred by a missing right incisor.

"Wondered when you'd ask. Nope, and she 'bout drove a lot of men crazy when she wouldn't give 'em the time of day. Said her man goin' come fetch her sooner or later—her man Titus, she said."

It was not possible. Nothing so perfectly fulfilling ever happened to anyone, Herman thought. White or black or red. Nobody was that lucky. He said nothing as he looked through unseeing eyes at the hitching post.

Bear said nothing as well.

Finally, Herman sat down on the bunkhouse steps. Raucous snores pouring out the door assured their privacy. Bear dug a stubby pipe from a vest pocket, packed it with tobacco from a leather tobacco pouch, and lit up, the aromatic smoke hanging in the unusually still night air.

Herman's thoughts were consumed by the need to get to Irene without delay. He would have to draw his wages. How much? About thirty dollars. How much did he have in his poke from the army? Another fifty-two dollars. Eighty-two dollars.

Hell, he could get back to Africa with that much money. Except he didn't want to go to Africa. He wanted to get to east Texas, some place called Emmons Landing. He wanted to look at Irene—not hold her, just behold her. How long would it take to get across this damn big state anyways?

To his surprise, Clairborne entered his thoughts. What would he say to the Virginian? Did he even have to say anything? Why not just pack as quietly as possible tonight, draw wages as early as possible in the morning, and ride away as fast as possible thereafter? Why not? Why even think about the white man?

Because he was decent. Because he was the first white man he'd come to know. Because he didn't act like the masters he'd known in Carolina. Because of Spanish Wells and a lot of lesser things before and after, like Clairborne cooking for both, picking up buffalo chips, scouring the skillet. Because he felt so good, so full of possibilities. Because he could. So he would.

Herman stood.

"I got to pack up. You can have my bunk, you want. Ain't no way I can sleep tonight."

"Much obliged. You know where Emmons Landing is, do you?"

"No, but I can ask, closer I get. Anything I should know you learned coming out here?"

"Well, I went back to Georgia after I mustered out. Found out my Ma died, so I headed west. Black folks in all the towns and most of the big ranches. They'll steer you 'round trouble they know of. You just got to be careful of white boys in town at night. They get a snootful of rotgut and, well, you know."

"Indians?"

"Why hell, don't expect they's much I can tell a famous Indian fighter such as yourself," Bear said with a gap-toothed grin.

—∿∿—

Clairborne was not the first in the bunkhouse to awaken. Three others were almost fully dressed and walking toward the door when he emerged from the depths of sleep only the hardest of work can plumb.

Pulling on his trousers, socks, and boots, and his shirt over his head, tucking it in, and buttoning up his fly, Clairborne was consumed with thoughts of breakfast. He emerged to find Titus Herman sitting on his ex-army mount, packhorse in tow.

"Just wanted to say adios," Herman said.

Clairborne was shocked and more than a little disconcerted by the sadness that coursed through him. He wondered if he'd misunderstood or missed something in the planning of the drive north, the part that said one of the wranglers would ride ahead scouting for the best grass and water, something that would explain Herman's imminent and unexpected departure.

Herman extended his ungloved hand. Clairborne moved closer and took it in his own.

"Got some good news, and I'm going to see if it's true. Been good knowing you."

"Likewise, for sure," Clairborne said.

"Well..." Herman shoved his hand into his gauntlet, adjusted his hat, and turned his horse toward the bright pink light painting the bottoms of scattered clouds on the eastern horizon. He said nothing more, lightly spurred his horse, and waved once before riding off.

Clairborne watched him go as the cowboys walked around him to the dining hall, some of them turning to see what had so riveted Clairborne's attention. But nobody asked.

He watched Herman until he disappeared over the crest of a knoll and stood looking at the spot for long moments after he was gone. Scenes of the recent past came and went. He tried to recall conversations with Herman but could not retrieve anything but vague generalities, polite banter without depth or substance. So how was it then that he felt so suddenly bereft of the man's presence? They were not friends, per se. Not in the old definition of the word.

His stomach growled audibly. He felt hollow. Physically and emotionally empty. The first he understood. The second mystified him. It mystified and saddened him to think of how little he knew about the man who had just ridden off, how few were his efforts to understand Herman the way one should understand a man who had shared hardships and danger with him.

Perhaps that was it. They'd gone through a lot together, emerged from a life-or-death struggle together. Challenge, discomfort, fear, privation, courage. You share those with a man and you are forever linked to him, conjoined by an invisible bond unaffected by class or race, space or time, and indescribable to anyone lacking a similar experience.

He recalled his favorite play, Henry V.

"We few, we happy few, we band of brothers; For he to-day that sheds his blood with me shall be my brother."

He moved to the dining hall feeling as lonely as he'd ever been in his life.

After breakfast, he met with the Caudills and Isaac Steiner in the ranch office. Everyone else was in a good mood, excited by the beginning of the drive. Clairborne was still weighted down by Herman's sudden departure. He forced himself to pay attention to the detailed planning about an endeavor that was both military in nature and totally new to him.

The list of supplies alone was mind boggling, and getting it right—determining what was needed and leaving what was not—made the difference between acceptable hardship and unacceptable suffering, between muttering and mutiny. While it was clear that nothing could make a cattle drive "comfortable," there were some things, such as burlap bags of dried fruit, that could improve a camp meal and the drovers' morale.

Pounds of bacon and sugar and flour and coffee beans, a keg of nails, sheets of canvas, crates of tin plates, cups and cutlery, boxes of ammunition, a medicine kit, salt, lard, vinegar, baking soda, rolling tobacco, chewing tobacco (can be used as a poultice), jugs of molasses and castor oil and calomel, needles for stitching clothes and cowboys, a coffee grinder, lanterns (and two tins of coal oil), a shovel and a pick (for burying dead cowboys), an axe for splitting firewood (if and when any was encountered), a jar of sourdough starter, a massive cast-iron skillet, and a dutch oven.

All of this, along with the bedrolls belonging to the drovers and wranglers, was stuffed into an invaluable piece of equipment called a "chuck wagon." Over the last several days, Clairborne had watched the cook loading supplies into the strange-looking contraption, and on the morning before the drive, he took the opportunity to compliment Caudill on his practical invention.

"Gosh, I wish I could take credit for it. That alone would guarantee my place in Texas history. Nah, it was old Charlie Goodnight come up with it," Caudill said. "Tell you what, Tucker. Let's us go take a look at it."

Behind the kitchen, the Rocking C's cook, the perennially surly man called Biscuit fiddled with the coffee grinder.

"How's it going there, Biscuit?" Caudill asked, to which the cook replied, "Oh, it could be worse, I s'pose."

As Caudill walked around the wagon pointing out its innovations and attributes, Clairborne recognized the chuck wagon as the heart of the drive. If anything bad happened to it, the entire enterprise would be affected. According to Caudill, his friend Charlie Goodnight adapted an iron-axled army wagon by adding bentwood bows to support the canvas covering that blocked both sun and rain. The right side supported a barrel holding a two-day water supply. Most important was the large box, the "chuck box," at the rear of the wagon. Its trays and drawers and swing-down tables reminded Clairborne of the large desks that dominated the studies and libraries of the grand homes along the James River, an impression heightened when he saw Steiner open a small drawer into which he placed tally books, several pens and pencils, and two bottles of India ink.

On the drive, the chuck wagon would be at or near the head of the column, both to keep it out of the dust cloud the cattle generated and to allow its positioning at the site of each night's camp.

Clairborne also learned that when it came to dust, he and the younger Caudill would be eating a lot of it. While Steiner would ride at the head of the column in his capacity as foreman and trail boss, Clairborne and Caudill would each take a side of the herd and spend their days riding up and down its length, from head to tail; past riders at the point, the swing, the flank, and those miserable souls bringing up the rear, the cowboys riding "drag."

The drive north to the new rail yards would follow ancient game and Indian migration routes, pathways used by Texans like trader John Chisum, whose name would eventually forever be associated with cattle drives he never himself led. The Rocking C plan was straightforward: head north-northeast for a month, then send a scout ahead to locate Abilene. They would push thousands and thousands of cattle across the Red River, the Canadian, the North Canadian, the Cimarron, and finally the Kansas. Those were the watercourses with names. For each of them, a score more anonymous rivers, streams, and creeks flowed west to east across their route, each with its quicksands and bogs, water moccasins, and potential ambuscades.

Clairborne looked at the crude map Caudill spread on the chuck wagon's tailgate and noted two things: the amount of the map's surface that was empty, devoid of names or geographic detail, and the distances. After he'd ridden from Abilene, Kansas, to the Rocking C, the idea of repeating the trip rekindled the reservations he'd harbored and rehashed so many times. To make matters more problematic, this time he would make the trip without the company of the laconic, reliable Titus Herman.

"Damn," Clairborne thought. "This is not going to be fun."

August 13
North West Texas

End of the first day. I am writing in the twilight after wolfing down my dinner of biscuits, beans, a decent son of a bitch stew, and a slice of vinegar pie. I have to hand it to Biscuit since he somehow gets it all done by himself, from starting the fires to cleaning the utensils.

We've come 13 miles more or less since starting at about 5 am. We stopped at about 6:30 pm. It is now about 8 pm, and I am to ride around the herd once again before retrieving my bedroll from the chuck wagon and seeing how much shut-eye I can get. Not much, I bet.

One very pleasant surprise is the singing. It seems most of the hands have pretty fair voices and a range of ballads in their respective repertoires. It's quite pleasant to hear the soft voices of the hands tending the herd at night, called "night-hawking." Their singing is as calming to me as it is to the herd and the remuda, perhaps even more so.

One thing of concern: I don't know when I will get the chance to practice with my firearms, since any sudden report within earshot of the cattle could start a stampede, and I can't really just sneak away to do it. Oh, well.

I wonder how old Buck and Ajax are doing. I wonder if they miss me. Heck, I wonder if anybody misses me.

———✳———

Despite his fatigue, already great and bound to increase, Clairborne had no trouble opening his eyes before dawn on the sixth day of the drive.

He donned his hat before he raised himself up on his elbows and then raised his head to the heavens to find them obscured by solid cloud cover. The morning was cool. The only sounds came from Biscuit, derby askew on his bald pate, plug of chewing tobacco already firmly lodged in his cheek.

Clairborne looked around.

Most of the hands were taking advantage of their final five or six minutes of sleep. They were invisible, tucked under the folds of their bedrolls, from which they emitted a cacophony of snores.

As he finished surveying the sleeping cowboys, something caught his eye. In a single fluid motion, Clairborne reached for his gun belt, lifting the Colt halfway out of the holster and letting it fall back to reduce the friction.

What was it? What anomaly in this evanescent tranquility had snagged his awareness, whispering, "All is not as it should be?"

When he saw it, Clairborne could not connect the vision with his intellect. He simply could not believe his eyes.

On the first night of the drive, D. A. Bodeen had opened himself to merciless kidding about his fear of snakes when he carefully laid his horsehair lariat on the ground around his bedroll to form what he'd insisted was a foolproof perimeter against the intrusions of any and all serpents, particularly rattlesnakes.

"It's a natural fact," he insisted in his reedy, slightly irate voice. "Mr. No-Shoulders won't crawl over no horsehair rope 'cause it itches his belly too much. It's a natural fact, and y'all boys ought to follow my lead, less'n you wake up to find you got yourself some company during the night."

Some of the hands agreed and put down their ropes as well. Most did not and joshed their snake-fearing friends with sharp-edged humor for the first few days.

Of all the drovers, the large western diamondback rattle-snake had selected D. A. Bodeen's bedroll on the far side of the camp as its resting place. Even in the weak light, the distinctive black diamonds stood out against the mottled olive green body with its fist-sized, triangular head.

The serpent rested in the depression formed by Bodeen's sprawled legs.

Clairborne's mind raced even as his body was paralyzed.

"I can't move or yell. I can't shoot it without hitting Bodeen. If I try to get a shovel...Christ, what can I do?" he asked himself.

Events overtook deliberations.

A cowboy three away from Bodeen awakened and sat up, his motion and noise stirring the serpent, which immediately sent the easily recognizable signal that it was perturbed.

The dry rattle quickly accelerated into a buzz as more cow-boys awoke and scrambled from their bedrolls.

In the depths of his dream, Bodeen's gentle and beloved grandfather morphed into a snake, but a snake with his grand-father's voice. So disturbing was the transformation of whom he loved most into what he hated most, Bodeen's mind willfully

terminated the hideous dream. The arrival of full consciousness brought with it simultaneous awareness—and disbelief.
His body involuntarily heaved before he regained control,
thinking, "I gotta be still so's somebody can get it off 'o me."

But it was too late.

Bodeen's sudden start triggered the rattler's panic, and its
rapid slither over the cowboy's right leg was more than he could
stand. Grasping the bedroll from the inside, he tried to rip it away
from his body, using the tarp and blankets to shield himself from
the fangs he knew were bared if not already arcing toward him.

The rattler's first strike hit the bedroll as it was lifted from
the ground, fangs piercing the layers of fabric but not reaching
Bodeen's flesh. The snake was thrown into the air as Bodeen's
body emerged amid inchoate cries and curses, and onto the
empty ground around him that had been hurriedly vacated
by his buddies. His right foot snagged in the folds. He saw the
rattler, its black-rimmed yellow eyes less than two feet away.
Without thought of consequences, Bodeen lashed out with his
right hand to push the snake away, made contact with its muscular, dry body, and instinctively gripped it to heave it anywhere
but where it was. His fingers closed around the rattler two feet
below its head, which was less than two feet away from Bodeen's
face. It struck again, both fangs penetrating the taut skin of the
right side of Bodeen's neck, one fang finding the carotid artery.

The rattler's first strike had been "dry," a defensive maneu-
ver meant to discourage a foe and conserve its supply of diffi-
cult-to-produce venom.

The second strike was meant to kill. Constriction of muscles
surrounding the venom glands on each side of the rattlesnake's

head pumped the entire store of hemotoxic poison into D. A. Bodeen's circulatory system.

He broke free of the bedroll and scrambled backward on his hands and feet like some ungainly land crab.

"It got me, boys! Oh lord, I'm a goner. It got me. It got me good," he said, coming to rest against a keg, the serpent separating and seeking its escape.

Four cowboys and Clairborne aimed their weapons at the snake but held their fire lest they stampede the cattle. The hand nearest the chuck wagon grabbed a shovel and pursued the fleeing serpent, missing it with his first three swings, connecting on the fourth, fifth, sixth, and seventh.

The cowboys rushed to Bodeen as he sank into shock even before the venom began breaking down his blood cells.

"Oh boys, this is a dastardly fate," he said, looking up at his friends, tears coursing the deep creases radiating from his soft gray eyes.

"Dilly, you get my saddle. Vern, see that Ma gets my wages. Oh boys, oh boys, I'm so sorry to go this way."

Cowboys knelt around him, trying to make him comfortable. Biscuit arrived with the medicine box, looked at the small punctures oozing droplets of Bodeen's blood, made eye contact with Steiner and Clairborne, and slowly shook his head.

There was nothing to be done.

Bodeen knew that as well.

"Dang, but I hate to go out this way. A snakebite. Dang." He looked at his friend Dilly. "Lord, I hate not saying goodbye to old Sam. I'd surely like to ride that old horse one last time. We come all the way from Indiana together. Take care of him, Dilly. Please."

He choked and convulsed.

Clairborne took Steiner's sleeve.

"We could give him laudanum, enough laudanum to, ah, to make him comfortable."

Steiner understood Clairborne's implicit suggestion. Better for Bodeen to slide into permanent, eternal peace from an overdose of narcotic than to endure the agony that would wrack him with prolonged, unimaginable pain.

He nodded at Clairborne. "Get the laudanum, Biscuit," Steiner said softly to the cook, who retrieved the brown, corked bottle from the medicine box.

Steiner knelt beside the stricken cowboy, now wrapped in a blanket and held by his pals Dilly and Vern.

"D. A., I'm sorry, but there ain't anything we can do to help you. That old snake got you good, just like you said."

Bodeen nodded. "I know. I just hate to go this way is all."

Steiner used the fingers of his left hand to wipe away the droplets of blood from the puncture wounds. In his right hand, he held the bottle in front of Bodeen's face.

"Know what this is, D. A.? It's laudanum."

"Don't know laudanum. Will it make me better?"

"No, D. A. You're a goner. This'll just make it easier for you to go, probably a lot easier, but it's up to you."

"How's that, boss?"

"I can't give this to you less'n you ask me to, you understand. I just can't do that without you asking me."

Understanding visibly transformed D. A. Bodeen's sunburned features.

"Oh. Oh sure. Mighty fine of you, boss. Wouldn't happen to have any rye for me to wash it down with, I suppose," Bodeen said with an incongruous smile.

"Sorry, D. A."

"OK. Well then." Bodeen looked around at the bareheaded cowhands encircling the spot of Texas plains where he would lie for the rest of time.

"Adios, boys. Feller never rode with a better bunch than y'all, that's for dead certain." Again, the incongruous smile. "As many times I said it, 'at's the first time it actually was—dead certain, that is."

Bodeen looked at Steiner.

"Well, I done talked myself thirsty, boss. Guess I'm ready for that drink you offered."

"Sure, D. A."

Steiner raised Bodeen's head and tipped the bottle into the cowboy's parted lips.

Bodeen gagged.

"Hoooeee. Worse 'n Ma's castor oil."

He'd swallowed nearly a third of the bottle.

Steiner laid him back down, stood, and handed the bottle back to the cook.

In a matter of minutes, D. A. Bodeen, in his nineteenth year and out of French Lick, Indiana, died, but not before saying in a voice barely audible to his friends who cradled him, "Old Sam. Old Sam."

—*∿*—

Eight days after burying Bodeen, two days after crossing the first major river, and one day after killing two wolves shadowing the herd, Clairborne left camp after breakfast and rode a little more than a mile to the rear of the column.

Pulling up to a low rise offering a sweeping perspective of the plains, the herd, and the riders dotted around its amorphous edge, Clairborne stopped and leaned forward in his saddle.

Early morning was his favorite time of day. The dew-damp earth smells, the calls from largely unseen birds, the respite from constant winds, and, of course, the coolness refreshed him physically and mentally—emotionally too. When he did think of it, at times like this one, alone on a hilltop, Clairborne recognized that the whole early morning experience was really about optimism. "We made it through yesterday. We're one day closer to Abilene. I am healthy and wealthy." He was also aware of how unusual it was for a man of his age to give much thought to health, since most didn't until it was gone. The death and discomfort he'd seen since crossing the Mississippi provided such a sharp contrast with health and happiness, he'd be a fool not to be aware of it.

"Now what is that?" he said aloud to himself. Standing in his stirrups, he reached back, unfastened the flap on the right saddlebag, and removed the telescope case, then the telescope itself.

Raising the polished brass tube to his eye, he focused on the distant anomaly that caught his attention. Smoke. Very light but clearly smoke rising in a thin, straight column that would not be visible in a few more minutes when the angle of light from the rising sun changed from ninety degrees to something less acute.

"Campfire. White men for sure. No Indian would give himself away like that. But who?" he asked himself. "Could be innocent coincidence, buff hunters, maybe a cavalry unit; hell, maybe just a bunch of settlers wandering across the plains. Maybe," he thought, "maybe." But the tickle at the bottom of his hairline, the slightly accelerated pulse said otherwise. There was only one way to deal with uncertainty out here. Determine firsthand the nature of the issue. But not without first consulting men with a lot more experience.

Clairborne studied the terrain. He would need to relate precisely where he'd seen evidence of someone on their back trail—for that was where they were, he'd realized. The smoke was rising from a spot they'd passed yesterday, about midafternoon, he judged from the distance, a half day's plod with the herd, maybe three hours for unencumbered riders.

He turned and spurred, wanting to catch Caudill and Steiner before they rode off for the day.

Riding at a brisk trot so as not to spook the cattle, he arrived at the chuck wagon to find Caudill already gone but Steiner standing beside Biscuit, sipping the last of his morning coffee.

In keeping with cow camp etiquette, Clairborne dismounted a respectful distance from the chuck wagon and walked the last thirty feet.

"You look like a man who's seen something, Tucker," Steiner said with a rare grin.

Accepting a cup of steaming brew from the cook, Clairborne pointed back in the direction from which he'd come.

"Smoke. Small fire, but smoke for sure. On our back trail, say maybe three, four hours away."

Other hands, bringing their dirty plates to the chuck wagon before starting their shifts, paused to listen. Steiner wasn't having it.

"You boys go on. You ain't getting paid to beat your gums nor stretch your ears. Get on, now."

Turning back to Clairborne, he said, "Let's you and me go find Sam."

On the way, Steiner listened to what few additional details Clairborne could provide. Then he asked what Clairborne thought should be done.

"Well, I just don't like getting a crick in my neck looking back all day. I'd rather just know what's back there one way or the other, I guess."

"So you'd do what, exactly?"

"Send two men back to scout it."

And those two would be?"

"Well, seems to me I'm about the most expendable," Clairborne said with a smile. "Baca's a dang good tracker, so he seems a good choice."

"Tell that to Sam," Steiner said with a brisk nod. "I agree."

It wasn't exactly praise, but Clairborne felt as if it were. He liked that Steiner asked his opinion and didn't beat around the bush when he liked what he heard.

Sam was riding toward them on the west side of the herd after checking the man riding point.

He waved at the two familiar horsemen, and as the distance closed enough to allow conversation, he leaned forward and said, "What's up, gentlemen?"

"Tell him, Tucker," Steiner said.

Caudill listened quietly as Clairborne repeated what he'd seen and how he proposed to deal with the development.

"You know, we just can't ignore something like this, hoping it's OK," Caudill said. Turning to Steiner he asked, "You don't think the boys'll think less of me for not going back myself, for sending Tucker and Baca to do it?"

Steiner snorted. "I don't. You're the boss. You're supposed to make the good decisions, not do everything yourself. Sorry. No disrespect meant."

"No, no. None taken, Isaac. I appreciate your candor. It's just that I really do want to go myself."

"'Course you do. Heck, so do I, but that's why we got this here experienced plainsman with us," Steiner said with a second rare smile and a sweep of his gauntleted hand toward Clairborne. "We'll just send our trusty scout back there and sip a cool lemonade while we wait for his report."

Caudill and Clairborne laughed.

"Well, aside from the fact we ain't got no lemonade nor any way to cool it if we did, that sounds like a mighty fine plan," Caudill said.

Clairborne wheeled his horse. "I'll get Baca and get started then."

"He's riding north-side flank. Hey, Tucker," Steiner said. "One other thing. Get back here before nightfall one way or the other even if it means you gotta break it off before you got all the answers. I don't want to stop the drive to come looking for you."

"Sure thing, boss. Sure thing. Save me some stew."

Luis Baca stopped and waited for Clairborne to ride up the rise.

"Morning, Luis. Como estas?"

"Bien. Bastante bien," he said as he retrieved his canteen.

"Wonder if you'd care to ride back a ways with me to, ah, do a little scouting, see who might be following us."

Baca shrugged and looked south, back at their massive and unmistakable trail.

"You see something?"

"Smoke."

"No a prairie fire?"

"No. Campfire. White man's campfire, but not a real big one."

Baca understood that Clairborne was not formally asking if he would go with him. It was an order wrapped in the courtesy of a theoretical option to refuse. He also understood that Clairborne had cleared the break in routine with Steiner or Caudill, maybe both.

"Sure," he said. "We need to take enough water, I think. No water back there. And rifles. Better go back to camp and get them."

Baca was right. Clairborne mentally berated himself for not thinking of it. "Dang it," he thought. "That's just a stupid oversight, you dumb-ass greenhorn."

But he contained his self-disgust, saying only, "Yeah, I gotta fetch my Henry and a box of cartridges. Let's go."

On any endeavor as monotonous as a cattle drive, a deviation from routine is instantly noted by everyone. The hands saw a brisk trot back to the chuck wagon, the filling of canteens, and the retrieval of a long gun rested across Clairborne's saddlebow.

Rumors of what was up spread through the ranks of the Rocking C cowboys like a dose of castor oil. Anything that could be equated with a threat raised the level of awareness, and each hand swiveled his head more than normal to detect anything amiss.

Clairborne and Baca trotted to the south end of the herd and then spurred into a canter once clear of the man riding drag. Several of the hands stood in their stirrups to watch then go, earning a rebuke from Steiner to "keep your eyes on the cows. You ain't gettin' paid to sight-see."

A mile and a half on the back trail, the two riders slowed to a trot. Two hours later, they stopped and dismounted on the north side of a low rise. Leading their horses, the two walked to just below the crest, where Clairborne grasped his Henry and handed his reins to Baca, who understood that he was to remain in place while Clairborne crawled to the top with his spyglass.

Just before topping the rise, Clairborne looked for the largest bush, and seeing one to his left, crawled up to its base, flattened on his stomach, and started to raise his telescope before he realized he didn't need to.

Four riders were heading toward the herd at a brisk walk. Mexicans. Absolutely no doubt about it. Leading two packhorses as well. Raising the telescope to his eye, he easily picked out the man in charge. Not only was he riding slightly in front of the other three, but his clothing and his tack were far more elaborate, albeit just as practical as that of the others. Three of the four were wearing side arms. He couldn't see the outside of the fourth but assumed he was heeled as well. This didn't square with what he'd learned from Antonio, that Mexican vaqueros didn't always carry pistols as did their American counterparts. Bandits? Not likely. But who, then? Clairborne had casually observed the Rocking C's Mexican riders, noting few wore pistols away from the bunkhouse as did the Americans. Most of the vaqueros, Clairborne observed, Antonio included, didn't even own one.

Clairborne quickly recalled where Baca fit into that issue, just as quickly remembering the Remington Navy with the bone grips he'd seen Baca strap on each morning. Baca also had that big-bore Remington rolling block rifle he'd used so effectively at Spanish Wells.

"OK," Clairborne thought. "Four of them. Two of us. We got the surprise and high ground at least for a little while longer." He also recognized that the intent of the Mexicans was clear. They were following the herd. Why was not evident, but Clairborne's instinct told him to suspect the worst—just as, he recalled, Wild Billy Martin had counseled with his dying breath.

Clairborne considered shooting them from ambush.

"Drop two of them if I'm lucky, then shoot their horses. They got no cover. It'd be easy."

He focused again on the leader. He was a fine-looking man who sat his bay as if born to the saddle. His refined attire spoke of elegance even through its coat of trail dust. The ivory grip of a pistol worn butt forward flashed from under the rider's short jacket, the edges of which were heavily embroidered.

The more he observed the group, the more certain he was that it represented trouble, and the more certain he was that when that trouble came, it would not be in the form of an attack from cover of either terrain or darkness. He was certain the man he watched would make his casus belli known; therefore, he was just as certain, for reasons purely instinctual, that the man was honorable. To shoot him from ambush would be dishonorable.

Clairborne crawled back a few feet, stood, and motioned Baca forward.

"Four riders. Mexican. Coming right ahead. Armed. Looks to me like they've been riding a pretty far piece. Two packhorses."

Baca kicked the dirt with the toe of his boot. "This don't feel good to me. I don't know why, but this don't feel good to me."

"Me neither. Go back and get Steiner and some boys and get back here quick as you can."

Baca's eyes bulged. "What? You damn crazy? What are you going to do?"

"Talk to them. Stall them till you come back with a party. Now get going."

Baca mounted.

"Jesus, Maria, and Jose. I tell you, this is stupid. They shoot you."

"I don't think so, and I can't think of anything else to do, so just get the hell back here as quick as you can."

Baca turned his horse and bolted, quirting his horse hard, not the normal, perfunctory, painless taps. The horse reacted with frantic speed.

Clairborne watched him go for a moment, mounted, and rode to the top of the hill, where he'd be exposed to the riders but could make a sudden retreat if he detected hostile intent.

The Mexicans slowed the instant he appeared. While still a half mile away, the leader saw Clairborne's raised right hand and spurred forward, leaving the others sitting their horses. Clairborne held his position above as the leader approached.

Just before they were within speaking distance, Clairborne berated himself for retaining his rifle, rested across the saddle, instead of returning it to the scabbard and relying on his Colt for any fast, short-range work. Too late now.

"Hola," he said.

The leader smiled and stopped his horse.

"Usted habla espanol, entonces." It was a statement rather than a question.

"Muy poco. Ingles y frances pero muy poco espanol."

The man's smile broadened, and he said in excellent French, "And where would a gringo learn French? New Orleans, perhaps?"

Clairborne was amazed and delighted with this unexpected encounter with culture.

"Paris, Normandy. Rouen, Chartres."

The man rode forward and removed his gloves. He held out his right hand and continued in flawless French. "Elfredo Sanchez Gonzales y Fermin, at your service, monsieur...?"

"Clairborne. Tucker Lightfoot Clairborne, late of Virginia by way of Paris."

Unbidden to do so, the man secured his canteen in his left hand and extended it to Clairborne, who instantly told himself, "if I take it with my right hand, I can't swing the Henry to defend myself."

Accepting the canteen with his left hand, he raised it to his lips but not high enough to block his view of the Mexican.

"Merci," he said returning the canteen. "You are a long way from home, it seems."

The Mexican drank, plugged the canteen, and nodded.

"Yes. Unfortunately, I am. But soon, God willing, we go back."

Clairborne wondered what "soon" meant. A day, a week, a month? But he strongly sensed the answer had something to do with the herd.

"Well, as you know, my herd is just ahead. I invite you to join us for dinner if you'd care to partake of our meager fare."

"A very gracious invitation. Most appreciated."

An awkward silence ensued before Clairborne asked, "It's presumptuous of me to inquire, but may I know where you acquired your excellent French?"

"Not at all. A Jesuit monastery near Salamanca. I was five years studying for the priesthood."

"Salamanca, Spain?"

"Yes. You know of it?"

"Only by legend. A beautiful place, rich with history and culture, I believe."

The Mexican removed his black, richly embroidered sombrero and ran his hand through his gleaming black hair. Clairborne noted that aside from the man's mustache and goatee, his unlined face was clean shaven, unlike his own.

Five years of Jesuit training. That was a significant commitment, a large chunk of the young man's life to date. What could have happened to cause such a dramatic change of direction? It would be impolite to inquire.

"Shall we return to the herd, monsieur?"

"But of course."

They engaged in idle banter until they saw the dust announcing the arrival of the Rocking C cowboys led by Steiner.

Clairborne turned to his "guest" and said, "We didn't know your intentions, so we thought it best to expect the worst. If you'll excuse me, I will inform them there is no danger so they may return to their duties."

The Mexican smiled. "I would do the same. Please don't delay on my account."

Steiner reined in at Clairborne's casual approach.

"Let the boys go back, Isaac. We won't need them."

"Good. You heard him, boys. Get back to the herd." Turning back to Clairborne and looking over his shoulder at the party of Mexicans, he asked, "Where are they going?"

Clairborne wiped his brow.

"I don't know exactly. If I were a betting man, I'd say they're interested in something or someone..."

It came to him in a flash.

"Son of a bitch," he said softly. "Antonio. I bet they've come for Antonio."

Steiner turned to face him. "What? What'd you say?"

"They've come for Antonio. To kill him. He killed the brother of the leader."

"They tell you that?"

"No. But Antonio told me once he came north because he killed his patron's son—over a woman, of course."

Both men lapsed into silence. Both thought about the consequences of a gunfight. Both furiously sought an alternative. Neither could come up with one.

"Well, I sure can't let them have him," Steiner said. "Mexican justice is same as ours. Hang 'em or shoot 'em. And we're already one man short of what we started with."

Clairborne shook his head slowly.

"Isaac. There's something here we're missing."

"Like what?"

"I don't know. I mean, why'd they just ride up—to a bigger bunch than their own? Why not just pick him off while he's night-hawking?"

The Mexicans sat their horses while Clairborne and Steiner talked out of earshot. When Clairborne looked over at them, he made eye contact with Gonzales, who reacted by riding over to them.

In French, Clairborne said, "Monsieur, this is our foreman, Isaac Steiner." Then in English, he said, "Isaac, this gentleman is Elfredo Sanchez Gonzales y Fermin." The two solemnly shook hands.

"Monsieur Clairborne," Gonzales said, "would you tell this gentleman I would like to have a private conversation with him, and if he agrees, would you be so good as to translate for us?"

"He wants to parlay and wants me to translate," Clairborne said matter-of-factly, withholding his opinion that it was the best course of action.

"Good idea," Steiner said, dismounting.

"It feels good to walk a little. We have been in the saddle for three months," Gonzales said. Clairborne translated.

"What brings you here?" Steiner asked with characteristic directness.

"That is what I want to discuss. I came for one of your men." Before Clairborne could translate, Gonzales added, "A man who killed my brother."

Clairborne wanted to blurt out, "After your brother molested his woman" but decided to hold his piece and let Steiner talk. He noticed the Mexican held Steiner's eyes and spoke with a distinct sadness, even weariness.

"Well, I'm sorry about your brother for sure, but I can't let you just ride up and take one of my men," Steiner said.

"You have already lost one man, I know. We saw the grave. I understand. That is why I have a bargain to make with you."

Clairborne was intrigued. He looked at Steiner, who half-smiled as he absent-mindedly dug the dirt with the toe of his boot.

"I don't think there's any deal to be made about this, senor. I'm not giving up one of my men."

The Mexican, using his quirt, pointed to the three men who came with him.

"You see those three? They are the best vaqueros in all Northern Mexico. Born on my family's ranch. Any one is as good as your Antonio. The old one there," he singled out the only one of the wiry riders with gray hair flowing out from his sombrero. "That one taught Antonio horses and cows and la riata."

"Why are you telling me this?" Steiner asked.

Gonzales folded his arms across his chest and turned away to face the horizon. He was quiet for moments before he spoke again.

"I was training for the church; being the second-oldest son, I was to go into the church. Then this. I have two younger brothers, but now I am the oldest. In our land, when someone kills your brother, there is no choice. I was called home, first to learn my new responsibilities at the ranch. Then, once I had learned them, it was time to find my brother's killer."

"And do what with him?" Steiner asked.

Gonzales turned to face the Americans. He smiled, but it was a smile of infinite, palpable resignation. "I have two brothers, sir. If I do not do this, they will come, one after the other, until it is done."

Like the sun emerging from a cloud, it became clear to Clairborne the man did not want to be here and that he did not want to kill anyone, even the man who had killed his brother.

Steiner put his hands on his hips and looked down. "Like I said, I'm just sorry as hell about your brother, but I cannot allow one of my hands to be taken away. Sorry. Just can't."

"What if I didn't take him?"

"What do you mean?"

"We fight. Right here."

Clairborne interrupted. "Antonio doesn't have a gun."

"I know. We would use the weapon he and my brother fought with: knives." Gonzales moved to stand directly in front of Steiner. "We fight with knives. No one else around. Just the two of us. He wins, my vaqueros bury me here and go back to tell my brothers. I win, I leave Hernando with you. He goes with you in Antonio's place. You pay him Antonio's wages. I give you my word, he is a better vaquero, and he will stay. My word."

Clairborne felt his gut surge. This was about honor—the Mexican's honor, Steiner's honor. But the offer seemed almost reasonable. Especially considering that there seemed no alternative. He could see Steiner was seriously considering it, turning over every possible benefit and liability of a deal that would inevitably result in death.

Clairborne looked back at Gonzales for a moment, just in time to see the Mexican stiffen. Turning to see what had caused the man to go rigid, he saw and immediately understood. Antonio was dismounting fifteen feet away, holding the reins to his horse.

No one spoke.

Reacting to their individual instincts and experience, Clairborne and Steiner straightened, consciously slowed their breathing, and flexed their fingers. Both also slowly moved their eyes to fix the positions of each man within relevant range.

Finally Antonio broke the awkward silence.

"You have come a long way, Senor. I expected you."

"Yes, and now I am here."

Clairborne's Spanish was good enough for him to follow the exchange.

Another period of silence, and dread ensued.

Steiner slapped the tongues of his quirt against his chaps.

"Gentlemen, let's be clear about one thing. I'm the trail boss of this outfit, and there will be no gunplay anywhere around this herd. And as I said, Mr. Gonzales, you are not taking one of my hands. It's just not going to happen. Do you understand that?"

Clairborne started to translate, but Gonzales held up his hand and said in French, "I understand even with my poor

English. I understand what you have to do, Mr. Steiner. I would do exactly the same in your place. But I ask you to recognize that any man of honor such as yourself, Monsieur Clairborne, or your hands for that matter, would do precisely what I am doing, what I have to do, as well."

When Clairborne finished translating, Steiner removed his hat and rubbed his forehead, a gesture Clairborne had come to realize as an indication the foreman was aggravated.

Then Sam Caudill rode up and dismounted.

The young Texan understood before a word was said that something bad was taking place. He could tell by posture alone.

When no one spoke, Caudill said, "Somebody want to tell me what's going on? Isaac?"

Steiner shook his head. "This man has come here to kill Antonio. Antonio killed his brother. I told him we won't give up one of our men, so here we are."

Caudill looked at the trim Mexican, his men, their horses and instantly understood the situation. He also instantly recognized a counterpart in the other young man, who, like him, was greatly blessed and greatly burdened.

He removed his glove and extended his hand. "Sam Caudill of the Rocking C."

Gonzales took the extended hand, introduced himself, and slightly bowed his head.

Caudill looked around. "I propose we discuss matters over coffee, perhaps in a location that allows some privacy. You are my guest if you care to stay."

Clairborne translated, surprised and impressed by the extemporaneous diplomacy unfolding in the Texas cow camp.

It seemed to Clairborne that Gonzales was relieved, whether because of a welcome delay of the inevitable or some vague chance it could be avoided. Whatever the reason, Gonzales accepted.

Caudill smiled.

"Tucker, I'm going to need you to translate. Isaac, I need you too." Turning back to Clairborne, he said, "Please inform my guest that he is welcome to bring along two of his men if he feels the need."

Again, Clairborne was impressed by the impromptu diplomacy. It was clear Gonzales was as well.

"No. Thank you, but that will not be necessary. We are all men of honor."

Caudill led the group to a small seep about a mile from the herd. The constant wind was warm; the herd-trampled, sunbaked grasses emitted a sweet, dry bouquet. Caudill and Clairborne picketed their horses. Gonzales and Antonio allowed their mounts to graze freely.

No one spoke. Caudill sat down. Clairborne waited to see what Gonzales would do. Clairborne recalled the term "hidalgo" and had to think a moment before he remembered why the word came to mind.

"Hidalgo," he recalled, was short for "hijo de algo," son-of-someone, a catch-all term for aristocracy, landed gentry, someone with hereditary claim to special status. It occurred to him that up until three years ago, the definition of hidalgo also applied to him.

Finally, Gonzales turned and sat. Antonio remained standing, unsure of what to do or say. Caudill said, "Antonio, join us."

No one spoke.

Finally, Caudill said, "Senor, I understand how important honor is to your people. It is important to any self-respecting man, but I really do understand that you Mexicans feel compelled to seek redress in such matters."

Before Clairborne finished translating, Gonzales smiled.

"And 'my people,' as you call them, understand how bellicose you Americans are, how you feel compelled to fight when you think your honor has been slighted in any way."

Caudill looked confused.

"What do you mean? I don't see the relevance of what you said."

Gonzales shrugged. "It's that you said you think all Mexicans are driven by honor above all else. I wanted you to understand that we think Americans are driven by the need for war."

The three Americans present imperceptibly stiffened.

"How so?"

"Well, first you fought the British, then you fought the British again, no? Then you almost fought the French, then you fought the Barbary pirates, then you fought us, and when you ran out of foreigners to fight, you fought each other. All this within little more than half a century. It is impressive, no?"

Caudill looked at Steiner and Clairborne. Each smiled sheepishly and resisted the urge to nod in reluctant agreement.

"We could sit here till doomsday talking about history, I guess, but we need to resolve the issue we face here," Caudill said.

"I agree, senor," Gonzales said. "May I suggest that we define our objective as clearly as possible, and in that regard, may I suggest that our objective is resolution of the issue with the least violence and bloodshed."

Caudill shook his head. "No. I cannot accept that there will be violence no matter what. We need to avoid getting anybody hurt here."

"Alas. Would that it were possible."

"Senor Gonzales, I have almost forty men. You have three. Let's be realistic."

Antonio, speaking halting English and no French but understanding the subject and drift of the negotiations, raised his hand. "Senores, may I speak?"

Caudill and Gonzales nodded in unison.

"I am the problem, no? I know, el Senor Gonzales is right when he says his brothers each will come in time if he fails to recover his family honor." He stroked his quirt slowly. "There is no other way. We must fight. I win, I live and can go farther away. I die, you get a fine vaquero to take my place." Antonio shrugged. "There is no dishonor in this." He faced Caudill. "No one will think you failed to protect your men. They will understand."

Caudill looked at Steiner, who didn't raise his eyes from the ground.

Caudill asked, "You mean you want to fight, Antonio?"

An abrupt laugh burst from the young vaquero. "No, Senor. It is the last thing I want, but it is the only thing I can do, he and I can do."

Caudill looked at Gonzales and was briefly hopeful a peaceful resolution was still possible because he saw open admiration of the Mexican's face as he regarded and clearly understood his countryman, Antonio.

"You are a man, Antonio," Gonzales said softly in Spanish.

Antonio shrugged. "We are all men here."

No one spoke.

Caudill, Clairborne, and Gonzales gazed at the countryside. Steiner and Antonio stared at the ground.

Caudill stood and put his hands on his hips. "You two are telling me you can't settle this any other way. You gotta go hacking and slicing on each other to settle this."

No one spoke.

"All right. How are you going to do this? Thunder and lightning! This is crazy," Caudill yelled, yielding to his frustration.

Gonzales stood. "I need to speak to my men. Then..." he nodded at Antonio, "he and I ride to someplace where we can resolve our differences."

Clairborne studied the impact of the Mexican's words on Caudill's countenance. He was surprised when Caudill sighed and shrugged.

"All right. OK. You two want to make peace with your maker," he said, and then waved his hand in frustration. "I'm not telling you to. I just assume you want to is all."

"Of course. Before and after," Gonzales said. Facing Clairborne, he added, "So years of study in Holy Mother Church comes to this. Someone dies in agony in this godforsaken..."

The unfinished sentence, begun with an ironic tone that trailed off into infinite sadness, spoke to Clairborne of the churning, the clash of values, and the notions of duty and honor grinding silently but perceptibly in the Mexican's heart. Duty to family or the teachings of the church? Honor to his father or to his Father? Was this killing or murder? Clairborne understood that ultimately, for the young Mexican patrician, it was a matter of eternity, of heaven or hell.

A feeling of utter impotence drained Clairborne of both physical and emotional strength. He knew one of these two men would soon be dead. He liked them both. Truly liked them both. He gripped his palms into fists, slowly beating them on his thighs.

"I go to speak to my men," Gonzales said.

The Rocking C men watched him go.

Antonio retrieved his horse and walked it back to where the others stood.

He removed his sombrero and hung it over the saddle horn. Clairborne realized how infrequently he had seen the young Mexican without his battered hat. He also realized Antonio was almost pretty, that his features were soft and well formed, his facial hair sparse but not scraggly, his cheekbones high and prominent, his eyes almost equine in their liquid darkness.

Antonio removed his fringed gauntlet and extended his hand to Caudill.

"I'm sorry, senor. I know this is losing you a day. I am sorry." He also wanted to say that he appreciated the way he'd been treated at the Rocking C, that he had thought he would stay with the Caudills for a long, long time. But he decided not to say anything more. To do so might acknowledge that he expected to die. On reflection, he really didn't want to die, but the truth was, in his gut, he suspected there was a very good chance this was the day. His last day.

He thought of his mother and quickly forced her from his mind lest the sadness weaken him.

The voice of his young boss brought him back to the present.

"You still don't have to do this, Antonio."

"Thank you, senor, and no disrespect, but I do." Wanting to avoid further discussion with Caudill, Antonio turned to Steiner and shook his hand. He smiled as he said, "This is trouble, but not so much as last winter's snows, I think."

Steiner nodded. "Not that bad, I guess. Just get this over with and get back to the cows, OK?"

Finally, Antonio turned to Clairborne. "Watch your fingers when you take a dally, Tucker," he said with a wan smile.

"Oh I got that lesson. Trust me on that," Clairborne said. "Like Isaac said, just get this over. I got lots more to learn, hombre."

Abruptly, Antonio swung into his saddle. "I'll wait for him there," he said, pointing to a low knoll a quarter mile away. He rode off at a walk. Clairborne thought it odd that Antonio never donned his sombrero.

The three Americans mounted and waited for Gonzales's return.

Less than five minutes later, he rode toward them, but when he saw Antonio sitting his horse in the distance, Gonzales turned to ride directly toward him, waving once at the Americans.

He and Antonio seemed to have a brief conversation before disappearing over the top of the knoll.

"How much time we give them?" Caudill asked no one in particular.

"Much time as they need, boss," Steiner said, stating precisely what Clairborne believed to be the right response.

Since none of them had a timepiece available, they had only the angle of the sun to tell how much time passed. It was not long before the tension mounted, going rapidly from underlying to overt.

"Isaac, I want you to get back to the herd. Make sure everything's OK," Caudill said. It was the last thing Steiner wanted to do, but he knew it was the right thing to do. Rumor control, if nothing else, required an authority figure at the herd.

"OK, boss."

Long minutes later, Caudill said, "Tucker, what do you think?"

Clairborne was thinking about an alley in Nashville, about how the only knife fight he'd known was over in mere seconds.

"I think it's over. It can't be still going on."

"Oh lord, that's just what I was thinking. Oh lordy, this is bad," Caudill said as he spurred his horse to a flat-out gallop.

They slowed at the summit.

The Mexicans were both on their backs; less than five feet separated their prostrate forms. Antonio's intestines were already covered with flies. The Toledo-steel dagger that had slit open his stomach dully glinted on the ground beside him.

A five-inch-long laceration of Gonzales's chest had transformed his handmade cambric shirt into a carmine, sticky mass. Antonio's bone-handled, double-edged blade protruded from the inside of Gonzales's left thigh.

Antonio was clearly dead. Gonzales was moving, although just barely, his right foot seeking a purchase on the grass slick with dark, drying blood.

The Americans hurriedly dismounted and moved to his side, Clairborne slipping his hand under the Mexican's curly locks.

Gonzales's eyes were unfocused and showed no awareness of their arrival.

Clairborne looked at the chest wound, long but shallow, thus not deadly. The thigh was another matter. The blade had found an artery. It was almost over.

He wiped some of the speckled blood from Gonzales's forehead and cheek. The man's eyes focused on the American, a connection was made, a spark in the gathering darkness of the Mexican's Jesuit-trained mind.

In flawless French, Elfredo Sanchez Gonzales y Fermin said, "Please mark my grave so my family can find me." A small sigh, and the eyes slowly dilated.

Clairborne gently closed the lids.

"Adieu, mon frere," he said.

He stood. He looked at Antonio, then back at Gonzales, then at the sky. Numbers filled his thoughts, odds, calculations, percentages. He wished he were better at numbers. If he could manipulate numbers more efficiently, he could use them to answer the question gnawing at him with sudden, persistent relentlessness. "Is this normal?" he thought. "Is all this death normal? How long since I left Virginia? How many people have I seen die since then? What does that work out to on a daily average? If it continues at this rate, how many more people will I see die in the next year, decade?

"I don't think you can get used to death like you get used to dust or dryness or dreariness," he thought. "Being lonely, sad, scared all the time is one thing. Being around death all the time is something else."

He realized no one had spoken for quite some time and felt no compunction to break the silence. The wind flipped Gonzales's sombrero over, then flipped it up on its brim and sent it rolling across the short grass. Clairborne wondered how long it would be identifiable as a hat before the elements turned it back into elements. He really wanted to sit down and put his arms on his knees for a while.

"We got to get these men buried. We got a herd to move," Caudill said.

Clairborne liked the young man for his focus on what had to be done, for the order of his thoughts. Work, attention to details, would allow them to leave behind the bodies as surely as the wind would remove the sombrero from the scene.

There was a problem, though, one that had no immediate solution. Gonzales had asked that his resting place be marked in a way that someone could find it later. Clairborne looked around. No rocks or stones. No trees, no downed timber.

"We need to mark his grave," Clairborne said. "That's what he asked me. I don't see how we can do that, what we can use that'll last a couple of years or so."

"His saddle. We'll wrap his saddle in a spare tarp and put it on the grave. Best marker a horseman could hope for," Caudill said.

Clairborne marveled at the speed and logic of the decision.

"And just in case somebody should come upon it before his family, we'll put a note in a jar tellin' folks to leave it be."

They rode back to the herd, where Caudill sent for Luis Baca to translate for Gonzales's men.

August 1868
Indian Territory

Elfredo Sanchez Gonzales y Fermin lies beneath the prairie grass, his resting place marked by his beautiful saddle. Antonio Jimenez rests beneath a mound of dirt that will disappear within a few months. Honor took both of them before their time. No, perhaps not. Who am I to say how much time each was allotted in this veil of tears?

In rereading my entries, I find monotonous themes of dismay, despair, confusion, and anger. Every now and again, I've written something that sounds optimistic or even gay. But most of it, most of my recorded thoughts, seem alien to me when I review them. So it is that I decline to record what I feel about these most recent deaths, these violent, unnecessary deaths. Ha! Even in passing reference to them, I cannot refrain from venting the anger seething inside me.

Antonio was an illiterate vaquero with amazing skills and an innate gentleness. He was with me in one of the most traumatic events of my life, with me to provide whatever succor he could.

Gonzales I knew less than a day, and yet I felt that a compelling if not inexplicable fraternal bond linked us somehow.

We are a little more than halfway to Abilene. How many incidents await us? More than we've seen so far? It is certain something else will rend our spirits in the weeks to come. It has been months since

I have regarded my face in a mirror. I have this feeling I would hardly recognize myself, which is not surprising since when I contemplate my deepest feelings, I am surprised such sentiments reside within me.

So many of the hands seem so happy, so carefree. They laugh and josh one another when I can barely bring myself to smile. I must try to be more like these simple souls. I have been surprised by how many hail from my country, Virginia, Tennessee: more than half our company. At first, they seem quite similar to one another. Hard, poor, ignorant, and frankly, violent, or at least ready to resort to violence seemingly as a first resort. They work like dogs, enduring privation without complaint and for a pittance. Their only permanent demand is for respect. I find myself thinking often that few if any of them would ever have been invited to dinner at Warwick, and this is almost embarrassing to me in that I also recognize that these were the men who filled the gray-clad ranks and died by the tens of thousands for the Cause.

It's ironic that now it is I who seeks the approval of these rawhide ruffians, and while they are invariably polite in their roughhewn fashion, I perceive there to be some distance between us that is not of my choosing. Perhaps the best course is not for me to be accepted by these men but respected by them.

—~~—

Clairborne removed his glove and used the corner of his bandana to dab at the dust irritating his right eye.

He watched a rider named Vogel trot out to take the point at the head of the herd, realizing he couldn't recall the man's first name. A while later, he watched another man, this one called Dutch Albrecht, ride back toward the chuck wagon after Vogel relieved him.

Dutch seemed to be holding his stomach with his right hand, but he rode with the fluid grace of a man who sat a horse with less thought than he gave to drawing breath. So what was he doing with his hand? Clairborne decided to find out, spurring to a trot and veering toward the upwind side of the herd where the chuck wagon rolled slowly forward.

By the time he got there, Dutch had dismounted, and Biscuit stood facing him with his hands on his hips. Dutch smiled, and Biscuit, who stood with his back toward Clairborne, shook his head, faced Clairborne as he walked up, and said, "Well, that's all we need."

He stepped back to reveal that Dutch held a puppy no bigger than both of the hands that cupped the canine against the cowboy's faded flannel shirt.

"Where in blazes did you find that?" Clairborne said, resisting the urge to reach for the bundle of black-and-tan fur.

"Some wagons crossed the trail about four miles north," Dutch said with a nod. "I stopped 'cause I seen some furniture just sticking out, and when I rode up, I seen it was from a wagon train. Must o' been lightening the load, I guess. Kind o' nice furniture. A chest of drawers, chairs. A desk."

"What about the pup?"

"Well, I was lookin' around, and I heard this here whinin', and I couldn't see where it was a-comin' from, so I got down on my hands and knees, and it was under the desk. Just a-sitting there all by its lonesome."

Biscuit pushed his derby up to his receding hairline. "So you decided to just pick it up and carry it back, knowing we got milk and time to play bitch, did you?"

"Why no, Biscuit," Dutch responded, clearly hurt by the implication that retrieving the puppy was irresponsible. "I do believe it's weaned already."

"I don't care if it can do sums and sing. It's a puppy, and it ain't got no chance of making it, so you ought to just put it out of its misery quick-like," Biscuit said.

Dutch's mouth dropped open. He looked at Biscuit, shifted his dumbfounded gaze to Clairborne, and then looked at the puppy, its tiny pink tongue bobbing as it panted.

"I can't...hell, I can't hurt a puppy, nor any dog less'n it got the hydrophobie or some such ailment. I ain't going to kill no puppy."

"Well then, what the hell are you going to do with it, dumb-ass?"

Dutch looked at Clairborne, clearly seeking a suggestion on how to avoid doing what hard-boiled logic demanded.

Clairborne tried not to look at the dog.

"Boy or girl?" he asked.

" Dunno, never checked." Dutch held the puppy up to examine it. "It's a boy. Got him a nice little set of stones for sure," he said with a grin.

Steiner rode up, dismounted, and walked over to the threesome.

"That a dog you got there, Dutch?"

"Yup. Found him in a old wagon camp about four miles up yonder."

Steiner reached over and scratched the mutt behind its ear. The dog responded by trying to chew the tips of his glove.

"Feisty little fella. What'd you plan on doing with him?"

Dutch looked sheepish. "Don't rightly know, boss. Just didn't seem right to ride off and leave him all by his lonesome, though. Guess I didn't think about it much," he said with a shrug.

Biscuit harrumphed. "A damn puppy. What next?"

"Oh heck, I'll take it," Clairborne said, only slightly less surprised by his words than were the other three.

Steiner regarded Clairborne with a look of amused curiosity but said nothing, letting the Virginian live with his impulsive sentimental gesture and its consequences—such as even less sleep than normal on a cattle drive.

Dutch held the puppy out with both hands. Clairborne hesitated to take it for a moment, long enough to transmit to Steiner—and himself—that he wished he could retract his words. But he couldn't.

He took the dog and looked at it for a few moments before raising his gaze to take in the three men, two of whom were smiling.

"Well, got work to do," Clairborne said, turning back to his horse. As he approached the mild-mannered gray gelding called Mouse, he held up the puppy and slowed his pace.

Mouse flicked his ears forward, raised his dewy muzzle, and flared his nostrils. The puppy wagged its tiny tail and licked Mouse's muzzle. Mouse didn't seem to mind but shifted his eyes to Clairborne without moving his head, and Clairborne imagined the horse saying, "What the hell is that?"

"It's company, that's what, and I appreciate your being hospitable," he said aloud.

Moving to Mouse's hindquarters, he dug in his saddlebag for his enameled cup, poured some water, and offered it to the dog, who responded by slurping eagerly.

He untied his wool jacket from on top of his slicker behind his saddle, put his boot into the stirrup, and mounted Mouse, who slowly swung his head around as if to ask, "Your really expect me to carry the furry little whatever?"

Clairborne arranged his jacket between his crotch and the pommel, put the puppy down, and folded a sleeve over it.

"Please don't cause me trouble, OK?" he said, suddenly thinking of the hounds he'd grown up with and taken for granted. He'd loved them but had never had a specific animal he considered his own. And now this. He stroked its neck. It looked up at him with black, shoe-button eyes.

Clairborne had absolutely no idea how he was going to make this work, but he was absolutely certain he would find a way.

—⚬⚬—

August, 1868
Indian Territory

It is past two o'clock in the morning, and I am in a dream realm, half asleep and half awake. No, more than half asleep. In three hours, I must mount up and begin another day on the trail, but I find myself the victim of a problem of my own creation. Nestled in the crook of my leg is a puppy, yet to be named.

I am mystified by my own actions in adopting this tiny creature. It makes no sense to give it the attention it must have to survive until it can take care of itself. Most of the events, major and minor, that have caused pain, time, and loss of equipment so far are attributable to the blurring of focus wrought by fatigue and monotony. So why take on unnecessary responsibility? Because this innocent being would die without my ministrations. Because I have seen so much death in the last few months, so much random suffering, that I cannot ignore the opportunity to tend the needs of this little creature. So concerned am I that it should wander off while I sleep (ha), I've tied its hind leg to my ankle with a piece of twine. I must acknowledge the impact the pup has had on our company. First, within an hour of my taking it, D. D. Dalghren rode up and held out a cup of milk. I was surprised on two counts: first, that D. D. knew of a single heifer in the entire herd still making milk, and second, that riding on the far side of the herd, he learned about the puppy so quickly. The little guy lapped up the milk and rewarded D. D. with a lick of his hand. D. D. told me that in his family, he was the one out of six children who took care of each litter of their coon hounds. I asked him if he wanted the pup, and he declined after thinking about it. So little lonesome boy is mine for the foreseeable future.

That's it! "Lonesome." Dutch said he found him sitting under a desk "all by his lonesome," so "Lonesome" it is.

Yesterday, I rode out to where Dutch found Lonesome. I wanted to see the place and, specifically, the furniture he said was left there. It was an odd experience. The pieces, a chest of drawers, two chairs, and a desk, are finely crafted oak. They sit upright on the prairie, visible from a distance. Indeed, their silhouettes reminded me of Stonehenge in southern England. I was reluctant to dismount, much less to open drawers and search for clues as to who left these monuments to a different life. To do so seemed like intruding on the sanctity of a graveyard.

Apparently Dutch had felt the same reservations because when I opened the desk, it seemed no one else had done so since it was abandoned. While the pigeonholes and small drawers were empty, the main drawers held two books and a neatly folded letter written in a fine, bold hand. The books are Paradise Lost and William Blackstone's Commentaries on the Laws of England. I had to read Paradise Lost because my tutor required it. The Commentaries I've only heard about. I made a decision, absurd on the face of it, to retrieve the leather-bound, gold-engraved tomes, each of which carries the name of the person whom I perceive to be its previous owner: Herbert A. Snyder, Esq., Indiana, Pennsylvania.

The letter evoked in me a sadness and a simultaneous admiration for Mr. Snyder. I shall keep it inside the Commentaries in the hopes of his travails being remembered long after his family's fine furniture has turned to dust.

I just paused to look around before trying to close my eyes and realized I have been making this entry in darkness without so much as a lantern or the afterglow of a campfire. The full moon is setting, but there is no evidence of the dawn to the east just yet. Everything seems cast in silver—no, more like pewter. I can hear one of the night-hawkers singing to the herd but can't make out the words since the snores around me drown out any distant dulcet tones.

I look at tiny Lonesome once more and will try again to get some shut-eye. Lord, I am tired...but strangely happy.

—∿∿—

Eight monotonous days later, the Rocking C ran into another problem.

At first, Danny Keller, who was riding point, thought the rider he saw in the distance was an outlaw, a rustler, clearly someone up to no good. Why else would the stranger turn his horse and ride off unless it was to advise his fellow banditos of the herd's proximity? Keller rode back to inform Caudill and Steiner, along the way telling Micky Aubochon to move up to point from his flank position and to keep his eyes peeled.

Clairborne, riding swing with Fritz Dornheim on the upwind side of the herd, saw the dust from Keller's hurried movement.

"What now?" he said aloud, fully expecting the answer to be negative, but he waited to be summoned.

Within minutes, Steiner trotted back to the rear, stopping at each rider along the way. When he got to Clairborne and the German, he frowned and recounted what Keller had seen.

"We gotta assume we're headed for trouble," he said, retrieving his canteen as he spoke. "Damn, it's hot."

"Maybe about to get hotter," Clairborne said, nodding toward the head of the herd, where Mickey Aubochon galloped back to where Caudill sat his horse.

"Let's get up there and see what's going on," Steiner said.

He and Clairborne cantered back to the chuck wagon, where Caudill awaited them.

"Farmers. Sodbusters," Caudill said with a sigh.

"What? What do they want?" Steiner asked.

"Don't know yet, but I can guess, and I'm guessing this has something to do with what they call Texas fever."

"Probably right, boss." Steiner shrugged.

"What's that?" Clairborne asked before recalling he'd heard it discussed over dinner in Saint Louis.

"Well, these folks up here, the farmers coming in, homesteaders and the like, seem to think our cattle carries what they call Spanish Fever—and that they lose stock when we pass through."

"We even heard they're trying to get a law passed to keep us from bringing our cattle to the railheads. And remember, daddy told you back in Saint Louis that Missouri passed a law against Texas cattle coming there."

Clairborne was stunned.

"They can't do that." He looked around. "How can they even try to do such a thing...? All this land..." he stammered, ready to get angry but holding back because he knew he must be missing something.

"Oh, they ain't got the votes in Topeka to get a quarantine. Too much money's involved to just stop the drives, but it's damn worrisome," Caudill said. Clairborne looked at the young man, surprised to hear him curse for the first time.

"Isaac, I want you to collect the reps from the other spreads and bring 'em up," Caudill said. "I want witnesses for what's going to happen, plenty of witnesses, and get 'em up here pronto, please."

Caudill was facing south, away from their direction of march, so he didn't see the farmers until Clairborne said, "Here they come."

A knot of wagons and riders spread out laterally a half mile distant from the herd.

"Yep, they aim to stop us, I reckon," Caudill said. "Dang. Tucker, bring up everyone but drag and swing and the wranglers with the remuda. And have 'em draw long guns. Dang, I hate this. I really do."

Caudill rode off.

Clairborne turned his horse to collect the riders, but not before he handed the puppy down to Biscuit and said, "He won't be any trouble, and I don't want him getting in the way...or hurt."

Biscuit put the pup under the chuck wagon bench. "He'll be here. Don't worry."

Moving off to gather the riders, Clairborne wrapped his reins around the saddle horn to free both hands. He drew the Colt, eased the hammer to half cock, and rotated the cylinders, looking closely to see that each cylinder had a percussion cap and that dust had not accumulated where it might jam the mechanism. Returning the Colt to its holster, he leaned back and unbuckled the right saddlebag, reached in, and retrieved the other long-barreled Colt, which he stuck into his waistband under his belt.

All of this he did reflexively. The only conscious thought, when it came, was his wish that he had his shotgun.

Five minutes later, he and fourteen other heavily armed men joined Caudill, Steiner, and the three representatives of the smaller ranches with cattle in the drive.

"Boys, here's what I'm thinking," Caudill said, his back to the gaggle of homesteaders blocking the trail.

"We're taking our cattle to Abilene. Period. I don't intend to let those sodbusters stop us or even slow us any. I'll give 'em my word we'll tighten up the herd as much as we can till we're away from their places, and we'll try to keep the herd out of their crops. But we're taking our cattle to Abilene. They got no right to stop us, and if they try to use Spanish Fever as a reason, there ain't no dang proof our cattle hurt their livestock, so I ain't buying it. We're taking our cattle to Abilene. Anybody got anything they want to say? No? All right, then. Let's go."

Almost as an afterthought, Caudill turned to Clairborne. "Tucker, stay close and keep that hogleg loose. Where's Speight?" Caudill asked, seeking the man considered the Rocking C's best shot before Clairborne's arrival.

"Here, boss," Speight said, moving his horse from the middle of the group.

"OK, Leonard. I want you over there on the left. Keep yourself on the higher ground to their right."

Clairborne approved. One known shooter in the middle, the other on the farmer's flank, slightly above them.

Clairborne was surprised by the last thing Caudill said before turning to confront the farmers.

"Nobody gets hurt, boys," he shouted. "I want us to just ride on after a little parlay."

The Rocking C men rode slowly, line abreast, toward the farmers who had lined up their wagons and carts hub to hub. Single riders on a motley assortment of horses and mules arrayed themselves on the flanks of the wagons. Several of the farmers' animals snorted and stamped as if they sensed something alien, an unfamiliar essence in the atmosphere that crackled with anxiety, radiating from one group to the other, from tense cowboy to nervous farmer.

Clairborne studied the farmers intently. Who was the leader? Who was the best marksman, the most likely to panic? If it came to it, who needed to be shot first? That his mind automatically and methodically focused on such mortal concerns was of no importance to him. It simply occurred. He removed his gloves and wedged them into the opening in the pommel beneath the saddle horn

"That one," he thought. "The fellow with the red flannel shirt and the yellow galluses. He's in the middle. Got the best-looking rig. His mules not only look well fed, they're well groomed. Kid sitting beside him's probably his son, and the two in the back of the wagon maybe sons too. Don't see weapons on any of them except the kid in the front."

The young man in question held a double-barreled shotgun. From where Clairborne sat his horse, it seemed both hammers of the shotgun were cocked. On the bench between them, a Remington Navy .36 pistol rested on a rag.

"Good call to go with the shotgun first, boy," Clairborne thought. "Wish I'd a brought mine."

As his eyes swept the line of farmers to the right and left, he saw several more shotguns, some Springfield muskets, a

Spencer carbine, and three trapdoor rifles. The latter surprised Clairborne in that the army had only adopted the .50 caliber trapdoor two years earlier, so how did farmers get any of them so soon? He also noted that several of the men aligned in front of the Rocking C had pistols stuck into waistbands, none in holsters.

"All right. Let's see who speaks up first, and then, while the leader's jawin', watch the rest."

Caudill walked his horse forward, Steiner on his right, Clairborne on his left.

"Howdy, gents," he said in a tone that sounded genuinely genial.

"You're not taking that herd across our land," said the man Clairborne thought was the leader. As he spoke, the man stood up in the wagon boot, holding the reins in his left hand, and shook his right fist. The young man beside him stood up as well, holding the shotgun in both hands across his chest.

"Well, he's right handed, and he left the pistol on the seat to his left," Clairborne thought. "If he swings the scattergun and I drop him, the old man or one of the boys behind him'll go for the pistol."

"Now look, mister, we don't want any trouble," said Caudill, "so let's just see if we can work out an agreement here."

"Nothing's negotiable except you turn that herd around and take 'em somewheres else."

"Now, friend—" Caudill said.

"I'm not your friend. I lost damn near half my livestock last year after you bastards brought your cattle across my place. Had to pick up and move west, start all over, and I'll just be damned if I'm going to let you yahoos run over me again."

"You mind not swearin'," Caudill said calmly.

The man seemed disconcerted by the request.

"What? Well, I don't see..."

Caudill moved a few steps closer.

"I just think it's bad luck to swear and curse and blaspheme. Bad luck. You don't think we can work an agreement?"

The farmer hesitated and shifted his weight. "No, I don't. Those cattle are like the plague."

Caudill looked back over his shoulder. "Mister, that there's darn fine beef. Should fetch top dollar in Abilene. These men and a lot others been working hard for years to get these beeves together and headed to market. So getting them on the train's pretty much a sure thing one way or the other, I reckon."

"Over my dead body," the farmer yelled.

Caudill said nothing for a long moment.

"These all your men, are they?" he said with a nod toward the line of farmers.

"No, but I speak for them all. We all got stock to lose from Texas Fever."

"Well, how about this," Caudill said. "How about we agree to work out a route that'll keep the herd away from your stock, and I even pay some of your men to keep the herd compacted until we get shy of your lands?"

Clairborne was fascinated by the contrast between the farmer's barely controlled anger and Caudill's calm attempts at negotiation. In the back of his mind, Clairborne could see how the unfolding dialogue might play out later in a court of law.

"Mister, the only thing we got to talk about is how long you got to turn that herd around," the farmer yelled.

Caudill was quiet for a moment before he looked up and down the line of farmers and asked, "Anybody want to help us protect your stock and get a little hard cash in the process?"

Silence.

Then a man riding bareback on a mule asked, "How much you payin'?"

"Grogan, you bastard. Shut your mouth! We agreed we're all in this together," the lead farmer shouted.

"Doesn't look that way, now does it?" Caudill said. Turning to the inquisitive man on the mule, he answered, "Same as I pay my men. A dollar a day, cash money."

The farmer next to the man named Grogan leaned over to talk with him but did so in a voice that didn't carry.

The leader sensed he might be losing control and consensus. On the high plains, the only thing scarcer than a reliable crop was cash. A few dollars could well mean the difference between staying or folding for almost all of these men and their families.

"You turn that herd," the leader yelled.

He slapped the reins, and his mules lurched forward. The young man with the shotgun swung the weapon from across his chest and reached down with his left hand to keep from falling backward. He never took his eyes off Caudill. The shotgun discharged the first barrel, sending a jet of flame, a cloud of smoke, and a clap of sound in the direction of the cowboys.

Clairborne's reflexive move sent a .44-caliber bullet into the young farmer's chest, propelling him over the bench and into the two men standing behind him.

All along the two lines, weapons flashed in the sun as they were presented, an array of muzzles eyeing each other across ten yards of contested ground.

Miraculously, no one fired.

Caudill, who had not drawn his weapon, stood in his stirrups and screamed, "Easy, easy, easy! Please, boys, no more bloodshed!"

The lead farmer dropped the reins and vaulted into the back of the wagon, where one of the other men held the convulsing body. Then the convulsing stopped.

At first, no one could hear what the farmer said. Then he stood up and raised his clenched fists to the cloudless sky and screamed, "Oh, the treachery! Murder, bloody murder. You've slain my son, my boy! I'll, I'll..."

His eyes fell on the revolver on the wagon bench in front of him.

Everyone knew what was about to happen.

Caudill yelled, "Don't, don't!"

Steiner shouted, "Please, mister. Hey please!"

The farmer in the next wagon jumped to his feet. "Lem, enough! Enough!"

Lem leaned toward the gun so slowly Clairborne recognized he had a margin of time to react, that he could give the man a few seconds to change his mind before he shot him in the heart, an action he prepared for by adjusting his aim at the center of the farmer's chest as he moved.

"Lem! In the name of God. Enough!" the adjacent farmer screamed again. "Enough, Lem!"

Lem straightened. He looked down at his dead son, knelt beside the body, and began sobbing. One of the two young men in his wagon slowly reached forward, used his thumb and forefinger to pick up the pistol by its muzzle, and just as slowly put it down on the wagon floor.

All the while, his eyes remained focused on Tucker Clairborne.

The prairie wind provided the only sound except for the occasional nickering of a horse or the stamping of a hoof. And the sobbing coming from the wagon bed.

Finally, Caudill said in a loud but even voice, "This didn't have to happen. We wanted to talk, to figure out a way. This didn't have to happen."

Steiner edged his horse forward and spoke to one of the older farmers.

"Why don't we just go back to our jobs? We'll do our best to avoid your stock and crops. Let's just call it a day, men. We all got work to do."

The elderly farmer looked at the men to his left and right then nodded. He turned his wagon and rode off without a word, as did the rest of the men who had come with him, including Lem, who stayed in the wagon bed with his dead boy while another son, the one who picked up the revolver, took the reins and turned the mules for home.

Steiner turned to the drovers. "Best get back to the herd, boys. Get 'em moving." He walked his horse back to where Caudill and Clairborne sat in silence.

"I thought he was trying to shoot you, Sam," Clairborne said. "Now, I'm not so sure. Maybe he didn't mean to shoot."

Caudill didn't immediately reply. His mind was whirling, trying to reconstruct the sequence, the words that had led to the death of a young farmer.

It seemed clear to him that the kid was knocked off balance when his father jerked the reins. It was even clearer that when the twin barrels of the shotgun whipped toward him, Caudill flinched and closed his eyes in anticipation of the weapon being discharged into his face. At that point, it had mattered not one whit whether the trigger was pulled accidentally or intentionally.

He looked at Clairborne, who was looking down, resting both hands on his saddle horn, not moving.

Caudill focused on what Clairborne had done. No, not what he had done but how he had done it. A chill arced down his spine like a bolt of cold lightning. The Virginian had recognized the threat, cleared leather, thumbed back the hammer, aligned his aim and pulled the trigger so quickly, Caudill was unable to separate the steps in his mind as he reviewed the incident.

Clairborne was very, very fast. And very accurate. And now it seemed he was remorseful. Caudill looked away, almost embarrassed by Clairborne's silence and his cast-down countenance.

"I think I had better leave," Clairborne said in a voice so soft that Caudill and Steiner had to analyze what they thought they'd heard before Steiner said, "To go where, Tucker?"

"I'm thinking I ought to go to Abilene and turn myself in."

"To who?" Caudill asked. "I don't think there's any law in Abilene, at least none that I've heard of."

"Sam's right," Steiner said. "Look, Tucker, even if there is a sheriff or a constable in Abilene, this is out of his jurisdiction, and the nearest federal law is probably back at Fort Riley or Junction City."

Clairborne raised his head. "I have to be practical. I think it best if I bring word of this to Abilene instead of the farmers getting their story out first. And then there's the opportunity to tell McCoy to get space ready for the herd in the rail yards, maybe even give the brokers time to get the cash together if they need to."

Caudill resisted the urge to shake his head in admiration of what he'd just heard. Clairborne wasn't just remorseful. He was also thinking about possible consequences and alternatives. While images of blood and gunfire had been swirling around in Caudill's head like so much wind-driven dust, Clairborne was planning out the next step—the next two or three steps, actually. Caudill looked into Clairborne's unblinking hazel eyes and thought, "You are one cold operator, my friend." Never had he known such a combination of white-hot reflex and icy pragmatism. He resolved then and there to avoid making an enemy of the Virginian.

Caudill looked at Steiner, who was looking back at him. "What do you think, Isaac?"

"It's a good plan. For all the reasons he says, it makes sense. Think there's any lawyers in Abilene yet?"

Caudill snorted. "Cow dung and carrion draw blowflies. Money and greed's got to draw lawyers. Tucker, you go straight to Joseph McCoy. He's bound to be in town this time of year, and he'll help you if anyone can. Heck, it's his town."

ABILENE

He knew where Abilene was before he saw it.

He'd followed cattle trails discernible to a blind man to the place where he sat his horse this early September afternoon, four and a half days after he'd ridden away from the Rocking C herd. The spot on the Kansas prairie occupied by Abilene was marked by a seemingly permanent cloud of yellow-brown dust to which puffs of gray-white locomotive smoke were drawn from the east like iron filings to a magnet. Clairborne stayed out of the town for nearly an hour before reluctantly, gently pressing his spurs to his mount's flank.

Dust and smoke, the first visible signs of human activity, were joined by the hooting of train whistles, clanging bells, and nonstop bawling of thousands and thousands of cattle. A shift of the Kansas wind wrapped him in the ineffable bouquet of stockyards full to overflowing with cattle having only four things to do: drink, defecate, urinate, and wait. Clairborne stopped to consider the town, which had grown noticeably since his last visit mere months earlier. The main rail line extended through to the west, and there were sidings that allowed more than one train to load at a time. He passed the sprawling cattle yards and wondered if there would be room for the Rocking C herd when it arrived.

Cattle moved up loading chutes into slatted cars, a process expedited by young men straddling the railings, each wielding a long, pointed pole to prod recalcitrant animals up the ramps. "What a job," he thought. "Poking cows in the butt all day...." He would recall his observation in days to come when he learned that in the social order of the cattle business, cowboys held the men they called "cowpokes" in great disdain.

More structures had gone up on Abilene's main street, and there were houses on what appeared to be side streets. There was even a separate building with a cross atop its purpose-built steeple.

Clairborne marveled at the crowds as he rode toward the Drover's Cottage, the interior of which he was happy to see was as clean and cool as he recalled.

The clerk behind the counter loved his job. With any luck, he would rise to assistant manager within another year or so if business held up. And why wouldn't it now that the cattle yards were completed and filling up as planned? Mr. McCoy had hired him personally in Chicago and brought him to Abilene as a member of the Drover's Cottage staff charged with delivering the level of service expected for top dollar.

He was used to dust-covered cowboys wandering in off the street to gawk at oriental carpets and crystal chandeliers, but this man's disheveled, trail-worn shabbiness was exceptional.

Tall, trim, and sunburned, the man walking toward the clerk wore an assortment of clothing presenting a distinct impression of better days. The cut of the jacket and trousers, the style of the hat and boots were originally eastern and expensive, but the patches and stitches covering elbows, knees, and cuffs, along with the hat's frayed brim and the badly scuffed boots, said that things had not been going all that well of late for the man who dropped his saddlebags on the carpet in front of the counter.

The man's gloves, quirt, and kerchief said "cowboy," but the tooled gun belt and holster supporting the ivory-handled Colt said something else. Just what was not clear to the clerk, who prided himself on figuring out guest particulars in the time it took for them to sign the green leather register.

Facing the effusive and efficient clerk, Clairborne pondered his next step. Should he surrender to the allure of a hot bath or try to find McCoy? He smiled at the realization that personal hygiene ranked nearly as high as preparing a defense against a possible murder charge.

With a shrug, he asked about McCoy, and in so doing, solved his dilemma. McCoy was not in town but was expected back shortly.

"I need to get word to Mr. McCoy that I must meet with him immediately. Can you get word to his office for me?"

"Oh yes, sir, but would you care to telegraph him as well? Mr. McCoy checks his telegrams at every stop," said the clerk.

"Fine," Clairborne replied. "Now how about getting the biggest tub and the hottest water to my room and lining up the best barber. Oh, yes, and another thing: Who's the best haberdasher in town? Send him up too. I need new duds, from sombrero to boots."

The clerk's eyes lit up at the prospect of commissions to be had from each of the services rendered and congratulated himself for not judging this apparently affluent "book" by its tattered cover. Since coming west, he'd long since learned that many such a vagabond was likely to pull gold coins from frayed pockets to pay for the best a facility had to offer.

Reading the fine penmanship upside down as the guest signed, the clerk asked "Would you care for a libation and some sustenance while you bathe, Mr. Clairborne?"

Clairborne raised his gaze to the lobby's elaborate ceiling and thought, "Priorities, priorities? What happens with the law will play out later, so what do I need right now?" He closed his eyes a second before answering, "A couple of good cigars."

Thirty minutes later Clairborne opened his eyes and watched wisps of vapor slowly rise from the hot, soapy water nearly overflowing the copper tub that rested squarely in the middle of his hotel room. His pink flesh, that which he could see, seemed almost iridescent. He lifted his right hand and examined his nails, finding them cracked and snagged but completely clean even though he hadn't scrubbed them. Next, he studied his four-fingered left hand, specifically the small, pink nub where his index finger had been. Until that moment, he had given no thought to how fast he'd adapted to having one less finger. He luxuriated in the tub, eyes closed, breathing subdued. At one point, his head slid to the side and water entered his mouth when he succumbed to slumber's irresistible influence.

Archimedes. The name of the Greek mathematician bolted out of mental nowhere to the forefront of his thoughts.

Archimedes, whose legendary bathtub revelation on the weight of pure gold brought him eternal fame. Clairborne smiled at recognition that the revelation he'd just had would have no impact on mankind, as did the Greek's discovery, but only on the course of his own future.

462

Reclining up to his lips in the hot bath in a hotel in a rawhide cattle town, he discovered, recognized, realized that forever more, he would avoid discomfort whenever possible.

Clairborne flicked his finger at a soap bubble,

"So, am I so soft that I can't handle the cowboy life?" he asked himself.

It was more than five minutes later before the answer materialized. It was not that he couldn't handle hard physical labor and Spartan living conditions, it was that he simply and strongly didn't prefer them. His would be a different path, a route defined by clean sheets, hot baths, good food and drink, books, music, and...and what? Something else, he sensed, was important to the quality of life he would seek, but try as he did, Clairborne could not nail it down.

He glanced over at the brass bed, the plump pillows enshrouded in soft pillowcases. The marble-topped table beside the bed supported a crystal decanter of whiskey and a cut-glass tumbler beside which a cedar cigar box supported a note from "A. M. Horton, Haberdasher to Gentlemen of the Plains" requesting that Mr. Clairborne "accept these cigars with our compliments in the hopes we will have the opportunity of serving you in the nearest of futures."

But as the water slowly cooled, Clairborne began to sense something dark and sharp-edged intruding on his euphoria, something so palpable that he conjured up the image of a beast, something threatening, an alligator or perhaps a water moccasin lurking beneath the soapy surface of his bath. That anything would intrude on his hard-earned bliss irritated him, caused him to shift his position, to sit up straight and focus on what it was.

His Colts were laid out on the crocheted bedspread.

What about them?

Slowly but sequentially, it occurred to him that if he stayed out west, he would have to retain the hard edge developed during the last several months. If he reverted to idle softness, bad things would happen to him. Inevitably. He had worked too hard, had seen and suffered too much to waste the lessons accrued since he crossed the "father of all waters," as the Indians called the Mississippi.

As he ruminated, the dark and menacing imminence took shape.

Clairborne recognized what he had become, what first Beekman had said and what he'd seen in the eyes of others afterward, after Spanish Wells and Charlie Guthrie and the farm boy. He could not deny it. He was a gunman, a pistolero, a shootist, whatever term applied to a man who used a handgun to kill someone else. More than once.

His saw that this train of thought had two tracks leading in opposite directions. He could stay out west, knowing his life would be punctuated by conflict. Or he could go home to Virginia. He was startled by how quickly he dismissed the thought of returning to Warwick—or Chicago or Saint Louis. No, the east was not for him. This was for him. The west was for him, but in what capacity? There was only one certainty at this point: not as a cowboy.

His comfort began to dissipate as if the copper tub's smooth bottom were supplanted by rough-edged rocks.

His thoughts were not logical.

He seemed to be telling himself that the east was too easy, too soft, and too predictable, while the west, at least as he knew it so far, was unpredictable, difficult, and perilous. But preferable.

He swirled his finger in the soapy water and decided it was too cool for comfort. He reached for the thick towel folded over the rack on the side of the polished copper tub and stood. Vigorous chafing with the scented cotton brought blood to the surface of his skin, emphasizing the contrast between the pinkish-white areas protected from the relentless sun and his brick-red wrists, neck, face, and forehead up to his hat line. Water dripping from his arms and feet blotched the wool carpet, marking his path to the bed, where he flopped on his still-moist back and closed his eyes.

"All right. That's it, then. It'll be hard as hell from time to time, maybe even most of the time. Who knows? But when I can, I'll live well, damn well. Or die trying."

He smiled and fell asleep, his bare feet suspended an inch above the carpet that slowly absorbed the last vestiges of his almost sinfully pleasant bath.

—◆◆◆—

September 17, 1868
Abilene, Kansas

> *Dearest Mother,*
>
> *Of course, I express my remorse for the interval between this letter and my last. My only legitimate excuse is that for months, I have been in a part of this vast country bereft of regular post. I am*

writing you on my arrival here and will certainly correspond more frequently in the future.

How are you? How is Amy? How is Warwick? You could fill a volume with information about subjects near to my heart. Alas, I fear that I may not be here in Abilene long enough to receive mail, but I will endeavor to let you know the instant I become aware of the likelihood of staying in one location for a period of time sufficient to both send and receive correspondence.

As I write, my mind is swirling with events and names and places to share with you. It is important to me that you know, above all else, that I am well. The rigors encountered to date I believe have made me a better man, at least in the sense of my taking care of myself. I have also learned oh so well how very blessed I was to be born to you and father and to have been raised in a home defined by gentility, duty, and education. Life here is quite Spartan for the most part, although one encounters erudition and grace where one least expects it. The other side of that coin is that one also encounters hard and inexplicable episodes just as suddenly.

It is with that information that I tell you of my plans for the foreseeable future. While I think of home, of you and Amy, of Warwick, every day— indeed, several times each day—I will remain out here for a while longer. Truth be told, I am exhilarated by the very unpredictability to which

I referred earlier. Matching my abilities to challenges that arise from nowhere gives me a sense of accomplishment I had not known until I ventured west.

Mother, I have been delaying what I wish to say next. I am so very aware of the difficulty of accurately conveying what I feel, of being able to share feelings without unduly alarming you. Let me reiterate that I am well—very well, actually. I repeat those words so that you may place what I am about to say in what I hope will be the best context.

Mother, I have been surprised at the violence, at the random eruption of events resulting in pain and suffering, that seem to be a primary thread in this vast tapestry that is life in the West. I refer not only to conflict between men but also to the violent, dangerous aspects of Nature itself. In that, I include such things as a colleague of mine, an excellent equestrian, whose mount kicked him as he passed behind it, killing him instantly. I've seen men swept away by river currents never to be seen again and others die of snakebites. I just realized that one example of how common such events are is that of four mortal episodes to which I just referred, I recorded only two in my journal, the other two being so mundane as to not motivate me to overcome my extreme fatigue enough to record them.

Again, Mother, these experiences have caused me to value life all the more in that I now fully understand how fleeting, how evanescent it is.

I also frequently compare my life to that of Father and Peyton, the men I admire most. Both of them witnessed death on a monstrous scale, while I have seen men pass as individuals. I wonder which is the harder to fathom, to reconcile with one's understanding of God's plan for us. Why does the Lord cause 10,000 men to die in the face of massed artillery and another to die when thrown from his horse on the road to dinner at a hotel? Does He intend to teach us one thing by contemplation of mass graves in eastern fields of battle and another by digging a single grave in unmapped prairie? And what does God want us to learn from the death of a sweet boy awakened by a deadly serpent in his blanket?

I appreciate only too late how very much I value your wisdom, Mother. It is only since I left your side that I have come to recognize your sagacious calm, to understand the depth of your knowledge, your compassion, and your patience—and yes, your strength. I so wish I were at your knee.

I will close now but promise to write again soon, tomorrow evening after I have posted this letter to you. Ha, two letters in two days!

I almost forgot to tell you that I had to leave Bucephalus at the Rocking C ranch, as there are very strict rules barring the presence of stallions on a cattle drive. I will endeavor to recover him as well as my possessions left there as soon as I can.

Goodness! This last entry made me realize I have not told you why I am here in Abilene. I wonder what my tutors would think of such random, disorderly thinking?

Ah well, as I said, there is so much to share.

I arrived in Abilene in advance of a herd of nearly 7,000 cattle driven north from west Texas to this sprawling railhead, from which they will be shipped to eastern markets. I say "in advance of the herd" in that my employer, Mr. Sam Caudill, entrusted me to arrange the logistics before the cattle actually arrive, things such as ensuring that there are pens to hold them, trains to ship them, and money to pay for them. Yes, your son has been entrusted with those responsibilities. Are you not amazed, Mother? I am.

I know I should have reversed the order of this letter, but I will do better next time, when there will be less pressure on the champagne cork and more time to pour.

I pray you are well. I embrace you in my dreams. I love you with all the gratitude only a son can feel for his dear mother.

Your Devoted Son,
Tucker L. Clairborne

Clairborne and McCoy took less than ten minutes to address details related to shipping the Rocking C herd.

McCoy was ebullient. Things were simply swell in every respect. But McCoy was nothing if not prescient, and he quickly sensed an unusual reserve in the sunburned man in the trail-worn clothes sitting across from him. He decided to say nothing, to see if Clairborne would fill the ensuing silence.

After less than a minute, he did.

"Do you know a man named Lemuel Boniface?" Clairborne asked.

"Ah Boniface, Boniface. Can't say as I do. Kind of an unusual name, so I expect I'd recall it. Why?"

"I killed his son."

Even for a man who believed he'd seen and heard it all, McCoy was momentarily stunned.

"Boniface, his boys—at least I think they were his boys, three of them—and about twenty other farmers tried to stop the herd. Tried to keep us from getting to Abilene. They—"

McCoy stood. "When was this? Where?" He sat back down and leaned forward.

"Ten days ago now. Said our cattle would kill their livestock and trample their crops, and they wouldn't allow it. Sam tried to reason with them, even offered to hire some to help keep the herd away from their spreads as much as possible."

"So what happened?"

"This man Boniface seemed to be the leader. When some of the others started...well, it looked like some were considering Sam's offer, and he slapped his mules, his wagon jolted, the kid swung his shotgun at us and fired it, and I shot him."

McCoy exhaled. "Why, damnation, Tucker. That's self-defense. You have nothing to worry about. We can take care of this."

"Well, there's a complication."

"A complication?"

"I'll be as straightforward as I can be. I've thought about nothing else since it happened. It may be that the kid just lost his balance, that he didn't mean to shoot us, that it was just an accident."

McCoy rubbed his chin. "These farmers were trying to block your—the herd's—movement?"

"Yes."

"Well, that's illegal right there. And you say Sam tried to reason with them?"

"Not only that, but before we rode out to meet them, he told us all he didn't want anybody hurt."

"And he, this kid, fired first—in your direction?"

"Yes."

"Tucker, I'm a gambling man, but only when I know the odds. I'd put money, a lot of money, on a wager that nothing's going to come of this. Nothing bad, that is. Nothing bad for anyone but this Boniface character."

Clairborne looked at the floor. "Nothing legal, you mean? Nothing like jail or worse?"

McCoy laughed. "Exactly. No damn jury is going to penalize you for what is clearly self-defense, as unfortunate as the whole thing is."

"Even if the jury is all farmers?" Clairborne said, looking up.

McCoy stood and walked to the sideboard holding several decanters of liquor. "Care to join me?" he asked, and then with a smile added, "I should have mentioned that this is your liquor I'm serving, delivered by Great Western as defined in a sales contract signed about a week after you headed south to Texas."

Clairborne smiled in spite of his dour mood. "A sip, then."

McCoy poured himself three fingers of whiskey and one for his guest and returned to the table with the glasses.

"Look, Tucker. There's going to be a day when farmers, homesteaders, and such will not only outnumber those in the cattle business, but most important, their sheer numbers will change politics. It will happen. But not for a while. Certainly not now. I don't know how legitimate their land claims are. Hell, I don't even know if they filed claims and hold title to anything. But I do know they have no damn right to stop a cattle drive."

He sipped his whiskey before continuing. "And they sure as hell don't have the right to threaten anyone with bodily harm, much less to blast a shotgun at you."

Clairborne nodded. "I've been reading about self-defense in Blackstone's—"

"What?" McCoy exclaimed. "You've been reading law books? Where?"

Clairborne explained how he had come into possession of the legal tome, eliciting McCoy's guffaws in the process.

"Lord above, Tucker. You probably know more about criminal law than anyone within hundreds of miles of this place. We don't even have a lawyer in town, much less a sitting judge, only a circuit rider who comes through twice a year." McCoy laughed again. "Hell's bells, boy, you've got the bona fides to hang a shingle on main street and be Abilene's first lawyer. I'm serious. Look, for the last month, a group of us have been meeting to figure out how this town will grow. I'll be honest with you. There is pressure coming from the newly arrived ladies, the wives of some of our leading figures, who demand, ah, 'improvements' in the town's reputation. I'd like you and your law books to join the discussion. What do you say?"

Clairborne sat back in his chair and thought a moment. He raised the whiskey to his lips and drained it.

"I'll just have another taste after all, Joe," he said. As McCoy poured, Clairborne shook his head and ran his hands through his freshly pomaded hair. "Tucker Lightfoot Clairborne, Esq., Attorney at Law." Who would have imagined such a thing? Certainly not Tucker Lightfoot Clairborne.

McCoy's liquor was excellent and, arriving as it did in an empty stomach, contributed significantly and quickly to Clairborne's mood.

Earlier in the day, A. M. Horton, haberdasher, had visited his hotel room with his son, Arthur Michael Junior, who toted the bags of fabric samples and catalogues of clothing styles.

When he met with McCoy, his old clothes were cleaned and mended, which, combined with the bath, haircut, and shave, made him realize just how filthy and noisome he had become.

Because McCoy was dining that night with potential investors from Europe, Clairborne was free to make his own dinner plans. The prospect of a meal served at a table featuring clean flatware and starched linen stimulated his appetite. He also recognized the incipient alcohol-induced euphoria washing through his circulatory system and thought it best to fill his stomach with food to counter the effects of whiskey after months of enforced abstinence.

After his meal, Clairborne pushed back his chair and looked around the hotel dining room. No doubt about it. This was preferable to freezing, broiling, soaking, or thirsting on the plains. He'd never considered himself to be fastidious, but he found himself staring at his clean fingernails and asking himself why he would ever get them dirty again if he had a choice.

Outside on the street, it was cooler than he'd ever experienced in Abilene, undoubtedly the result of the thunderstorm that swept through the town the day he arrived, a storm that drove the summer's miasma before it while pulling cool, dry air in its wake.

He stood on the porch and lit a cigar. Looking up as he extinguished the match, he beheld the building across the street and realized that it had not there mere months ago.

It was, of course, a saloon, a saloon bearing a gilt-lettered sign identifying it as the Rooster.

Clairborne crossed the street, dividing his attention among piles of horse manure and the riders, wagons, and other pedestrians crowding the hundred-foot-wide expanse.

The Rooster was crowded. It featured not only a planked floor and a painted ceiling, but also a dark wood bar replete with brass footrail and evenly spaced spittoons. The ends and the center of the bar offered patrons displays of free food—hard-boiled eggs, pickled pigs' feet, raw onions, slabs of dark bread, sliced sausages, and crocks of mustard and butter. The bartenders, three in number, wore clean aprons, striped shirts with cellulose collars, neckties, and sleeve garters. Clairborne stepped aside at the batwing doors to let others enter while he surveyed the smoke-filled room.

To the right rear, a roulette wheel held the attention of six men whose attire said "cowboy." The left rear of the room was the domain of the faro and poker games, again pursued with varying degrees of enthusiasm by mostly young men not intimately acquainted with soap and water.

More to the point, every man he saw was heeled.

Clairborne didn't feel like sitting. He moved to the near end of the bar and was quickly served by a redheaded, freckled, wire-thin young man with a smile broader than his shoulders.

Since he'd already downed corn whiskey with McCoy and a hoppy beer with his steak, he hesitated when asked what he wanted.

"Umm, I guess a beer would be fine." He realized after the fact that as he walked to the rear of the room to observe the games of chance, he held the beer mug in his left hand to keep his gun hand free. The realization amused him.

One game in particular seemed to be drawing a crowd. Clairborne found and took the last open space against the rear wall a few feet from the table.

He quickly understood why it had drawn an audience. Arrayed in its center was an unusually large amount of money. Only three of the five players were still in the game. Leaning against the wall, Clairborne soaked in the relevant details of the situation, the players, the others standing around watching the house gambler steadily adding to his winnings at the direct expense of one man in particular, the one seated directly in front of Clairborne, the one who, although more than three feet away, emitted a stink that caused Clairborne to breathe through his mouth.

On losing the last of his stash visible on the green baize table, the player threw in his hand muttering, "Well, shit."

The remaining two were a study in contrasts. One was older and reserved, well-dressed, winning and sober, to judge from the cash in front of him. The other gambler was not a cowboy, and after a few seconds of analysis, Clairborne pegged him for a teamster—young, tattered, sweat stained, losing, and on the blurred edge of inebriation.

The older man placed fifteen silver dollars in the pot. "See your five and raise you ten. Fifteen to stay," he said matter-of-factly.

The young gambler slammed his fist onto the table so hard he bounced his whiskey glass into the air.

"You can see I ain't got it, goddamn it. You're just buyin' the pot." He looked up at the man standing next to Clairborne. "Willy, give me seven dollars."

"Table stakes," the older gambler said in an even tone.

"My ass! My ass! You got four months of my wages, goddamn it. You can't just take my last dollar without'n you show me your hand."

The older gambler said nothing. The young man knocked over his chair as he leaped to his feet and raised his fists over his head, shouting, "Busted, broke. Four months of mules' asses and eating dust, and it's all gone in a hour. It ain't fair, goddamn it, and I ain't havin' it!"

The older gambler said nothing, maintaining his gaze on the young gambler's midsection.

Clairborne lowered his right hand from his vest pocket to the top of his belt, inches from his pistol.

The youth swept his eyes around the circle of spectators and stopped at his buddy, Willy, standing next to Clairborne.

"Willy, I just need seven dollars."

"Table stakes," the older gambler repeated.

"Shut your damned mouth, son of a bitch!"

"C'mon, Fergy," Clairborne's neighbor said. "Let's go back to camp."

"I'm broke, goddamn it. I ain't got a dime for a drink."

Clairborne felt the urge to admonish the young loudmouth rising like magma and resisted it, telling himself, "It's none of your affair, Tucker."

But there must have been something in his expression that radiated his disdain. Or perhaps it was mere propinquity to Willy. Either way, the young man switched his bloodshot eyes to Clairborne and leaned forward. "You see something funny, do you?"

"Not particularly funny, no."

The young gambler straightened and stood in front of Clairborne with less than two feet between them.

"Something else, is it? Something making you smile, mister?"

Clairborne's pulse pounded in his ears, and he opened his mouth slightly to relieve the pressure he felt building. A voice behind his eyes said slowly and loudly, "Don't do this, Tucker. He's drunk and angry. Find another way."

Willy reached out for the young gambler's arm. "C'mon, Fergy. Let's get the hell out o' here."

"Keep your damn hand off o' me," the young man screamed at Willy. "Ain't goin' nowheres without my money and this sumbitch tells me what he's smilin' at."

"Well, friend," Clairborne said evenly. "Looks as if you're going to leave without either. I doubt that gentleman's going to contribute his winnings to a charity case, and I'm not inclined to parlay with a drunk."

The young gambler drew back his right arm to cock the blow he intended to deliver to Clairborne's face, but before he finished winding up, Clairborne raised his right boot and slammed his heel into the top of the young man's arch, producing an audible crunching noise instantly overridden by a shriek of pain.

The young gambler folded over his smashed foot only to meet Clairborne's rising knee impacting his face between his top lip and his nose, bouncing him backward in a spray of blood.

Howling and holding his face with both hands, the young gambler didn't resist as Clairborne grabbed the back of his collar and his belt and then dragged him to the front door through the crowd, which parted like the Red Sea for Moses. Through the door, Clairborne swung to his left, dropped the groaning form into a water trough, wiped his hands on his trousers, and walked back to the hotel, ignoring the Rooster's patrons jamming the door and windows behind him.

Up the stairs and into his room, he sat on the edge of his bed, searching for an outlet for the adrenaline coursing though him, turning his tongue to brass, and making his fingers quiver. His eyes swept the room and came to rest on the leather-bound law book on the sideboard.

Clairborne walked over and picked up the heavy repository of legal knowledge and hefted it twice. He turned to the table, pulled out a chair, sat down, opened the book to a random page, and started reading: *"Resolution of Property Disputes Lacking Written Documentation."*

Two hours later, he closed the book, rose, washed his face, and changed into his nightshirt. He dropped to his knees and recited the Lord's Prayer aloud, then slid himself into the envelope of cool, starched sheets. Five minutes later, he was asleep.

———

September 18, 1868
Abilene, Kansas

> *Dear Mother,*
>
> *Are you amazed? So long between letters from your vagabond son, and now two in as many days.*
>
> *Probably you did not put much credence in my avowal to improve the frequency and quality of my correspondence, and if that is the case, I could not blame you.*
>
> *I want you to know that I write not because of some sense of duty or obligation but rather because I find it so enjoyable. You see, as I sit here in my hotel room, pen in hand, my mind's eye is filled with visions of Warwick as I hope it is these days. I see you and Amy bustling about to deal at once with the burgeoning social calendar for the oncoming season as well as with what I dearly hope is the challenge of successfully managing the myriad aspects of life at Warwick.*

On that note, Mother, I trust you will never hesitate to apprise me of your situation. While I know we have never considered discussion of financial obligations and the ability to meet them as fodder for polite conversation, the times in which we find ourselves have changed that. By dint of my labor, good luck, and good advice, I am in a position to address any monetary challenges that may vex you—and Amy. It is my duty to do so, and it would give me pleasure as well to feel that I have finally contributed something tangible, something about which you could brag, if such an act were in your nature.

I will remain here in Abilene for a while yet, as there are services I can render to the Caudills and perhaps some other tasks I can do as well. The Rocking C herd should arrive in two or three days, so we'll see what comes next.

The other opportunity arises from the fact that Abilene is so new and is growing so rapidly, it has yet to address its civic structure in even so much as a theoretical manner. Mr. McCoy is the founding father in a very real sense of the word, but Abilene is run on consensus among those with a demonstrable stake in the issue du jour. Most involved in civic affairs are shop owners and tradesmen.

While I do not wish to sound naive, Mother, I find myself thinking often of my ancestors who carried civic virtue and the rule of law on their backs from the old world to the new and who built the society we so love. I see no irony in what I have just written, no collision of my logic with the adamant abolitionists who say our society was built on the backs of slaves, by the sweat of their brow. Jamestown, Harrison's Landing, Westover, Carter's Grove, Shirley, Warwick were not launched into the unknown with the assistance of slaves. That, as you know, came later.

Be that as it may, there are no slaves here, only free men seeking to make their fortune by dint of their fortitude and their intelligence. I am proud to be one of them, and Mother, I hope you are proud of me as well.

I love you dearly. Affection to little Miss Amy.

Your Obedient Son,

Tucker

Journal Entry
September 19, 1868
Drover's Cottage,
Abilene, KA.

As the beneficiary of recent developments, I should feel much better about them than I do, or at best, understand my feelings when they are so contradictory. Neither is the case.
It seems there may be no legal consequences arising from the death of Benjamin Boniface.

McCoy sent a lengthy telegram to the nearest federal authority, a Marshall Thomas Blinding, at Fort Riley, detailing the events as

I recounted them. McCoy and other civic leaders sent a messenger to summon Lemuel Boniface to Abilene along with any witnesses he cared to bring. It will be at least another week before we learn of his response. In the interim, this morning, Marshall Blinding responded with an endorsement of the approach taken by McCoy and the others to date as well as an injunction from a judge in Kansas City to record the developments as they occur and send them to judicial offices for review and archiving.

So here I sit in my room recording these events and my sentiments, curiously ambivalent about my future. McCoy has asked me to dine with him and the other gentlemen he convened to consider the death of the Boniface boy. He has told me only that they wish to discuss with me a topic unrelated to the boy. When I pressed him, he smiled, slapped my back, and said that I should trust him, that folks think well of me here and wish to discuss what he characterized as an "arrangement." My watch tells me I will learn more in less than three hours.

Should I be apprehensive? I think not. But we shall see soon enough.

William Bigelow was the wealthiest resident of Abilene, Kansas. Joseph McCoy was wealthier but didn't reside full-time in the boomtown. As befitting a wealthy merchant and soon-to-be banker, Bigelow and his family occupied the town's largest home, an unfinished two-story structure of stone and brick with a flint shingle roof. Its yard was graced by newly planted elm and oak saplings, and a flower bed bordered the wide front veranda.

Clairborne dismounted and tied his horse to the hitching post beside the flagstone walkway leading to the house from the street. Seeing several horses already tethered, he wondered if he was late, if he'd misread the time on the handwritten invitation delivered to his room shortly after his conversation with McCoy.

Glancing down at his new boots, he grinned at the glow produced by the boot maker's skill, good leather, and hand-rubbed wax. Before he finished climbing the steps to the porch, the front door opened to reveal the stout, well-dressed form of William Bigelow as he strode forward and extended his hand.

"Mr. Clairborne, so very good to meet you. I've heard so many things about you. Welcome to my home."

Clairborne responded to the effusive greeting by doffing his new hat and shaking his host's hand. "The pleasure is mine, sir. Thank you for your hospitality. I'm honored. I'm sorry, but I have no calling card to present."

"No, no, no. It's we who are honored, sir, and calling cards are not yet so common hereabouts. Do come in."

The parlor was carpeted and full of leather furniture and sepia photographs suspended by cords on the striped wallpaper. Clairborne marveled at the combination of tasteful furniture and the smell of paint and freshly sawn lumber. The stone fireplace was cold, and the damask drapes were pulled back, allowing the setting sun to illuminate the room. Aromas of beef and bread and soups, potatoes, butter, gravy, and pies suffused the layers of cigar and pipe smoke suspended a foot below the ten-foot high tongue-and-groove ceiling.

Bigelow took Clairborne's elbow, steering him toward the woman who emerged just then from the dining room.

"Mr. Clairborne, may I present my wife, Emmaline. Mother, this is Mr. Tucker Clairborne of Virginia."

Clairborne instantly sensed that Emmaline Bigelow had to be one of the forces pushing for law and order in Abilene to which McCoy had referred. Thin, pinch-faced, and unsmiling, dressed in black silk, her hair parted in the middle and drawn into a severe bun, she held out her tiny hand and said, "We have high hopes for you, Mr. Clairborne. Welcome to our home."

Disconcerted by the greeting and momentarily nonplussed, Clairborne bowed and said, "My honor, ma'am."

The rest of the room was occupied by a collection of Abilene's civic leaders, nearly all of whom were young to middle aged and energetic. Some were bald, some florid, but all shared a distinct similarity of language and interest that made it hard for Clairborne to recall individual names. They each told Clairborne how glad they were to meet him and how much they looked forward to working with him, a message that thickened his feeling that something involving him had already been decided. He was not certain he liked the feeling all that much.

McCoy and Bigelow were clearly the leaders of the pack, the others deferring to their opinions and laughing a little too hard at their witticisms. Clairborne engaged in the dinner table banter but was careful to maintain a mental fence around his thoughts and words, at least until it became clear to him just what his hosts had in mind. He paid even more attention to his alcohol consumption, limiting it to one whiskey before dinner and opting for apple cider rather than wine with the meal.

At the meal's conclusion, Bigelow stood.

"Gentlemen, let's retire to the library for our postprandial libation and discussion of the topic du jour, shall we?"

"Here it comes," Clairborne told himself.

On the way to the library, he couldn't help but notice Mrs. Bigelow hovering at the edge of the men as they sauntered out of the dining room. She glared at her husband, who ignored her as he retrieved a decanter of whiskey from a sideboard.

"So the little biddy doesn't approve of alcohol," Clairborne mused. "I'll bet she'd like to see every saloon in town turned into a schoolroom."

Once drinks were poured and cigars were lit, Bigelow asked Clairborne to stand beside him.

"Gentlemen," he intoned. "This is a fine day for Abilene, the town of the future. We'll look back at this day and remember it as the first formal step we took to make Abilene realize its potential, to turn it from a rawhide, roughhewn spot in the prairie to a prosperous place with all of the attributes of civic virtue, a place where decent women can walk the streets in safety and children can go to school, a place where the Sabbath is respected and peace is the rule rather than the exception."

Clairborne looked around as the men exclaimed, "Hear, hear" and raised their glasses.

Bigelow put down his whiskey and cigar and grabbed the peaked satin lapels of his black frock coat.

"Uh oh," Clairborne thought. "This is going to be a stem-winder."

"So what have we agreed on in our meetings? What's the first step we agree to take? A peace officer is what we need. A sworn officer of the law to see to it that ruffians, desperadoes, and drunks are dealt with quickly, that Abilene's reputation as a law-abiding town, safe for business and families, is well established."

Bigelow put his hand on Clairborne's shoulder and smiled.

"Tucker, we want you to accept the position of constable. We want you to help us bring Abilene to its rightful place in our great country's future. What do you say?"

He was stunned. A couple of days ago, he worried about getting hanged, and now he was being offered a job as a lawman. The cheers gave him a few seconds to recover.

His mind whirled. "Do I want the job? Can I even say no? Do I owe it to McCoy? Does this place even have laws to enforce?" An element of ire manifested itself in the tangle of his emotions. "How presumptuous of these people...."

He realized his hosts were waiting for his response.

"I am deeply honored, deeply honored, but I must add that I feel unqualified for the post." When Bigelow started to protest, he raised his hand. "Folks, the truth is I know nothing about the law and am inclined to avoid conflict whenever possible."

McCoy moved to the front of the men facing Clairborne and Bigelow.

"That's why we want you for the job, Tucker. We'll provide the law for you, and we don't want a bully wearing a badge. You've shown us you can handle ruffians and drunks without automatically resorting to gunplay. That's what we're looking for. What do you say?"

Clairborne lowered his gaze to the oriental carpet. He could say no to Bigelow but not McCoy. He didn't know anything about law enforcement, had never considered it for a second, and now...

"Oh, we didn't tell you," Bigelow interjected. "Pay's seventy-five dollars a month and a room at the Drover's."

"That tears it," Clairborne told himself. "They just painted me into a corner I can't get out of." He looked around at his smiling hosts and shrugged.

"Well, gentlemen. I guess you just hired yourself a constable."

———⚬⚬⚬———

Journal entry
Sept 20, 1868
Abilene, Kansas

I am an officer of the law as of tomorrow morning, when I am to take my oath. It couldn't be done today because nobody had written it down yet, so there is nothing for me to repeat.

To say that I am dubious about this turn of events is a grand understatement. In my gut, I do not want this job, and given the opportunity to do so, I would decline the offer.

I would do so because I am not seasoned enough to be ready for contingencies. My temper is short, and my hand is quick. Neither is of my doing, but I fear the combination could be my undoing.

———⚬⚬⚬———

He slept badly and rose early.

He dressed deliberately, choosing each item of attire carefully. He didn't want to look too different from the cowboys and teamsters and farmers he expected to be his clientele, yet he wanted to present the town's elders with visual assurances that he was not a cowboy, a teamster, or a farmer, even though they already knew that.

Clairborne also suspected that being well dressed would give him an element of implicit authority that, most times, would be to his advantage, especially with men who worked with their hands.

Regarding his reflection in the full-length mirror beside the washstand, Clairborne recalled the words of Wild Billy Martin. "Be ready for anything."

It was getting cooler, so his long jacket would be comfortable. It made him look a little more substantial, serious. It also covered his holster. He decided that was good. It would cause him to think a little—just a little—before drawing his Colt. He decided to ride out of town later in the day to practice drawing the pistol from beneath the black broadcloth, to determine the most natural, efficient movements. He wanted to have a second handgun on his person as well. One of the short-barreled Colts almost fit into his inside left breast pocket but not quite, and the bulge it produced told all but the blind that Tucker Clairborne packed a pocket gun. "Too bad," he said aloud. He'd rather have it than not have it. He also decided to consult with Mr. Horton, the tailor, to redesign the interior pocket, to reinforce it and realign it to facilitate carrying and withdrawing the short-barreled Colt.

He straightened his shoulders and put on the new hat, but not before turning it over in both hands to admire it: dark-gray 10X beaver, silk lined, five-inch crown, four-and-a-half inch brim with a kettle curl. His initials were embossed in gold letters in the leather sweatband.

The image reflected back at him was of a young man trying to be taken seriously. A mustache? Would a mustache, a beard, some facial hair help? Couldn't hurt. Start with a mustache. He'd discovered he very much enjoyed his daily shave. Two thoughts followed contemplation of hot towels and bay rum: Don't go at the same time every day. Matter of fact, don't do anything at the same time every day. Don't make it easy for somebody to lie in wait. Also, barbershops were even better than saloons for picking up the latest rumors, the comings and goings of notable personalities. Good. A daily shave. For free. Tony Rigetti told him this morning, "You no pay, Mr. Clairborne. You come here, others come here too, and that's a good for me."

He looked down at his new boots, which rose almost to his knees. Beneath the patina of unavoidable dust, the black leather fairly glowed from three applications of wax rubbed in by the cobbler's apprentice. Clairborne raised his right foot to wipe off the dust on the section of trouser leg between knee and boot top and then repeated the procedure with the left.

Retrieving a clean handkerchief from the sideboard, he ran it over his upper lip and then tucked it into his right inside pocket.

No more delay. Time to go. He studied his reflected image. First he smiled, and then he shook his head.

"I'm no lawman," he mumbled as he opened the door. "Just make sure nobody else knows that."

———<>———

From a distance of little less than mile, Abilene, Kansas, reminded Sam Caudill of an anthill. The closer he got, the more accurate the analogy became. It seemed to be a study in opposites: frenzy on one hand, order on the other, and above it all, a mantle of dust that seemed impervious to prairie wind.

Caudill pulled gently on the reins and leaned forward on the saddle horn. Although he'd never been to Abilene, he had no doubt that he could find whatever passed as the main thoroughfare and the commercial enterprises he sought. The question was finding Tucker Clairborne. Loosening the reins and clicking his tongue was all it took to get his mount moving. At the edge of the cattle yard, a knot of men leaned against a rail, their backs to Caudill's approach. He dismounted and walked up to them, offering his hand to the first man who noticed his approach.

"Sam Caudill, Rocking C. Pleasure to meet you."

"Why it's a dang pleasure to meet you Mr. Caudill. We heard you was a comin' with more 'n five thousand head. Oh. Tim Plougher's my handle."

"When are you fellas loading?" Caudill asked.

"Tomorrow. Should take two days, then we're done, and it's back to San Antone."

Caudill smiled. "Thought you boys looked like Texicans."

"Sure enough," Plougher replied. "Your herd close, is it?"

"A day south. Say, any of you boys know a fella name of Clairborne? Tucker Clairborne?"

Another cowboy leaned back from the rail and said, "You mean the new sheriff? Fella missin' a finger?"

Caudill's jaw dropped. "Well...it...no. What do you mean 'the new sheriff'?"

The cowboy ejected a stream of tobacco juice into the dirt.

"Fella from down Texas way got hisself appointed sheriff yestiddy. Word is he lost a finger taking a dally. Ollie's the only one seen him, though."

"That's 'cause today's his first day on the job," an unusually large and ugly cowboy ventured. "And we're all takin' bets on when's gonna be his last," the man said, drawing laughs and nods from the others.

"It can't be," Caudill told himself, and then he smiled. "Sure it can, and dang if that don't beat all. That old boy rides in with a gun and a lawbook and, bam, he gets a badge. If that don't beat all!"

Another of the hands, the one called Ollie, spoke up. "'Less I miss my guess, that's him right there," he said, nodding toward the rider approaching from town.

Caudill swung his head around. Sure enough, it was Clairborne riding at a trot into the face of a strong breeze and the sun. The breeze blew back his jacket. The sun glinted off the brass badge pinned to his vest.

Caudill felt a surge of affection as he contemplated the familiar form and face, a face creased by a wide smile, a form clad in fine, expensive new clothes.

Clairborne swung down and shook Caudill's extended hand.

491

"Tucker Clairborne, you rascal. What's this they tell me about you being a sheriff?" He laughed.

"Constable actually." Clairborne smiled back. "Pretty strange, I admit." Aware of the cowhands observing the reunion, he faced them and said, "Howdy, boys. Ya'll doing OK, are you?"

"You bet, sheriff," said the man who had introduced himself as Tim Plougher. "We're collecting our wages tomorrow, and we're all looking forward to washin' the trail dust off'n our backs and flushin' it down our gullets."

"Well, have fun," Clairborne said. "Just have fun. Since I just finished pushing a herd up from Texas myself, I know ya'll've earned it."

Clairborne faced Caudill. "How far out's the herd?"

"Be here tomorrow for sure."

"Let me show you where to drive them. McCoy's got pens ready and waiting, along with everything else," Clairborne said, not wanting to mention cash money specifically.

Caudill mounted. "Good. You can tell me how you got that star on the way."

———

Three days later it was done.

At four thirty in the afternoon, the men of the Rocking C stood in line to collect their wages in front of a folding table behind which sat Sam Caudill and Isaac Steiner. As a subtle sign of their return to civilization, Biscuit had loosened one side of the wagon's canvas cover to make an improvised sun screen under which the wages were dispensed and ledgers were signed.

Before he started the process, Caudill climbed on a crate and looked at the tattered cowhands for a long moment.

"Boys, let's us thank our Lord and savior."

Each man removed his hat and bowed his head.

"Lord, we just thank you for being with us through this drive. We know you have a plan for each of us, and we just ask that you help us to understand it. We ask that you receive the souls of the five fine young men what didn't make it. They were good boys, each of 'em, but I expect you know that already. So we just thank you, Lord. Thanks for everything you done for us and everything you're going to do. Amen."

Caudill replaced his hat and cleared his throat.

"Boys, I don't guess I need to say thanks for what you done. The money you're about to pocket says that better'n anything. But you done dang good these last months, and all but five of us 'at started are standin' here today. You can leave your bedrolls in the wagon if you care to instead of lugging 'em into town, which is where I assume you're headed. We're bound for home in five or six days, and I truly hope most of you ride with us. 'Em as don't, I just want you to know my daddy and me appreciate what you done. Well, I expect you all want me to quit beating my gums and get on with your wages. Let's get you boys paid."

Caudill had given some thought to his speech, and he'd wanted to add a plea for each man to think of his immortal soul before and during the visit to Abilene. He decided not to get too religious, thinking that it might rankle some of the men even though not doing so would have disappointed his father.

And, he had to admit to himself, right about now a beer and a pretty girl were running down the homestretch about neck and neck with a hot bath and a dinner, even though he'd never known either the product of a brewer's art or the blissful frustration of young love.

He chided himself for thinking of alcohol and carnal knowledge, for letting Lucifer slip into his thoughts like a foot into an old boot. Nevertheless, he was in a hurry to get to Abilene and test his self-discipline. According to Clairborne, at last count the expanding town offered more than eight boarding houses, three hotels, two bathhouses, three general stores, six stables, and twelve saloons, more than enough for a test of his will.

—⁂—

There were no rules.

The town council—which was self-appointed—had yet to write down the ordinances it wanted enforced. That made it pretty much up to the judgment of the twenty-one-year-old Virginian.

Clairborne finished his second cup of coffee, wiped his lips with a napkin, pushed back from the table, and donned his hat. With a nod at Dominic the waiter, he walked through the lobby and out to the sidewalk, where he paused to fish his Breguet out of his vest pocket. Three minutes before eight. He looked to his right, then to his left, tipping his hat to the two women passing in a buckboard. Thirty yards to his left on the same side of the street, he spotted a body in the dirt beside which sat a man holding his head.

Clairborne approached slowly, swiveling his head, noticing others passing without so much as a glance at the two inert forms. Less than ten feet away from the duo, Clairborne heard snoring, great, ragged roars punctuated by what almost sounded like hiccups. Closing to within five feet, he observed that the man lying in the street was on his side, his head rolled forward toward the ground, drool from his open mouth flowing steadily into the sand, which he periodically inhaled, triggering the small coughs that sounded like hiccups. The man sitting on the side of the horse trough held his head in his hands without moving. Between his legs was a platter-sized circle of vomit that had also spattered his mule-ear boots.

Clairborne resisted the urge to touch the man's shoulder.

"You all right there, partner?" he asked.

No response.

"Hey, fella. You OK?"

The man squinted up at Clairborne, gobs of vomit suspended in his beard, the visible portion of his eyes so bloodshot Clairborne winced in sympathy. Apparently, the combination of head movement and looking into the sun was all it took to activate the man's gag reflex. He lowered his head, retched, and mumbled something incoherent.

Clairborne looked around. A man exited the saloon, walked a short way to his horse, mounted, and rode off without so much as a backward glance. Two other men, deep in conversation, walked past on the boardwalk and showed no awareness of the self-inflicted suffering. Clairborne followed their example and walked away to check the recently constructed holding cell wherein he was to deposit all miscreants.

He was alarmed and amused by what he observed. Tucked behind the room on Front Street that was to be his office, the rectangular structure of roughhewn lumber ten feet wide, twenty feet long, and eight feet high seemed more appropriate for livestock than people. It had neither windows nor doors. Access to its interior was gained by climbing a ladder to its roof and then using another ladder to descend into the jail. Once a miscreant had lowered himself into the interior space, the ladder was pulled up, and the opening was covered with a sturdy hatch secured by two beams slipped through purpose-made latches. Four evenly spaced air holes provided the only ventilation for what would be oven-like in the summer and arctic-like during the winter. Clairborne found the structure to be an interesting combination of function, economy, and simplicity.

But as he stood looking into the unoccupied, dirt-floored interior, his thoughts returned to the two drunks. How in the coon-dog blazes could you get a drunk, a passed-out, dead-weight body, up one ladder and down another? It mattered; it mattered a great deal since it dawned on him that a lot of his work would involve drunks, and a lot of that work with drunks would entail getting them into the jail to safely sleep off their inebriation. He thought of the drunk with puke in his beard. There was no possibility that Clairborne would do anything that would transfer such foul substances to his own clothes.

And then another thought occurred.

Far more important than his clothes was his safety.

He had a vision of trying to help a drunk to his feet and the drunk responding by slipping Clairborne's Colt from its holster and putting a .44 slug into his liver.

"I'm going to need a deputy," he decided quickly, recognizing that the demand taking shape in his mind might well get

496

him out of the job he really didn't want in the first place. He also recalled Bigelow's recent observation that the town elders were drafting codes and ordinances he would enforce in addition to keeping the peace.

"Things get pretty quiet in the winter," Bigelow told him. "That's when we'd want you to be collecting our new municipal taxes, and as soon as we get a court set up, it'll be your job to serve papers and such."

Although he'd understood the need for a growing town to have such institutions and related revenues, Clairborne had not liked that list of duties at all. "They don't give me a deputy to help with all that stuff, I'll hand 'em my badge."

Then what? Looking up at the thin strata of clouds scudding east toward the rising sun, he knew the answer.

"Head to Wyoming to check my inheritance." Contemplation of property and income made dealing with drunks and cowboys blowing off steam even less appealing. Heading back to Front Street, Clairborne adjusted his cravat and looked fleetingly at the four digits of his left hand. It was curious that no one had asked him about it since he came to town. Confident that his demand for a deputy would be denied, he considered checking the train schedules to see what was smoking and then decided that would be a little premature.

"That can come later," he thought, "after I've quit."

Continuing his rounds, Clairborne considered whom he should hit with his request, McCoy or Bigelow, and decided on Bigelow. McCoy was too accommodating. Bigelow, on the other hand, was not only "new money" but also clearly full of himself, to the point of being unable to modify a given position for fear of looking weak. He knew right where to look for Abilene's second wealthiest man: the construction site at the corner of Buckeye and Third, where the town's first bank was taking shape. Bigelow was to be the president of the bank; six other Abilene property owners constituted the board of directors, and rumor had it that Joseph McCoy was a primary investor—and silent partner—as well.

Nearing the site, Clairborne slowed to watch the work in progress, The bank would be the first of the town's commercial structures to have a true foundation consisting of stone and mortar paving for its basement and primary vault. Swarms of workers had already completed the framing and were busily raising rafters to support a pitched roof. Three wagons full of flagstones and bricks waited in line behind the site where stacks of lumber were depleted as quickly as the town's new sawmill—half-owned by Joseph McCoy—and freight trains could deliver its green, unseasoned wood from eastern forests.

Bigelow stood to one side of the site, a rolled-up set of plans tucked under one arm. He noticed Clairborne's approach and extended his hand.

"Morning, Constable. Another fine day in Abilene, isn't it?"

Clairborne had to admit it was. The autumn weather of the last week had brought crisp nights and cool, sunny days.

"Mr. Bigelow, there's something I need to discuss with you. Business."

Bigelow regarded the newly minted lawman with a broad grin.

"You looking for an opportunity to invest in Abilene, perchance?"

"Oh no, no. Not that kind of business. My new business. I require a deputy. We have to have at least two full-time sworn officers to keep the peace and do the other things you folks are talking about," Clairborne said. Then he added, "At the rate this place is growing."

Bigelow scratched his chin and looked up at the ragged clouds skimming over the rooftops.

"Actually, I see your point, Constable. I do. Anyone in mind?"

Clairborne had not anticipated Bigelow's response.

"Ah, no. I just know...Well, among other things, think about how one person would get a drunk cowboy into the jail if he didn't want to go. If he resisted, don't think one man could do it. And if you want the office to be responsible for tax collection and such, that means being out in the county, out of town for a stretch at time."

"Heck, never even thought of it." Bigelow smiled. "You know, the fact that you identify such things makes me sure you're the perfect man for the job. I can't speak for the others, but I think the case for a deputy's pretty strong with even a cursory examination of the particulars." He put his hand on Clairborne's shoulder. "Why don't you start looking for candidates, and I'll see what I can do."

Clairborne tipped his hat. "Thanks for giving it some thought, Mr. Bigelow. Appreciate it."

Walking away from Bigelow, who quickly shifted his attention back to the bank construction, Clairborne was angry with himself. "Now what?" he asked himself. "I'll tell you now what, now you've got to find somebody to do the job, and not just anybody. Even if you plan to light a shuck out of here as soon as you can, you still have to pick somebody who can—and will—cover your back until then. And I'm sure not going to be a tax collector. Damnation."

He quickly realized there was only one potential source of manpower he could consider: the men of the Rocking C. Just as quickly he realized that while every one of them had done his job, he knew few of them well enough to analyze their temperament, judgment, or their abilities with fists and weapons. Stopping to observe Front Street's morning traffic, he decided to seek recommendations from Sam Caudill and Isaac Steiner. If they could just agree on two or three names, he could take it from there.

Over dinner that same night, they did.

John Toombs, Dutch Albrecht, and Findley McComb.

"Each of those boys is hard as woodpecker lips and as reliable as the sunrise," Caudill said while Steiner nodded. "I think any of them could do the job if they wanted."

"Which one would you recommend of the three? Like I said, main consideration for me is watching my back in times of trouble, that and being able to keep the peace while I'm catching some shut-eye."

"Isaac, you haven't said much. What do you think?" Caudill asked.

Steiner used his fork to push sweet peas through the congealed butter on his plate. "Well, if I had to choose one and only one to take to a shin-kickin' contest, I think it'd be McComb."

Caudill leaned back from the table.

"Really? I thought you and him had words a couple of times."

"Did," Steiner said. Turning to Clairborne he added, "McComb's from Virginia too, one of Jackson's foot cavalry, I hear."

"Really? You know where in Virginia?" Clairborne said. "I've shot the breeze with him a few times during the drive, but I didn't recognize his accent as Virginia." He shook his head and continued. "Guess the most relevant question is what'd you have words with him about?"

Clairborne thought one of Steiner's most admirable traits was the way the man considered his words before uttering them. Steiner's Teutonic reserve gave added credence to his opinions. Clairborne watched Steiner turn his glass of apple cider in his hand while he thought.

"Tucker, I hope you don't take this the wrong way, but it doesn't surprise me you haven't heard of McComb's family."

"How so?"

"He's from some hardscrabble farm in the Blue Ridge. You're from a big plantation in the tidewater. How many folks did you know before the war that farmed their own land, that didn't have slaves?"

Clairborne was quiet. He couldn't see much connection between his question and Steiner's answer.

"You ever spend much time in the mountains, the Blue Ridge?" Steiner asked.

"Ah, no."

"McComb and I've known each other long enough to talk about our homes. I don't think there could be a bigger difference between his situation and yours, especially considering you both hail from the same state."

501

Steiner went on to say that McComb was one of the hardest-working men he'd ever known but also one of the "prickliest," by which he meant "I think he'd rather eat a horse turd than take any guff."

"But he'll do what needs to be done, and brother, can that boy fight. I've seen him in more brawls than any other two men I know. He just doesn't tolerate disrespect, for sure."

Clairborne demurred. "Heck, Isaac, I don't want to spend time separating my deputy from folks he thinks insulted him."

"Oh, he's not that bad, Tucker," Caudill said. "A might touchy, yes, but a dang good fella to have around, all things considered. Don't you think, Isaac?"

Steiner smiled. "Sure, boss. All things considered."

"Tell you what," Clairborne said. "Don't say anything to him until I get a chance to watch him for a while, get a feeling for how he handles things in town," he said.

Caudill and Steiner both grinned, and then Caudill said, "That's a wise step to take."

The next morning, Clairborne rode out to the Rocking C camp, where most of the cowboys were relaxing between visits to the town. He was looking for Findley McComb but learned that he was in Abilene getting his saddle repaired.

Sitting on an empty water keg, Clairborne realized how much he liked the men around him. He may not ever ride with them again, but he'd spent months with them in the most challenging situations he'd ever known, and now it was over. These boys would go home and restart the cycle of caring for cattle, collecting them, driving them north to market. He considered each man. They smiled and laughed. They were young, and as Caudill had observed, each was as "hard as woodpecker lips," be they white or Negro or Mexican, Yankee or Southern boy. It occurred to him that he would actively miss their company. Then he saw D.D. Dalghren riding into camp. Trailing behind, tongue lolling and tail wagging, Lonesome broke into a run when he saw Clairborne. The puppy tried to jump into Clairborne's lap but Clairborne suddenly stood and just as suddenly made a painful decision.

"D.D., looks like you and this old pup pretty much belong together. Why don't you take him back to Texas with you?"

Dalghren looked surprised and delighted. "You mean that Tucker? I can keep him? I surely would like that but he's your hound."

"Not really," Clairborne said, suddenly wanting to terminate the conversation and leave lest he change his mind. As he mounted his horse, Clairborne said, "you found him and he's spent more time with you than with me. Besides, I can't keep an eye on him in town. I'm not saying I won't miss the little scruff but it's better this way. Adios."

As he rode away, Clairborne resisted a nearly overwhelming urge to turn his head to see if Lonesome was following him.

—⁓—

Journal entry
September, 1868
Abilene, Kansas

For better or worse, I have a deputy to assist me in my efforts to enforce the law, such as it is, in this town.

Findley McComb is a fellow Virginian, although I would say that is the only thing we have in common. He hails from Elkton in the Shenandoah Valley, served with Jackson, and was twice wounded, once grievously. From what I have been able to gather, his family had a small farm in the Blue Ridge above Elkton but lost it shortly after the war. One of three boys, only he survived the war, his father having died before the onset of hostilities.

Although I met him in Texas and rode north to Abilene in his company, I did not get to know him all that well. After observing him for two consecutive nights as he made the rounds with other Rocking C hands and other Texicans blowing off steam, I offered him the job.

Small and lean as a rope, McComb seems to possess two desirable attributes—three actually, considering the reliability he manifested as a Rocking C hand. He has both a great sense of humor and an equally great sense of honor. In two nights of watching him, I've seen him mediate to prevent a fight twice and also pound flat a man who mistook McComb's small stature as representative of his grit.

When I offered him the post of deputy this afternoon, his immediate response was that he didn't "have much use for rules and laws and such." He told me that it seemed to him "if folks just heeded the words in the Good Book about treatin' others the way you want to be treated, there wouldn't be a need for all them other laws tellin' me how to behave."

I won him over by agreeing with him. He seemed intrigued by my proposition that since Abilene didn't really have all that much law, he and I would pretty much decide on our own how we would go about keeping folks from getting hurt and cowboys out of trouble.

So here we are, two Virginians with no experience as lawmen about to take on the responsibility for keeping the peace in a town full of rowdy cowhands intent on drinking, gambling, whoring, and fighting—and losing their wages as fast as they can. On the other side of the coin is the handful of ladies equally intent on seeing all such activity halted immediately and replaced by Bible meetings, temperance leagues, and garden clubs. And although there are a lot more cowboys than bluenoses, I've already seen how much sway these flinty biddies hold over their starched-collar, dry-goods-peddler husbands. Actually, I feel kind of sorry for the husbands. On one hand, they know who benefits most from cowboys throwing money around. But at the end of their day counting cash, they have to go home and explain just why it is they haven't shut down all the saloons, gambling parlors, and related dens of inequity.
I don't envy them one bit. When I see one of them getting his ear chewed by his shrewish wife, I want to pull his other ear and tell him to get some self-respect. That sure as blazes is never going to happen to me.

It occurs to me that I should be careful about thinking in absolutes when it comes to my future. Today, I received telegrams from my bank and my business partner. It seems my investments have done well. With a little study, I've come to understand the concept of net worth, and in that regard, my situation exceeds anything I could have imagined less than a year ago. But I have much more study ahead if I am to chart my own financial course. The bank requested direction regarding my earnings, asking whether I preferred shares, bonds, commodities, real estate, gold, or cash reserves. Since I have such paltry understanding of the options offered, I've opted for gold until I can knowledgeably consider the alternatives.

It simply does not seem real to me, but thousands of dollars in hard currency secured in my name and available at the speed of the telegraph is slowly but surely altering my perspective. For the better. Definitely for the better.

—◦◦◦—

The ensuing week was far less eventful than Clairborne had feared.

He and McComb worked out a routine based on trial and error. The saloons being open twenty-four hours a day complicated the work schedule somewhat, but both agreed they had to be on duty during the night, when the saloons were busiest.

Clairborne started his day midmorning, with McComb joining him six or so hours later. Their rounds rotated them at opposite sides of Front Street. They knew that the sound of gunplay would carry and they'd be able to reinforce each other within seconds from just about anywhere in town.

After eight days on the job, there had been no shooting worth noting, which pleasantly surprised Clairborne, who'd expected at least a "hoorah" or two, cowboys blowing off steam by firing into the air as they entered or exited town.

Instead, there were just a lot of drunks. Drunks fighting each other. Drunks falling off horses, drunks getting run over by a farm wagon, and one drunk who fell out of the second-story window of Abilene's only two-story whorehouse, a place Clairborne avoided as much as possible after his earlier experience there.

McComb was a source of fascination.

Three times in as many days, McComb, all by himself, had jailed men much larger than he was. On two of those occasions, McComb knocked out his foe, one by battering him with a spittoon as the two rolled around the saloon floor.

Another surprise came when Clairborne entered the Alamo saloon one evening. McComb, leaning against an upright piano, was singing "Sweet Peril" in a fine tenor, a performance that had several lean, gun-toting, inebriated cowboys dabbing tears at the couplet "Alas, how easily things go wrong. A sigh too much, a kiss too long...."

Clairborne watched in amazement as the place erupted in cheers when McComb finished and worked his way to the front door.

"Findley, you have a fine singing voice indeed."

"Thanks, but where I come from, everyone can sing a ballad and dance a shivaree."

Afterward, Clairborne tried to recall similar experiences at Warwick. Balls and cotillions, yes. Hymns, yes. Carols, yes. But routine singing and dancing with family, friends, neighbors? Never. It was another example of the fact that while they were born in the same state, they might as well have hailed from different countries.

It didn't take long before Clairborne also understood the subtle and not-so-subtle influence money played in his work. Not money as in wages, but money as in business, ownership, shares. And it affected even him.

Within the first week, Clairborne learned who owned which saloons, who had interests in them. It explained a lot about why saloons were thriving despite the insistence of certain women in town that they be shut down. He'd known of McCoy's ownership interests since they met. What he'd learned since was that nearly every one of Abilene's civic leaders owned outright or had significant interests in one or more of the town's drinking parlors and "entertainment pavilions."

He also quickly noted which saloons plied their clients with whiskey bought from Great Western supply, the company in which he'd invested while in Saint Louis. Not many. In contrast to Great Western's line of goods, most of Abilene's whiskey mills sold "tonsil varnish" that was locally produced, very bad and cheap. It seemed that the few selling Great Western libations also were the less rowdy, probably, he decided, because they were inherently more expensive. Cowboys could drink more for less and get "knee-crawlin' drunk" faster in the saloons offering local rotgut. And that meant he and McComb spent more time in the dives than in the "high-class" drinking emporia.

Two weeks into the job, the last of the large Texas herds of 1868 straggled into Abilene's stockyards.

On a crisp morning, Clairborne sat in a chair on the porch of his one-room office at the end of the main thoroughfare. Boots propped against a post, he leaned the chair back on its two rear legs and observed the comings and goings. A steady westerly wind kept the smell of horse urine and feces at bay, not that he would have noticed if it were otherwise, having long since become inured to the prevailing stench.

McComb rode up and dismounted.

"You been out to the yards, talked with them newcomers yet?" he asked as he stepped up on the porch.

"No. Why?"

McComb removed his hat, withdrew a kerchief from his vest pocket, and wiped his brow. "Was I a betting man, I'd put a month's wages there's trouble coming."

"How so?"

"I can't recall but one other bunch of men as sorry looking, as sour, and as downright angry as them boys. Us at Appomattox."

Clairborne was paying attention from the beginning of the conversation. McComb's observation focused his thoughts at the exclusion of all else.

Replacing his hat and rubbing his chin, McComb said, "Here's what I think's gonna happen. Them boys'll collect their wages, ride into town, and swallow everthing that's liquid, including horse piss if it's in a glass, all of which is normal. But these boys is raw. They been on the short end of the stick for months, and what they been through makes our drive look easy. They're gonna be looking for asses to kick. For sure."

Clairborne immediately thought of shotguns and conversation.

Wild Bill had advised him about the value of a scattergun. His intuition told him a talk with the trail boss might help mitigate events to come.

Then he thought the better of it. What would he say, even obliquely, to the leader? "Talk to your men about good manners?"

No. Best to just get ready for the worst then be pleasantly surprised if it didn't happen.

In the cattle pens, the new arrivals sat their horses in silence, staring into the distance as if unaware that their travails were over.

Consisting of cattle from six smaller ranches, the herd had been dogged by misfortune and bad decisions from the start. Inexperience and argument led to changes in plans that resulted in delayed departure north across prairies parched to desperate dryness. Stampedes caused by weather, rustlers, and Indians angered at the trail boss's refusal to pay a toll resulted in the loss of fifteen percent of the herd. Death by thirst took another five percent. An unusually vicious storm front swept over the plains almost a hundred miles northwest of the herd, giving it not so much as the scent of rain but dumping a flood surge into the Canadian River that swept downstream just as the herd began to cross. Another four percent and two cowboys were lost.

By the time they dragged into Abilene, frustration compounded by exhaustion ground the drovers down to the nubbin of their patience, abrading the last vestige of civility from men who valued manners.

Clairborne watched them from a distance.

Red-eyed, rail-thin, and raw-boned, they rode into town with an eerie silence, teetering on the knife-edge of collapse.

They rode at a walk instead of at the gallop as had every other bunch he'd seen, including the Rocking C. They sat their horses in front of the saloons and general stores, silent and specter-like as if confused by the options before them.

Clairborne thought he'd better get himself another cup of coffee. It was going to be a long night for certain. Then he decided he didn't need caffeine. Tonight, when alcohol met exhaustion and the realization dawned on the cowboys that they'd actually made it, that their suffering was over, there would be more than enough adrenaline to go around.

———

Keeping an eye on the late arrivals was easy because most of the cowboys up from Texas had gone home, reducing the number of itinerant drovers in Abilene by almost three-quarters from the late summer peak.

The first night for the latecomers was not all that exceptional, primarily because most of the hands had not yet been paid and remained in camp on the outskirts of town. The eight men who did come in with cash in their pockets, predictably enough, headed straight for the saloons nearest the stock-yards and drank themselves into oblivion—quietly, by Abilene standards.

Two days later, a fall storm wandered in from the west, fit-fully shifting from cold to warm so quickly as to complicate deci-sions on what to wear. Any time it rained in Abilene, the streets became treacherous pahways at best and muddy morasses at worst, with some puddles more like small ponds. Horses hitched to rails stood mostly on three legs with their heads down, ears back, manes dripping.

In late morning, Clairborne had met with Bigelow and other Abilene civic leaders in one of what were becoming reg-ular meetings to discuss civic matters. He sat against the wall listening to the town fathers' discussion for about forty-five minutes and then gradually lost interest after learning a jus-tice of the peace was to be appointed, a criminal code had been passed, and he was now expected to keep a record of every arrest and its outcome. His mind shifted to the coming eve-ning and what to expect, so he was surprised when he heard his name.

"Sorry," he said.

Bigelow smiled. "Mr. Pelletier has a question for you, Constable."

"Sir?" Clairborne said, shifting his gaze to the corpulent, wheezing, bald and heavily bearded man he liked least of all the group.

"Now that we've provided a set of codes, I wanted to know what you think could best be done to enforce them, to...ah,

guarantee our town's reputation, to stop all gunplay and drunk-
enness, all the lewd behavior?"

Clairborne's peripheral vision took in the others' reaction to
the question. There was much examination of fingernails and
pocket watches. Only one man looked at Clairborne and smiled.
Pelletier hooked his thumbs under his violet silk lapels and
waited for the answer, his fat lower lip protruding from beneath
the compressed upper.

"Well, let's see," Clairborne said. "Number one, ban the wearing of guns inside town limits. Number two, shut down all the
saloons. Number three, shut down all the whorehouses. That
ought to just about do it."

Silence.

He looked around the room. Most of the faces registered stu-
pefaction quickly replaced by furious calculation of the financial
impact such actions would have on their respective portfolios.

Mr. Hogworth, outright owner of a dry goods store and silent
partner in three of the town's saloons, was the first to speak.

"Well, thank you for your forthright answer, Constable. We
do appreciate it, and I'm sure you've provided us with grist for
the mill in the future. Now gentleman, I suggest we move from
the theoretical to the pragmatic and discuss our water supply
and construction of public privies."

Clairborne smiled. He nodded at Bigelow when he caught
his eye, stood, and left the smoke-filled room.

He paused under the porch roof to consider the rain falling
hard and straight down, his slicker hanging from a peg in his
office across the submerged street.

He smiled again. "Bet that's the last time I get asked for an opinion by those folks," he thought, grin getting wider.

It didn't take a Swiss timepiece to know it was close to dinnertime and getting closer by the minute to whatever this night would bring.

It stopped raining just before Clairborne finished his meal, walked to his office, and lit up a cigar on the porch, watching traffic pick up once people realized the clouds had emptied.

McComb strolled up, sat on the other chair, and used his jack-knife to scrape mud from his boots. Neither spoke, Clairborne absorbed with his smoke, McComb with the particularly vis-cous mass covering his boots from ankle down.

They watched two separate bunches of cowboys lope into town five minutes apart. Each group rode abreast taking up nearly the entire width of the street and forcing some wagons and riders coming the other way to yield to their passage. The cowboys shouted at one another as they passed, egging one another on to see who could drink the most in the shortest time.

"Well, I don't much like the looks of the way this evening's headed," Clairborne said softly, examining the inch-long ash glowing on the end of his panatela.

"Nope," McComb replied.

Neither spoke again during the twenty minutes it took Clairborne to finish and lay the still-burning cigar on arm of his chair.

"Well, reckon we'd better get about keeping the peace," Clairborne said.

They stood and headed off in opposite directions, paying as much attention to where they were stepping as they did to the human activity around them. In the ensuing three hours, Clairborne and McComb passed each other twice, trading no more than a nod each time. Clairborne had watched two men whale away at each other in the middle of a saloon, their pugilistic ineptitude precluding the need to intervene. McComb had held the reins of another man's horse while he struggled to help his soused companion find his seat in the saddle. A few minutes later, he chided another cowboy for hurling dinner and several pints of beer into a water trough.

When the cowboy finished emptying his stomach, McComb stood in front of him with his hands on his hips.

"Mister, that's about the damn dumbest thing I've seen this week. Why'd you foul the water when you got the whole damn street to puke on?"

The cowboy looked around, dazed and confused by the question. His buddies laughed so hard they had to lean on a hitching rail to keep from falling into the mud.

"Hell, Deputy. Shorty's so pie eyed he couldn't hit the ground with his hat."

"Well, he should o' hit it with his puke," McComb said. Bending at the waist to look the cowboy in the eye, he said, "Now, I'll tell you what. Shorty, is it?"

The cowboy nodded as he wiped the stomach residue off of his chin whiskers.

"Shorty, I want you to pull the bung and drain this here trough, then get yourself a bucket and refill it with fresh water. OK, pardner?"

He turned to Shorty's buddies.

"You boys can help him or not, makes no nevermind to me, but I'm serious about that trough being cleaned out."

"Don't worry, Deputy," said Shorty's buddies. "We'll just a-set here and have ourselves a smoke while Shorty cleans up. No problem at all."

McComb smiled at Shorty's friends and said, "Much obliged."

———————

Clairborne had just left the Sunflower Saloon when he heard a pistol shot, shouts, and another shot.

He sprinted back, drawing his Colt as he ran.

Two men ran into the night, paused to look up and down the street as if to remember where they'd tied their horses, and then saw Clairborne. Each carried a pistol at the ready.

Clairborne slowed to a walk.

"Where you boys going in such a rush?" he asked.

The cowboy farthest away from him, the one partially shielded from Clairborne's view by the body of the closest man, leaned around his buddy and said, "None o' yer goddamn business!"

As he delivered his defiant message, a third man blew out of the saloon. Hatless and holding his pistol at eye level, he almost collided with the two on the boardwalk.

He fired into the man closest to Clairborne, the ball from his .36-caliber Remington sending the man sprawling into the muddy street. The cowboy who had cursed Clairborne fell backward to get away from the shooter, firing at him as he tumbled to the boardwalk. The round missed, smashing into the saloon wall and showing Clairborne with splinters. The hatless shooter flinched and then swung his Remington at the recumbent form scrambling crab-like to get away and get to his feet.

Clairborne's brain worked furiously. The only two things he knew for certain were that hatless cowboy had shot the first in the back and that he, Clairborne, would shoot anyone who pointed a gun at him and decide legal niceties later.

"You son of a bitch. You goddam assassin!" the hatless cowboy screamed at the man who had cursed Clairborne. Thumbing back the hammer, he stepped forward to close the gap between him and his recumbent prey.

"Hold your fire there," Clairborne yelled.

The hatless man whirled and pulled the trigger at precisely the same second Clairborne exerted the requisite pressure on his. The difference was that Clairborne's pistol was already aimed.

Clairborne's mind registered the hatless man falling on the other cowboy and the horses tied to the hitching rails frantically rearing, neighing, yanking loose, and racing away in the night, one of them stepping on the back of the hapless cowboy lying face down in the muck.

The hatless man thrashed and screamed. The cowboy who had cursed Clairborne struggled frantically to free himself from his assailant's frenzied convulsions. Rolling to his hands and knees, he saw his pistol on the boardwalk and lunged.

"Leave it! Leave it, goddamn it!" Clairborne yelled, deciding there was too little time and too much distance to kick it away. Turning to expose only his right side, fully extending his arm and aiming his Colt, he yelled again, "Leave it lay! Leave—"

The cursing cowboy accelerated his movements, seizing the gun and swinging it up, rolling on his right side.

The muzzle flash illuminated the frieze. Clairborne's shot hit him in his right ear.

The cowboy dropped straight down and didn't quiver. Beside him, the hatless cowboy's reflexive movements wedged his body against the wall, but he continued to push with his right boot, again and again, each time slipping in the blood slathering the rough pine planks. He was silent. His hands and arms, his head were still. Only his right leg moved. Slower. Suddenly his spurs began a furious, staccato pounding, involuntary signals of panic and pain and inchoate recognition that the end was near. Blood seeped from his mouth and nose. His boot and spur thudded twice more, and he was gone.

Clairborne shuddered.

A muffled groan from the street pulled him back to reality. Moving to the inert form in the mud, he hesitated, turned to face the doorway, and yelled, "Butch. Butch. This is Constable Clairborne. What the hell's going on in there?"

The voice of Butch the bartender echoed back, "Nothing now. It's over in here, Constable. Couple of shot men, though."

"Well, get the hell out here and help me," Clairborne yelled back. His call triggered an avalanche of men falling over themselves to see what had transpired outside. Some actually did fall, as the first ones out pulled up to avoid the bodies on the boardwalk and were run over by the mob behind them. Regaining their feet and wiping the sticky, already-congealing blood off their hands on their trousers, the spectators gaped and exclaimed.

"Lord above," said the man closest to Clairborne.

"Somebody see to that man in the street yonder," Clairborne said, pointing at the form with his pistol.

McComb pushed through the crowd, stopped when he saw the bodies, and then lurched forward when he located his boss.

"You OK? You shot?" he blurted.

"No," Clairborne said.

McComb looked around.

"Godawmighty! Two, no, three men down. You get 'em? What happened? You sure you're not shot?"

Clairborne holstered his Colt. "Yeah, Findley," he said, suddenly tired, suddenly very much desiring a cup of coffee. "I don't even...Anybody know these men?"

An unusually thin boy stood up from beside the body of the man who had cursed Clairborne. He raised both hands to his unruly hair and wept.

"Oh, Sheriff, this here's a good man. Just a good, good man. Why'd he have to die anyhow? It was just a darn argument over a Spanish bit."

Butch the bartender stepped forward.

"He's right, Constable. They was just arguing about breaking horses. Then that one," he said, pointing his chin at the cowboy who'd sworn at Clairborne, "slapped leather and hit Toby with his gun." He nodded inside. "His piece went off when he hit him, killed him right then. Don't know that he meant to kill anybody, though. Then Toby's brother jumped up and drew, and Orie shot him too."

Another man in the crowd stepped forward.

"We're all from Texas, Constable. We all know each other, been together these last three months." He looked down at the bodies.

"These men, their families, been a' feuding off and on for a while. We put all that behind us for the drive, but it was hard, Constable. It just wore off all the, all the...I don't know. It just don't seem right to get through all that then to set about killing one another after we made it."

"So two dead in there and two dead, one wounded out here?" Clairborne asked Butch.

The cowboy who was weeping beside the body of the second man Clairborne shot sobbed louder, drawing everyone's attention. He stood and put his hands on top of his head.

"Where's Orie's head?" he cried. "I can't take Orie home to his ma without his head. I can't. I just can't," he sobbed.

Clairborne looked down at the carnage wreaked by his single shot and understood the boy's lament. His bullet had removed a chunk of the cowboy's skull.

"Butch, go get the undertaker," Clairborne said. "You fellas," he said, facing the others, "better get on back to camp, and I don't want any more trouble, hear?"

McComb moved to his side as the crowd slowly and quietly dispersed.

Butch the bartender and a boy who'd materialized out of nowhere splashed buckets of water from the horse troughs on the blood and body matter drying inside on the floor and outside on the saloon wall and boardwalk. Then they attacked the stains with stiff brooms. An hour later, Clairborne saw only wet spots and fresh sawdust where earlier there had been evidence of slaughter. After supervising the undertaker's bonanza, Clairborne pulled out his watch: 3:47 in the morning.

Cowboys and others, teamsters and some farmers mostly, rode or walked in knots up and down the street under solid but thin clouds rendered a pearly translucent by the full moon above them.

Titus Herman entered Clairborne's mind, but he couldn't figure out why.

Clairborne started at the realization that he had not reloaded his Colt. One or two rounds could make the difference, and it would be stupid to get hurt or worse for want of two bullets. Inside his office he replaced Thunder with Lightning in his holster; placed Thunder on his desk; disassembled it; cleaned the powder residue from the barrel, cylinder, and exterior surfaces; and reloaded. Then he held the Colt in both hands and examined it in the light of the single coal-oil lantern keeping darkness at bay in the Abilene constable's office. Wild Bill Martin.

What would Wild Bill Martin think of what had transpired since that day in the Missouri woods? Why was he thinking of Wild Bill Martin just now instead of his father? That seemed strange.

A shot rang out, then another, another, then a veritable fusillade.

Clairborne stuffed Thunder into his waistband and bolted for the door. Outside, he paused. It sounded as if the shooting had come from his right, from the eastern end of the street. He started running, passing men leaning out from behind cover and peering in the direction he took.

Each open saloon cast a patch of oily yellow light out of its front doors onto the sidewalk and mud, but Clairborne wasn't counting how many he traversed as he ran down Front Street, slowing only at the sight of a group of men gathered outside the Bucket of Blood, split evenly on both sides of the door.

"What's going on?" Clairborne shouted.

"Your deputy's got his hands full, that's for sure," said an older cowboy who recognized Clairborne.

The message galvanized Clairborne. He drew and cocked both Colts. He could hear shouting from inside. Then the voice of his deputy.

"I ain't gonna say it again, goddamn it. Put it down!"

Clairborne peeked around the corner of the door.

Findley McComb, his back to the door, held his pistol at arm's length, aiming it at the head of a cowboy with flaming red hair and beard. The redhead, in turn, held his pistol at another cowboy who looked even younger and was sitting on the floor with his back against the bar. Blood covered his face and hands, which were held palm up. Another cowboy lay moaning in a heap under an overturned table. Several others lined the walls, all facing in, all holding their hands conspicuously clear of their weapons. Cards, poker chips, dice, coins, glasses, and beer pitchers were scattered across the sawdust-covered floor.

Clairborne slowly entered, moving to McComb's right as he said, "All right, boys. There's two of us law dogs here now, so everyone else needs to put down their pieces real slow like." Then, for reasons he could never explain, he added, "It's time to think about mamma."

The faces that weren't already turned his way joined the ones that were, several mouths dropping open at the same time. One man at the back of the room turned to the three-card monte dealer standing next to him. "What the hell did he say?" he asked from the corner of his mouth. The gambler shook his head, holding his hands out all the while. "Something about his mother."

The redhead looked at Clairborne, quickly focusing on the two Colts aimed at his chest. He lowered his piece to the floor and raised his hands.

"Findley, get some rope and tie up anyone that needs it. We'll give 'em a night in the hoosegow while we sort this out."

Two hours later, Clairborne and his deputy sat across from each other in their office. Clairborne was in a state of amazement. Leaning back in his chair and sipping coffee from a cup he held in both hands, he contemplated McComb's verbal report.

"So Findley, you're telling me that this whole thing started over cards. That one cowboy hit another with a beer mug just as you walked in. You fired a round in the air to get everyone's attention. That started more fireworks, and the only injuries are one cowboy with a broken jaw from the beer mug, another who cut himself on a whiskey glass when he was diving for cover, and some joker who broke his wrist when he tripped on the steps? Damn, how many shots fired and nobody got hit?"

"Several," McComb said. "A lot. I emptied my piece, I know that."

Clairborne leaned his chair forward and put both hands on the desk blotter.

"You emptied your gun and didn't hit anyone?"

McComb looked at the floor before raising his eyes to Clairborne.

Then he shrugged. "Hell, Tucker. I never said I could shoot."

—◊◊◊—

Emmaline Bigelow hefted the oriental carpets over the clotheslines, straightened them out, and proceeded to whack them with the heavy wire rug beater, being careful to stand upwind so the dust, dog hair, and cigar ashes would blow away from her unsmiling face. Lips compressed more than usual, she whaled the rugs as if to teach them a lesson. Another series of shootings, several dead in one night, and most upsetting of all were her husband's words that nobody would be punished for the carnage.

"The instigators lost their lives, Emmaline. There's no one alive that's to blame for it," he said over breakfast.

But to Emmaline Bigelow, that simply did not seem possible. Four men dead—no, five as of an hour ago—and nobody has to face any consequences? Impossible. More to the point, unacceptable. Her anger and frustration increased. The impact of the rug beater increased accordingly.

"Shootings are becoming commonplace." Whack.

"We now have not one but two officers of the law." Whack.

"And more shootings now than ever." Whack.

"This cannot continue." Whack.

"It will not." Whack. Whack. Whack.

Lugging the heavy rugs back into the house and unrolling each in its designated place did nothing to reduce Emmaline Bigelow's energy level. When she entered her husband's office off the parlor, she beheld his narrow-shouldered back as he sat at his desk bent over large accounting ledgers, seemingly unaware of her presence.

Hands on her skinny hips, she waited to see how long he would continue to pretend she wasn't there. A minute was long enough.

"William, we need to talk."

Bigelow swiveled around to face her. "Ah, Emmaline, my dear. What's on your mind?" he asked, knowing full well the topic du jour would involve gunplay.

"I'm asking you again what you and the others are going to do about all the shooting."

"What are we going to do?"

"Is your hearing failing already, William?"

"No. Well, it seems to me that—"

"William," Emmaline said, moving closer and shaking her right index finger. "The situation is outrageous. Outrageous! Four or five men dead in a single night, and you sit here toying with accounts. What are you going to do about it?" Her voice rose to a level of shrillness that made her husband want to flee the premises.

"Well, I don't think it's fair to say I'm 'toying' with my accounts, Emmaline. I mean this is what makes our life so comfortable, after all," he said, waving his hand at his desktop.

"Don't try to change the subject, William. I'm talking about law and order in Abilene, and you know it. We have two—two!—peace officers and more carnage than ever. Are you going to speak to Constable Clairborne or not?"

Bigelow sounded hurt when he replied, "And just what would I say to him? I mean, he was at the scene of both shootings immediately while we were all safe in our beds, after all, my dear."

"Safe? Safe?" she shrieked. "Is anyone in Abilene safe when random violence has become so commonplace? Am I safe in my own bed these days?"

Bigelow made the mistake of not immediately responding, thereby creating a vacuum Emmaline quickly filled with supposition.

They had not slept together in so long that she could not remember their last intimacy. That normally didn't bother her at all. William was fat. He snored, his breath composed of equal parts cigar, alcohol, coffee, and bits of meat wedged between his molars. Furthermore, his attentions to her were selfish at best. No. She didn't miss intimacy with her husband at all. But she was hurt and more than a little shocked to realize that the feeling was mutual. She read into his silence "What man would want you?" She wanted to go outside and plant bulbs or scour pots or carry coal up from the cellar, something physical and hard. But she felt that she was in yet another contest of wills with her husband, and she could not cede the field and flee.

So she stood her ground and glared.

"Of course you are safe, Emmaline. Nothing ever happens this side of town, nothing bad. You know that."

"Not yet," she said. "But I'm telling you that the ladies of Abilene are looking to their men to get control of this town again before some innocents are harmed by those barbarians. We're not going to stand for this William, not for a minute more," she said, spinning abruptly and leaving.

Bigelow stared at the doorway through which his wife of sixteen years had stormed away.

"What in God's name?" he asked himself before emitting a huge sigh. The money was to be made in the short span, three to four more years at most, that Abilene was the beef-shipping center of the plains. When the railroads moved west, the herds would follow, and Abilene would then prosper or fail on the basis of the farms he knew would replace cattle herds. But that would be years from now, and in the interim, there would be more cattle, more cowboys, and more violence. It was inevitable.

As would be the mounting ire of Emmaline Bigelow.

William Bigelow looked up at his new Elgin office clock. Not even ten a.m. He looked back at the doorway as he slid a silver flask from his coat pocket and took a long pull. The thought of leaving entered his mind. Again.

Every day since his oldest boy died, choking on his own blood, in his father's arms, Lemuel Boniface remembered the face of the man who killed his son.

He made sure everyone else in his family not only remembered the loss but focused on the need for revenge as well. At morning prayers and evening meals, Boniface beseeched the Lord to reserve special ire for his son's killer. He prayed aloud for prolonged suffering, for agony to precede the man's transition to the torments of eternal damnation.

Vengeance consumed his thoughts the morning he walked with his two sons to the barn where, out of the steady, freezing rain, they would regrease the wagon axles—a laborious, time-consuming task, but one that had to be done periodically.

The Boniface males were halfway through the job when it simply dawned on Lemuel that it was time do what needed to be done. Crops were harvested, almost enough fuel and forage for the winter stored, and now they were down to maintenance items. No more essential tasks blocked the path to his highest priority: killing the man he'd learned was named Tucker Clairborne. That this Clairborne was deadly with firearms was important to know but not a deterrent. He would just have to be killed in a manner that removed his advantage. Boniface had spent a good amount of time studying the issue and had decided to confront Clairborne at a time and place where he was most likely to have his weapon holstered, to be relaxed and less vigilant. An ambush. He would assassinate an assassin.

The vision of Clairborne's face as he recognized Boniface and the fact that Boniface had the drop on him provided the only reliable salve to his relentless anguish. As he slid the left rear wheel off the nearly dry axle, Boniface even smiled at the image of a dumbfounded, soon-to-be-dead Tucker Clairborne.

In the split second between his lubricated fingers losing their grip on the axle and the imminent, inevitable result of his loss of concentration, Boniface understood what was about to happen.

Seeing it coming did not lessen the excruciating pain erupting through him when the falling axle crushed his hand, pinning it against the massive tree-stump supporting the wagon while the wheel was removed.

Shrieks of pain brought his wife and daughters racing to the barn, where they helped his sons lift the wagon enough to slide out his hand, mangled flat, blue-white bone shards protruding at odd angles from flesh covered with axle-grease and blood.

So great was the hatred Lemuel Boniface felt for Tucker Clairborne that even at the apogee of his agony, wavering at the edge of consciousness, his thoughts alternated between consternation that he had again evoked God's displeasure and awareness that he personally could not avenge his son's death.

Thrashing, involuntarily resisting frantic efforts of sons and daughters and wife to restrain him, Boniface saw the angelic face of his oldest surviving boy and blurted his first coherent words.

"Joshua," he croaked. "Joshua, avenge your brother."

Sixteen-year-old Joshua straightened and stared at his father. Always stern, always religious, always hard working, his father had been a different man since the loss of his oldest son in the confrontation with the cowboys. Now he was sullen and bitter. Since they buried his brother behind the house, he had become obsessed with revenge and talked of little else. No one in the Boniface household disagreed with the need for justice. It was just that Joshua, middle boy, gangly and sweet natured, wished that every now and again, the family could talk about something else. In the back of his mind, Joshua had worried that he would lose his father too, that the cowboy—no, the man was a gunman—who shot his brother would be too fast for his father unless his father shot the man from ambush, which he knew his father would never do.

Now his father had passed the fiery brand to him, had ordered him to carry it until there was no more need for revenge and the flame could be extinguished. Joshua Boniface had never once disobeyed his father. He frequently delayed compliance with an order from either one of his parents, testing how long he could put off some unpleasant task, but the answer was always the same: not long. One or both of the Boniface parents tracked each child with amazing efficiency. Joshua sensed that this momentous task, his sudden, unanticipated appointment as the instrument of vengeance for the Boniface family, would be unavoidable and could be put off no longer. The realization shot raw fear through his adolescent frame.

His mother looked up at him and snapped, "Help us carry your father into the house, Joshua. What's the matter with you?"

Inside the spartan Boniface residence, they laid the injured patriarch on the trestle table and slipped a corn-husk-filled pillow under his head. Boniface stifled the pain by turning the situation into a contest of wills, his against that of Satan, who wanted him to curse God, denounce God, not just for the jolts of pain flashing up from his smashed hand, but also for the difficulties yet to come. Coaxing crops out of the Kansas soil was hard enough for an able-bodied man. For a man with one hand and a stump, it was probably impossible.

Job.

He thought of Job as his family scurried around trying to ease his pain and figure out what to do with what was left of his hand. Specifically, he considered Job 2:10: "But he said unto her, Thou speakest as one of the foolish women speaketh. What? shall we receive good at the hand of God, and shall we not receive evil?"

Wasn't the lesson of Job that God just wanted to test Job's faith? Hadn't God rewarded Job for his refusal to "denounce God and die" as Job's wife had recommended? "Accept the Lord's will," Lemuel Boniface told himself. "Accept the Lord's will," he repeated again and again until unconditional acceptance of his pain-filled plight expanded to fill every corner of his waking mind. It took hours and agony-filled hours, but as he hoped, the word of God eventually brought the solace he needed.

―――

Autumn breeze slipped under the partially open window of Tucker Clairborne's room, bringing with it coolness that deepened his reveries. But it also carried street noises that prodded him awake. Rolling over and pulling his quilt up over his ears, Clairborne slipped back into fitful sleep and fleeting images. His mother entered an unfamiliar room where he sat. She silently and solemnly approached him with a clear but undefined purpose. "Hello, Mother," he said, but his greeting elicited no verbal response. Instead, she leaned over and picked up a puppy Clairborne hadn't realized was in his lap and carried it out of the room. He wanted to call her back, to protest the loss of the dog, but he could neither speak nor stand. A pathetic, incoherent croak leaked from his mouth, and his legs were as heavy as waterlogged tree stumps. He remained seated, clenching his fists in impotent anger, not knowing who should be the object of his frustration, his mother or himself.

———

A few days later, Clairborne sat at his desk absent-mindedly studying the bottom of his coffee cup. He wanted more but didn't stand and walk the five feet to the coal-fired potbelly stove warming the room and the coffee pot alike. Something was wrong. He had no energy, no desire to do anything. His life was ruled by routine. Eat, walk his rounds, visit the privy, walk his rounds, eat, have a drink or two, sleep. No journal entries or pistol practice or lively conversations or active planning for the future. A shroud of fog had descended over him so dense and dark it snuffed out emotion and denied him a sense of purpose or direction. He'd even snapped at his deputy more than once, causing the normally gregarious McComb to avoid him as much as possible.

Once again, his wandering mind collided with Hamlet, his least favorite of Shakespeare's plays. Each time he read or saw it performed, he liked the Danish prince even less, his antipathy even corroding his respect for the playwright whose other characters all seemed so believable to Clairborne, so acutely drawn, so balanced in their foibles and fortes. But Hamlet seemed to him unbalanced in his anxiety and self-pity.

"Kind of like me," he thought, a sour smile spreading across his lips. "Of course I don't like Hamlet. I'm too much like him."

McComb pushed open the door and entered, heading straight for the coffee pot. Clairborne was glad to see his deputy and fellow Virginian.

"Want to freshen that up?" McComb asked, holding the coffee pot and nodding at Clairborne's cup.

"Yeah, sure. Thanks," Clairborne answered. "What's Elkton like?" he asked McComb, who was startled by both the subject and the friendly tone of voice.

"Elkton? Lord above, I haven't thought of it in a coon's age. How come you asked?"

"Oh, I don't know. I guess I was just thinking about how much of Virginia I never saw, how much of it I don't know, and it struck me as kind of strange is all."

They chatted for another hour, letting the ebb and flow of inconsequential matters smooth some of the rough edges that had started to snag their relationship, both men aware of what was going on. Both men found themselves thinking, "This is better."

"Heard something last night you might find interesting," McComb said.

"What was that?"

"Well, I was talking to that fella Tilton Angley, faro dealer over to the Rosebud."

"And?"

"Well, you know how some folks want to let you know about things but don't want lots of other folks to know they're talking to lawmen all that much?"

"And?"

"Well, Angley told me he heard your reputation's kind o' spread. Actually, he said Abilene's reputation's kind o' spread."

"That's not a bad thing," Clairborne said. "Town fathers ought to like hearing that. Good for business."

"Not so sure about that," McComb said.

"How so?"

"Well, it seems that—and I ought to tell you Angley's not the onliest one I heard this from—but it seems word's getting out that Abilene's the place to go for action and for making your name as a bad actor. You know, a pistolero."

Clairborne's attention sharply focused on the potential importance of McComb's words. "You put much stock in that kind of talk, Findley?"

McComb blew on his coffee even though it was lukewarm.

"I do. It just seems likely. There's money and whiskey and women. And there's folks drifting in and out. Word is it's a place to go to find work, all kinds of work. And maybe some folks just lookin' for a chance to make a name. Gotta remember, sitting here in Abilene, it's easy to lose sight of how this place looks from outside of town."

"Anything specific?"

"Ever hear of Bentley Rogers? Or Newt Boyce?"

Clairborne thought for a moment. "Nope. Can't say as I have."

"Well, no disrespect, Constable, but maybe you ought to. They're both bad actors, and word is they're both somewheres in Kansas. Odds are, they'll show up here sooner or later."

"Thanks for the information," Clairborne said, fishing his watch from his vest pocket. "Better be making my rounds."

In truth, it was a little earlier than he usually started evening patrols, but after hearing McComb's intelligence, he wanted to be alone. He wanted to contemplate the possibility that the worst that could happen was edging measurably from the realm of theoretical to that of distinctly possible. As he'd been warned, his reputation with a gun would attract men willing to test their reflexes and courage against his. Since he thought of himself as more lucky than skillful, he'd wondered what would happen should he encounter someone simply better with a gun than he was.

He thought about saddling up and riding off to someplace where nobody knew him but quickly dismissed the notion. Men such as he left a scent that could be followed by anyone willing to put his nose to the wind. No, it would be better to stay on his home ground, such as it was, and see who came looking for him in Abilene, Kansas.

—w—

Bentley Rogers sat on a rock and studied his horse. He'd not purchased the lovely black gelding with a white blaze. It was his by right of possession. He'd killed its former owner, a gambler who lost a great deal of money to Rogers and then decided two days later to retrieve the $107. He'd come after Rogers and made three mistakes, any one of which could have been fatal in and of itself.

He didn't consider the fact that Rogers had been unsuccessfully pursued by others for a variety of reasons. That those efforts failed and the failures were widely discussed should have caused the gambler to give some thought to the effort. It didn't because of the other two mistakes. He was mad and got madder every passing day that he recalled the money he lost. He was also a heavy drinker and told himself he wasn't.

The gambling problem with Rogers began at a poker table where the two sat across from each other in a game lasting nearly two days. For a long time, the gambler had usually prevailed in games of chance, particularly poker, but a few years before he met Rogers, things began to slowly unravel in a sequence all too common. Whiskey eroded his judgment, his memory, and his concentration. When he started to lose more than he won, the gambler made more large bets to recoup losses in one fell swoop. His losses accelerated, as did his frustration. So he followed Bentley Rogers west from Kansas City and finally caught up with him in Hays City, where he fired on Rogers from ambush, missed, and was quickly dispatched to wherever failed gamblers and would-be assassins go.

After a cursory investigation by the Hays City marshal, Rogers got the gambler's horse and his saddlebags, which contained dirty clothes. It was a beautiful and very well-mannered horse, and Rogers liked it. He hadn't named the animal for the first week but then decided to call it Chance. He traded the gambler's side arm, a poorly maintained 1858 Remington Navy revolver, to a dry-goods store proprietor for two pounds of coffee, five pounds of beans, a slab of bacon, and a tin of Mott's Chemical Pomade. Rogers kept what he believed was the gambler's primary weapon, a well-cared-for, two-barreled Derringer in .41 caliber the gambler had worn in a spring-loaded rig up his right coat sleeve.

In Kansas City, Rogers heard much talk about the money to be made at the burgeoning railhead called Abilene. Fortunes and reputations reportedly popped out of the soil like sunflowers. While not a professional gambler, Rogers preferred covering his expenses from a seated position at a poker table rather than in, God forbid, any that resulted in perspiration. He'd never cared for hard labor, which had caused endless conflict with his farmer father in Ohio, conflict of such intensity that his father frequently accused his mother of adultery, yelling, "No son of mine could be so goddamned worthless."

Rogers could read and do numbers but disdained "clerking." His gun hand developed early and effortlessly. A man of moderate courage, Rogers was also "prickly," easily offended and instinctively aware that backing down once meant backing down forever. So he never considered backing down. By the autumn of 1868, nine men, the last of whom was the gambler in Hays City, had cashed in their chips as a result of crossing Bentley Rogers.

Rogers was ambivalent about his reputation as a shootist. On one hand, it got him excellent service in saloons, hotels, and eateries; good seats at variety and vaudeville shows; and relative assurance that no one would try to cheat him in games of chance. On the other, he was obliged to advance awareness of his name. Stasis was not an option. Either he was deadly, or people would start to speculate about why he'd seemed to avoid any given confrontation. Was it weakness, fear, failing eyesight, involuntary tremors, something—anything—debilitating?

West of the Mississippi, there was an emerging phenomenon at the center of which Bentley Rogers and his ilk found themselves. Reputations fed on themselves, and just as decay drew maggots, a "name" attracted men in search of a name for themselves.

In Kansas City, they said there was no law whatsoever in Abilene. Then in Hays City, he'd heard that there was, that the town fathers had hired a constable or a sheriff. Somebody had mentioned the man's name and implied the Abilene lawman had some sand, but he couldn't recall the specifics, only that the man in question had been a player at Spanish Wells. No matter. It was unlikely he would get directly involved with a lawman. Never had. And if he did, it was unlikely the lawman was as capable as he was.

So, on to Abilene.

At the Alamo, Abilene's largest saloon, Clairborne slipped inside and to the right of the door, nodded at the nearest bartender, and leaned against the wall. The place was warm—stuffy, actually—and wore the standard mantle of blue-gray tobacco smoke nearly obscuring the ceiling. The bouquet of stale beer, sweat, leather, dirty clothes, and dirtier bodies mingled with the bracing sweet scent of the day's layer of fresh sawdust scattered on the floor. The musicians were taking a break, so the predominant murmur of conversation punctuated by laughter told him things were OK in the Alamo. Clairborne was about to turn and leave when a thought from nowhere caused him to pause and lean back against the wall.

His right hand went to the bulge under his coat caused by the silver-plated Colt with its eight-inch barrel. For a while now, Clairborne had considered the benefits of carrying the two Colts with the three-inch barrels, one on his hip in place of the long-barreled model, the second in the left inside breast pocket his tailor had reinforced to serve as a covert holster. He asked himself why he was suddenly so focused on gun size. The answer he came up with was "for the same reason a carpenter pays attention to his hammer. The Colts are my tools."

—◈—

Riding into Abilene, Bentley Rogers attracted little if any notice, which was fine with him. His first impression of the place was very favorable. It exuded the kind of constant motion bordering on frenzy he associated with making easy money and having fun.

He considered a bath and then thought of a haircut even though he didn't care all that much for the tonsorial arts. Like most men of the time, he faced a choice: wear his hair long or cut it to a "Prussian." His vanity and his reflection in the mirror caused him to opt for the former. Even though long hair got messy between monthly ablutions and the dirtier it got, the more it itched, Rogers liked the look of his straight brown hair covering his ears and cut straight across his neck as if his infrequent barbers used a draw knife rather than scissors. Unlike most of his contemporaries, Bentley Rogers preferred to shave his face as often as possible, thus minimizing the irritation arising from the unavoidable combination of sweat, dirt, and whiskers.

Reining up in front of McMillan's Hotel on an unnamed side street, Rogers was met by a man wearing an apron over his striped, collarless shirt the sleeves of which sported maroon silk garters.

"Looking for a room for a couple of days. This place got a vacancy?" Rogers asked.

"You bet, mister," the man said. "Give you a hand with them saddlebags," he said, stepping down from the boardwalk.

"No. I'll get them," Rogers replied. He didn't care for anyone touching his possessions, except for his horse, which always got the best feed and care a local livery could provide.

Two hours after signing the register, Rogers had bathed, dropped off his laundry, and eaten a steak-and-potato lunch washed down with two mugs of beer. The meal, the beer, and the autumn sun had the unexpected impact of making him so tired he could barely keep his eyes open, so a nap was just the ticket.

Sitting on his bed to remove his boots, Rogers thought of his father and smiled. "You old bastard. What would you think of a man who napped in the middle of a weekday? Not much. Well, the feeling's mutual, you old goat."

Their parting surfaced in his thoughts.

As he rode away from the farm bareback on his mule, Rogers had tried unsuccessfully to block his father's imprecations from his hearing, eventually kicking the mule into a trot and not looking back. If he had, Rogers would have seen his father trotting as well, his fist punching the air as he hurled curses at the back of his middle child. The last words Rogers heard were "Don't you never come back," to which Rogers had mumbled, "Don't you worry about that."

Hanging his gun belt over the bedstead next to his head, Rogers also thought of his mother and was again surprised by the emotion she evoked in him: disdain. Rogers simply could not fathom anyone putting up with the verbal and physical abuse his mother absorbed without complaint. He looked at his holstered, nickel-plated Smith & Wesson.

"I'd a shot him a long time ago, Ma," he said aloud.

Then he slid effortlessly into deep, untroubled sleep.

An hour later, Rogers heard hammering, voices, and the clatter of lumber being off-loaded from wagons. It irritated him. He had a headache. He pushed up to a sitting position, ran his hands through his hair, and pondered the next step. Through his closed window, Rogers observed a work gang engaged in construction of a building less than fifty feet from his room. How the hell was a man supposed to sleep with all that racket? He pulled on his boots, donned his gun belt and hat, and went to the front desk.

"How the hell can I sleep with all that racket right next to my room?" he asked the clerk, a man whose only distinguishing characteristic was his swanlike neck.

The clerk made a study of hotel clientele. This one was not to be toyed with, even if he made stupid complaints about noise in the middle of the day. After all, he told himself, a lot of folks made their living at gaming tables, and this fellow didn't look like a cowboy or an itinerant drummer. The clerk's habitual politeness swiftly morphed into obsequiousness in the face of the man's irritation and his large gun.

"I do apologize for the inconvenience, Mr. Rogers. It's just that, well, Abilene is growing so fast, it's hard to find peace and quiet anywhere these days. Price of progress," he said, attempting a laugh.

Rogers locked his light-gray, deep-set eyes on the clerk. "You expect me to pay for a room so noisy I can't sleep in it?"

The clerk didn't care at all for the direction this conversation was taking.

"Why, sir, I can't be responsible for what others are doing on their property. Surely we can find some way of addressing your discomfort. Perhaps a free drink at one of our sister establishments?"

Rogers stared at the clerk and said, "Tell you what. Here's what you can do. You go out there and tell them to stop disturbing your guests, you move me to a room where I can't hear them, or I break your damn nose. How's that sound?"

The clerk was affronted but fearful. Would this fellow really break his nose?

"Perhaps I could find you a hotel with less activity around it. I could—"

Rogers sensed fear, and the sensation stirred him. "I'm not going to move. I'm here, and I want quiet. The only question is how are you going to deliver it?"

The clerk felt sweat trickle down his ribs.

"Surely, sir, you can't expect me to tell those men to stop working," the clerk said, his unspoken words being "just so you can nap."

The warmth in Roger's belly didn't counter the worsening discomfort behind his right eye. Without saying anything further, he walked to the door, exited, and moved to the construction site.

Seven men and three boys. One was the boss. Two boys unloaded raw lumber from a wagon. Another boy carried buckets of nails up ladders to the framers, who promptly pounded them into the aromatic wood. The six other men were enjoying their work, laughing and singing ditties. None wore firearms. Or knives. At least not in sight.

Rogers strolled over to the boss, a ruddy, bearded man, the only one not working.

The man looked up at Rogers as he approached.

"Howdy," the man said.

"How much longer you boys gonna be doing all that goddamn hammering?"

The man was confused by the question and the snarl with which it was delivered.

"What? What the hell do you mean?"

"Figures you'd be hard of hearing," Rogers said, "what with all that goddamn hammering and all. I asked you how much longer you're going to be making that noise."

The foreman straightened up to his full five-foot-nine-inch height and put his fists on his hips. "As long as it goddamn takes to finish this job, bucko. That's how long."

Rogers moved closer but not within range of the foreman's fists.

"Tell those boys to go get a drink and come back tomorrow."

The foreman's eyes bulged.

"Who the hell are you to be telling me what to do? Get the hell out of here," he said just as he became aware of the unnatural way the man's hands hung straight down at his sides.

The man just stared at him.

The foreman turned and shouted, "Murray, come over here quick," which caused a very large, heavily muscled man to descend the ladder supporting his considerable bulk.

Rogers smiled at his approach.

"You want me, boss?" the man called Murray asked, wiping his palms on his hips.

"This here boyo just saunters up to me and tells me we have to quit so's he can have some peace and quiet, Says we should go have a drink and come back tomorrow, so he says."

Murray shifted his gaze to Rogers and smiled at the prospect of pounding him into a grease spot.

Rogers read his mind.

"Here's the deal. I just want a little quiet. I came here with a simple request that you boys call it a day and go for a drink. Hell, I'll even buy the first round." Rogers smiled a broad, tooth-displaying but clearly mirthless smile.

"But you make one move toward me, and I'll kill you dead before you take a full step."

Murray's eyes flicked to Rogers's pistol and then to his boss. Rogers held his smile and didn't move.

The foreman looked at Rogers, then at Murray, then at his crew.

"Aw shit, this ain't worth nobody getting hurt, but you can't just sashay up and tell people what to do. We'll go, mister, but you ain't heard the last of this. We got law here in Abilene."

"So I've heard," Rogers said. "So I've heard."

———*∿*———

Clairborne rode out of town just before noon to get in a little more practice with his short-barreled Colts. He had yet to decide which of the two would be his primary and which his under-the-armpit backup.

Findley McComb went to the office a little after noon to make coffee and take it easy before starting his rounds.

Still wearing his hat, he was standing by the stove, coffee pot in hand, when the door slammed open and an obviously agitated man entered and began shouting before he closed the door behind him. McComb had never seen the man before and didn't care a bit for his manner.

"You need to go down to my work site and clap a son of a bitch in irons who just threatened to kill me 'cause I interrupted his goddamn nap," the man yelled.

McComb's first impulse was to laugh. Instead he offered the man a cup of coffee.

"I don't want any damned coffee. I want you to arrest that crazy bastard. Get him off the by-God streets."

"Now hold on there, partner." McComb said. "How about sitting down, taking a breath, and telling me from the beginning what's got you so fired up," he said as he put the coffee pot down on the stove and took a seat behind the desk.

The man started to bluster and then thought better of it. He pulled a chair up to the front of the desk and sat, leaning forward and putting his hands on the desk, palms down.

"Deputy, me and my crew was working on the new livery over behind McMillan's, and this crazy bastard come out and told me we was making too much noise and we was to quit and go home so's he could go back to sleep. Said he'd kill me if I didn't shut down."

McComb leaned forward. "He said he'd kill you if you didn't stop work? That he'd kill you?"

"That's what he said. Now what the hell are you going to do about it's what I want to know."

"He's staying at McMillan's?"

"Yeah. I seen him go back there on my way here."

"OK. What's this villain look like, anyways?"

The man stood up and held his right hand up to his forehead.

"'Bout this tall. Slim. Got like a bowler hat but got a wider brim than a bowler. Got long hair down over his ears. Wearin' a kind of yellow shirt, black trousers over his boots. No spurs. Looked more like a city fella than a cowhand. Oh yeah, and he was packin'—a Smith & Wesson. Nickel-plated."

"Well, thanks," McComb said as he stood and extended his hand while he wondered when Clairborne would be back and what to do in the interim.

The man stood and shook hands but seemed unsure of what to do next.

"Your name?" McComb asked.

"Peter Sheridan's the name. Best damned carpenter in Abilene, too. I'm staying over to Ellie's boarding house in case you need me to swear out a affidavit or some such thing."

"Thanks," McComb said. "I'm sure we'll be in touch shortly."

The man turned to leave and then stopped at the door.

"I appreciate your looking into this." He paused and then said, "Deputy, I'm sure you know your business and all, but you ought to be careful with this rattlesnake. He ain't right in the head. Can't be, so you might want to be real careful, if you know what I mean."

McComb watched Sheridan leave and remained standing. He knew exactly what Sheridan meant. Even if Sheridan were exaggerating, which was likely, this didn't sound at all rational. He looked at the Elgin Regulator wall clock. Ten minutes after two p.m. What kind of hoot owl would demand work stoppage in the middle of the day so he could catch up on his sleep?

Damn. Where was Clairborne anyway?

McComb really didn't want to confront the napper, but he could find no solid reason for procrastination other than fear of getting shot, and fear was not a solid reason for not doing his job. So he sighed and poured a half cup of coffee, drank it, opened the stove, and threw in the coffee grounds, which hissed and sparked and released a cloud of heavily scented steam. He looked around and thought how much he liked the office, how functional and, well, comfortable it was. He and Clairborne kept it neat as a pin. Even the papers they'd begun to process were stacked, one stack awaiting review and signatures, the other waiting to be filed— once they got around to creating a file system.

McComb realized he was delaying the inevitable. He lifted his dragoon from his double loop holster, pulled the hammer to half cock, and rotated the cylinder to check the percussion caps. He held the Colt in both hands, noting that the bluing was almost worn off and the walnut grips scratched, but the piece was rust free and as deadly as the day it emerged from the Hartford, Connecticut, factory. After sliding the gun into the holster, lifting it halfway out, and then letting its weight pull it back home, he retrieved his jacket from the coat rack, pulled it on but left it unbuttoned then left the office.

At the hotel's front desk, McComb described the man for whom he was searching.

"You must mean Mr. Rogers," the clerk said. "That would be Mr. Bentley Rogers. He's in room eleven, and he is in. I saw him come back about a half hour ago."

"Son of a bitch. Bentley Rogers. Here. Son of a bitch. Now what do I do?" McComb asked himself.

His stomach felt as if he'd just swallowed a tin cup of ice water. He needed to massage his abdomen. He cursed Tucker Clairborne for his absence. He was aware of the clerk staring at him. Duty called. Son of a bitch. Son of a bitch.

"'Room eleven?" he asked the clerk.

"Yes, sir. Upstairs. First door on the left."

Bentley Rogers had not been asleep more than twenty minutes when someone knocked slowly but firmly on his door.

"What?" he yelled, rolling to his elbow, unholstering his pistol and resting his thumb on its hammer.

"Deputy McComb. We'd like to speak with you about a complaint filed with the constable's office, Mr. Rogers."

Rogers's immediate irritation was tempered by immediate caution. Did the deputy say "we" wanted to talk? If so, how many men were with him? Probably plenty. He was angry with himself for not hearing their approach, what with the walls so thin, so very thin they wouldn't even slow down a fusillade fired through them—from either side.

"All right. Just a minute." Rogers said.

He slipped on his boots, stood, put the Smith & Wesson back into the holster, strapped it on, opened the door, and was surprised to see Findley McComb standing by himself off to the left side of the door, out of the obvious line of fire.

McComb's pistol was holstered.

"What can I do for you?" Rogers said with a smile.

"How's about you and me having a little chat downstairs so I can hear your side of things, your take on what happened a while ago?"

Rogers hesitated. He didn't relish following what he perceived to be an order, couched as it was in a request. He didn't want to go downstairs. He wanted to finish his nap. But the man in front of him radiated the aura of someone both confident and capable.

"Oh, what the hell," Rogers said. "Let me get my hat." He noted that McComb stepped into his room when he turned to retrieve his hat and then waited for him to leave first, following him downstairs instead of walking in front.

In the small lobby, they sat across from each other at the single table.

"So what's this all about there, Deputy?"

"Well, Mr. Rogers, in a nutshell, fella complained to me that you told him to stop work because it was keeping you awake. Said you threatened to kill him if he didn't."

McComb was pleasantly surprised by Rogers's response. Rogers threw back his head and laughed.

"Why, hell no, Deputy. I'll bet you dollars to doughnuts that mick didn't tell you I offered to buy him and his crew drinks if they'd shut down early and that he called an even bigger mick over and told his gorilla to pound me into grease. Didn't tell you that, did he?"

"Well no, actually he didn't. You saying you didn't threaten to kill him?"

"When he sicced the big fella on me, I told him I'd plug 'em both if they tried it. That I did, but, hell, it was the best way to make sure things didn't get out of control, and it worked, right? I mean here we're talking about it rather than trading lead."

McComb leaned back in his chair.

"OK, Mr. Rogers. I'm going to tell the constable what I've heard from the both of you, and he'll decide what needs to be done, if anything. You sticking around for a while?"

Rogers smiled. "Haven't had a chance to get to know Abilene yet. Thought I might, though. After I finish my nap."

"Well, fine. May want to consider the town's growing like a weed. Lots dust and noise. Pretty unavoidable."

Rogers appreciated the deputy's tact, his implicit and therefore easier to accept message.

"Why, sure, Deputy," he said. "Once I get caught up on my shut-eye, I'm sure things'll be just hunky-dory."

"Be seeing you around there, Mr. Rogers," said McComb, standing and offering his hand.

"Count on it, Deputy. Count on it."

Back at the office, Clairborne hung up his hat and coat, walked to the stove, threw in some some scrap lumber, and opened the top of the coffee pot. Empty. He glanced at the wall clock and decided to make another pot before starting his rounds. When the door opened, he turned to see McComb. In place of his usual grin, McComb looked downright dour, and after hanging his hat, he plopped down in a chair and rubbed his temples.

"Something up?" Clairborne asked.

"Yes. Bentley Rogers is up. Remember me asking you if you heard of him?"

"I do."

"Well, he's here, and less than an hour after he rode in, he got into a pissing contest with a construction crew working on the new stable, the one behind McMillan's."

"The whole crew? How many hurt?"

"None. Nobody hurt. Yet. But there will be. Interesting fella. Seemed downright civil to talk with, which I just did, but there's no doubt he walked up to the boss and told him to send everybody home so he could finish his nap."

Clairborne stared at McComb for a long moment and then shook his head. "I know you're not joshin' me, Findley, but that's one of the damnedest things I ever heard."

They sat in the office for the next forty-five minutes discussing the phenomenon called Bentley Rogers. They pondered proactivity: deputizing five or six more citizens and then running Rogers out of town. They discussed the benefits of conversation, quiet, subtle negotiation to let Rogers know he could stay so long as he kept the dust down but that they'd be watching him like hawks over a chicken coop.

At one point in their consultation, Clairborne found his thoughts drifting to a different but related topic, one that had come to mind during each of his last few pistol practice sessions. He'd long since noticed that after firing the first few rounds, his hands began to perspire, and the more sweaty they got, the more difficult it was to retain his grip on the ivory stocks during recoil. He wondered if changing them to checkered walnut would improve his control.

When McComb got up to get more coffee, Clairborne reached under his left armpit and withdrew one of the two short-barreled Colts he now carried. Seemed a shame to get rid of the ivory. Running the tip of his finger over the smooth, off-white surface, he marveled at the process that had brought this piece of elephant tusk from somewhere in Africa all the way to Abilene. Holding the Colt in his left hand while he traced the ivory with his right, Clairborne's eye went to the pink stub where his left index finger had been until that day in west Texas. He didn't like to look at his left hand.

Then it dawned on him. Gloves. Kid-leather gloves. Gloves would absorb the sweat and enhance the tackiness between gun and hand, and kid gloves were thin enough not to impair fine movements such as those required to reload or fish change from a vest pocket to pay for a drink. And the left glove could have only three fingers, so he wouldn't have to see the mangled nub all the time. Funny how something such as a new pair of gloves improved his mood in the middle of a conversation about a deadly threat.

For the next two days and nights, Clairborne and McComb watched Bentley Rogers. By the third day, it was clear to both of them that Rogers was a fastidious creature of habit: rising at the same time, making his early afternoon ablutions, dropping off his laundry, eating at the same place—Evans's Eats—and even ordering the same thing for his first meal of the day. He began with an apple fritter and coffee, then consumed a plate of eggs and a ham steak and a dollop of calf brains, biscuits and preserves, and, of course, more coffee.

He preferred the Alamo but also spent time in the Blue Bison and the Long Horn. His favorite game of chance was keno, and from what Clairborne and McComb could tell, Rogers seemed to win more than he lost, which was unusual because the odds favored the house and the dealer. He also didn't drink all that much, three drinks of whiskey and one beer in the course of a night at the tables. A teetotaler by local standards. The beer he consumed midway through the evening. He helped himself to the "free lunch" offered at each end of the bar at the Alamo—hard-boiled eggs and pickled pigs feet and a salami sandwich washed down by a mug of ale held him until "dinner" at dawn: steak and potatoes, apple pie, and a glass or two of apple cider.

After the second day, Clairborne and McComb stopped detailing their observations of Rogers when they met, implicitly deciding to mention only deviations from what appeared to be the norm if and when they occurred. Still, Clairborne and McComb retained their personal reservations about him, each feeling that it was only a matter of time before something happened, something unpleasant, something requiring response on their part.

Both men also independently arrived at the same emotional state at about the same time. Knowing something would happen sooner or later, they began to resent Rogers for keeping them on tenterhooks. They quietly contemplated provoking him but doing so in a public place and in such a manner that they could later argue in front of a magistrate or jury that Rogers had initiated the event in question.

McComb envisioned a confrontation involving fisticuffs and began planning accordingly, calculating distances, first blows, proximity to items such as beer mugs or spittoons or chairs that could be used as weapons.

Clairborne was convinced it would be a matter of gunplay, and where his deputy was confident that he would prevail in a slugfest, Clairborne felt a looming sense of dread.

The evening of the day Clairborne took delivery of his black goatskin gloves, he slipped inside the Longhorn and looked around to see Rogers at a keno table near the back of the room. Rogers sat with his back to the wall. He was smiling at the man facing him, a teamster Clairborne had seen around but didn't know. Clairborne could tell the man was unhappy and quickly wondered if his anger was directed at Rogers. It wasn't. The teamster was yelling at his friend, another teamster, this one named Olafson, whose wagon had brought the new furniture to the constable's office.

Clairborne saw that Rogers was amused at the argument. Clairborne also noted Rogers's hands were in view. Clairborne moved slowly to the rear of the room, positioning himself behind the yelling teamster, whose large knife had slipped around on his belt almost to the middle of his back.

It was a replay of a common theme. Somebody losing at a game of chance wanted a loan from a friend, who refused to give it. It happened almost every night, rarely ending in anything more than heated words.

Olafson stood and started to leave. The other teamster grabbed his arm. "Give me the money you owe me, Ollie. I need it now, not payday. Now!"

"You'll just lose it for sure. No more loans for you," Olafson said calmly, putting his hand on that of his colleague in an attempt to disengage.

"You cheap bastard!" the teamster shouted. Clairborne saw the teamster release his grip on Olafson's arm and shift to his right hip, his gnarled hand searching for the big knife with the stag-horn handle.

Just as the teamster's fingertips found the scabbard, Clairborne, reflexively wishing he had his larger gun, drew his short-barreled Colt and slammed it into the teamster's right ear. The man howled and wheeled around, hands cupping his lacerations. Clairborne had expected his blow to send the teamster to the floor. When it didn't, he took two steps back, thumbed the hammer back, and aimed the muzzle at the middle of the teamster's contorted face.

"There'll be no swinging that pig sticker tonight, buster. Keep your paws up. Merkel," Clairborne said to the keno dealer, "pull that toothpick out of the scabbard and put it somewhere for safekeeping."

Flicking the muzzle of his Colt in the direction of the door, Clairborne said, "You just earned a night in the hoosegow. You know where it is, so get moving."

"What about my ear? My ear's split wide open," the teamster yelled.

Clairborne's voice was calm by comparison.

"Too bad, buddy. Better your ear than Olafson's belly. Now, I'm not going to tell you again. Get moving."

As they started to the door, Clairborne reflexively looked back at the keno table and the men sitting around it.

Bentley Rogers was smiling at him.

—◈—

Winter comes in fast and hard on the plains.

Sleet whipped sideways, stinging man and beast alike, driving men inside and causing horses to turn their rumps to the storm. From morning to midafternoon, the temperature dropped seventeen degrees, hovered for an hour as if to collect its nerve, and then plunged another ten degrees in the next five hours.

Clairborne stood at his hotel window and contemplated the tempest, wondering how to offset his distaste for cold and wet with his obligations to venture out into the cold and wet. Moving to the carved pine wardrobe to ponder his choices, he realized he'd not yet purchased either woolen long underwear or a scarf or a buffalo coat. He did have a black wool overcoat with a roll collar and flapped pockets, however. Slipping it on, he looked in the mirror and decided to wait another day to get a shave. Glancing outside again, Edgar Allen Poe materialized in his thoughts. Edgar Allen Poe and hot chocolate. How nice it would be to return to his bed and trim the lamp wick until its soft yellow light invited rest and reading. He could sink into the pages of a good yarn, sip chocolate, rest the book on his chest, and wrap himself in the arms of Morpheus.

How nice indeed.

Clairborne wore a necktie every day, something he didn't have to do since western style was fairly relaxed for men. He never gave a thought to why he automatically wrapped the black silk cravat around his neck, adjusting the knot until it looked just right, the way his father had taught him. If Clairborne had ever asked himself why the tie, he would realize it implicitly implied power, enhanced gravitas. It wasn't just the tie. It was the combination of the cut of his coat and vest, his starched linen, the dignified hat with the kettle-roll brim, and the shine on the straight-laced shoes he wore around town instead of boots.

And of course there was also his reputation. On a fairly regular basis, he'd observed men pointing him out on the streets or in a saloon. He was getting used to it but was still ambivalent about whether it was a net benefit or liability.

Well, time to go. Another glance outside. Damn, but it looked nasty.

He reached for the door, paused, and then turned and went back to the mirror. Pulling open his coat, Clairborne watched his hand move over the hammer of his Colt. He let the coat close and made a decision. Opening the coat again, he drew the Colt and slid it into the large right front pocket, noting with satisfaction that it produced only a modest bulge, something hard to detect.

Clairborne smiled. It was a good decision.

Four hours later, he met McComb inside the American Eagle, Abilene's second-largest saloon.

They stood just inside and to the left of the door, surveying the room.

"Never seen this place this quiet," McComb said, removing his hat and wiping sleet from its brim. "Glory be, but it's ugly out there."

Clairborne nodded. "Yeah. This is the quietest night I've seen since I got here. Makes sense, though. Man's got to be darn thirsty to brave such a dastardly night for a shot of whiskey."

The American Eagle's two bartenders stood behind the bar chatting. Five of their six customers engaged in a card game, and the sixth watched the proceedings with his back against the bar, thumbs tucked into his vest pockets.

"Tell you what, Findley. No reason for both of us to be freezing our tails tonight. Why don't you call it a day and get some shut-eye?"

"You serious, boss?"

"I am indeed. Like I said, no need for both of us tonight. This place is as dead as every other hooch palace in town. Go on. See you tomorrow."

"Don't have to tell me twice," McComb said.

"I just did," Clairborne said.

After McComb left, Clairborne moved to the bar and spoke to the older of the two bartenders.

"Hey, Frankie. How about pouring me a cup of coffee while I make myself a ham sandwich," he said, lifting the fly screen off the platter of cold cuts and condiments at the end of the bar.

"Let me get you some fresher bread there, Constable. That's been out since noon. Probably stale." Frankie unwrapped the cheesecloth to unveil thick, aromatic rye bread, which Clairborne quickly sliced and layered with slabs of ham and coats of mustard. It wasn't Smithfield ham from Virginia, but its salty cure was finely balanced by thin veins of sweet fat. Clairborne devoured it and made another.

Frankie polished a shot glass with the bottom of his apron and watched the constable enjoy the fare.

"Fella was in here asking about you tonight," he said.

Clairborne looked up from his midnight snack. "Who?"

"Bentley Rogers. Just asked if I'd seen you tonight. Told him no. That's all. Then he sat over yonder for about an hour," Frankie said, nodding at the back of the room. "Didn't eat nor drink nothin'."

"Well, thanks, Frankie. Appreciate it."

Clairborne's eyes went over Frankie's shoulders to the mirrored backbar. His own reflection spoke to him through the set of its jaw and its unblinking eyes.

Tonight.

Tonight it will happen. Clairborne sensed the symmetry of the situation. McComb was gone. The streets were empty. He understood that even as he and his deputy had been studying Rogers, Rogers was observing him, cataloguing his movements. Clairborne took his coffee and sat down at a table just inside and to the left of the door. He unbuttoned his coat and arranged it to allow easy access to the Colt in the pocket and the other concealed and suspended beneath his left armpit. He listened. It was still blowing. Sleet still assaulted the saloon's shake roof.

The other bartender moved to both of the potbellied stoves and threw in more coal. Clairborne decided to stay put. He didn't think about how long, about when he would venture outside or where he would go when he did. He was operating on pure gut feel. And why not? What the hell else was there to go on?

No more coffee. He didn't want the jitters. No problem staying awake. Not tonight, with Bentley Rogers somewhere out there. Why wasn't he afraid or even nervous? It struck him as odd. He imagined Rogers entering and wondered if he would start blazing away immediately or engage in polite conversation prior to opening the ball. Based on his observation that Rogers was right-handed, Clairborne quickly decided he'd chosen the best spot. Forcing Rogers to shoot to his weak side gave Clairborne an advantage, if only a slight one. By now, Clairborne understood that contests between evenly matched men came down to luck and slight advantages. "Assuming," he told himself, "that we're evenly matched."

The card players laughed, traded friendly insults, stretched, and yawned. Standing, scratching armpits, and putting one last squirt into the spittoons, they headed for the door, nodding to Clairborne as they passed.

When the door closed, Clairborne drew the Breguet and snapped open the elaborately engraved gold case. The Roman numerals under the thin hands said 5:27. Clairborne lifted the masterpiece to his ear and listened to the rhythmic, reliable beating of its bejeweled heart and would have bestowed a kiss on the heirloom were it not for the presence of the two bartenders. Did they know what was about to happen? How could he be so certain someone was about to die while these two men standing within the range of conversational voice seemed so oblivious, so bored?

"Wind the Breguet some more? No. Don't. You could damage the mainspring. Leave it."

Another hour passed. Clairborne stood and stretched, buttoned his coat, and carried his coffee cup over to Frankie, who said, "You didn't have to do that, Constable."

"Oh, just thought I'd save you the hike," Clairborne said. "And thanks for the tip."

He was startled by what he saw when he stepped outside.

It was as if he'd been transported somewhere else. In place of the howling tempest he'd fled to the sanctuary of the saloon, utter calm prevailed. Already, mud puddles the size of small ponds had congealed into striated ice reflecting the soft, peach-hued streaks of cloud limning the eastern horizon.

Clairborne's breath vaporized when he exhaled and stung his nose when he inhaled. He looked up. Dawn had not yet overwhelmed the points of crystal still visible above the darker western horizon.

Stepping off the boardwalk onto the street, his shoes crunched the frozen soil that only hours earlier had squished beneath his weight.

It was one of the most beautiful mornings Clairborne had ever seen.

He looked up again.

"Is this a sacrilege on a day like this?" he asked himself.

He looked to his right, then to his left.

Windows gaped back at him, not one offering so much as the glow of a cigarette to indicate the presence of another man.

Three columns of smoke rose vertically in the still air; one from the back of a dry goods store, one from the livery office, and another from a bakery on a side street. He felt mildly cheated that the aroma of burning wood and baking bread was denied him by the still, freezing air. Suddenly, his stomach growled. He thrust his hands into his coat pockets, shrugged his shoulders, and stamped his feet. He wondered if he should buy more substantial gloves than the new kid-leather pair utterly failing to warm his hands.

Just as suddenly, he saw Bentley Rogers. A hundred yards away, but no doubt about it. Walking at a steady pace toward Clairborne, wearing a long, unbuttoned coat. Without analysis, Clairborne recognized that Bentley Rogers was calm; his breathing produced small puffs of vapor backlit by the eastern glow.

Forty yards.

"Well, maybe switching to the short Colts wasn't such a good idea," Clairborne thought. "Five more inches of barrel might be a good thing right about now."

Wrapping his right hand around the ivory grips of his snub-barreled Colt concealed in his coat pocket, he thumbed back the hammer as surreptitiously as possible.

Clairborne took one step farther into the street and turned to face Bentley Rogers, who had closed the distance to twenty yards, close enough for Clairborne to see the man was smiling.

"His coat's buttoned," Bentley Rogers thought. "Bad luck for you, Constable, and good luck for me."

At fifteen feet Bentley Rogers stopped and grasped his coat lapels with both hands, pulling them ever so slowly apart and then lowering his hands toward his waist, stopping at midchest.

Without a word, a nod, or a blink, Clairborne raised the muzzle to horizontal in his pocket and squeezed the trigger. The powder flash ignited his wool coat but sent the .44 lead ball into the belly of Bentley Rogers. Clairborne withdrew the Colt from his pocket and fired again.

The first ball hit Bentley Rogers's sternum, deflecting to the left and tearing through his heart. The second took off his right ear, but the Ohioan's will was so strong, his right hand withdrew his pistol just enough to send it tumbling onto the frozen mud alongside its owner.

Clairborne held his Colt at "present," two punctuation points of gun smoke hanging in the frozen air.

"Christ in heaven," he thought. "Am I that good?" Looking down at the smoldering hole in the front of his coat, Clairborne cursed the need to replace a garment only a month old. Without identifying the reason for doing so, he took off the jacket and dropped it on the street. Later, he would realize he was intuitively hiding evidence of the deception leading to the demise of Bentley Rogers.

He moved slowly to the body of the gunman, who'd fallen first to his knees and then onto his back, head turned to the right so visual evidence of his damaged ear was minimal, aside from the pool of congealing blood beneath it.

The corpse's eyes were half open. Clairborne leaned over the body. He felt pity. He felt for this dead human the same sensation he had felt when he beheld deer he'd hunted in the James River bottomlands. He felt the need to apologize. He felt absurd.

Another sensation flooded through him like a torrent. Without his realizing it, Clairborne's brain had reviewed the encounter and delivered its findings: correct decision to place the pistol in the pocket, tricky to align the gun and target center mass with the gun still in his pocket. Excellent withdrawal and presentation, superb accuracy, all of which combined to produce a dead opponent. The sensation produced by the automatic analysis was pride—deep, unprecedented pride that pounded through his system as if he'd just finished a sprint. He, Tucker Lightfoot Clairborne, had deliberately chosen to confront a mortal threat and had prevailed as a result of his inordinate abilities – leavened by a modicum of deceit.

At the squeak of a hinge behind him, Clairborne turned to see Frankie and the other bartender peering around the edge of the door.

Clairborne returned his Colt to its holster, and said, "Go get McComb. And better get the undertaker too, please, Frankie."

"Sure thing. You OK, Constable?"

"Yeah," Clairborne said calmly. "I'm fine."

Frankie moved to Clairborne's side.

"Christ almighty. You got two shots into him before he got one off. We heard two reports and feared the worst. Christ, Constable. I never seen such shooting as this. Never."

Clairborne looked up from the body and for a moment considered the perfect clarity of the morning sky marred only by the three columns of chimney smoke.

He looked at Frankie. "Well, it's just unfortunate, but it's done. Please get my deputy and the undertaker so we can clean this up."

Frankie took off running. The other bartender appeared at Clairborne's side with a steaming cup of coffee in one hand and a shot glass of bourbon in the other.

"Thought you might want one of these, but hell, why not both?" the bartender said.

Clairborne tossed down the whiskey and then sipped the hot coffee, wincing at its flow down his gorge and into his belly. He didn't quite know what to do next. Nobody else had come to see what the shooting was all about. They had probably just rolled over and pulled up the covers. "That's what I'd do," Clairborne thought. "If shots woke me up and I noticed how cold it was, I'd just lie back down and pull the blankets over my head."

As he picked up his coat, visions of bedsteads and down pillows and quilts changed his focus. Enervation replaced energy, and fatigue flooded through him.

———

The inquiry was mercifully short. William Bigelow presided over the group of five civic leaders who made up the Abilene Town Council, although Clairborne was unaware of any election that had yet taken place to produce legal or official capacity. Clairborne found it interesting that there was no lawyer present, that as yet there was no attorney-at-law practicing in Abilene. One of the five was Joseph McCoy's agent in

Abilene, an earnest young accountant McCoy trusted to over-
see things in his absence, which was increasingly frequent of
late, rumors being that McCoy was already looking to repli-
cate his Abilene successes somewhere along the railroad lines
inching inexorably westward, ever closer to the heart of cattle
country.

The council met in the Alamo, closed to the public for the
duration of the proceedings, which concluded in less than
two hours. Two days after the shooting, Bigelow and his colleagues summoned, listened to, and questioned McComb, Peter
Sheridan, the two bartenders working the American Eagle on
the night in question, the clerk at the McMillan Hotel, and, of
course, Tucker Clairborne.

In the interim between the incident and the inquiry,
Clairborne did little else but ponder the events of the night winter came to Abilene. He might become something else should he
live long enough, but as of late October, 1868, he was a man who
earned his living with a firearm. He was not particularly happy
about it. He had also pored over his Blackstone, reading and
rereading the sections on murder, manslaughter, and battery.

When it came time to testify, Clairborne took his seat in front
of a table behind which the six men sat, Bigelow in the center. To
his relief and surprise, nobody asked him if Rogers had drawn first.
Clairborne had decided that if they did, he would tell them no, that
he hadn't waited, that he knew Rogers wanted to kill him, that he
feared for his life if he gave Rogers the initiative, that Rogers had
killed others and Rogers had threatened to kill law-abiding citizens
right here in Abilene within hours after he rode into town.

And he was getting paid by the citizens of Abilene, Kansas, to maintain peace and order. Clairborne wanted to make it as easy as possible for the civic leaders to agree quickly and without reservations that he'd done the right thing. He knew it was their individual and collective desire to do that, and his goal was not to do or say anything that would impede their momentum. His yes and no answers achieved that goal.

When the hearing was over, drinks were consumed, hands shaken, and cigars smoked. William Bigelow excused himself to return to his office. As he walked briskly to minimize his exposure to the cold, Bigelow found himself pondering how to get Tucker Clairborne to leave town. The longer he stayed, the more of society's dregs would be drawn to the opportunity to make a name for themselves by taking him on. That would not be good for the town or business. No doubt about it, Clairborne would have to go.

The shooting of Bentley Rogers changed things. People were different, people Clairborne knew by name. They treated him with a forced hardiness he interpreted as ineffective cover of their discomfort around him. People he didn't know were less willing to engage him in conversation. They also stared at him longer than was the case before.

At least that was the way he felt about things.

Two weeks after the Rogers incident, the door of the constable's office opened to admit a short, rotund, jocular fellow who identified himself as Cornelius Jaakman, reporter for the *Kansas City Star*.

Clairborne, alone in the office, stood and extended his hand as Jaakman recited his bona fides, handed over his business card, and removed his bowler and his plaid wool overcoat.

Clairborne looked at the wall clock and figured Jaakman must have made a bee-line to his office from the train station, since the express from Kansas City had arrived only eleven minutes ago if it was on time.

Moving to the stove, Clairborne offered Jaakman a cup of coffee, poured one for himself, and asked, "Now what can I do for you?"

Jaakman smiled, revealing large, prominent yellow teeth that instantly reminded Clairborne of a beaver.

"I come to tell our readers about the famous Abilene, the straight stuff. There's so much fantastic talk about this place, Gomorra of the Plains and all. Lots of interest, believe you me."

"So you want to write about Abilene?"

"That I do. I wouldn't be surprised if my stories get picked up on the wires and sent east. That's how much interest there is in Abilene."

Clairborne returned to his chair behind the desk.

"You should've come a couple of months ago. Things have quieted down a lot since the drives. Other thing is you need to talk to a fella named William Bigelow and also to Joe McCoy. Those two are kind of the powers that be in Abilene."

Jaakman nodded vigorously. "Oh, indeed I will, Constable. Indeed I will, but I also want to talk to you." He paused, looked at the floor, and then raised his moon face and continued. "I need to talk with you, Constable. In truth, you are why I'm here in Abilene."

Clairborne was perplexed. "Me? You came all this way to talk to me? Surely you jest, sir." His obvious consternation amused Jaakman, who rested his elbows on the arms of the chair and steepled his fingertips.

"Is it possible, sir, that you are unaware of your renown?"

Clairborne did not, could not answer.

His mind raced. He could see no benefit from this "renown," only liabilities.

"Oh Lord," he thought. "What if my mother were to read about me? That can't happen. It would be too grave a shock for her to learn of my lot through the newspapers. She'd be ashamed of me."

Clairborne abruptly stood.

"I'm sorry, Mr. Jaakman, but it would be most inappropriate for me to talk with you. I do not wish to continue this conversation. I urge you to focus your efforts on the success of this town and the good people behind it, but I will not submit to any interrogation on the subject of me." Leaning forward he added, "I would deem it a most hostile act for you to talk with others about me behind my back. Do I make myself clear, sir?"

Now it was Jaakman's turn to be astonished. Hauling his corpulent form to his feet, he blurted, "Surely, sir, I am mistaken for taking your words as a threat. You cannot prevent the press from seeking the truth about you, a noted shootist, a survivor of Spanish Wells, a man who performed a self-amputation—a man,

I might add, now a public employee. Surely, sir, we can find a mutually satisfactory way to tell your story."

Clairborne struggled to hold his temper. The more he thought about it, the less he liked the idea of his name appearing in the newspapers, anywhere.

He moved to the coat rack and donned his new overcoat and hat. Turning to Jaakman he said, "I'm not going to say this again. My position is that I do not want to be the subject of your story. It could only be bad for me, but I don't expect you to understand that. It's a free country, Mr. Jaakman. I can't stop you, I guess, but I can damn sure make it hard for you if I read any lies or calumnies about me under your name."

Jaakman moved after Clairborne as he opened the door. "But Constable, don't you see that the best insurance against such inaccuracies is your cooperation? If you won't talk to me, how can I get things right?"

"That, Mr. Jaakman, is your problem. Adieu."

—⁓—

Nine miles away, Joshua Boniface shivered and blew on a pathetic campfire so small it couldn't warm his coffee, much less his hands. He'd been on the trail to Abilene for two days and nights and had never been so cold and uncomfortable in his sixteen years of hard life. With his mittened hands, he tried to lift the battered enamel coffee pot to pour its lukewarm contents into the dented cup only to drop the pot into the fire, effectively drowning the anemic flickers of heat he'd managed to generate.

He plopped to his rump and began to cry.

More than anything he'd ever wished for, he wanted to go home. No, more than anything he'd ever wished for, he wanted to be able to go home. Anger swift and heated rose from the pit of his empty stomach, but it was not anger at the man who'd shot his brother, the man he'd been dispatched by his father to kill. It was his father who sparked the coals, who blew them to life. It was his hard, demanding, unbending, unaffectionate father whom Joshua wanted to curse aloud. But he did not. His attention was distracted by the strand of snot hanging from his reddened nose. He wiped his sleeve across his nose and upper lip and considered the glistening mass.

Why hadn't his mother tried to stop him from going? Why hadn't his brother or his sisters protested his designation as angel of death, this fool's errand on which he'd been dispatched? He knew the answer. Because they would have been beaten. His father never struck to get attention or administer a mild physical rebuke. He sent his gnarled fist or his open palm into the soft flesh of his wife and children to inflict pain, to teach a lesson only pain could teach.

Joshua Boniface briefly considered turning the mule away from Abilene and heading somewhere, anywhere else. He had one dollar and thirty-two cents in his pocket, a good mule, saddle and bridle, two good blankets, a Remington Navy revolver, a surplus Springfield .58-caliber musket, and the shotgun his brother was holding when he died. Surely that was enough to get a leg up on a new start. Surely.

The fleeting optimism was replaced by the certainty that any deviation from his father's plan would bring his father off his sickbed to track him down and administer a punishment too horrible to consider. No, it was best just to ride into town and get it over with, one way or the other. He looked at his mule, its head hanging low, its long, soft ears back. Tears flowed from his eyes, and his nose ran, and his butt was cold from the frozen ground. Delaying the inevitable by staying out here was not an option. Going home was not an option, nor was running away. He was freezing and shivering. He stood and walked to the mule, stroked its neck, and fed it a dried carrot retrieved from the gunnysack tied behind the worn saddle. He replaced his coffee pot and cup into the same sack and then put his foot into the stirrup and pulled himself onto the mule's broad back but hesitated to nudge it with his heels.

It just didn't seem fair. It just didn't seem at all fair.

Joshua Boniface stopped three times to rest his mule and give it some sustenance from his gunnysack. He used his boot heel to break the ice on small streams for the mule to drink. He himself didn't drink at all. The water was too cold to scoop up with his bare hand, and it felt like iron shards in his stomach. Besides, he never got thirsty.

The northeasterly wind carried the scent of Abilene to him even before he saw it. Wood smoke. Food cooking. Maybe also raw wood being sawed. Something else too, but he couldn't really tell what. Maybe it was unwashed people. Maybe livestock.

A scattering of outbuildings, shacks, and small houses with sod roofs seemed to rise reluctantly from the frozen turf. As he rode past, the odd human barely looked up from the marathon of tasks, menial and critical, necessary merely to survive winter on the plains. He stopped to gaze in amazement at the spread of vacant stock pens to his west. Never had he seen man-made structures as vast, as orderly. He felt small and insignificant in the presence of such enterprise.

There were far fewer people on the streets of Abilene than he's expected. Instead of the thoroughfares jammed with the teamster wagons, buckboards, boisterous cowboys, and ambling pedestrians his brother had breathlessly described, there were only a few men and women scampering about, clutching their hats or the collars of their coats and shawls.

Where would he find the man he'd come to kill?

He could ask around, but what would he say? How would he describe his brother's killer? Joshua Boniface knew what the man looked like for sure. He would never forget the angular face and broad shoulders, the insolent eyes, and the blindingly fast hands. Best not to dwell on the speed of the hands.

In their bucolic isolation, he and his father did not know of Tucker Clairborne's elevation to peace officer, a development that would have embittered Lemuel Boniface even more, if that were possible. Nor did they know whether the man they sought was even in Abilene. It was only the place to start the quest to find him.

Joshua's brother said that people visiting Abilene paid for rooms in places called hotels and boarded their horses in livery stables. It occurred to Joshua that he should find one of these places and begin asking around there. He stopped at the first two-story building he came to, a clapboard structure with a loft and a pulley suspended from an opening on the second floor.

The writing above the two wide doors on rails identified the place:

Obermann's Livery
Horses Boarded and Let
Carriages, Wagons, Surreys and Buckboards for Occasions

But Joshua Boniface could not read, so he dismounted and entered, encountering a large, bearded man with a leather apron stretched over his ample belly, a man engaged in labor of such intensity that steam rose from his bald, exposed pate.

"What can I do for you, sonny?"

"I'm looking for a livery stable."

Klaus Obermann hesitated and studied the wan youngster, recognizing quickly the boy was unlettered, the rule rather than the exception of the times.

"Well, you found one, sonny. You want to put up your mule for a while? Outside with oats, a nickel a day. Inside's a dime."

The boy was mortified by the thought of depleting his pocket change to care for his mule.

"No, sir. No, sir," he stammered. "I'm just looking for someone, and I thought maybe liveries were a good place to start."

"All right," Obermann said, wiping his sweaty palms on his greasy apron. "Who would that be?"

"Well, I don't know his name. He was riding with the Rocking C up from Texas a couple of months ago. Don't know if'n he's still here or not. Tall fella. Astride a bay mare. Oh, and he's missing a finger on his left hand."

Obermann threw back his massive head and guffawed.

"Why, sonny, he's not only here. Sounds like you're talking about Tucker Clairborne. Constable Tucker Clairborne. Office is on Main Street. Just keep heading in the same direction till you come to Main, turn east, and it's on the right between Elmore's Dry Goods and the land office."

The boy's shock at hearing Clairborne's title registered immediately with Obermann, who wanted to ask why the boy sought the town's resident peace officer. His curiosity was trumped by western etiquette. A man's—or a boy's—business was nobody else's business.

The boy hesitated and looked outside over his shoulder.

"You look plumb froze there, sonny. Care for a cup of coffee before you venture off?"

The boy nodded enthusiastically. "Oh that'd be mighty fine, sir. I'm just about done in. Coffee'd be just the thing."

On the way into his office, Obermann cast a professional eye on the youngster's mount, noting approvingly that the mule's coat was thick, its muscles well formed. There was something else that caught his attention. Both of the mule's flanks sported what were clearly long guns, wrapped in blankets in place of proper scabbards, lashed to the saddle with thick rawhide thongs. Odd, but still none of his business.

As the boy sat in his office, holding the coffee cup with both of his red-knuckled hands, Obermann rested his bulk on the edge of the battered table that served as his desk.

"You heard anything about Constable Clairborne since he come to town?"

"No sir."

"Turns out, we got ourselves quite a shootist as our lawman," Obermann said. "Yeah. Danged if he ain't but shot two men in two months and banged up a couple more dumb enough to treat him rudely," he added, closely watching the boy's reaction to his words. "And the last fella he shot, about two weeks ago now, danged if the fella wasn't another shootist, name o' Bentley Rogers, come to Abilene to butt heads with our constable. Bad choice on his part."

As pale as the boy was when he arrived, Obermann noticed the blood drain from his face as he processed the information.

"Something's up here," Obermann thought, "and it ain't good."

Joshua Boniface put down his coffee cup. "Thanks ever so much for the coffee, sir. I, well, I can't afford to put up my mule here, but what would the charge be for a bate of oats while I'm looking for the constable?"

The implied brevity of the boy's visit confirmed Obermann's suspicion that he was observing something unsettling unfolding before him. "He's looking for Clairborne to use one of those long guns on him," Obermann knew with sudden certainty. And just as certain was his knowledge that the skinny, shivering kid sitting with blond curls tumbling from his hat would die in any contest pitting him with a long-gun against Tucker Clairborne and his Colt.

"Tell you what, son. I got to go into town anyways. Why don't you stay here and warm up, and I'll ask around for the constable? Save you the searchin'."

The boy's eyes flashed concern. "Oh, I want to surprise him." He paused and then continued, "You see, he lost his fine folding knife at our place when he visited, and I found it, and my daddy told me I had to give it back to him, so I wanted to kind of surprise him."

Obermann smiled in appreciation of the boy's quick mind, at his ability to spin such an elaborate fabrication out of thin air.

"OK," Obermann said. "What if I just see where you can find him and don't say anything to anybody. And you can get comfortable here while I'm asking around. Feed your mule too."

The boy considered the offer for a few moments in front of the hot stove and then looked up. "That'd be mighty fine for sure, sir. Thanks. Thanks a lot."

Obermann took off his leather apron and donned his buffalo coat and his sweat-stained hat. "You just make yourself comfortable for a hour or so, and I'll be back," he said.

Swinging up onto the back of his favorite gray gelding, Obermann decided to look for Deputy Finley McComb. He'd had a drink or two with McComb and found him decent and reasonable. He'd never spoken with Constable Clairborne and didn't care to, considering the man's reputation. No, Findley McComb would know how best to handle developments.

Obermann kicked the gelding into a canter and hoped for the best.

He found McComb in the first place he looked, the dining room of his boarding house, where the deputy was pouring gravy onto his mashed potatoes. Obermann stood in the doorway opposite him, holding his hat in his hands. McComb looked up and recognized the large man but was irritated with himself when he couldn't instantly recall his first name.

"Help you, sir?" McComb asked as the other boarders turned to see whom he was addressing. One of them was

Anton Borsheim, a traveling salesman who'd played cards with Obermann enough to know his name.

"Hey, Klaus," he said. "How you doin'? What brings you here, a quest for the best biscuits in Abilene?" he said, casting a quick glance at Sara, the comely cook, as she carried a tureen of steamed collards into the room.

"Oh, hey there, Anton. No, I come to talk with Deputy McComb."

McComb stood and wiped traces of gravy from his mustache with a gingham napkin that matched the tablecloth. "Dang it. My meal's gonna get cold," he thought as he walked around the table and extended his hand. "Let's go into the parlor," he said.

Once there, McComb asked, "So what can I do for you?"

Obermann, suddenly not so sure of his initial suspicions, hesitated. "Well, there's this boy showed up at my place today. Seems nice and polite enough, but he's trying to find Constable Clairborne. Had a kind of strange reason, seemed to me. Anyhow, he's got two long guns lashed to his mule, no side arms that I could see. I dunno, he's nervous, and his story seemed kinda far-fetched. Just seemed strange is all."

McComb pointed to a rocking chair behind Obermann as he sat himself down on the settee.

"How old?"

"Hard to tell. About maybe fifteen, maybe."

"What's his story?"

"Said the constable visited their farm on the drive and lost his folding knife. Said they found it, and his father sent him to return it. Said he wanted to surprise the constable with it, so I wasn't to let on to anyone."

McComb leaned back and rubbed his chin.

"Fishy all right. I don't think any of us visited any farm, and as you maybe heard, we had a set-to with a bunch of farmers instead of making a social call. Clairborne kinda settled things. Kid's at your place?"

"Thawin' out."

"All right. Let me finish my meal, and I'll ride back with you. If'n he's got the knife, I'll take him to the constable."

Left unsaid was what he would do if the boy couldn't produce the subject of his alleged mission.

———

Joshua Boniface innately understood the element of surprise.

Standing over the hot potbellied stove in the livery stable office, he realized that it could be the difference between life and death, and when that understanding took form in his conscious thoughts, he grabbed his coat and hat and mittens, ran to his mule, and headed for Main Street.

He knew Obermann would either talk directly to this Clairborne fellow or to someone who would alert Clairborne to his presence in Abilene. No question about that.

In his haste and inexperience, Joshua Boniface made three mistakes that led to his death.

Each decision was logical yet flawed. Combined, they were fatal.

His first mistake was coming to Abilene instead of going anywhere else on the continent.

His second bad choice was to continue his quest during daylight. Had he waited for darkness, which came early in late autumn, it was unlikely that Clairborne would have seen the boy's reflection in the side window of the claims office. Clairborne's attention was triggered by the boy's quick movement back into the side street after he spotted Clairborne walking in his direction. Clairborne slowed, catching the reflection in the last light of the day, the image of someone pulling a long gun from under his coat and raising it to his shoulder.

The third error came from nerves. Nerves and caution. Boniface had decided to use the shotgun rather than the pistol or the musket. But he didn't carry the shotgun with the hammers back and cocked. He'd seen what happened when his brother lost his balance with two handfuls of cocked side-by-sides. So while he hugged the walls and moved slowly toward the center of town, he left the hammers down.

The prospect of catching Claiborne off guard flushed his adrenal glands. A pounding pulse obliterated his memory of the need to cock the crosshatched hammers.

Clairborne made no such mistake.

When he saw the boy, he pulled his Colt and looked around for bystanders, of which there were none. He stopped ten feet away from the corner and waited, watching the reflected image with lupine intensity. Hearing footsteps behind him, he raised his left hand, palm facing backward in the universal sign to stop whatever you're doing—in this case, ambling down a boardwalk.

"What's going on?" the man behind him asked.

Clairborne thrust his left hand back toward the pedestrian and said nothing. The man reacted by standing on his tiptoes to see over Clairborne's shoulder, curiosity trumping caution and common sense.

Joshua Boniface heard the man's question and didn't hear an answer. He was aware of the situation collapsing around him, aware that the slightest deviation from his impromptu ambush had to favor his foe—his experienced, deadly foe. He wondered if he could make it back to his mule.

Two voices screamed in his head. One cried, "See what's going on."

The other roared, "Run."

Peeking around the corner, he came face to face with the man who killed his brother. Fury at his miserable lot in life blazed up, blinding him to everything but the face of Tucker Clairborne. That his foe was to his right forced Joshua Boniface to step fully onto the sidewalk to bring his gun to bear as quickly as he could even as Clairborne shouted, "Drop it! Drop it!"

But Joshua Boniface could not move fast enough. He was looking directly into the unblinking eye of Clairborne's short-barreled Colt, the shotgun suddenly heavy, and even worse, not doing what it should when its triggers were tightly squeezed.

The boy's fifteen-year-old brain made the connection even as it shut down.

The shotgun failed to fire because he hadn't cocked it.

He recognized no sequence of the physical and mental consequences resulting from the bullet's impact with his body. Tumbling backward, limbs flailing like those of a marionette whose strings have been cut, Joshua Boniface thought: "Fool."

—◈—

Again, an inquiry was held.

Again Tucker Claiborne was exonerated. The testimony of Obermann, McComb, and teamster Fred "Stinky" Sackhause, who'd walked up behind Claiborne on the sidewalk, made it abundantly clear that Abilene's constable had acted with due caution and legitimate cause. The hearing was over in less than an hour.

Unlike the first such hearing, however, this one was open to the public as a result of a unanimous vote by the inquisitors. The audience included journalist Cornelius Jaakman, who could hardly believe his good fortune, which had begun three days earlier when he heard the single report of the Colt and arrived at the scene in the first wave of gawkers.

Having served in the quartermaster corps of the Union Army, Jaakman had seen more than his share of dead men, although he'd never been involved in combat, had never even heard gunfire. He had, however, seen battlefields within a few days of the slaughter, before the swollen bodies of men and horses were dealt with, the men interred, the horses burned.

He'd never looked closely at any of the hundreds if not thousands of corpses strewn about the fields of glory. Repelled by the stench and the flies, he and the other clerks had rushed by as rapidly as possible. Aside from the indescribable odor, the only thing he remembered was how surprisingly monochromatic the corpses were, all gray and dark when one would think guts and brains and bone would be more colorful.

Joshua Boniface was the first corpse, the first victim of violent death he chose to observe closely, and his first impulse was to weep.

Although he told no one and would not write the words, he thought the boy to be positively angelic. So pale, so drawn. Curly blond hair framing his face, eyes closed, impossibly long lashes evoking an almost feminine countenance. Jaakman thought it odd that any male could be so compellingly beautiful and was flustered by his desire to straighten the boy's hair, to rearrange his coat to cover the wine-dark blood on his thin chest, a circular stain centered on an even darker hole the size of a nickel. The angles of the boy's lips, now blue and closed, hinted at neither fear nor terror. The image was that of tragic waste, sadness, inequity. It just didn't seem fair. It just didn't seem at all fair. But it was all legal, absolutely legal, even logical that things turned out as they had. And that, ultimately, was what journalist Jaakman knew was his challenge: to take this treasure trove of disparate elements and forge them into a story, a read that would knock the socks off his editors, peers, and publisher and elevate him above the ranks of ink-stained wretches praying for just such an opportunity. Jaakman was just good enough to realize the need for restraint, to understand that the components of his story were so powerful in and of themselves, he could go easy on the adjectives. His hands trembled in anticipation.

Tucker Clairborne also thought of Joshua Boniface, although he tried not to. He wondered why Rogers had evoked so little self-analysis of events, while this boy would not vacate his thoughts and dreams.

When he'd moved to the boy lying on the boardwalk, he'd not recognized him, feeling instead a discomforting certainty that he should. He stood over the boy and was struck dumb by the exquisiteness of the face he beheld. In the Louvre, in Florence, in Spain; in chapels, palaces, chateaux, he'd seen the faces of cherubim as imagined by Leonardo, Donatello, Rubens, Caravaggio, and Velasquez. This was such a face. But thinner.

Then it came to him.

"I killed his brother."

The pain of biting off a fingernail down to the quick brought William Bigelow back to reality. He examined his left index finger and sucked the tiny trickle of blood secreted from his self-inflicted wound.

It was not just about blood. No, it was about...well, to be honest, it was about money. It was about the reputation of Abilene, Kansas, and its ability to attract capital and upstanding citizens of all social classes, from bankers to livery boys. There was also a personal advantage to be gained from the step he'd just recognized as necessary and inevitable. By getting Tucker Clairborne to leave, he could not only remove what had become an unexpected, complex, and convoluted problem, he could also appease his wife, who had made his life truly miserable since the shooting of the boy at the corner of Front and First Streets. He rehearsed the words he would use after the deal was done.

"My dear, I want you to be one of the first to know that at my suggestion, the town fathers have terminated our contract with Constable Clairborne and that he will be departing our fair Abilene in a matter of days." He should be standing when he delivered the information, standing with his hands on his lapels, and he must get the news to her so expeditiously she could have the pleasure of breaking it to the brigade of biddies with whom she consorted.

But what if the town council didn't go along? What if a majority or even a vocal minority thought it was just fine, desirable even, to have Clairborne enforcing law and order in the local environs? Quickly reviewing the makeup of the council and the arguments supporting his case, Bigelow decided the odds favored him, especially since Joseph McCoy was not in town.

He was right.

A special—and closed to the public—meeting of the town council convened that evening in his parlor resulted in a unanimous vote to produce and execute a resolution terminating the employment of Tucker Clairborne as constable of Abilene, Kansas.

Now for the hard part: telling Clairborne.

Bigelow decided he must be the messenger. It would look very good indeed if he were to quietly and professionally handle such an unpleasant and, God forbid, potentially dangerous undertaking. If any one thing would lead to the mayoralty—and whatever elected or appointed post might lie beyond—this would have to be it. So Bigelow closed the meeting by telling his colleagues, "Gentlemen, I will depart now to find the constable and tell him of our decision, if you will excuse me."

They did. Relieved by Bigelow's move, every one of them felt an indebtedness as well, since he'd not asked anyone to accompany him to provide moral support.

Clairborne entered the Alamo at the beginning of his evening rounds just as the meeting of the city fathers ended. He was still there twenty minutes later when Bigelow found him. At Bigelow's request, they moved to the table farthest away from the establishment's few other clients, and Bigelow wasted no time on social niceties.

"Constable, I have the most unpleasant duty to inform you that the town council is asking for your resignation. We can discuss the reasons for that, but first I want to say two things. We are indebted to you for what you have done here, for sending the message to all and sundry that there is law in Abilene. You have accomplished what we asked of you in that regard. And that leads me to my second point: because we believe you've done such a excellent job and because our action is unilateral, we are prepared to pay you a good-faith sum in the amount of two hundred dollars if you agree to comply with the council's decision. Well, there it is."

Clairborne hadn't expected this but was neither upset nor inconvenienced by the offer. It had the effect of catalyzing his own feelings, which had become more and more unsettled since he put a bullet into Joshua Boniface. It was as if the notion of leaving Abilene had been hiding behind a screen and whispering seductively. Now, it simply stepped into the open and revealed its attractiveness. It made sense. For everyone. He knew exactly where he would go, again an idea lurking in the back of his mind that leaped to the fore as he considered Bigelow's offer.

It was time to go to Wyoming. Rawlins, Wyoming, to be exact. Thanks to Billy Martin, he owned property there, and it was time to visit his inheritance.

Bigelow was slightly unsettled by Clairborne's smile.

"Bank notes or coin?" Clairborne asked. "I prefer coin. When can you have it together?"

Recognizing that Clairborne had accepted the offer without argument, without even minor haggling, Bigelow felt a flood of relief smooth the edges of anxiety that had been rubbing his guts since the council meeting.

"Tomorrow evening. Thursday morning at the latest."

"Excellent. That'll do," Clairborne said, and paused before he added, "I have one condition."

Bigelow felt as if he'd been kicked in the stomach. "Here it comes," he thought.

"I want your guarantee that Findley McComb will be promoted to constable."

Bigelow held his breath until it became clear that was Clairborne's only condition.

Jumping to his feet and extending his hand, he exclaimed, "Done and done" so loudly he attracted the attention of the Alamo's other denizens.

"Just let me find him so I can tell him myself," Clairborne said from his chair.

"Done and done!" Bigelow repeated.

Clairborne stood and shook Bigelow's hand.

"You are a man of honor, sir," Bigelow gushed, "and it is my honor to know you."

Clairborne couldn't resist saying, "And it will be your delight to see my heels."

Bigelow laughed nervously, turned, and left the Alamo.

Clairborne wanted to sit down and have a drink, to consider his next move, but his sense of obligation to Findley McComb drove him into the night to find his deputy.

There would be time for a drink and consideration of the future.

November 18, 1868
Abilene, Kansas

> *Dearest Mother,*
>
> *This may be the most difficult letter to compose I have ever attempted.*
>
> *I undertake it knowing I have been dishonest. My failure to inform you of drastic events and experiences is as morally indefensible as lying about them. So much has happened, so serious are the ramifications of each event in question, that I must make a choice: either endeavor to provide you with all of the details you may need to place them in context, or recognize that no effort to do so could ever succeed, so alien is my existence compared to anything you could even imagine.*
>
> *I begin.*
>
> *I have killed men with my own hand. I have not murdered. I am not a hired assassin. I believe each time I took a life, there was no alternative, certainly*

not "turning the other cheek." I am not proud of this. I wish most strongly that it were not the case. I have discovered that I have an inordinate ability to defend myself in that my hand moves in synchrony with my thoughts. Do not worry about any of this resulting in my being considered an outlaw, a felon. On the contrary, I was appointed constable by the city fathers of Abilene, and it was in that capacity that the latest of these unfortunate incidents occurred.

I must also inform you that I have been maimed. I lost the index finger of my left hand in a roping accident in Texas last summer. It has proven to be the mildest of inconveniences, especially since I am right-handed, as you well know.

In a very short time, a day or two, I am leaving Abilene for a place called Rawlins in Wyoming Territory. As I wrote to you some time back, I own property there as a result of my providing solace to a dying man I encountered by purest coincidence. Oh, Mother. As I reread these words I can imagine the grief and pain they will cause you, but I cannot deceive you about my life since I know you would hear things about me one way or the other. Then your shock would be compounded by disappointment that you had not learned of your son's life from your son himself. I would do anything, dearest Mother, to shield you from even more distress than you have already suffered, but

I will not deceive you any longer. You may read something in the papers or talk with someone who has done so, since Abilene has been the subject of interest to a number of reporters from the East. I urge you not to believe any of these accounts, as these people are without honor and are not worthy of Christian charity. They fabricate events and present them as facts.

In closing, please know that I really am well, that I read and pray daily. Unfortunately, there is no Episcopal church this side of Kansas City, so I have not had the comfort of communion in far too long.

You should also know that my investments seem to be doing well thanks primarily to luck on my part and the acumen and honesty of my distant business partners.

Again, I am reluctant to post this, but I simply must reestablish contact with you. I promise I will write within a day or two of my arrival in Rawlins. Please give my dearest affections to Sister Amy.

Adieu, Tucker Lightfoot Clairborne, Esq.

WYOMING

Had Clairborne undertaken his trip to Rawlins, Wyoming, even two months earlier, he could have simply ridden north from Abilene until he encountered the Union Pacific tracks in Nebraska at Grand Island, Cozad, or somewhere in between. It would have been challenging and dangerous to cross open prairie by himself but not any more so than what he'd already been through. There were trails and known sources of water, and due caution coupled with hard-earned experience could balance the threats posed by Indians.

But starting the trip in November meant that riding horseback from Abilene to the westbound Union Pacific was out of the question. The blizzards and bone-cracking cold ushered in by the calendar meant that Clairborne faced a rump-numbing train ride: east to Kansas City, then north to Omaha, and then west along the Union Pacific's brand-new line that had reached Wyoming Territory only six months earlier.

Fitful snow began falling before he arrived in Kansas City, the kind of snow optimists thought was not so bad and that pessimists saw as a skirmish line for murderous storms already on the march. Using his forearm to rub condensation from the railcar window, Clairborne saw only shades of gray so soft and so pervasive he could not discern the horizon even at two o'clock in the afternoon. The potbellied stove at the end of the car sup-plemented the moist heat generated by his fellow passengers. The coach's interior was comfortable but noisome. Most of his fellow travelers either slept, stared ahead without focus, or tried to observe the passing countryside through the steamed-up windows.

In Kansas City and Omaha, Clairborne spent the time between connections luxuriating in the best hotels each city had to offer. He also decided without any forethought to use an alias when signing the registers. When he did think about it, Clairborne recognized the act for what it was: a necessary, wise step to obviate unwanted conflict. His choice of pseudonyms was a source of mild amusement; "Lee Jackson" in Kansas City and "Stuart Hood" in Omaha.

When the much-delayed Union Pacific train inched into the Rawlins depot, its bell clanged weakly, and a single shriek from its whistle seemed an admission that it was embarrassed by its tardiness.

Clairborne swung down to the raw planks of the unfinished platform, saddlebags over his shoulder, a valise in each hand. Later-afternoon Rawlins was devoid of all color. How could any place be so gray? he asked himself in dismay. He saw seven wooden buildings, each draped with icicles. He didn't count the tents, all of which seemed to be furiously belching smoke from stovepipes poking through the canvas. He wiped his nose on the back of his glove.

"This is the worst place I've ever seen," he said aloud. "Lord above, what a godforsaken exile I've sent myself into." His second thought on setting foot in Rawlins, Wyoming, was to buy a ticket on the next train out.

"Beg pardon, sir," said a man whom Claiborne hadn't noticed, a short man wearing a double-breasted navy wool coat that dropped below his knees and a matching navy-blue, brimmed hat bearing a polished brass badge that said "Station Master."

"You say something, sir? Sorry. Didn't catch it."

"Just talking to myself," Clairborne said.

"You wouldn't happen to be Mr. Stuart Hood, would you?"

Clairborne nodded. It was the name written on the tags affixed to his trunk being wrestled from the baggage car onto a handcart by a scrawny old man barely up to the task.

"Yeah, that's me," Clairborne said absent-mindedly, still dazed by the desolation of the place.

"You want to hold your baggage in the depot, or you got someplace else you want 'em?"

Clairborne didn't immediately answer. Slowly swiveling his head, he continued to process Rawlins, its evidence of multiple works in progress, each mantled with a foot of snow.

He ignored the station agent before saying, "Sorry. Sorry. I didn't mean to be rude. It's just that, ah, just that.... What was your question again?"

"What would you like me to do with your baggage, Mr. Hood?"

"Palace Hotel. Is that it?" he asked with a nod at the largest building he saw, a two-story wooden structure on the corner of the only two discernible streets, a wrap-around veranda fronting the second story.

"That's it, all right. Damn fine place. Pride of Rawlins, is the Palace. Even got rooms with their own stoves, and two of 'em's got a bath tub right in the room."

"OK. Bring my things there," Clairborne said. He headed down the street toward the Palace, counting exactly six people, all men, one appearing to be oriental, all scurrying to destinations offering light and warmth. He saw only four horses tied to hitching posts and one wagon pulled by two mules stopped in front of a large tent covered with a series of neatly painted signs identifying the owner and his businesses: "T. A. Kent & Co. Wines and Liquors. Groceries. Chicago Ale. Bank."

Clairborne's mood improved the moment he stepped inside the Palace Hotel.

The lobby was surprisingly illuminated, large, and carpeted. A circular maroon leather settee surrounding a potted palm anchored the middle of the room, the marble-and-carved-oak registration desk to the right, open doors to the dining room on the left. It was also warm, the freezing cold effectively held at bay by a fireplace and a large stove on opposite sides of the room.

A well-dressed boy jumped to his feet and ran to greet Clairborne. "Allow me to take those, sir. Welcome to the Palace Hotel, Mr...."

"Ah, Hood. I don't have a reservation. Hope that's not going to be a problem."

The desk clerk wiped his chin with a napkin as he emerged from his office.

"Only two paying guests tonight other than yourself. Mr. Hood, is it? How long will you be with us?"

Clairborne smiled. "Don't know. A while. Rumor has it you have rooms with their own heat and bath."

The clerk beamed. "Indeed we do. Best accommodations this side of Omaha. The presidential suite is available."

Again Clairborne smiled. He'd long since become used to western hyperbole, but the notion of a presidential suite in the middle of nowhere was amusing.

"How much?"

"Seasonal rates are in effect. You can have the suite and its amenities for seventy-five cents a night. That includes breakfast, two hot baths a week, and a daily shave if you're so inclined."

Since the peak rate at Abilene's Drover's Cottage was fifty cents a night, the Palace at first struck him as almost extortionate until he remembered half of the profits were supposed to be his.

Signing the register, he said, "Send up a bottle of the best whiskey in town, and I want clean glasses every day. I'd also appreciate a pot of coffee each morning at seven. What newspapers are available?"

The clerk reeled off the names of papers published in Chicago, Saint Louis, Kansas City, and Omaha, adding proudly that they were delivered to Rawlins only two days after they hit the streets, "so their news is still as fresh as mother's potato salad."

The suite, larger than his room in Abilene, was immaculate and well appointed and did indeed have a small cast-iron stove. The bellboy quickly set about igniting its pine knots and adjusting the flue.

Clairborne walked to the surprisingly large window and pulled back the curtains to peer at the darkening main street. Not a soul in sight. In the ten minutes since he had entered the hotel, the sky had surrendered its last bit of light. He ran his bare hands around the window frame, detecting only the slightest of drafts. "Somebody did this place right," he thought. He walked to the stove and warmed his hands while he looked around the room. Maybe, just maybe he'd stay in Rawlins, Wyoming, a little longer. At least he was warm.

—

Time for a drink, a drink followed by dinner. Clairborne changed into fresh clothes but decided not to bathe. Too cold, and it had been only four days since his last bath. He shaved with his father's silver-handled Sheffield straight razor and ran his monogrammed, silver-backed, boar-bristle brush through his hair. Examining one of his short Colts, Clairborne decided he would buy some leather dressing and work it into his belts and holsters within the next day or two. Although he was only going to the next building, he donned his kettle-brim hat and left his room in a good mood.

The Bon Ton saloon was almost as impressive as the Palace Hotel. Rawlins's second-largest "permanent" structure, it had a second-floor balcony accessed by a staircase in the rear. It also featured a mirrored backbar and an elevated but empty stage. Standing to the left of the door, Clairborne counted ten tables, all but one of them full. Two bartenders served the thirsty. Two gamblers ran their tables, faro and blackjack. At the right rear of the room, Clairborne saw something of great interest.

On a chair perched on a platform reached by three steps sat a well-dressed man with a full beard, a gray hat on the back of his head. But what impressed Clairborne was not the man's attire. It was the huge double-barrel shotgun resting across his ample lap that drew Clairborne's attention. Had to be a ten-gauge. The full-length barrel meant its load could be directed better than if the barrels were sawed off.

"This must be a hell of a rowdy place if they need a full-time shotgun," Clairborne told himself.

He studied the crowd. Boisterous, but no more so than the clientele of most drinking holes. Couple of loudmouths. A few drunks on the verge of collapse. Nothing out of the ordinary. Still...somebody—namely his business partner—thought it necessary to have that flinty-eyed shotgunner on the payroll.

At the bar, Clairborne ordered "best whiskey you got there, friend" and watched the barkeep tap a small keg at the left of the mirrored backbar. Raising the cut glass to his nose, he sniffed the amber liquid and put it back on the bar.

"Where'd you get this?" he asked.

"Omaha. How come?" the bartender said.

"Kind of rough around the edges," Clairborne said.

"Ah, well then, a man of refined taste," the bartender said with a smile. "I've been suggesting to the boss that we procure a better pour for folks such as yourself, but he doesn't think it's worth it. At least not yet. And not during the winter."

Clairborne sipped. He grimaced. "Damn. Lots of room for improvement there. Damn." He coughed. Then he and the bartender chuckled.

In the mirror, Claiborne saw a man approach from his right rear.

"Pour me another shot o' panther piss, there, Clyde." The man threw a nickel on the bar, and the bartender took the man's glass jar and filled it with a cloudy yellow liquid from a large barrel resting on its side.

As Clyde poured, the man turned to study Clairborne, who studiously ignored him. The man's wavering movement, slurred speech, and foul breath had announced his state of inebriation before he'd arrived at bar's edge.

"Hey, greenhorn," the man said. "You the new Sunday school teacher? You need to be careful you don't get them fine duds dirty," he said, turning to ensure his friends picked up on his baiting the newcomer.

Clairborne thought: "Not again. Here we go."

"Don't talk much for a Sunday school teacher, there, do ya?" the drunk asked.

His drinking buddies chuckled.

Clairborne said nothing. His eyes made contact with those of Clyde the bartender, whose eleven years of pushing drinks from Paducah to Rawlins told him the newcomer was not amused. He wondered if he should move closer to the oaken club suspended under the bar in front of him.

Clairborne sipped his whiskey.

"Least he ain't drinking sasparilla," the man said to his friends. "I still think he's a girly though."

Clairborne couldn't see a gun on the man's reflected image.

"What kind o' damn hat does a girly wear anyhow?" the man said.

Clairborne ignored him. The man leaned over to get closer to his face. His breath smelled as if he'd been eating carrion. Then the man knocked Clairborne's hat to the floor and turned to make a face at his friends, evoking more laughter.

Clairborne whipped the short-barreled Colt up under the man's chin and pushed it into the soft, stubble-covered flesh.

"On your knees, mule turd. On your knees," Clairborne hissed through clenched teeth. The man dropped to his knees and began to whimper.

"Shut up," Clairborne said. "Open your mouth."

The man hesitated a second before complying. Clairborne shoved the Colt muzzle as far into the man's mouth as it would go.

The man gagged. Then he closed his eyes and wet himself.

"Clyde," Clairborne said.

"Yes sir?"

"What's the shotgun's name over there?"

"Morton," Clyde said evenly.

Keeping his eyes on his kneeling tormentor, Clairborne said, "Now Clyde, slide real easy like up here beside me." And when Clyde did so, Clairborne raised his voice and said, "Morton, you pretty fair with that scattergun, are you?"

"Fair enough," Morton said calmly.

"Well, then, that being the case, you'll have noted that Clyde here is now in your line of fire should you decide to interrupt my conversation with this jackass, and since Clyde is innocent of any wrongdoing, we wouldn't want Clyde to get hurt, now would we?

"No, we wouldn't," Morton said.

"Excellent," Clairborne said.

He stole a glance at the mirror to see what was going on behind him. Nobody moved. Leaning slightly down to the quivering man whose clenched eyes were streaming tears, he said, "Open your eyes."

The man did.

"Pick up my hat."

The man felt around on the sawdust-covered floor until he found the hat and offered it to Clairborne.

"Wipe off the sawdust."

The man held the hat up high enough to see and cleaned its crown and brim.

Clairborne took the hat in his left hand and cocked the hammer, the sound of which carried to the farthest corner of the tomb-quiet room.

The man closed his eyes and groaned, his body quivering.

"What's that stench?" Clairborne said. "Did you just shit yourself, jackass?" Turning slightly to face the man's friends, he said, "You don't think that's funny?"

Their only response was downcast eyes.

"Now, jackass. You crawl out of here and don't ever, ever come back. Do you understand?" Clairborne asked, pushing the barrel for emphasis.

The man gagged again, nodded as best he could, and something garbled that could have been "yes, sir" slipped from his lips.

"I mean it. I see you here again, I might get upset." Removing the Colt, he said, "Now git."

When the man scrambled through the door, Clairborne reholstered his Colt and turned to face the room.

"Gentlemen, I apologize for this unpleasantness, but I simply won't tolerate rudeness." He withdrew a twenty-dollar gold piece from his vest pocket and ostentatiously flipped it on the bar.

"As the bard said, 'all's well that ends well,' so allow me to make up for this episode by picking up the tab."

The crowd reacted with instant enthusiasm, cheers replacing their frigid, fearful silence.

Clairborne turned around to face the bartender and lowered his voice.

"Sorry this happened, Clyde. You and Morton split any change left after these folks drink their fill."

Before Clyde responded, Clairborne turned and walked through the crowd rushing the bar and for the most part ignoring him as he departed the scene.

From a door cracked open on the second floor, a woman watched him go. She had never been so repulsed and so attracted to a man in her life.

—⁓—

Genevieve LaBelle never forgot that evening for two reasons. It was the first time she laid eyes on Tucker Clairborne, and it was also the day she discovered her first gray hair.

"Jenny" LaBelle closed the door and leaned against it, raising her right hand to her slim, long throat rising from the taupe Belgian lace collar of her green taffeta dress.

"I hope he doesn't stay."

But she knew he would be around long enough for them to meet even if she tried to avoid him. The town was too small and the trains too infrequent.

She sat down on the stool in front of her vanity and regarded the reflected image.

Pursing her lips, she ran through a series of facial expressions, each of which affected a different set of muscles and section of skin. She put her fingertips in front of both ears and gently pulled back the flesh to see if there was any detectable reduction of a nonexistent sag under the chin or around the green eyes.

She examined her makeup, deciding the dusting of powder successfully hid the bridge of freckles crossing her nose. She turned to examine her face in profile and studied her jawline, reassured by the absence of excess skin.

She rotated on the stool and brought her torso into profile, automatically sucking in her breath and straightening her back. An expensive French whalebone corset accentuated her thin waist and modest breasts, reflecting the fashion of the times, as did her hairstyle. Parted in the middle, swept back over her small ears, and bunched in a mass of tight curls at the back of her head, Jenny LaBelle's thick, gleaming auburn tresses were one of her finest features. She picked up a tortoiseshell hand mirror and moved it skillfully around her head in the final step of her twice-a-day toilette.

She stopped dead and sucked in her breath. Leaning forward to bring her head closer to the vanity mirror, she focused on the part line, and there it was: a single gray hair slapping her silly, crushing any aspiration of permanent or even prolonged youth.

It was not fair. Twenty-four years old and turning gray? Working her fingertips to separate the offending strand, she reflexively yanked it out and used both hands to hold it up in better light. Frieda, her diminutive German maid, had prepared her hair that morning and not mentioned it. How could this happen? How could something this life changing take place in less than a day?

Without a conscious decision to do so, she began reviewing her finances, racing through the numbers she checked almost daily, numbers that told her how long her money would last when—not if—her looks no longer produced it.

The sum she came up with sent a shiver down her spine. Looking into the mirror, she saw a woman facing disaster, displacement, discomfort, degradation, and hunger. She saw poverty and all of the apocalyptic demons that rode in poverty's posse intent on dragging destitute females into a hell no man could imagine.

She would not go back there.

With a strength she never analyzed, Jenny LaBelle had never succumbed to the cushioning effects, the powerful allure of either narcotics or alcohol, refuges from reality calming the fears of so many young women she'd known on the road from Louisiana to Wyoming. She drank sparingly but had never allowed laudanum or opium or cocaine to enter her body after the first experimentation.

She had to retain control of her excellent mind, especially when she was selling her exquisite body.

She stood and walked to the window, pulled back the curtains, and regarded the empty vastness behind the hotel. She always had a plan in the back of her mind, a "next step," a "just in case" that had served her well more than once when things suddenly went sideways.

Moving to the full-length mirror in front of the modesty screen behind which she undressed, she regarded her image. She could not afford to be self-deluding, literally could not afford it.

"Good enough for a while longer, young lady," she said, smoothing a nonexistent wrinkle from her dress. She moved to her oaken armoire, pulled open the bottom drawer, and extracted a slim book bound in brown leather with a green leather spine bearing gold embossed letters that spelled A-C-C-O-U-N-T-S. She sat on the four-poster bed and rested the ledger in her lap.

"Time to get serious, Jenny, my girl," she said. Opening the book and running her manicured fingertips over the familiar ciphers, she sighed. "So far to go and so little time."

—⁓—

Back at his room, Clairborne took off his hat, turned it over in his hands, and said, "Well, that didn't take long."

For a moment he leaned against the door and then moved to the window and pulled back the curtains. It was snowing. Fat, soft, pale-blue flakes the size of quarters drifted straight down, absorbing all sound.

He leaned forward and rested his forehead on the ice-glazed windowpane. He leaned back, scratched his initials into the frozen filigree, and stared at his handiwork.

"How could I come so far and still be so lost?"

There would be no staying in Rawlins, Wyoming, now. Something bad would happen sooner than later in the wake of his most recent conflict, something sucked to the surface of this maelstrom that had become his life.

He didn't waste time asking himself why such things continued to happen. They just did. The only question reverberating in his head was, where next? Winter snows had halted Union Pacific construction a hundred miles from Rawlins at a place called Evanston. He took off his coat, unbuckled his shoulder holster, and hung it on the bedstead. His hand slipped to the cold, checkered grip, and his fingertips traced the silver-plated contours.

"Am I using you or are your using me?" he asked Mr. Colt's masterpiece.

He sat on the quilted bedspread and lowered his head into his hands.

"Where did this begin?" he wondered and reached into his valise for his tattered journal to reread its earliest entries. He retrieved his pen and bottle of India ink.

November 26, 1868

I cannot explain to myself what I have become. Who I am today is so different from who I was mere months ago, and I view with trepidation who I will be a year hence.

I try not to think of my parents, the responsibilities to them, and the life they bequeathed me. Would Father turn his face from mine were he still alive and aware of what I have done since leaving beloved Warwick? When I allow myself to think of him, of Mother as well, I cannot believe they would disown me. But there is no doubt they would be distressed and disappointed, and for me, that is worst of all.

So now? I carry my name and my reputation as a dead weight rather than with pride. I join the company of men whom I do not know and hope not only that they do not know me but also that they do not know of me. I fear this continent is not large enough for me to get away from myself. There is no going back. There is only going on, and so I will.

Finally, I must ask myself why it is I continue to attract the attention of men like the drunk in the bar tonight. He seemed to note my attire and assume that it signified a dandy, a coward. In his inebriated state, did he consider the consequences of his actions? Probably not. I was stone sober, and yet I didn't consider the possible consequences of my reaction. What were my options? To ignore him and pick up my hat? No, in this part of the world the consequences of ignoring such an insult would be worse, much worse, than reacting as I did. My reactions will deter others from such rude behavior. Ignoring him would encourage others to think they can amuse themselves at my expense. I would never treat another man in such a manner. I will not tolerate being treated that way myself.

He stared at the journal's leather binding, amused by the hubris of any individual's recorded thoughts. Who would ever read them? Who would care?

James River bottomland. His father's voice. His mother's scent. Like falling dominoes, the individual aromas of sun-warmed jasmine and rain-damp autumn leaves, beeswax, Smithfield ham, stables, hay, and horses led one to the other, replacing esoteric philosophic questions.

Home.

Home was a possibility. Why not? Take his money home to Warwick. Restore house and grounds. Regain influence. It was his duty to return.

The room had become stifling. He adjusted the stove flue and opened the window. He leaned out into the frozen silence, seeing not so much as a single horse, much less another human. Clairborne inhaled, to the limits of his lungs' capacity, the sub-zero Wyoming winter air searing his nose and trachea.

But it was a startling reality that watered his eyes.

There it was.

He would never go back to Virginia. Never. Every time he thought of it, the answer was the same, only clearer. He was no longer a Virginian, a gentleman. That was over, done. It was not a matter of place nor even a matter of money. It was a matter of fit.

His words took physical form in the shape of crystalized vapor. "I don't know where or how this ends. I don't know where to go." He closed the window and gazed through the frosted panes, seeing nothing, yet seeing all.

"It can only be west of here..."

—◦◦◦—

The silence awakened him the next morning. He retrieved the Breguet from the nightstand and brought it to his ear. His breath fogged its face and condensed over his quilt. He glanced at the wood stove and considered the discomfort required to even begin heating the room. Too much. He rolled over and pulled the down comforter over his head.

In the adjacent building, Jenny LaBelle leaned into the mirror and squinted. Looking for telltale lines seeping from the corners of her eyes, she found none and smiled. Her gaze went to her cleavage, shadowed by the lace trim of the mauve peignoir she wore under the heavy blue wool robe.

Frieda approached, carrying a tray with tea, cream, sugar, and toast. Jenny decided to conduct a test. She would not mention the gray hair to Frieda. She would watch Frieda as she ran the brush through her hair, a hundred strokes per side. She asked herself again whether Frieda was being discrete or careless. She knew the answer. Frieda was dedicated to her and was undoubtedly shielding her from the shock all women feared, particularly those whose welfare depended on youth and beauty.

Then she thought of the stranger who had caused such a ruckus in the saloon the night before, her shiver instantly detected by her maid.

"You are cold, Miss? A shawl perhaps?"

"No, Frieda. It's not the cold."

After a few seconds, she added, "It's a man."

Freda stopped her brushing and stared at Jenny's reflected image, startled by such an uncharacteristic personal revelation, the first she'd ever heard from her employer in the seven months they'd known each other.

Jenny herself was startled as well, startled that the man had this residual impact and startled that she had verbalized it to Frieda. She sipped her tea, grimacing at its bitterness, realizing she'd neglected to add cream and sugar.

She was displeased with herself. She could not recall having this reaction before, and it was an unpleasant sensation. For the last decade of her life, Jenny LaBelle had exercised a rigid control over her emotions, putting rational decision making ahead of all else. Determining the best possible option had long since been her daily, hourly focus, and it had worked. She had money and a room of her own, fine clothes, decent food, a handmaid, and protection from ruffians and drunks. The cost, being a "kept woman," the occasional sex with the owner of the hotel and saloon, was payable. He was not a bad man, at least not with her, and no more self-focused in bed than most men. He had never hit her, and on the rare occasions when he drank too much, he was a happy drunk, not a mean one.

Yes, the cost of her situation was worth it indeed—almost enviable, everything considered. Things had been a lot worse at other times in her twenty-four years. A lot worse.

And no man who walked into the Bon Ton saloon and stuck his pistol into the mouth of a drunk railroad man was going to jeopardize her situation. Not if Jenny LaBelle could help it.

Her eyes shifted down and to her right, to the slightly open drawer of the vanity in front of which she sat. The nickel-plated, stubby barrels of the Remington .41-caliber derringer winked up at her, its pearl handle lustrous in the morning light. It gave

West from Yesterday

her solace. Its hefty presence in the small pockets artfully concealed in her dresses, her riding attire—yes, even her robe—provided a confidence, an equilibrium she hadn't had before the small but deadly implement became part of her life.

As Frieda resumed her brushing, Jenny recalled the first time she'd seen such a weapon used by a woman, another "soiled dove," most of whom carried edged weapons of some sort, firearms being too expensive and hard to conceal.

What was that girl's name? Well, hardly a girl. Her weathered face, her mended dress, even her dirty gray hair came to mind, but not her name.

She recalled how, in a steaming, rancid saloon in Natchez, she'd watched a beefy boatman slap the woman and then reach down and grab her hair, yanking her to her feet. The woman winced but uttered not a sound. The boatman held her hair with his left hand and drew back a fist the size of a small ham and laced with scars, scabs, and evidence of more than one long-since broken knuckle. The woman spoke in a voice so low only Jenny and the boatman heard her.

"I'll kill you," she said.

The boatman froze and tried to focus his alcohol-besotted brain on the absurdity of what he'd just heard.

"Huh? What?" He turned to his fellow boatmen sitting at a nearby table. "You hear that? She gonna kill me. This itty-bitty rat bitch gonna kill me."

Jenny yelled, "You're a goddamned coward! Beating on a woman. Coward!"

The woman turned enough to make eye contact with her, her eyes telling Jenny not to get involved. Then the woman

faced the boatman just as he turned away from his friends and cocked his arm for the blow to follow.

He never launched it.

Jenny heard a muffled "pop" and saw the boatman release the woman and move backward as if he'd been pushed hard.

Except that he hadn't been pushed.

In a move so subtle no one had noticed, the woman had withdrawn her nickel-plated, pearl-handled, twin-barreled Remington derringer and shoved it against the boatman's belly, depressing the trigger the instant the muzzle touched his shirt. The .41-caliber, soft-lead bullet plowed into the boatman, pushing him backward, the pain and uncommanded movement confusing him.

The boatman looked down. Flames ignited by burning grains of gunpowder confused him. "How did my shirt catch fire?" he wondered. A dark stain spread rapidly from the hole three inches above the rope belt that held up his grimy britches. The spreading flames fed on the grease-impregnated fabric, taking the boatman's attention away from the horrendous pain in his belly. He looked up at the woman who had shot him, bewilderment replacing anger. His legs trembled. He dropped his hands to his side and slowly sat down.

"Gonna hit me again, was you?" the woman said as she lowered her gun to his forehead.

"Not now. Not never."

She pulled the trigger. This time, the report was louder, the muzzle flash small but bright. Men scrambled for cover, knocking over tables, sending cards and coins, bottles and glasses flying in all directions. They just wanted to get the hell away from this woman, unaware that she'd fired the only two rounds the derringer held.

The woman slid the gun back into her pocket and turned to Jenny.

"Thanks."

She walked slowly out the back door, and Jenny never saw her again.

As Frieda resumed her brushing, Jenny studied her reflected image. "What was that woman's name?"

———

Disconcerting silence. Silence so total that, on waking, he momentarily wondered if something was wrong with his hearing. Lying on his back, he rubbed his ears with both hands, relieved at the sound of skin on skin.

The ceiling was pressed tin. He hadn't noticed it yesterday, had not really noticed much of anything about the room. It occurred to him that he would be here awhile unless he got on a train bound back east. Unlikely. This would be his abode for the foreseeable future—days, weeks, who knew? Who cared? He turned his head to study the details of the room, quickly realizing that someone had spent a lot of money, an unlikely amount of money, on the construction and furnishing of this hotel literally on the ragged edge of civilization. Why? Only one possible reason. Someone had big plans, plans that must be based on the assumption of significant returns for such a significant investment.

"Well, why not?" he asked himself out loud. "The railroad's already here. Land's probably cheap—although I can't imagine what anybody would do with land here. Too cold for livestock."

He thought about Abilene. People had made big money there very quickly. He smiled. "I'm thinking about how to make money? What's happened to me?"

An hour later, he returned to his room after a breakfast of calf brains, scrambled eggs, biscuits, blackberry jam, and coffee—three large cups of black coffee. Good coffee. Before mounting the stairs, he asked the clerk for stationery, pen, and ink. In his room, he hung up his coat, threw two pieces of dry fir into the stove, and sat down at the small desk beside a window. Reaching over to pull back the heavy brocade drapes, he glanced at the frozen tableau and noted the absence of any life form, human or otherwise. He let the drape fall back into place and turned to the blank sheets.

"Where is my money?"

Two days later, when telegrams to his bankers and business partners were still unanswered, Clairborne's pent-up energy overflowed. Over his wool union suit, he donned the heaviest wool pants he owned along with a wool vest, wool jacket, and wool scarf. He strapped on a long-barreled Colt; slid its short-barreled relative into the shoulder holster; picked up his buffalo coat, hat, rabbit-fur-lined gloves, and Henry rifle; and left the room, slowly descending the staircase, already questioning the sanity of his impromptu plans.

A clerk he didn't recognize looked up from the ledger at the reception desk.

"Sir?"

"Fetch me a horse, will you? Just going to take a little mosey around."

Involuntarily glancing at the door and the frigid bleakness on the other side, the clerk stammered, "Sir?"

"A horse. This place has a livery, doesn't it? Oh, just tell me where the livery is, and I'll get it myself."

Outside, still but frigid air slapped his exposed cheeks. Clairborne surveyed the empty street and saw two livery stables, one on the right and one on the left, the latter being slightly larger. He headed toward it, slogging slowly through the driest snow he'd ever encountered, so dry he knew he didn't have to worry about its soaking his boots and the bottom of his trousers.

In the office, a glowing coal-oil lantern hanging from the ceiling cast a small circle of dim, amber light on the battered plank floor. The office was neat but empty. Clairborne moved into the gloom of the barn. Steam pulsed from the noses of the horses studying him from their stalls. A few snorted. One stamped its hoofs in the dry, clean straw. Clairborne recognized the place was well managed. Everything was in order. Blended aromas of hay and leather, horse breath and feed grain pleased him, softened the slight irritation caused by the absence of the owner or hired hand.

"Anybody here?" he shouted.

A black man emerged from the corner of the loft, pitchfork in hand.

"Sorry, friend. Should 'a heard you come in, but hearing ain't what it used to be. What can I do for you?"

Clairborne studied the man as he descended the ladder. Slight but muscular. Graceful movements. White hair and beard.

"This your place?" Clairborne asked.

"Ah, no, sir. Wish it was, but wishin' ain't getting'. No, I run the place for the owner. Now what was it you need?"

"A mount. Going to take a little meander around. Been cooped up in my room since I got here. Probably won't be more than an hour or so."

The man studied Clairborne. He cocked his head and said, "Sir, hope you don't mind my saying it, but being as how you're new and all, you might want to reconsider. It...well, you ride out a piece, it snows some more, and you may not be able to retrace your tracks. Lord only knows what could happen then."

"Why mister," Clairborne smiled, "just about every livery horse I ever heard of could find its way back to the barn come hell or high water. Just what kind of cayuses you renting here if that's your concern?"

The man smiled back and shook his head.

"Oh, I ain't worried about the horses. I never worry about the horses. It's the riders I fret over, specially them as want to wander off into a by-God blizzard."

"What's your name?"

"Robert McMannis at your service."

"Well, Robert, tell you what. I just have to get my blood flowing, so you pick a sure-footed little mare for me, and I promise to have her back in about an hour. How's that?"

"Well, it's your funeral, but you want to take a ride, ain't my job to stop you. I'll just stoke up my stove so's I can throw your frozen carcass on it when you get back. If you get back."

It had been weeks since Clairborne was last astride.

The mare picked her way through the drifts with an intelligence and grace that kindled Clairborne's affection. The long buffalo coat draped over her flanks trapped her body heat, radiating it up and around Clairborne's form, surprising him with its unexpected comfort.

Above him, the last of the solid overcast crept toward the east, the sun, low on the horizon, putting in a token appearance to remind those who noticed that it had not entirely abandoned Rawlins, Wyoming.

Cresting a low ridge, Clairborne pulled up and leaned his forearms on the saddle horn. Beyond, a vastness bathed in blue-white snow beckoned, daring him to ride into its void. He looked back at the tattered town-in-progress, smoke from scores of chimneys rising in straight columns as if they too were frozen solid.

He grinned and shook his head.

"Hell of a place," he said aloud, his frozen breath visible before him. His mount turned her head back just enough to make eye contact with him, her ears rotated to meet his voice.

"A hell of a place," he repeated. Left unsaid was the certainty that he didn't want to be anywhere else.

Back at the stable, he handed the reins to Robert McMannis. "Fine little filly. Plenty of bottom for sure," he said.

McMannis nodded. "Just like I told you."

"You said you don't own the place. Who does?"

"That'd be Mr. Price, same as owns the hotel and the other livery too. Same as owns just about everything hereabouts."

Clairborne was not surprised to learn his partner had such extensive holdings in Rawlins. In fact, it made sense. On arrival in Abilene, he'd begun to learn that money begets money.

Standing in the livery door and regarding the town, he heard his stomach rumble and felt it twist. He was almost as hungry as he was cold.

—⁓—

The hotel lobby was empty of humans but full of an irresistible aroma emanating from the dining room.

Looking over Marcus Price's left shoulder, she saw him enter. Adrenaline flamed in her gut and colored her face, triggering immediate anger with herself that a man had affected her so. Instantaneous assessment of the situation led to the realization that his expression changed when their eyes met. She had seen that expression before, several times. It gave her instant pleasure. It meant the man she had seen earlier, the man who radiated danger, was just that—a man, a man completely taken by her appearance. But this one was different. This one caused things to happen against her will, such as her right hand rising involuntarily to the cameo broach at her neck.

Clairborne stopped at the dining room threshold. There were only three people in the room—four if the waiter was counted—but Clairborne had eyes locked on only one. She was the most beautiful woman he'd ever seen. Anywhere.

Auburn hair pulled back in a jumble of curls. A pert chin with the slightest of clefts. Lips full and moist, slightly parted showing just a hint of perfect teeth. But it was the eyes, the eyes that snared him. Only once before had he seen such luminescent green, and that was in Paris, an atelier in Paris on a warm summer evening. That was a pretty girl. This was a beautiful woman. Clairborne hesitated. Instinct told him that the large, well-dressed man seated at the table with her was Price, his partner.

Looking up from his coffee, Marcus Price saw her expression change, and his first thought was self-protection. Someone approaching from behind. Stupid, stupid to take a seat with his back to the door. Stupid. But don't overreact, he told himself. Turning slowly in his chair, Price saw a man being helped with his coat, gloves, and hat by the waiter. Expensive clothes cut in the latest eastern fashion. Money. The large silver buckle visible under the man's jacket said "pistol belt." The man was not looking at him. He was staring at Jenny, as nearly all men did, but Price allowed none to stare for more than a moment. This was no cowboy or railroad gandy dancer, so Marcus Price would allow him a few more seconds to appreciate the beauty of his woman before interrupting. Then he realized this was the hotel guest who'd made such a splash.

He looked across the table at the woman and saw something in her face both irritating and unprecedented. Her color was up, her lips slightly parted, her breasts visibly rising beneath the damask bodice. She was interested.

"Excuse me, my dear," Price said, rising to his feet, dabbing his lips with a starched napkin.

Clairborne shook himself from his befuddlement and moved into the room, shifting his eyes to the man turning to meet him, who extended his hand and spoke in a high, thin voice, surprising in a man of such outsized proportions.

The top of Marcus Price's Prussian-cut hair was five feet ten inches from the soles of his feet, clad as they were in woolen stockings and polished shoes. The brown coat over green silk vest over starched white shirt were eastern in style and quality, but the expensive cut and cloth did not entirely disguise the spherical nature of his physique, widest at the waist and tapering above and below. The hand extended to Clairborne was muscular. Clairborne wondered at the source of such strength in a man who clearly spent most of his time under a roof.

"Marcus Price, sir. At your service."

"Tucker Clairborne. A pleasure to make your acquaintance, I'm sure," said Clairborne, instantly regretting that he'd given his real name rather than the one he'd signed into the register on arrival. He blamed the woman for his carelessness.

"Be careful, boy," flashed through his thoughts.

Marcus Price checked that register every morning. He knew something was amiss. This was the man who'd arrived two nights ago, who'd caused a ruckus unusual even by local standards and was now giving a different name. Not all that unusual out here, but worth noting.

"New to Rawlins, sir. Welcome. Would you join us for breakfast?" Price said, sweeping his hand at the table and the woman.

"Most grateful, sir, but I wouldn't think of intruding. Please continue your repast."

"Nonsense. Join us," Price said in a tone with sufficient edge to elicit Clairborne's instant resentment. However, this was not the time. Perhaps he was overreacting, and there were two empty chairs at the table anyway, and she was sitting there looking at him. What the hell.

Price took Clairborne's right elbow in his hand, steering him to the table.

"Allow me to introduce Miss Genevieve LaBelle. Jenny, this is Tucker...I'm sorry, was it Claiborne?" Price asked.

"Clairborne, with an *r.*"

Jenny raised her hand, bringing with it a subtle scent of rosewater, and Clairborne raised it to his lips.

At that moment each of them knew everything had changed, and each reacted in the same way, replacing fascination, petulance, confusion with a solid wall of caution. Each had heard the ice crack under the weight of their respective emotions. Each understood the need to reassess, to think, to consider what next. Suppress feelings. Engage reason. Think.

Each instinctively sought refuge in civility. Polite and idle banter bought time and space.

Clairborne responded to the predictable question about what brought him to Rawlins with an equally predictable and vague answer, something about "just heading west, taking in the country."

Jenny LaBelle concentrated on her tea. Anything to avoid making eye contact with Clairborne, who, sharing the same objective, focused his words and concentration on Marcus Price—who was not in the least deceived.

Breakfast consumed and plates cleared, Clairborne thanked Price for his hospitality and glanced at Jenny.

"You've both been so generous with your time; I shouldn't take any more of it. By your leave, then," he said, rising to his feet. Price also stood.

"Dinner tonight. I insist. Eight of the clock. Here. I really do insist."

In an instant before replying, Clairborne decided the course he would take. He would spend the day learning as much as he could about Rawlins and Marcus Price, his allies, associates, enemies. Where was the nearest judge or magistrate? Did Price own them? Then after dinner, over drinks and cigars, he would show Marcus Price the last will and testament of Guillaume Martin.

"I accept, sir, but only on the grounds that I provide the evening's libations."

"Eight of the clock, then. Good day."

Clairborne faced Jenny LaBelle and bowed from the waist. "A pleasure meeting you, ma'am."

"Likewise," she responded with a smile so subtle that Clairborne flushed, thinking his callow display of attraction amused her.

—⁓—

His Breguet informed him it was 7:15 and that, invisible above the solid clouds, a new moon ignored all things human.

He was ready, almost giddy with anticipation. Marcus Price owned almost everything of value in Rawlins. How much he'd acquired with Wild Bill's money was unknown, as was how to determine that very salient fact.

Clairborne retied his cravat for the third time, centering the knot and adjusting his father's stickpin. Without conscious effort, his eyes took in the left side of his jacket. "Good," he told himself. "No bulge."

And what about Price? No one had heard of Price ever tangling with anyone—physically anyway. That, of course, did not mean he didn't carry somewhere on his person. There was no law in Rawlins except the most compelling law of all: self-interest. Price would have to fend for himself unless scatter-gun-toting Morton also got paid to watch Price's back.

Again, a glance at the Brequet. 7:18. What the hell.

The waiter bowed slightly and led Clairborne to an immaculately set table for two at the back of the dining room, from which it was shielded by a silk screen. Clairborne didn't recognize the pattern of the china but knew it was European—Daulton or Limoges, Sevres perhaps. He slid into the chair pulled out by the waiter, who filled his wine glass. Clairborne raised the goblet to his nose, the bouquet pulling his mouth into another smile. He looked up at the waiter.

"Excellent."

Things were not "excellent" for Marcus Price. Things were, in fact, very bad. He'd learned who Tucker Clairborne was without much trouble. Tucker Clairborne was trouble. Price didn't know exactly what kind of trouble to expect from the Virginian's sudden appearance; he just knew that even if it was solely his manifest interest in Jenny, that would be trouble enough. His primary source of information, his banker in Kansas City, had responded to his telegram within three hours, telling Price that a newspaper that very morning had featured a front-page article about "the cavalier shootist, the man who tamed Abilene." Price stood in front of his dressing mirror, fidgeting with his vest and watch chain. Looking up at his face, Price saw forty-seven years of relentless toil. He saw a man with enough money to keep a beautiful woman, at least for a while. He saw a man who believed until that morning that he had made it, that his train had come in, that he was about to capitalize on his bet that owning land before anyone else appreciated its value would exponentially expand his already appreciable net worth. His confidence had been growing steadily in the months since he'd learned through prairie grapevine and newspaper articles that his erstwhile business partner had conveniently died in a riding accident. Price didn't think Martin had any relatives, and if so, he doubted that Martin had left any legal record of his desires regarding his estate.

His relationship with Martin had been one of convenience. Martin had given him unlimited leeway regarding investments. Price knew that if he crossed Martin, he would die as a result.

Lately, Price had entertained notions of eventual political office before deciding it was better to own politicians than to be one. Price didn't take the word of others on financial matters. He looked for himself at the mountains to the west, understanding intuitively the minerals waiting out there to be found and taken. He knew that while not the best cattle country in America, the grass and water could accommodate vast herds of breeds imported from Europe. He'd participated in conversations with learned men about the benefits of importing these hardy breeds, bovine species more accustomed to harsh Northern European winters than the rangy longhorns of Texas. But what Price knew best of all was the opportunity represented by two-legged animals. Humans. Settlers. Homesteaders. Waves of them washed out of the stagnant city slums back east, bursting with the kind of energy it takes to survive, to prosper west of the Mississippi. And Marcus Price was there ahead of that tide, getting ready to receive it, to sell not only land but the tools to beat that land into submission, everything from axes to plowshares, butter churns to guitar strings, bullets to dress patterns. Yes, sir. He was ready.

And now that son of a bitch shows up.

"Well," Price said as he contemplated his cigar, "let's go find out just what it is that brings Mr. Clairborne to Rawlins." He tapped the ash into an ashtray, straightened his coat, and turned for the door.

—⁊⁄⁄⁊—

Reflecting on the dinner later that night, Clairborne smiled. It had gone very well. The fare was delicious, the spirits first rate, the tone excruciatingly polite. He likened it to national diplomacy on a personal level—two countries wary of each other, trying as discretely as possible to determine the other's goals and ability to attain them. He had enjoyed it immensely, especially its conclusion.

Placing his puro on the crystal ashtray, he'd reached into his breast pocket and withdrawn a certified copy of Wild Bill's last will and testament.

"Marcus, there is something I want to show you, something you need to know about without further delay."

Price received the proffered document between two fingers, holding it as if it were a noxious insect, immediately understanding his life was about to change. Clairborne would have been shocked by just how much information Price had collected in less than one day thanks to his telegraphic connections to his eastern associates. It was the reason he'd been so very careful with his words during dinner. The man sitting across from him was a mortal threat. Not in the rattlesnake way, but even more dangerous because he could strike without warning.

Price unfolded the document and silently read every word. Adrenaline burst into his stomach and throat, boosting his heartbeat and respiration, cascading beads of sweat over the folds of fat beneath his armpits.

His first thought was a blasphemous curse of his former business partner. He actually envisioned Billy Martin roasting in hell. He looked up from the will but said nothing for a long moment while he tried to control his words, his voice.

"Well, so we are to be partners. No, we are partners, then. My, how quickly things change. What are your thoughts?"

Clairborne smiled. "Golly, I haven't really got any. Not really. I just wanted to let you know about this, then get a handle on what it means, you know. What is involved. Where Bill's shares are. What my obligations are."

Long ago, Price had learned that the best approach to almost everything, be it a fight or a business deal, was to be underestimated by one's opposite number.

"I'm no businessman, for sure, so I just thought we could, you could kind of teach me what I need to know. How's that sound?" Clairborne said, leaning back in his chair.

"Like a load of hot horseshit," Price thought. "I know what you're up to, you miserable whelp. You think I'm that dumb, do you? We'll see about that."

Price smiled. The anger surging through him replaced the fear and uncertainty spawned by the damned document, anger that boiled away extraneous notions and left only a clear broth of essential concerns. He would deal with Tucker Clairborne the same way he'd dealt with every other obstacle. He'd take his time. He'd learn the man's strengths and weaknesses. Then he would strike. There was no option. Too much was at stake—so much, in fact, that mere seconds of thinking about it sent another surge of fear through his corpulent mass, causing him to shiver.

"Why, Tucker, I think that is a capital idea. We put our heads together, take a look at the possibilities and, damn, we'll make our famous fortunes. For sure. Let's drink to fortunes made and shared." He waved his arm expansively. "Hell, there's enough out here to make a thousand men rich as Croesus."

Their snifters clinked. They shook hands. They finished their smokes and talked of nothing of consequence. There was no need to do so. Each understood the other. Each was amused at his dawning respect for the man sitting across the table. This was going to be a challenge. Someone was going to get run out of town. At a minimum. Probably, someone was going to die. Damn, but this was exhilarating.

—◆◆◆—

Jenny LaBelle sat in front of her mirror motionless and so lost in thought that she looked through her own reflection. Dread weighed on her like a cloak of stone. Something bad was going to happen just as things were going so well. Since her unspoken agreement with Price a few months earlier, she no longer had to consort with bar patrons other than to make brief, infrequent appearances to "class up the joint," as Marcus had laughingly told her.

She pondered the situation, reviewing it from the moment she'd met Marcus Price, from the moment she realized he might provide a refuge of sorts, a physical sanctuary from a lover—Frankie Monaghan—who'd turned obsessive and whom she'd grown to fear as she'd never feared anyone. She'd left other men. Some had left her. She fled Frankie Monaghan in a mortal panic.

When she met Marcus Price, he raised her gloved hand to his lips while his eyes took in her form, her hair, the way nearly every man did, but she'd appreciated that Price had been more discreet.

He was finely dressed, so much so that his attire almost masked his girth. When he moved, it seemed he launched his stomach in the direction he wanted to go and the rest of his body followed, reminding her of a full milk bucket being carried from the barn to the house, contents sloshing even when the bucket was held steady.

And then he'd offered her work as a "hostess," only to tell her the first night on the job that she was not to "entertain" any customers, that her mere presence would draw men into the Bon Ton, where they would imbibe his beer and whiskey along with the "free" lunches.

He was right. Word spread instantly around Rawlins that "a prairie rose" had blossomed in the Bon Ton. The nightly take went up within twenty-four hours, and on the third evening, she sat at the out-of-tune piano, slender fingers dancing over the keys, her lilting voice silencing the routine cacophony, and men twisted in their chairs and stood to hear "I'll Remember You, Love, in My Prayers." All over the room, miners, cowboys, railroad workers, laborers, even hardened card dealers, dabbed their eyes at the familiar opening lines.

And when she trilled,

As if on the wings of a beautiful dove,
In haste with the message it bears
To tell you I miss you and give you my love
And remember you, love, in my prayers...

more than one weather-beaten hardcase openly sobbed. Price knew he'd struck gold, that men would ride through blizzards to hear Jenny LaBelle sing and, if they were fortunate enough, to actually inhale her fragrance as she glided past, bestowing smiles and greetings to men bereft of female company.

Within a week, she had her own tastefully furnished room. Within a month, Price sent Frieda to her. Then he began regular distribution of her "pin money." A month after that, he'd collected what she reckoned was the cost of her comfort.

She shrugged. It wasn't so bad, all things considered. A glance at her account book underscored the feeling.

But this fellow Clairborne troubled her. No. That wasn't true. He'd done nothing to "trouble" her except show up in Rawlins. Her reaction to him troubled her. She shook her head and pushed away the tumbler of whiskey. "Think," she told herself.

A man that good looking, that dapper, that wealthy simply had to be trouble, had to be accustomed to women falling all over him. Expect that they would. Expect that she would. She shook her head so hard her curls whipped around her face.

"Damned if I will. I'll be damned if I will," she snapped at her reflection.

<hr />

Clairborne retrieved his Colt from his jacket pocket and put in on the nightstand. He took off his vest, laid his Breguet on the sideboard, loosened his cravat, and poured himself a finger of whiskey. When he raised the glass to his nose, the scent of its contents shifted his thoughts to Price. He had to give the man credit. When he'd stepped off the train less than seventy-two hours ago, the last thing he expected to find buried under the snow and monochromatic scenery was cut crystal, oriental carpets, decent food, and almost decent whiskey. All thanks to the ambitions and tastes of Marcus Price. He sat down in the rocking chair in front of the wood stove, which nearly glowed. A sense of accomplishment, satisfaction, perhaps even pride caused him to exhale slowly. He sipped and smiled. He raised his glass and said aloud, "Don't know how this will pan out, but it's starting just fine."

He wondered what the definition of "making oneself" really was. Money? Possessions? Fame? A family?

He yawned and stretched.

"I'll think about it later," he said, standing and sliding his braces off his shoulders.

—⁓⁓⁓—

Price contemplated the decanter on the sideboard and then looked at his watch instead of reaching for the whiskey.

"Too late. Too much to do tomorrow."

A sudden, slow wave of sadness washed over him. It would never be the same. He was certain things would never be as good as they'd been twenty-four hours ago, much less as good as he'd been certain they would be next year and the years to come. He'd even begun to entertain hopes that Jenny might stay with him for a while, a long while. It could happen.

He sat down heavily in the maroon leather wing chair that had arrived from Saint Louis a week earlier. He'd ordered it two months earlier in celebration of another hunch paying off. The man in charge of the Union Pacific work had mentioned in passing that his crews were encountering vast amounts of coal right on the surface as they dug the grades west of town. "Good coal," the engineer had said. "Pretty sure it's anthracite. Never heard of it being so close to the surface."

Price poured the man another drink and asked one question. "You report this to Chicago?"

"Hell no," the engineer said. "I got a damn railroad to build."

Price acted immediately, securing samples and sending them east for analysis. It was anthracite. Very good anthracite. Price took steps to secure mining rights for hundreds of square miles, a move that elicited only head shaking from others who saw the action as foolhardy.

Price ran the numbers in his head, the money to be made from this combination of pure luck and predatory intelligence. He sighed. Complications. His vision blurred. Suddenly he couldn't focus on money. Instead, he realized that he didn't feel hatred for the interloper, the agent of change who'd arrived along with the worst blizzard of the season.

"Maybe I will have a drink," he thought. He rose from his chair, incipient rheumatism tugging at the base of his spine, and moved slowly, almost hesitantly, to the decanter, raising his right hand for the tumbler beside it, the left hand beginning to move toward to crystal container of Kentucky whiskey.

He froze. He was going to vomit. "What the hell?"

The porcelain washbasin rested on the marble-topped dresser across the room. Too far. He was irritated. Now he would have to call someone to clean his puke from the carpet.

Sweat rolled off the slope of his forehead and burned his left eye. Price began to raise his left hand to rub away the pain in his eye, but another pain, this one excruciating and unprecedented, erupted from his armpit halfway down his arm and, an instant later, exploded in the opposite direction up to his jaw.

His knees buckled. He looked for something to break his fall. Nothing within reach. Marcus Price did not understand what was happening to him as his face hit the floor at the edge of the braided rug. The pain in his chest. A short croak. A longer moan.

"Please don't hurt her," he whispered.

—⁘—

Jenny LaBelle sat at the window of her room looking at the frenzied activity below. A watery sunlight failed to draw any appreciable color from the natural environment, the humans, or their structures. Tents and buildings alike billowed thick ropes of gray smoke from stoves kept hot to fend off the still-frigid air normal for early March. The piles of snow mantling the town for the last four months were now mounds of gray, mud-spattered ice and slush. The streets were so muddy that men routinely had their boots sucked off when crossing. One thing was different. The smoke had the tang of coal instead of the sweeter aroma of wood. Rawlins residents were taking advantage of the more abundant fuel that was also easier to recover and use than wood.

Frieda entered with morning tea, which she poured and sugared, and then set about laying out Jenny's clothes. They talked very little. Their friendship had begun to build, nurtured by the security each had felt in the world they'd been constructing with Marcus Price. Since his death and subsequent replacement by the young Virginian, the bond had been replaced by a reserve. Jenny and Frieda were unsure of many things but certain of only one. Things would change.

Three months ago—eighty-nine days, to be precise—they'd buried Marcus in the new cemetery. It seemed more like three centuries. The arrival of spring with its violent, capricious weather, the resumption of construction on the railroad—each contributed to Jenny's disquiet, her inability to relax. She spent every waking hour planning for contingencies, discreetly moving her money to caches both corporate and improvised. Clairborne confused her by not asking questions about Price's dealings, and she wasn't sure whether it was because he assumed that being a woman, she knew nothing about them or, even more irritating, that anything she knew would be either inaccurate or irrelevant or both. But she knew a lot, almost everything about income and expenses, who owed what to whom, what deals were done and what deals were done but not yet legally recorded. It hadn't been hard for her to accumulate such knowledge. Price talked casually about such things over their meals and in more intimate settings. All men did that. She'd also watched him make entries in his accounting books and overheard conversations with associates, employees, and sources. It was enough. She knew a lot. None of which she'd mentioned to Clairborne.

She realized that her tea had gone cold while, yet again, her thoughts meandered over the landscape of concerns. She also realized that she had, again, suppressed the biggest concern of all: her attraction to Tucker Clairborne and her certainty that he was just as strongly attracted to her.

Ever since the discovery of Price's remains, Clairborne had treated her with excruciating politeness, his manners so impeccably correct as to be maddening. He'd quickly assured her that he had no intention of changing the status quo regarding her domicile or domestic situation. He declined to call her by her first name but gently insisted she address him by his. He also studiously avoided eye contact.

Since that first night, there had been no further evidence that he had a violent nature, perhaps because his reputation precluded it. But she'd decided that it was more likely the change stemmed from the other side of his character. He was unfailingly courteous, solicitous of others, generous to a fault, and, as a result, very well thought of around Rawlins. It didn't hurt that he was also the wealthiest man in the territory.

—◦◦◦—

Just how wealthy he was, Tucker Clairborne had yet to determine in the three months since Marcus Price so conveniently simplified things. Information, formal and otherwise, came in almost daily. The most important came from the territorial court reaffirming the legitimacy of Wild Bill's last will and testament and informing him that despite the fact that Price had died intestate, probate should be settled within another few months.

He had communicated none of this to his mother.

A month ago, he sent her a birthday greeting notably lacking in details of his situation. Clairborne tried to convince himself that he'd chosen discretion because nothing regarding his finances was absolutely certain and that it would be better to wait until it was.

He knew better. In truth, he didn't write about the details of his situation because he didn't know what to tell his mother about Jenny LaBelle. And he didn't know what to tell his mother because he didn't know what to tell himself. There were only two indisputable facts: He was in love with her. She was a whore. The two facts were irreconcilable, and thus, he told himself, so were he and Jenny.

Unable to get her out of his mind, Clairborne stood up from the rolltop desk in Price's office and raised his arms over his head. An unusually large pile of the day's mail offered distraction, so he began absent-mindedly sorting though it. A thick envelope addressed to Genevieve LaBelle caught his attention. He held it in both hands. He looked at the regulator wall clock just as the minute hand clicked past 6:17. Shifting his gaze to the window, he realized it was dark. Pale yellow lantern light leaked out of the windows across the street, briefly silhouetting passersby. Without thought, Clairborne retrieved his coat and hat from the rack beside the office door, donned them, walked out of the warm office, turned right onto the board sidewalk, greeted two railroad men loading a wagon, and entered the Bon Ton Saloon. Nodding to the bartenders and Morton the shotgunner, he moved to the staircase at the back of the room and climbed the steps two and a time.

A thin ribbon of light from under her door told him she was there. He raised his right hand to knock, removing his hat with his left, which also held the envelope. He hesitated, suddenly realizing the abrupt, impromptu nature of the acts that had brought him to her door from the safe, comfortable confines of the office. He realized that he was holding his breath and exhaled as he tapped on the oaken doorjamb.

Immediately, he wished he hadn't.

"Maybe she's not inside. Maybe I should bolt," he thought, only to extinguish such a foolish thought on consideration of the image of her opening the door to see him fleeing down the staircase.

Jenny Labelle opened the door, oil lamps casting her form in a soft radiance, her scent of lavender tipping successive dominos of sensibility and caution. He was lost, and he knew it. An adrenaline blaze ignited his innards and took his breath away. He stammered and raised his left hand.

"I, um, I brought you this. Thought you might be expecting it."

She looked down to see his hat and looked up with a puzzled expression.

He looked down and understood her confusion.

"Oh, not the hat. This," he said, taking the envelope from under his hat with his right hand.

"Yes, I was expecting it. A catalogue from back east. How considerate of you to deliver it."

She didn't want to seem forward, but what else could she do? she asked herself, her mind racing to find a socially acceptable alternative to the only thing she could think to do. Jade green eyes unblinking, she looked at Clairborne. "Won't you come in?"

Clairborne was seized by panic. Traversing her threshold amounted to a personal Rubicon.

She held his gaze. His mind went blank.

"I'd be honored," his voice a low croak.

She stepped back and aside.

"So would I."

———∽∾∽———

She'd known men who were enthusiastic. She'd known men who were young and innocent. She'd known some who were mean and some who were just plain ignorant. Lying beside Tucker Clairborne, suspended in a dream state made of equal parts fatigue and disbelief, she realized that she had, for the first time in her life, experienced pure pleasure. She moved her head just enough to see his face but not enough to wake him. His hair was down over his forehead, his lips parted, his breathing slow and deep.

What single thing about him made being with him for the last four hours so different, so new?

The answer came in a flash once she focused her mind on its pursuit.

Consideration.

He asked if he could kiss her. He asked for permission to remove the ribbon from her hair. He asked if she would like him to brush it out. At each step down the irreversible path, he'd explicitly or implicitly sought her agreement to proceed. When he knelt to untie her shoes as she sat on the edge of her bed, the gentleness with which he unlaced and removed them, setting them upright on the carpet, brought tears to her eyes.

Now, floating on a millstream of comfort and hope and affection, Jenny LaBelle resigned herself to a new experience. She would face each day in love for the first time in her life and know it was, it must be, impossibly finite. How could it be anything else? How could happiness prevail against such odds? She was what she was. He was from a society so different, everything he'd done and said in the last few hours underscored that they might as well have hailed from different planets. The memory of men she'd known momentarily saddened her. She wished she were something other than what she was and thought about how that could have been. She came up with no answers.

She turned her head to stare blankly at the ceiling, just enough for Clairborne to see her in profile when he surfaced from the depths of what must have been delirium.

Somewhere outside, a horse nickered in the darkness. Inside the room, there was enough ambient light for Clairborne to make out her eyelashes, her pert nose, and her full lips. Her eyes were open.

"I would love to know what you're thinking," he said, but before she could answer, he chuckled and added, "or maybe I wouldn't."

Propping herself up on her right arm, she touched his cheek with her left hand, using the tips of her nails to trace the contours of his mouth.

"I'm thinking about what to say to you. There are things I want to say to you, but because I've never said them before, I don't know if I should, if it would be right. Or wise."

Clairborne smiled. "Me too. Jenny, I just had some of the most marvelous dreams, dreams that come on the heels of...well, I don't know, marvelous moments. That sounds so inadequate." He shook his head. "I sound like an idiot."

"No, you don't."

"Yes, I do. All right. I'll just say it, Jenny." Clairborne sat up and pulled the blankets around her shoulders, another act of spontaneous consideration.

"This is a different world out here. You and I are both here for the same reason: to start a new life. We left everything behind, and we're looking for, for..."

"Happiness?" she said.

Clairborne hesitated. "For sure, but I don't know, maybe something else. Happiness, yes, but an old dog lying in the sun is happy. I don't know. I just feel there is something I have to do with my life."

He looked at her.

"I started caring for you the first time I saw you, Jenny. I know that you are used to that. But I really didn't want to get tangled up, to become obligated, because I don't think I will be staying all that long in Rawlins."

He lifted her chin.

"Now I can't imagine being away from you, and I don't know what that means."

She smiled.

"It may mean you care for me as much as I care for you, Tucker."

His stomach growled deeply, and he flushed with embarrassment. "I'm sorry. How humiliating."

"I know what you need," she said. "Coffee, steak, potatoes, eggs, biscuits, and more coffee." As she rose from the other side of the bed, Jenny gathered the top blanket and wrapped it around her body. Clairborne turned away in respect for her modesty, but the momentary vision of her form flamed in his mind.

He lay back on the goose-down pillows and closed his eyes.

He started with surprise when he realized he'd gone back to sleep. Jenny opened the door carrying an outsized tray; the aromas wafting from it triggered another growl from his guts and a smile.

Watching her set the tray on the bed and lift the covers from the serving plates, Tucker Clairborne understood that he had entered a realm bereft of trails or roads, a realm lacking even charts to map the way ahead.

Never in his twenty-one years had he felt this good.

———

WESTERN UNION

TO: JOSEPH MCCOY ABILENE KS.   MARCH 2, 1869

FROM: TUCKER CLAIRBORNE RAWLINS WYO 11:03 AM

SUBJECT: REQUEST

AM IN DIRE NEED OF CAPABLE, TRUSTWORTHY ACCOUNTANT STOP MUST BE ABLE TO MANAGE DIVERSE AFFAIRS WITH LITTLE SUPERVISION STOP WILL PAY IN ACCORDANCE WITH QUALITY OF SERVICE AND INTEGRITY STOP LETTER TO FOLLOW STOP

TUCKER

———

WESTERN UNION

TO: TUCKER LIGHTFOOT CLAIRBORNE

RAWLINS WYO   MARCH 3, 1869

FROM: JOSEPH MCCOY ABILENE KS   0817 AM

SUBJECT: RECOMMENDATION

HAVE CANDIDATE IN MIND STOP PERSONAL RELATION STOP DETAILS IN SPECIAL DELIVERY LETTER POSTED TODAY STOP

JOSEPH MCCOY

—✐—

Rawlins, Wyoming Territory
March 5, 1869

Dear Joe,

How very much I look forward to learning more about your nominee. I find myself in the ludicrous position of not knowing either the extent or the nature of holdings that have come into my possession through little or no effort on my part.

With your excellent sources of information, you may have already learned the relevant details of my situation, so in recognition of that likelihood, I will be brief. Except for the terrain and the climate, Rawlins is in many ways similar to Abilene. It is raw and wooly and replete with potential. In addition to the obvious benefits accruing to the advent of Union Pacific service, there is ample evidence of significant coal deposits, which I have been told are unusually easy to extract. I have also been told that the coal is called anthracite, the type preferred by the steel industry. The immediate question is one of profits after investment in the infrastructure to recover it. Would those costs be low enough to successfully compete with mines much closer to the eastern steel mills, or is there another potential market in which our coal would have an inherent cost advantage?

Forgive me, for I'm getting ahead of myself. Coal is a theoretical subject at this point, but now on to a practical one. As you know, Billy Martin bequeathed me his estate, most of which consists of holdings and interests here in Wyoming Territory. His partner, Marcus Price of Ohio, had parlayed his and Billy's money into investments quite similar in scope and nature, if not total value, to those accrued to you by dint of your acumen and initiative. Within a week of my arrival, Mr. Price suddenly passed from this world from apoplexy while alone in his quarters. As a result of his dying intestate, the courts in Omaha have determined I am his sole beneficiary. That means I own nearly everything around here.

You once said, "A man should know his limitations," and that is why I sent the request for your recommendation on someone to manage things for me. An accountant would be sufficient for the time being, but Joe, to be completely honest, I would benefit most from the services of someone whose knowledge transcends mere bookkeeping and extends into estate management or perhaps even law.

I confess that even the prospect of wealth and comfort is insufficient to overcome my desire to see more of this great country. The idea of wasting my time behind a desk is, frankly, mortifying to me.

I must also tell you that I am giving serious consideration to matrimony. Please treat that news with discretion, as I have yet to formally take that step. Should I do so, we shall explore the possibilities of residence west of here, in, say, San Francisco or possibly even the Oregon Territory. Why not?

So I finish by saying my trust in your judgment and integrity is such that I am inclined to hire anyone you should recommend and in so doing acknowledge yet another debt I owe you. I look forward to repaying those obligations.

I remain, sir, your most obedient servant,
Tucker L. Clairborne

———

Abilene, KS.
March 27, 1869

Dear Tucker,
Rarely have I been so singularly delighted as I was on reading your letter. Such wonderful news! My most sincere congratulations on your estates fiscal and domestic.

You do me great honor with your request for such an important post as that which you have

defined. I shall be straightforward with my rec-
ommendation. The man I believe would best fit
your bill is my brother-in-law. He is a successful
attorney in Chicago, where he has done quite well
with his very substantial clientele. His situation
has taken a tragic turn of late in that his wife, my
younger sister, and their children, my nephew and
two darling nieces, were taken from him in a fire
that destroyed not only his family but also their
abode. This occurred nearly six months ago, and he
remains so stricken with grief that he seems to have
lost interest in life itself.

On receipt of your wire, I contacted him imme-
diately and have been most pleasantly surprised by
his interest in offering you his services. It would be
the proverbial "clean break," would it not? You need
know little of Chicago to know how rare it is for a
man to be both financially successful and widely
respected for integrity. Algernon (Haas) is both. He
is a college man matriculating from Yale University.
He was born in Bavaria but came to this country
with his parents when he was an infant. He met
my sister through the machinations of our mother
and the approval of our father, who also engaged
Algernon as his counselor.

If you agree, I will have Algernon (I address
him as Al) contact you forthwith in hopes you find
him as agreeable and capable as do I.

Again, Tucker, you have honored me with your request, for which I thank you most sincerely.

With greatest respect,
Joseph R. McCoy, Esq.

———

The razor slid under his chin and down to his Adam's apple without so much as a nick. His skin was soft and pink from the steaming Turkish towel Jenny had wrapped around his face, the first evidence of her skill in the tonsorial arts. She took his silver-handled shaving brush and lathered his face with the sandalwood shaving soap that had come from Chicago in the morning mail. At breakfast, he'd complained about the absence of a barber in Rawlins. Jenny had smiled and said, "I'll take care of that."

Now, his chair tilted back against the washstand in his room, he was enjoying the best shave he could remember. And Jenny was giving it to him. He congratulated himself on not voicing the slightest trepidation when she picked up his straight razor. She clearly knew what she was doing, stropping the Sheffield blade with a smooth, rhythmic motion that conveyed expertise surprising in a woman.

Where had she come by this skill, yet another in a growing list of unlikely talents and unexpected knowledge he'd noted since stepping over her threshold? He quickly decided he didn't want to know.

She shushed him when he began to speak.

"Just relax," she said. "Don't move your lips unless you want them shaved too...and don't smile. You're impossible," she said, standing back from him when a grin creased his features.

She wore an apron over her green taffeta dress, the sleeves of which were rolled up to protect them from the soap and water spots.

He closed his eyes, and she moved to his side and resumed the slow, methodical stroking of his facial contours. Hints of her rosewater commingled with notes of sandalwood. Clairborne sighed and rested his woven fingers on the towel covering his lap.

"If there's a heaven..." he thought. He absorbed her essence through his barely opened eyes. She toweled the remaining soap from his face and then reached for the bottle of bay rum. She dabbed a few drops in her palm and rubbed them together, then patted the bracing liquid on his cheeks, her fingers running lightly but firmly over his lips, under his jaw, and down the front of his throat, slipping under the open collar of his shirt and then rising to his temples where, splayed then closed, they carried him to the soft edge of slumber. She kissed the top of his head.

"Rest on the bed, dear. I'll fetch something to eat."

Clairborne rose from the chair, moved to the bed, sat down, removed his shoes, and ran his hands over his face. Lying back on the pillows, he closed his eyes and let the bay rum scent flood his nose. Euphoria seeped into his awareness, trickling slowly but noticeably enough for him to recall just how many whiskeys he'd consumed. One; only one, and he had sipped it during the hour it took for Jennie to complete her ministrations. So what he was feeling was not alcohol induced, nor even alcohol influenced.

"If there's a heaven..." he thought.

———

Rawlins, Wyoming Territory
June 1, 1869

> *My Dear Mother,*
>
> *I fear that on reading this long-delayed letter, you may well believe that I am playing the fool, but I assure you that is not so. I am happy, indeed delighted, to report to you that your son has never found himself in better circumstance, at least not since I left Warwick and your loving embrace.*
>
> *Not only am I physically well, but I am also enjoying that unique and most desirable state of deep affection and commitment to a woman who has won my heart. Her name is Genevieve LaBelle of Boissier Parish, Louisiana. While her family is not landed, they are successful merchants of long standing in those parts. I have not met them since Genevieve (I call her Jenny) has come out here in pursuit of her dreams to bring culture to this raw, unlettered land, to teach music and, eventually, to start a school of music and fine art.*
>
> *I know that you must instantly be less than enamored by the prospect of a single female*

traveling alone and being surrounded as she is by so many unattached men, most of whom are little better than ruffians. You would be amazed at the respect she is given by those selfsame ruffians as well as the few gentlemen hereabout. That is not just because of her astonishing beauty, which quite dumbfounds men on first beholding her. No, it is for the most part due to two separate factors. On the frontier, men are even more conscious of chivalric standards than is the case in the East. I believe that's because women are so rare as to be venerated and protected more here than elsewhere.

Also, Jenny has been so kind and unselfish with her time, teaching piano and voice to the few children, organizing holiday festivities, caring for the ill and dying—we have as yet no physician—that in this roughhewn locale, she commands the affection and respect of a Florence Nightingale.

We are not betrothed. I have not broached the subject with her. Yet. The distance separating her family and you from us precludes formal introductions and solicitation of permission to proceed with matrimony. Yes, Mother, I am that serious. And while that distance might indeed mitigate against physical introduction, it should not prevent our receiving the requisite blessings from our respective families over time to come.

It just occurred to me that an itinerant photographer is to come to Rawlins within a fortnight from Omaha, and I shall have him photograph both of us so that you may see my health and my love.

You should also know that just as was the case with you, Father, and Warwick, Jenny provides a daily dose of wisdom on how best to manage the affairs that have fallen to me by pure fortune. I speak of the happenstance of my finding Guillaume Martin in that glade in Missouri where he had taken his mortal tumble from his horse. As I relayed to you, M. Martin decided that the paltry succor that I provided in his last hours warranted his naming me heir to his estate and all his earthly possessions, him having no living relatives.

On arrival here, I found his estate to include half of the businesses and real properties here in this boomtown of Rawlins. And then, Mother, in an equally unlikely turn of events, M. Guillaume's business partner, Mr. Marcus Price of Ohio, expired of natural causes within a week of my arrival and the very night of our first discussion of how best to advance our new partnership.

That was in November. For the succeeding months, I have been struggling to understand and administer my holdings. I have yet to fully identify them and it is in the latter that Jenny suggested an idea I am pursuing. She counseled me to retain the services of an accountant or attorney to act as steward of my interests. I am doing so through the good offices of Mr. Joseph McCoy of Abilene and

Chicago, who knows more about opportunity and how best to exploit it than anyone I know.

All this is to say I am furiously busy and deliriously happy and totally lacking in comprehension of just how and why all this has come to pass.

You will be happy to know that two of my dearest friends have rejoined me here in Rawlins. Bucephalus and Ajax arrived on the train two days ago from Texas. As you could guess, Bucephalus is alarmingly rank, not being ridden for these last six months. Ajax is still as sweet natured as always.

Before I forget, I have formally petitioned the Episcopal diocese in Kansas City to designate Rawlins as a new parish and to send us a priest. I understand my request is being favorably considered. I must also tell you that Jenny suggested the need for a church building, which I have undertaken to construct on a beautiful site with a Christian cemetery adjacent to it.

In closing, I pledge to write to you every week from now on. I do so in full understanding of how monstrous has been my failure to correspond and thus to alleviate your natural concern.

Please give my love to Amy and fill me in on all things Warwick and Virginia.

I close with Affirmation of my Love and Affection,
Your Son,
Tucker Lightfoot Clairborne

—*m*—

Six months into the year, things had progressed to the degree that Clairborne rode a crest of success, waves, a veritable tide of successes. Although Algernon Haas had been in Rawlins only seventeen days, he'd already revised the ledgers, filed documents in federal court in Omaha, set up new accounts with banks in Omaha and Chicago, and met with each man and the one woman responsible for Clairborne's holdings—the bars, the liveries, the stores, and the bordello—to institute standard bookkeeping practices. His daily reports to Clairborne were clinical and succinct. His recommendations fell in line with everything else Haas did as well. He always began with a brief summation of the issue, a definition of why he proposed a change, what was to be gained at what risk of loss, and then closed with a rank order of proposals.

Clairborne couldn't have been happier with either Haas or his work, the results of which brought order out of confusion along with a significant increase in a phrase Clairborne learned from Haas: net worth.

Newcomers arrived on every train. They also came in wagons and astride horses, mules, and even oxen. Some showed up on foot. The nature of the newcomers was changing as well, just as it had in Abilene. The raw-edged, overwhelmingly male population of gamblers, gandy dancers, grifters, drifters, and owl hoots was leavened by a broader diversity of denizens. Now entire families were arriving, many of them deciding to make a go of it in Rawlins or thereabouts. For Jenny, it meant securing an organ for the newly completed church and organizing volunteers to build a stone wall and erect a wrought-iron gate for the adjacent cemetery. Her energies also produced a one-room schoolhouse, a carton of McGuffey Readers, a blackboard, chalk, and a reproduction of Gilbert Stuart's unfinished portrait of George Washington, all paid for anonymously by Clairborne.

She'd begun her classes in an army tent erected next to the schoolhouse construction site. She then demanded that the tent be moved farther away to protect the children's ears from carpenters' and framers' incessant profanities. Jenny focused her time on teaching, working even during evening hours to grade tests and papers.

No census was taken in Rawlins. Things changed too much day to day to make such an effort worthwhile, but it was generally thought the town was home to nearly thirty school-age children, only seventeen of whom attended class regularly. Clairborne would have been interested in the advent of formal education along the rough edge of the frontier even without his relationship to Jenny. Probably even without the urging of the young Austrian cavalry officer, Gunther Rall, whose toast called on Clairborne to be a missionary of culture and refinement. So it was not unusual for him to become aware of the reason not all of the town's youngsters went to school.

For a few, it was a labor issue. Their hands and strong backs were needed in their families' endeavors to put food on the table and keep a roof over their heads. But for others, there was a more unsettling issue: Jenny LaBelle's matrimonial state, or more to the point, the lack thereof.

Clairborne learned via the rumor mill that a number of Rawlins families refused to expose their children to the ministrations of a kept woman. Sitting alone in his office one warm afternoon, shortly after first hearing that news, he decided he agreed with them. He wouldn't send his offspring to a school run by a kept woman either.

What to do?

Glancing around the office with new oak rolltop desks, file cabinets, a braided rug, glass windows, and a now-cold stove, Clairborne pondered his situation. The thought of Jenny LaBelle added to his elation, an emotion becoming so constant it dragged in its wake a cautionary note: "This too shall pass."

But not just now. Just now, life was as sweet as sorghum syrup and as rich as melted butter.

"I'm going to marry her," he said aloud.

His mind's eye was instantly occupied by his mother, standing expressionless, hands clasped in front of her black-clad form.

"What will I tell her? What can I tell her?" He'd already asked himself those questions a thousand times since acknowledging the depth and immutability of his affection for Jenny. But it was simply impossible to ever inform his mother of Jenny's past. His mother was the strongest woman he knew, but such a revelation might well kill her. It wasn't enough that he'd abandoned his home and family and attendant responsibilities, and now he proposed to give the family name to a woman of ill repute?

From his mother's perspective, simply impossible. He couldn't blame her.

The chaos of his desires, possibilities, problems, and potential consequences fell naturally into the ordered structure he'd absorbed from participating in his accountant's processes.

The proposal was, therefore, simple. Marry Jenny, lie to his mother. Keep them apart. Forever. Never again see his mother? Ever? He sighed. Details of Warwick's architecture, its terrain, places where he used to hide from his older brother, Christmas, the coolness of his bed linen sequentially materialized, rotating out of memory and passing into oblivion.

Ever since he rode away, he'd told himself he would return, self-confidence restored, pockets full. Reflections on his return had cushioned the privations and the shocks he encountered more than he'd realized until this moment.

"Oh, Mother. Oh, Jenny," he sighed. He stood up and wiped his eyes, realizing the routinely frenetic pace of visitors was bound to bring someone unannounced through the door at any second. In the moments before that happened, he told himself aloud, "I'll ask her tonight."

The flutter in his stomach and the shortness of breath went on so long that Clairborne finally took notice. He wondered if he'd consumed too much coffee on an empty stomach but not only couldn't recall how many cups he'd downed, he also couldn't remember if he'd eaten anything at all.

Walking down the street to the hotel from Price's office, he passed several people he knew, some by name, others by face, but his mind was in such an unsettled state that he passed others without acknowledging their greetings, which struck them as strange, since the Virginian was unfailingly polite. It was also puzzling because he had such a large smile on his face.

He bounded up the steps and across the boardwalk, bursting into the office Haas occupied. Frieda was there as well. He hung his hat on the coat rack, paused, and turned back to his manager. Haas was smiling. It was the first time Clairborne had seen him smile. They exchanged greetings. Frieda blushed and lowered her eyes. Haas also looked away sheepishly. Clairborne's elation ratcheted up several notches more.

"This is too good," he thought. "Something is going on between those two. Lord, Lord, I hope so, anyways."

Frieda hurriedly took her leave. Clairborne sat on the edge of Haas's desk, pulled his cigar holder from his breast pocket, offered one to Haas, cut it, lit it, and as the thick curls of aromatic smoke floated upward, he said, "I have something very important and very confidential to tell you, Algernon."

Haas nodded.

"Tonight I am going to propose to Jenny. I've already booked two tickets on the midnight eastbound. Here is what I want you to do. I have no idea how long we'll be away." Clairborne laughed. "Hell, I don't even know for sure where we'll go. Get married in Omaha or Ogalala, whichever one has the first preacher we can find. Then, who knows?"

Haas beamed and nodded.

"I want you to take care of everything, everything for me. I'll wire you every time we're somewhere you can wire back, but you don't need to send weekly reports or updates. Do you need me to sign anything to give you a free hand?"

Haas stood and reached for Clairborne's hand.

"I'm so happy for you. Congratulations and best wishes. And no, there is no need for further documentation of my responsibilities."

Clairborne's eyes flooded.

"I trust you, Algernon. I couldn't take this step in this way without your minding affairs here. Thank you."

"Everything will be fine, Mr. Clairborne. Don't worry about anything. You just treat Jenny to the time of her life."

"I intend to do just that," Clairborne said. "Oh," he exclaimed, slapping his forehead. "She doesn't know anything about this. I'm going to ask her at dinner. That'll give her time to pack. At least I think it will. Who cares? I'll just buy her a new wardrobe wherever we wind up."

Clairborne paused at the door and turned back to face Haas.

"Algernon, your being here makes this possible, makes it OK to bolt, to just leave, and I appreciate that more than I can say."

Haas rose from his chair.

"Mr. Clairborne, your trust in me, coming here, it has changed my...well, I wish you joy, Mr. Clairborne. I give you joy."

Clairborne put his hat high on his brow and turned for the door, stopping just before he exited.

"Lord, I almost forgot. I'm going to need to money. I ah, I'm embarrassed to ask, but how much do we have on hand?"

Cash—bank notes or coin—was scarce as hen's teeth on the frontier. Before Haas arrived, Clairborne had taken minimal amounts from his cash flow and made a concerted effort to track revenue and expenses in the leather-bound ledgers inherited from Price. He'd hated every minute of it. After Haas came to town, Clairborne paid even less attention, relieved of the need to mess with numbers, his major expenses, meals, lodging, and horse care absorbed by the enterprises he now owned.

He couldn't recall Haas's last weekly report, which always accounted for cash on hand to the penny.

"How much would you like, all of it? Why not? In two days rents are due," Haas said as he withdrew the cash box and flipped open its heavy lid.

"Oh gosh. How about, say, two hundred dollars?" Clairborne said, his voice and his mannerisms conveying his expectation that Haas would chide him for extravagance.

"Why not seven hundred? Two hundred in gold and the rest in bank notes. Easier to carry."

Clairborne laughed as he took the gray canvas bank bag. Things were just getting better and better.

Yesterday, Rawlins was stifling, far too early for such heat. Before dawn, a cold front roared down over the escarpment, bringing hail and hard rain before rolling on east over the plains. Clairborne stood on the boardwalk in front of his office, looking east to the lush green horizon, then west to the distant mountains mantled with a layer of late snow. Across the sea of mud and to his right, four men guffawed and slapped each other on the back. A woman—was it Mrs. Childress?—snatched a boy by his ear and dragged him off, reading him the riot act on the way home.

Clairborne loved them all, each and every one. He pivoted on his boot heel and headed off at a brisk pace, almost a trot, to find the one he loved most of all. "No, no, don't get ahead of yourself, Tucker. So get that done, then go get her...."

———

She knew it was Tucker pounding up the steps and down the hallway. She stood and glanced at her image in the mirror as she moved to the door to open it on the second soft knock. As she reached for the knob, a sudden tremor shook her, a premonition, an unwanted interloper in the realm of happiness she'd known these last few months. She was certain Tucker was going to propose matrimony and tried not to think of it, lest her hopes were dashed on the rocks of reality. They were simply too far apart in their origins and experiences for marriage to happen, for it to last if it did happen. Still, she hoped it would. She opened the door, and he embraced her so hard it took her breath away.

"It is going to be today, then," she told herself. "Lord, give me guidance."

He led her to the red settee he had bought a month earlier and sat down beside her.

"You look wonderful, Jenny. Have I told you today how very beautiful you are? No? Well, shame on me, then."

She laughed and kissed him softly, holding his tanned face in her hands just inches from her own.

"Jenny, I have something to ask you, something I've wanted to ask you for a while, and—"

In a flash, Jenny knew what was about to happen. Exhilaration. Just as suddenly, fear. She stood abruptly and turned her back to him. She raised both hands to her mouth and turned around, her eyes brimming with tears. In a voice as low and as soft as the one he heard only when they were entwined, exhausted, she said, "Tucker, I must tell you somethings before we go further."

Clairborne stood and reached for her, but she backed away.

"No, Tucker. I mean it. There are some things you have to know."

With a wave of his hand and a smile, Clairborne said, "Jenny, do you know why it's taken me this long to get around to asking you what I'm about to ask? Because I not only looked for every possible reason not to but I looked at those reasons repeatedly. Trust me. There's not a thing you can say that will change my mind about the future, our future."

She looked up at him and said in a calm, matter-of-fact tone of voice, "Tucker, my mother's mother is a Negro. My grandmother is a Negro, a house servant. She was...well, it doesn't matter how things happened."

She held his eyes with hers, unblinking, dry. "Dear Lord, Tucker, I hope it doesn't matter to you, but I had to tell you."

His cousin's axe handle impacting his ribs...Billy Creech dropping through the gallows trapdoor...

Clairborne couldn't breath. He raised both hands to rub his temples and squeezed closed his eyes. It wasn't imaginary. She'd said it. To his face. No way to deny this new knowledge. He saw his mother standing at the foot of the grand staircase, hands folded in front of her. He could not tell her he was about to bestow the family name on a prostitute, but was eager to do so even though the marriage would permanently sever the ties to the east, to the old, to the First Families of Virginia.

But this.

He didn't want to look at her. Her beauty, her calm demeanor, her intelligence, common sense, would only confuse him more, and she would see his torment.

"Why isn't she emotional? Why isn't she weeping? Can she not be aware of what she just told me? Who cares? Who the hell cares?" he asked himself and shuddered when the answer came in an instant.

"God help me. I do."

Retrieving his hat and gloves from the sideboard, he kept his eyes on the floor planks.

"I have to think," he said. "I have to think about why you told me this, Jenny. I, ah, just have to think." He closed the door quietly behind him.

Jenny LaBelle sat on her bed and stared at the door. The pain at the back of her throat was such that it almost constricted the tears suddenly and silently staining the breast of her taffeta dress. Creeping up from her heart, slowly at first and then accelerating, was the certainty she would never again see Tucker Clairborne.

It was easy because he'd already packed. An hour and seventeen minutes after he walked out of Jenny LaBelle's suite,

Tucker Clairborne handed a twenty-dollar gold piece to the stable hand, swung onto the broad black back of his beloved stallion, tugged the rope connected to the bridle of faithful Ajax, and rode out of Rawlins.

—✦—

Two days out, then three days up. The fifth day brought him to the timberline with a temperature that forced him to retrieve his woolen muffler and his gloves from his pack. The weather held. Game was plentiful, and the creeks were noisy with snowmelt and splashing trout. When he ate, which was only once a day on most days, it was only when he stopped to care for the horses. His own hunger had left him. But she hadn't. She was a presence, ubiquitous, a chimera hovering around him, beside him. He didn't like it but invested no energy in trying to banish her to oblivion. He knew she would not leave. He understood this was part of his penance.

Lying on the rocky ground again after months of feather beds relegated deep sleep to the same folds of memory that held full stomachs, laughter, purpose, and all the good things in his life, good things he'd assumed would only get better. Each pleasant recollection took on a cutting edge, puncturing and lacerating his thoughts with their random appearances.

And then the dreams began.

He was plowing a field, knowing he had no business doing so and that if anyone saw him, he'd be expected to explain what he was doing. Only he didn't know. And instead of following a team of his father's prize mules, it was his beautiful black Bucephalus struggling, snorting with equine disdain, turning his head to regard the one who had humiliated him with a plow harness. The horse sank to its hocks in the glutinous black soil, lurching against the harness, stumbling forward, evoking pity in Clairborne, who wanted to voice encouragement but could not find the words.

As the plowshare turned the soil, Clairborne beheld that it was not the rich black bottomland of his James River home. It was dry and red and hard, resisting the plow and the efforts of the stallion pulling it, and when the plow broke through, it revealed not dirt awaiting seed but faces and bodies, faces of people he knew were dead: his father, his brother, the man he killed in the Nashville alley. Others he didn't know, but all of them reached out with fleshless fingers to grasp his legs, his feet. He kicked them away and looked behind him to behold a score of silent hellions rising from the plowed furrow, all facing him, each moving toward him as best it could. Panic, sheer terror engulfed Clairborne as he whipped the reins and screamed at the stumbling horse, whom he realized could not run away, anchored to the massive plow as it was, but as he knelt to unfasten the plow, the hands rising from the soil grabbed him, and he smelled death and corruption of rotting flesh, tried to stand to run away, leaving the horse to his fate, but he could not break free, and he realized these devil's minions were going to devour him whole.

Variations of these ghastly visions visited his slumber the next night as well, until he avoided sleep with the same vigor he avoided sustenance. The contagion of his dreams spread to his waking hours, contaminated his thoughts, and overrode his effort to focus on something, anything else.

Little sleep and less food. Confusion and apathy, guilt and anger filled every corner of his conscience, randomly careening off one side of his mind to impact on another. He became numb, unaware and uncaring, cut off from his surroundings, signals from his horses, signs on the grasses, the sandbars of creeks and small rivers beside which he camped.

So it was that when he looked up from his small fire, he was startled by the presence of the two riders sitting their lathered mounts across the creek less than twenty feet from where he squatted. That he allowed two strangers to ride up to his fire, to enter his camp unbidden ignited another small flame to the guttering glow of self-contempt.

"Hello the fire," said one of the riders, a small, wiry man with a long, dirty yellow beard.

Clairborne stood, slowly, instinctively turning his right side toward the riders.

"Smelt your fire. We was heading up for this creekside to camp, good water and all. You mind we throw down for the evenin', do you?" Yellow Beard asked.

After a pause that could have been taken for impoliteness, Clairborne said, "I guess there's room for you—over there."

The riders looked at each other but said nothing.

"All right, then. Over here it is," Yellow Beard said as he dismounted.

Clairborne shrugged.

"Don't mean to be unsociable. Just that I got some thinking to do, and I'm not good company just now. Nothing personal."

The second rider never took his eyes off Clairborne. Of medium build, he emitted a quiet menace so strong it was almost an odor. It occurred to Clairborne that the man's unblinking stare could warrant a comment about rudeness.

Although he felt no hunger, Clairborne busied himself with a meal, making a point of putting more wood on the fire, filling a pot with creek water, and then filling the pot with dried beans before hanging it over the flames.

The riders began preparing their camp across the creek at the base of huge boulders. After chiding himself for his lack of alertness when they appeared, Clairborne studied them closely out of the corner of his eye.

Yellow Beard carried what appeared to be an 1858 Remington Army model pistol in a jockstrap holster. The stock protruding from his saddle scabbard looked to be that of a shotgun, not a rifle.

The second rider's patched coat fell away just long enough for Clairborne to see something rare. The man was double-heeled. Gun belts crossed at the waist supported backward-holstered Colts with walnut grips. He recalled seeing only one other man carrying double-rigged cross-draw.

After removing his coat, Crossbelts gathered wood and built a structure out of rocks and small drift logs, in front of which he laid the fire. Clairborne quickly understood its purpose was to reflect the fire's heat into the space between it and the wall of boulders, at the base of which the newcomers unfolded their bedrolls.

"Smart," Clairborne said to himself, recalling how cold the last two nights had been.

When he'd finished his simple meal and washed his cook pot and tin plate, he checked the picket rope to which his horses were tied and decided to give each of them another handful of oats. As he retrieved their feed bags, remorse arose from the back of his mind. He'd been rude to the riders, just plain rude. Walking back to the water's edge, he held up the oat bag and called to the men hunched over their fire.

"Noticed you didn't feed your mounts. Got some extra feed if you'd like it."

Yellow Beard jumped to his feet and trotted to the creek.

"Downright neighborly of you, friend. Thanks a bunch."

Clairborne heaved the half-empty sack across the creek, where Yellow Beard caught it with both hands.

"Sorry about my lack of hospitality. Like I said, got a lot to think on, but that's no excuse for rudeness."

"Oh, hell, don't worry none about it. You go on ahead and think yourself into a lather," Yellow Beard chuckled. "We won't bother you none at all. We'll be gone afore daybreak."

Clairborne returned to his bedroll, sat, and removed his boots, then his coat and hat. But not his pistol belt. He was not sure why. Whatever the reason, as he lay back and pulled his coat over him, ostensibly for its warmth, his hands slid unobtrusively into the inner pocket and withdrew the short-barreled Colt, sliding it down to where it would rest on his left side. Then, reaching down with his right hand, he slowly withdrew the long-barreled revolver from the holster and with cold deliberation thumbed the hammer back to full cock before carefully laying the gun on the blanket. It was a dangerous move. The Colt had a finely honed hair trigger, but Clairborne knew the risk of an accidental discharge was outweighed by the split seconds he'd gain by its already being fully cocked.

Within an hour, his sixth-sense suspicions hardened to certainty.

At first he wasn't sure what he was hearing. The two men were at least thirty feet away from him, but as he lay on his back with the bedroll pulled up around his neck, his head resting on his saddle, he heard the men talking, clearly talking as if they were just on the other side of his dying campfire instead of the other side of the creek. For a few moments, the acoustic aspects of the situation got more of his focus than the words he was hearing, but once those words sank in, Clairborne responded by retrieving both pistols and working the bedroll down in the darkness.

"I'm tellin' you, I think that's him."

Clairborne recognized the nasal, high-pitched tones of Yellow Beard.

"Don't care who he is. They's one of him and two of us. We can take him without breakin' a sweat," came the deeper, hoarse intonations of the rider sporting the crossbelts.

"Well, Bobby, I'm purty certain that's him, but I ain't about to lose a handful of brains to find out for sure."

"All right then, by gawd, I'll take him by my lonesome, but don't you come to me later wantin' none of his stuff."

"How're you gonna do it?" asked Yellow Beard.

"Gonna wait to just before daybreak, gonna sit up and wait for him to take his mornin' piss, then when he got his hands full, I'm gonna shoot him so full o' holes he'll be empty before he hits the ground."

"Oh, all right," Yellow Beard said. "Guess there ain't much can go sideways, as simple as that'll be. I'm in."

Clairborne watched the men lay back on their blankets.

It took only seconds for him to determine the best course of action.

Kill them first.

Start with the one who wanted to shoot the piss out of him. Then Yellow Beard. Smaller. Ought to go down with fewer rounds than it's going to take for the bigger fellow. Shoot Yellow Beard with the short barrel. Use Thunder on the other one.

Thinking of Crossbelts's overheard tactics, Clairborne formed his own.

His fire had died down. They had built theirs up. Its light would blind them to movements on his side of their campfire. He would slowly remove his bedroll, then edge himself down to the creek, then stand, then shoot. Shoot every bullet in his Colts, twelve rounds for two men. That ought to do it.

"Give it some time," he told himself. "No hurry. They're not going anywhere." He could hear them talking, not as clearly as before, but the tone of their conversation led Clairborne to believe the topics had shifted from murder to something more mundane. Women. Horses. Money.

———⁓———

He woke with a start. "Jesus. How could I fall asleep?" he asked himself, almost gagging on the brassy taste of fear clogging his throat. A quick glance showed his two assailants propped against their saddles, staring into the campfire flames.

Clairborne looked up at the heavens and took a deep breath.

"Maybe I want to die. Maybe that's why I went to sleep. Maybe I just wanted them to come over and do me in without my knowing, without my seeing it coming."

Had it come to this? To suicide? Had such depths been obtained that his life had become an insult to God? Fear of hell filled his mind.

He didn't want to go to hell, but he was pretty certain that if he were to die in his present state, that was where he would wind up. He remembered a painting he'd seen in the Louvre. *The Triumph of Death*, it was called, painted by Pieter Breugel The Elder. It scared him then. It filled him with panic now, in his camp high in the Wyoming Rockies. He connected the horrifying visions of his recent dreams with the images created long ago by the Flemish master.

It cleared his mind.

"I can't die now. I've got to live long enough to get back on the path to righteousness. I've got to do those two in to buy myself some time, time to get right again."

He pulled the blanket aside, gripped the two Colts, stood up, and walked to the creek.

Yellow Beard saw him first, a phantom emerging from the darkness, each arm fully extended, each hand holding a Colt gleaming in the reflected firelight.

Yellow Beard started to say something, but Clairborne shot him in his open mouth before he could speak.

His next shot, fired from the long barreled pistol in his right hand, missed its target altogether. Instead of plowing through Crossbelts's torso, it smashed into a boulder behind him and ricocheted the now-deformed chunk of soft lead into Crossbelts's back.

The thunk of lead striking rock was lost in the rapid reports of Clairborne's Colts, his third shot striking Crossbelts below his ribs as the impact of the ricochet on the left side of his back swung him to his right.

Crossbelts had been slow, too slow to understand what was happening and so was still sitting, then reaching for his pistols when Clairborne loomed out of the darkness preceded by spurts of flame. Unaware of how badly he'd been wounded, he raised his empty hands in front of him and wondered why his partner didn't shoot this fellow.

Clairborne's fourth round hit him in the chest, and his fifth shot took out Crossbelts's left eye.

Gun smoke fogged the campsite. Clairborne fired again and then collapsed in agony when a ball impacted the right side of his rib cage, tore through his shirt, shredded flesh, and snapped his bottom true rib. He dropped his pistols and broke his fall with his right hand, severely spraining his wrist. He was aware of sand in his mouth and stars dancing in his eyes. Pain over-rode his senses, all except the sense of survival. He didn't know if the two men were dead, only wounded, or, worst of all, coming for him.

Clairborne rolled and tried to push up, nearly passing out from the pain radiating from his side and his wrist.

"Why can't I breathe? Damn. Where are my guns?"

Then he understood. He'd been shot.

"Oh," he murmured as he lay back on the soft sand.

"Finally," he said and then fainted.

671

It was almost light when he opened his eyes.

"I must have got them" was his first thought. "Otherwise I wouldn't be seeing that tree."

He didn't move, didn't even try to. As he lay in the cold sand, pain wracked him, immobilized him with fear of how much worse it could be should he move.

He'd been shot. How badly he didn't know, but ultimately, having a bullet hole in him a long, long ride from Rawlins was as good as having a bullet through his brains or heart. He would wind up dead either way. One way was just quicker.

A raven landed on a branch above him. Clairborne and the raven studied each other. He recalled reading about ravens in an account of the battle of Agincourt—or was it Crecy? The field was littered with so many corpses, the victors couldn't keep the ravens off the bodies. He remembered the soldiers hated the ravens because of their appetite for eyeballs.

"Not mine, goddamit," he croaked, scaring the raven into flight.

Steeling himself for the inevitable increase in pain he was about to initiate, Clairborne sat up, nearly swooning in the process.

In a few seconds, his mind cleared, and he saw what he was looking for: two dead men.

"Goddam, I got them both," he exclaimed, instantly regretting his words.

"I apologize, Lord. Forgive my blasphemy, please."

He tried to stand and failed. He took a breath and raised his right arm trying to get a look at his wound. The entire right side of his shirt was almost black with dried blood, only the ragged tear in the fabric showing him where to look for the wound itself. Pain didn't tell him. His entire torso throbbed so badly he ignored his wrist. Gently, carefully, he slid his left hand across his stomach and as lightly as possible ran his fingertips over the damage and was confused by what they told him. There didn't seem to be a hole in him, only a...a what? A crease. A gouge, a hell of a gouge for certain. He looked at his fingertips and noted the blood that covered them. He was still bleeding. That had to stop and stop soon. He looked around the campsite.

Both of his foes were sprawled on their backs. He studied them for moments before realizing what was nagging at the back of his mind. Neither man had drawn his weapons. The pistols were wedged into the holsters.

"So who shot me?" he wondered aloud. White scars on the massive gray boulder behind Crossbelts's body answered his question. A ricochet.

"Sweet Jesus," Clairborne croaked. "I shot myself."

He wanted to lie down again, to contemplate the irony, but his pain demanded his attention.

Yellow Beard was sprawled on his back but on the left side of his gun belt, Clairborne saw a knife handle protruding from a fringed sheath.

It took him almost an hour to move the six feet to the body and retrieve the knife, a skinning blade, not a fighting tool, a skinner that was often used but rarely cleaned, to judge from the dried blood and bits of crusty tissue at the base of the quillon. Never mind; he didn't intend to use the blade for surgery on himself, only to cut away his shirt, the shreds of which he immersed in the creek and then used to wash his wound. The yellow-purple contusion from the gash on his side had spread all the way to his navel.

Two other shirts retrieved from his bag became bandages he wrapped as tightly as he could bear around his midsection. His mind focused on the ride back to Rawlins, and it dawned on him.

"Wait a minute. I don't have to get back to Rawlins. I just have to get to the rail line." If he headed south, he would hit it. Couldn't miss it. Two, maybe three days. Then it was just a matter of time before a passing train would pick him up and take him back to Rawlins.

No. Not back to Rawlins. Back to Jenny.

They carried him on a cot from the freight car to the hotel. By the time they got to the door, half the population was jostling to see him. Enveloped by a fever, Clairborne wasn't sure what was happening, what the source of the buzzing sound was, and why the steady rhythm of the train had morphed into bouncing and swaying. He was lifted onto his bed. Pillows were fluffed under his head. Someone he didn't know unwrapped his viscous, reeking bandages. Someone else touched his wound. Clairborne passed out.

Algernon Haas was humming tunelessly, sitting in a cane-backed chair beside the bed, reading a newspaper.

"Where's Jenny?" Clairborne croaked. "Algernon, where's Jenny?"

Haas jumped to his feet and felt Clairborne's brow with the back of his hand.

"Still too much fever," he said.

"Where's Jenny?"

Despite the fact that Haas knew Clairborne would ask the question, he still didn't know what to say or how to say it, but there was no point in delay or obfuscation.

"She's gone, Tucker."

"What? What do you mean 'gone'? Gone where? When?"

"Tucker, she is gone. Get your strength back and we can discuss this further, but right now only two things are certain. Jenny is gone, and you need to recover."

Clairborne was stunned into momentary silence. Ignoring the pain, he raised his head off the pillow. The room seemed to tilt, forcing him to grip the sides of the bed to prevent his falling to the floor.

"Do you mean she left, or that she's, that she's..."

"She left, Tucker. On the train east. I don't know where. Four days ago."

That meant he could find her when he recovered, and by God, he would.

—∿—

Two days later, just after dawn, the fever broke, Clairborne sat up in bed, and Haas brought him a bowl of beef broth. The windows were open, but no breeze mitigated the heat that baked the room.

Haas sat beside the bed and watched silently as Pennington Filmore, who had been a hospital corpsman for the Union Army and was now Rawlins's only undertaker, changed Clairborne's bandages and washed his wound. Clairborne didn't like him. He talked too much, talked incessantly, talked drivel, but since his ministrations didn't seem to make matters worse, Clairborne concentrated on being polite. It was difficult because beads of sweat dripped from Filmore's forehead to splat on Clairborne's face.

Admiring his handiwork, Filmore straightened up and wiped his hands on the dirty apron he wore over his brown suit.

"Nice. Nice, if I do say so myself...and I do. It is healing nicely, sir. Beneficent pus and decreased discoloration. Now you will have a dandy scar, sir. The wound was too ragged for me to stitch, but fortunately, being on your side and all, it won't be visible and shouldn't be too uncomfortable beyond stiffness once it heals. Yes sir, nice work, if I do say so."

Haas, understanding Clairborne's growing impatience with the fussy Filmore, guided Filmore to the door, thanking him and assuring him of immediate payment for his services. Haas closed the door and turned to Clairborne, who stared at the ceiling for moments before speaking.

"Did Frieda go with her?"

"No. Frieda is here, Tucker."

"Why hasn't she come to see me?"

Before Haas could respond, Clairborne said, "Stupid question. She probably hates me for leaving the way I did. I understand. Please give her my regards."

Haas sighed. "I will, Tucker, but that's not why she didn't come to see you. I asked her not to."

"Why?"

"Because there is something you must know, something only I should tell you."

A sense of dread so strong it almost nauseated him flooded Clairborne.

Haas crossed the carpet, reached down, and took Clairborne's hand, a gesture that was almost feminine and completely different from Haas's normal stiff formality.

"Jenny was pregnant. She lost the child two days after you left. I'm sorry. I'm so sorry." His grip tightened. He touched Clairborne's cheek with his other hand.

Clairborne's guts went stone cold.

"I killed it" was his only thought. "It's my fault. I killed my..."

"What was it? Was it a boy or a girl?"

"I don't know. I think it was too early to tell," Haas said softly.

"Why didn't she tell me? Clairborne said. Then he remembered their last meeting. She said there were "some things" he had to know. "Some things," not "something," and he'd left before he heard the rest of what she wanted to tell him: that she was pregnant. With his child.

It didn't matter. Nothing mattered. Nothing. Not now. Not ever.

"We buried the baby in the cemetery. I'll take you when you want, when you can," Haas said.

"All right," Clairborne murmured. "I'd like to be alone if I may."

———

At first light the next day, in the first rain to cool Rawlins in almost a month, Tucker Clairborne rode under the cemetery's wrought-iron gate and dismounted slowly, the pain in his side an afterthought. He led his horses up the gentle grade, his eyes sweeping the ground for the new grave.

It shouldn't have surprised him to realize how small it was, but it did—mere handfuls of dirt packed into a mound beneath which rested the baby.

There was no headstone. Haas said one had been ordered from Omaha. Instead, the grave was marked by a rough plank on which had been carved the words "Our Infant Child."

Clairborne removed his hat and knelt. He took a handful of the moist, freshly turned earth and raised it to his nose. It smelled good. Rich. He wondered if his child's body was already part of it.

It seemed odd that he was not weeping. He tried to understand why but found no answers. Never before had he felt such emptiness. He had not slept nor had any coffee, but he was not tired. Only empty. He wondered who had carved the simple words on the plank. It was nicely done. Maybe Hank Straughn, the best framer in town.

Then an awareness emerged with an insistent forcefulness.

"I am worthless. Without worth or value to anyone. No, worse than that. I am a bringer of death and despair. That is what I am."

He sensed his horse, its soft muzzle low, next to his shoulder.

He stood, absent-mindedly donned his hat then brushed mud from his trousers.

He turned to put his boot into the stirrup but stopped. He leaned over and gently kissed the piece of pine that marked the spot where his issue would rest forever.

"Good-bye, my child," he said.

He mounted and turned downhill. Passing under the gate, the black stallion—without a word or so much as a tug on the reins—turned away from town and headed west.

The End

Acknowledgments

On November 26, 1968, these four men risked their lives to rescue me and my six comrades from certain death. Without their guts and skill it would have ended then.

Jim Fleming
Fred Cook
JJ Jensen
Paul McClellan

Kith and Kin

All creative endeavor rests on the shoulders of others. *West from Yesterday* is no different. In "blood kin," my wife, Stephanie weakened the bonds of inertia that for too long kept me comfortably idle. My sons Tyler and Spencer were constantly encouraging. My cousin Bill (William Allen Harrison III) rode this trail with me in more ways than one, often taking the lead when I was unsure of the path ahead. My "true friends" know who they are but cannot know how much they mean to me. "Good dogs," beloved Lola and goofy Burfoot were at my feet as I wrote and ready to play when I wasn't. And as for "blind luck," I can only acknowledge my inability to comprehend why I continue to be so blessed.

And others who encouraged, corrected, and instructed...

For their diplomatic observations and encouragement

Joe and Sibella Giorello

Ben Le

Ron Pedee

Michael Kanady

For their expertise

Chance Bowers, cowboying and ranching

Dane Burns, guns

Dave Clark, horses

Warren Stricker, Director of Archives, Plains-Panhandle Historical Museum, Canyon, Texas.

Anne Davidson, Director, White Deer Land Museum, Pampa, Texas.

The staff of the Museum of the Plains, Perryton, Texas

The staff of Palo Duro State Park, Palo Duro, Texas

The staff of Hutchison County Historical Museum, Borger, Texas

Bibliography

Adams, Ramon F. *The Cowboy Dictionary*. New York, NY: Putnam, 1993.

Blevins, Win. *Dictionary of the American West*. Seattle, WA: Sasquatch Books, 2001.

Clasrud, Bruce A. Searles, Michael N. *Buffalo Soldiers in the West:* College Station, Tx.: Texas A&M University Press, 2007.

Gwynne, S. C. *Empire of the Summer Moon*. New York, NY: Scribner, 2010.

Hamalainen, Pekka. *The Comanche Empire*. New Haven, Conn: Yale University Press, 2008.

Peterson, Harold L., Elman, Robert. *The Great Guns*. New York, NY: Grosset and Dunlap, 1971.

Merrill, James M. *Spurs to Glory*. New York, NY: Rand McNally & Company, 1966.

Rollins, Phillip Ashton. *The Cowboy*. Norman, OK: University of Oklahoma Press, 1936.

Russell, Charles M. *The Western Art of Charles M. Russell*. New York, NY: Ballantine Books, 1975.

Thomason Jr., John W. *Stars in Their Courses*. New York, NY: Berkley Publishing, 1958.

Venturino, Mike. *Shooting Colt Single Actions.* Livingston, MT: MLV Enterprises, 1995.

Von Schmidt, Harold. *The Western Art of Harold Von Schmidt.* New York, NY: Bantam Books, 1976.

Ward, Geoffrey C. *The West.* Boston, New York, Toronto, London. Little, Brown and Company, 1996.

Randolph Carter Harrison has had three careers: officer in Army Special Forces, foreign correspondent and spokesman for one of the world's largest corporations.

Today, Harrison lives on the side of Squak Mountain in Washington State.

West from Yesterday is Harrison's first novel.

Made in the USA
Charleston, SC
12 December 2013